C...

Clive Barker wa...
is the worldwide...
novels including...
Show, *Sacrament* and *Galilee*. In addition to his work
as a novelist and short story writer, he also illustrates,
directs and produces for the stage and screen. Clive
Barker lives in Los Angeles.

'To call Clive Barker "a horror novelist" would be like
calling The Beatles "a garage band". Always creating
and always pushing into the furthest reaches of the
human mind, he is an artist in every sense of the
word. He is the great imaginer of our time. He not
only knows our deepest fears, but also what delights
us, what turns us on, and what is truly holy in the
world. Haunting, bizarre, beautiful. These are the
only words we can use to describe Clive Barker until
we invent new, more fitting, adjectives.'

QUENTIN TARANTINO

'Clive Barker is Hell's anatomist, and with each
scalpel brilliance dissects Hollywood, twisted gut to
heart of darkness.'

WES CRAVEN, Director of *Scream*

'Coldheart Canyon unfolds with genuine momentum,
in the vigorous style of a fully engaged storyteller.'

New York Times

Also by Clive Barker

The Books of Blood, Volumes I–VI
The Damnation Game
Weaveworld
Cabal
The Great and Secret Show
The Hellbound Heart
Imajica
The Thief of Always
Everville
Incarnations
Forms of Heaven
Sacrament
Galilee
The Essential Clive Barker

Clive Barker

COLDHEART CANYON

HarperCollins*Publishers*

HarperCollins*Publishers*
77–85 Fulham Palace Road,
Hammersmith, London W6 8JB

www.harpercollins.co.uk

This paperback edition 2002

First published in Great Britain by
HarperCollins*Publishers* 2001

A catalogue record for this book
is available from the British Library

ISBN 0 00 777275 0

Typeset in Meridien by
Palimpsest Book Production Limited,
Polmont, Stirlingshire

Printed in Great Britain by
Clays Ltd, St Ives plc

For David Emilian Armstrong

ACKNOWLEDGEMENTS

There are a lot of people to thank for helping me bring this one home. It was a devil of a book to write, for a host of reasons. For one thing, I began writing it the week before my father passed away, and inevitably the long shadow of that event dimmed the joy of writing, at least for the first six months or so, slowing it to a crawl.

Paradoxically, even as my production of useable text diminished, I could feel the scale of the story I wanted to tell getting bigger. What had originally begun life as an idea for a short, satiric stab at Hollywood began to blossom into something larger, lusher and stranger: a fantasia on Hollywood both in its not-so-innocent youth and in its present, wholly commercialized phase, linked by a sizeable cast and a mythology which I would need to create and explain in very considerable detail.

I don't doubt that this second incarnation of the book will be much more satisfying a read than the first – which I had written almost in its entirety before changing direction – but Lord, it was a son of a bitch to get down onto the page.

Forgive me, then, if the list of people I'm thanking is longer than usual. And believe me when I tell you every one of them deserves this nod of recognition, because each has helped get *Coldheart Canyon* out of my head and into print.

Let me begin with the dedicatee of this book, David Emilian Armstrong, my husband and in every sense of the word my partner: the one who was with me when one of our five dogs, Charlie, passed away (Charlie's loving presence, and the sadness and frustration of losing him, is recorded in this novel). David always has faith in my capacity to go one step further: to make the tale I'm telling a little richer, the picture I'm painting a little brighter, the photograph I'm taking a little sexier.

My thanks to Craig Green and Don MacKay, to whom I first gave the handwritten pages to be typed; and most especially to David John Dodds – my oldest and dearest friend – who worked through much of the Christmas period (with the Seraphim offices deserted around us) polishing the text, then polishing the polishes, so that the immense manuscript would be ready to be dispatched to my publishers before I went to recuperate in Kauai.

To Bob Pescovitz, my researcher, and Angela Calin, my translator, my thanks.

To Michael Hadley, Joe Daley and Renée Rosen, who run all the various aspects of my creative life outside writing and painting (films, television, theme park mazes and toy-lines, web-sites, photographs – and the endless business of promoting the above), my gratitude. In the last year and a half, I have often been an absentee boss, because I've been in the wilds of *Coldheart Canyon*. During that period, they have worked together to make our businesses prosper. Let me not forget Ana Osgood and Denny McLain, to whom fall the very considerable responsibilities of organizing and archiving my visual work, especially the many enormous paintings for my next books, *The Abarat Quartet*.

Then there are the two people – Toya Castillo and Alex Rosas – who make the homes in which we work run smoothly. Who feed David and myself, and wash our clothes; who make sure there's shampoo in our shower and our dogs smell sweet. Again, I have been something of a phantom of myself for much of the last year, passing through the house on my way to write or paint with a distracted look. They kindly indulge my craziness, and my endless calls for cups of hot sweet tea.

I also owe a great debt of gratitude to Dr Alex del Rosario, and his assistant Judy Azar. I recently described Alex as the perfect 'artist's doctor'. He has guided me through some lengthy periods of sickness in the last couple of years, understanding as no other physician in my history has the fierce and sometimes self-wounding passion that makes artists attempt to do the impossible: to paint another world into being, while writing a two hundred thousand word novel while producing a couple of movies, for instance. For me, this is my natural, albeit obsessive, behaviour. But my body isn't that of a thirty-year-old any longer (or even that of a forty-year-old!). It complains now when I drive it hard; as I do daily. It has taken a massive contribution of sympathetic counsel, medication and alternative therapies to keep body and spirit together since my father's death and I owe Alex a huge debt of thanks for my present good health.

Finally, the powers that be. First, my love and thanks to Ben Smith, my Hollywood agent, who has been a true visionary in a job that is often maligned (in this book, for instance) as being for cold, artistically disinterested men and women. My thanks and great admiration go to the lawyer who has helped shape my business life in the last two years, David Colden. The *Abarat* deal with the Disney Company was the largest literary deal made in Hollywood last year, and it covers every possible shape and permutation that my invented world might take, in the hands of Disney's imagineers. To give you a taste of what kind of wordage David Colden has minutely analysed on my behalf: the Disney contract had three pages alone devoted to listing its *contents*!

On the literary side, my dear Anne Sibbald, who has surely the tenderest heart of any agent who ever represented an unreformed maker of monsters like myself, has been a constant source of encouragement, and a fearless champion when – on occasion – the machinations of the corporate world proved painful and incomprehensible.

And last – but oh, you both know, never least – my editors.

In New York, Robert Jones (who's had his own wars to fight of late, and has still always been there with a witty word of support; or some wonderfully dry remark at the expense of the many idiocies of the publishing world).

And finally we come to Jane Johnson. *My* Jane, I insist, the Editor of Editors, who is never far from my mind when I set pen to paper. Increasingly, Jane, I think I write to entertain *you*, to please *you*. We have survived for many years together on a raft of shared beliefs about the necessity of dreams, tossed around in the tumultuous seas of modern publishing. In that time, Jane has lost countless colleagues to exhaustion, frustration and despair, and yet she manages to be a mistress of beautiful prose as well as an editor of a stable of authors, who, like me, could not imagine their literary lives continuing without her.

I would have given up the increasingly problematic ambition of having a broad audience for my work, and fled into the minor, the hermetic and the oblique, without her tireless encouragement.

My love to you, my Jane; and, as always, my heartfelt thanks.

Here's another tale for you, saved from the flood.

C.B.

CONTENTS

PROLOGUE

THE CANYON

I t is night in Coldheart Canyon, and the wind comes off the desert.

The Santa Anas, they call these winds. They blow off the Mojave, bringing malaise, and the threat of fire. Some say they are named after Saint Anne, the mother of Mary, others that they are named after one General Santa Ana, of the Mexican cavalry, a great creator of dusts; others still that the name is derived from *santanta*, which means Devil Wind.

Whatever the truth of the matter, this much is certain: the Santa Anas are always baking hot, and often so heavily laden with perfume that it's as though they've picked up the scent of every blossom they've shaken on their way here. Every wild lilac and wild rose, every white sage and rank jimsonweed, every heliotrope and creosote bush: gathered them all up in their hot embrace and borne them into the hidden channel of Coldheart Canyon.

There's no lack of blossoms here, of course. Indeed, the Canyon is almost uncannily verdant. Some of the plants here were brought in from the world outside by these same burning winds, these Santa Anas; others were dropped in the faeces of the wild animals who wander through – the deer and coyote and racoon; some spread from the gardens of the great dream palace that lays solitary claim to this corner of Hollywood. Alien blooms, this last kind – orchids and lotus flowers – nurtured by gardeners who have long since left off their pruning and their watering, and departed, allowing the bowers which they once treasured to run riot.

But for some reason there is always a certain bitterness in the blooms here. Even the hungry deer, driven from their traditional trails these days by the presence of sightseers who have come to see Tinseltown, do not linger in the Canyon for very long. Though the deer venture along the ridge and down the steep slopes of the Canyon, and curiosity, especially amongst the younger animals, often leads them over the rotted fences and toppled walls into the secret enclaves of the gardens, they seldom choose to stay there for very long.

Perhaps it isn't just that the leaves and petals are bitter. Perhaps there are too many whisperings in the air around the ruined gazebos, and the animals are unnerved by what they hear. Perhaps there are too many presences brushing against their trembling flanks as they explore the clotted pathways. Perhaps, as they graze the overgrown lawns, they look up and mistake a statue for a pale fragment of life, and are startled by their error, and take flight.

Perhaps, sometimes, they are not mistaken.

Perhaps.

The Canyon is familiar with perhaps; with what may or may not be. And never more so than on such a night as this, when the winds come sighing off the desert, heavy with their perfume, and such souls as the Canyon hosts express their longing for something they dreamed they had, or dreamed that they dreamed, their voices so tenuous tonight that they're inaudible to the human ear, even if there were someone to hear them, which there never is.

That's not entirely true. On occasion somebody will be tenacious enough to find their way into this vale of luxury and tears; a tourist, perhaps even a family of tourists, foolishly determined to discover what lies off the prescribed route; looking for some famous heart-throb's love-nest, or a glimpse of the idol himself, caught unawares as he walks with his dog. There are even a few trespassers over the years who have found their way here intentionally, guided to this place by hints dropped in obscure accounts of Old Hollywood. They venture cautiously, these few. Indeed there is often something close to reverence in the way they enter Coldheart Canyon. But however these visitors arrive, they always leave the same way: *hurriedly*, with many a nervous backward glance. Even the crassest of them – even the ones who'd claim they don't have a psychic bone in their bodies – are discomfited by something they sniff here. Their sixth sense, they have discovered, is far more acute than they had thought. Only when they have outrun the all-too-eager shadows of the Canyon and they are back in the glare of the billboards on Sunset Boulevard, do they wipe their clammy palms, and wonder to themselves how it was that in such a harmless spot they could have been so very afraid.

PART ONE

THE PRICE OF THE HUNT

1

'Your wife did not want to look around the Fortress any further, Mr Zeffer?' Father Sandru said, seeing that on the second day the middle-aged man with the handsome, sad face had come alone.

'The lady is not my wife,' Zeffer explained.

'Ah . . .' the monk replied, the tone of commiseration in his voice indicating that he was far from indifferent to Katya's charms 'A pity for you, yes?'

'Yes,' Zeffer admitted, with some discomfort.

'She's a very beautiful woman.'

The monk studied Zeffer's face as he spoke, but having said what he'd said, Zeffer was unwilling to play the confessee any further.

'I'm her manager,' he explained. 'That's all there is between us.'

Father Sandru, however, was not willing to let the issue go just yet. 'After the two of you departed yesterday,' he said, his English coloured by his native Romanian, 'one of the brothers remarked that she was the most lovely woman he had ever seen . . .' he hesitated before committing to the rest of the sentence '. . . in the flesh.'

'Her name's Katya, by the way,' Zeffer said.

'Yes, yes, I know,' said the Father, his fingers combing the knotted grey-white of his beard as he stood assessing Zeffer.

The two men were a study in contrasts. Sandru ruddy-faced and rotund in his dusty brown habit, Zeffer slimly elegant in his pale linen suit.

'She is a movie star, yes?'

'You saw one of her films?'

Sandru grimaced, displaying a poorly-kept array of teeth. 'No, no,' he said. 'I do not see these things. At least not often. But there is a little cinema in Ravbac, and some of the younger brothers go down there quite regularly. They are great fans of Chaplin, of course. And there's a . . . *vamp* . . . is that the word?'

'Yes,' Zeffer replied, somewhat amused by this conversation. 'Vamp's the word.'

'Called Theda Bara.'

'Oh, yes. We know Theda.'

In that year – which was 1920 – everybody knew Theda Bara. She had one of the most famous faces in the world. As, of course, did Katya. Both were famous; their fame tinged with a delicious hint of decadence.

'I must go with one of the brothers when they next go to see her,' Father Sandru said.

'I wonder if you entirely understand what kind of woman Theda Bara portrays?' Zeffer replied.

Sandru raised a thicketed eyebrow. 'I am not born yesterday, Mr Zeffer. The Bible has its share of these women, these *vamps*. They're whores, yes; women of Babylon? Men are drawn to them only to be destroyed by them?'

Zeffer laughed at the directness of Sandru's description. 'I suppose that's about right,' he said.

'And in real life?' Sandru said.

'In real life Theda Bara's name is Theodosia Goodman. She was born in Ohio.'

'But is she a destroyer of men?'

'In real life? No, I doubt it. I'm sure she harms a few egos now and again, but that's about the worst of it.'

Father Sandru looked mildly disappointed. 'I shall tell the brothers what you told me,' he said. 'They'll be very interested. Well then . . . shall I take you inside?'

*   *   *

10

Willem Matthias Zeffer was a cultured man. He had lived in Paris, Rome, London and briefly in Cairo in his forty-three years; and had promised himself that he would leave Los Angeles – where there was neither art nor the ambition to make art – as soon as the public tired of lionizing Katya, and she tired of rejecting his offer of marriage. They would wed, and come back to Europe; find a house with some real history on its bones, instead of the fake Spanish mansion her fortune had allowed her to have built in one of the Hollywood canyons.

Until then, he would have to find aesthetic comfort in the *objets d'art* he purchased on their trips abroad: the furniture, the tapestries, the statuary. They would suffice, until they could find a château in the Loire, or perhaps a Georgian house in London; somewhere the cheap theatrics of Hollywood wouldn't curdle his blood.

'You like Romania?' the Father asked as he unlocked the great oak door that lay at the bottom of the stairs.

'Yes, of course,' Zeffer replied.

'Please do not feel you have to sin on my account,' Sandru said, with a sideways glance.

'Sin?'

'Lying is a sin, Mr Zeffer. Perhaps it's just a little one, but it's a sin nevertheless.'

Oh Lord, Zeffer thought; how far I've slipped from the simple proprieties! Back in Los Angeles he sinned as a matter of course; every day, every hour. The life he and Katya lived was built on a thousand stupid little lies.

But he wasn't in Hollywood now. So why lie? 'You're right. I don't like this country very much at all. I'm here because Katya wanted to come. Her mother and father – I'm sorry, her stepfather – live in the village.'

'Yes. This I know. The mother is *not* a good woman.'

'You're her priest?'

'No. We brothers do not minister to the people. The Order of St Teodor exists only to keep its eyes on the

11

Fortress.' He pushed the door open. A dank smell exuded from the darkness ahead of them.

'Excuse me for asking,' Zeffer said. 'But it was my understanding from yesterday that apart from you and your brothers, there's nobody here.'

'Yes, this is true. Nobody here, except the brothers.'

'So what are you keeping your eyes on?'

Sandru smiled thinly. 'I will show you,' he said. 'As much as you wish to see.'

He switched on a light, which illuminated ten yards of corridor. A large tapestry hung along the wall, the image upon it so grey with age and dust as to be virtually beyond interpretation.

The Father proceeded down the corridor, turning on another light as he did so. 'I was hoping I might be able to persuade you to make a purchase,' he said.

'Of what?' Zeffer said.

Zeffer wasn't encouraged by what he'd seen so far. A few of the pieces of furniture he'd spotted yesterday had a measure of rustic charm, but nothing he could imagine buying.

'I didn't realize you were selling the contents of the Fortress.'

Sandru made a little groan. 'Ah . . . I'm afraid to say we must sell in order to eat. And that being the case, I would prefer that the finer things went to someone who will take care of them, such as yourself.'

Sandru walked on ahead a little way, turning on a third light and then a fourth. This level of the Fortress, Zeffer was beginning to think, was bigger than the floor above. Corridors ran off in all directions.

'But before I begin to show you,' Sandru said, 'you must tell me – are you in a buying mood?'

Zeffer smiled. 'Father, I'm an American. I'm *always* in a buying mood.'

*   *   *

12

Sandru had given Katya and Zeffer a history of the Fortress the previous day; though as Zeffer remembered it there was much in the account that had sounded bogus. The Order of St Teodor, Zeffer had decided, had something to hide. Sandru had talked about the Fortress as a place steeped in secrets; but nothing particularly bloody. There had been no battles fought there, he claimed, nor had its keep ever held prisoners, nor its courtyard witnessed atrocity or execution. Katya, in her usual forthright manner, had said that she didn't believe this to be true.

'When I was a little girl there were all kinds of stories about this place,' she said. 'I heard horrible things were done here. That it was human blood in the mortar between the stones. The blood of children.'

'I'm sure you must have been mistaken,' the Father had said.

'Absolutely not. The Devil's wife lived in this fortress. Lilith, they called her. And she sent the Duke away on a hunt. And he never came back.'

Sandru laughed; and if it was a performance, then it was an exceptionally good one. 'Who told you these tales?' he said.

'My mother.'

'Ah,' Sandru had shaken his head. 'And I'm sure she wanted you in bed, hushed and asleep, before the Devil's wife came to cut off your head.' Katya had made no reply to this. 'There are still such stories, told to children. Of course. Always stories. People invent tales. But believe me, this is not an unholy place. The brothers would not be here if it was.'

Despite Sandru's plausibility, there'd still been something about all of this that had made Zeffer suspicious; and a little curious. Hence his return visit. If what the Father was saying was a lie (a sin, by his own definition), then what purpose was it serving? What was the man protecting? Certainly not a few rooms filled with filthy tapestries, or

13

some crudely carved furniture. Was there something here in the Fortress that deserved a closer look? And if so, how did he get the Father to admit to it?

The best route, he'd already decided, was fiscal. If Sandru was to be persuaded to reveal his true treasures, it would be through the scent of hard cash in his nostrils. The fact that Sandru had raised the subject of buying and selling made the matter easier to broach.

'I do know Katya would love to have something from her homeland to take back to Hollywood,' he said. 'She's built a huge house, so we have plenty of room.'

'Oh, yes?'

'And of course, she has the money.'

This was naked, he knew, but in his experience of such things subtlety seldom played well. Which point was instantly proved.

'How much are we talking about?' the Father asked mildly.

'Katya Lupi is one of the best-paid actresses in Hollywood. And I am authorized to buy whatever I think might please her.'

'Then let me ask you: *what pleases her*?'

'Things that nobody else would be likely – no, could *possibly* – possess, please her,' Zeffer replied. 'She likes to show off her collection, and she wants everything in it to be unique.'

Sandru spread his arms and his smile. '*Everything* here is unique.'

'Father, you sound as though you're ready to sell the foundations if the price is right.'

Sandru waxed metaphysical. 'All these things are just objects in the end. Yes? Just stone and wood and thread and paint. Other things will be made in time, to replace them.'

'But surely there's some sacred value in the objects here?'

14

The Father gave a little shrug. 'In the Chapel, upstairs, yes. I would not want to sell you, let us say, the altar.' He made a smile, as though to say that under the right circumstances even that would have its price. 'But everything else in the Fortress was made for a secular purpose. For the pleasure of dukes and their ladies. And as nobody sees it now . . . except a few travellers such as yourselves, passing through . . . I don't see why the Order shouldn't be rid of it all. If there's sufficient profit to be made it can be distributed amongst the poor.'

'There are certainly plenty of people in need of help,' Zeffer said.

He had been appalled at the primitive conditions in which many of the people in the locality lived. The villages were little more than gatherings of shacks, the rocky earth the farmers tilled all but fruitless. And on all sides, the mountains – the Bucegi range to the east, to the west the Făgăras Mountains – their bare lower slopes as grey as the earth, their heights dusted with snow. God knew what the winters were like in this place: when even the earth turned hard as stone, and the little river froze, and the walls of the shacks could not keep out the wind whistling down from the mountain heights.

The day they'd arrived, Katya had taken Willem to the cemetery, so that she could show him where her grandparents were buried. There he'd had proof aplenty of the conditions in which her relatives lived and died. It was not the resting places of the old that had moved Willem; it was the endless rows of tiny crosses that marked the graves of infants: babies lost to pneumonia, malnutrition and simple frailty. The grief that was represented by these hundreds of graves had moved him deeply: the pain of mothers, the unshed tears of fathers and grandfathers. It was nothing he had remotely expected, and it had made him sick with sorrow.

For her part, Katya had seemed untouched by the sight,

talking only of her memories of her grandparents and their eccentricities. But then this was the world in which she'd been raised; it wasn't so surprising, perhaps, that she took all this suffering for granted. Hadn't she once told him she'd had fourteen brothers and sisters, and only six of them were left living? Perhaps the other eight had been laid to rest in the very cemetery where they'd walked together. And certainly it would not be uncommon for Katya to look coldly on the business of the heart. It was what made her so strong; and it was her strength – visible in her eyes and in her every movement – that endeared her to her audiences, particularly the women.

Zeffer understood that coldness better now that he'd spent time here with her. Seeing the house where she'd been born and brought up, the streets she'd trudged as a child; meeting the mother who must have viewed her appearance in their midst as something close to a miracle: this perfect rose-bud child whose dark eyes and bright smile set her utterly apart from any other child in the village. In fact, Katya's mother had put such beauty to profitful work at the age of twelve, when the girl had been taken from town to town to dance in the streets, and – at least according to Katya – offer her favours to men who'd pay to have such tender flesh in their bed for the night. She had quickly fled such servitude, only to find that what she'd had to do for her family's sake she had no choice but to do for herself. By the age of fifteen (when Zeffer had met her, singing for her supper on the streets of Bucharest) Katya had been a woman in all but years, her flowering an astonishment to all who witnessed it. For three nights he'd come to the square where she sang, there to join the group of admirers who were gathered around to watch this child-enchantress. It hadn't taken him long to conceive of the notion that he should bring her back with him to America. Though he'd had at that time no experience in the world of the cinema (few people did; the year was 1916, and film was a fledgling), his instincts told him there was something special in the face and bearing of this creature. He had influential friends on the West Coast – mostly men who'd grown tired of Broadway's petty disloyalties and piddling profits, and were looking for a new place to put their talents and their investments – who reported to him that cinema was a grand new frontier, and that talent scouts on the West Coast were looking for faces that the camera, and the public, would love. Did this child-woman not *have* such a face, he'd thought? Would the camera not grow stupid with infatuation to look into those guileful yet lovely eyes? And if the camera fell, could the public be far behind?

He'd inquired as to the girl's name. She was one Katya Lupescu from the village of Ravbac. He approached her; spoke to her; told her, over a meal of cabbage-rolls and cheese, what he was thinking. She was curiously sanguine about his whole proposal; practically indifferent. Yes, she conceded, it sounded interesting, but she wasn't sure if she would ever want to leave Romania. If she went too far from home, she would miss her family.

A year or two later, when her career had begun to take off in America – she no longer Katya Lupescu by then but *Katya Lupi*, and Willem her manager – they'd revisited this very conversation, and Zeffer had reminded her how uninterested she'd seemed in his grand plan. Her coolness had all been an illusion, she'd confessed; a way in part to keep herself from seeming too gauche in his eyes, and in part a way to prevent her hopes getting too high.

But that was only part of the answer. There was also a sense in which the indifference she'd demonstrated that first day they'd met (and – more recently – in the cemetery) was a real part of her nature; bred into her, perhaps, by a bloodline that had suffered so much loss and anguish over the generations that nothing was allowed to impress itself too severely: neither great happiness nor great sadness. She

17

was, by her own design, a creature who held her extremes in reserve, providing glimpses only for public consumption. It was these glimpses that the audience in the square had come to witness night after night. And it was this same power she would unleash when she appeared before the cinematographic camera.

Interestingly, Katya had shown none of this quality to Father Sandru the previous day.

In fact, it was almost as though she'd been playing a part: the role of a rather bland God-fearing girl in the presence of a beloved priest. Her gaze had been respectfully downcast much of the time, her voice softer than usual, her vocabulary – which often tended to the salty – sweet and compliant.

Zeffer had found the performance almost comical, it was so exaggerated; but the Father had apparently been completely taken in by it. At one point he'd put his hand under Katya's chin to raise her face, telling her there was no reason to be shy.

Shy! Zeffer had thought. If only Sandru knew what this so-called *shy* woman was capable of! The parties she'd master-minded up in her Canyon – the place gossip-columnists had dubbed *Coldheart Canyon*; the excesses she'd choreographed behind the walls of her compound; the sheer filth she was capable of inventing when the mood took her. If the mask she'd been wearing had slipped for a heartbeat, and the poor, deluded Father Sandru had glimpsed the facts of the matter, he would have locked himself in a cell and sealed the door with prayers and holy water to keep her out.

But Katya was too good an actress to let him see the truth.

Perhaps in one sense, Katya Lupi's whole life had now become a performance. When she appeared on screen she played the role of simpering, abused orphans half her age, and large portions of the audience seemed to believe that this was reality. Meanwhile, every weekend or so, out of sight of the people who thought she was moral perfection, she threw the sort of parties for the other idols of Hollywood – the vamps and the clowns and the adventurers – which would have horrified her fans had they known what was going on. Which Katya Lupi was the real one? The weeping child who was the idol of millions, or the Scarlet Woman who was the Mistress of Coldheart Canyon? The orphan of the storm or the dope-fiend in her lair? Neither? Both?

Zeffer turned these thoughts over as Sandru took him from room to room, showing him tables and chairs, carpets and paintings; even mantelpieces.

'Does anything catch your eye?' Sandru asked him eventually.

'Not really, Father,' Zeffer replied, quite honestly. 'I can get carpets as fine as these in America. I don't need to come out into the wilds of Romania to find work like this.'

Sandru nodded. 'Yes, of course,' he said. He looked a little defeated.

Zeffer took the opportunity to glance at his watch. 'Perhaps I should be getting back to Katya,' he said. In fact, the prospect of returning to the village and sitting in the little house where Katya had been born, there to be plied with thick coffee and sickeningly sweet cake, while Katya's relatives came by to stare at (and touch, as if in disbelief) their American visitors, did not enthral him at all. But this visit with Father Sandru was becoming increasingly futile, and now that the Father had made his mercenary ambitions so plain, not a little embarrassing. There wasn't anything here that Zeffer could imagine transporting back to Los Angeles.

He reached into his coat to take out his wallet, intending to give the Father a hundred dollars for his troubles. But before he could produce the note the Father's expression changed to one of profound seriousness.

'Wait,' he said. 'Before you dismiss me let me say this:

19

I believe we understand one another. You are looking to buy something you could find in no other place. Something that's one of a kind, yes? And I am looking to make a sale.'

'So is there something here you haven't shown me?' Zeffer said. 'Something special?'

Sandru nodded. 'There are some parts of the Fortress I have not shared with you,' he said. 'And with good reason, let me say. You see there are people who should not see what I have to show. But I think I understand you now, Mr Zeffer. You are a man of the world.'

'You make it all sound very mysterious,' Zeffer said.

'I don't know if it's *mysterious*,' the priest said. 'It *is* sad, I think, and human. You see, Duke Goga the man who built this Fortress – was not a good soul. The stories your Katya said she had been told as a child –'

'Were true?'

'In a manner of speaking. Goga was a great hunter. But he did not always limit his quarry to animals.'

'Good God. So she was right to be afraid.'

'The truth is, we are *all* a little afraid of what happened here,' Sandru replied, 'because we are none of us certain of the truth. All we can do, young and old, is say our prayers, and put our souls into God's care when we're in this place.'

Zeffer was intrigued now.

'Tell me then,' he said to Sandru. 'I want to know what went on in this place.'

'Believe me please when I tell you I would not know where to begin,' the good man replied. 'I do not have the words.'

'Truly?'

'Truly.'

Zeffer studied him with new eyes; with a kind of envy. Surely it was a blessed state, to be unable to find words for the terribleness of certain deeds. To be mute when it came to atrocity, instead of gabbily familiar with it. He found his curiosity similarly muted. It seemed distasteful – not to mention pointless – to press the man to say more than he expressed himself capable of saying.

'Let's change the subject. Show me something utterly out of the ordinary,' Zeffer said. 'Then I'll be satisfied.'

Sandru put on a smile, but it wasn't convincing. 'It isn't much,' he said.

'Oh sometimes you find beauty in the strangest places,' Zeffer said, and as he spoke the little face of Katya Lupescu came into his mind's eye; pale in a blue twilight.

2

Sandru led the way down the passageway to another door, this one rather smaller than the oak door they'd come through to get to this level. Out came his keys. He unlocked the door, and to Zeffer's surprise he and the priest were presented with another flight of steps, taking them yet deeper into the Fortress.

'Are you ready?' the Father asked.

'Absolutely,' Zeffer said.

Down they went. The stairs were steep, the air becoming noticeably more frigid as they descended. Father Sandru said nothing as they went; he glanced back over his shoulder two or three times, to be sure that he still had Zeffer on his heels, but the expression on his face was far from happy, as though he rather regretted making the decision to bring Zeffer here, and would have turned on his heel and headed back up to the relative comfort of the floor above at the least invitation.

At the bottom of the stairs he stopped, and rubbed his hands together vigorously.

'I think before we proceed any further we should take a glass of something to warm us,' he said. 'What do you say?'

'I wouldn't say no,' Zeffer said.

The Father went to a small cubby-hole in the wall a few yards from the bottom of the stairs, from which he brought a bottle of spirits and two glasses. Zeffer didn't remark on the liquor's proximity; nor could he blame the brothers for needing a glass of brandy to fortify them when they came down here. Though the lower level was supplied with electricity (there were lengths of electric lamps looped along the walls of the corridor) the light did nothing to warm the air nor comfort the spirit.

Father Sandru handed Zeffer a glass, and took the cork out of the bottle. The pop echoed off the naked stone of walls and floor. He poured Zeffer a healthy measure of the liquor, and then an even healthier measure for himself, which he had downed before Zeffer had got his own glass to his lips.

'When I first came here,' the Father said, 'we used to brew our own brandy, from plums we grew on our own trees.'

'But not now?'

'No,' the Father said, plainly saddened at the fact that they were no longer producers of liquor. 'The earth is not good any longer, so the plums never ripen properly. They remain small and sour. The brandy made from such fruit is bitter, and nobody wants to drink it. Even *I* will not drink it, so you can judge for yourself how bad it must be!' He laughed at his self-deprecation, and used the laughter as a cue to fill his glass up again. 'Drink,' he said to Zeffer, tapping his glass against Zeffer's glass as though this was the first he'd had.

Zeffer drank. The brandy was stronger than the stuff he'd had at the hotel in Brascov. It went down smoothly, warming his belly when it arrived.

'Good, yes?' the Father said, having downed his second glass.

'Very.'

'You should have another before we go on.' And he filled Zeffer's glass without waiting for a reply. 'We're a long way below ground here, and it gets hellishly cold . . .' Glasses were filled, and emptied. The Father's mood was noticeably better now, and his tone chattier. He put the glasses and the bottle back in the hole in the wall, and then led the way down the narrow corridor, talking as he went. 'When the Order first came to the Fortress, there were plans to found a hospital here. You see, there are no hospitals within a hundred and twenty miles of here. It would be very practical. But this is not a place for the sick. And certainly not the dying.'

'So: no hospital?'

'Well, we made preparations. You saw yesterday one of the wards –'

Zeffer remembered. He'd glanced through an open door and there'd been two rows of iron beds, with bare mattresses.

'I thought it was a dormitory for the brothers.'

'No. We each have our own cells. There are only eleven of us, so we can each have a place in which to meditate and pray . . .' He offered Zeffer a glance, accompanied by a small smile. 'And drink.'

'I can't imagine it's a very satisfying life,' Zeffer said.

'Satisfying?' The idea was obviously a little confounding to Sandru. 'Meaning what?'

'Oh, just that you don't get to work in the community. You can't help people.'

They had come to the end of the passageway, and Sandru sorted through his collection of keys in order to open the third and final door.

'Who can truly be helped?' he said, his face turned down to the labour of sorting. 'I suppose perhaps children can be comforted, sometimes, if it's dark and they're afraid. You can tell them you're with them; and that will sometimes stop them crying. But for the rest of us? Are there really any words that *help*? I don't know of any.' He had found the right key, and now slipped it noisily into the antiquated lock. As he did so, he glanced up at Zeffer. 'I think there's more comfort to be had from seeing beautiful women on the cinema screen than in any prayer I know. Well, perhaps not comfort. Distraction.' He turned the key in the lock.

'And if that sounds like heresy, well so be it.'

*　　*　　*

24

Sandru pushed the door open. The room was in darkness, but despite that fact there was a warmth in the air; at least in contrast to the chilly air of the passageway. Perhaps the difference was no more than two or three degrees, but it felt significant.

'Will you wait here a moment?' Sandru said. 'I'll just bring a light.'

Zeffer stayed where he was, staring into the darkness, enjoying the slight rise in temperature. There was enough illumination spilling from the passageway behind him to light the threshold. There, carved into stone beneath his feet, was a curious inscription:

Quamquam in fundis inferiorum sumus, oculos angelorum tenebimus.

He didn't linger to puzzle over this for more than a few seconds, but instead let his eyes drift up and into the room itself. The chamber before him was large, it seemed; and unlike the rest of the rooms and corridors, which were simply constructed, far more elaborate. Could he make out pillars, supporting several small vaults? He thought so. There were chairs and tables within a few yards of where he stood, and what appeared to be lamps or the like heaped on top of them.

The confusion inside was explained a moment later, when the Father returned with a bare bulb, attached to a length of electric cord.

'We use this as a storeroom,' he said. 'Many of the items we found in the Fortress when we arrived we put down here, just to get them out of the way.' He lifted the light to give Zeffer a better view.

Zeffer's estimation of the size of the place, and of the complexity of its construction, had been conservative, it now turned out. The chamber was fully thirty-five feet long; and almost as broad, the ceiling (which was indeed divided into eight elaborately-vaulted sections, divided by pillars) higher than the passageway by six feet or more.

The floor was littered with furniture and crates; the place plainly filled by hands that had little or no respect for the objects they were moving; wishing only to put them quickly out of sight. It occurred to Zeffer that if indeed there were treasures here the chances of finding them – or indeed of their being in reasonable condition when discovered – were remote. Still, the Father had brought him this far at no little inconvenience to himself; it would be discourteous to now show no interest in what the chamber contained.

'Did you have a part in moving all of this?' he asked Sandru, more out of a need to fill the silence between them than because he was genuinely curious.

'Yes, I did,' the Father replied. 'Thirty-two years ago. I was a much younger man. But it was still a back-breaking labour. They built things big here. I remember thinking that maybe the stories were right . . .'

'Stories about –'

'Oh . . . nonsenses. About this furniture having been built for the retinue of the Devil's wife.'

'The Devil's wife.'

'Lilith, or Lilitu. Sometimes called Queen of Zemargad. Don't ask me why.'

'This is the same woman Katya spoke about?'

Sandru nodded. 'That's why the locals don't have much hope for the sick if they stay here. They think Lilith's curse is on the place. As I say: nonsenses.'

Whether it was nonsense or not, the story lent some flavour to this banal adventure. 'May I look more closely?' Zeffer asked.

'That's what we're here for,' Father Sandru replied. 'I hope there's *something* that catches your eye, for your sake. All these stairs and doors. I'd forgotten how far down it was . . .'

'I'm sorry to have made this so burdensome,' Zeffer said, quite sincerely. 'If I'd known you were going to go to so much trouble I wouldn't have –'

'No, no,' Sandru said. 'It's not a trouble to me. I only thought there might be an item here that pleased you. But now I'm down here I doubt it. To be truthful I believe we should have taken all this trash up the mountain and thrown it in the deepest gorge we could find.'

'Why didn't you do just that?'

'It wasn't my choice. I was just a young priest at the time. I did as I was told. I moved tables and chairs and tapestries, and I kept my counsel. Our leader then was Father Nicholas, who was very clear on the best thing to be done – *the safest thing for our souls* – and would not be moved on the subject. So we did as we were told. Father Nicholas, by the way, had the foulest temper of any man I ever knew. We all lived in fear of him.'

Zeffer moved into the room, talking as he went: 'May I say something that I hope won't offend you?'

'I'm not easily offended, don't worry.'

'Well . . . it's just that the more I hear about your Order, the less like priests you seem to be. Father Nicholas's temper and the brothers all familiar with Theda Bara. And then the brandy.'

'Ah, the sins of the flesh,' Father Sandru said. 'We do seem to have more than our share, don't we?'

'I *have* offended you.'

'No. You've simply seen the truth. And how can a man of God be justly offended by that? What you've observed is no coincidence. We are all . . . how shall I put this? . . . men who have more than our share of flaws. Some of us were never trusted with a flock. Others, like Father Nicholas, *were*. But the arrangement was never deemed satisfactory.'

'His temper?'

'I believe he threw a Bible at one of the parishioners who was sleeping through the good Father's sermon.' Zeffer chuckled; but his laughter was silenced a moment later. 'It killed the man.'

'Killed –?'

'An accident, but still . . .'

'– with a Bible. Surely not.'

'Well, that's how the rumour went. Father Nicholas has been dead twenty years, so there's no way to prove it or disprove it. Let's hope it isn't true, and if it is, hope he's at peace with it now. The fact is, I'm glad I was never trusted with a parish. With a flock to tend. I couldn't have done much for them.'

'Why not?' Zeffer asked, a little impatient with Sandru's melancholy now. 'Do you have difficulty finding God in a place like this?'

'To be honest Mr Zeffer, with every week that passes – I almost want to say with every hour – I find it harder to see a sign of God *anywhere*. It would not be unreasonable, I think, to ask Him to show himself in beauty. In the face of your lady-companion, perhaps . . . ?'

Katya's face as proof of God's presence? It was an unlikely piece of metaphysics, Zeffer thought.

'I apologize,' Sandru said. 'You didn't come here to hear me talk about my lack of faith.'

'I don't mind.'

'Well I do. The brandy makes me maudlin.'

'Shall I take a look then?' Zeffer suggested. 'At whatever's in here?'

'Yes, why don't we?' Sandru replied. 'I wish I could give you some kind of guidance, but . . .' He shrugged; his favourite gesture. 'Why don't you start looking, and I'll go back and get us something more to drink?'

'Nothing more for me,' Zeffer replied.

'Well, then for me,' Sandru said. 'I'll only be a moment. If you need me, just call. I'll hear you.'

Zeffer took a moment, when the man was gone, to close his eyes and let his thoughts grow a little more orderly. Though Sandru spoke slowly enough, there was something mildly chaotic about his thought processes. One minute he was talking about furniture, the next about the mad Duke and his hunter's habits, the next about the fact that they couldn't make a hospital here because the Devil's wife had cursed the place.

When he opened his eyes his gaze moved back and forth over the furniture and the boxes without lingering on anything in particular. The bare bulb was stark, of course, and its light far from flattering, but even taking that fact into account there was nothing in the room that caught Zeffer's eye. There were some finely-wrought things, no question; but nothing extraordinary.

And then, as he stood there, waiting for Sandru to return, his gaze moved beyond the objects that filled the chamber, and came to rest instead on the *walls* beyond.

The chamber was not, he saw, made of bare stone. It was covered with tiles. In every sense, this was an understatement, for these were no ordinary tiles. Even by so ungenerous a light as the bare bulb threw upon them, and viewed by Zeffer's weary eyes, it was clear they were of incredible sophistication and beauty.

He didn't wait for Father Sandru to return; rather, he began to push through the piles of furniture towards the designs that covered the walls. They covered the floor, too, he saw, and ceiling. In fact, the chamber was a single masterpiece of tile; every single inch of it decorated.

In all his years of travelling and collecting he'd never seen anything quite like this. Careless of the dirt and dust laden webs which covered every surface, he pushed on through until he reached the nearest wall. It was filthy, of course, but he pulled a large silk handkerchief out of his pocket, and used it to scrub away some of the filth on the tiles. It had been plain even from a distance that the tiles were elaborately designed, but now, as he cleared a swathe across four or five, he realized that this was not an abstract pattern but a *representation*. There was part of

29

a tree there, on one of the tiles, and on another, adjacent to it, a man on a white horse. The detail was astonishing. The horse was so finely painted, it looked about ready to prance off around the room.

'It's a hunt.'

Sandru's voice startled him; Willem jerked back from the wall, so suddenly that it was as though he'd had his face in a vacuum, and was pulling it free. He felt a drop of moisture plucked from the rim of his eye; saw it flying towards the cleaned tiles, defying gravity as it broke on the flank of the painted horse.

It was a strange moment; an illusion surely. It took him a little time to shake off the oddness of it. When he looked round at Sandru, the man was slightly out of focus. He stared at the Father's shape until his eyes corrected the problem. When they did he saw that Sandru had the brandy bottle back in his hand. Apparently its contents had been more potent than Zeffer had thought. The alcohol, along with the intensity of his stare, had left him feeling strangely dislocated; as though the world he'd been looking at – the painted man on his painted horse, riding past a painted tree – was more real than the old priest standing there in the doorway.

'A hunt?' he asked at last. 'What kind of hunt?'

'Oh, every kind,' Sandru replied. 'Pigs, dragons, women –'

'Women?'

Sandru laughed. 'Yes, women,' he said, pointing towards a piece of the wall some yards deeper into the chamber. 'Go look,' he said. 'You'll find the whole thing is filled with obscenities. The men who painted this place must have had some strange *dreams*, let me tell you, if this is what they saw.'

Zeffer pushed aside a small table, and then pressed himself between the wall and a much larger piece of furniture, which looked like a wooden catafalque, too large to move. Obliged to slide along the wall, his jacket did the job his handkerchief had done moments before. Dust rose up in his face.

'Where now?' he asked the Father when he'd got to the other side of the catafalque.

'A little further,' Sandru replied, uncorking the brandy and shamelessly taking a swig from the bottle.

'I need some more light back here,' Zeffer said.

Reluctantly, Sandru went to pick up the lamp. It was hot now. He rummaged in one of the nearby boxes to find something to protect his palm, found a length of cloth and wrapped it around the base of the lamp. Then he tugged on the light-cord, to give himself some more play, and made his way through the confusion of stuff in the room, to where Zeffer was standing.

The closer Sandru came with the light the more Zeffer could make out of the painting on the tiles. There was a vast panorama spread to left and right of him; and up above his head; and down to the ground, spreading beneath his feet. Though the walls were so filthy that in places the design was entirely obliterated, and in other places there were large cracks in the tiles, the image had an extraordinary reality all of its own.

'*Closer*,' Zeffer said to Sandru, sacrificing the arm of his fur coat to clean a great portion of tiled wall in front of him. Each tile was about six inches square, perhaps a little smaller, and set close to one another with a minimum of grouting, so as to preserve the continuity of the picture. Despite the sickly light of the bulb, its luminescence still showed that the colour of the image had not been diminished by time. The beauty of the renderings was perfectly evident. There were a dozen kinds of green in the trees, and more, sweeter hues in the growth between them. Beneath the canopy there were burnt umbers and siennas and sepias in the trunks and branches, skilfully highlighted to lend the impression that light was falling through the foliage and catching the bark. Not all the tiles were rendered with the same expertise, he saw.

Some of the tiles were the work of highly sophisticated artists; some the work of journeymen; some – especially those that were devoted to areas of pure foliage – the handiwork of apprentices, working on their craft by filling in areas that their masters neither had the time nor perhaps the interest to address.

But none of this spoiled the power of the overall vision. In fact the discontinuity of styles created a splendid energy in the piece. Portions of the world were in focus, other parts were barely coherent; the abstract and the representational sitting side by side on the wall, all part of one enormous story.

And what *was* that story? Plainly, given the kind of quarry Sandru had listed, this was more than simply a hunt: it smacked of something far more ambitious. But what? He peered at the tiles, his nose a few inches from the wall, trying to make sense of what he was seeing.

'I looked at the whole room, before we put all the furniture in here,' Sandru said. 'It's a view, from the Fortress Tower.'

'But not realistic?'

'It depends what you mean by *realistic*,' Sandru said. 'If you look over the other side –' he pointed across the room '– you can see the delta of the Danube.' Zeffer could just make out the body of water, glittering in the gloom: and closer by a mass of swampy land, with dozens of inlets winding through it, on their way to the sea. 'And there!' Sandru went on, 'to the left –' again, Zeffer followed Sandru's finger '– at the corner of the room, that rock –'

'I see it.'

The rock was tall, rising out of the ocean of trees like a tower, shrubs springing from its flank.

'That's called the May Rock,' Sandru said. 'The villagers dance there, on the first six nights of May. Couples would stay there overnight, and try to make children. It's said the women always became pregnant if they stayed with their men on May Rock.'

'So it exists? In the world, I mean. Out there.'

'Yes, it's right outside the Fortress.'

'And so all those other details? The delta –'

'Is nine miles away, in *that* direction.' Sandru pointed at the wall upon which the Danube's delta was painted.

Zeffer smiled as he grasped what the artists had achieved here. Down in the depths of the Fortress, at its *lowest* point, they had recreated in tile and paint what could be seen from its pinnacle.

And with that realization came sense of the inscription he'd read on the threshold.

Though we are in the bowels of Hell, we shall have the eyes of Angels.

This room was the bowels of Hell. But the tile-makers and their artist masters, wherever they'd been, had created an experience that gave the occupants of this dungeon the eyes of angels. A paradoxical ambition, when all you had to do was climb the stairs and see all this from the top of the tower. But artists were often driven by such ambition; a need perhaps, to prove that it could even be done.

'Somebody worked very hard to create all this,' Zeffer said.

'Oh indeed. It's an impressive achievement.'

'But you hide it away,' Zeffer said, not comprehending the way the room had been treated. 'You fill the place with old furniture and let it get filthy.'

'Who could we show it to?' the Father replied. 'It's too *disgusting . . .*'

'I see nothing –' he was about to say *disgusting*, when his eye alighted on a part of tile-work that he'd cleaned with his arm but had not closely studied. In a large grove a round stadium had been set up, with seating made of wood. The perspective was off (and the solution to the perspective changed subtly from tile to tile, as various hands had contributed their piece of the puzzle. There were perhaps twenty tiles that had some portion of the stadium represented upon them; the work of perhaps five artists). The steep benches were filled with people, their bustle evoked with quick, contentious strokes. Some people seemed to be standing; some sitting. Two more groups of spectators were approaching the stadium from the outside, though there was no room for them inside.

But what drew Zeffer's eye, and made him realize that the Father had been right to wonder aloud who he might show this masterwork to, was the event these spectators had assembled to witness. It was an arena of sexual sport. Several performances were going on at the same time, all unapologetically obscene. In one section of the arena a naked woman was being held down while a creature twice her size, his body bestial, his erection monstrous, was being roped back by four men who appeared to be controlling his approach to the woman. In another quarter, a man had been stripped of his skin by three naked women. A fourth straddled him as he lay on the ground in his own blood. The other three wore pieces of his skin. One had on his whole face and shoulders, her breasts sticking out from beneath the ragged hood. Another sat on the ground, wearing his arms and pulling on the skin of his legs like waders. The third, the queen of this quartet, was wearing what was presumably the *pièce de résistance*, the flesh which the unhappy owner had worn from mid breast-bone to mid-thigh. She was cavorting in this garish costume like a dancer and, by some magic known only to the maker of the mystery, the usurped skin still boasted a full erection.

'Good God . . .' Zeffer said.

'I told you,' Sandru said, just a little smugly. 'And that's the least of it, believe me.'

'The least of it?'

'The more you look, the more you see.'

'Anywhere in particular?'

'Go over to the Wild Wood. Look amongst the trees.'

Zeffer moved along the wall, studying the tiles as he went. At first he couldn't make out anything controversial, but Sandru had some useful advice.

'Step away a foot or so.'

In his fascination with the details of the stadium, Zeffer had come too close to the wall to see the wood for the trees. Now he stepped back and to his astonishment saw that the thicket around the arena was alive with figures, all of which were in some form or other monstrous; and all unequivocally sexual. Erections were thrust between the trees like plum-headed branches, women dangled from overhead with their legs spread (a flock of birds, thirty or more, swooped out of the sex of one; another was menstruating light, which was splashing on the ground below the tree. Snakes came out of the scarlet pool, in bright profusion).

'Is it like this all over?' Zeffer said, his astonishment unfeigned.

'All over. There are thirty-three thousand, two hundred and sixty-eight tiles, and there is obscene matter on two thousand, seven hundred and ninety-eight of them.'

'You've obviously made a study,' Zeffer observed.

'Not I. An Englishman who worked with Father Nicholas did the counting. For some reason the numbers remained in my head. I think it's old age. Things you want to remember, you can't. And things that don't mean anything stick in your head like a knife.'

'That's not a pretty image, with respect.'

'With respect, there's nothing pretty about the way I feel,' Sandru replied. 'I feel old to my marrow. On a good day I can barely get up in the morning. On a bad day, I just wish I were dead.'

'Lord.'

Sandru shrugged. 'That's what living in this place does

35

to you after a while. Everything drains out of you somehow.'

Zeffer was only half-listening. He was exhilarated by
what he saw, and he had no patience with Sandru's melancholy; his thoughts were with the walls, and the pictures
on the walls.

'Are there records documenting how this was created?
It *is* a masterpiece, in its way.'

'One of a kind,' Sandru said.

'Absolutely one of a kind.'

'To answer your question, it's believed to have been
funded by Duke Goga, who had lately returned from the
Crusades with a large amount of booty, claimed from the
infidel in the name of Christ.'

'But to build a room like this with money you'd made
on the Crusades!' Zeffer said incredulously.

'I agree. It seems like an unlikely thing to do in the name
of God. Of course none of this is proved. There are some
people who will tell you that Goga went missing on one of
his hunts, and it wasn't him who built this place at all.'

'Who then?'

'Lilith, the Devil's wife,' the Father said, dropping his
voice to a whisper. 'Which would make this the Devil's
Country, no?'

'Has anybody tried to *analyse* the work?'

'Oh yes. The Englishman I spoke of, George Soames,
claimed he had discovered evidence of twenty-two different styles amongst the designs. But that was just the
painters. Then there were the men who actually *made*
the tiles. Fired them. Sorted out the good from the bad.
Prepared the paint. Cleaned the brushes. And there must
have been some system to align everything.'

'The rows of tiles?'

'I was thinking more of the alignment of interior with
the exterior.'

'Perhaps they built the room first.'

'No. The Fortress is two-and-a-half centuries older than this room.'

'My God, so to get the alignment so perfect –?'

'Is quite miraculous. Soames found fifty-nine geographical markers – certain stones, trees, the spire of the old abbey in Darscus – which are visible from the tower and are also painted on the wall. He calculated that all fifty-nine were correctly aligned, within half a degree of accuracy.'

'Somebody was obsessive.'

'Or else, divinely inspired.'

'You believe that?'

'Why not?'

Zeffer glanced back at the arena on the wall behind him, with all its libidinous excesses. 'Does that look like the kind of work that somebody would do in the name of God?'

'As I said,' Sandru replied, 'I no longer know where God is and where He isn't.'

There was a long silence, during which Zeffer continued to survey the walls. Finally he said: 'How much do you want for it?'

'How much do I want for what?'

'For the room?'

Sandru barked out a laugh.

'I mean it,' Zeffer said. 'How much do you want for it?'

'It's a *room*, Mr Zeffer,' Sandru said. 'You can't buy a room.'

'Then it's not for sale?'

'That's not my point –'

'Just tell me: is it for sale or not?'

Again, laughter. But this time there was less humour; more bemusement. 'I don't see that it's worth talking about,' Sandru said, putting the brandy bottle to his lips and drinking.

'Let's say a hundred thousand dollars. What would that be in lei? What's the leu worth right now? A hundred and thirty-two-and-a-half to the dollar?'

'If you say so.'

'So that's what? Thirteen million, two hundred and fifty thousand lei.'

'You jest.'

'No.'

'Where would you find such money?' A pause followed. 'If I may ask?'

'Over the years, I've made some very lucrative investments on behalf of Katya. We own large parts of Los Angeles. Half a mile of Sunset Boulevard is in her name. Another half mile in mine.'

'And you would sell all that to own *this*?'

'A little piece of Sunset Boulevard for your glorious Hunt? Why not?'

'Because it's just a room covered with filthy tiles.'

'So I have more money than sense. What does it matter to you? A hundred thousand dollars is a great deal of money.'

'Yes, it is.'

'So, do we have a deal or not?'

'Mr Zeffer, this is all too sudden. We're not talking about a *chair* here. This is part of the fabric of the Fortress. It has great historical significance.'

'A minute ago it was just a room covered with filthy tiles.'

'Filthy tiles of *great* historical significance,' Sandru said, allowing himself a little smile.

'Are you saying we can't find some terms that are mutually satisfying? Because if you are –'

'No, no, no. I'm not saying that. Perhaps we could eventually agree on a price, if we talked about it for a while. But how would you ever get it back to California?'

'That would be my problem. This is the twenties, Father. Anything's possible.'

'And then what? Suppose you *could* get everything back to Hollywood?'

38

'Another room, the same proportions –'

'You have such a room?'

'No. I'd build one. We have a house in the Hollywood Hills. I'd put it in as a surprise for Katya.'

'Without telling her?'

'Well if I told her it wouldn't be a surprise.'

'I'm just astonished that she would allow you to do such a thing. A woman like that.'

'Like *what*?'

The question caught Sandru off-balance. 'Well . . . so . . .'

'Beautiful?'

'Yes.'

'I think our conversation's come full-circle, Father.'

Sandru conceded the point with a little nod, lifting the brandy bottle as he did so.

'So she's not as perfect as her face would suggest?' he asked at last.

'Not remotely. Thank God.'

'This place, with all its obscenities, would *please* her?'

'Yes, I think it would. Why? Does that make you more open to the idea of selling it to me?'

'I don't know,' Sandru replied, frowning. 'This whole conversation hasn't turned out the way I thought it would. I expected you to come down here and maybe buy a table, or a tapestry. Instead you want to buy the walls!' He shook his head again. 'I was warned about you Americans,' he added, his tone no longer amused.

'What were you warned about?'

'Oh, that you thought nothing was beyond your grasp. Or beyond your pocket.'

'So the money isn't enough.'

'The *money*, the *money*.' He made an ugly sound in the back of his throat. 'What does the *money* matter? You want to pay a hundred thousand dollars for it? Pay it. I'll never see a leu so why should I care what it costs you? You can steal it as far as I am concerned.'

39

'Let me understand you clearly. Are you agreeing to the sale?'

'Yes,' Father Sandru said, his tone weary now, as though the whole subject had suddenly lost all trace of pleasure for him. 'I'm agreeing.'

'Good. I'm delighted.'

Zeffer returned through the maze of furniture to the door, where the priest stood. He extended his hand. 'It's been wonderful dealing with you, Father Sandru.'

Sandru looked down on the proffered hand, and then – after a moment of study – took it. His fingers were cold, his palm clammy. 'Do you want to stay and look at what you've bought?'

'No. I don't think so. I think we both need a little sun on our faces.'

Sandru said nothing to this; he just turned and led the way out along the corridor to the stairs. But the expression on his face, as he turned, was perfectly clear: there was no more pleasure to be found above as there was down here in the cold; nor prospect of any.

There were ten thousand things Zeffer had not witnessed, or even glimpsed, in his brief visit to the vast, mysterious chambers in the Fortress's bowels; images haunting the tiles which he would not discern until the heroic labour of removing the masterwork from the walls and shipping it to California was complete.

He was a literate man; better educated than most of his peers in the burgeoning city of Los Angeles, thanks to parents who had filled the house with books, even though there was often precious little food on the table. He knew his classics, and the mythologies from which the great books and plays of the ancients had been derived. In time he would discover dozens of images inspired by those same myths on the tiles. In one place women were depicted like the Maenads immortalized by Euripides; maddened souls in service of the god of ecstasies, Dionysus. They raced through the trees with bloody hands, leaving pieces of male flesh scattered in the grass. In another place, single-breasted Amazons strode, drawing back their mighty bows and letting fly storms of arrows.

There were other images – many, many others – that were not rooted in any recognizable mythology. In one spot, not far from the delta, huge fishes, which had sprouted legs covered with golden scales, came through the trees in solemn shoals, spitting fire. The trees ahead of them were aflame; burning birds rose up from the canopy.

In the swamp, a small town stood on long limbs, its

presence appearing to mark the position of some place that had existed there once but had been taken by time, or a prophecy of some settlement to come. The artists had taken liberties with the rendering, foreshortening the scene so that the occupants of the city were almost as big as their houses, and could be plainly seen. There were excesses here, too; perversities just as profound as anything the Wild Wood was hosting. Through one of the windows a man could be seen spread-eagled on a table, around which sat a number of guests, all watching a large worm enter him anally and then erupt from his open mouth. Another was the scene of a strange summoning, in which a host of black birds with human heads rose up from the ground, circling a girl-child who was either their invoker or their victim. In a third house a woman was squatting and shedding menstrual blood through a hole in the floor. Several men, smaller than the woman above by half, were swimming in the water below and undergoing some calamitous transformation, presumably brought on by the *menses*. Their heads had flowered into dark, monstrous shapes; demonic tails had sprouted from their backsides.

As Father Sandru had warned (or was it *boasted*?) to Zeffer, there was no part of the landscape depicted there on the walls that was not haunted by some bizarre sight or other. Even the clouds (innocent enough, surely) shat rains of fire in one place, and evacuated skulls in another. Demons cavorted unchallenged over the open sky, like dancers possessed by some celestial music, while stars fell between them; others rose over the horizon, leering like emaciated fools. And in that same sky, as though to suggest that this was a world of perpetual twilight, teetering always on the edge of darkness and extinction, was a sun that was three-quarters eclipsed by an exquisitely rendered moon, the latter painted so cunningly it seemed to have real mass, real roundness, as it slid over the face of the day-star.

In one place there was painted a line of crowned figures

– the kings and queens of Romania, back to ancient times – painted marching into the ground. The noble line rotted as it proceeded into the earth, carrion birds alighting on the descending lineage, plucking out regal eyes and law-giving tongues. In another place a circle of witches rose in a spiral from a spot marked by standing-stones; their innocent victims, babies whose fat had been used to make the flying ointment in which they had slathered themselves, lay scattered between the stones like neglected dolls.

And all through this world of monstrous hurts and occasional miracles, the Hunt.

Many of the scenes were simply documents of the vigorous beauty of the chase; they looked as though they could have been painted from life. There was a pack of dogs, white and black and pie-bald (one bitch charmingly attending to her suckling pups); some being muzzled by peasants, others straining on their leashes as they were led away to join the great assembly of hunters. Elsewhere, the dogs could be seen accompanying the hunters. Where the Duke had chosen to kneel and pray, a white dog knelt beside him, his noble head bowed by the weight of shared devotion. In another, the dogs were splashing in a river, attempting to catch the huge salmon outlined in the stylized blue waters. And in a third place, for no apparent reason but the playfulness of the artists, the role of dogs and men had been reversed. A long, beautifully decorated table had been set up in a clearing amongst the trees, and at it sat a number of finely-bred dogs, while at their booted feet naked men fought over scraps and bones. Closer examination showed the arrangement of figures to be even more anarchic than it first appeared, for there were thirteen dogs at the table, and in their centre sat one dog with a halo perched between his pricked ears: a canine Last Supper. An informed observer, knowing the traditional positions of the Apostles, could have named them all. The writers of the Gospels were there in their accustomed seats; John sitting closest to his master,

Judas sitting at the perimeter of the company, while Peter (a Saint Bernard) brooded at the other end, his furrowed brow suggesting he already knew he would betray his master three times before the long night was over.

Elsewhere in the landscape, the dogs were painted at far crueller work. Tearing rabbits apart in one place, and ripping the flesh from a cornered stag in another. In a third they were in a contest with a lion, and many had been traumatically injured by the battle. Some crawled away from the place, trailing their bowels; one had been thrown up into the trees, and its corpse hung there, tongue lolling. Others lay sprawled in the grass in pools of blood. The hunters kept their distance, no doubt waiting for the lion to become so weakened by blood-loss that they could close in and claim the heroic moment for themselves.

But the most perverse of all the scenes were those in which erotic love and hunting were conjoined.

There was, for instance, a place where the dogs had driven a number of naked men and women up a gorge, where they had encountered a group of hunters armed with spears and nets. The terrified couples clung to one another, but the netters and the spearers knew their business. Men were separated from women and the men were run through with spears, the women all bundled up in the nets, heaped on carts, and carried away. The sexual servitude that awaited them was of a very particular kind. Reading the walls from left to right the viewer's eye found that in an adjacent valley the women were freed from the nets and strapped beneath the bodies of massive centaurs, their legs stretched around the flanks of the animals.

The women's response to this terrible violation was something the artists had taken some trouble to detail. One was screaming in agony, her head thrown back, as blood ran from the place where she was being divided. Others appeared to be in ecstasy at this forced marriage, pressing their faces joyously to the necks of their deflowerers.

But this part of the story did not finish there. If the 'reader', scanning these walls, had continued his enquiry, he would have found that some of the men had survived the massacre in the gorge, and returned, on a later sequence of tiles, to hunt the creatures that had their wives in sexual thrall. These were some of the most brilliantly painted sequences on the walls: the surviving lovers returning on horseback, so as to match their speed to that of the centaurs. Lassoes circling in the air over their heads, they closed on the centaurs, who were slowed down by the very women they carried around to pleasure them. Several were brought down by ropes around the neck, others were speared in the throat or flank. The women they carried were not always lucky in these encounters. Though no doubt their rescuers intended to free them, it was often the case that they perished beneath the weight of their violators, as the dying centaurs rolled over, crushing them. Perhaps there was some moral here – some lesson about the vulnerability of the innocent women when two tribes of males were set against one another; but the artists seemed to take too much grisly pleasure in their depictions for this to be the case. Rather, it appeared to be done for the pleasure of the doing; of the imagining, and of the rendering. There was no moral from one end of this world to the other.

It would be possible to go on listing at great length the horrors and the spectacles of the scenes laid out on the tiles: the fields of dancing demons, the fairy races, the succubi squatting on roofs, the holy fools draped in coats of cow-dung, the satyrs, the spirits of graveside, roadside and hearthside; the weasel-kings and the bloated toads; and so on, and so on, behind every tree and on every cloud, sliding down every waterfall and lingering beneath every rock: a world haunted by the shapes of lust and animal lust and all that humanity called to its bosom in the long nights of its despair.

45

Though Hollywood – even in its fledgling years – was presenting itself to the world as the very soul of the imagination, there was nothing going on before the cameras there (nor would there be, ever) that could compete with what the master tile-painters and their apprentices had created.

It was, as Sandru has said, the Devil's Country.

Zeffer went to Brascov to hire men, at prices five or six times what he would have paid locally, because he wanted hands that could do the job with some finesse, and minds that could count to a higher number than their fingers. He devised the means by which the masterpiece could be removed himself. The tiles were meticulously numbered on the reverse sides and a huge legend made of the room by three cartographers he had also hired in the city, so that there would be a meticulous record of the way the design had been laid out; and an obsessive accounting of how the tiles were numbered, stacked and packed away; including a detailed description of which tiles were cracked or damaged before they were packed, which had been mislaid by the original tilers (there were a hundred and sixteen such tiles; most turned ninety or a hundred and eighty degrees by an artisan too tired, too bewildered or perhaps too drunk to realize his error); all so that when the tiles were unpacked at the house in Coldheart Canyon there would be no difficulty reordering them into the original design.

It was a long process; a total of eleven weeks were to pass before the crated tiles were finally transported from the Fortress.

All the work had drawn much attention of course; from the brothers themselves, who knew what was going on because Father Sandru had told them, and from the villagers, who had only the vaguest of ideas of what all this was about. There were rumours flying around that the removal was being undertaken because the tiles had put the souls of the Fathers in spiritual jeopardy, but precise details of this jeopardy changed from account to account.

The vast sum of money that was now in the possession of the Order did very little to transform the lives of the priests, apart from inspiring some of the most embittered exchanges in the history of the brotherhood. Several of the priests were of the opinion that the tiles should not have been sold (not because of their merit, but because it was not wise to loose such unholy images on the secular world). To this, Father Sandru – who was more often, and more publicly, drunk by the day – offered only a sneering dismissal.

What does it matter?, he said to the complainers: *they are only tiles, for God's sake.*

There were a good number of shaken heads by the way of response, and a very eloquent riposte from one of the older Fathers, who said that God had put the tiles into their protection, and it was cynical and careless of him to let them go. What damage might they not do, out there in the world, he said; what hurt to innocent souls?

Sandru was unmoved by all this. There *were* no innocent souls in Hollywood, he had learned; nor was there any sin or excess painted in the tiles that the people of that city were not intimately familiar with. He spoke with an authority which he didn't in truth possess, but it sufficiently impressed the brothers – or at least a greater number of them – so that the nay-sayers were finally silenced.

There was much debate about what should happen to the money. One faction, led by the older men, believed it had been acquired by dubious means, and the only uncorrupted way to dispose of it was to distribute it amongst the poor. Surprisingly, very few voices supported this solution; *some* part of the money might be given to the needy in the village, the priests agreed, but there were other causes that should be attended to. There was some lobbying for a complete removal of the Order to some other place than the Fortress; a more comfortable place, where they could find their way to God without the Devil's shadow falling across their path. It was Sandru who was the most eloquent advocate of their staying in the Fortress. His tongue well lubricated with brandy, he explained that he felt no sense of regret that he'd sold the tiles; it was a once-in-a-lifetime opportunity, and he was glad he'd taken it. Now, he said, they should use the money to rejuvenate the place. Get the hospital up and running, as had always been the plan; see what they could do about refertilizing the land, so that the vineyards would prosper as they had in the old days.

'Our path is perfectly clear!' he said to the brothers. 'Whether our faith in the Lord is secure or not, we can heal here, and we can grow the grape, and pass our lives with purpose.'

He smiled as he spoke. That word – *purpose* – had not been on his lips for many years, and it gave him pleasure to speak it. But even as he spoke the smile started to die away, and the colour shrank from his ruddy face.

'I beg you to excuse me,' he said, putting his hand to his belly, 'I am sickened by too much brandy.'

With that he pulled out of his robes the bottle from which he had been drinking since early morning, and set it clumsily down on the table in front of him. Then he turned and stumbled out to get a breath of fresh air. Nobody went after him; he had no friends left in the Fortress. His old allies were too embarrassed by his excesses to publicly share his opinions; fearful that his behaviour might reflect poorly on them, and keep them from advancement. So he was alone as he wandered giddily through the ruins of the dead vines. It was evening, and now that the summer was past, the air was beginning to get chilly. But the sky overhead was a perfect blue, and there was a new moon, its pallid crescent just clearing the mountains.

Sandru tried to let the sight of the sky and moon calm him; have them placate the pain of his heart, give life back to his numbed fingers. But the trick was beyond them. He realized suddenly that this was not a spasm brought on by too much brandy. He was dying.

The brothers had medicines for weakness of the heart, he knew; it would not be the end of him if he got back to them quickly enough. He turned on his heel, attempting to voice a shout of alarm. But his panicked chest would provide no breath for him to cry for help. His legs began to fail him, and down he went, face first, into the earth. He tasted the soil in his mouth, bitter and unappetizing. He spat it out; and with the last of his strength he pushed himself up out of the filth and let gravity roll him over.

He could not move, but it didn't matter. The darkening sky overhead was spectacle enough. He lay there for six or seven shortening gasps, while a star, lonely in its solitude, brightened at his zenith. Then he let life go.

The brothers did not find him until the middle of the night, by which time a frost had settled on the old vineyard, the first frost of that autumn. It glittered on the bulk of the dead Father; on his bulbous nose and in the knots of his beard. It had even inscribed its filigrees on his unblinking eyes.

4

There was no hospital established at the Fortress; then or ever. Nor was there any attempt to replant the vineyard, or make the grounds around the Fortress in any way flourish. With Father Sandru's passing (at the relatively tender age of sixty-two), what little enthusiasm there had been for change withered. The younger men decided to leave the Fortress; three of them left the Order entirely and became members of the secular community. Of the three, one – a young man by the name of Jan Valek took his own life less than a year later, leaving a long suicide note, a kind of epistle to his sometime brothers, in which he wrote of how he'd had a dream after the death of Father Sandru, in which *I met the Father in the vineyards, which were all burning. It was a terrible place to be. Black smoke was filling the sky, blotting out the sun. He said to me that this was Hell, this world, and there was only one way to escape it, and that was to die. His face was bright, even in the darkness. He said he wished he'd died earlier, instead of going on suffering in the world.*

'I asked him if they allowed him to drink brandy wherever he was now. He said he had no need of brandy; his existence was happy; there was no need to conceal the pain with drinking.

'Then I told him I still had a life to live in the world, whereas he had been an old man, with a weak heart. I was strong, I said, and there was a good chance I'd be alive for another thirty, maybe forty years, which was an agony to me, but what could I do?

' "So take your own life," he said to me. He made it sound so simple. "Cut your throat. God understands."

' "He does?" I said to him.

' "Certainly," he told me. "This world is Hell. Just look around.
What do you see?"

'I told him what I saw. Fire, smoke, black earth.

' "See?" he said. "Hell."

'I told him, though of course I was still dreaming, I was going
to take his advice. I was going to go back to my room, find a sharp
knife, and kill myself. But for some reason, as often happens in
dreams, I didn't go home. I went into Bucharest. To the cinema
where Brother Stefan used to bring me sometimes, to see films.
We went inside. It was very dark. We found seats and Stefan had
me sit down. Then the film began. And it was a film about some
earthly paradise. It made me weep, it was so perfect, this place.
The music, the way the people looked. Beautiful men and women,
all so lovely it took my breath away to look at them. There was
one young man in particular – and it makes me ashamed to write
this, but if I don't do it here, in my last confession, where will I
do it? – a young man with dark hair and light-filled eyes, who
opened his arms to me. He was naked, on the screen, with open
arms, inviting me into his embrace. I turned to Father Stefan in
the darkness, and he said the very thing that was going through
my mind. "He wants to take you into his arms."

'I started to deny it. But Stefan interrupted me and said: "Look
at him. Look at his face. It's flawless. Look at his body. It's perfect.
And there – between his legs –"

'I covered my face in shame, but Stefan pulled my hands from
my face and told me not to be ashamed, just to look, and enjoy
looking. "God made all of this for our pleasure," he said. "Why
would he give us such a hunger to look at nakedness unless he
wanted us to take pleasure in it?"

'I asked Stefan how he knew it was God's work. Perhaps the
Devil had made nakedness, I said, to tempt us and ensnare us.
He laughed, and put his arm around me, and kissed me on the
cheek as though I was just a little child.

' "This isn't the Devil's work," he said. "This is your invitation
to paradise." Then he kissed me again, and I felt a warm wind

51

blowing, as though it was spring in whatever country they had created on the screen. And the wind made me want to die with pleasure, because it smelled of a time I remembered from long ago.

'So now I have come back to my room. I have a knife. When I have finished writing this I will leave what I have written on the table, and I will go out into the field, and cut my wrists. I know we are taught that self-slaughter is a sin, and that the Lord does not wish us to harm ourselves, but if He does not wish me to end my life, why is this knife within reach of my hand, and why is my heart so much at peace?'

His body was found about a hundred yards from the place where Sandru's frost-covered body had been discovered. Coming so soon upon the death of the old priest, the death of Jan Valek undid the Brotherhood completely. Orders came from Bucharest, and the Brotherhood was disbanded. There was no need to guard the Fortress any longer, the Archbishop said. The brothers would be more useful to the Church if they worked with the sick and the dying, to offer the Lord's comfort where it was most needed.

Within a week, the Order of St Teodor had left the Fortress Goga.

There were those among the villagers who felt that the Fortress had invited its abandonment, and began its own process of self-slaughter. Superstition, no doubt; but it was certainly strange that after five centuries of life, during which span it had remained strong, a quick process of disintegration should begin as soon as the community of caretakers departed.

True, the winter immediately following was particularly severe. But there had been heavier snows on the roofs and they had not bowed beneath the weight; there had been stronger winds through the casements and they'd not broken open and smashed, there had been more persistent floodings of the lower floors, and the doors had not been carried off on their rotted hinges.

By the time the spring came round – which was late April that year – the Fortress had effectively become uninhabitable. It was as though its soul had gone out of it, and now all it wanted was to allow the seasons to take their steady toll. They were guileless collaborators. The summer was as violently hot as the winter had been bitter, and it bred all manner of destroyers in the fabric of the building. Worm and fly and wasp contributed to the baking heat of the sun with their burrowings and layings and nestings. Beams that had taken ten men to lift them became dusty, hollow things, as delicate as the bones of immense birds. Unable to support their own weight, they collapsed upon themselves, bringing down entire floors as they fell. By the time September arrived, the Fortress was open to the elements. The ward where the brothers had optimistically laid out rows of beds now had a ceiling of cloud. When the first rains of autumn came the mattresses were soaked; fungus and mildew sprouted where the sick would have lain. The place stank of rot from end to end.

And finally, somewhere in the middle of the second winter in its empty state, the floorboards cracked and opened up, and the lowest level of the Fortress, the level where Father Sandru had brought Zeffer to show him the tiled chamber, became available to sky and storm. If anyone had ventured into the Fortress that winter they would have witnessed the most delicate of spectacles. Through the eight vaults above the once-tiled room – which were now all cracked like eggs – snow came spiralling down. It fell into a room denuded. The workmen Zeffer had hired to do the work of removing the tiles had first been obliged to empty the room of all the monks had left in there. Some of the furniture had subsequently been stolen, some broken up for firewood, and the rest – perhaps a quarter of the bounty – simply left to decay where it had been piled up. The snow settled in little patches on the floor; patches which would not melt for the next four months, but only get wider and deeper as the winter's storms got worse, the snow heavier.

Just before the thaw, in the middle of the following April, the weight of snow and ice finally brought the vaults down, in one calamitous descent. There was nobody there to witness it, nor anyone within earshot to hear it. The room which had contained the Hunt was buried in the debris of all the vaults, plaster and wood and stone filling the chamber to the middle of the walls. Nobody who visited the Fortress in subsequent years – and there were a few explorers who came there every summer, usually imagining they'd stumbled on something darkly marvellous – a Fortress, perhaps, belonging to Vlad the Impaler, whose legendary territories lay only a few hundred miles off to the west, in Transylvania – none of these visitors dug through the overgrown ruins with any great enthusiasm; certainly none ever asked themselves what function the half-buried room might have once served. Nor, should it be said, would they have been able to guess, even the cleverest of them. The mystery of the ruined chamber had been removed to another continent, where it was presently unfolding its dubious raptures for the delectation of a new and vulnerable audience. Men and women who – like the tiles – had in many cases lately left their homelands; and in their haste to be famous left behind them such talismans as hearth and altar might have offered by way of protection against the guileful Hunt.

PART TWO

THE HEART-THROB

1

There's a premiere in Los Angeles tonight, at Grauman's Chinese Theatre. The Chinese has been housing such events since 1923, but of course the crowds were much larger back then, tens of thousands of people, sometimes even hundreds of thousands, would block Hollywood Boulevard in their hunger to see the star of the moment. Tonight's event is nowhere near that scale. Though the studio publicists will massage the numbers for tomorrow's *Variety* and *Hollywood Reporter*, claiming that a crowd of four thousand people waited in the chilly evening air for the appearance of the star of tonight's movie, Todd Pickett, the true numbers are in fact less than half that.

Still, a third of the Boulevard is barricaded off, and there are a few cop cars in evidence, just to give the whole event more drama.

As the limos approach the red carpet, and the ushers, who are dressed in the black leather costumes of the villains in the movie, step forward to open the doors a few 'screamers', paid and planted in the crowd by the studio publicity people to get a little excitement going, start to do their job, yelling even before the face of the limo's passenger has been seen. There's a large contingent of A-list names on tonight's guest-list, and plenty of faces that elicit screams as they appear. Cruise isn't here, but Nicole Kidman is; so is Schwarzenegger, who has a small role in the picture as the retiring Gallows, a vengeful, mythological character whom our hero, played by Todd Pickett, must either choose to embody when his time comes round, or – should he refuse – be pursued by the ghosts of several generations of former incarnations of the character, to persuade him otherwise. Sigourney Weaver plays the woman who has broken the curse of Gallows once before, to whom Pickett's character must go when the phantom pursuers are almost upon him. Her arrival at Grauman's is greeted by a genuine roar of approval from the fans, who are devoted to her. She waves, smiles, allows a barrage of photographs to be taken, but she doesn't go near the crowd. She's had experiences with overly-possessive fans before: she walks straight down the middle of the red carpet, where she's out of reach of their fingers. Still they shout, '*We love you Ripley!*', which is the character she plays in the *Alien* movies, and with which she will be identified until the day she dies. She waves, even when they call the name Ripley, but her eyes never focus on anybody in the crowd for more than a moment.

The next limo in the line contains the bright new star of *Gallows*, Suzie Henstell, named by this month's *Vanity Fair* one of the Ten Hottest Names in Hollywood. She is petite (though you'd never know it on the screen), blonde and giggly; she's shared a little marijuana with her boyfriend in the limo, and it was a bad move. She stumbles a little as she steps onto the red carpet, but the crowd has been prepped, thanks to several months of puff pieces and photo-spreads and in-depth interviews, to think of this woman as a full-blown star, even though they have yet to see more than a few frames of her acting ability from the trailer for *Gallows*. So what do they care if she looks a little out of it? Unlike Ms Weaver, who wisely chooses to be elusive, allowing the photographers just a minute or two to catch her, the new girl is still hungry for adulation. She goes straight to the barricades, where a number of young women with souvenir programmes for *Gallows* are waving them around. She signs a few, giving her boyfriend, who is a six-foot Calvin Klein model hunk, a goofy 'gee-I-must-be-famous!' look. The model looks back vacantly, which is the only look in his repertoire. He can give it to you vacantly with a semi hard-on in his jeans, or vacantly with his ass hanging out of his Y-fronts. Either way, it is heart-achingly beautiful; almost troublingly so.

The wind comes in gusts along Hollywood Boulevard, and the security men start to look a little worried. It was some bright publicist's idea to build two gallows, as a kind of gateway through which the audience for the premiere will need to come. Not, it now seems, a clever notion. The gallows are made to be trashed tomorrow morning, so they're made of light timber and foam-core. The wind is threatening to topple them; or worse, pick them up entirely and deposit them on top of the crowd. Light though they are, they could do some serious damage if they fell.

Four of the ushers from inside the theatre are summoned from their duties and told to go and stand beside the gallows, two on either side, holding on to them as casually as possible. Security is told that the publicity people only need five more minutes. As soon as Suzie Henstell can be persuaded to move on up the carpet and into the building (which at present she is showing no desire to do), the director's, Rob Neiderman's, limo can be brought to the carpet, followed by the last and most important of the bunch, Todd Pickett.

The wind is getting worse; the gallows sway giddily. An executive decision is made to bring Neiderman's limo in, and if Suzie's screaming fans are visible waving like lunatics behind Neiderman in his press pictures, so be it. This isn't a perfect world. It's already 8:13p.m. At this rate the picture won't be able to begin until half past the hour, which wouldn't be a problem if the damn thing weren't so long, but Neiderman's cut came in at two hours and forty-three minutes, and though the studio appealed to Pickett to get him to shave the thing down to a tight two hours, Todd came back saying he liked the picture pretty much as it was, so only four minutes were going out of it. That means it'll be past eleven before the picture's finished, and almost midnight by the time everybody's assembled at the party venue. It's going to be a long night.

Neiderman has persuaded the easily-distracted Miss Henstell away from her fans and down the carpet to the door. The big moment is at hand. The ushers cling to the gallows, their jobs depending on the perpendicularity of their charges. The largest of the limos comes up to the kerb. Even before the door has opened, the fans – especially the women – are in a state of ecstasy, shrieking at the top of their voices.

'Todd! Todd! Oh God! Todd!'

The cameras start to flash, as though the incomprehensible semaphore of their flashes is going to summon the man in the limo.

And out comes Todd Pickett, the star of *Gallows*, the reason why ninety-five percent of its audience will be there when it opens next Friday (it is now Monday); Todd Pickett, one of the three biggest male action-movie-stars in the history of cinema. Todd Pickett, the boy from Cincinnati who failed in all his grades but ended up the King of Hollywood.

He raises his hands like a presidential candidate, to acknowledge the shouts of the crowd. Then he reaches back into the limo to catch hold of the hand of his date for the night, Wilhemina Bosch, a waitress-turned-model-turned-actress-turned-model again, with whom he has been seen at parties and premieres for the past four months, though neither will say anything about the relationship than that they're good friends.

He gathers Wilhemina to him, so that the photographers can get pictures of them together. Then arm in arm, through the blizzard of lights and the barrage of *We love you, Todd*! coming at them from every side, the pair make their way to the cinema doors, which – having gathered their most

60

important guests into the fold, then close rather defiantly, as if to divide the important from the unimportant, the stable and the solid from those who are simply objects of the night's wind.

Gallows is an irredeemable piece of shit, of course, and everyone involved with it, from the executives who green-lit it (at a cost of some ninety-million dollars, before prints and advertising costs add another thirty-seven to the bill) to the humblest publicist, knows.

It is, in the words of Corliss's review in *Time*, '*an old fashioned action-horror picture which lacks the full-bone theatrics of grand guignol, and the savvy, John-Woo-style action piece audiences have come to expect. One minute Schwarzenegger is camping it up, the next Todd Pickett, as his unwilling successor, is playing his scenes as though he's Hamlet on a particularly dreary night in Denmark. From beginning to end,* Gallows *is bad noose.*'

Everybody going up the red carpet that Monday night already knows what *Time* is going to say; Corliss had made his contempt for the picture very plain in a piece about the state of action movies he wrote two weeks before. Nor does it take an oracle to predict that there will be others who will not like the picture. But the extent of vitriol will prove astonishing, even to those who expected the worst. In the next forty-eight hours, *Gallows* will garner some of the most negative reviews of the last twelve months, the vehemence of the early news reviewers empowering minor names to pull out the stops. Besides the incomprehensible script, everyone agrees, there is a lacklustre quality to the picture that betrays the cast's indifference to the entire project. Performances aren't simply uneven, they seemed designed for entirely different movies: a hopeless mismatch of styles. The worst culprit in this regard? There is no question about that. All the reviewers will agree that the most inadequate performance comes from its star, Todd Pickett.

People writes that: '*Mr Pickett is plenty old enough to know better. Thirty-something-year-olds don't act the way Mr Pickett acts here: his trademark "young man with a chip on his shoulder and a thousand-watt smile," which was looking stale the second (all right, the third) time he did it, seems particularly out-of-place here. Though it seems incredible that time has passed so fast since America first swooned to the charms of Mr Pickett – he's now simply too old to play the twenty-something Vincent. Only Wilhemina Bosch, as Vincent's Prozac-chewing sister, comes out of this mess with any credibility. She has an elegant, beautifully-proportioned face, and she can turn a line with the snappy, East-coast smarts of a young Katharine Hepburn. She's wasted here. Or, more correctly, our time would be wasted here were she not in the movie.*'

The premiere audience didn't seem to mind it. On occasion there were audible gasps and loud laughter (perhaps in truth a little *over*-loud, a little fake) for the jokes, but there were several long stretches in the Second Act, when the movie seemed to lose their interest. Even in the Third Act, when the action relocates to the orbiting space station, and the special effects budget soared, there was very little real enthusiasm. A few scattered whoops of nihilistic delight when the villain's planet-destroying weapon actually went off, against expectation, and Washington DC is fried to a crisp. But then, as the smoke cleared and Todd, as the new Gallows, proceeded to finish off the bad guys, the audience became restless again.

About fifteen minutes before the end credits rolled a member of the audience got up from his seat on the aisle and went to the bathroom. A few people caught a look at the man's face as he looked back at the screen. It was Todd Pickett, lit by the light of his own face. Nobody got up to ask for his autograph.

Pickett stared at the screen for a moment only, then he turned his back on it and trudged up and out of the cinema. He didn't go to the restroom. Instead he asked one of the ushers if he could be allowed out of the back of the building. The usher explained that the area around the back had no security.

'I just want a quiet smoke with nobody watching me,' Todd explained.

The usher said, sure, why not, and led Todd down a passageway that ran behind the screen. Todd looked up at his reversed image on the screen. All he could remember about the scene that was playing was how damn uncomfortable his costume had been.

'Here you go,' the usher said, unlocking the doors at the end of the corridor, and letting Todd out into an area lit only by the ambient light from the Boulevard.

'Thanks,' Todd said, giving him a twenty-buck bill. 'I'll be back out front by the time the credits roll.'

The usher thanked him for the twenty note and left him to himself.

Todd took out a cigarette, but it never got to his lips. A wave of nausea overtook him, so powerful and so sudden that it was all he could do not to puke down his own tuxedo. Up came the scotches he'd had in the limo as he drove on down to the premiere, and the pepperoni pizza, with three cheeses and extra anchovies, he'd had to add ballast. With the first heave over (something told him there were more to come) he had the presence of mind to look around, and confirm that this nasty little scene was not being spied on, or worse, photographed. Luckily, he was alone. All he had for company back here was the detritus of premieres past; piles of standees and gaudy scenery pieces designed to advertise movies gone by: Mel Gibson against an eruption of lurid flame; Godzilla's eye; the bottom half of a girl in a very short dress. He got to his feet and stumbled away from the stench of his vomit, making his way through this graveyard of old glories, heading for the darkest place he could find in which to hide his giddy head. Behind him, through the still-open door, he could hear the sound of gunfire, and the muted sound of his own voice:

'Come on out, you sonofabitch,' he was yelling to somebody. By now, if the movie had been working, the audience would have been yelling and screaming, wild with bloodlust. But despite the over-amped soundtrack, nobody was yelling, because nobody gave a damn. The movie was dying on its feet.

Another wave of nausea rose up in him. He reached out to catch hold of something so that he didn't fall down and his outstretched hand knocked over a cardboard cut-out of Tom Cruise, which toppled backwards and hit a cardboard *Titanic*, which in turn crashed against a cardboard *Mighty Joe Young*, and so on and so forth, like a row of candy-coloured dominoes, stars falling against ships falling against monsters, all toppling back into a darkness so deep they were an indistinguishable heap.

Luckily, the noise of his vomiting was covered by the din of his own movie. He puked again, twice, until his stomach had nothing left to give up. Then he turned his back on the vomit and the toppled idols, and stepped away to find a lungful of clean air to inhale. The worst was over. He lit his cigarette, which helped settle his stomach, and rather than returning inside, where the picture was two minutes from finishing, he walked along the side of the building until he found a patch of street-light where he could assess himself. He was lucky. His suit was unspattered. There was a spot of vomit on his shoes, but he cleaned it off with his handkerchief (which he tossed away) and then sprayed his tongue and throat with wintergreen breath-cleanser. His hair was cropped short (that was the way it was in the movie, and he'd kept the style for public appearances), so he had no fear that it was out of place. He probably looked a little pale, but what the hell? Pale was in.

There was a gate close to the front of the building,

guarded by a security officer. She recognized Todd immediately, and unlocked the gate.

'Getting out before it gets too crazy?' she said to him. He smiled and nodded. 'You want an escort to your car?'

'Yeah, thanks.'

One of the executive producers, an over-eager Englishman called George Dipper, with whom Todd had never worked before, was standing on the red carpet, his presence ignored by the press, who were standing around chatting to one another, or checking their cameras before the luminaries reappeared. George caught Todd's eye, and hurried over, dragging on his own cigarette as though his life depended on its nicotine content.

There was scattered applause from inside, which quickly died away. The picture was over.

'I think it played brilliantly,' George said, his eyes begging for a syllable of agreement. 'They were with us all the way. Don't you think so?'

'It was fine,' Todd said, without commitment.

'Forty million, the first weekend.'

'Don't get your hopes up.'

'You don't think we'll do forty?'

'I think it'll do fine.'

George's face lit up. Todd Pickett, the man he'd paid twenty million dollars to (plus a sizeable portion of the back-end) was declaring it *fine*. God was in His Heaven. For a terrible moment Todd thought the man was going to weep with relief.

'At least there's nothing big opening against it,' Todd said. 'So we've got one weekend clear.'

'And your fans are loyal,' George said. Again, the desperation in the eyes.

Todd couldn't bear to look at him any longer.

'I'm just goin' to make a quick getaway,' Todd said, glancing towards the theatre doors.

The first of the crowd were emerging. If the expressions

on the first five faces he scanned were an omen, his instincts were right: they did not have a hit. He turned his back on the crowd, telling George he'd see him later.

'You *are* coming to the party?' George said, hanging on to him as he headed down the carpet.

Where was Marco? Todd thought. Trusty Marco, who was always there when he was needed. 'Yes, I'll pop in later,' he said, glancing back over his shoulder at George to reassure him.

In the seconds since he'd turned away the audience spilling from the theatre door had jumped from five to a hundred. Half of them saw him. In just a few seconds they'd be surrounding him, yelling his name, telling him they loved this and they hated that, touching him, pulling on him –

'*Here, boss!*'

Marco called to him from the kerb. The limo door was open. God bless him! Todd raced down the carpet as people behind him started to call his name; cameras started to flash. Into the limo. Marco slammed the door. Todd locked it. Then Marco dashed around to the driver's seat with a remarkable turn of speed given his poundage, and got in.

'Where to?'

'Mulholland.'

Mulholland Drive winds through the city like a lazy serpent for many miles; but Marco didn't need to know where along its length his boss wanted to be taken. There was a spot close to Coldwater Canyon, where the undulating drive offers a picture-perfect view of the San Fernando Valley, as far as the mountains. By day it can be a smog-befouled spectacle, brown and grey. But by night, especially in the summer, it is a place of particular enchantment: the cities of Burbank, North Hollywood and Pasadena laid out in a matrix of amber lights, receding to the dark wall of the mountains. And moving against the darkness, the lights of planes circling as they await their instruction to land at Burbank Airport, or the police helicopters passing over the city, spitting a beam of white light.

Often there were sightseers parked at the spot, enjoying the scene. But tonight, thank God, there were none. Marco parked the car and Todd got out, wandering to the cliff-edge to look at the scene before him.

Marco got out too, and occupied his time with wiping the windshield of the limo. He was a big man with the bearded face of a bear recently woken from hibernation, and he possessed a curious mixture of talents: a sometime wrestler and ju-jitsu black belt, he was also a trained Cordon Bleu cook (not that Todd's taste called for any great culinary sophistication) and a twice-divorced father of three with an encyclopaedic knowledge of the works of Wagner. More importantly, he was Todd's right-hand man; loyal to a fault. There was no part of Todd's existence Marco Caputo did not have some part of. He took care of the hiring and firing of domestic staff and gardeners, the buying and the driving of cars, and of course all the security duties.

'The movie's shit, huh?' he said matter-of-factly.

'Worse than.'

'Sorry 'bout that.'

'Not your fault. I should never have done it. Shit script. Shit movie.'

'You want to give the party a miss?'

'Nah. I gotta go. I promised Wilhemina. And George.'

'You got something going with her?'

'Wilhemina? Yeah. I got something. I just don't know whether I want to. Plus she's got an English boyfriend.'

'The English are all fags.'

'Yeah.'

'You want me to swing by the party and bring her back up to the house for you?'

'Suppose she says no?'

'Oh *come on*. When did any girl say no to you?'

67

Todd said nothing. He just stared out over the vista of lights. The wind came up out of the valley, smelling of gas fumes and Chinese food. The Santa Anas, hot off the Mojave, gusted against his face. He closed his eyes to enjoy the moment, but what came into his head was an image of himself: a still from the movie he'd fled from tonight. He studied the face in his mind's eye for a moment.

Then he said: 'I look tired.'

Todd Pickett had made two of his three most successful pictures under the aegis of a producer by the name of Keever Smotherman. The first of them was called *Gunner*; the kind of high concept, testosterone-marinated picture Smotherman had been renowned for making. It had made Todd – who was then an unknown from Ohio a bona fide movie star, if not overnight then certainly within a matter of weeks. He hadn't been required to turn in a performance. Smotherman didn't make movies that required actors, only breath-taking physical specimens. And Todd was certainly that. Every time he stepped before the cameras, whether he was sharing the scene with a girl or a fighter-plane, he was all the eye wanted to watch. The camera worked some kind of alchemy upon him; and he worked the same magic on celluloid.

In life, he was good-looking, but flawed. He was a little on the short side, with broad hips; he was also conspicuously bandy. But on the screen, all these flaws disappeared. He became gleaming, studly perfection, his jaw-line heroic, his gaze crystalline, his mouth an uncommon mingling of the sensual and the severe. His particular beauty had suited the taste of the times, and by the end of that first, extraordinary summer of coming-to-fame his image, dressed in an immaculate white uniform which made poetry of his buttocks, had become an indelible piece of cinema iconography.

Over the years, other stars had risen just as high, of

course, and many just as quickly. But few were quite as ready for their ascent as Todd Pickett. This was what he'd been polishing himself for since the moment his mother, Patricia Donna Pickett, had first taken him into a cinema in downtown Cincinnati. Looking up at the screen, watching the parade of faces pass before him, he'd known instinctively (at least so he later claimed) that he belonged up there with those stars, and that if he willed it hard enough, willed and worked for it, then it was merely a matter of time before he joined the parade.

After the success of *Gunner*, he fell effortlessly into the labours of being a movie star. In interviews he was courteous, funny and self-effacing, playing the interviewers so easily that all but the most cynical swooned. He was confident about his charms, but he wasn't cocky; loyal to his Mid-Western roots and boyishly devoted to his mother. Most attractive of all, he was honest about his shortcomings as an actor. There was a refreshing lack of pretension about the Pickett persona.

The year after *Gunner*, he made two pictures back to back. Another action blockbuster for Smotherman, called *Lightning Rod*, which was released on Independence Day and blew all former box-office records to smithereens, and then, for the Christmas market, *Life Lessons*. The latter was a sweetly sentimental slip of a story, in which Todd played opposite Sharon Campbell, a Playboy model turned actress who had been tabloid fodder at the time thanks to her recent divorce from an alcoholic and abusive husband. The pairing of Pickett and Campbell had worked like a charm, and the reviews for Todd's performance were especially kind. While he was still relying on his physical gifts, the critics observed, there were definitely signs that he was taking on the full responsibilities of an actor, digging deeper into himself to engage his audience. Nor was he afraid to show weakness; twice in *Life Lessons* he was required to sob like a baby, and he did so very convincingly. The picture was a huge hit, meaning that both of the big money-makers of the year had Todd's name above the title. He was officially box-office gold.

For most of the following decade he could do no wrong. Inevitably, some of his pictures performed better than others, but even the disappointments were triumphs by comparison with the fumbling labours of most of his contemporaries.

Of course, he wasn't making the choice of material on his own. From the beginning he'd had a close relationship with his manager, Maxine Frizelle, a short, sharp bitch of a woman in her mid-forties who'd once been voted the Most Despised Person in Hollywood, and had asked, when the news had reached her, if the awards ceremony was full evening dress. Though she'd been representing other clients when she first took Todd on, she'd let them all go once his career began to demand her complete attention. Thereafter she lived and breathed the Pickett business, controlling every element of his life, private and professional. The price she asked studios for his services rapidly rose to unheard-of heights, and she drove the deal home every single time. She had an opinion about everything: rewrites, casting, the hiring of directors, art-directors, costume designers and directors of photographers. Her only concern was the best interests of her wonder-boy. In the language of an older but similarly feudal system, she was the power behind the throne; and everyone who worked with Todd, from the heads of studios to humble hair-stylists, had some encounter with her to relate, some scar to show.

Needless to say, the Pickett magic couldn't remain unchallenged forever. There were always new stars in the ascendancy, new faces with the new smiles appearing on the screen every season, and after ten years of devotion the audience that had doted on Todd in the mid-to-late eighties began to look elsewhere for its heroes. It wasn't that his pictures performed less well, but that others performed even better. A new definition of a blockbuster had appeared; money-machines like *Independence Day* and *Titanic*, which earned so much so quickly that pictures which would once have been called major hits were now in contrast simply modest successes.

Anxious to regain the ground he was losing, Todd decided to go back into business with Smotherman, who was just as eager to return to their glory days together. The project they'd elected to do together was a movie called *Warrior*: a piece of high concept junk about a street-fighter from Brooklyn who is brought through time to champion a future earth in a battle against marauding aliens. The script was a ludicrous concoction of clichés pulled from every cheesy science-fiction B-movie of the fifties, and an early budget had put the picture somewhere in the region of a hundred million dollars simply to get it on screen, but Smotherman was confident that he could persuade either Fox or Paramount to green-light it. The show had everything, he said: an easily-grasped idea (primitive fighting man outwits hyper-intelligent intergalactic empire, using cunning and brute force); a dozen action sequences which called for state-of-the-art effects, and the kind of hero Todd could perform in his sleep: an ordinary man put in an extraordinary situation. It was a no-brainer, all round. The studios would be fools not to green-light it; it had all the marks of a massive hit.

He was nothing if not persuasive. In person, Smotherman was almost a parody of a high-voltage salesman: fast-talking, short-tempered and over-sexed. There was never an absence of 'babes', as he still called them, in his immediate vicinity; all were promised leading roles when they'd performed adequately for Smotherman in private, and all, of course, were discarded the instant he tired of them.

72

Preparations for *Warrior* were proceeding nicely. Then the unthinkable happened. A week shy of his forty-fourth birthday, Smotherman died. He'd always been a man of legendary excess, a bottom-feeder happiest in the gamier part of any city. The circumstances of his death were perfectly consistent with this reputation: he'd died sitting at a table in a private club in New York, watching a lesbian sex show, the coronary that had felled him so massive and so sudden he had apparently been overtaken by it before he could even cry out for help. He was face down in a pile of cocaine when he was found, a drug he'd continued to consume in heroic quantities long after his contemporaries had cleaned up their acts and had their sinuses surgically reconstructed. It was one of the thirty-five illegal substances found in his system at the autopsy.

He was buried in Las Vegas, according to the instructions in his will. He'd been happiest there, he'd always said, with everything to win and everything to lose.

This remark was twice quoted at the memorial service, and hearing it, Todd felt a cold trickle of apprehension pass down his spine. What Smotherman had known, and been at peace with, was the fact that all of Tinseltown was a game – and it could be lost in a heartbeat. Smotherman had been a gambling man. He'd taken pleasure in the possibility of failure and it had sweetened his success. Todd, on the other hand, had never even played the slots, much less a game of poker or roulette. Sitting there listening to the hypocrites – most of whom had despised Smotherman – stand up and extol the dead man, he realized that Keever's passing cast a pall over his future. The golden days were over. His place in the sun would very soon belong to others; if it didn't already.

The day after the memorial service he poured his fears out to Maxine. She was all reassurance.

'Smotherman was a dinosaur,' she said as she sipped her

vodka. 'The only reason people put up with his bullshit all those years was because he made everybody a lot of money. But let's be honest: he was a low-life. You're a class act. You've got nothing to worry about.'

'I don't know,' Todd said, his head throbbing from one too many drinks. 'I look at myself sometimes . . .'

'And what?'

'I'm not the guy I was when I made *Gunner*.'

'Damn right you're not. You were nobody then. Now you're one of the most successful actors in history.'

'There's others coming up.'

'So what?' Maxine said, waving his concerns away.

'Don't do that!' Todd said, slamming his palm down on the table. 'Don't try and placate me! Okay? *We have a problem*. Smotherman was going to put me back on top, and now the son of a bitch is dead!'

'All right. Calm down. All I'm saying is that we don't need Smotherman. We'll hire somebody to rework the script, if that's what you want. Then we'll find somebody hip to direct it. Somebody with a contemporary style. Smotherman was an old-fashioned guy. Everything had to be big. Big explosions. Big tits. Big guns. Audiences don't care about any of that any more. You need to be part of what's coming up, not what happened yesterday. You know, I hate to say it, but perhaps Keever's dying is the best thing that could have happened. We need a new look for you. A new Todd Pickett.'

'You think it's as simple as that?' Todd said. He wanted so much to believe that Maxine had the problem solved.

'How difficult can it be?' Maxine said. 'You're a great star. We just need to get people focussed on you again.' She pondered for a moment. 'You know what? We should set up a lunch with Gary Eppstadt.'

'Oh Jesus, why? You know how I hate that ugly little fuck.'

'An ugly little fuck he may be. But he is going to pay

for *Warrior*. And if he's going to put twenty million and a slice of the back-end on the table for your services to art, you can make nice with the son of a bitch for an hour.'

3

It wasn't simply personal antipathy that had made Todd refer to Eppstadt so unflatteringly. It was the unvarnished truth. Eppstadt was the ugliest man in Los Angeles. Charitably, his eyes might have been called reptilian, his lips unkissable. His mother, in a fit of blind affection, might have noted that he was disproportioned. All this said, the man was still a narcissist of the first rank. He hung only the most expensive suits on his unfortunate carcass: his fingernails were manicured with obsessive precision; his personal barber trimmed his dyed hair every morning, having shaved him first with a straight razor.

There had been countless prayers offered up to that razor over the years, entreating it to slip! But Eppstadt seemed to live a charmed life. He'd gone from strength to strength as he moved around the studios, claiming the paternity of every success, and blaming the failures on those who stood immediately behind him on the ladder, whom he promptly fired. It was the oldest trick in the book, but it had worked flawlessly. In an age in which corporations increasingly had the power, and studios were run by committees of business-school graduates and lawyers with an itch to have their fingers in the creative pie, Eppstadt was one of the old school. A powermonger, happiest in the company of somebody who needed his patronage, whom he could then abuse in a hundred subtle ways. That was his pleasure, and his revenge. What did he need beauty for, when he could make it tremble with a smiling *maybe*?

He was in a fine mood when he and Todd, with Maxine in attendance, met for lunch on Monday. Paramount had carried the weekend with a brutal revenge picture that Eppstadt had taken a hand in making, firing the director off the project after two unpromising preview screenings, and hiring somebody else to shoot a rape scene and a new ending, in which the violated woman terrorized and eventually dispatched her attacker with a hedge-cutter.

'Thirty-two point six million dollars in three days,' he preened. 'In *January*. That's a hit. And you know what? There's nobody *in* the picture. Just a couple no-name TV stars. It was all marketing.'

'Is the picture any good?' Todd asked.

'Yeah, it's fucking *Hamlet*,' Eppstadt said, without missing a beat. 'You're looking weary, my friend,' he went on. 'You need a vacation. I've been taking time at this monastery –'

'Monastery?'

'Sounds crazy, right? But you feel the peace. You feel the tranquillity. And they take Jews. Actually, I've seen more Jews there than at my nephew's Bar Mitzvah. You should try it. Take a rest.'

'I don't want to rest. I want to work. We need to set a start-date for *Warrior*.'

Eppstadt's enthusiastic expression dimmed. 'Oh, Christ. Is that what this little lunch is all about, Maxine?'

'Are you making it or not?' Todd pressed. 'Because there's plenty of other people who will if you won't.'

'So maybe you should take it to one of them,' Eppstadt said, his gaze hooded. 'You can have it in turnaround, if that's what you want. I'll get business affairs on it this afternoon.'

'So you're really ready to let it go?' Maxine said, putting on an air of indifference.

'Perfectly ready, if that's what Todd wants. I'm not going

to stand in the way of you getting the picture made. You look surprised, Maxine.'

'I *am* surprised. A package like that . . . it's a huge summer movie for Paramount.'

'Frankly I'm not sure this is the right time for the company to be making that kind of picture, Maxine. It's a very hard market to read right now. And these expensive pictures. I mean, this is going to come in at well north of a hundred thirty million by the time we've paid for prints and advertising. I'm not sure that makes solid fiscal sense.' He tried a smile; it was lupine. 'Look, Todd: I want to be in business with you. Paramount wants to be in business with you. Christ, you've been a gold-mine for us over the years. But there's a generation coming up – and you know the demographics as well as I do – these kids filling up the multiplexes, they don't have any loyalty to the *past*.'

Eppstadt knew what effect his words were having, and he was savouring every last drop of it.

'You see, in the good old days, the studios were able to *carry* stars through a weak patch. You had a star on a seven-year contract. He was being paid a weekly wage. You could afford a year or two of poor performance. But you're expensive, Todd. You're *crucifyingly* expensive. And I've got Viacom's shareholders to answer to. I'm not sure they'd want to see me pay you twenty million dollars for a picture that might only gross . . . what did your last picture do? Forty-one domestic? And change?'

Maxine sighed, a little theatrically. 'I'm sorry to hear that, Gary.'

'Look, Maxine, I'm sorry to be having to *say* it. Really I am. But numbers are numbers. If I don't believe I can make a profit, what am I doing making the movie? You see where I'm coming from? That simply doesn't make sense.'

Maxine got up from the table. 'Will you excuse me a minute? I've got to make a call.'

Eppstadt caught the fire in Maxine's voice.

'No lawyers, Maxine. *Please*? We can do this in a civilized manner.'

Maxine didn't reply. She simply stalked off between tables, snarling at a waiter who got in her way. Eppstadt ate a couple of mouthfuls of rare tuna, then put down his fork. 'It's times like this I wish I still smoked.' He sat back in his chair and looked hard at Todd. 'Don't let her start a pissing competition, Todd, because if I'm cornered I'm going to have to stand up and tell it like it is. And then we'll *all* have a mess on our hands.'

'Meaning what?'

'Meaning . . .' Eppstadt looked pained; as though his proctologist was at work on him under the chair. 'You can't keep massaging numbers so your price looks justified when we all know it isn't.'

'You were saying I'd been a gold-mine for Paramount. Just two minutes ago you said that.'

'That was then. This is now. That was Keever Smotherman, this is post-Keever Smotherman. He was the last of his breed.'

'So what are you saying?'

'Well . . . let me tell you what I'm *not* saying,' Eppstadt replied, his tone silky. 'I'm not saying you don't have a career.'

'Well that's nice to hear,' Todd said sharply.

'I want to find something we can do together. But . . .'

'But?'

Eppstadt seemed to be genuinely considering his reply before he spoke. Finally, he said: 'You've got talent, Todd. And you've obviously built a loyal fan-base over the years. What you *don't* have is the drawing power you had back in the old days. It's the same with all of you really expensive boys. Cruise. Costner. Stallone.' He took a moment, then leaned closer to Todd, dropping his voice to a conspiratorial whisper. 'You want the truth? You look weary. I mean, *deep down* weary.' Todd said nothing. Eppstadt's observation was like being doused in ice-cold water. 'Sorry to be blunt. It's not like I'm telling you something you don't already know.'

Todd was staring at his hand, wondering what it would feel like to make a fist and beat it against Eppstadt's face; over and over and over.

'Of course, you can have these things fixed,' Gary went on chattily. 'I know a couple of guys older than you who went to see Bruce Burrows and looked ten years younger when he was finished working on them.'

Still idly contemplating his hand, Todd said: 'Who's Bruce Burrows?'

'Well, in many people's opinion he's the best cosmetic surgeon in the country. He's got an office on Wilshire. Very private. Very expensive. But you can afford it. He does it all. Collagen replacements, lifts, peels, lipo-sculpture . . .'

'Who went to see him?'

'Oh, just about everybody. There's nothing to be ashamed of: it's a fact of life. At a certain age it's harder to get the lovehandles to melt. You get laugh-lines, you get frown lines, you get those little grooves around your mouth.'

'I haven't got grooves around my mouth.'

'Give it time,' Eppstadt said, a touch avuncular now.

'How long does it take?'

'I don't know. I've never had any of it done. If I went in there, I'd never get out again.'

'Too much to fix.'

'I think it's bad taste to jump on somebody else's self-deprecation, Todd. But I forgive you. I know it hurts to hear this. The fact is, I don't have to have my face out there fifty feet high. You do. That's what they're paying for.' He pointed at Todd. '*That face.*'

'If I was to get something done . . .' Todd said tentatively, 'about the lines, I mean?'

'Yes?'

80

'Would you make *Warrior* then?'

He had opened the door to Eppstadt's favourite word: '*Maybe*. I don't know. We'd have to see. But the way I look at it, you haven't got much to lose getting the work done anyway. You're a heart-throb. An old-fashioned heart-throb. They want to see you kick the shit out of the bad guy and get the girl. And they want their heart-throb perfect.' He stared at Todd. '*You need to be perfect*. Burrows can do that for you. He can make you perfect again. Then you get back to being King of the Hill. Which is what you want, I presume.'

Todd admitted it with a little nod, as though it were a private vice.

'Look, I sympathize,' Eppstadt went on, 'I've seen a lot of people just fold up when they lose their public. They come apart at the seams. You haven't done that. At least not yet.' He laid a hand on Todd's arm. 'You go have a word with Dr Burrows. See what he can do for you. Six months. Then we'll talk again.'

Todd didn't mention his discussion about Dr Burrows to Maxine. He didn't want the decision process muddied by her opinion. This was something he wanted to think through for himself.

Though he didn't remember having heard of Burrows before, he was perfectly aware he was living in the cosmetic surgery capital of the world. Noses were fixed, lips made fuller, crow's feet erased, ears pinned back, laugh-lines smoothed, guts tucked, butts lifted, breasts enhanced. Just about any piece of the anatomy which gave its owner ego problems could be improved, sometimes out of all recognition. Traditionally of course, it had been women who were the eager and grateful recipients of such handiwork, but that had changed. One of the eighties muscle-men, who'd made a fortune parading a body of superhuman proportions some years before, but had begun to lose it to gravity, had returned to the screen last year looking more pumped than ever, his perfect abdominals and swelling pectorals – even his sculpted calf muscles – surgically implanted. The healing had taken a little while, given the extensiveness of the remodelling. He'd been out of commission for five months – hiding in Tuscany, the gossip went – while he mended. But it had worked. He'd left the screen looking like a beaten-up catcher's mitt, and come back spanking new.

Todd began by making some very circuitous inquiries, the sort of questions which he hoped would not arouse suspicion. The word came back that the procedures were far from painless. Even legendary tough guys had ended up wishing they'd never invited the Drs to mess with them, the process had been so agonizing. And of course once you began, if you didn't like what you saw you had to let Burrows make some more fixes; wounds on wounds, pain on pain.

But Todd wasn't discouraged by the news. In fact in a curious way it made the idea of undergoing the procedures more palatable to him, playing as it did both into his machismo side and a deep, unexplored vein of masochism.

Besides, was there any pain on God's green earth as agonizing as reading *Daily Variety* and finding that once again you *weren't* in its pages? That other actors – names sometimes you'd never heard of – were getting the scripts, the parts and the deals that would once have dropped into your lap as a matter of course? There was no pain as sharp or as deep as the news of somebody else's success. If it was an actor older than himself that was bad enough. But if it was a contemporary – or worse, somebody *younger*, somebody *prettier* – it made him so crazy he'd have to go pop a tranquillizer or three to stop himself getting morose and foul-tempered. And even the happy pills didn't work the way they had in the old days. He'd taken too many; his body was too used to them.

82

So: what to do, what to do?

Should he sit on his slowly-expanding ass and start to avoid the mirror, or take the bull by the horns and get an appointment with Dr Burrows?

He remained undecided for about a week. And then one evening, sitting at home alone nursing a drink and flipping the channels of his sixty-inch TV, he came upon a segment from the telecast of last year's Oscar ceremony. A young actor, whom he knew for a fact was not one of the smartest bunnies in town, was receiving his third Oscar of the night, for a picture he had – at least according to the credits – written, directed and starred in. The latter? Well there was no disputing that. He was in every other frame of the damn picture, back-lit and golden. He was playing a stuttering, mentally unstable poor boy from the Deep South, a role which he claimed he had based on the life of his father's brother, who had died tragically at the hands of a lynch mob that had mistaken him for a rapist. It was all perfect Oscar-fodder: the ambitious young artist bucking the star system to tell a tale of the human spirit, rooted in his own family history.

Except that the truth was neither so moving nor so magical. Far from having been lynched, the 'dead' uncle was still very much alive, (or so gossip around town went) having spent twenty-two years in jail for a rape that he did not to this day contest. He had received a healthy pay-back from the studio that released the picture to stay conveniently quiet, so that his story could be told the Hollywood way, leaving the Golden Boy with his ten-thousand-watt smile to walk off with three Oscars for his mantelpiece. Todd had it on good authority that his directorial skills extended no further than knowing where his Winnebago was parked.

He wasn't the only one aspiring to snatch Todd's throne. There were plenty of others, chirpy little cock-suckers swarming out of the woodwork to play the King of Hollywood, when Todd had yet to vacate the role.

Well fuck 'em. He'd knock them off their stolen pedestals, the sons of bitches. He'd have the limelight back in a heartbeat – all that glory, all that love – and they'd be back on the casting couch in a week with their fannies in the air.

So what if it cost him a few weeks of discomfort? It would be worth it just to see the expressions on their pretty little faces when they realized they'd got greedy a decade too early.

Contrary to recent opinions, the King of the Heart-throbs was *not* dead. He was coming home, and he was going to look like a million dollars.

4

On the day Todd had booked to see Burrows for a first consultation, he had to cancel at the last minute.

'You're not going to believe my excuse,' he told the receptionist, 'but I swear it's the truth.'

'Go on.'

'My dog's sick.'

'Well that's not one we hear very often. So, gold star for originality.'

The fact was that Dempsey, his mutt, was not looking too good that morning; he'd got up to go out into the back yard for his morning piss and he'd stumbled, as though one of his legs was numb. Todd went down to see if he was okay. He wasn't. Though he still put on a happy face for his boss, his expression looked strangely dislocated, as though he was having difficulty focussing on Todd.

'What's wrong with you, boy?'

Todd went down on his haunches in front of the dog, and stroked his ears. Dempsey growled appreciatively. But he felt unsteady in Todd's arms; as though at any moment he might keel over.

Todd called Maxine and told her he'd be at the vet's for the next few hours.

'Something wrong with that flatulent old dog of yours?'

'You'll be flatulent when you get to his age,' Todd said. 'And yeah. There *is* something wrong. He keeps falling over.'

*　　*　　*

He'd had Dempsey eleven years. He'd bought the dog as a pup just before he'd started to shoot *Gunner*. As a consequence the dog's first real experience of life beyond his mother's teat was being carried around a movie studio by his owner and *adored*; all of which he thereafter took as his God-given right. Dempsey had been with Todd on every set since; the two were inseparable. Todd and Dempsey; Dempsey and Todd. Thanks to those early experiences of universal affection he was a confident dog; afraid of nobody, and – unless somebody was afraid of him – predisposed to be friendly.

The vet's name was Dr Spenser; an ebullient black woman who'd been looking after Dempsey since puppyhood. She did a few tests and told Todd that yes, there were definitive signs that Dempsey was having cognitive difficulties.

'How old is he now?'

'He'll be twelve next March.'

'Oh that's right – we didn't know his birthday so we said –'

'– Oscar Night.'

'What's wrong, boy?' Dr Spenser said to Dempsey, ruffling him under the chin. 'He's certainly not his usual happy self, is he?'

'Nope.'

'Well, I'd like to keep him in here for a few tests.'

'I brought a stool sample like you asked.'

'Thanks.'

Todd produced a small Tupperware container of dog poop. 'Well we'll have that analysed. You want the container back? Just kidding. Don't look so grim, Todd –'

'I don't like seeing him like this.'

'It's probably a virus he's picked up. We'll give him a few antibiotics and he'll be good as new.'

'But there's something weird about his eyes. Look. He's not even focussing on us.'

Dempsey had raised his head, knowing full well he was being talked about, but plainly he was having some difficulty fixing his gaze on whoever was doing the talking.

'This couldn't just be old age, could it?'

'I doubt it. He's been a very healthy dog so far, and it's my experience that a mutt like Dempsey is going to last a lot longer than some over-bred hound. You leave him with me. Check in with me at the end of the day.'

Todd did that. The news was there was no news. The stool sample had gone to the lab to be analysed, and meanwhile Dempsey was looking weak, perhaps a little disorientated, but there'd been no noticeable deterioration in his condition.

'You can either take him home tonight or leave him here. He'll be perfectly fine here. We don't actually have anybody monitoring the dogs from eleven p.m. till six in the morning, but the chances of –'

'I'm going to come and collect him.'

Despite Spenser's reassurances that there had been no deterioration, Todd disagreed. Usually when he arrived at the vet's after Dempsey had stayed in for a couple of hours, either for a shot, or his six-month check-up, he was greeted by the dog in crazy mode, yapping his delight at seeing his boss again, and ready to be out of the door before they could stick another damn needle in his backside. But today, when Dempsey came round the corner it seemed to take a moment before the dog even realized it was his master at the door, calling to him. And when he came, though some of his old enthusiasm returned, he was a shadow of his former self. Dr Spenser had already gone off-duty for the night. Todd asked if he could have her home number, but there were some things, it seemed, even being Todd Pickett couldn't get you.

'She's got kids to take care of,' the male nurse said. 'She likes to keep this place and her home-life very separate.'

'But if there's an emergency?'

'I'd recommend going to the twenty-four-hour animal hospital on Sepulveda. There'll be doctors there all night if anything were to happen. But honestly, I think it's some virus he's picked up out at the dog park, and it'll just take a course of antibiotics.'

'Well can I take some antibiotics then?' Todd said, getting a little irritated with the casual way Dempsey's case was being treated.

'Dr Spenser doesn't want to give Dempsey anything till she's got some results from the stool sample, so I'm afraid there'll be no drugs for Dempsey until tomorrow.'

Dempsey didn't eat. He just looked at the bowl of food Marco had prepared for him, and turned up his nose at it.

Then he went to lie on the back step and stayed there for the rest of the evening.

In the middle of the night Todd was woken by what sounded like the effects track from *The Exorcist*, a stomach-wrenching series of mumblings and eruptions. He switched on the bedroom light to find Dempsey at the bottom of his bed, standing in a pool of bright yellow puke. He looked horribly ashamed of having made a mess, and at first wouldn't come to Todd to be petted, but when he did – and Todd had his arms around the dog – it was clear he was in a bad way. Dempsey's whole body was cold, and he was trembling violently.

'Come on, m'man,' he said. 'We're gonna take you to get some proper Dring.'

The noise had woken Marco, who got dressed to drive while Todd held onto Dempsey, who was wrapped in his favourite comforter, a quilt Todd's grandmother had made for her grandson. The dog lay sprawled over Todd's knee, all one hundred pounds of him, while Marco drove through the almost empty streets to Sepulveda.

It was five minutes after five in the morning when they

arrived at the animal hospital, and there were just two people waiting with their pets to be helped. Even so it took twenty-five minutes before a doctor could be freed up to see Dempsey, during which time it seemed to Todd that Dempsey's condition worsened. His shaking became more violent than ever, and in the midst of one of his spasms, he convulsively shat brown gruel, mostly on the floor, but on Todd's leg and shoe too.

'Well now,' said the night doctor brightly, 'what seems to be the trouble?'

Todd gave him an exhaustive run-down on the events of the last day. He then asked Todd to pick Dempsey up and put him on the examination table – choosing this particular instant to remark what a fan of Todd's he was, as though Todd could have given a damn at that moment.

Then he examined the dog, in a good and thorough manner, but making asides throughout as to which movies of Todd's he and his wife had particularly enjoyed and which they hadn't. After about five minutes of this, seeing the expression of despair and anger on Todd's face, Marco quietly mentioned that Mr Pickett was really only interested right now in the health of his dog. The doctor's mouth tightened, as though he'd just been badly offended, and his handling of Dempsey (at least to Todd's eyes) seemed to become a little more brusque.

'Well, you have a very sick dog,' he said at the end of the examination, not even looking at Todd but talking to Marco. He was plainly embarrassed by his earlier show of fanboy enthusiasm, and was now over-compensating for it wildly.

Todd went to sit on the examination table to cradle Dempsey, which put him right in the doctor's line of sight.

'Look,' he said quietly, 'I'm sorry if I'm not being quite as appreciative of . . . your support of my pictures as I would normally be, Doc. It's nothing personal. I'm sure we could have a great conversation about it under different circumstances. But I'd like Dempsey comfortable first. He's sick and I want him better.'

Finally the doctor managed a little smile, and when he spoke his voice had also quieted, matching Todd's: 'I'm going to put Dempsey on a saline drip, because he's obviously lost a lot of fluids in the last twelve to twenty-four hours. That should make him feel a whole lot happier. Meanwhile, you said Dr Spenser over at Robertson VCA was doing stool checks?'

'She said it could be a virus.'

'Well . . . maybe. But looking at his eyes, it seems more systemic to me. If he were a younger dog I'd say parvo or heartworm, which is a parasite. But again, we commonly see toxo in pound dogs or strays, and I'm sure he's had his heartworm medications. Anyway, we'll see from the stool results tomorrow.'

'Wait, wait. You're saying it could be parvo or heartworm, but you don't really think it's either of these?'

'No.'

'So what do you think it is?'

The doctor shook his head. 'I'd say there's a better than fifty-fifty chance he's got some kind of tumour. On the brain or on the brain-stem.'

'And if he has?'

'Well, it's like a human being. You can sometimes fix these things –'

At this juncture, as though to demonstrate that things were not in a very fixable state right now, Dempsey started to shudder in Todd's arms, his claws scrabbling against the metal table as he tried to stay upright.

'It's okay, boy! It's okay!'

The doctor went for a nurse, and came back with an injection.

'What's that for?'

'Just to calm him down a little, so he can get some sleep.'

'Are you sure?'

'Yes, I'm sure. It's a mild tranquillizer. If you don't want me to give it to the dog, Mr Pickett . . .'

'Yes. Yes. Give it to him.'

The injection did indeed subdue Dempsey's little fit. They wheeled him away into another room to be given an intravenous infusion, leaving Todd with the quilt.

'Damn dog,' he said, now Dempsey was out of earshot. 'More trouble than he's worth.' Tears very close.

'Why don't we get a cup of coffee?' Marco suggested. 'And we can talk to the doctor more when we get back?'

There was a little donut shop in the mini-mall at the top of Sepulveda, and it had just opened. They were the first customers of the day. Todd knew the instant he walked in that both the women serving recognized him, so he turned round and walked out again rather than risking getting caught in a conversation: Marco brought out two coffees and two Bear Claws in greaseproof paper, still warm from the oven. Though he hadn't thought he had an appetite, the pastry was too good not to be eaten; so he ate. Then, coffee in hand, they walked down to the hospital, the eyes of the women in the donut shop glued to Todd until he had disappeared from sight.

They said nothing as they walked. The day was getting underway; the traffic on Sepulveda backing up as it waited to take its turn to get onto the freeway. These were people with two-hour commutes ahead of them before they got to their place of work; people with jobs they hated, houses they hated, and a pay-cheque at the end of the month that wouldn't even cover the cost of the mortgage, the car payments, the insurance.

'Right now,' Todd said, 'I'd give my eye teeth to be one of them, instead of having to go back in there.'

91

'I can go in for you.'

'No.'

'Dempsey trusts me,' Marco said.

'I know. But he's my dog.'

5

A gain, there was no news. Dempsey had been hooked up to a saline drip, and looked as though the tranquillizer had taken its effect. He wasn't quite asleep, but he was dazy.

'We'll do an X-ray today, and see how he looks,' the doctor said. 'We should have the results back by the end of the day. So why don't you two go home, we'll keep Dempsey here and see what we can do to get him well?'

'I want to stay.'

'Well that's going to be very uncomfortable for you, Mr Pickett. We don't have a room we can put you in, and frankly you both look as though you didn't get a full night's sleep. Dempsey's mildly sedated, and we'll probably keep him that way. But it's going to be six or seven hours before we get any answers for you. We share our X-ray technician with our hospital in Santa Monica, so she won't even be in to look at Dempsey until eleven at the earliest.'

'I still want to stay. You've got a bench out there. You're not going to throw me out if I sit on that are you?'

'No. Of course not.'

'Then that's where I'll be.'

The doctor looked at his watch. 'I'll be out of here in half an hour and the day-doctor, Dr Otis, will be taking over Dempsey's case. I will of course bring her up to speed with everything we've done so far and if she feels there's something else she wants to try –'

'She'll know where to find me.'

'Right.'

The doctor gave up a wan smile, his second and last of the night. 'Well, I sincerely hope you have good news with Dempsey, and that by the time I come in again tonight you've both gone home happy.'

Todd would not be dissuaded from staying on the bench, even though it was situated a few steps away from the front counter, next to the soda machine, and would leave him in full view of everyone who came through the next few hours. Marco said that he would come back with a Thermos of good coffee and something to eat, and left Todd there.

The parade of the needy began early. About two minutes after Marco had gone a distraught woman came in saying that she'd struck a cat with her car, and the victim was now in her car, alive, but terrified and badly hurt. Two nurses went out with well-used pairs of leather gloves and a syringe of tranquillizer to subdue the victim. They came back with a weeping woman and a corpse. The animal's panicked self-defences had apparently used up what little energies its broken body had possessed. The woman was inconsolable. She tried to thank the nurses for their help but all she could do was cry. There were six more accidents that rush hour, two of them fatalities. Todd watched all this in a dazed state. Lack of sleep was beginning to catch up with him. Every now and then his eyes would flicker closed for a few seconds, and the scene in front of him would jump, like a piece of film which had had a few seconds' worth of action removed and then been spliced back together again. People moved abruptly from one place to another. One moment somebody was coming in, the next they were engaged in conversation (often tearful, sometimes accusatory, always intense), with one of the nurses; the next they'd gone, or they were on their way out.

Much to his surprise, nobody gave him more than a cursory glance. Perhaps, they thought, that can't *possibly* be Todd Pickett, sitting on a broken-down old bench next to a broken-down old soda machine in a twenty-four-hour animal hospital. Or perhaps it was just that they saw him, recognized him, and didn't care. They had other things to think about right now, more pressing than the peculiar presence of a weary-looking movie star on a broken-down bench. They had a rat with an abscess, a cat that had had six kittens but had got the seventh stuck, a guinea pig in a shoe box that was dead when the box was opened; a poodle that kept biting itself; a problem with fleas, a problem with mange, two canaries that hated one another, and so on and so forth.

Marco came back with coffee and sandwiches. Todd drank some coffee, which perked him up.

He went to the front desk and asked, not for the first time, to see the day-doctor. This time, he got lucky. Dr Otis, a pale and slight young woman who looked no more than eighteen, and refused to look Todd in the face (though this, he realized was her general practice: she was the same with Marco and with the nurses, eyes constantly averted), appeared and said that there was nothing to report except that Dempsey would be going for X-rays in about half an hour, and they would be available for viewing tomorrow. At this point, Todd lost his temper. It happened rarely, but when it did it was an impressive spectacle. His neck became blotchy-red, and the muscles of his face churned; his eyes went to ice-water.

'I brought my dog in here at five o'clock this morning. I've been waiting here – sitting on that bench – that bench right there, you see it? Do you see that bench?'

'Yes, I –'

'That's where I've been since six o'clock. It is now almost eleven o'clock. I've asked on several occasions for you to have the common decency to come out and tell me what's happening to my dog. Always politely. And I've been told, over and over again, that you're very busy.'

'It's been a crazy morning, Mr –?'

'Pickett is my name.'

'Well, Mr Pickett, I'm afraid I can't –'

'Stop right there. Don't say you can't get the X-rays until tomorrow because you can. You will. I want my dog looked after and if you won't do it I'll take him some place where he can be taken care of and I'll make sure every damn newspaper in the State of California –'

At this moment an older woman, obviously the hospital manager, stepped into view and took Todd's hand, shaking it. 'Mr Pickett. My name's Cordelia Simpson. It's all right, Andrea, I'll take care of Mr Pickett from here.'

The young woman doctor retreated. She was two shades whiter than she'd been at the beginning of the conversation.

'I heard most of what you were telling Andrea –'

'Look, I'm sorry. That's not my style. I don't like losing my temper, but –'

'No, it's okay. I understand. You're tired and you're concerned about –?'

'Dempsey.'

'Dempsey. Right.'

'I was told he'd be X-rayed today and we'd have the results back this afternoon.'

'Well, the speed of these things all depends on the volume of work, Mr Pickett,' Cordelia said. She was English, and had the face and manner of a woman who would not be pleasant if she were riled, but was doing her best right now to put on a gentler face. 'I read a piece about you in the *LA Times* last year. You were on the cover with Dempsey, as I remember. Clearly you're very close to your dog. Here's what I'm going to do.' She consulted her watch. 'Dempsey is being seen by the radiographer right now, and I guarantee that we'll have the results back by . . . six. It *might* be earlier but I think six we can guarantee.'

'So how long before I can take him home?'

'You want to take him now?'

'Yes.'

'You'll find him rather dopey. I'm not sure he could walk.'

'I can carry him.'

Cordelia nodded. She knew an immovable object when she saw one. 'Well I'll have one of the nurses come fetch you when he's ready. Is that his?'

She pointed to the quilt on the bench. Quite unconsciously, Todd had been nursing it while he waited. No wonder people had kept their distance.

'Yes.'

'Do you want me to have him wrapped up in it?'

'Thank you.'

Cordelia picked up the quilt. 'And my apologies, Mr Pickett, for any difficulties you may have had. Our Drs are horribly overworked. And, I'm afraid to say, often people who are wonderful with animals aren't always terribly good with human beings.'

Ten minutes later a burly Latino appeared with a sleepy-eyed Dempsey, wrapped in his quilt. His ears pricked up just a little at the sight of Todd, enough for Todd to know that his holding the dog, and whispering to him, meant something.

'We're going home, old guy,' Todd murmured to him, as he carried him down the steps into the street and round to the little parking lot behind the building, where Marco was backing out the car. 'I know you didn't like it in there. All those people you didn't know with needles and shit. Well, fuck them.' He put his nose into the cushion of baby fur behind Dempsey's ear, which always smelled sweetest. 'We're going home.'

For the next few hours Dempsey slept in the quilt, which Todd had put on his big bed. Todd stayed beside him, though the need for sleep caught up with him several times, and he'd slide away into a few minutes of dreamland: fragments of things he'd seen from his bench in the waiting room, mostly. The box containing the dead guinea pig, that absurd poodle, nipping its own backside bloody; all just pieces of the day, coming and going. Then he'd wake and stroke Dempsey for a little while, talk to him, tell him everything was going to be okay.

There was a sudden rally in Dempsey's energies about four o'clock, which was when he was usually fed, so Todd had Marco prepare a sick-bed version of his usual meal, with chicken instead of the chopped horse-flesh or whatever the hell it was in the cans, and some good gravy. Dempsey ate it all, though he had to be held up to do so, since his legs were unreliable. He then drank a full bowl of water.

'Good, good,' Todd said.

Dempsey attempted to wag his tail, but it had no more power in it than his legs had.

Todd carried him outside so he could shit and piss. A slight drizzle was coming down; not cool, but refreshing. He held onto the dog, waiting for the urge to take Dempsey, and he turned his face up to the rain, offering a quiet little prayer.

'Please don't take him from me. He's just a smelly old dog. You don't need him and I do. Do you hear me? Please . . . hear me. Don't take him.'

He looked back at Dempsey to find that the dog was looking back at him, apparently paying attention to every word. His ears were half-pricked, his eyes half-open.

'Do you think anyone's listening?' Todd said.

By way of reply, Dempsey looked away from him, his head bobbing uneasily on his neck. Then he made a nasty sound deep in his belly and his whole body convulsed.

Todd had never seen the term projectile vomit displayed with such force. A stream of chewed chicken, dog mix and water squirted out. As soon as it stopped, the dog began to make little whining sounds. Then ten seconds later, Dempsey repeated the whole spectacle, until every piece of nourishment and every drop of water he'd been given had been comprehensively ejected.

After the second burst of vomiting he didn't even have the strength to whine. Todd wrapped the quilt around him and carried him back into the house. He had Marco bring some towels and dried him off where the rain had caught him.

'I don't suppose you care what's been going on all day, do you?' Marco said.

'Anything important?'

'Great foreign numbers on *Gallows*, particularly in France. Huge hit in France, apparently. Maxine wants to know if you'd like to do a piece about Dempsey's health crisis for one of the woman's magazines.'

'No.'

'That's what I told her. She said they'd eat it up, but I said –'

'No! Fuck. Will these people never stop? No!'

'You got a call from Walter at Dreamworks about some charity thing he's arranging, I told him you'd be back in circulation tomorrow.'

'That's the phone.'

'Yeah. It is.'

Marco went to the nearest phone, which was in the master bathroom, while Todd went back to finish drying the dog.

'It's Andrea Otis. From the hospital. I think it's the nervous young woman you saw this morning.'

'Stay with him,' Todd said to Marco.

He went into the bathroom, which was cold. Picked up the phone.

'Mr Pickett?'

'Yes.'

'First, I want to say I owe you an apology for this morning –'

'No that's fine.'

'I knew who you were and that threw me off –'

'Dempsey.'

'– a little. I'm sorry.'

'Dempsey.'

'Yes. Well, we've got the X-ray results back and . . . I'm afraid the news isn't very good.'

'Why not? What's wrong with him?'

'He is riddled with cancer.'

Todd took a long moment to digest this unwelcome news. Then he said: 'That's impossible.'

'It's in his spine. It's in his colon –'

'But that can't be.'

'And it's now spreading to his brain, which is why we've only just discovered it. These motor and perception problems he's having are all part of the same thing. The tumour's spreading into his skull, and pushing on his brain.'

'Oh God.'

'So . . . I don't know what you want to do.'

'I want this not to be happening.'

'Well yes. But I'm afraid it is.'

'How long has he got?'

'His present condition is really as good as things are going to get for him.' She spoke as though she was reading the words from an idiot-board, careful to leave exactly the same amount of space between each one. 'All that is really at issue is how quickly Dempsey becomes incapacitated.'

Todd looked through the open door at the pitiful shape shuddering beneath the quilt. It was obvious that Dempsey had already reached that point. Todd could be absurdly optimistic at times, but this wasn't one of them.

'Is he in pain?' he asked the doctor.

'Well, I'd say it's not so much pain we're dealing with as anxiety. He doesn't know what's happening to him. And he doesn't know why it's happening. He's just suffering, Mr Pickett. And it's just going to get worse.'

'So you're saying I should have him put down?'

'It's not my place to tell you what to do with your dog, Mr Pickett.'

'But if he was your dog.'

'If he was my dog, and I loved him as you obviously love Dempsey, I wouldn't want him suffering . . . Mr Pickett, are you there?'

'Here,' Todd said, trying to keep the sound of tears out of his voice.

'So really it's up to you.'

Todd looked at Dempsey again, who was making a mournful sound in his sleep.

'If I bring him back over to the hospital?'

'Yes?'

'Would there be somebody there to put him to sleep?'

'Yes, of course. I'll be here.'

'Then that's what I want to do.'

'I'm so very sorry, Mr Pickett.'

'It's not your fault.'

Dempsey roused himself a little when Todd went back to the bed, but it was barely more than a sniff and a half-hearted wag.

'Come on, you,' he said, wrapping Dempsey tightly in the quilt, and lifting him up, 'the sooner this is done the sooner you're not an unhappy hound. Will you drive, Marco?'

It was four-thirty in the afternoon, and though the drizzle had ceased, the traffic was still horrendous. It took them fifty-five minutes to get down to the hospital, but this time – perhaps to make up for her unavailability the last time he'd been there – Dr Otis was at the counter waiting for him. She opened the side door, to let him into the non-public area.

101

'You want me to come in, boss?' Marco asked.

'Nah, it's okay. We'll be fine.'

'He looks really out of it,' the doctor remarked.

Dempsey had barely opened his eyes at the sound of Todd's voice. 'You know, I realize this may seem like a strange thing to say, but in a way we're lucky that this caught him so fast. With some dogs it takes weeks and months . . .'

'In here?' Todd said.

'Yes.'

The doctor had opened a door into a room not more than eight by eight, painted in what was intended to be a soothing green. On one wall was a Monet reproduction and on another a piece of poetry that Todd couldn't read through his assembling tears.

'I'll just give you two some time,' Dr Otis said. 'I'll be back in a few minutes.'

Todd sat down with Dempsey in his arms. 'Damn,' he said softly. 'This isn't fair.'

Dempsey had opened his eyes fully for the first time in several hours, probably because he'd heard the sound of Todd crying, which had always made him very attentive, even if the crying was fake. Todd could be rehearsing a sad scene from a picture, memorizing lines, and as soon as the first note of sadness crept into his voice Dempsey would be there, his paws on Todd's knees, ready to give comfort. But this time the animal didn't have the strength to help make the boss feel better. All he could do was stare up at Todd with a slight look of puzzlement on his face.

'Oh God, I hope I'm doing the right thing. I wish you could just tell me that this is what you want.' Todd kissed the dog, tears falling in Dempsey's fur. 'I know if I was you I wouldn't want to be shitting everywhere and not able to stand up. That's no life, huh?' He buried his face in the smell of the animal. For eleven years – whether Todd had had female company or not – Dempsey had slept on his bed; and more often than not been the one to wake him up, pressing his cold nose against Todd's face, rubbing his neck on Todd's chest.

'I love you, dog,' he said. 'And I want you to be there when I get to heaven, okay? I want you to be keeping a place for me. Will you do that? Will you keep a place for me?'

There was a discreet knock on the door, and Todd's stomach turned. 'Time's up, buddy,' he said, kissing Dempsey's burning hot snout. Even now, he thought, I could say *no, I don't want you to do this*. He could take Dempsey home for one more night in the big bed. But that was just selfishness. The dog had had enough, that was plain. He could barely raise his head. It was time to go.

'Come in,' he said.

The doctor came in, meeting Todd's gaze for the first time. 'I know how hard this is,' she said. 'I have dogs myself, all mutts like Dempsey.'

'Dempsey, did you hear that?' Todd said, the tears refusing to abate. 'She called you a mutt.'

'They're the best.'

'Yeah. They are.'

'Are you ready?'

Todd nodded, at which point she instantly transferred her loving attention to the dog. She lifted Dempsey out from Todd's arms and put him on the steel table in the corner of the room, talking to him all the while, 'Hey there, Dempsey. This isn't going to hurt at all. Just a little prick –'

She pulled a syringe out of her pocket, and exposed the needle. At the back of Todd's head that same irrational voice was screaming: 'Tell her no! Knock it out of her hand! Quickly! Quickly!' He pushed the thoughts away, wiping the tears from his eyes with the back of his hand, because he didn't want to be blinded by them when this happened. He wanted to see it all, even if it hurt like a knife.

He owed that to Dempsey. He put his hand on Dempsey's neck and rubbed his favourite place. The syringe went into Dempsey's leg. He made a tiny little grunt of complaint.

'Good boy,' Dr Otis said. 'There. That wasn't so bad now, was it?'

Todd kept rubbing Dempsey's neck.

The doctor put the top back on the syringe and pocketed it. 'It's all right,' she said. 'You can stop rubbing. He's gone.'

So quickly? Todd cleared away another wave of tears and looked down at the body on the table. Dempsey's eye was still half-open, but it didn't look back at him any longer. Where there'd been a sliver of bright life, where there'd been mischief and shared rituals – where, in short, there'd been Dempsey – there was nothing.

'I'm very sorry, Mr Pickett,' the doctor said, 'I'm sure you loved him very much and speaking as a doctor, I *know* you did the right thing for him.'

Todd sniffed hard, and reached over to pluck a clump of paper handkerchiefs from the box. 'What does that say?' he said, pointing to the framed poster on the wall. His tears made it incomprehensible.

'It's a quote by Robert Louis Stevenson,' Andrea said. 'You know, who wrote *Treasure Island?*'

'Yeah, I know . . .'

'It says: *"Do you think dogs will not be in heaven? I tell you, they will be there long before any of us."*'

6

He waited until he got home, and he'd governed his tears, to make arrangements for Dempsey's cremation. He left a message with a firm that was recommended by the Animal Hospital for their discreet handling of these matters. They would pick Dempsey's body up from the Hospital Mortuary, cremate him and transfer his ashes, guaranteeing that there was no mingling of 'cremains' – as they described them – but that the ashes they delivered to the owner would be those of their pet. In other words they weren't putting canaries, parrots, rats, dogs and guinea pigs in the oven for one big bonfire and dividing up the 'cremains' (the word revolted Todd) in what looked to be the appropriate amounts. He also called his accountant at home and made arrangements for a ten thousand dollar donation to the Hospital, the only attendant request being that five hundred of that money be spent on putting in a more comfortable bench for people to sit on while they waited.

He slept very well with the aid of several Ambien and a large scotch, until about four thirty in the morning when he woke up and felt Dempsey moving around at the bottom of the bed. The drugs made his thought processes muddy. It took him a few seconds of leaning over and patting the coverlet at the bottom of the bed to bring his consciousness up to speed. Dempsey wasn't there.

Yet he'd felt the dog, he would have sworn to it on a stack of Bibles, getting up and walking around and around on the same spot, padding down the bed until it was comfortable for him.

He lay back on the pillow and drifted back to sleep, but it wasn't a healthy sleep thereafter. He kept half-waking, and staring down at the darkness of the bottom of the bed, wondering if Dempsey was a ghost now, and would haunt his heels until the dog had the sense to go on his way to heaven.

He slept in until ten, when Marco brought him the phone with a woman called Rosalie from the Pet Cremation Service. She was pleasant in her no-nonsense way; no doubt she often had people in near hysteria at the other end of the telephone, so a little professional distance was necessary. She had already been in contact with the Hospital this morning, she said, and they had informed her that Dempsey had a collar and quilt with him. Did Todd want these items returned, or were they to be cremated with his pet?

'They were his,' Todd said, 'so they should go with him.'

'Fine,' said Rosalie. 'Then the only other question is the matter of the urn. We have three varieties –'

'Just the best you've got.'

'That would be our Bronze Grecian Style.'

'That sounds fine.'

'All I need now is your credit card number.'

'I'll pass you back to my assistant. He can help you with all that.'

'Just one other question?'

'Yes.'

'Are you . . . *the* Todd Pickett?'

Yes, of course, he was the real Todd Pickett. But he didn't feel like the real thing; more like a badly bruised lookalike. Things like this didn't happen to the real Todd Pickett.

106

He had a way with life that always made it show the bright side.

He went back to sleep until noon then got up and ate some lunch, his body aching as though he was catching a heavy dose of the flu. His food unfinished he sat in the breakfast nook, staring blankly at the potted plants artfully arranged on the patio; plants he'd never persuaded Dempsey not to cock his leg against every time he passed.

'I'm going back to bed,' he told Marco.

'You don't want to put a holding call into Maxine? She's called nine times this morning. She says she has news about a foreign buyer for *Warrior*.'

'Did you tell her what happened to Dempsey?'

'Yes.'

'What did she say?'

'She said: *oh*. Then she went back to talking about the buyer.'

Todd sighed, defeated by the woman's incomprehension. 'Maybe it's time I got out of this fucking business,' he said to Marco. 'I don't have the balls for it any longer. Or the energy.'

Marco put up no protest at this. He hated everything about the business, except Todd, and always had. 'Why don't we go down to Key West like we always promised ourselves? Open a bar. Get fat and drunk —'

'— and die of heart attacks at fifty.'

'You're feeling morbid right now.'

'A little.'

'Well it won't last forever. And one of these days, we'll have to honour Dempsey and get another dog.'

'That wouldn't be honouring him, that'd be replacing him. And he was irreplaceable. You know why?'

'Why?'

'Because he was there when I was nobody.'

'You were pups together.'

This got a smile out of Todd; the first in forty-eight hours.

'Yeah . . .' he said, his voice close to breaking again. 'We were pups together.' He tried to hold back the tears, but they came anyway. 'What is *wrong* with me?' he said. 'He was a dog. I mean . . . *come on*. Tell me honestly, do you think Tom Cruise cries for a day if one of his dogs dies?'

'I don't think he's got dogs.'

'Or Brad Pitt?'

'I don't know. Ask 'em. Next time you see 'em, ask 'em.'

'Oh sure, that's going to make a dandy little scene. Todd Pickett and Brad Pitt: "Tell me, Brad, when your dog died did you wail like a *girl* for two days?"'

Now it was Marco who laughed. *'Wail like a girl?'*

'That's how I feel. I feel like I'm in the middle of some stupid weepie.'

'Maybe you should call Wilhemina over and fuck her.'

'Wilhemina doesn't do fucks. She does lovemaking with candles and a lot of wash-cloths. I swear she thinks I'm going to give her something.'

'Fleas?'

'Yeah. Fleas. You know, as a last act of rebellion on behalf of Dempsey and myself I'd like to give fleas to Wilhemina, Maxine and –'

'Gary Eppstadt.'

Both men were laughing now, curing the hurt the only way it could be cured, by being included in the nature of things.

Speaking of inclusion, he got a call from his mother, about six o'clock. She was at home in Cambridge Massachusetts, but sounded ready to jump the first plane and come visit. She was in one of her 'I've a funny feeling' moods.

'What's going on?'

'Nothing.'

'Yes there is.'

She was inevitably right; she could predict with startling accuracy the times she needed to call her famous son and

108

the times when she should keep her distance. Sometimes he could lie to her, and get away with it. But today wasn't one of those days. What was the point?

'Dempsey's dead.'

'That old mutt of yours.'

'He was not an old mutt and if you talk about him like that then this conversation ends right here.'

'How old was he?' Patricia asked.

'Eleven, going on twelve.'

'That's a decent age.'

'Not for a dog like him.'

'What kind of dog would that be?'

'You know –'

'A mutt. Mutts always live longer than thoroughbreds. That's a fact of life.'

'Well, mine didn't.'

'Too much rich food. You used to spoil that dog –'

'Is there anything else you want besides lecturing me about how I killed my dog with kindness?'

'No. I was just wanting to chat, but obviously you're in no mood to chat.'

'I loved Dempsey, Mom. You understand what I'm saying?'

'If you don't mind me observing something –'

'Could I stop you?'

'– it's sad that the only serious relationship you've had is with a dog. It's time you grew up, Todd. You're not getting any younger, you know. You think about the way your father aged.'

'I don't want to talk about this right now, okay.'

'*Listen to me.*'

'Mom. I don't –'

'You've got his genes, so listen for once will you? He was a good-looking man your father, till he was about thirty-four, thirty-five. Now granted he didn't take care of himself and you do – I mean he smoked and he drank a lot more than was good for him. But his looks went practically overnight.'

'Overnight? That's ridiculous. Nobody's looks go –'

'All right, it wasn't overnight. But I was there. I saw. Believe me, it was quick. Five, six months and all his looks had gone.'

Even though this was an absurd exaggeration, there was an element of truth in what Patricia Pickett was saying. Todd's father had indeed lost his looks with remarkable speed. It would not have been the kind of thing a son would have noticed, necessarily, but Todd had a second point-of-view on his father's sudden deterioration: his best friend Danny had been raised by a single mother who'd several times made her feelings for Merrick Pickett known to her son. The rumours had reached Todd, of course. Indeed they'd become practically weekly reports, as Danny's mother's plans to seduce the unwitting subject of her desires were laid (and failed) and re-laid.

All this came back to Todd as his mother went on chatting. Eventually, he said, 'Mom, I've got to go. I've got to make some decisions about the cremation.'

'Oh, Lord, I hope you're keeping this quiet. The media would have a *party* with this: you and your dog.'

'Well all the more reason for you to clam up about it,' he warned. 'If anybody calls, saying they want a quote.'

'*I know nothing.*'

'You know nothing.'

'I know the routine by now, honey. Don't worry, your secret's safe with me.'

'Don't even tell the neighbours.'

'Fine! I won't.'

'Bye, Mom.'

'I'm sorry about Brewster.'

'Dempsey.'

'Whatever.'

*   *   *

110

It was true; when Todd gave the subject some serious thought: Merrick Pickett had indeed lost his looks with startling speed. One day he'd been the best looking insurance agent in the city of Cincinnati, the next (it seemed) Danny's mother wouldn't look twice at him. Suppose this was hereditary? Suppose *fifty percent* of it was hereditary?

He called Eppstadt's office. It took the sonofabitch forty-eight minutes to return the call and when he did his manner was brusque.

'I hope this isn't about *Warrior*?'

'It isn't.'

'We're not going to do it, Todd.'

'I get it, Gary. Is your assistant listening in on this conversation?'

'No. What do you want?'

'When we had lunch you recommended a guy who'd done some work for a few famous names.'

'Bruce Burrows?'

'How do I get hold of him? He's not in the book.'

'Don't worry. I'll hook you up.'

'Thanks.'

'You're making a good call, Todd. I hope we can get back in business as soon as you're healed.'

Once he had the number, Todd didn't leave himself further room for hesitation. He called Burrows, booked the consultation, and tentatively chatted over some dates for the operation.

There was one piece of outstanding business before he could move on: the disposal of Dempsey's ashes. Despite the reassurances of Robert Louis Stevenson, Todd did not have any clear idea as to the permanence of any soul, whether animal or human. He only knew that he wanted Dempsey's mortal remains to be placed where the dog had been most happy. There was no doubt about where that was: the back yard of the Bel Air house, which had been, since his puppyhood, Dempsey's unchallenged territory: his stalking ground, his school-yard when it came to learning new tricks. And it was there, the evening before Todd put himself into the hands of Bruce Burrows, that he took the bronzed plastic urn provided by the Cremation Company out into the yard. The urn contained a plastic bag, which in turn contained Dempsey's ashes. There were a lot of them; but then he'd been a big dog.

Todd sat down in the middle of the yard, where he and Dempsey had so often sat and watched the sky together, and poured some of the ashes into the palm of his hand. What part of this grey sand was his tail, he wondered, and which his snout? Which part the place behind his ear he'd love you forever if you rubbed? Or didn't it matter? Was that the point about scattering ashes: that in the end they looked the same? Not just the snout and the tail, but a dog's ashes and a man's ashes. All reducible, with the addition of a little flame, to this mottled dust? He put his lips to it, once, to kiss him goodbye. In his head he could hear his mother telling him that it was a gross, unhealthy thing to do, so he kissed them again, just to spite her. Then he stood up and cast Dempsey's ashes around, like a farmer sowing seeds. There was no wind. The ash fell where he threw it, evenly distributed over the mutt's dominion.

'See you, dog,' he said, and went back into the house to get himself a large bourbon.

PART THREE

A DARKER TIME

1

For four months, in the summer of his seventeenth year, Todd had worked at the Sunset Home for the Elderly on the outskirts of Orlando, where he'd got a job through his Uncle Frank, who worked as an accountant for Sunset Homes Incorporated. The place was little more than a repository for the nearly-dead; working there had been the most depressing experience of his young life. Most of his duties did not involve the patients – he had no training as a nurse, nor intended to get any. But the care of one of the older occupants, a man by the name of Duncan McFarlane, was given over to him because McFarlane was prone to unruliness when he was being bathed by the female nurses. McFarlane was no great trouble to Todd. He was just a sour sonofabitch who wasn't going to make anybody's life one jot easier if he could possibly avoid it. The ritual of giving a bed-bath to his patient was Todd's particular horror; the sight of his own body awoke a profound self-disgust in the old man. Asking around, Todd had discovered that McFarlane had been an athlete in his prime. But now – at the age of eighty-three – there was no trace of the strength or the beauty his body had once possessed. He was a pallid sack of shit and resentment, revolted by the sight of himself.

Look at me, he would say when Todd uncovered him, *Christ, look at me, Christ, look at me*. Every time it was the same murmured horror. *Look at me, Christ, look at me.*

To this day, the image of McFarlane's nakedness remained

with Todd in all its grotesque particulars. The little beard of dirty white hair that hung from the old man's scrotum; the constellation of heavy, dark warts above his left nipple; the wrinkled folds of pale, spotted flesh that hung under his arms. Todd felt guilty about his disgust, and kept it to himself, until one day it had been the subject of discussion in the day-room, and he'd discovered that his feelings were shared, especially by the male members of the nursing staff. The female nurses seemed to have more compassion, perhaps; or were simply indifferent to the facts of creeping senility. But the other men on the staff – there were four of them besides Todd – were afterwards constantly remarking on the foulness of their charges. One of the quartet – a black guy from New Orleans called Austin Harper – was particularly eloquent on the subject.

'I ain't endin' up like any o' these ol' fucks,' he remarked on more than one occasion, 'I'd blow my fuckin' brains out 'fore I'd sink that fuckin' low.'

'It won't happen,' Todd had said.

'How'd you reckon that, white boy?' Austin had said. He'd patted Todd on his backside; which he took every possible opportunity to do.

'When we're as old as these folks there'll be ways to fix it,' Todd replied.

'You mean we'll live forever? Bullshit. I don't buy any of that science-fiction crap, boy.'

'I'm not saying we'll live forever. But they'll have figured out what gives us wrinkles, and they'll have a way to smooth them out.'

'Will they now? So you's goin' to be all smoothed out, is you?'

'I sure as hell am.'

'You'll still die, but you'll die all smoothed out an' pretty?' He tapped Todd's ass appreciatively again.

'Will you quit doin' that?' Todd said.

'I'll quit when you quit wavin' it in my nose.' Austin

116

laughed, and slapped Todd's ass a third time, a stinging swat.

'Anyways,' Todd said, 'I don't give a shit what you think. I'm going to die pretty.'

The phrase had lingered. To die pretty; that was the grand ambition. To die pretty, and not find yourself like poor old Duncan McFarlane, looking down at his own nakedness and saying, over and over: *Oh Christ, look at me. Oh Christ, look at me. Oh Christ . . .*

Two months after Todd had left Florida to go to Los Angeles for a screen-test, he'd got a scrawled note from Austin Harper, who – given that it was more or less certain that they'd never see one another again, figured it was okay for Todd to know that if Austin had had a chance he would have ploughed Todd's ass 'all the way to Key West and back'. 'And *then* you'd be all smoothed out, baby,' Harper had written.

'Oh, and by the way,' he'd added. 'That old fuck McFarlane died a week ago. Tried to give himself a bath in the middle of the night. Drowned himself in three inches of water. That's what I call a damn fool thing to do.

'Stay smooth, m'man. You're going to do great. I know it. Just remember to thank me when they gives you an Oscar.'

2

'Kiddo?'

Todd was floating in a blind black place, his body untethered. He couldn't even feel it.

'Kiddo? Can you hear me?'

Despite the darkness all around, it was a comfortable place to be in. There were no predators here in this no-man's-land. There were no sharks circling, wanting ten-percent of his flesh. Todd felt pleasantly removed from everything. Except for that voice calling him.

'Kiddo? If you can hear me, move your finger.'

It was a trick, he knew. It was a way to get him to go back to the world where once he'd lived and breathed and been unhappy. But he didn't want to go. It was too brittle that place; brittle and bright. He wanted to stay where he was, here in the darkness, floating and floating.

'Kiddo . . . it's Donnie.'

Donnie?

Wait, that couldn't be right. His older brother, Donnie? They hadn't talked in months. Why would he be here, trying to seduce him out of his comfortable hideaway? But then, if not Donnie, then who? Nobody else ever called him Kiddo.

Todd felt a dim murmur of anxiety. Donnie lived in Texas, for God's sake. *What was he doing here?*

'Talk to me, Kiddo.'

Very reluctantly, Todd forced himself to reply to the

summons, though when he finally coaxed his lips to shape it the sound he made was as remote as the moon.

'Donnie?'

'Well, howdy. I must say it's good to have you back in the land of the livin'.' He felt a hand laid on his arm. The sensation, like Donnie's voice, and his own, felt distant and dulled.

'You had us a bit stirred up for a while there.'

'Why's . . . it . . . so *dark* in here?' Todd said. 'Will you have someone turn on the lights?'

'Everything's going to be okay, buddy.'

'Donnie. *Please*. Turn on the lights.'

'They *are* on, Kiddo. It's just you've got some bandages over your face. That's all it is. You're going to be just fine.'

Bandages on his face.

Now it all started to come back to him. His last memories. He'd been going under Burrows' knife for the big operation.

The last thing he remembered was Burrows telling him to count backwards from ten. Burrows had been smiling reassuringly at him, and as Todd counted – had thought: I wonder how much work *he's* had done on that face of his? The nose for sure. And all the lines gone from around his eyes –

'Are you counting, Todd?' Burrows had said.

'Ten. Nine. Eight –'

There hadn't been a seven. Not that Todd could remember. The drugs had swept him off to their own empty version of La-La land.

But now he was back from that dreamless place, and Donnie was here at his bedside, all the way from Texas. Why? And why the bandages over his eyes? Burrows hadn't said anything about bandages.

'My mouth's so dry,' Todd whispered.

'No *problemo*, buddy,' Donnie replied gently. 'I'll get the nurse in here.'

'I'll have a vodka . . . straight up.'

Donnie chuckled. 'I'll see what I can do.'

Todd heard him get up and go to the door, and call for a nurse. His consciousness wavered, and he felt himself slipping back into the void from which he'd just been brought by Donnie's voice. The prospect of that lush darkness didn't seem quite as comforting as it had a few moments before. He started to panic, scrambling to keep hold of the world, at least until he knew what had happened to him.

He called out to Donnie:

'Where are you? Donnie? Are you there?'

Footsteps came hurriedly back in his direction.

'I'm still here, Kiddo.' Donnie's voice was tender. Todd couldn't remember ever hearing such tenderness in it before now.

'Burrows didn't tell me it'd be like this,' Todd said.

'There's nothing to get worked up about,' Donnie replied.

Even in his semi-drugged state, Todd knew a lie when he heard one.

'You're not a very good actor,' he said.

'Runs in the family,' Donnie quipped, and squeezed Todd's arm again. 'Just kidding.'

'Yeah . . . yeah . . .' Todd said. As he spoke a spasm of pain ran from the bridge of his nose and spread across his face in both directions. He was suddenly in excruciating agony. 'Jesus,' he gasped. 'Jesus. Make it stop!'

He felt Donnie's reassuring hand go from his arm; heard his brother crossing to the door again, yelling as he went, his voice suddenly shrill with fear: *'Will somebody get in here. Right now! Christ!'*

Todd's panic, momentarily soothed by his brother's voice, started to rise up in him again. He raised his hand to his face. The bandages were tight and smooth, like a visor over his head, sealing him in. He started to hyperventilate. He was going to die in here, if he didn't get this smothering stuff off his face. He began to claw at the bandages. He needed air. Right now!

Air, for Christ's sake, air –

'Mr Pickett, don't do that! Please!'

The nurse caught hold of Todd's hands, but the panic and the pain made him strong and she couldn't prevent him from digging his fingers beneath the bandages and pulling.

There were flashes of light in his head, but he knew it wasn't the light of the outside world he was seeing. His brain was overloading; fear was leaping like lightning across his skull. His blood roared in his ears. His body thrashed around in the bed as though he was in the grip of a seizure.

'All right, nurse. I've got him now.'

Suddenly, there were hands around his wrists. Some body stronger than the nurse was gently but insistently pulling his fingers away from his face. Then a voice came to find him through the sound of his own sobs.

'*Todd?* This is Dr Burrows. Everything is fine. But please *calm down*. Let me explain what's going on. There's nothing to worry about.' He spoke like a hypnotist, the cadence of his sentences even, his voice completely calm. And while he went on speaking, repeating the same information – that everything was fine, all Todd had to do was breathe deeply, deeply – he held Todd's arms against the bed.

After a few moments, the bright bursts of light began to become less frequent. The din of blood began to recede. So, by degrees, did the waves of panic.

'There,' Dr Burrows said, when the worst of it was over. 'You see? Everything's fine and dandy. Now why don't we get you a fresh pillow? Nurse Karyn? Would you please get Mr Pickett a nice fresh pillow?'

Oh so gently, Burrows raised the upper half of Todd's body off the bed, talking to him all the while: the same calming monologue. All the strength to resist, indeed all

121

need to do so, had gone out of Todd. All he could do was abandon himself to Burrows' care.

Finally he said: 'What's . . . wrong . . . with me?'

'First let's get you comfortable,' Burrows replied. 'Then we'll talk it all through.'

Todd felt the motion of the nurse as she slipped the fresh pillow into place behind him. Then, with the same tenderness as he used to lift him up, Burrows carefully lowered Todd back down upon the pillow.

'There. Isn't that better?' Burrows said, finally letting his patient go. Todd felt a pang of separation, like a child who'd been abruptly deserted. 'I'm going to let you rest for a while,' Burrows went on. 'And when you've slept, we'll talk properly.'

'No . . .' Todd said.

'Your brother Don's here with you.'

'I'm here, Todd.'

'I want to talk now,' Todd said. 'Not later. Now. Donnie! Make him stay.'

'It's okay, Kiddo,' Donnie said with just the right edge of threat, 'Dr B's not goin' anywhere. Answer his question, Doc.'

'Well, first things first,' Burrows said. 'There's absolutely nothing wrong with your eyes, if that's what you're worried about. We just have to keep the dressings in place around your eye-sockets.'

'You didn't tell me I'd be waking up in the dark,' Todd said.

'No . . .' Burrows replied. 'That's because the procedure didn't go *quite* as we planned. But every operation is a little different, as you'll remember I explained to you. I'm sorry I wasn't here when you woke . . .'

Now that he was calmer, Todd began to recall some of the things about Burrows that had irritated him. One of them was that voice of his: that fake *basso profundo* that was a practised attempt to conceal his queeniness, and to match

122

his voice to the heroic proportions of his body. An artificial body, of course. The man was a walking advertisement for his craft. He was fifty-five at least, but he had the skin of a baby, the arms and the chest of a body-builder and the wasp-waist of a show-girl.

'Just tell me the truth,' Todd said to him. 'Did something go wrong? I'm a big boy. I can take it.'

There was a pin-drop silence. Todd waited. Finally, Burrows said: 'We had a few minor complications with your procedure, that's all. I've explained it all to your brother Donald. There's nothing – *absolutely nothing* – for you to be concerned about. It's just going to take a little more time than we'd –'

'What *kind* of complications?'

'We don't need to go into that now, Todd.'

'Yes, we do,' Todd said. 'It's my *face*, for fuck's sake. *Tell me what's going on*. And don't screw around with me. I don't like it.'

'Tell him, Doc,' Donnie said, quietly but firmly.

Todd heard Burrows sigh. Then that studied voice again: 'You'll remember that during the preparation evaluation I did warn you that on occasion there were reactions to chemical peels which could not be predicted. And I'm afraid that's what happened in your case. You've had an extreme, and as I say completely unpredictable allergic response to the peel. I don't believe for one moment there's going to be any significant damage in the long term. You're a healthy young man. We're going to see some swift epidermal regeneration –'

'What the fuck's that?'

'Your skin's gonna grow back,' Donnie replied, his Texan drawl turning the remark into a piece of cold comedy.

'What do you mean?' Todd said.

'The effect of the procedure we use – as I explained in our evaluation, and is fully described in the literature I gave you –'

'I didn't read it,' Todd said. 'I trusted you.'

'– the procedures we use may be likened to a very controlled chemical burn, which produces changes in the *dermis* and the *epidermis*. Damaged or blemished skin is removed, and after forty-eight hours at the most, new, healthy skin is naturally generated, which has pleasing characteristics. The client regains a youthful –'

This time it was Donnie who interrupted Burrows' molassic flow. 'Tell him the rest,' Donnie said, his voice thick with anger. 'If you don't tell him, I will,' Donnie went on. He didn't give Burrows a chance to make the choice. 'You've been out of it since you had the operation, Kiddo. In a coma. For three days. That's why they sent for me. They were getting worried. I tried to have you moved to a proper hospital, but that bitch of a manager – Maxine, is it? – she wouldn't let me. She said you'd want to stay here. Said she was afraid the press would find out if you were transferred.'

'We're perfectly capable of looking after Mr Pickett here,' Burrows said. 'There isn't a hospital in California that could give him better care.'

'Yeah, well, maybe,' Donnie said. 'Seems to me he'd still be better off in Cedar Sinai.'

'I really resent the implication –' Burrows began.

'*Will you just shut the fuck up?*' Donnie said wearily. 'I don't give a monkey's ass *what* you resent. All I care about is getting my brother properly fixed up and out of here.'

'And as I say –'

'Yeah. As you say. Tell you what, why don't you and Nurse Karyn there step out for a few minutes and let me have a private word with my brother?'

Burrows didn't attempt any further self-justification, and Todd knew why. He could imagine Donnie's expression in perfect detail: both brothers got colour in their faces when they were riled up; and a cold eye. Burrows duly retreated, which was the wisest thing he could have done.

'I want to get you out of here, Kiddo,' Donnie said as soon as they had gone. 'I don't trust these people as far as I could throw 'em. They're full of shit.'

'I need to talk to Maxine before we do anything.'

'What the fuck for? I don't trust her any more than I trust these sons of bitches.'

There was a long silence. Todd knew what was coming next; so he just waited for it.

'Just so you know,' Donnie said, 'you've done some damn-fool things in your life, but this whole deal is the stupidest idea I ever heard. Gettin' yourself a fuckin' face-lift? What kinda thing is that? Christ. Does Momma know about this?'

'No. I put you down as next of kin. I thought you'd understand.'

'Well I can't say I do. It's a mess. It's a goddam mess. And I've got to go back to Texas tomorrow.'

'Why so soon?'

'Because I've got a court appearance at eight o'clock on Thursday morning. Linda's tryin' to take away my weekends with Donnie Junior, and if I'm not in court her lawyer's going to get the judge to rule against me. I've been up before him a couple of times, and he doesn't like me. So, I'm going to have to love you and leave you, which I don't much like doin'. I guess I could call Momma and –'

'*No!* No, Donnie, please. I don't want her here.' Todd reached out blind; caught hold of Donnie's arm. 'I'll be okay. You don't have to worry about me. I'll be just fine.'

'All right. I hear you. I won't call Momma. Besides, the worst's over. I'm sure that's right. But listen to me, you get yourself the hell out of here and go to a proper hospital.'

'I don't want the press finding out about this. If Maxine thinks –'

'Have you heard a fuckin' word I said?' Donnie said, his voice getting louder. 'I don't trust that bitch. She's out for herself. That's all she cares about. Her piece of the action.'

'Don't start shouting.'

'Well, what the fuck do you expect? I've been sitting here for seventy-two hours straight wondering how I was going to tell Mom that you died having plastic fucking surgery on your fucking face –' He paused for a breath. 'Christ, if Dad was alive . . . he'd be so damned ashamed.'

'Okay, Donnie. I get the message. I'm a fuck-up.'

'You're surrounded by so many ass-kissers, you're not getting good advice. It makes me wanna puke. I mean, these people. They're all puttin' on some show – tellin' me this, tellin' me that – and meanwhile you're lying there at death's door.

'And will they give you a straight answer? Will they *fuck!*' He paused to draw sufficient breath to launch in afresh. 'What happened to you, Kiddo? Ten years ago you would have laughed your butt off at the thought of getting a face-lift.'

Todd let go of Donnie's arm. He drew a deep, sorrowful breath. 'It's hard to explain,' he said. 'But I got to stay on top of the heap somehow. Younger guys keep coming along . . .'

'So let 'em. Why do you need to stay on top? Why not walk away from it? You've had a good run, for Christ's sake. You've had it *all*, I'd say. All and more. I mean fuck! What more do you want? Why do this to yourself?'

'Because I *like* the life, Donnie. I like the fame. I like the money.'

Donnie snorted. 'How much more money do you damn well need? You've got more than you can spend if you –'

'Don't tell me what I've got and I haven't got. You don't know what it costs to live. Houses and taxes.' He stopped his defence; took a different track. 'Anyhow, I don't hear you complaining –'

'Wait –' Donnie said, knowing what was coming. But Todd wasn't about to be stopped.

'– when I send you money.'

'Don't start that.'

'Why not? You sit there tellin' me what a fuck-up I am, but you never said no to the cash when you needed it. Which is all the time. Who paid your last legal bills, Donnie? And the mortgage on the house so you could start over with Linda, for the third time or fourth time or whatever it was? Who paid for that mistake?'

He let the question hang there, unanswered. Eventually, very quietly, Donnie said: 'This is so fucked. I came here –'

'– to see whether I was dead or alive.'

'– to look after you.'

'You never cared before,' Todd said, with painful bluntness. 'Well did you? All these years, when have you ever come out here and spent time with me?'

'I was never welcome.'

'You were *always* welcome. You just never came because you were too fucking jealous. Why don't you admit it? At least once, between us, say it: you were so fucking jealous you couldn't stand the idea of coming out here.'

'You know what? I don't need to hear this,' Donnie said.

'You should have heard it years ago.'

'I'm outta here.'

'Go on. You did your gloating. Now you can go home and tell everyone what an asshole your brother is.'

'I'm not going to do that,' Donnie said. 'You're still my brother, whatever you do. But I can't help you if you surround yourself –'

'– with ass-kissers. Yeah. You said that.'

Todd heard Donnie get up and cross to the door, dragging his feet as he always had.

'What are you doing?' Todd said.

'I'm leaving. Like I said I would. You're going to be fine. That faggot Burrows will take very good care of you.'

'Don't I get a hug or something?'

127

'Another time. When I like you better,' Donnie said.

'And when the hell will that be?' Todd yelled after him.

But all he got by way of reply was the echo of his own voice off the opposite wall.

3

Maxine turned up a little after seven, and after a few perfunctory expressions of relief that Todd was 'back from the dead', as she indelicately put it, quickly moved on to the news she was here to debate.

'Somebody in this place has a big mouth,' she said. 'I got a call from the editor of the *Enquirer* this afternoon, asking if it was true that you'd been admitted to a private hospital. I told him absolutely not; this was a lie, garbage etc. etc. And I said that if he published that you were in hospital or anything vaguely resembling that, we'd sue him *and* his wretched rag. Ten seconds later I've got Peter Bart calling from *Variety*, asking the same damn question. And while I'm on with Peter, trying not to tell him an out-and-out lie 'cause he has a nose for bullshit, I have a call from *People* on the other line, asking the same question. Coincidence? I don't think so.'

Todd moaned behind his mask of bandages.

'I've told Burrows we have to move you,' Maxine went on.

'Wait, Donnie said yesterday you told him that you wanted me to stay here.'

'That was before I got the calls. Now it's just a matter of time before some photographer finds his way in here.'

'Shit. Shit. Shit.'

'That would make a nice little picture, wouldn't it?' Maxine said, just in case Todd hadn't already got a snapshot in his mind's eye. 'You lying in bed with your face all bandaged up.'

'Wait!' Todd said, 'They'd never be able to prove it was me.'

'The point is: it *is* you, Todd. Whoever's put out the word about your being here is working in this building. They've probably got access to your records, your charts –'

Todd felt a spasm of the same panic that had seized him when he'd first woken up. The horror of being trapped. This time he governed it, determined not to let Maxine see him losing control.

'So when are you getting me out of here?' he said.

'I've got a car coming at five tomorrow morning. I've told Burrows I want the security in this place tripled 'til you leave. We'll take you to the beach house in Malibu until we find somewhere more practical.'

'I can't go home?' Todd said, knowing even as he floated the idea that it was out of the question. That would be the first place the journalists and the paparazzi would come looking for him.

'Maybe we should fly you out of state when you're feeling a little better. I'll call John; see if I can get him to fly you up to Montana.'

'I don't want to go to Montana.'

'You'd be a lot more secure up there than here. We could arrange for round-the-clock nursing –'

'I said *no*. I don't want to be that far away from everything.'

'All right, we'll find some place here in the city. What about your new lady-friend? Miss Bosch? She's going to be asking questions too. What do you want me to tell her?'

'She's gone. She's shooting something in the Cayman Islands.'

'She was fired,' Maxine said. ' "Creative differences" apparently. The director wanted her to show her tits and she said no. Though God knows some of her runway work has left little to the imagination. I don't know why she's got coy all of a sudden. Anyway, she wants to talk to you. What do I say?'

'Anything you like.'

'So you don't want her in on this?'

'Fuck no. I don't want anybody to know.'

'Okay. It's going to be difficult, but okay. I've got to go. Do you want me to send a nurse in to give you something to help you sleep?'

'Yeah . . .'

'We'll find a place for you, until you mend. I'll ask Jerry Brahms. He knows the city back to front. All we need's a little hideaway. It needn't be fancy.'

'Just make sure he doesn't get wind of what's going on,' Todd said. 'Jerry *talks*.'

'Give me a little credit,' Maxine replied. 'I'll see you tomorrow morning. You get some sleep. And don't worry, nobody's going to find out where you are or what's happened. I'll kill 'em first.'

'Promise.'

'With my bare hands.'

So saying, she was out of the room, leaving Todd alone and in the dark.

Donnie was right, of course. This was undoubtedly the stupidest thing he had ever done. But there was no going back on it. Life, like a movie, only made sense running in one direction. What could he do but go with the flow, and hope to hell there was a happy ending waiting for him in the last reel?

A storm moved in off the Pacific in the middle of the night; the seventh storm of that winter, and the worst. Over the next forty-eight hours it would dump several inches of rain along the coast from Monterey to San Diego, creating a catalogue of minor disasters. Storm-drains overflowed and turned the streets of Santa Barbara into white-water rivers; two citizens and seven street-people were swept away and drowned. Power-lines were brought down by the furious winds, the most badly struck area being Orange County, where a number of communities remained without power for the next three days. Along the Pacific Coast Highway, where the wildfires of the previous autumn had stripped the hillsides of vegetation, the naked earth, no longer knitted together by roots, turned into mud and slid down onto the road. There were countless accidents; fourteen people perished, including a family of seven Mexicans, who'd only been in the promised land four hours, having skipped over the border illegally. All burned up together, trapped in their overturned truck. In the Pacific Palisades, the deluge carried away several million dollar homes; in Topanga Canyon, the same.

Of course all this made the business of getting Todd from the hospital to Maxine's beach house both more lengthy and frustrating than it would have been otherwise, but it may have helped to keep the endeavour secret. Certainly there were no photographers at the hospital door when they left; nor anybody waiting for them in the vicinity of the beach house. But that didn't mean they were out of danger. Calls to Maxine's offices inquiring about Todd's condition had multiplied exponentially, and they were now coming in from further afield – several from Japan, where *Gallows* had just opened – as the rumours spread. One of the German reporters had even had the temerity to suggest that Todd was undergoing plastic surgery.

'I gave him hell. Fucking Kraut.'

'Aren't you German on your mother's side?'

'He's still a fucking Kraut.'

Todd was sitting in the back of Maxine's Mercedes, with Nurse Karyn – who had been thoroughly investigated by Maxine and judged reliable – at his side. The nurse was a woman of few words: but those she chose to utter usually carried some punch.

'I don't see why y'all give a damn. I mean, what does it matter if somebody gets wind of it? He just got a chemical

132

peel and a few nips and tucks. What's the big deal?'

'It's not something Todd's fans need to know about,' Maxine replied. 'They've got a certain idea of who Todd is.'

'So they'd think it wasn't too *masculine*?' Nurse Karyn said.

'Shall we just move on from this?' Maxine said, catching Nurse Karyn's gaze in the driving mirror, and shaking her head to indicate that the conversation – or at least this portion of it – was at an end. Todd, of course, saw none of this. He was still bandaged blind.

'How are you doing, Todd?' Maxine said.

'Wondering how soon –'

'Soon,' Maxine said. 'Soon. Oh, by the way, I had a word with Jerry Brahms, and told him exactly what we needed. Two hours later he came back to me, said he had the *perfect* house for you. I'm going to see it with him tomorrow.'

'Did he tell you where it was?'

'Somewhere up in the hills. Apparently, it was a place he used to go and play when he was a kid. I guess this is in the forties. He says it's completely secluded. Nobody's going to come bothering you.'

'He's full of shit. They have fucking bus tours up in the hills. Every other house has somebody famous living in it.'

'That's what I told him. But he swore this house was ideal. Nobody even knows about the Canyon it's in. That's what he said. So we'll see. If it isn't any good for you, I'll keep looking.'

Later that afternoon, Burrows came out to the beach house to change Todd's dressings. It was a surreal ritual for all concerned: Todd semi-recumbent on the deco sofa in the large window overlooking the beach, Maxine sitting at a distance, nursing an early vodka stinger, Burrows – his confidence tentatively back in place after the prickly

133

exchanges of the previous day – chatting about the rain and the mud-slides while he delicately removed the bandages.

'Now the area around your eyes is going to be a little gummed up,' he warned Todd, 'so don't try and open your eyes until I've done some cleaning.'

Todd said nothing. He was just listening to the boom of his heart in his head, and outside, the boom of the storm-stirred waves. They were out of step with one another.

'I wonder,' Burrows said to Maxine, 'if you'd mind closing the blinds a little way? I don't want it to be too bright in here when I uncover Todd's eyes.'

Todd heard Maxine crossing to the window; then the mechanical hum of the electric blinds as they were lowered.

'I think that'll be far enough,' Burrows said. A click, and the hum stopped. 'Now, let's see how things look. Hold *very* still, Todd, please.'

Todd held his breath as the dressing which the bandages had kept in place was gently teased away from his face. It felt as though a layer of his skin was coming away along with the gauze. He heard a little intake of breath from Maxine.

'What?' he murmured.

'It's okay,' Burrows said softly. 'Please hold still. This is a very delicate procedure. By the way, when I put the new dressing on, I'll be leaving holes for your eyes, so you'll be able to . . . very still, please . . . good, good . . . so you'll be able to see.'

'Maxine . . . ?'

'*Please*, Todd. Don't move a muscle.'

'I want her to tell me what it looks like.'

'She can't see yet, Todd.'

Burrows said something to his nurse, half under his breath. Todd didn't catch the words. But he heard the gauze, which had now been stripped from his face completely, dropped with a wet plop into a receptacle. He

134

imagined it soaked with his blood, shreds of his skin stuck to it. His stomach turned.

'I want to puke,' he said.

'Shall I stop for a moment?' Burrows asked.

'No. Just get it over and done with.'

'Right. Well then I'm going to start cleaning you up,' Burrows said. 'Then we'll see how you're healing. I must say, it's looking *very* good so far.'

'I want Maxine to take a look.'

'In a minute,' Burrows said. 'Just let me –'

'*Now*,' Todd said, nausea fuelling his impatience. He raised his hand blindly and pushed at Burrows. The man moved aside. 'Maxine?' Todd said.

'I'm here.'

Todd beckoned in the direction of Maxine's voice. 'Come and look at me, will you? I want you to tell me what I look like.'

He heard Maxine's heels on the polished wood floor.

'*Hurry*.' Her step quickened. Now she was close by him. 'Well?' he said.

'To be honest, it's hard to tell till he –'

'Christ! I knew it! I fucking *knew* it! He fucked me up!'

'Wait, wait,' Maxine said. 'Calm down. A lot of it's just the ointments he put on you. Let him clean it off before we get hysterical.' Todd reached out to her. She caught hold of his hand. 'It's going to be okay,' she said, though her grip was clammy. 'Just be patient. Why can't men be patient?'

'*You're* not patient,' he reminded her.

'Just let him work, Todd.'

'But you're not. Admit it.'

'All right. I'm not patient.'

Burrows set to work again, meticulously swabbing around Todd's eyes, cleaning his gummed lashes. The stink of cleaning fluid was sharp in his nostrils, his sinuses ran, and his eyes, when he finally opened them, were awash.

'Welcome back,' Maxine said, unknitting her fingers from his, as though a little embarrassed by the intimacy. It took a couple of minutes for Todd's sight to clear, and another two for his eyes to become accustomed to the dimmed light in the room. But part by part, face by face, the world came back to him. The large, half-blinded window, and the rain-lashed deck beyond it. The expensive ease of the room; the Indian rug, the leather furniture, the Calder mobile, in yellow, red and black, which hung below the sky-light. Burrows' knitted brow, and fixed, nervous smile. The nurse, a pretty blonde woman. And finally Maxine, her face ashen. Burrows moved away, like a portrait painter stepping back from a canvas to check the effect he'd achieved.

'I want to see,' Todd said to him.

'Give yourself a minute,' Maxine said. 'Are you still feeling sick?'

'Why? Is it going to make me heave?'

'No,' she said. He almost believed her. 'You just look a little puffy, that's all. And a little *raw*. It's not so bad.'

'You used to be such a good liar.'

'Really,' she insisted. 'It's not so bad.'

'So let me look.' Everyone in the room remained still. 'Will somebody get me a mirror? Okay –' He started to push himself up out of the chair. 'I'll get one myself.'

'Stay where you are,' Maxine said. 'If you really want to see. Nurse? What's your name?'

'Karyn.'

'Go up into the bedroom, and you'll find a little hand mirror there on the vanity. Bring it down.'

It seemed to Todd the girl took an eternity to fetch the mirror. While they waited, Burrows stared out at the rain. Maxine went to refresh her stinger.

Finally, the girl returned. Her eyes were on Burrows, not on Todd.

'Tell her to give it to me,' Todd said.

'Go on,' Burrows said.

The nurse put the mirror into Todd's hand. He took a deep breath, and looked at himself.

There was a moment, as his eyes fixed on his reflection, when reality fluttered, and he thought: *none of this is real*. Not the room, nor the people in it, nor the rain outside, nor the face in the mirror. Especially not the face in the mirror. It was a figment, fluttering and fluttering and –

'Jesus . . .' he said, like Duncan McFarlane, *'look at me –'*

The strength in his hand failed him, and the mirror dropped to the ground. It fell face down. The nurse stooped to pick it up, but he said: 'No. Leave it.'

She stepped away from him, and he caught a look of fear in her eyes. What was she afraid of? His voice, was it? Or his face? God help him if it was his face.

'Somebody open the blinds,' he said. 'Let's get some light in here. It's not a fucking funeral.'

Maxine went to the switch, and flipped it. The mechanism hummed; the blind rose, showing him an expanse of rain-soaked deck, some furniture; and beyond the deck the beach. One solitary jogger – probably some famous fool like himself, determined to preserve his beauty even in the pouring rain – was trudging along the shore, followed by two bodyguards. Todd got up from his chair and went to the window. Then, despite the presence of strangers, he laid his hand against the cold glass and began to weep.

4

Burrows had brought both painkillers and tranquillizers that Todd supplemented with a large order from Jerome Bunny, a ratty little Englishman who'd been his supplier of illicit pharmaceuticals for the last four years. Under their influence, Todd spent the next twenty-four hours in a semi-somnambulant state.

The rain was unrelenting. He sat in front of Maxine's immense television screen and watched a succession of images of other people's pain – houses gone, families divided – dreamily wondering if any of them would exchange their misery for his. Every now and then a memory of the visage he'd seen in the mirror – vaguely resembling somebody he'd known, but horribly wounded, filled with pus and blood – would swim up before him, and he'd take another pill, or two or three, and wash it down with a shot of single malt, and wait for the opiates to drive the horror off a little distance.

The new dressings Burrows had put on, though as promised they indeed left his eyes uncovered, were still oppressive, and more than once Todd's hands went up to his face unbidden, and would have ripped the bandages off had he not governed himself in time. He felt grotesque, like something from a late-night horror movie, his face – which had been his glory – become some horrible secret, festering away beneath the bandages. He asked Maxine what movie it was – some Rock Hudson weepie – in which a man was covered up this way. She didn't know.

'And stop thinking about yourself for a while,' she said. 'Think about something else.'

Easily said; the trouble was thinking about himself came naturally to him. In fact, it had become second-nature to him over the years to put all other considerations out of sight: to care only about Todd Pickett, and (on occasion) Dempsey. Not to have done so would have meant a diminution of his power in the world. After all, he'd been playing a game which only the truly self-obsessed had a chance of victory. All others were bound to fall by the wayside. Now, when it would have been healthier to direct his attention elsewhere, he'd simply lost the knack. And he had no dog by his side to love him for being the boss, whatever the hell he looked like.

Late in the day Maxine came back from her visit to the Hideaway, as she had now dubbed it, with some good news. The house in the hills was just as Jerry Brahms had advertised.

'It's the only house in the Canyon,' she said.

'Which Canyon?'

'I don't even think it's got a name.'

'They've all got names, for God's sake.'

'All I can tell you is that it's somewhere between Cold-water and Laurel. To be perfectly honest I got a little lost following Jerry up there. He drives like the Devil. And you know my sense of geography.'

'What is the house like?'

'Right now it's practically empty. There's some old stuff in there – looks like it goes back to the fifties, maybe earlier – but nothing you'd want to use. I'll have Marco choose some furniture from the Bel Air house and move it over. Get you comfortable. But really it's ideal for what we need right now. By the way, Ms Bosch has been calling my office. She got quite pushy with Sawyer. She's absolutely certain you're in Hawaii screwing some starlet.'

'If that's what she wants to think.'

'You don't care?'

'Not right now.'

'You're certain you don't want to see her?'

'*Christ*. See her? No, Maxine. I do not want to see her.'

'She was pretty upset.'

'That's because she wanted a part in *Warrior*, and she thought I'd get it for her.'

'Okay. End of discussion. If she calls again –?'

'Tell her she's right. I'm in Hawaii fucking the ass off anyone you care to name. Manipulative little bitch.'

'So here,' Maxine said. She proffered an envelope.

'What's this?'

'They're the pictures I took of the Hideaway.'

He took the envelope. 'It'll be fine,' he said before he'd even looked at the photographs.

'You might be there for a few weeks. I want you to be comfortable.'

Todd pulled out the photographs.

'They're not the best, I'm afraid,' Maxine said. 'It's one of those throwaway cameras. And it was raining. But you get the idea.'

'It looks big.'

'According to Jerry they used to call them dream palaces. All the rich stars had them. It's hokey, but it's got a lot of atmosphere. There's a huge master-bedroom with a view straight down the Canyon. You can see Century City; probably the ocean on a clear day. And the living room's as big as a ballroom. Whoever built it put a lot of love into it. All the mouldings, the door-handles, everything is top of the line. Of course it gets campy. There's a fresco on the ceiling of the turret. All these faces leaning over looking down at you. Famous movie stars, Jerry said. I didn't recognize any of 'em but I guess they were from silent movies.' She paused, waiting for judgment. Todd just kept looking at the pictures. 'Well?' Maxine finally said. 'Too Old Hollywood for you?'

'No. It's fine. Anyway, isn't that what I am now?'

'What?'

'Old Hollywood.'

J erry Brahms had been a child-actor in the late thirties, but his career hadn't lasted into puberty. He'd been at his 'most picturesque', as he liked to put it, at the age of nine or ten, after which it had all been downhill. Todd had always thought of Brahms as being slightly ridiculous: with his overly-coiffed silver hair, his mock-English diction, and his unforgiving bitchiness about the profession to which he'd once aspired.

But Jerry knew his Hollywood, there was no doubt of that. He lived and breathed the place: its scandals, its triumphs. He was most informed about the Golden Age of Tinseltown, which coincided, naturally enough, with the years of his employment. In matters relating to this period his knowledge was encyclopaedic, as he'd proved three years before, when Todd had been looking for a new house. Jerry had volunteered his services as a location scout, and after a week or two had taken Todd and Maxine on a grand tour of properties he thought might be suitable. Todd had not wanted to go; he found Jerry's chatter grating. But Maxine had insisted. 'He'll be heartbroken if you don't go,' she'd said. 'You know how he idolizes you. Besides, he might have found something you like.'

So Todd had gone along; and it had turned out to be quite a trip. Jerry had organized the tour as though he was entertaining royalty (which perhaps, as far as he was concerned, he was). He'd hired a stretch, supplied a champagne-and-caviar hamper from Greenblatt's in case they wanted to picnic along the way, and a map of the city, on which he'd meticulously marked their route. They went down to the Colony in Malibu, they wound their way through Bel Air and Beverly Hills; they looked at Hancock Park and Brentwood, their route plotted by Jerry so that he could show off his knowledge of where the luminaries of Hollywood had lived and died. They passed by Falcon Lair on Bella Drive, which Valentino had built at the height of his fame. They went to the Benedict Canyon Drive home where Harold Lloyd had spent much of his life, and past Jayne Mansfield's Pink Palace, which was as gaudy as ever, and the house where Marilyn and DiMaggio had briefly lived in wedded bliss. They visited homes occupied, at one time or another, by John Barrymore ('It *still* smells of liquor,' Jerry had remarked), Ronald Colman, Hearst's widow, Marion Davies, Clara Bow, Lucille Ball and Mae West. Not all the houses were for sale, nor open for inspection; in some cases Jerry's research had simply turned up a property close by, or one that resembled the house in which some luminary had lived. Other properties were located in areas that had become shadows of their glamorous selves, but Jerry didn't seem to care, or perhaps even notice. The fact that stars whose faces had become legendary – whose names evoked lives of elegance and luxury – had lived in these homes blinded him to the fact that there was often decay around them. They were like sacred sites, and he a pilgrim. Todd had found the tenderness with which he talked about these places, and about the people who'd once occupied them, curiously touching.

Four or five times during the trip Jerry had directed the driver to a certain spot, invited Maxine and Todd to get out of the limo in order to show them a certain view, then presented them with a photograph taken on precisely the same spot sixty or seventy years before, when many of the places they visited had been little more than an expanse

143

of cactus and sand. It had been an education for Todd. He hadn't realized until then how recent Los Angeles was, nor how tenuous its existence was. The greenery was as artificial as the stucco walls and the colonial facades. The city was one enormous back-lot, fake and fragile. If the water ever ceased to pump then this verdant world, with its palaces and its swooning falls of bougainvillaea, would pass away.

As it turned out, Todd hadn't ended up buying any of the properties Jerry had shown them that day, which was probably for the best. He finally decided to stay in his house in Bel Air, but substantially remodel it. It didn't matter, Jerry had said, apparently reserving his opinion on whether Todd would join the pantheon of guests, nobody legendary had ever lived there.

Once Todd had said yes to the house in the hills, it took a day to get the move to the Hideaway properly organized; a day which left Todd spent sitting at the window of the Malibu house, staring at the pale reflection of his bandaged face in the rain-spattered glass. Technically, the painkillers Burrows had given him should have left him without any discomfort whatsoever, *but* for some reason, even when supplemented by some of Bunny's specials – not a minute of that day passed without his being acutely aware of the pressure of the gauze and the bandages on his face. He morbidly wondered if perhaps he wouldn't be left with this residue of feeling for the rest of his life; he'd heard of people who'd had certain operations who were made much worse by the surgeon's knife, and indeed were never the same again. The thought terrified him: that he'd done something completely irreversible. But there was no use in regretting it. All he could do now was hope to God that this unavoidable complication, as Burrows insisted it was, would be quickly cured, and he'd have his face back intact. He wasn't even hoping for improvement at this point. Just the old, familiar Todd Pickett face would do fine; creases, laugh-lines and all.

Later, Marco came to pick Todd up, having spent the morning moving some essentials over to the new house. Todd went with him in the sedan, Maxine followed on.

'I got lost twice this morning,' Marco said, 'going back and forth from the old house to the new one. I don't know why the hell it happened, but twice I got all turned round and found myself back onto Sunset again.'

'Weird,' Todd said.

'There are no street signs up there.'

'No?'

'There aren't many houses, either, which is what I like. No neighbours. No tour buses. No fans climbing over the walls.'

'Dempsey used to get them!'

'Oh yes, old Dempsey was great. Remember that German? Huge guy? Climbs over the wall, gets Dempsey's teeth clamped in his ass and then –'

'Tries to sue me.'

'– tries to sue you.'

They chuckled at the incident for a moment, then rode in silence for a while.

6

'So what exactly did Jerry tell you about this place?' Todd asked Maxine as they stood outside the Hideaway.

'Not much. I told you he'd played here as a kid? Yes, I did. Well, he said he had wonderful memories of the house. That was about all.'

Maxine hadn't taken any pictures of the exterior, it had been raining so hard that day. Now, seen clearly for the first time, the house appeared much larger than Todd had anticipated; perfectly deserving of the term 'dream palace'. He couldn't get a complete grasp of its size because the vegetation around it had been left to run wild. A large grove of bamboo to the right of the front door had grown fully thirty feet, its tallest stalks standing higher than the chimney-stacks. Bougainvillaea grew everywhere in lunatic abundance, purple, red, pink and white; and even the humble ferns, planted in the shade of the perimeter wall, had flourished there, and grown antediluvian. There was room beneath the fronds to stand with your hands raised and still not touch the nubby spores on their underbellies.

The house itself was palatial Spanish in style, with more than a hint of Hollywood fantasy in its genes. The stucco was a washed-out pink, the roof a washed-out red. There was a great deal of elaborate tilework at the front steps, and around the windows, the tiles themselves still bright blue and turquoise and white, the complex interplay of their patterns lending a touch of Moorish beauty to the façade. The front door looked as though it had been purloined from the set of a medieval epic; the kind of door Douglas Fairbanks Senior might have slammed and bolted shut to keep out an army of evil-doers. It would have sufficed too, in its enormity. Maxine had to push hard to open it; and when it finally swung wide it did so not with a gothic creak but with a deep rumble, as a system of counterweights hidden in the wall aided her labour.

'Very dramatic,' Todd remarked, playing it off. In truth, he was impressed by the scale of the place; by its scale and theatricality. But guileless enthusiasm he'd had shamed out of him long ago. It wasn't cool to like anything too much, except yourself.

Maxine led the way through the turret, with its grandiose spiral staircase and its trompe l'oeil ceiling, into the house. The photographs she'd taken had come nowhere near doing the place justice. Even stripped of most of its furniture, as it was, and in need of repair, it was still nothing short of magnificent. There was everywhere evidence of master craftsmen at work: from the pegged wood floors to the elegantly carved ceiling panels; from the exquisite symmetry of the marble mantels to the filigree of the wrought iron handrails, only the best had been good enough for the man or woman who'd owned this place.

Marco had artlessly arranged a few items of Todd's furniture in the living room, a little island of brittle modernity in the midst of something older and more mysterious. Todd made a mental note to give everything he owned away, and start again. In future, he was going to buy antiques.

They went through to the kitchen. It was built on the same heroic scale as everything else: ten cooks could have happily worked in it and not got in one another's way.

'I know it's all ridiculously old-fashioned,' Maxine said. 'But it'll do for a little while, won't it?'

'It'll do just fine,' Todd said, still surprised at how much the place pleased him. 'What's out back?'

'Oh the usual. A pool. Tennis courts. And a huge koi pond. Probably a polo field for all I know.'

'Any fish in the pond?'

'No. You want fish?'

'It's no big deal.'

'I can get koi for you if you want them. Just say the word.'

'I know. But it's not worth it. I'll be here a month and gone.'

'So take them with you.'

'And where would I put them?'

'Okay,' Maxine shrugged. 'No fish.' She went to the kitchen window and continued her description of the real estate. 'The whole Canyon belongs to the house, as far as I can see, but the gardens spread down the hill an acre and a half and all the way up to the top of the hill behind us. There's a guest-house up there. Perhaps two. I didn't go look: I figured you wouldn't be having any visitors.'

'Does Jerry know anything about the history of the place?'

'I'm sure he does, but to be honest I didn't ask.'

'What did you tell him about me?'

'I told him you had a stalker, and she was getting dangerous. You needed to get out of the Bel Air house for a while until the police had caught her. Frankly, I'm not sure he bought it. He's got to have heard the rumours. I think we'd be best letting him in on what's been happening –'

'We've had this conversation once –'

'Hear me out, will you? If we make him feel like he's part of the conspiracy, he'll stay quiet, just because he wants to please you. He'll only get chatty if he thinks we kept him out because we didn't trust him.'

'Why the hell would he want to please me?'

'You know why, Todd. He's in love with you.'

Todd shook his bandaged head, which was a mistake. The room around him swam for a moment, and he had to grab hold of the table.

'You okay?' Maxine said.

He raised his hands, palms out, in mock surrender. 'I'm fine. I just need a pill and a drink. I sent Marco out to get some supplies.'

'But Todd . . . it's barely gone noon.'

'So? If I stay here and get shit-faced every day for the next month who's going to care? Find me something to drink, will you?'

'What about Jerry? We didn't finish –'

'We'll talk about Jerry some other time.'

'Am I telling him or not?'

'I said I don't want to talk about it any more.'

'All right. But if he starts to gossip, don't say I didn't warn you.'

'If he tells the fucking *National Enquirer* it's my fault. Happy?'

Todd didn't wait for a reply. Leaving Maxine to search for the liquor, he wandered out to the back of the house. The lawn – which lay at the bottom of a long flight of steps from the house, their railings entirely overtaken by vines – was the size of a small field, but it had been invaded on every side by the offspring of the plants, shrubs and trees which surrounded it, many of them in premature flower. Bird of Paradise trees twenty feet tall, sycamore and eucalyptus, rose bushes and fox-gloves, early California poppies shining like satin in the grass; meadowfoam and corn lily, hairy honeysuckle and wild grape, golden yarrow, blue blossom and red huckleberry. And everywhere, of course, the ubiquitous pampas grass; soft, fleecy plumes swaying in the sun. It was uncommon, even uncanny, verdancy.

Todd strode across the lawn, which was still wet from the rain, down to the pool. Dragonflies flitted everywhere;

bees wove their nectar trails through the balmy air. The pool was a baroque affair, descending from the relatively restrained style of the main house into pure Hollywood kitsch. The model, perhaps, was B de Mille Roman. A large mock-classical bronze fountain was set at the back of the pool, the intertwined limbs of its figures – a sea-god and his female attendants – rendered more baroque still by the tracery of living vines which had crept up over it. A sizeable conch in the sea-god's hands had once been a source of rejuvenating waters for the pool, but those waters had ceased to flow a long time ago. Todd was mildly disappointed. He would have liked to have seen sparkling blue water in the pool instead of the few inches of bottle green rain-water that were there at the bottom.

He turned and looked back towards the house. It was still more impressive from this side than it had been from the front, its four floors rising like the tiers of a wedding cake, its walls lush with ivy in places, and in others naked. Beyond it, further up the hill, Todd could just see a glimpse of one of the guest-houses that Maxine had mentioned. Altogether, it really was an impressive parcel of land, with or without the buildings. Had Jerry shown it to him as part of the grand tour Todd might well have been tempted to invest. The fact that Jerry hadn't done so probably meant that it had not belonged to anyone of significance, though that seemed odd. This wasn't just any Hollywood show-place: it was the crème de la crème, a glorious confection of a residence designed to show off all the wealth, power and taste of a great star.

By the time he'd made his way back inside, Marco had turned up from Greenblatt's with a car-load of supplies. He welcomed his boss with his usual crooked smile and a generous glass of bourbon.

'So what do you think of the Old Dark House?'

'You know . . . in a weird way I like it here.'

'Really?' said Maxine. 'It's nothing like your taste.' She

was plainly still mildly irritated by their earlier exchange, though for Todd it was past history, soothed away by his wanderings in the wilderness.

'I never really felt comfortable in Bel Air,' he said. 'That house has always been more like a hotel to me than a home.'

'I wouldn't say this place was exactly *cosy*,' Maxine remarked.

'Oh, I don't know,' Todd said. He sipped on his bourbon, smiling into his glass. 'Dempsey would have liked it,' he said.

7

On Thursday, 18th of March, Maxine got a call that she knew was coming. The caller was a woman called Tammy Lauper, who ran the International Todd Pickett Appreciation Society, which despite its high falutin' title had its headquarters, Maxine knew, in the Laupers' house in Sacramento. Tammy was calling to ask a very simple question, one that she said she was 'passing on' to Maxine from millions of Todd's fans worldwide: *Where was Todd?*

Maxine had dealt with Tammy on many occasions in the past, though if she possibly could she ducked the calls and let Sawyer deal with them. The trouble was that Tammy Lauper was an obsessive, and though in the eight years she'd been running the 'Appreciation Society' – (she'd once said to Maxine she hated to hear it called a *fan club*. 'I'm not an hysterical teenager,' she'd said. This was true: Tammy Lauper was married, childless, and, when last spotted, an overweight woman in her middle thirties) – she'd done a great deal to support Todd's movies, and could on occasion be a useful disseminator of deliberately erroneous information, she was not somebody Maxine had much time for. The woman annoyed her, with her perpetual questions about trivia, and her unspoken assumption that somehow Todd belonged to her. When she *was* obliged to speak to the Lauper woman – because there was some delicate matter in the air, and she needed to carefully modulate the flow of news – she always aimed to keep the exchanges brief. As courteous as possible – Tammy could be prickly if she didn't feel as though she was being given her due – but brief.

Today, however, Tammy wasn't about to be quickly satisfied; she was like a terrier with a rat. Every time Maxine thought she'd satisfied the woman's curiosity, back she'd come with another enquiry.

'Something's wrong,' she kept saying. 'Todd's not been seen by *anyone*. Usually when he goes away, members of the Society spot him, and they report to me. But I haven't heard *one word*. Something's wrong. Because I *always* hear.'

'I'm sure you do.'

'So what's going on? You've got to tell me.'

'Why should anything be going on?' Maxine said, doing her best to maintain her equilibrium. 'Todd's tired and he needs a break, so he went away for a few weeks.'

'Out of state?'

'Yes. Out of state.'

'Out of the country?'

'I'm afraid he asked me not to say.'

'Because we've got members all over the world.'

'I realize that, but –'

'When he went on his honeymoon to Morocco,' Tammy went on, 'I had six reports of sightings.' (This was a reference to the event which had caused Maxine more publicity problems than any other in Todd's life: his short-lived marriage to the exquisitely emaciated model Avril Fox, which had been strewn with potentially image-besmirching scenes: adulteries, a couple of ménages-à-trois involving Avril's sister, Lucy, and a spot of domestic violence.)

'Sometimes,' Maxine said, a trace of condescension creeping into her voice now, 'Todd likes to be out in public. Sometimes he doesn't.'

'And right now?'

'He doesn't.'

'But *why* would he mind being seen?' Tammy went on. 'If there's nothing wrong with him . . .'

153

Maxine hesitated, wondering how best to calm the suspicions she was clearly arousing. She couldn't just make an excuse and jump off the phone; that would make the Lauper woman even more curious than she already was. She had to manoeuvre the conversation away from this dangerous area as carefully as possible.

'I'll tell you why,' she said, dropping her voice a little, as though she was about to share something of real significance with Tammy. 'He's got a secret project in the works.'

'Oh?' Tammy said. She didn't sound persuaded. 'This isn't *Warrior*, is it? I read that script, and –'

'No, it isn't *Warrior*. It's a very personal piece, which Todd is writing himself.'

'He's writing it? Todd is writing something? He said in an interview with *People* last July he hated writing. It was too much like hard work.'

'Well, I lied a little,' Maxine said. 'He's not doing the actual writing. He's working with somebody on the project. A very well-respected screenwriter, actually. But he's pouring out his heart, so it'll be a very personal project.' There was a silence. Maxine waited. Had Tammy taken the bait or not?

'So this is autobiographical, this movie?'

'I didn't say it was a movie,' Maxine said, taking some petty pleasure in catching Tammy out. 'It may end up on the screen, but right now he's just working hard to get his feelings down. He and the writer, that is.'

'Who is the writer?'

'I can't say.'

'You know it would make all this very much more *believable* if you gave me some more details,' Tammy said.

That was it. Maxine lost her composure. How dare this little bitch suggest her lies weren't believable?

'You know I've really said more than I should already, Tammy,' she snapped. 'And I've got six calls waiting. So if you'll excuse me –'

'Wait – What am I going to tell the members?'

'What I just told you.'

'You *swear* Todd's fine?'

'Good God, how many times? *Yes*. Todd is perfectly fine. In fact, he's never been better.' She drew a deep breath, and attempted to calm herself a little before she ended up saying something she regretted. 'Look, Tammy, I really wish I could tell you more. But this is a matter of Todd's privacy, as I'm sure you understand. He needs a little time away from the pressure of being a celebrity, so he can work on this project, and when he's finished I'm sure you'll be one of the first to hear about it. Now really, I've got to go.'

'One more question,' Tammy said.

'Yes.'

'What's it called?'

'What's what called?' Maxine replied, playing for time.

'The script. Or the book. Or whatever it's going to be. What's it called?'

Oh shit, Maxine thought. Now she was in deep. Well, why the hell not give the damn woman a title? She'd lied herself into a hole as it was, one more shovelful wouldn't hurt. She pictured Todd in an image now indelibly inscribed in her mind's eye, sitting waiting for Burrows to start cutting away the bandages. And the title came:

'*The Blind Leading the Blind*,' she said.

'I don't like that,' Tammy said, already proprietorial.

'Neither do I,' Maxine replied, thinking not just of the title, but of this whole, sprawling, exhausting mess. 'Trust me, Tammy. Neither do I.'

Tammy Jayne Lauper lived on Elverta Road in Rio Linda, Sacramento, in a one-storey ranch-style house fifteen minutes from the Sacramento International Airport, where her husband had worked for eight years as a baggage handler. They had no kids, nor any hope of having any, this side of a miracle of Biblical proportions. Arnie had a zero sperm count. Tammy didn't mind much. Just because God had given her breasts the size of watermelons didn't mean she was born for motherhood. And of course the absence of children left plenty of space in the house for all the files relating to what Arnie sneeringly called 'Tammy's little fan club'.

'It isn't a fan club,' Tammy had pointed out countless times, 'it's an *Appreciation Society*.' Arnie said Tammy wasn't no appreciator, she was a fan, plain and simple, and he knew every time they'd used to sleep together and she closed her eyes it was that dickhead Pickett she'd been imagining on top of her fat ass, and that was the whole unvarnished truth of it. When Arnie got to talking like that, Tammy would just tune him out. He'd stop eventually, when he knew she wasn't listening; go back to sitting in front of the TV with a beer.

The main centre of the Todd Pickett Appreciation Society's operations was the front bedroom. The room she and Arnie slept in was considerably smaller, but as she'd pointed out to him, it didn't really matter since all they did was sleep in it. They still had a double bed, though God knows why; he never touched her; and a couple of years back she'd stopped wanting him to. The third bedroom (and all the closets), were used for storage: files of clippings, issues of the fanzine (quarterly for the first year, then monthly, now quarterly again), photographs and biographies to be distributed to new members, copies of press kits from every film Todd had ever made, in twenty-six languages. Downstairs, in what would have been the family room, she kept the Collection. This was made up of items related to Todd and his career, all of them relatively rare, some one-of-a-kind items. Hanging in zipped-up plastic laundry bags were articles of clothing made for the cast and crew of his pictures. On the mantelpiece, still sealed in their boxes were six Todd Pickett dolls that had been the hot thing to own during his teen-idol period, the boxes signed by Todd. Preserved in a vacuum pack were several unused latex makeup pieces for his Oscar-nominated performance as the maimed firefighter in *The Burning Year*. She didn't ever look at those. She'd been warned that they deteriorated when they were exposed to sunlight.

The collection also contained a comprehensive library of scripts for his movies, with all their addenda, including one marked up in Todd's handwriting, along with a complete set of novelizations of the movies, leather-bound with gilt lettering. There were also credit-listings on all the crews who worked with him, costume sketches and call-sheets, and of course, posters of every size and nationality. If the Smithsonian ever wanted to open a wing dedicated to the life and career of Todd Pickett, Tammy had once boasted, they need look no further than her front room. Once, she'd attempted to enumerate the items she owned. It was something in the region of seventeen thousand three hundred, not including those pieces of which she had more than one copy.

It was to this shrine that Tammy had come after her frustrating exchange with Maxine Frizelle. She closed and locked the door (though Arnie would not be back from work and his after-hours carousing for some time), and sat down to think. After a few minutes, turning over the conversation she'd just had, she went to the very back of the room, and took from its place amongst the treasure-trove a box of photographs. These were her special pride and joy: pictures of Todd (fourteen of them in all) which she'd managed to buy from somebody who'd known the still photographer on Todd's third picture, *Life Lessons*. This was Todd's coming-of-age picture: the one in which he'd changed from being a Boy to being a Man. Of course, his smile would always be a boy's smile, that was part of its magic, but after *Life Lessons* he went on to play tougher roles: a homecoming soldier, a firefighter, a man wrongfully accused of his own wife's murder. Here then, caught in the moment before his cinematic adulthood, was the boy-man of Tammy's dreams. She had even purchased the negatives from which the series of pictures had been printed, and along with them the assurance from the person she'd got them from that they had been 'lost' in the production offices before they were ever seen by the director, the producer or by Todd himself. In short, she had the only copies.

Their rarity wasn't the reason she valued them so highly however. What made them her special treasure – the quality that made her return to them over and over, when Arnie was out at work, and she knew she had time for reverie – was the fact that the photographer had caught his subject unawares. Well, shirtless and unawares. Todd was sleek and pale, his body not heavy at all, not all muscle and veins popping out, just a nice, ordinary body; the body of the boy next door if the boy next door happened to be perfect. She had never seen a body she thought so beautiful. Then there was his face. Oh that face! She'd seen literally thousands of photographs of Todd in the last eleven years – and to her adoring eyes he was handsome in every single one of them – but in these particular pictures he was something more than handsome. There was a certain lost look in his eyes, that allowed her to indulge the belief that if she'd been there at that moment – if he'd seen her and looked at her with the same forsaken feeling in his heart as was in his eyes – everything in her life would have been different; and maybe, just maybe, everything in his.

When she was thinking clearly, she knew all this was romantic nonsense. She was a plain woman; and, even though she'd shed thirty-two pounds in the last two years, was still thirty overweight. How could she hope to compare with the glossy beauties Todd had romanced, both on screen and off? Still she allowed herself the indulgence, once in a while. It made life in Sacramento a little more bearable to know that her secret glimpses of Todd were always there, hidden away, waiting for her. And best of all, nobody else had them. They were hers and hers alone.

There was one other wonderful thing about the fourteen pictures: they had been snapped in such quick succession that if she leafed through them fast enough she could almost create the illusion of movement. She did that now, while she thought about the way Maxine had talked to her on the phone. That nonsense about Todd going away to write his life-story, or whatever she'd said it was going to be; it didn't ring true. It simply wasn't like Todd to be so inaccessible. Every vacation he'd taken – in India, in New Guinea, in the Amazon, for God's sake – he'd been spotted. Somebody had had a camera, and he'd posed; smiled, waved, goofed around. It just wasn't like him to disappear like this.

But what could she do about it? She wasn't going to get any answers out of anybody close to Todd: they'd all trot out the same story. She'd already exhausted her contacts at the studios, all of whom claimed not to have seen Todd in a while. Even over at Paramount, where he was supposedly making his next picture, nobody had seen him in many months. Nor, according to her most reliable source over there, the secretary to Sherry Lansing's assistant, were there any meetings on the books, either with Todd or any of his production team. It was all very strange, and it made Tammy afraid for her man. Suppose they were covering something up? Suppose there'd been an accident, or an assault, and Todd had been hurt? Suppose he was in a hospital bed somewhere on life-support, his life slipping away, while all the sons of bitches who'd made fortunes off his talent were lying to themselves and anyone who'd listen, pretending it was going to be okay? Things like that happened all the time; especially in Hollywood. Everyone lied there; it was a way of life.

Her thoughts circled on these terrible images for an hour or more, while she sat amongst her treasures. At last, she came to a momentous decision. She could do nothing to solve this mystery sitting here in Sacramento. She needed to go out to Los Angeles, and confront some of these people. It was easy to tell somebody a lie on the telephone. It was harder to do when you were face to face with someone; when you were looking into their eyes.

She took one last look through the sequence of photographs, lingering on the last of the fourteen, the one in which Todd's gaze was closest to making contact with the camera. Another shot, and he would have been looking directly at her. Their eyes, as it were, would have met. She smiled at him, kissed his picture, then put the photographs away, tucked the box out of sight and went through to the kitchen to call Arnie at the airport, and tell him what she planned to do. He was in the middle of his shift, and couldn't come to the phone. She left a message for him to call her; then she made a reservation on Southwest for the flight to Los Angeles, and booked a room in a little hotel on Wilshire Boulevard, which she'd stayed in once before when she'd come into LA for a Todd Pickett convention.

The flight was scheduled at 3:10 that afternoon, and was to get into Los Angeles at 4:15, but the departure was delayed for almost two hours, and then they circled over LAX for almost three quarters of an hour before they could land, so it wasn't until half-past seven that she stepped out of the airport into the warm, sweet-smog air of her beloved's city.

She didn't know what she was going to do, now she was here; how or where she was going to begin. But at least she wasn't sitting at home brooding. She was closer to him, here, whatever Maxine Frizelle had said about him being off in some faraway place. That was a lie; Tammy knew it in her bones. *He was here*. And if he was in any trouble, then by God she would do her best to help him, because whatever anybody might say she knew one thing for certain: there wasn't a soul on earth who cared for the well-being of Todd

Pickett more than she. And somewhere, tucked away in a shameful corner of her head she almost hoped that there was some conspiracy here; because that would give her a chance to come to his rescue; to save him from people like Frizelle, and make him understand who really cared about him. Oh, wouldn't that be something! She didn't dare think about it too much; it made her sick with guilt and anticipation. She shouldn't be wishing anything but the best for her Todd. And yet the same thought kept creeping back: that somewhere in this city he was waiting for her – even if he didn't know it yet; waiting to be saved and comforted. Yes, she dared think it: perhaps even loved.

8

Todd and Marco had settled into life at the Hideaway in the Canyon quite easily. Todd occupied the enormous master bedroom which had (as Maxine had boasted) an extraordinary view down the canyon. On clear days, of which there were many in that early March, Todd could sit at his window and watch the ocean, glittering beyond the towers of Century City. On exceptional days, he could even make out the misty shape of Catalina Island.

Marco had taken a much smaller bedroom on the top floor, with an adjacent sitting room, and did much as he had in the Bel Air home: that is, served with uncanny prescience the needs of his boss, and having provided such services as were required, then retreated into near-invisibility.

The area was much quieter than Bel Air. There seemed to be no through traffic on the single road that wound up through the Canyon, so apart from the occasional sound of a police helicopter passing over, or a siren drifting up from Sunset, Todd heard nothing from the city that lay such a short distance below. What he did hear, at night, were coyotes, who seemed to haunt the slopes of the canyon in significant numbers. On some nights, standing on one of the many balconies of his new mansion nursing a drink and a cigarette, he would hear a lone animal begin its urgent yapping on the opposite slope of the canyon, only to hear its call answered from another spot, then another, the din rising into a whooping chorus from the darkness all around him, so that it seemed the entire canyon was alive with them. They'd had coyotes up in Bel Air too, of course. Their proximity to the house would always send Dempsey into a frenzy of deep-chest barking, as though to announce that the dog of the house was much larger than he was, in reality.

'I'm surprised we've got so many coyotes up here,' Marco said, after one particularly noisy night. 'You'd think they'd go somewhere with a lot more garbage. I mean, they're scavengers, right?'

'Maybe they like it here,' Todd observed.

'Yeah, I guess.'

'There's no people to fuck with them.'

'Except us.'

'We won't be here long,' Todd said.

'You don't sound too happy about that.'

'Well I guess I could get used to it here.'

'Have you been up on the ridge yet?'

'No. I haven't had the energy.'

'You should go up there. Take a look. There's quite a view.'

The exchange, brief as it was, put the thought of a trip up the hill into Todd's head. He needed to start exercising again, as Maxine had pointed out, or he was going to find that his face was all nicely healed up and his body had gone to fat. He didn't believe for a minute that his face was anywhere near being healed, but he took her point. He was drinking too much and eating too many Elvis Midnight Specials (peanut butter, jelly, crispy bacon and sliced banana on Wonder Bread sandwiches, deep fried in butter) for the good of his waistline. His pants were feeling tight, and his ass – when he glimpsed it in the mirror – was looking fleshy.

In a while he'd have to get back to some serious training: start running every morning; maybe have his gym equipment brought over from the Bel Air house and installed in the guest-house. But in the meantime he'd ease back into the swing of things with a few exploratory walks: one of which, he promised himself, would be up the top of the hill, to see what the view was like when you got to the end of the road.

Burrows and Nurse Karyn came every other day to change the dressings and assess the condition of his face. Though Burrows claimed that the healing process was going well, his manner remained subdued and cautious: it was clear that the whole sorry business had taken a toll upon his confidence. His sun-bed tan could not conceal a certain sickliness in his pallor; and the skin around his eyes and mouth, taut from a series of tucks and tightenings, had an unnatural rigidity to it, like a teak mask under which another, more fragile man, was trapped. Superficially, he remained unfailingly optimistic about Todd's prognosis; he was certain there would be no permanent scarring. Indeed he was even willing to chance the opinion that things were going to work out 'as planned', and that Todd was going to emerge from the whole experience looking ten years younger.

'So how long is it going to be before I can take off the bandages?'

'Another week, I'd say.'

'And after that . . . how long before I'm back to normal again?'

'I don't want to make any promises,' Burrows said, 'but inside a month. Is there some great urgency here?'

'Yeah, I want people to see me. I want them to know I'm not *dead*.'

'Surely nobody believes *that*,' Burrows said.

Todd summoned Marco. 'Where are those tabloids you brought in?' he asked. 'The doctor's not been reading the trash in his waiting-room recently.'

Marco left the room and re-appeared with five magazines, dropping them on the table beside Burrows. The top one had a blurred, black and white photograph of a burial procession, obviously taken with an extremely long-distance lens. The headline read: *Superstar Todd Pickett Buried in Secret Ceremony*. The magazine beneath had an unsmiling picture of Todd's ex-girlfriend, Wilhemina Bosch, and announced, as though from her grieving lips: *'I never even had a chance to tell him good-bye.'* And underneath, a third magazine boasted that it contained *Todd Pickett's Last Words! 'I saw Christ standing at his death-bed, claims nurse.'* Burrows didn't bother with the others.

'Who starts bullshit like this?'

'You tell me,' Todd replied.

'I hope you're not implying that it was somebody in my surgery, because I *assure* you we've been vigorous –'

'Yeah, yeah, yeah,' Todd said. 'You're not responsible for anything. I know. See? I *finally* got smart. I read the small print.'

'Frankly, I don't see where your problem lies. All you'd have to do is make one call, tell them who you are, and the rumours would be laid to rest.'

'And what would he say?' Marco asked.

'It's obvious. He'd say: I'm Todd Pickett and I'm alive and well, thank you very much.'

'And *then what?*' Todd said. 'When they want to come to take a photograph to confirm that everything's fine? Or they want an interview, face-to-face. Face. To. Face. With *this?*'

His face was presently unbandaged. He stood up and went to the mirror. 'I look like I went ten rounds with a heavyweight.'

'I can only assure you that the swelling is definitely going down. It's just going to take time. And the quality of the new epidermis is first-rate. I believe you're going to be *very* pleased at the end of everything.'

Todd said nothing for a moment. Then, with a kind of simple sincerity he'd seldom – if ever – achieved in front of a camera, he turned and said to Burrows: 'You know what I wish?' Burrows shook his head. 'I wish I'd never laid eyes on you, you dickhead.'

9

Tammy knew only a very few people in Los Angeles, all of them members of the Appreciation Society, but she decided not to alert anybody to the fact that she'd come into town. They'd all want to help her with her investigations, and this was something she preferred to do alone, at least at the outset.

She checked herself into the little hotel on Wllshire Boulevard, within a few hundred yards of the Westwood Memorial Park, where a host of stars and almost-stars were buried or interred. She'd made her rounds of the famous who rested there on her last visit. Donna Reed and Natalie Wood were amongst them, so was Darryl F. Zanuck and Oscar Levant. But the Park's real claim to fame – the presence that brought sightseers from all over the world – was Marilyn Monroe, who was laid to rest in a bland concrete crypt distinguished only by the number of floral tributes it attracted. The crypt beside it was still empty, kept – so it was said – for the mortal remains of Hugh Hefner.

Tammy had not much enjoyed her visit to the Park. In fact it had depressed her a little. She certainly had no intention of going back this time. It was the living she was concerned with on this visit, not the dead.

When she was settled in she called Arnie, gave him her room number in case of emergency, and told him she'd be back in a couple of days at most. She heard him pop a can of beer while she was talking – not, to judge by his slightly slurred speech, his first of the night. He'd be fine without her, she thought. Probably happier.

She ordered up some room-service food, and then sat plotting how she'd proceed the next day. Her first line of enquiry would be the most direct: she'd go up to Todd's home in Bel Air and try to find out whether or not he was there. His address was no secret. In fact she had pictures of every room in the house, including the ensuite bathroom with the sunken tub, taken by the realtor when the house was still on the market, though it had been remodelled since and its layout had probably changed. Of course, her chances of even getting to the front door – much less of seeing him – were remote. But it would be foolish of her not to try. Maybe she'd catch him going out for a jog, or spot him standing at a window. Then all her concerns would be laid to rest and she would be able to go back to Sacramento happy, knowing that he was alive and well.

She'd hired a car at the airport, and had planned to drive up to Bel Air the evening she arrived, but after the hassles of the delayed flight she was simply too tired, so she went to bed at ten and rose bright and early. The room service offered at the hotel was nothing special – and she liked a good breakfast – so she crossed over Wilshire and went into Westwood Village, found herself a diner, and ate heartily: scrambled eggs, bacon, hash browns, white toast and coffee. While she ate she skimmed *People* and *USA Today*. Both had pieces about the up-coming Oscars, which were now only three days away. Todd had never won an Oscar (which Tammy believed to be absolute proof of the corruption of the Academy) but he'd been nominated four years ago for *Lost Rites*, one of his less popular pictures. She'd been very proud of him: he'd done fine work in the movie and she'd thought he had a crack at winning. Watching the ceremony had been nearly impossible. Her heart had hammered so hard as Susan Sarandon, who'd been presenting the award, had fumbled with the envelope; Tammy thought she was going to pass out from anticipation before the winner was even named. And then of course, Sarandon had named the winner, and it hadn't been Todd. The cameras had been on him throughout the whole envelope-fumbling routine, and there'd been a moment between the naming of the winner and his applauding when his disappointment had been perfectly clear: at least to someone who knew the language of his face as well as Tammy.

She'd only seen one of the movies in this year's race, and she'd only gone to that because Tom Hanks was in it, and he seemed such a likable man. She skimmed the articles rather than reading them, hoping maybe there'd be some reassuring mention of Todd. But there was nothing.

Breakfast finished, she walked back to the hotel, left a message for Arnie at the airport, just to say all was fine, and then picked up a map at the front desk in case her sense of direction failed her. Thus prepared, she set off for Todd's home.

It took twenty-five minutes driving through the heavy morning traffic to get up into the narrow, winding streets of Bel Air. There wasn't much to see; most of the mansions were hidden behind high walls, bristling with spikes and video cameras. But there was no doubting the fact that she was in a very select neighbourhood. The cars parked on the narrow thoroughfares were all expensive (in one spot she manoeuvred past a coffee-and-cream Rolls Royce on the left and a red Porsche on the right). On another street she encountered some glamorously-hooded superstar out running, a black limo following close behind, presumably carrying the bottled water and the granola bars.

What must it be like, she wondered as she drove, to be so pampered and cosseted? To know that if there was no toilet paper in the house, no ice cream in the freezer, then it was somebody else's damn job to go and get it. Never to have to worry about taxes or mortgage payments. Never to wake up at three in the morning and think: *Who am I? I'm nobody. If I died tomorrow nobody would really notice, nobody would really care.*

Of course she knew there were plenty of responsibilities that came along with all this wealth and comfort. And they took their toll on some folks: it drove them to drink and drugs and adultery. It was hard to be idolized and scrutinized. But she'd never had much sympathy for the complainers. So, people paid you millions to see you smile, and it made you feel inadequate. Tough shit.

She found Todd's house readily enough. There was no number, but she recognized the castellated wall and the square lamps on either side of the gate. She drove on up the street, found a parking spot, and wandered back towards the house, trying to look as inconspicuous as any two hundred and three-pound woman in orange polyester pants could. When she reached the gates she saw that there was a car parked in the driveway, twenty yards inside the gates, its trunk open. There was no sign of anyone loading or unloading. She watched from the street for a minute or two, her courage alternately rising then failing her. She couldn't just go up to the gate and ring the bell. What would she say? Hello, I'm Todd's Number One Fan, and I was wondering if he was feeling okay? Ridiculous! They'd think she was a stalker and have her arrested. In fact they might be watching her right now, on a hidden camera: calling the police.

She stood there, quietly cursing herself for not having thought this through properly before she came up here. She didn't know whether to stand her ground, and make the best of this nightmarish situation, or attempt to casually slip away.

Then a door slammed, somewhere out of sight. She wanted to make a run for it, but she was too far from the car to make a quick retreat. All she could do was stand there and hope to God there was nobody looking at the security monitors at that particular moment.

170

Now came the sound of somebody whistling, and seconds later the whistler himself stepped into view. Tammy recognized him instantly. It was Marco Caputo, Todd's assistant and body-guard. She'd encountered the man twice before, once at the premiere party for *The Burning Year*, and the second time in Las Vegas, when Todd had been named Actor of the Year at ShoWest. She'd very politely presented her credentials as the President of the Appreciation Society, and politely asked Caputo if she could have a minute to talk with Todd. On both occasions he'd been rude to her. The second time, in fact, he'd called her 'a crazy bitch', which she'd complained to Maxine Frizelle about. Maxine had apologized in a half-hearted way, and said it would never happen again, but Tammy wasn't about to put Caputo's temper to the test a third time, especially under these dubious circumstances.

Before he could look up and see her she backed off into the thicket of blackberry bushes that grew unchecked on the other side of the street. She kept her eyes on him at all times; he was too busy with his present labours to notice her, thank God; and now, hidden in the bushes, she had the perfect vantage point from which to observe him as he went back and forth between the house and the car. He was loading his vehicle up with an odd assortment of things: including several awards she knew belonged to Todd. He was also removing some other items: a variety of fancy ornaments, a marijuana plant in a pot, some framed photographs. All this, plus nine or ten sealed cardboard boxes, carefully placed in the trunk or on the back seat of his car. There was no sign of Todd through the process; nor did she hear any exchange from inside the house. If Todd was here, he was not engaged in conversation with Marco. But her instincts told her he was *not* here.

For fully a quarter of an hour she watched him work and finally – putting all the evidence together – she came to the conclusion that she was witnessing an act of theft. Of course, her dislike of the thief factored into her assessment, but there was no doubt that Caputo looked furtive as he went about his labours. Every now and then he'd glance up as if he was afraid he was being watched (perhaps he sensed that he was); and when he did she saw that his face was ill-shaven, and his eyes heavy. Sleep wasn't coming too easily of late.

She had already decided what she was going to do well before he'd finished with his felony. She'd follow him when he departed and find out where he was dropping off all his booty. Then she'd call the police and have him arrested. Hopefully that would improve Maxine's low opinion of her. She might even find herself trusted enough to be invited into the charmed circle around Todd. Well, perhaps that was a little too much to hope for. But at the very least she'd be stopping Caputo profiting from his theft.

With the car now filled to capacity, Caputo slammed the trunk, and headed back to the house, presumably to lock up. Once he'd gone Tammy disentangled herself from the blackberry bushes and hurried back to her own car. It was getting warm. She felt sweat running from beneath her breasts, and her underwear was bunched in the groove of her butt. She turned the air-conditioning to its coldest setting, then drove on up the street a little way until she had sufficient room to turn around, and came back down in time to see Caputo's black Lexus easing out of the driveway. He was the only occupant of the vehicle.

Keeping her distance, she followed the Lexus down through the maze of Bel Air's walls and cameras to Sunset Boulevard. She almost lost her quarry at the lights, but luckily the eastbound traffic on Sunset was heavy, and with a little discourteous driving she was able to keep him in sight, finally catching up with him again. He drove with ease and impatience, slipping lanes to overtake tardy drivers; but she was a match for him. Wherever he was going, she was going to be on his thieving tail.

She had no time to consult the maps she'd picked up, she was too busy keeping her eyes on him. So when he suddenly swung a left, and took off up into the hills again, she instantly lost all sense of where they were headed. The traffic soon grew sparse, the streets narrow and serpentine.

Once he halted at a stop sign and he looked back over his shoulder. She was certain he'd realized he was being followed, and prepared herself for a confrontation. But no; something he'd laid on the back seat had moved, it seemed, and he was simply leaning over to reposition it. The job done he then proceeded on his way, and she continued to follow, at a discreet distance.

The road wound so tightly on itself as it ascended that she let him slip out of sight several times rather than risk his realizing he was being pursued. But she didn't fear losing him. Unlike Bel Air, which was made up of a warren of small streets, the Canyon into which they were climbing seemed to have only one thoroughfare, and they were both on it. What little sign of habitation she saw – a wall, and occasionally a gate in a wall – suggested this was not particularly well-fancied real estate, which was surprising given its location. The trees had been allowed to grow over the road, in some places intertwining their branches to form a leafy vault overhead. In one spot, where a number of tall palm trees grew close to the road, fallen fronds lay in a brittle carpet on the pot-holed tarmac.

She began to get just a little anxious. Although she reassured herself that she was just a couple of minutes' drive away from Sunset, this felt like a very different world; a backwater, where who knew what went on? That very fact, of course, supported her shadier suspicions. This was a perfect place for an illegal transaction: there didn't appear to be anybody here to witness Caputo's dealing. Except, of course, herself.

The black Lexus had been out of sight for quite a while

when, as she turned a corner, she came upon it parked so badly that she might have ploughed into the back of it had she not acted quickly to avert the collision. She swung wide of it, glancing back to see Caputo manually opening a pair of immense gates. The thief started to look round at her, but she put her foot on the accelerator and was out of sight before he could fix his gaze. She drove on a considerable distance, but the road came to a dead-end, which left her with two options. One, to turn round and make a conspicuous retreat past the gates, so that he was certain she'd gone; or to hope that the urgency of his mission would make him careless about her presence, and by the time she'd trekked back to his thieves' lair she would have been forgotten. She decided on the latter. She'd come too far to turn and run off now with her tail between her legs.

The first thing she noticed when she got out of her car was the deep hush of the Canyon. Though the Bel Air house was nicely situated, away from the din of any major thoroughfare, she'd still been aware that she was in the middle of a city. But here the only sound was the music of birds, and insects in the grass. She was careful not to slam the door. Leaving the key in the car, and the door just slightly ajar in case she needed to make a fast getaway, she headed back down the street to the gate.

There were no cameras mounted along the perimeter this time, which surprised her; but then perhaps she was walking into a nest of infamous felons, and everyone in the vicinity knew to keep their distance. If so – if the people Marco was doing business with were real villains – then she was in trouble. She was alone up here; and nobody knew where she'd gone.

This is insanity, she thought to herself as she walked. But she kept on walking. The prospect of coming out of this the unlikely heroine was simply too attractive to be turned down. Yes, there was a risk. But then perhaps it was time she took a few, instead of hiding away in her house and doting on her picture collection. She was in the thick of things now, and she wasn't going to allow herself to turn her back on this adventure. If she did – if she got in her car and drove away – wouldn't she always wonder how different things might have been if for once in her life she'd had the courage of her instincts?

Arnie had always called her a dreamer, and maybe he was right about that. Maybe she'd been living in a dream world for too long, with her little museum of photographs to dote on; hoping – though it could never happen, of course – that one day, when she flicked through the pictures, Todd would look at her and smile at her and invite her into his world, to stay. It was a silly dream, and she knew it. Whereas being here now, walking on the hard street in the hot sun, with an old cracked wall to the left of her – all that was real, perfectly real. So perhaps today was the day when the photographs became real too; the day when she finally found her way to a man of flesh and blood; to a Todd who would return her look, finally; see her and smile at her.

The thought made her quicken her step; and she arrived at the gates breathing a little faster, exhilarated by the prospect that with the hazards she imagined the house contained there was one possibility she could not properly imagine (though Lord knows she'd tried to conjure it over and over): the image of her idol, appearing before her, and her with so much to say she wouldn't know where to begin.

10

S he scanned the area around the gates (the bars of which were exquisitely interwoven with both wrought iron vines and the living variety), in search of the inevitable security cameras, but to her surprise found none. They were either extremely well concealed, or else the owners of this house were so certain that their Canyon was safe from visitors that they didn't feel the need of them. More surprisingly still, the gates had no locks; she was able to push one of them open wide enough for her to slip through.

She could see some of the house from where she stood, though it was mostly hidden by the great riot of shrubs and trees that lined the curving driveway. Caputo's car was parked close to the front door. The trunk was open, and he was now unloading his loot. She wished she'd brought a camera; then she could have simply photographed him in the middle of his illicit transaction, and left with her evidence. But as it was, she felt obliged to get a little closer, and find out who he was dealing with. If she didn't have some further evidence, it was going to end up being his word against hers; and she, after all, was the trespasser here. Her accusations weren't going to carry much weight unless she could be very specific about what she had witnessed.

She waited until Caputo had gone into the house, and then crept towards the front door, covering perhaps half the distance between door and gate before the thief strode out of the house again, and returned to the car. She ducked for cover behind a Bird of Paradise, its sickly sap gummy beneath her heels. From there she watched while Caputo hauled another load of booty up out of the trunk. As he did so there was a shout from inside the house; the voice curiously muted.

'Marco! This picture's cracked.'

'Shit.'

Marco set down the box he was lifting from the trunk, and went back to the doorstep. As he did so, the owner of the picture, and of that curiously muffled voice, came out of the house. The sight of him made Tammy's heart quicken. First, he was shirtless, his slacks hanging low on his hips. His torso was tanned, but far from trim. He looked to have a body that had once been well cared for but was now quickly going to seed. The muscles of his upper arms were soft, and he had the beginnings of love-handles spilling over his belt. His face was swathed in bandages. They weren't tight to his skull, like the bandaging on a mummy. They were more irregular; patches of gauze held against his cheeks and brow and jaw and neck, with lengths of bandaging running all the way around his head to secure them and locks of his lush dark hair stuck up out of the bandages like tufts from the pate of a clown. All in all, that was what he resembled, with his ill-fitting pants, and his little paunch: something from a circus. Part clown, part freak.

He lifted up the picture for Marco to see. 'Look.'

'It's just the glass that's cracked. Easy fix.'

'You're careless.'

'I said I'd get it fixed, boss.'

'That's not the point. You're fucking careless.'

Only as the clown returned into the house, dropping the offending picture against the door-jamb for Marco to pick up, did Tammy realize who she'd just seen.

It was Todd. Oh my Lord . . .

It was Todd standing there on the doorstep, with his face all bandaged up and his stomach hanging over his trousers.

Tammy heard herself gasping. She put her hand over her mouth to silence the sound, but she needn't have bothered. The men's fractious exchange had escalated into an argument loud enough to drown out any noise she might make.

'You're so fucking clumsy.'

'Some of the stuff slipped off the back seat, that's all. No big deal. It was an accident.'

'Well, there's too many fucking accidents around here for my liking.'

'Hey . . . I said I'm sorry.'

'It's a picture of the house where I was born.'

'Yeah? Well I'll get a new frame for it on Monday.'

The exchange about the broken glass apparently came to a halt there. Tammy watched while Caputo stood on the step, staring into the house, muttering something under his breath. Whatever it was, it wasn't for Todd's ears; he was just quietly letting off steam. He leaned on the car, lit a cigarette and soothed himself with a smoke.

Tammy didn't dare move. Even though Caputo wasn't looking directly at her, there was a better than even chance that he'd catch sight of her if she broke cover. All she could do was stay where she was, her mind filled with feverish explanations for what she'd just seen.

Obviously something horrible had happened to Todd, but what? Her first thought was that one of his ex-girlfriends had tried to harm him (he'd always had poor judgment when it came to women). Either that or there'd been some kind of accident (was that what his remark about 'too many accidents' had meant?). Whatever it was, he was in terrible pain, or else why would he be acting the way he just had? Her heart went out to him. And to be stuck up here in this God-forsaken place with only that cretin Caputo for company: it would drive anybody crazy.

Finally, Caputo dropped his cigarette, ground it out, and went back to his work. Tammy waited until he'd disappeared inside the house and stepped out of her hiding place. What now? Back to the gate, up the street to her car, and away? Clearly that was the most sensible thing to do. But that would mean leaving without finding what was wrong with her poor Todd. She couldn't do that. It was as simple as that. She couldn't do it.

She was going to have to find a way into the house, and then discover some means to speak to him before Caputo intervened. Obviously the front door wasn't the way to go; not with the thug standing right there. She was going to have to try around the back. She retraced her sticky steps a few yards, and then crossed to the corner of the house. A paving stone path led down the flank of the house. It was a narrow, steep descent, and it plainly hadn't been used in many years. Roots had cracked the stones, and shrubbery choked the path in several places. It took her fully ten minutes to make her cautious descent, but it delivered her into a far more beautiful spot than she'd expected. Somebody had once created a wonderful garden back here; and now, with spring early this year throughout the state, the place was glorious. Everywhere there were bursts of brilliant colour – and hummingbirds, going from flower to flower, and butterflies, drying their newly-exposed wings in the sun.

The beauty of the place put all thoughts of jeopardy out of Tammy's head, at least for a few moments. She made her way through the bushes to what had once been an enormous lawn – though there were so many wild flowers in the tall grass, and so much grass sprouting in the border, that lawn and border had become virtually indistinguishable – and looked back up at the house, her gaze going from window to window, balcony to balcony, to see if there was anybody watching her. She saw nobody, so she grew a little more confident and strode out into the middle of the lawn so that she could get herself a good look at the house. It was much larger than she'd assumed from the front, and even in its dilapidated state it was an elegant place, the curves of its balconies echoing one another, the ironwork of its railings delicate.

That said, it was a strange house for Todd to be living in. She knew how hard he'd worked to perfect his residence in Bel Air (four architects; two interior designers; millions of dollars spent): so why was he here? There could only be one explanation. He was in hiding. He didn't want anyone to see him in his wounded state. She understood the logic of that. There were some people – some of his *fans* – who wanted to think he was perfect. Luckily, she wasn't one of those people. Far from it. The fact that he was here, all locked away, hurting and angry, made her feel all the more love for him. If she got a chance, she'd tell him so. If he'd let her, she'd peel those stifling bandages off his face. She didn't care what he looked like underneath; it was still her Todd, wasn't it? Still the man she idolized. For once the fact that her breasts were too big would be a Godsend. They'd be a comfortable place for him to lay his hurt head. She could rock him and keep him there, safe and sound.

From the corner of her eye, she saw something move in the foliage. The blissful imaginings fled. Very slowly, she looked towards the shrubs where she'd seen the motion. The sun was bright; the shadows dark and solid. The leaves shook in the light breeze. Was that what she'd seen? The leaves shaking? Apparently so, for there was nothing else visible.

She returned her gaze to the house, looking for the best way for her to get in. There were no open windows on the garden level – at least none that she could see – and the doors all looked to be securely locked. She pushed her way through a line of shrubs so as to see if the house was any more vulnerable elsewhere, but the foliage grew thicker around her as she proceeded, and then she somehow managed to become disorientated, because when she turned back to try another way she found that she'd lost sight of both the lawn and the house. She felt like Alice, suddenly shrinking away; the flowers around her were huge, like sunflowers, only purple and scarlet, and the scent they gave off was achingly sweet. They grew so tall, however, and in such preternatural numbers, that she could not see the house at all – not a chimney pot, not a balcony. Her only hope was to make a guess at the direction in which the house lay, which she did, plunging on through the enormous blooms. But her guesswork was hopelessly amiss. The shrubbery simply thickened, the sunflowers giving way to bushes whose branches carried bell-shaped yellow blossoms, almost the size of her head. She couldn't yell for help, of course; that would bring Caputo running. She had no choice but to head on in the same hopeless fashion, until at last the thicket cleared somewhat, and she had sight of the sky again.

Emerging from the shrubbery she was instantly on her guard, in case she'd come to a place where she could be spotted. But she needn't have worried. Her travels had brought her down the hill, and put a line of cypress trees (which she could not remember moving through) between herself and the house. Only one reasonably sensible option presented itself. Directly ahead of her was a narrow path-way – as overgrown as the one that had brought her down the side of the house. She had no idea where it led, but it *was* a pathway; it implied that others had been here before her, perhaps in the same predicament, and this trail of trodden ground marked their exit. If it had worked for them, why not for her? Pulling pieces of twig and blossom from her hair and blouse as she went, she followed the path.

She suddenly had a mental picture of herself in her present state. What a sight she must be, stumbling out of the greenery like some crazed explorer. What the hell was she thinking of? Out there on the open street it had been easy to talk herself into this trespass. Now she was beginning to think the whole idea wasn't so smart. It wasn't the fact that she was lost in the environs of the house that discomfited her: she'd find her way back to the street eventually. Nor was she particularly concerned about the threat posed by Caputo; not now that she knew Todd was here. Caputo might yell a bit, and threaten her with the police if she didn't leave; but he was more bark than bite. No, what had brought her to a halt was the distinct sense that she wasn't alone out here in the undergrowth. There was somebody close by. She couldn't see anybody, but the feeling was too strong to be ignored.

She slowly started to turn on her heel, viewing the scene around her.

'Whoever you are . . .' she said, doing her best to keep her voice as quiet and non-confrontational as possible, 'please show yourself.'

There was a motion in the undergrowth, five or six yards from where she stood. Somebody – or something – had apparently moved from their hiding place. There was more than one creature in the vicinity, she guessed; it was several. There was foliage moving all around her now, as though those hiding in the shrubbery were getting ready to show themselves.

She started walking again, faster than before, and her walking brought her into a place where the shrubbery cleared a little, presenting her with a most unexpected sight. There were perhaps seven or eight cages, arranged on either side of a wide, flagged walkway. They varied in size. The largest might have housed two horses and left some room for manoeuvre, the smallest was perhaps half that size. Vines had wrapped themselves around the bars and fell here and there, in tattered green curtains, as though to conceal what lay inside the cages. In fact, there was nothing to conceal. The occupants of this menagerie had long since disappeared.

She moved down the walkway cautiously, increasingly certain that her stalkers were matching her motion step by step on the other side of the cages. Some of the cages had high wooden bars, which suggested they'd housed small monkeys. Others were built more robustly, their bars twice or three times the thickness. What kind of animal had been held in a cage like this? It was too small to comfortably accommodate a rhinoceros, or even a bear or tiger. And in a day rife with unanswered questions, here was another one: what had happened to the occupants of this tawdry private zoo? Was there a graveyard somewhere in the thicket where the animals had been laid to rest? Or had their owner set them free to roam the Canyon?

She was almost at the end of the walkway now. The final cage on her right was in a much better state than the others. Foliage had been interwoven with the bars so cunningly that there was practically nothing of the interior visible. Its gate, which was similarly covered, stood a little ajar. Tammy peered in. The air inside smelled of some subtle perfume, its source the candles which were set in a little cluster at the far end of the cage. There was a small cot set against the wall to her right, somewhat incongruously made up with two oversized red silk pillows and a dirty yellow comforter. There was a chair and a tiny table on the other side of the cage, and on the table paper and pen. Beside the cot there was an upended wooden box, which also functioned as a table. Books were piled high upon it. But her attention didn't linger on the books. It was drawn to the cluster of candles at the far end of the cage. There was a kind of altar there, roughly made; set on a few pieces of wood raised up on rocks. In the middle of the altar was what Tammy first thought was a piece of sculpture, representing the face of a beautiful young woman. When she got closer to it, however, she saw that it was a life-mask. The mouth carried an oh-so-subtle smile; and there was a slight frown on the subject's otherwise perfect brow. Such beauty! Whoever this woman was – or had been – it was easy to understand why she'd been elected for this place of honour in the candlelight. It was the kind of face that made you gape at its perfection. The kind the camera loved.

Ah now; the mysteries of this house and place began to seem more soluble. Was this beauty the owner of this once-great house; remembered here by some obsessive fan? Was this shrine made out of devotion for a woman who'd walked in these gardens, once upon a time?

Tammy took another step towards the altar, and saw that besides the life-mask there were a number of other, smaller items set there. A scrap of red silk, one edge of it hemmed; a cameo brooch, with the same woman's face carved in creamy stone; a little wooden box, scarcely larger than a matchbox, which presumably held some other treasure; and lying flat beneath all of these a cut-out paper doll, about twelve inches tall of a woman dressed in the frilly underwear of a bygone era. The paper from which the doll was made had yellowed, the colours of the printing faded. It was something from the twenties, Tammy guessed. Her knowledge of that era of cinema was sketchy, but the three faces, one of cardboard, one of plaster, one of stone, teased her: she *knew* the woman whose image was thricefold copied here. She'd seen her flickering black and white picture on some late-night movie channel. She tried to put a name to the face, but nothing came.

Despairing of the puzzle, she took a step back from the altar, and as she did so she felt a rush of cool air against the back of her neck. She turned, completely unprepared for what met her gaze. A man had come into the cage behind her, entering so silently he was literally a foot from her and she hadn't heard his approach. There were places in the leafed and barred roof where the sun broke through, and it fell in bright patches upon him. One of them fell irregularly upon his face, catching both his eyes, and part of his nose, and the corner of his mouth. She saw immediately that it wasn't Caputo. It was a much older man, his eyes, despite the sun that illuminated them, grey, cold and weary, his hair, what was left of it, grown out to shoulder length and quite white. He was gaunt, but the lack of flesh on his skull flattered him; he looked, she thought, like a saint in her grandmother's old Bible, which had been illustrated with pictures by the Old Masters. This was a man capable of devotion; indeed addicted to it.

He raised his hand and put a homemade cigarette to his lips. Then, with a kind of old-fashioned style, he flicked open his lighter, lit the cigarette and drew deeply on it.

'And who might you be?' he said. His voice was the colour of his eyes.

'I'm sorry,' Tammy said. 'I shouldn't be here.'

'Please,' he said gently, 'let me be the judge of that.' He drew on the cigarette again. The tobacco smelled more pungent than any cigarette she'd ever inhaled. 'I'd still like your name.'

'Tammy Lauper. Like I said —'

'You're sorry.'

'Yes.'

'You don't mean to be here.'

'No.'

'You got lost, I daresay. It's so easy, in the garden.'

'I was looking for Todd.'

'Ah,' the stranger said, glancing away at the roof for a moment. The cigarette smoke was blue as it rose through the slivers of sun. 'So you're with Mr Pickett's entourage.'

'Well no. Not exactly.'

'Meaning?'

'I just . . . well, he knows me . . .'

'But he doesn't know you're here.'

'That's right.'

The man's gaze returned to Tammy, and he assessed her, his gaze, though insistent, oddly polite. 'What are you to our Mr Pickett?' he said. 'A mistress of his, once?'

Tammy couldn't help but smile at this. First, the very thought of it; then, the word itself. *Mistress*. Like the flick of his lighter, it was pleasantly old-fashioned. And rather flattering.

'I don't think Todd Pickett would look twice at me,' she said, feeling the need to be honest with this sad, grey man.

'Then that would be his loss,' the man replied, the compliment offered so lightly that even if it wasn't meant it was still beguiling. Out of nowhere she remembered a phrase her mother had used, to describe Jimmy MacKintosh, the man she'd eventually divorced Tammy's father to pursue. 'He could charm the birds of the trees, that one.' She'd never met a man with that kind of charisma before, in the flesh. But this man had it. Though their exchange so far had been brief and shallow, she knew a bird-charmer when she met one.

'May I ask . . .'

'Ask away.'

'. . . who are you?'

'By all means. One name deserves another. I'm Willem Zeffer.'

'I'm pleased to meet you,' Tammy said. 'Again, I'm sorry.' She made a half-hearted glance over her shoulder at the altar. 'I shouldn't have come in here.'

'You weren't to know. It's easy to get lost in this . . . jungle. We should have it all cut back.' He smiled thinly. 'You just can't get the staff these days.'

'That woman,' Tammy said. 'The one in the mask?'

'*In* the mask?' Zeffer said. 'Oh. I see. Yes. In the mask.'

'Who is she?'

He stepped to the side, in order to have a clear view of the altar and what was upon it. 'She was an actress,' he explained, 'many, many moons ago.'

'I thought I recognized her.'

'Her name's Katya Lupi.'

'Yes?' The name rang a bell, but Tammy still couldn't

186

name any of the movies this woman had been in.

'Was she very famous?'

'Very. She's up there with Pickford and Swanson and Theda Bara. Or she was.'

'She's dead?'

'No, no. Just forgotten. At least that's my impression. I don't get out into the world any more, but I sense that the name Katya Lupi doesn't mean very much.'

'You'd be right.'

'Well, she's lucky. She still has her little dominion here in Coldheart Canyon.'

'*Coldheart?*'

'That's what they called the place. She was such a heart-breaker, you see. She took so many lovers – especially in the early years – and when she was done with them, she just threw them aside.'

'Were you one of them?'

Zeffer smiled. 'I shared her bed, a little, when I first brought her to America. But she got tired of me very quickly.'

'What then?'

'I had other uses, so she kept me around. But a lot of the men who loved her took her rejection badly. Three committed suicide with bullets. A number of others with alcohol. Some of them stayed here, where they could be close to her. Including me. It's foolish really, because there's no way back into her affection.'

'Why would you want to be . . . back, I mean?' Tammy said. 'She must be very old by now.'

'Oh time hasn't staled her infinite variety, as the Bard has it. She's still beautiful.'

Tammy didn't want to challenge the man, given that he was plainly besotted with this Lupi woman, but the idol of his heart must be approaching a hundred years of age by now. It was hard to imagine how any of her beauty remained.

'Well, I guess I should be getting along,' Tammy said.

She gently pressed past Zeffer, who put up no resistance, and stepped out of the cage onto the walkway. It was so quiet she could hear her stomach rumble. Her Westwood breakfast seemed very remote now; as did the little diner where she'd eaten it.

Zeffer came after her, out into the open air, and she saw him clearly for the first time. He had been extremely handsome once, she thought; but his face was a mess. He looked as though he'd been attacked; punched repeatedly. Raw in places, pale and powdery in others, he had the appearance of a man who had suffered intensely, and kept the suffering inside, where it continued to take its toll. She couldn't make quite so hurried an attempt to abandon him now that she'd seen him plainly. He seemed to read her equivocation, and suggested that she stay.

'Are you really in such a hurry?'

He looked around him as he spoke; he seemed to be reading the peculiar stillness in the air.

'Perhaps we could walk together a ways. It isn't always safe up here.'

Before she could ask him what he meant by this he turned his back to the door of the cage and picked up a large stick that was set there. The way he wielded it suggested he'd used it as a weapon in the past, and had some expectation of doing so again now.

'Animals?' she said.

He looked at her with those sorrowful grey eyes of his. 'Sometimes animals, yes. Sometimes worse.'

'I don't understand.'

'Perhaps, with respect, it would be better not to try,' he advised. The stillness seemed to be deepening around them, the absence of sound becoming heavier, if that were possible. She didn't need any further encouragement from Zeffer to stay close to him. Whatever this stillness hid, she didn't want to face it alone. 'Just take it from me that

Coldheart Canyon has some less-than-pretty occupants.'

Something behind the cages drew Zeffer's attention. Tammy followed the direction of his gaze. 'What were the cages for?' she asked him.

'Katya went through a phase of collecting exotic animals. We had a little zoo here. A white tiger from India, though he didn't live very long. Later, there was a rhinoceros. That also perished.'

'Wasn't that cruel? Keeping them here, I mean? The cages look so small.'

'Yes, of course it was cruel. She's a cruel woman, and I was cruel for doing her bidding. I have no doubt of that. I was probably unspeakably cruel, in my casual way. But it takes the experience of living like an animal –' he glanced back at the cage '– to realize the misery they must have suffered.'

Tammy watched him scrutinizing the shrubbery on the far side of the cages.

'What's out there?' she said. 'Is it animals that –'

'*Come here*,' Zeffer said, his voice suddenly dropping to an urgent whisper. '*Quickly*.'

Though she still saw nothing in the shrubbery, she did as she was told.

As she did so there was a blast of icy air down the narrow channel between the cages, and she saw several forms – human forms, but distorted, as though they were in a wind-tunnel, their mouths blown into a dark circle lined with needle teeth, their eyes squeezed into dots – come racing towards her.

'*Don't you dare!*' she heard Zeffer yell at her side, and saw him raise his stick. If he landed a blow she didn't see it. The breath was knocked from her as two of her attackers threw themselves upon her.

One of them put a hand over her face. A spasm of energy passed through her bone and brain, erupting behind her eyes. It was more than her mind could take. She saw a white light, like the light that floods a cinema screen when the film breaks.

The cold went away in the same instant: sounds and sights and all the feelings they composed, gone.

The last thing she heard, dying away, was Willem Zeffer's voice yelling: '*Damn you all!*'

Then he too was gone.

In the passageway in front of Katya's long-abandoned menagerie, Willem Zeffer watched as the forces that had broken cover carried Tammy Lauper away into their own horrid corners of the Canyon, leaving him – as he had been left so often in this godless place – helpless and bereft.

He threw the stick down on the ground, his eyes stinging with tears. Then the strength ran out of him completely, and he went down on his knees at the threshold of his hovel, cursing Katya. She wasn't the only one to blame, of course. He had his own part to play in this tragic melodrama, as he'd admitted moments before. But he still wanted Katya damned for what she'd done, as he was damned: for the death of tigers and rhinoceros, and the murder of innocent women.

PART FOUR

LIFE AFTER FAME

1

Three days after Tammy had pursued Marco Caputo up Sunset Boulevard and into the mysterious arms of Coldheart Canyon was Oscar Night: the Night of Nights, the Show of Shows, when billions of people across the world turned their eyes on Tinseltown and Tinseltown did a pirouette and a curtsey and pretended it was a lady not a five-buck whore.

Todd had known from the start that there was no chance of his attending the ceremony. Though he could now see that his wounded face was indeed healing properly, it was plain that he was in no condition to step into the limelight anytime soon. He had briefly considered hiring one of the great makeup men of the city to disguise the worst of the discoloration, but Maxine quickly dissuaded him. Such a plan would require them to share their secret with somebody else (this in itself was risky: makeup personnel were legendary gossips) and there was always the chance that, however good the cover-up was, the illusion of perfection would be spoiled under the blaze of so many lights. All it required was one lucky photographer to catch a crack in the painted mask, and all their hard work would be undone. The rumour-mill would grind into motion again.

'Anyway,' she reminded him, 'you loathe the Oscars.'

This was indeed true. The spectacle of self-congratulation had always sickened him. The ghastly parade of nervous smiles as everyone traipsed into the Dorothy Chandler Pavilion, the shrill laughter, the sweaty glances. Then, once everyone was inside, the circus itself. The lame jokes, the gushing speeches, the tears, the ego. There was always a minute or two of choreographed mawkishness, when the Academy carted out some antiquated star and gave them a last chance to flicker. Occasionally, when the taste level plummeted further than usual, the Academy chose some poor soul who'd already been stricken by a stroke or was in the early stages of Alzheimer's. There'd be a selection of clips from the poor soul's great pictures, then, fumbling and bewildered, he or she would be led out to stand alone on the stage while the audience rose to applaud them, and you could see in their eyes that this was some kind of Hell: to have their finest moments thrown up on a screen – their faces strong and shining – and then have the spotlight show the world what age and disease had done to them.

'You're right,' he'd said to Maxine. 'I don't want to be there.'

So why, if he truly didn't want to be there, was he sitting at his bedroom window tonight, staring down the length of the Canyon towards the city, feeling so damn sorry for himself? Why had he started drinking, and drinking hard, at noon, and by two-thirty – when he knew the first limousines were beginning to roll up to the Pavilion – was he in the depths of despair?

Why, he asked himself, would he want to keep company with those hollow, sour people? He'd fought the battle to get to the top of the Hollywood Hill long ago, and he'd won it. He'd had his face plastered up on ten thousand billboards across America, across the world. He'd been called the Handsomest Man in the World, and believed it. He'd walked into rooms the size of football fields and known that every eye was turned in his direction, and every heart beat a little faster because he'd appeared. Just how much more adulation did a man *need*?

The truth?

Another hundred rooms, filled with people stupefied by worship would not be enough to satisfy the hunger in him; nor another hundred hundred. He needed his face plastered on every wall he passed, his movies lauded to the skies, his arms so filled with Oscars he couldn't hold them all.

It was a sickness in him, but what was he to do? There was no cure for this emptiness but love; love in boundless amounts; the kind of love God Himself would be hard-pressed to deliver.

As the cloudless sky darkened towards night he started to pick out the Klieg lights raking the clouds: not from the Pavilion itself (that lay to the west, and was not visible from the Canyon), but from the many locations around the city where his peers, both prize-winners and losers, would in a few hours come to revel. Members of the press were already assembling at these sacred sites – Morton's, Spago's, the Roosevelt Hotel – ready to turn their cameras on the slick and the stylishly unkempt alike. A smile, a witticism, a look of glee from those burdened with victory. They'd have it all in the morning editions.

Picturing the scene was too much for him. He got up and went down to the kitchen to fix himself another drink. By now he was on the second cycle of intoxication; having drunk himself past the point of nausea by mid-afternoon, he was moving inexorably towards a deep luxurious drunkenness; the kind that flirted with oblivion. He'd suffer for it for whatever part of tomorrow he saw of course, and probably the day after that. He was no longer young enough or resilient enough to shrug off the effects of a binge like this. But right now he didn't give a rat's ass. He simply wanted to be insulated from the pain he was feeling.

As he opened the immense fridge to get himself ice, he heard, or thought he heard, somebody, a woman, say his name.

He stopped digging for the ice and looked around. The kitchen was empty. He left the fridge open and went back to the door. The turret was also deserted, and the dining room dark, the empty table and chairs silhouetted against the window. He walked on through it into the living room, calling for Marco. He flipped on the light. The fifty-lamp chandelier blazed, illuminating an empty room. There were several boxes of his belongings sitting there, still unopened. Moved from Bel Air but still unpacked. But that was all.

He was about to go back to the kitchen, assuming the voice he'd heard alcohol-induced, when he heard his name called a second time. He looked back into the dining room. Was he going crazy?

'Marco?' he yelled.

There was a long empty moment. Somewhere in the darkness of the Canyon a solitary coyote was yelping. Then came the sound of a door opening, and he heard Marco's familiar voice: 'Yes, boss?'

'I heard somebody calling.'

'In the house?'

'Yeah. I thought so. A woman's voice.'

Marco appeared on the stairs now, looking down at his employer with an expression of concern. 'You okay?'

'Yeah. I just got unnerved, is all.'

'You want me to go check around?'

'Yeah, I guess so. I don't even know where it was coming from. But I heard somebody. I swear.'

Marco, who'd emerged from his bedroom in his boxers, headed back upstairs to get dressed. Todd went back to the kitchen, feeling a little stupid. There wasn't going to be anybody here, inside the house or out. Every stalker, every voyeur, every obsessive was canvassing the crowds around the Pavilion, looking for a way to slide past the security guards, under the velvet rope, and into the company of their idols. They weren't wasting their time stumbling around in the darkness hoping for a glance of Todd Pickett, all fucked up. Nobody even knew he was here, for Christ's sake. Worse; nobody cared.

As he returned to the business of making his drink, he heard Marco coming back down the stairs, and was half tempted to tell him to forget it. But he decided against it. No harm in letting one of them feel useful tonight. He dropped a handful of ice-cubes into his glass, and filled it up with Scotch. Took a mouthful. Topped it up. Took another mouthful –

And the voice came again.

If there had been some doubt in his head as to whether he'd actually heard the call or simply imagined it, there was now none. Somebody was here in the house, calling to him.

It seemed to be coming from the other side of the hallway. He set his drink down on the counter and quietly crossed the kitchen. The turret was deserted. There was nobody on the stairs either above or below.

He took the short passageway down to what Marco had dubbed the Casino, an immense wood-panelled room, lit by a number of low-slung lights, which indeed looked as though it had been designed to house a roulette wheel and half a dozen poker tables. Judging by the distance of the voice it seemed the likeliest place for whoever had spoken to be lurking. As he walked down the passageway it briefly occurred to him that to make this investigation without Marco at his side was foolishness. But the drink made him bold. Besides, it was only a woman he'd heard. He could deal with a woman.

The door of the Casino stood open. He peered in. The windows were undraped; a few soft panels of grey light slid through them, illuminating the enormity of the place. He could see no sign of an intruder. But some instinct instructed him not to believe the evidence of his eyes. He wasn't alone here. The skin of his palms pricked. So, curiously, did the flesh beneath his bandages, as though it were especially susceptible in its newborn state.

'Who's there?' he said, his voice less confident than he'd intended.

At the far end of the room one of the pools of light fluttered. Something passed through it, raising the dust.

'Who's there?' he said again, his hand straying to the light switch.

He resisted the temptation to turn it on, however. Instead he waited, and watched. Whoever this trespasser was she was too far from him to do any harm.

'You shouldn't be in here,' he said gently. 'You do know that, don't you?'

Again, that subtle motion at the other end of the room. But he still couldn't make out a figure; the darkness beyond the pool of light was too impenetrable.

'Why don't you step out where I can see you?' he suggested.

This time he got an answer.

'I will . . .' she told him. 'In a minute.'

'Who are you?'

'My name's Katya.'

'How did you get in here?'

'Through the door, like everybody else,' she said. Her tone was one of gentle amusement. It would have annoyed Todd if there hadn't also been a certain sweetness there. He was curious to see what she looked like. But the more he pressed her, he thought, the more she'd resist. So he kept the conversation off the subject, and casually wandered across the immaculately laid and polished floor as he talked.

'It must have been hard to find me,' he said.

'Not at all,' she said. 'I heard you were coming from Jerry.'

'You know Jerry?'

'Oh, yes. We go way back. He used to come up here

when he was a child. You made a good choice with him, Todd. He keeps secrets.'

'Really? I always thought he was a bit of a gossip.'

'It depends if it's important or not. He never mentioned me to you, did he?'

'No.'

'You see. Oh yes, and he's dying. I suppose he didn't mention that either.'

'No he didn't.'

'Well he is. He has cancer. Inoperable.'

'He never said a thing,' Todd said, thinking not only of Jerry but of sick, silent Dempsey.

'Well why would he? To you of all people. He idolizes you.'

Her familiarity with Jerry, and her knowledge of his sickness, only added to the puzzle of her presence.

'Did he *send* you up here?' Todd said.

'No, silly,' the woman replied. 'He sent *you*. I've been here all the time.'

'You have? Where?'

'Oh, I mostly stay in the guest-house.'

She spoke so confidently, he almost believed her. But then surely if she *were* occupying the guest-house, Brahms would have warned Maxine? He knew how important Todd's security was. Why would he let Maxine see the property, and not mention the fact that there was somebody else living in the Canyon?

He was about halfway across the room now, and he could see his visitor's outline in the darkness. Her voice had not misled him. She was a young woman; elegantly dressed in a long, silver gown, highlighted with sinuous designs in gold thread. It shimmered, as though it possessed a subtle life of its own.

'How long have you been staying here?' he said to her.

'A lot longer than you,' she replied.

199

'Really?'

'Well, of course. When I first met Jerry, I'd been here . . . twenty, twenty-five years.'

This was an absurd invention of course. Even without seeing her clearly, it was obvious she was less than thirty; probably considerably less.

'But you said Jerry was a boy when you met him?' Todd said, thinking he'd quickly catch the woman in her lie.

'He was.'

'So you can't have known him . . .'

'I know it doesn't seem very likely. But things are different here in the Canyon. You'll see. If you stay, that is. And I hope you will.'

'You mean buy the house?'

'No. I mean *stay*.'

'Why would I do that?' he said.

There was a moment's pause, then, finally, she stepped into the light. 'Because I want you to,' she replied.

It was a moment from a movie; timed to perfection. The pause, the move, the line.

And the face, that was from a movie too, in its luxury, in its perfection. Her eyes were large and luminous, green flecked with lilac. Their brightness was enhanced by the darkness of her eyeshadow, and the thickness of her lashes. Neither her nose nor her mouth were delicate; her lips were full, her chin robust, her cheekbones high; almost Slavic. Her hair was black, and fell straight down, framing her face. She wore plenty of jewellery, and it was all exquisite. One necklace lay tightly in the valley of her throat, another – much, much looser – fell between her breasts. Her earrings were gold; her bracelets – several on each wrist – all elaborately wrought. Yet she carried all this effortlessly, as though she'd been wearing a queen's ransom in jewellery all her life.

'I'm sure you could find plenty of company besides me,' Todd said.

'I'm sure I could,' she replied. 'But I don't want plenty of company. I want you.'

Todd was totally bewildered now. No part of this puzzle fitted with any other. The woman looked so poised, so exquisite, but she spoke nonsense. She didn't know him. She hadn't chosen him. He'd come up here of his own free will, to hide himself away. Yet she seemed to insinuate that he was here at her behest, and that somehow she intended to make him stay. It was all pure invention.

Still she didn't look crazy; anything but. She looked, in fact, as though she'd just stepped out of her limo at the Pavilion and was about to walk down the red carpet to a roar of adulation from the crowd. He wouldn't have minded being beside her, either, if she had been taking that walk. They would have made quite a couple.

'You haven't looked around the house very much,' she said.

'How do you know?'

'Oh . . . I have eyes everywhere,' she teased. 'If you'd been in some of the rooms in this house, I'd know about it, believe me.'

'I don't find any of this very comforting,' he said. 'I don't like people spying on me.'

'I wasn't *spying*,' she said, her tone going from pleasing to fierce in a heartbeat.

'Well what would you call it?'

'I'd call it being a good hostess. Making sure your guest is comfortable.'

'I don't understand.'

'No,' she said, more softly now, 'you don't. But you will. When we've had a chance to spend some time with one another you'll see what's really going on here.'

'And what's that?'

She half-turned from him, as though she might leave, which was the last thing he wanted her to do. 'You know

201

maybe we'd be better leaving this for another night,' she said.

'No,' he said hurriedly.

She halted, but didn't turn back.

'I'm sorry,' he said. They were rare words from his mouth.

'Truly?' she said. Still she didn't turn. He found himself longing to feel her gaze on him, as though – absurd as this was – she might go some way to filling the void in him.

'*Please*,' he said. 'I'm truly sorry.'

'All right,' she said, apparently placated. She looked back at him. 'You're forgiven. For now.'

'So tell me what I've missed. In the house.'

'Oh, all that can wait.'

'At least give me a clue.'

'Have you been downstairs? I mean all the way down to the bottom?'

'No.'

'Then don't,' she said, lowering her head and looking up at him with a veiled gaze. 'I'll take you there myself.'

'Take me now,' he said, thinking it would be a good opportunity to find out how real all her claims were.

'No, not tonight.'

'Why not?'

'It's Oscar Night.'

'So?'

'So it's got you all stirred up. Look at you. You think you can drink the pain away? It doesn't work. Everyone here's tried that at some point or other –'

'Everyone?'

'In the Canyon. There are a lot of people here who are feeling exactly like you tonight.'

'And how's that?'

'Oh, just wishing they'd had a few prizes for their efforts.'

'Well they don't give Oscars to actors like me.'

202

'Why not?'

'I guess they don't think I'm very good.'

'And what do you think?'

He mused on this for a moment. Then he said: 'Most of the time I'm just being me, I guess.'

'That's a performance,' Katya said. 'People think it's easy. But it's not. Being yourself . . . that's hard.'

It was strange to hear it put that way, but she was right. It wasn't easy, playing yourself. If you let your attention drop for a moment, there was nothing there for the camera to look at. Nothing behind the eyes. He'd seen it, in his own performances and in those of others: moments when the concentration lapsed for a few seconds and the unforgiving lens revealed a vast vapidity.

'I know how it hurts,' she said, 'not to be appreciated.'

'I get a lot of other stuff, you know.'

'The other stuff being money.'

'Yes. And celebrity.'

'And half the time you think: it doesn't matter, anyway. They're all ignoramuses at the Academy, voting for their friends. What do you want from them? But you're not really convinced. In your heart you want their worthless little statues. You want them to tell you they know how much you work to be perfect.'

He was astonished at this. She had articulated what he'd felt on a decade of Oscar Nights; an absurd mixture of contempt and envy. It was as though she was reading his mind.

'How did you figure all that out?'

'Because I've felt the same things. You want them to love you, but you hate yourself for wanting it. Their love isn't worth anything, and you know it.'

'But you still want it.'

'You still want it.'

'Damn.'

'Meaning yes?'

203

'Yes. That's it. You got me.'

It felt good, for once, to be understood. Not the usual nodding, whatever-you-say-Mr-Pickett bullshit, but some genuine comprehension of the mess inside him. Which made the mystery of its source all the stranger. One minute she was telling him lies (how could she possibly have known Brahms as a child?) the next she was seeing into his soul.

'If you really *do* own this house,' he said, 'why don't you live in it?'

'Because there are too many memories here,' she said simply. 'Good and bad. I walk in here and,' she smiled, though the smile was thin, 'it's filled with ghosts.'

'So why not move away?'

'Out of Coldheart Canyon? I can't.'

'Are you going to tell me why?'

'Another time. This is a bad time to tell that story.' She passed her delicate hand over her face, and for a moment, as the veil of her fingers covered her features, he saw her retreat from her beauty, as though for a moment the performance of selfhood was too much for her.

'You ask *me* a question,' he suggested.

Her hand dropped away. The light shone out of her face again.

'You swear you'll answer me truthfully if I do?'

'Sure.'

'Swear.'

'I said so.'

'Does it hurt behind the bandages?'

'Oh.'

'You said you'd answer me.'

'I know. And I will. It's uncomfortable, I'll tell you that. But it doesn't really hurt any more. Not like it used to. I just wish I'd never messed with this. I mean, why couldn't I be happy the way I was?'

'Because nobody is. We're always looking for something we haven't got. If we weren't, we wouldn't be human.'

'Is that why you came spying on me?' he said, matching her mischief with some of his own. 'Looking for something you haven't got?'

'I'm sorry. It was rude of me: watching you, I mean. Spying. You've as much right to your privacy as I have to mine. And it's hard to protect yourself sometimes. You don't know who's a friend and who's not. That can make you crazy.' Her eyes flashed, and the playfulness was back. 'Then again, sometimes it's *good* to be crazy.'

'Yes?'

'Oh sure. Sometimes it's the only thing keeps you sane.'

'You're obviously talking from experience.'

'Of getting crazy once in a while? Sure. I'm talking from intimate experience.'

'Care to give me an example?'

'You don't want to know. Really you don't. Some of the things I've done in this very room . . .'

'Tell me.'

'I wouldn't know where to begin.'

Her gaze flitted off around the room, as though she was looking for some cue for her memories. If it was an act, it was a very good one. In fact this whole performance was looking better and better.

Finally, she said: 'We used to play poker here. Sometimes roulette.'

'Marco and I figured that out.'

'Sometimes,' she said, her gaze returning to him, 'I was the prize.'

'You?'

'Me.'

'I don't think I understand.'

'You understand perfectly well.'

'You'd give yourself to the winner?'

205

'See? You understood. I didn't do it every night. I'm not *that* much of a slut.' She was smiling as she spoke, lapping up his disbelief. She began to walk towards him, slowly, matching her approach to the rhythm of her words. 'But on the nights when you need to be crazy –'

'What did you give them? A kiss!'

'Pah! A kiss! As if I'd be satisfied with so little. No! Down on the floor in front of the losers, that's what I'd give them. Like dogs, if we felt like it.'

The way she stared at the ground as she spoke, it was clear she was remembering something very specific. The subtlest of motions went through her, as though her body was recalling the sensation of pressing back against a man; to take him, all of him, inside her.

'Supposing somebody won that you didn't like?'

'There was no such man. Not here, in my house. They were all gods. Beautiful men, every single one. Some of them were crude at first. But I taught them.' She was watching Todd closely as she spoke, measuring his response. 'You like hearing this?'

He nodded. It wasn't quite the way he'd expected this conversation to go, but yes, he liked her confessions. He was glad his pants were baggy, now that she was so close to him, or she'd have seen for herself how much he liked them.

'So let me be sure I got this right. The winner would fuck you, right here on the ground –'

'Not on the bare boards. There used to be carpets. Beautiful Persian carpets. And there were silk cushions, red ones, which I kept in a heap over there. I like to make love amongst cushions. It's like being held in somebody's hand, isn't it?' She opened her cupped hand in front to demonstrate the comfort of it. 'In God's hand.'

She lifted the bed of her palm in front of his eyes, and then, without warning, she reached out and touched his face. He felt nothing through the bandages, but he had

206

the illusion that her hand was like a balm upon his cheek, cooling his raw flesh.

'Does that hurt?'

'No.'

'Do you want me to go on telling you?'

'Yes, please.'

'You want to hear what I did . . .'

'. . . on the cushions. Yes. But first, I want to know –'

'Who?'

'No, not *who*. Why?'

'Why? Lord in Heaven, why would I *fuck*? Because I loved it! It gave me pleasure.' She leaned closer to him, still stroking his cheek. He could smell her throat on the breath she exhaled. The air, for all its invisibility, was somehow enriched by its transport into her and out again. He envied the men who'd taken similar liberties. In and out; in and out. Wonderful.

'I love to have a man's weight bearing down on me,' she went on. 'To be pinned, like a butterfly. Open. And then, when he thinks he's got you completely under his thumb, roll him over and ride him.' She laughed. 'I wish I could see the expression on your face.'

'It's not pretty under there.' He paused, a chilling thought on his lips.

'The answer's no,' she said.

'The answer to what?'

'Have I *spied* on you while your bandages were being changed? No I haven't.'

'Good.' He took a deep breath, wanting to direct the conversation away from talk of what was behind his mask. 'Go back to the game,' he said.

'Where was I?'

'Riding the lucky sonofabitch.'

'Horses. Dogs. Monkeys. Men make good animals. Women too sometimes.'

'Women got to play?'

'Not in here. I'm very old-fashioned about things like that. In Romania a woman never played cards.'

'Romania. That's where you're from?'

'Yes. A little village called Ravbac, where I don't think any woman had ever had pleasure with a man.'

'Is that why you left?'

'One of many reasons. I ran away when I was barely twelve. Came to this country when I was fifteen. Made my first picture a year later.'

'What was it called?'

'I don't want to talk about it. It's forgotten.'

'So finish telling me –'

'– about riding the men. What else is there to say? It was the best game in the world. Especially for an exhibitionist, like myself. You too.'

'What about me?'

'You've done it in front of people. Surely. Don't tell me you haven't. I won't believe you.'

What the hell? This woman had him all figured out. Pinned. Like a butterfly. There didn't seem to be much purpose in denying it.

'Yes, I've had a few public moments at private parties.'

'Are you good?'

'It depends on the girl.'

She smiled. 'I think you'd be wonderful, with the right audience,' she said.

Her hand dropped from his cheek, and she started to walk back across the room, weaving between imaginary obstacles as she picked up her erotic tale.

'Some nights, I would simply walk naked amongst the tables while the men played. They weren't allowed to look at me. If they looked, I would thrash them. And I mean thrash. I had a whip for that. I still have it. The Teroarea. The Terror. So . . . that was one of the rules. No looking at the prize, no matter what it did to tempt them.' She laughed. 'You can imagine, I had a hundred ways. Once

208

I had a little bell, hooked through the hood of my clitoris. Tinkling as I walked. Somebody looked, I remember. And oh they suffered.'

She was at the mantelpiece now, reaching up and under the fireplace and took a long, silver-handled switch from its hiding place. She tested it on the air, and it whined like a vengeful mosquito. 'This is the Teroarea. I had it made by a man in Paris, who specialized in such things. My name is chased into the handle.' She passed her thumb over the letters: '*Katya Lupescu*, it says. Actually it says more. It says: "This is her instrument, to make fools suffer." I regret having that written there, really.'

'Why?'

'Because a man who takes pleasure in being given pain is not a fool. He's simply following his instincts. Where's the foolishness in that?'

'You're big on pleasure,' Todd said.

She didn't seem to understand what he meant; she cocked her head, puzzled.

'You talk about it a lot.'

'Twice I've mentioned it,' she said. 'But it's been in my mind a little more than that.'

'Why?'

'Don't be coy,' she said, a little sternly. 'Or I'll beat you.'

'I might not like that.'

'Oh, you would.'

'Really . . .' he said, with just a touch of anxiety in his voice. He could not imagine having that thing, her Terror, give him pleasure, however expertly it was wielded.

'It can be gentle, if I want it to be.'

'That?' he said. 'Gentle?'

'Oh yes.' She made a scooping motion with her free hand. 'If I have a man's sex in my palm, here.' He got an instant, and uncannily sharp picture of what she had in

209

mind. Her victim on all fours, and that scooping motion of hers; the taking up of his cock and balls, ready for her. Completely vulnerable; completely humiliated. He'd never let a woman do anything like that to him, however much she promised it was to give him pleasure.

'I can see you're not convinced,' she said, 'even when I don't have your face to look at. So you'll just have to take it on trust. I could touch men with this and they'd shoot like sixteen-year-olds. Even Valentino.'

'Valentino?'

'And he was queer.'

'Rudolph Valentino?'

'Yes. You didn't know he was that way?'

'No, it's just . . . he's been dead a long time.'

'Yes, it was sad to lose him so quickly,' she said.

She obviously had no difficulty agreeing with him about how long the Great Lover had been deceased, even though it made nonsense of her story.

'We had a great party for him, out on the lawn, two weeks after he'd been taken from us.' She turned away from him and laid the switch back on the mantelpiece. 'I know you don't believe a word of what I've told you. You've done the mathematics, and none of it's remotely possible.' She leaned on the mantelpiece, her chin on the heel of her hand. 'What have you decided? That I'm some kind of trespasser? A little sexually deranged but essentially harmless?'

'I suppose something like that.'

'Hmm.' She mused on this for a moment. Then she said: 'You'll change your mind, eventually. But there's no hurry. I've waited a long time for this.'

'This?'

'You. Us.'

She left the thought there to puzzle him a moment, then she turned, the dusting of melancholy that had crept into her voice over the course of the last few exchanges brushed away. She was bright again; gleaming with harm-less trouble-making.

'Have you ever done it with a man?'

'Oh, Jesus.'

'So you have!'

He was caught. There was no use denying it.

'Only . . . twice. Or three times.'

'You can't remember.'

'Okay, three times.'

'Was it good?'

'I'll never do it again, so I guess that's your answer.'

'Why are you so sure?'

'There's some things you can be that sure of,' he said. Then, a little less confidently, 'Aren't there?'

'Even men who aren't queer imagine other men some-times. Yes?'

'Well . . .'

'Perhaps you're the exception to the rule. Perhaps you're the one the Canyon isn't going to touch.' She started to walk back towards him. 'But don't be too certain. It takes the pleasure out of things. Maybe you should let a woman take charge for a while.'

'Are we talking about sex?'

'Valentino swore he only liked men, but as soon as I took charge . . .'

'Don't tell me. He was like a naughty schoolboy.'

'No. Like a baby.' Her hand went to her breast, and she squeezed it, catching the nipple in the groove between her thumb and forefinger, as though to proffer it for Todd to suckle.

He knew it wasn't smart to show too much emotion to the woman. If there was some genuine streak of derange-ment in her, it would only empower her more. But he couldn't help himself. He took half a step backwards, aware that the trenches of his mouth were suddenly running with spit at the thought of her nipple in his mouth.

'You shouldn't let your mind get between you and what your body wants,' she said. She took her hand from her breast. The nipple stood hard beneath the light fabric.

'I know what my body wants.'

'Really?' she said, sounding genuinely surprised at the claim. 'You know what it wants *deep down*? All the way down to the very darkest place?'

He didn't reply.

She reached out and took gentle hold of his hand. Her fingers were cold and dry; his were clammy.

'What are you afraid of?' she said. 'Not me, surely.'

'I'm not afraid,' he said.

'Then come to me,' she told him, softly. 'I'll find out what you want.' He let her draw him closer to her; let her hands move up over his chest towards his face.

'You're a big man,' she murmured.

Her fingers were at his neck now. Whatever she was promising about discovering *his* desires, he knew what *she* wanted; she wanted to see his face. And though there was a part of his mind that resisted the idea, there was a greater part that wanted her to see him, for better or worse. He let her hands go up to his jawline; let her fingers rest on the adhesive tape that held the mask of gauze against his wound.

'May I . . . ?' she asked him.

'Is this what you came here to do?'

She made a small, totally ambiguous smile. Then she pulled at the tape. It came away with a gentle tug. He felt the gauze loosen. He stared down into her face, wondering – in this long moment before it was done and beyond saving – if she would reject him when she saw the scars and the swelling. A scene from that same silent horror movie he'd seen in his mind's eye many times since Burrows had done his brutal work, flickered in his head: Katya as the appalled heroine, reeling away in disgust at what her curiosity had uncovered. He the

212

monster, enraged at her revulsion and murderous in his self-contempt.

It was too late to stop it now. She was pulling at the gauze, coaxing it away from the hurts it concealed.

He felt the cool air upon his wounds, and cooler still, her scrutiny. The gauze dropped to the floor between them. He stood there before her, more naked than he'd ever been in his life – even in nightmares of nakedness, more naked – awaiting judgement.

She wasn't horrified. She wasn't screaming, wasn't flinching. She simply looked at him, without any interpretable expression on her face.

'Well?' he said.

'He made a mess of you, no doubt about that. But it's healing. And if my opinion is worth anything to you, I'd say you're going to be fine. Better than fine.'

She took a moment to assess him further. To trace the line of his jaw, the curve of his temple.

'But it's never going to be perfect,' she said.

His stomach lurched. Here was the heart of it: the bitter part nobody had wanted to admit to him; not even himself. He was spoiled. Perhaps just a little, but a little was all it would take to shake him from his high perch. His precious face, his golden face, the beauty that had made him the idol of millions, had been irreparably damaged.

'I know,' Katya said, 'you're thinking your life won't be worth living. But that's just not true.'

'How the hell do you know?' he said, smarting from the truth, angered by her honesty.

'Because I knew all the great stars, in the silent days. And believe me, the smart ones – when they weren't making the money any longer – just shrugged and said okay, I've had my time.'

'What did they do then?'

'Listen to yourself! There's life after fame. Sure it'll

213

take some getting used to, but people have perfectly good lives –'

'I don't want a perfectly good life. I want the life I had.'

'Well you can't have it,' she said, very simply.

It was a long time since somebody had told Todd Pickett that he couldn't have something, and he didn't like it. He took hold of her wrists and pulled her hands away from his face. A quick fury had risen in him. He wanted to strike at her, knock her stupid words out of her mouth.

'You know, you are crazy,' he said.

'Didn't I tell you?' she said, making no attempt to touch him again. 'Some nights I'm so crazy I'm ready to hang myself. But I don't. You know why? I made this hell for myself, so it's up to me to live in it, isn't it?'

He didn't respond to her; he was still in a filthy rage about what she'd said.

'Do you understand what I'm saying?'

'I think I've had it with your advice for the night,' he said, 'so why don't you just go back wherever you came from –'

In mid-sentence he heard Marco calling.

'Boss? Are you okay? Where the hell are you?'

He looked towards the door, half expecting to see Marco already standing there. He wasn't. Todd then looked back at Katya, or whoever the hell she was. The woman was retreating from him, shaking her head as if to say: *don't tell*.

'It's okay!' he yelled to Marco.

'Where are you?'

'I'm fine. Go make me a drink. I'll meet you in the kitchen!'

Katya had already retreated to the far end of the room, where the shadows from which she had originally emerged were enclosing her.

'Wait!' Todd said, his fury not yet completely abated.

214

He wanted to make sure the woman didn't leave thinking she would be allowed to come back, come stalking him while he slept, damn her. But she had turned her back on him now, ignoring his instruction. So he went after her.

A door opened in the darkness ahead of him, and he felt a wave of night-air, cool and fragrant, come in against his face. He hadn't known that there was a door to the outside of the house at the far end of the Casino, but she was out through it in a heartbeat (he saw her silhouette as she flitted away along a starlit path), and by the time he reached the door she was gone, leaving the shrubs she'd brushed as she ran shaking.

He stepped over the threshold, and looked around, attempting to orient himself. The path Katya had taken led up the hill, winding as it went. Back to the guest-house, no doubt. That was where the crazy-lady was in residence. She'd made herself a nice little nest in the guest-house. Well, that was easily fixed. He'd just send Marco up there tomorrow to evict her.

'Boss?'

He walked back into the Casino and stared down at the expanse of floor where she'd had him picturing her making love. He'd believed her, too; a little. At least his dick had.

Marco was at the other end of the room.

'What the hell's going on?' he said.

Todd was about to tell him there and then – about to send him up the hill to oust the trespasser – but Marco was bending down to gingerly pick something up from the ground. It was Todd's discarded bandages.

'You took 'em off,' he said.

'Yeah.'

The rage he'd felt started to seep out of him now, as he remembered the tender way she'd looked at him. Not judging him, simply looking.

'What happened, boss?'

215

'I found another door,' he said rather lamely.

'Was there somebody here?' Marco said.

'I don't know,' he said. 'Maybe. I was just wandering around, and I came down here . . .'

'The door was open?'

'No, no,' Todd said. He closed the door with a solid slam. 'I just tried it and it was unlocked.'

'It needs a new lock then,' Marco said, his tone uncertain, as though he was suspicious of what he was being told, but playing along.

'Yes, it needs a new lock.'

'Okay.'

They stood for a moment at opposite ends of the room, in silence.

'Are you all right?' Marco said after a pause.

'Yeah. I'm fine.'

'You know pills 'n' liquor'll be the death of you.'

'I'm hopin',' Todd replied, his joviality as forced as Marco's.

'Okay. If you say you're okay, you're okay.'

'I'm okay.'

Marco proffered the bandages. 'What do you want me to do with *these*?'

'What do you think?' Todd said, getting back into the normal rhythm of their exchanges now. The door was closed. The woman and the path and the nodding shrubs were out of sight. Whatever she'd said, he could forget, at least for tonight. 'Burn them. Where's that drink? I'm going to celebrate.'

'What are you celebrating?'

'Me losing those damn bandages. I looked like God knows what.'

'Burrows might want you to keep 'em on.'

'Fuck Burrows. If I want to take the bandages off, it's my choice.'

'It's your face.'

216

'Yeah,' Todd said, staring again at the ground where the crazy woman had claimed she'd laid her body, imagining her there. 'It's my face.'

2

Maxine came up to the house the following afternoon to tell Todd about the Oscar festivities, reporting it all – the ceremony itself, then the parties – with a fine disregard for his tenderness. Several times he almost stopped her and told her he didn't want to hear any more, but the dregs of curiosity silenced him. He still wanted to know who'd won and who'd lost.

There'd been the usual upsets, of course, the usual grateful tears from the usual surprised ingénues, all but swooning away with gratitude. This year, there'd even been fisticuffs: an argument had developed in the parking lot at Spago's between Glenn Turner, a young, fast-talking filmmaker who'd made two movies, been lionized, and turned into a legendary ego all in the space of fifteen months, and Vincent Dinny, a vicious writer for *Vanity Fair* who'd recently profiled Turner most unflatteringly. Not that Dinny was a paragon himself. He was a waspish, embittered man in his late sixties, who – having failed in his ascent of the Hollywood aristocracy – had turned to writing about the town's underbelly. Nobody could have given a toss for his pieces had they not carried a certain sting of truth. The piece on Turner, for instance, had mentioned a certain taste for heroin; which was indeed the man's vice of choice.

'So who won?' Todd wanted to know.

'Glenn broke two fingers when he fell against his car, and Dinny got a bloody nose. So I don't know who won.

It's all so ridiculous. Acting like children.'

'Did you actually see them fighting?'

'No, but I saw Dinny afterwards. Blood all over his shirt.'
There was a pause. 'I think he knows something.'

'What?'

'He was quite civilized about it. You know how he is.
Shrivelled up little prick. He just said to me: I *hear* Todd's
had some medical problems, and now you've got him under
lock and key. And I just looked at him. Said nothing. But
he knows.'

'This is so fucked.'

'I don't know how we deal with it, frankly. Sooner or
later, he's going to suggest a piece to *Vanity Fair*, and they're
going to jump on it.'

'So fucked,' Todd said, more quietly. 'What the hell did
I do to deserve this?'

Maxine let the question go. Then she said. 'Oh, by the
way, do you remember Tammy Lauper?'

'No.'

'She runs the Fan Club.'

'Oh yeah.'

'Fat.'

'Is she fat?'

'She's practically obese.'

'Did she come to the office?'

'No; I got a call from the police in Sacramento, asking
if we'd seen her. She's gone missing.'

'And they think I might have absconded with her?'

'I don't know what they think. The point is, you haven't
seen her up here?'

'Nope.'

'Maybe over in Bel Air?'

'I haven't *been* over in Bel Air. Ask Marco.'

'Yeah, well I said I'd ask you and I asked.'

Todd went to the living-room window, and gazed out at
the Bird of Paradise trees that grew close to the house. They

hadn't been trimmed in many years, and were top-heavy with flowers and rotted foliage, their immensity blocking his view of the opposite hill. But it didn't take much of an effort of imagination to bring the Canyon into his mind's eye. The palm-trees that lined the opposite ridge; the pathways and the secret groves; the empty swimming pool, the empty koi-pond; the statues, standing in the long grass. He was suddenly seized by an overwhelming desire to be out there in the warm sunshine, away from Maxine and her brittle gossip.

'I gotta go,' he said to Maxine.

'Go where?'

'I just gotta go,' he said, heading for the door.

'Wait,' Maxine said. 'We haven't finished business.'

'Can't it wait?'

'No, I'm afraid this part can't.'

Todd made an impatient sigh, and turned back to her. 'What is it?'

'I've been doing some thinking over the last few days. About our working relationship.'

'What about it?'

'Well, to put it bluntly, I think it's time we parted company.'

Todd didn't say anything. He just looked at Maxine with an expression of utter incomprehension on his face, as though she'd just spoken to him in a foreign language. Then, after perhaps ten seconds, he returned his gaze to the Birds of Paradise.

'You don't know how wearying it gets,' Maxine went on. 'Waking up thinking about whether everything's okay with Todd, and going to sleep thinking the same damn thing. Not having a minute in a day when I'm not worrying about you. I just can't do it any more. It's simple as that. It's making me ill. I've got high blood pressure, high cholesterol –'

'I've made you a lot of money over the years,' Todd broke in to observe.

'And I've taken care of you. It's been a very successful partnership. You made me rich. I made you famous.'

'You didn't *make* me famous.'

'Well, if I didn't I'd like to know who the hell did.'

'*Me*,' Todd replied, raising the volume of his voice just a fraction. 'It's *me* people came to see. It's *me* they loved. *I* made myself famous.'

'Don't kid yourself,' Maxine said, her voice a stone.

There was a long silence. The wind brushed the leaves of the Bird of Paradise trees together, like the blades of plastic swords being brushed together.

'Wait,' Todd said. 'I know what this is about. You've got a new boy. That's it, isn't it? You're fucking some kid, and –'

'I'm not fucking anybody, Todd.'

'You fucked me.'

'Twice. A long time ago. I wouldn't do it today.'

'Well just for the record neither would I.'

Maxine looked at him coldly. 'That's it. I've said what I needed to say.'

She went to the door. Todd called after her. 'Why do it to me now? Why wait till I'm so fucking tired I can hardly think straight!' His voice continued to get louder, creeping up word on word, syllable on syllable. 'And then screw me up like this?'

'Don't worry, I'll find somebody else to look after you. I'll train them. You'll be taken good care of. It's not like I'm walking out on you.'

'*Yes you are.*'

He turned to look at her, finally. The blood had rushed to the surface of his half-mended face. It was grotesquely red.

'You think I'm finished, so you're leaving me to be crucified by every piece of shit journalist in the fucking country.'

Maxine ignored the outburst, and picked up what she was saying. 'I'll find somebody to take over, who'll protect you better than I can. Because I'm just as tired as you are, Todd. Then I'm going to have one last party down at the beach house, and get the hell out of this city before it kills me.'

'Well I'm not going to let you go.'

'Oh, now don't start threatening –'

'I'm not starting anything. I'm just reminding you. We've got a contract. I'm not going to allow you to make a fortune out of me and then just walk away when things get difficult. You owe me.'

'I *what*?'

'Whatever's on the contract. Another two years.'

'I can't do it. I won't do it.'

'Then I'll sue your ass, for every fucking cent you earned off me.'

'You can try.'

'And I'll win.'

'Like I said, you can try. If you want all our dirty washing dragged out for everyone to see, then do it. I guarantee you'll come out looking worse than I will. I've covered for you so many times, Todd.'

'And you signed a confidentiality agreement. If you break it, I'll sue you for breaking that, too.'

'Who cares? Nobody gives a rat's ass about me. I'm just a professional parasite. You're the movie star. You're the all-American boy. The one with the reputation to lose.' She paused. Then murmured, almost ruminatively: 'The tales I could tell . . .'

'I can tell just as many.'

'There's nothing anyone can call me that I haven't been called a *hundred* times. I know everyone says I'm a cunt. That's what they say right? "How can you work with that fucking cunt?" If I have to hear it in a courtroom one more time, I can take that, as long as when it's all over I don't have to hear your whining and complaining any more.'

'Okay,' Todd said. 'If that's the way you want to play it.'

Maxine headed for the door. 'For your information,' she said, 'I could go down to LAX right now, and I could fill a limo with kids who have ten times your talent. They're all coming here, looking to be the next Tom Cruise, the next Leonardo DiCaprio, the next Todd Pickett. Pretty boys with tight asses and nice abs who'll end up, most of 'em, selling their tight asses on Santa Monica Boulevard. The lucky ones'll end up waiters.

'If I wanted to, I could make any one of them a movie star. Maybe not a star like you. But then again maybe *bigger*. Right face, right time, right movie. Some of it's luck, some of it's salesmanship. The point is, I *sold* you, Todd. I told people you were going to be huge, and I said it so often that it became the truth. And you were so sweet back then. So . . . natural. You were the boy next door, and yes – for your information – I was a little in love with you, like everyone else. But it didn't last long. You changed. I changed. We both got rich. We both got greedy.' She put her hand to her mouth, and gently passed her fingers over her lips. 'But you know what, Todd? Neither of us was ever happy. Am I right? You were never happy, even when you had everything you'd ever dreamed of wanting.'

'What's your point?'

'I don't know what the point is,' she said softly. 'I guess that's the problem in a nutshell, isn't it? I don't know what the point is.' She stared into middle distance for a while. 'You'll be fine, Todd,' she said finally. 'Things will work out better without me, you'll see. I'll find someone to take care of you, Eppstadt'll find a movie for you, and you'll be back in front of the cameras in a few months, looking perfect. If that's what you want.'

'Why wouldn't I want that?' he said to her.

She looked at him wearily. 'Maybe because none of it's worth a damn.'

223

He knew he had a riposte for that; he just couldn't figure out what it was at that particular moment. And while he was trying to figure it out, Maxine turned her back on him and walked out.

He let her go. What was the use of a feud? That was for the lawyers. Besides, he had more urgent business than trading insults with her. He had to find Katya.

The afternoon sun was not just warm, it was hot, and the foliage was busy with hungry hummingbirds and the Canyon was quiet and perfect. He threaded his way through the overgrown bushes, past the tennis courts and the antique sundial, up towards the guest-house. The gradient became quite steep after a time, the narrow steps decayed by time and neglect, so that in some spots they'd collapsed completely. After a while, he realized the path had divided at some earlier point, and that he'd taken the wrong turning. The mistake took him on a picturesque tour of the gardens' hidden places, bringing him first to a small grove of walnut trees, in the middle of which stood a large gazebo in an advanced state of disrepair, and then into a garden within a garden, bounded by an unkempt privet hedge. Here there were roses, or rather the remains of last year's blooms, the bushes fighting for space, and strangling each other in the process. There was no way through the thorny tangle to pick up the path on the other side, so he was obliged to try and get around the garden from the outside, staying close to the hedge. It was difficult to do. Though the plants he was striding through didn't have thorns, they were still unruly and wild; twigs and dead flowers scraped at his face, his shirt was quickly soiled, his sneakers filled with stony earth. By the time he got to the other side of the garden, and took to the path again, he was short of breath and patience; and had two dozen little nicks and scratches to call his own.

His wanderings had brought him to a spot that offered

a spectacular view. He could see the big house below him surrounded by palms and Birds of Paradise; he could see the baroque weathervane on the top of the gazebo he'd passed on his way here, and the orchid house, which he had come upon on one of his earlier trips around the garden. All this, bathed in clear warm California light; the crystalline light which had brought filmmakers here almost a century before. Not for the first time since coming to the house he had a pleasurable sense of history; and a measure of curiosity as to the people who might once have walked here, talked here. What ambitions had they plotted, as they ambled through these gardens? Had they been sophisticates, or simpletons? What little he knew about Old Hollywood he'd heard from Jerry Brahms, which meant he'd only ever really been half-listening. But he knew enough to be certain those times had been good, at least for a man like himself. Douglas Fairbanks and Rudolph Valentino, Charlie Chaplin, the Barrymore clan, and all the rest had been like royalty, lording it over their new dominion in the West. A bean-counting prick like Eppstadt – with his demographics and his endless corporate manoeuvring – would have had no power in the world this Canyon still preserved.

Having caught his breath, he now continued his ascent. The shrubbery became denser the closer he got to the guest-house. He would have needed a machete to hack through it efficiently; but, lacking one, had to do with a branch he picked up on his way. The flowers gave up their perfume as he beat his way through them, and he recognized their scent. It was *her* scent. The scent on Katya's skin. Did she walk naked amongst them, he wondered, pressing the flowers against her body? Now that would be a sight to see.

The thought of this had stirred him up; he actually had a hard-on. Not an everyday order of hard-on either, but the kind that was so strong it actually hurt. It was a long time since he'd had a woodie so fierce, and it added immeasurably to his sense of well-being. With the guest-house now in view he pressed towards his goal, feeling curiously, happily, adolescent. So what the hell if Maxine was deserting him? What the hell if he'd never be a Golden Boy again? He was still alive and kicking, still had a stick in his hand, and a woodie in his pants, and the thought of Katya's flower bath in his mind's eye.

The thicket had finally thinned, and he was at last delivered onto a small unkempt lawn. The house before him was a two-storey affair, built in the same style as the main house, simply on a much more modest scale. Above the door, set into the stucco, was a single tile, with a man on a horse painted upon it. He glanced up at it for only a moment. Then he pressed his flattened hand down the front of his jeans to push his erection into a less obvious position on the clock, and knocked on the mad-woman's door.

3

There was no reply from within, nor any sound of movement in response to his knocking. He knocked a second time, and then – after a short pause – a third. Still there was no response, so he tried the latch. The door was unlocked. He pushed it open, and stepped out of the sunlight into the cool interior of the house.

At first glance he assumed that he'd misunderstood what Katya had told him, and the house was not occupied after all; merely used as a storage space of some kind. The room before him, which was large and high-ceilinged, was little more than a junk-room, filled with furniture and bric-a-brac. But as his eyes became more accustomed to the murky light, after the blaze of sun outside, he began to make sense of what he was seeing. Yes, the place was over-filled, but the contents of the room were far from junk. On the wall to the left hung an enormous tapestry depicting a scene of medieval revelry; on the wall opposite was a series of white marble bas-reliefs that looked to have been filched from a Roman temple. In the far corner, close to a great oak door, were more slabs of stone, these carved with hieroglyphics. There was an elegant chaise longue in front of the massive fireplace; and a table, its legs elaborately carved with baroque grotesqueries, stood in the middle of the room. All of this had presumably been removed from the big house at some point, but that hardly explained the strange confusion of periods and styles.

Moving deeper into the room, Todd called out to

announce his presence. There was no reply. He didn't linger now to study the furniture or the antiquities, but crossed the room to the large oak door. Here again he knocked, but receiving no reply, he turned the carved handle, and pushed the door open. Given its size, he'd expected it to be heavy, but it wasn't. On the other side was a wide hallway, the walls of which were hung with white masks. No, not masks, *life-casts*; white plaster faces, all caught with that expression of eerie, enforced repose that such masks always wore. He'd had similar things made of his own face, by special effects men. Once for the facewound in *Gunner*, once for a bullet wound. It was an eerie experience, to look at the finished work. *This is what I'll look like when I'm dead*, he'd thought when he'd been shown the final results.

There were thirty or forty masks displayed on the wall; mostly of men. He thought that he vaguely recognized some of the faces, but he couldn't have put names to any of them. They were all handsome; some of them almost beautiful. He remembered Katya's crazy talk about the parties she'd had in the house. How she'd seduced Valentino. Was this collection the inspiration for that fantasy? Had she dreamed of fucking the famous because she had plaster copies of their faces up on her wall?

The door at the other end of the wall of life-masks was, like the last, deceptively light. This time he paused to puzzle out why, and examining it a little more closely, had his answer. It was fake. The large rusted nails weren't iron at all, but carved and stippled wood; the patina of antiquity had been achieved by a skilled painter. It was a door from a movie-set; all illusion. And if the doors had been made that way, what about the tapestry and the bas-reliefs and table carved with grotesqueries? They were all most likely fakes. Stolen off a back-lot, or bought from a studio fire-sale. None of it was real.

He pushed the door open, and came into a second room,

this one much smaller than the first, but just as cluttered. On the wall opposite him hung a large mirror, its gilt frame elaborately carved with naked figures, men and women knotted together in configurations which looked both sensual and tormented. He seldom let a mirror go by without putting it to use, and even now – knowing he wouldn't like what he saw – he paused and assessed his reflection. He was a sad sight, his clothes in disarray from his trip through the shrubbery, his face like an inept copy of its finer self. He wondered if perhaps he shouldn't turn back; he was in no condition to present himself to Katya. Even as he was thinking about this the door to the left of the mirror creaked a little, and – caught by the wind – opened a couple of inches. Forsaking his sorry reflection, he went to the door and peered into the room beyond.

The sight before him put all thought of retreat from his mind. Inside was an enormous four-poster bed, its columns decorated in the same lushly erotic style as the gilded frame of the mirror. A swathe of dark purple velvet hung in ripe folds like a half-raised curtain. The red pillows heaped on the bed were just as excessive, creamy silk fringed with lace. The sheet, which was also silk, was pulled back, so that the sleeper was left uncovered.

It was Katya, of course.

There she lay, face-down; her hair unloosed, her body naked.

He stood at the door, enraptured. The pillow she lay on was so soft and deep that her face was almost concealed, but he could still see the high curve of her cheek, the tender pink of her ear. Was she awake behind her pale lids, he wondered, her nakedness a deliberate provocation? He suspected not. There was something too artless about the way her legs were splayed, too childlike about the way her hands were tucked up against her breasts. And the final proof? She was snoring. If this was indeed a performance then that was a touch of genius.

The perfectly human thing which made all the rest so believable.

His eyes went to the cleft of her buttocks; to the gloss of the hair that showed between her legs. He was suddenly stupid with lust.

He took a step towards the bed. The floor creaked under his weight, but thankfully the noise wasn't loud enough to stir her. He continued his approach, his gaze fixed upon her face, looking for the merest flutter of a lash. But there was none. She was deeply asleep; and dreaming. He was close enough now to see that her eyes were in motion behind her lids, watching something happening in another place.

At the bedside, he dropped down onto his haunches, his left knee popping loudly. There was a faint dusting of gooseflesh on her limbs, he saw. He couldn't resist the temptation to reach out and touch her skin, as though he might smooth the gooseflesh away with his fingertips. Surely she would wake now, he thought. But no, she slept on. The only sign that she might be surfacing from sleep was the slowing of the motion of her pupils. The dream was leaving her; or she was departing from the dream.

He was suddenly alarmed. What would she think, if she woke to find him this close to the bed, his intent so unquestionably voyeuristic? Perhaps he should go; quickly, before she woke. But he couldn't bring himself to move an inch. All he could do was kneel there, like a suppliant, his heart beating furiously, his face a furnace.

Then, in her sleep, she murmured something. He held his breath, trying to catch the words. It wasn't English she was speaking, it was an Eastern European language; probably her native Romanian. He could make no sense of what she was saying, of course, but there was a softness to the syllables; a neediness, which suggested they were supplications. She turned her face up from the pillow, and he saw that her expression was troubled. Her brow was furrowed, and there were tears welling beneath her lids.

The sight of her distress bothered him. It brought back memories of his mother's tears, which he'd watched her shed so often as a child. Tears of frustrated rage, sometimes; but more often tears of loneliness.

'Don't . . .' he said to her softly.

She heard him speaking, it seemed. Her entreaties grew quieter. Then she said: 'Willem?'

'No . . .'

The frown nicking her brow deepened and her lids began to flutter. She was waking up now, no doubt of that. He got to his feet, and began to retreat to the door, keeping his eyes fixed on her face. Only when he reached the door did he finally, regretfully, relinquish sight of her and turn away.

As he slipped through the door he heard her speak. 'Wait,' she said.

He was sorely tempted to exit rather than turn and face her, but he resisted his cowardice and looked back towards the bed.

She had pulled the sheet a little way up, to partially cover her nakedness. Her eyes were open, and the tears her dreams had induced were now running down her cheeks. Despite them, she was smiling.

'I'm sorry,' Todd said.

'For what?'

'Coming in here uninvited.'

'No,' she said sweetly. 'I wanted you to come.'

'Still, I shouldn't have stayed . . . watching you. It's just that you were talking in your sleep.'

'Well it's nice to have somebody listening,' she said. 'It's a long time since anyone was with me when I slept.' She wiped the tears from her cheeks.

'Are you all right?' he asked her.

'Yes, I'm fine.'

'Were you having a bad dream?'

'I can't remember,' she said, glancing away from him. He knew from his acting coach what such glances indicated: a

231

lie. She knew exactly what she'd been dreaming about; she just didn't want to tell him. Well, that was her business. God knows everybody was allowed their share of secrets.

'What time is it?' she said.

He glanced at his watch. 'Almost four-thirty.'

'You want to go for a walk before it gets too dark?' she said.

'Sure.'

She threw off her sheet, and got up out of bed, glancing up at Todd as she did so, as though to assure herself of his scrutiny.

'I'm going to bathe first,' she said. 'Would you do me a little favour in the meantime?'

'Sure.'

'Go back to the Gaming Room, where we met last night, and –'

'Don't tell me. Fetch your whip.'

She smiled. 'You read my mind.'

'As long as you promise not to be beating me with it.'

'Nothing could be further from my mind,' she said.

'Okay. I'll get it . . . but no beating.'

'Take your time. There's still plenty of light in the sky.'

He left her feeling oddly light-footed, pleased to have an errand from her. What did that say about their relationship, he wondered as he ran? That he was naturally subservient? Ready to do her will at the snap of her fingers. Well, if so, so.

He found his way back down to the big house without difficulty. Marco heard him in the Gaming Room, heavy-footed as ever, and came to see what all the noise was about.

'You okay?'

'That's all you ever ask. Am I okay? Yes. I'm better than okay.'

'Good. Only I heard from Maxine –'

232

'Fuck Maxine.'

'So it doesn't bother you?'

'No. We had a good run together. Now it's over.'

He picked up the switch from the mantelpiece.

'What the hell is that?'

'What does it look like?'

He beat the air two or three times. The switch was beautifully balanced; he could imagine learning how to use it with considerable cunning. Perhaps she would let him stroke her body with it.

Marco studied him in silence for a few moments; then he said: 'You never told me why you took your bandages off. Were they too tight?'

'I didn't take them off. *She* took them off.'

'Who's she?'

'The woman who owns this house. Katya Lupescu.'

'I'm sorry, you've lost me.'

Todd smiled. 'No more explanations,' he said. 'You'll meet her later. I gotta go.'

He left Marco standing at the door with a befuddled expression on his face, and headed out into the light again, climbing the slope towards Katya's house, aware that he was behaving like a man who'd just been given a new lease on life.

He didn't call her name as he entered this time. He simply made his way through the rooms of fake relics.

The sound of running water came from the room adjacent to the bedroom. Apparently, Katya was still running her bath.

He paused and looked around the bedroom. There were several enormous posters on the wall, which he had not noticed until now. Framed posters: one-sheets for movies, many decades old to judge by the stylized graphics, and the yellowing of the paper they were printed on. The same image dominated all seven posters: that of a woman's face. She was represented in two of them as a waif, a

233

child-woman lost in a predatory world. But in the others she'd matured beyond the orphan, and these were the images that reminded him of the woman he'd met last night – an exquisite femme fatale glowering from the frames as she planned her next act of anarchy. There was, of course, no question who the woman was. Her name was on the posters, big and bold. *The Sorrows of Frederick*, starring Katya Lupi. *The Devil's Bride*, starring Katya Lupi. *She is Destruction*, starring Katya Lupi.

What the hell was he to make of this new piece of evidence? Of course it was possible that Katya had paid to have seven posters representing fictitious films printed on aged paper and framed to look like objects of antiquity, but it wasn't very likely. Was it possible this Katya Lupi – who bore such a resemblance to the Katya he knew – was hardly the same woman at all but a granddaughter, with an uncanny resemblance to her older relative? It was a more plausible solution than any other he could think of. Certainly the flawless woman he'd seen naked minutes before, her face without so much as a wrinkle upon it, could not be the woman who'd starred in these movies. There had to be some other explanation.

He was about to call out and announce his presence when he heard a soft intake of breath echoing off the bathroom walls. He went quietly to the door, and glanced in. In a large, old-fashioned ceramic bath, half-filled with water, lay Katya, her legs spread, her hips lifted clear of the water so that he could see how her fingers slid inside her. Her eyes were closed.

Not for the first time this afternoon, Todd could feel the head of his dick tapping out the rhythm of his pulse against the inside of his pants. But he had no desire to interrupt Katya's game. He was perfectly happy to watch her: her face in ecstasy, her breasts clearing from the water as her body arched, her legs lifted up and straddling the sides of the bath. The mysteries of who she was and how she came to be here suddenly seemed absurdly irrelevant. What the hell did it matter? Look at her!

'Did you bring it?'

He'd had his eyes on her cunt; but when he looked back up at her face she was staring at him, her expression fierce with need.

'The Teroarea. Did you bring it?'

He was mortified with embarrassment, but plainly she couldn't have cared less. She had other priorities.

'Yes,' he said, showing her the switch. 'I brought it.'

'So use it.'

'What?'

She lifted her hips even higher, spreading her legs to give him a full view of her sex. It was ripened by her own touches; but also, he knew, from the anticipation of his return.

'Touch it,' she said. 'Lightly.'

His target stood proud of its hood, presented for his delectation.

'Please,' she begged.

He took four steps to the bottom of the bath, keeping his eyes fixed upon her. He felt the weight of the switch in his hand. He'd never done anything remotely like this before, but something about the way her body was contorted to offer her sex up to him lent him confidence.

'Are you ready?'

'*Just do it*!'

He lifted the Terror. Her clitoris looked as hard and as red as a ruby. He lay the switch on it with a short little stab that made her sob.

'Again!' she demanded immediately.

The ruby was already a little redder.

'*Again*!' she said.

He struck her again, twice, three times, four and five and six, while every muscle in her body went rigid so as to be his perfect target.

'More?' he said.

There were tears on her face, but she simply growled at him between gritted teeth. He took it to mean yes, and went to work again, until the sweat was running from his face, and down his back, his breath was rough with exertion. But she would not let him stop. Her gaze, her sneer, her offered body spoke the same demand, and he dutifully answered it, over and over and over and –

Suddenly her eyes rolled up in her head. Her mouth opened. He could barely make sense of the words, they were so thick with feeling.

'Again.' Her pupils had almost gone from sight. 'Once.'

He lifted the Terror, which for all its litheness, its lightness, suddenly felt brutal in his aching hand. Her body had started to shake. He was shaking too, now. But the Terror had its own imperative. Down it came once more.

She let out a cry that sounded more like something a bird would utter than a woman. Then her limbs lost their solidity, and her legs slipped gracefully off the sides of the bath. A tiny plume of crimson tinted the water.

He dropped the switch and retreated to the door, in a kind of childish terror at what he'd done; and at how much it had aroused him. Katya's eyes had closed. The expression on her face was one of childish contentment; an infant sleeping in the arms of innocence.

He slid down the door-frame into a squatting position, and there – exhausted by the intensity of the previous minutes, he must have briefly fallen asleep, because when he opened his eyes again the water was still moving, but Katya had vacated the tub. Vacated the bathroom too, in fact. He didn't have to get up to find her. He merely had to swing his head round, to see that she was sitting on the edge of the bed, her legs open, looking at her reflection in the long oval mirror. The expression of contentment had not left her face; but now there was a little smile on her lips too.

She had a wide repertoire of smiles, he thought; or at least it seemed he'd seen a lot in the short time they'd known one another. There was her teasing smile, her mischievous smile, her dark smile, her dry smile. This one had a little of everything in it. She knew he was watching her, so there was something of her performance smile in it. But it certainly wasn't phoney. How fake could someone be when she'd just let her body lead her into such extremes? Surely he was one of a rare order of men: those to whom she'd given herself in that profound way. He thought of the blood-tinted water rising up between her legs, and felt a peculiar mingling of retroactive alarm (what had he been doing, risking her most tender anatomy with nothing but the look on her face to guide him?) and exhilaration that they'd come through it together: their first shared insanity. Whoever she was, trespasser, lunatic, stalker, star, all other possible definitions paled before this: she was the woman who had taught him how insignificant the flesh between his legs was when it came to the pleasuring of certain women.

'Come here,' she said.

He pushed himself up off the doorframe and went over to her. 'Let me see,' she said, unbuckling his pants.

'I came . . .'

'I know.'

His trousers were massively too big, which was the way he liked to wear them. As soon as his belt was unbuckled, they fell down. He was afraid his dick would make a sorry show by now, shrivelled up in a crinkled skin of dried semen. But no. His erection had been so furiously hard it remained quite impressive, even though it was sodden. He could not imagine any other woman with whom he'd had sex taking such guileless pleasure in the perusal of his quarter-hard dick. Nor would any of those women have leaned forward, as Katya now did, and kissed it.

'May I look at you?' he said.

She assumed he didn't mean her face. She spread her legs. He hoisted his pants back up and went down on his knees.

'Does it hurt?' he said.

'Yes,' she said. She put her hand on the back of his head, gently pressing him towards her body. 'Look inside me,' she said. 'Don't be afraid. You did it. See what you did?'

He could see without opening her up. Her whole pubic region was puffy and inflamed.

'Go on, look,' she said. 'Enjoy what you did.'

He gently parted her labia, which were sticky beneath his fingertips. Not blood, not sweat. Just the natural juices of an aroused body.

'You see?' she said, pressing his fingers deeper into her. She was like a furnace in there. 'You've got thoughts going round in your head you never imagined having. Am I right?'

He replied by gently scooping her juices out on his fingers and putting them deep into his mouth.

'You want to lick me out?'

He shook his head.

'I'm afraid I'd draw more blood.'

'Maybe I'd like that.'

'Give me time.'

She took his fingers out of his mouth and replaced them with her tongue.

'You're right,' she said, when they'd finished kissing. 'We've got all the time in the world.'

She stood up. He stayed where he was, at her feet, still not quite believing they'd come so far so fast.

'It isn't a dream,' she said, reading his doubts as she'd read so many other thoughts of his in the last twenty-four hours. 'Sometimes it seems that way, but that's just the Canyon.'

He held onto her leg for a moment, kissing the inside of her thigh.

238

'We were going to walk, remember?' she said.

'You still want to?'

'Oh yes. I'd love to. It's a perfect night for introductions.'

PART FIVE

DESIRE

1

The Canyon had once been a kind of Eden for Zeffer; its bowers had been places of comfort, an escape from a world that was growing too tawdry too quickly for his taste. But that was many, many years ago. Now he hated his sometime paradise. It was a place of confinement and punishment; a lush hell, made all the more agonizing because he knew that just beyond the perimeters his mistress Katya had set were streets that he'd once driven around like a lord. The passage of years had transformed them, of course; probably out of all recognition. Seven decades was a long time. And if he climbed the southern flank of the Canyon, and stood on the ridge – which was on the very limits of his proscribed domain – then he could see the towers of what looked to him like a city within a city, where in his day there had been little more than a dirt road and some sagebrush. They had owned land down there, he and Katya, once upon a time. Probably the lawyers had taken their profits and died by now. But then he couldn't remember signing papers over to any other authority, so it was just possible then if someone was to question who owned the land on which that gleaming city stood, the paper trail would lead back to Katya Lupescu and Willem Matthias Zeffer.

There had been a time when Katya had been quite acquisitive: she'd been rich, and the land had been cheap, so she'd had him buy large plots of it, hundreds of acres in fact, as an investment. She'd got the idea from Douglas

Fairbanks and Mary Pickford, who had also made large purchases, saying, with considerable foresight, that as long as there was a hunger for people to be distracted from their unhappiness, there would be a need for this new world of theirs, this Hollywoodland. It followed, then, that the ground on which that New World was built would only grow in value.

Many times Zeffer had been tempted to leave the Canyon and venture down the hill to discover what it all looked like now, but he didn't dare. Katya had told him plainly what the consequences would be if he ever tried to leave. There would be no way back for him. She would see to it that he was torn limb from limb by those amongst the haunters of these hills who were loyal to her; the creatures she referred to as *los niños*: the children.

He didn't doubt that she would enforce the edict. She knew what power she held, and how to keep it. His death would be a fine lesson for those amongst the clans here who were less than loyal, and muttered their unrest in the ears of coyotes, and plotted the undoing of their mistress. They called her by many names, in many languages, being men and women who had come from all over the world, and now, in this strange afterlife, were returning to the tongue they knew best. To some she was *La Catin*, the Bitch; to others she was simply the Duchess of Sorrows. But none of these name-callers dared confront her. Whatever they whispered, whatever they plotted, they were too afraid of what they would lose if they went up against her and failed to win the day. Not only did they hope for her clemency at some time in the future, but they prayed with all their hearts that they'd be let back into the house, so that they could once more venture down the stairs into the Devil's Country, where they had once tasted something that was in their blood now permanently and could not be satisfied, except by more of the same.

He understood their hunger. He shared it. And if she

would let him back into the house then all the agonies of this half-life of his would be erased; all pain forgotten, all need dispatched. But Willem had few hopes of such clemency. Katya was crazy. She always had been, of course; indeed in earlier times it had been part of her glamour. Wasn't that part of what had made her so incredible to watch up there on the screen? A gleam of madness always lit up the eyes of her characters, whatever she was playing. Her innocents were crazy with their sinlessness; just as the vamps she played later were maddened by their sin. Of all the names that she was called, it was Cesar Romero's nickname that suited her best, *La Puta Enojada*, the Mad Bitch. That was the name Zeffer used when he talked about her. Katya, *La Puta Enojada*. But bitch or no, mad or no, she had the reins, and that was that. She was not going to wither any time soon, thanks to the machinations of that damnable room; nor was she likely to get up one morning and vacate her Canyon. She was just as afraid of the world beyond its perimeters as he was. In truth, for all her bombast and her brutality, it was fear that shaped her life.

Fear of living, fear of dying. Fear of staying, fear of going. Fear of remembering, and yes, fear of forgetting.

But every now and again, even in this despairing paradise, there would come a glimpse of hope; a hint of a chance that things might finally change for the better. Such hints and glimpses usually appeared in the form of interlopers; people whose unplanned presence in the Canyon had the potential to subtly change the balance of power in *La Puta Enojada*'s feudal realm.

There had been perhaps a dozen such opportunities during the time in which Zeffer had been a prisoner of the Canyon, all in their way dangers to the status quo, and all carefully managed by Katya, so as to prevent the destruction of her autocracy. The most notable, until now, had been the appearance of a runaway child, one

Jerry Brahms, who had fled his minders into the Canyon, ignorant of the mysteries he was treading amongst. He'd almost brought her down, that one, coming into the house without anyone realizing he was there, and getting his fingers into places they had no business being. Opening doors; letting the ghosts sniff the Hunt. The fact that he was a child had made her indulgent of his mistakes. Rather than have him killed, Katya had let him live; brought him to her bosom, in fact.

It was an act of trust that had served her well as the years had passed. Brahms the boy had become Brahms the man, and his loyalty had remained unwavering. Zeffer had never entirely understood what had happened between them, but he had his suspicions. Katya had shown Brahms pleasures that had marked him as hers forever. That meant, most likely, that she had taken him down to see the Hunt. Once you'd walked in the Devil's Country, smelt its ancient air, you belonged to that place, in some unspeakable way. It owned you. He didn't need to look any further than his own body for evidence of this. Since Katya had forbidden him to enter the house – keeping him from close proximity to the tiles – he had started to look and feel his true age. His hair had turned white, his bones and joints ached perpetually. Why was he surprised? Nobody lived forever. Not movie goddesses, nor the men who served them. And certainly not houses, however much rapture they contained. Every façade cracked, finally; and crumbled; and went away to dust. It was only a question of time.

Which thought brought him back to the newest trespasser in their sealed world: the most promising opportunity for an undoing of long-held certainties he'd seen in many years. She was a strong one, this big-boned, big-breasted woman with her unhappy eyes. She was trouble, thank God. Under the right circumstances a woman like that could do all kinds of mischief. If, of course, she was still alive. She'd been snatched away by *los niños*, the corrupt

246

children of the Canyon, offspring of unsavoury couplings between animals and ghosts. Zeffer had witnessed such intercourse many times over the years; vile marriages between ghost women and coyotes; ghost men and deer, or dogs; even once, a woman and a bird. Somehow, such consummations were often fruitful, though the birthings were not anything he could have imagined until he laid eyes on them. The animals who produced infants this way almost always died in the process; every now and again he would come upon one of their rotted carcasses on the hillside, and he'd know that another hybrid had been added to that unholy tribe. The revenant women who allowed such congress (some of them famous in their day, reduced in their frustration and madness to mating with wild animals), these women seemed to show no signs of trauma when the birth was over, their bodies being less than flesh and more than ether; malleable, mendable. But that was not to say their matings were without consequence. These ghosts were also the wildest, in his experience; the most prone to sudden violence. The beast had got into them in more ways than one. They were touched by a kind of rabidity, which was in distressing contrast to what remained of their elegance. Their glossy skins were pulled tight over something feral; and their beauty could not conceal it. Women who had once been household names – paragons of elegance and sophistication – walking on all fours, their gait crabbed, their speed uncanny; baring their perfect teeth in the thicket and yelping like coyotes who'd just come upon a fresh kill.

There was reason, then, for him to believe the interloper had not survived her abduction. If they'd caught up with her, *los niños* might have toyed with her for awhile, but they were stupid things, and their attention spans were short. It would not take them long to decide that there'd be more sport in hurting the woman than in teasing her, and once her blood began to run they'd become frenzied, and fall upon her, taking her limb from limb.

That was his fear.

The source of his hope? That he had not heard any death-cries in the Canyon since she'd been gone. It was a tiny reason to believe that something good might come of the woman's arrival here, but he had to have some little measure of hope, or there was nothing. So in the absence of hearing the woman's screams, he allowed himself to believe that there was one in the Canyon who might be the undoing of Katya Lupi.

2

Tammy was indeed alive. She knew she was alive because she was hungry. It was the only thing about her present condition which she really recognized; the rest was a kind of fever-dream, filled with blurred horrors; remote pieces of what might be real and what she hoped to God were not.

She had been carried by her abductors to the far end of the Canyon where there was no sign of any habitation. The area was pretty much jungle: dense thickets of barbed shrubs, overshadowed by stands of immense, shaggy palms. There was no way to climb up any of these trees, to escape those who'd brought her here (though even if she'd been able to do so, she was certain they would sniff her out); nor was there any way to move more than a few steps through the thicket. So she was left with only one option: she had to confront her abductors.

It was her mother's gift to her, this even-headedness. In circumstances that would have brought lesser minds to the point of collapse, Edith Huxley Lauper (Ma Edie to everyone who'd ever known her for more than a day), had been uncannily calm. And the more panicky people around her had become, the calmer she'd get. It made her an ideal nurse, which was the work she'd done all her life. She soothed the hurt, she soothed the dying, she soothed the bereft. Everything's fine, she would say in that soft voice of hers (another of her gifts to Tammy); and by some miracle everyone would believe her. Very often, because

249

people believed her, the panic ceased and everything was fine. It was a kind of self-fulfilling prophecy.

So now, sitting in the thicket, in the midst of this fever dream, with its voices and its faces and its stink, she repeated Ma Edie's mantra to herself, over and over: *Everything's fine, everything's fine, everything's fine,* waiting for it to turn out true.

Her head still throbbed from the white light that had wiped out the world before her abduction; and her stomach was certainly in need of filling, but she still had all her limbs, for which she was grateful, and a voice in her throat. So, once she'd calmed herself down, she started to talk to whatever it was that had come after her, (and was still there, in the vicinity) her volume quiet, but her tone insistent enough that she would not be mistaken for somebody who was afraid.

'I'd like to get back to the house now,' she said to them, 'so will one of you please escort me?' She scanned the bushes. They were watching her. She could see the glitter of their eyes, the gleam of their teeth. What *were* they? They didn't seem quite substantial; she had the feeling that their flesh was not as solid as hers, as *real* perhaps; yet they'd possessed enough strength to remove her from the vicinity of Zeffer's cage to this corner of nowhere, so they weren't to be disrespected.

'Do you understand me?' she'd said, keeping her tone even. 'I need to go back to the house.'

Off to her left she saw a motion in the thicket, and one of the creatures approached her, coming close enough that for the first time she'd had a proper view of one of the abductors. It was a female, no doubt of that, and vaguely related to a human being. The creature's naked body was scrawny, her ribs showing through flesh that seemed to be covered with light grey-silver hair. The front limbs were extremely delicate, and she surely had hands and fingers not pads and claws. But the back legs were as crooked as a dog's, and rather too large for the rest of her anatomy, so that squatting her proportions were almost frog-like.

But the head: that was the worst of her. Her mouth was nearly human, as was her nose, but then the skull curved and suddenly flattened so that her eyes, which were devoid of whites, and set to either side of the skull, like the eyes of a sheep, stuck out, black and shiny and stupid.

She turned her head and stared at Tammy with her shiny eyes. Then, from those human lips came the scraps of a voice. 'It's no use to beg,' she told Tammy. 'We eat you.'

Tammy took this in her stride; or at least did all she could to give that impression. 'I'm not begging you for anything,' she said, very calmly. 'And you're *not* going to eat me.'

'Oh?' said another voice, this time over to her right.

Tammy moved slowly, so as not to invite anything precipitous. She looked at the second speaker, who – like the female – had come closer to her. She guessed this was a male; one of the creatures who'd snatched her away from between the cages. He had a head of ungainly size and shape, his nose flattened out like the nose of a bat, his mouth wide and lipless. Only his eyes were human; and they were unexpectedly and exquisitely blue.

'What shall we do with you then?' he said to Tammy, the slits of his nostrils flattening as he inhaled her scent.

'Help me,' she said. The male lowered his lumpen head, and stared at her from under the weight of his brow. 'I need to get back to the house,' Tammy said.

'You know the Lady?' said the female.

'What Lady?'

'In the house?'

A third voice now; a thin, reedy voice in the darkness behind the female. 'Kat. Ee. A,' the voice said.

'Katya?' Tammy said.

'Yes,' said the male. 'Katya.'

He had come closer to her, and was now sniffing around

her hair. She didn't protect herself, even though flecks of his cold phlegm were hitting her neck and face. She just kept her focus, as best she could. Perhaps these freaks, for all their bizarrity, knew something about why Todd was here. If she was going to free him she had to know what she was freeing him from.

'What do you want with Katya?' Tammy said, keeping her options open as to whether she knew the woman or not.

At the mention of Katya's name a series of little convulsions had taken over the female. She threw back her head, showing a throat as lovely as Garbo's. After a moment, the convulsions subsided. Once they were governed, the woman gave Tammy her answer.

'She is the one who has the Hunt.'

There wasn't much illumination to be had from this. But Tammy pursued the questioning, not hoping for much. 'What hunt?' she asked, keeping her voice low and even.

'The Devil's Hunt,' said the male, still close to her.

'You seen it?' the female said.

'No,' Tammy replied.

'Liar.'

'If I'd seen it I'd tell you I'd seen it. But I haven't.'

'You been in the house?'

'No I haven't,' Tammy said. 'Why, is this hunt you're talking about *in* the house?'

'The Hunt's in the house.'

This part was even more puzzling than the earlier stuff. Plainly her sources were not terribly reliable. Were they referring to some sort of game that Katya played?

'Have *you* ever been in the house?' she asked them.

'No,' said the female.

'But you want to go?'

'Oh yes,' she said. 'I want to see how it is.'

'Well . . .' Tammy said. 'Perhaps I could help you get in . . . to the house.'

252

The female regarded her warily, moving her head back and forth to assess Tammy with both eyes.

'It's not possible,' she said.

'Why not?'

It was the male who answered, and the phrase he used was powerful but incomprehensible. 'Death at the threshold,' he said.

There were mutters and growls from others in the undergrowth at the mention of the threshold. She had no doubt that for all their apparent strength these creatures were deathly afraid of the house, and, no doubt, of its mistress.

'Has this woman Katya done you some harm?' she asked the female.

The creature shook its wretched head. 'Kill her one day.'

'You want to kill her?'

'Yes.'

'Why?'

The woman just stared, her stare containing a profound distrust. Not just of Tammy, or indeed of Katya: of the world, but of being alive. It was as though every breathing moment was conditional; an agony. And despite the brutal foulness of the thing's appearance, Tammy felt some measure of sympathy for it.

'Maybe I could get this Katya to come out,' Tammy suggested.

The male growled, deep in his chest. 'You'd do that?'

Tammy was ready to make any promise right now, to get out of her present predicament. She nodded.

There was a long moment, in which the freaks did not reply. Then, glancing around the company of her fellows, as if to check that she would not be challenged, the female caught hold of Tammy's wrist, and pulled her up out of the thicket.

'We're going?' Tammy said.

'Yes! Yes!' the female replied. 'Quickly, though. Quickly.'

She didn't get any argument from Tammy, who was happy to be on her way. Whatever dangers the house held they could hardly be worse than staying out here in the open. The day was quickly passing away. It would soon be dark. And judging by the repeated glances the woman gave the sky, she too was cognizant of the failing light. After the third or fourth glance Tammy couldn't help but ask her what she was so nervous about.

'Peacock,' she said.

A peacock? There had been peacocks here? It wasn't so surprising, on second thoughts. It fitted with the extravagance of the place. But they belonged on well-clipped lawns, not in this jungle of thorns and flowers. And even assuming the bird could push its way through the thicket without being stripped of all its finery, what could it do if it *did* catch up with them? They had bad tempers, she remembered reading once, but they were nervous things. She'd just shoo it away.

'Nothing to be scared of,' Tammy said.

The woman gave her another disconcerting sideways look. The male, meanwhile, came up beside Tammy and stared at her breasts. Not about to be intimidated, she stared back. There was something vaguely recognizable in this freak; a cast to his features which reminded her of somebody famous. Who the hell was it? Some movie star. Was it Victor Mature? Yes, it was. Victor Mature. It was uncanny.

The lookalike, meanwhile, leaned forward, hooked a long cold finger through a hole in Tammy's blouse and before she could do a damn thing about it, tore the light cotton blouse away from her skin.

'You keep away from me,' she told the offender.

He bared his teeth at her. 'Pretty boobies,' he said.

'What?'

The forbidding grimace had transformed into a weird version of a smile. 'Titties,' he said.

He reached out and touched the side of her breast with his open palm, stroking it. 'Jugs. Knockers –'

'Baby feeders,' Tammy added, figuring it was better to play along with the joke, however witless.

'*Fun bags,*' he grinned, almost moronically.

She wondered just for a moment if that was the answer to this mystery: that these pitiful remnants of humanity were cretins, mongols, retards; the children of Hollywood parents who could not bear the idea that they'd produced such freaks, and given them over to somebody who'd simply dumped them in the empty Canyon. No, that was ridiculous. Atrocities like that didn't happen in this day and age; it was unthinkably callous. But it did go some way to explaining the curious passages of starry flesh and bone she kept seeing: Garbo's throat on the woman, Victor Mature in this breast-obsessed male.

'Udders,' he said.

'Jigglies,' she countered. 'Chi-chis. Kazooms –'

Oh, she had a million. So presumably did every woman with larger than average breasts in America. It had started when she was twelve, when thanks to an unfortunate hormonal trick she was walking around with a bosom that would have looked just fine on a big-boned twenty-two-year-old. Suddenly men were looking at her, and the dirty words just came tumbling out of their mouths. She went through a phase when she thought every man in Sacramento had Tourette's Syndrome. Never mind that the girl with the hooters was twelve; men got diarrhoea of the mouth at the sight of large breasts. She had them called everything: 'the twins', 'skin-pillows', her 'rack', her 'set', her 'mounds', her 'missiles', her 'melons', her 'milk-makers'. At first it upset her to be the object of fun, but after a while she learned not to listen to it any more, unless some unusual name came along to swell the lexicon, like 'global superstars', or 'bodacious ta-tas', both of which had brought a despairing smile to her face.

Of course in two years' time all her girlfriends had got bosoms of their own –

'Wait.'

The female had halted, its body suddenly besieged by nervous tics.

'What's wrong?' Tammy said.

The woman governed her little spasms and stood still, listening. Then pointed, off to her right, and having pointed she quickly bounded away, dragging Tammy after her.

As they fled – and that's what it was suddenly, *fleeing* – Tammy glanced back over her shoulder. They were not taking this journey unaccompanied. There was a contingent of freaks coming after them, though they were keeping their distance. But it was not the freaks, however, that the female was so afraid of; it was something else.

'What?' Tammy gasped. 'What?'

'*Peacock,*' the woman replied. She didn't speak again. She simply let go of Tammy's arm and threw herself into the cover of the thicket. Tammy turned, and turned again, looking for the creature that had caused this unalloyed panic. For a moment, she saw nothing; and all she heard was the sound of the female racing off through the thicket.

Then, almost total silence. Nothing moved, in any direction. And all she could hear was a jet, high, high above her.

She looked up. Yes, there it was, crawling across the pristine blue, leaving a trail of vapour tinted amber by the setting sun. She was momentarily enchanted; removed from her hunger and her aching bones.

'Beautiful,' she murmured to herself.

The next moment something broke cover not more than ten yards from her.

This time Tammy didn't stand there mesmerized, as she

had at the cages. She threw herself out of the path of the shape that was barrelling towards her. It was the bizarrest of all the freaks she'd encountered. Like all its kin it had some of her own species in its genes but the animal it was crossed with – yes, *a peacock* – was so utterly unlike a human being that the resulting form defied her comprehension. It had the torso of a man, and the stick-thin back legs, scaly though they were, also belonged to a human being. But its neck was serpentine and its head no larger than a fist. Its eyes were tiny black beads, and between them was a beak that looked as though it could do some serious damage. Having missed her on the first assault it now turned around and came at her again, loosing a guttural shriek as it did so. She stumbled backwards, intending to turn and run, but it raised its body up and she saw to her disgust that its underbelly was made exactly like that of a man, and that it was in a state of considerable arousal. The moment of distraction cost her dearly. She fell back against a blooming rhododendron bush, and lost her footing in a midst of pink-purple blossom. She cursed loudly and coarsely, grabbing onto whatever she could – blossom, twig, root – to haul herself up. As she attempted to do so she saw the creature slowly lower its sleek turquoise head, and one of its scaly forelimbs – withered remnants of arms and hands – went to its chin, where it idly scratched at a flea.

Then, while she struggled like an idiot to get back on her feet, the creature lifted up its backside and spread its glorious tail. By some quirk of genetics, it had inherited its father's glory intact. The tail opened like God's own fan, compensating for every other grotesque thing about the beast. It was beautiful, and the creature knew it. Tammy stopped struggling for a moment, thinking perhaps she could talk some sense into this thing.

'Look at you,' she said.

Was there brain enough in that little skull to understand

that it was being flattered? She frankly doubted it. But the creature was watching her now, its head cocked to one side. She kept talking, telling it how fine it looked, while tentatively reaching around to find a branch large enough to carry her weight, so that she could pull herself to her feet. The creature shook its tail, the feathers hissing as they rubbed against one another. The iridescent eyes in their turquoise setting shimmered.

And then, without warning, it was on her. It moved so suddenly she didn't have a chance to clamber out of its way. She fell back into the blossoms for a second time, and before she could raise her arms to ward it off, the peacock came down against her body, trapping her.

She felt its erection against her body, and its wizened hands clawing at her breasts. Its beak snapped above her face, threatening her eyes.

For a moment she lay still, afraid of what it would do to her if she resisted it. But then it began to thrust its hips against her, and a spasm of revulsion overcame her better judgment. She reached up and caught hold of the thing's neck, just below the head, her fingers digging deep into its blotchy, corrugated flesh. Even so, it continued to grind its body against her. She raised her other hand to join the first, and started to strangle the thing. Still it pumped on, as though so stupefied with lust it was indifferent to its own jeopardy. She pressed hard on its throat, closing off its windpipe. Its grindings continued unabated. She pressed harder, and harder still. Then it seemed to reach a point of no return, and a series of shudders passed through its body. She felt something wet spurting on her belly, where its rhythms had pushed up the rags of her blouse.

'Oh *God*,' she said, 'You *filthy, dirty* –'

Its climax over, it belatedly seemed to realize that it couldn't breathe and started to thrash about. Its claws raked her breasts, which stung like fury, but she refused to let go of its scrawny throat. If she gave it an inch it would

258

surely kill her. Her only hope was to dig deep and hold on until the thing lost consciousness.

But it was easier said than done. The bird's orgasm hadn't exhausted its energies. It thrashed maniacally, beating its stunted wings against the blossoms, so that a blizzard of pink petals came down upon them like confetti. Tammy kept her teeth and her hands locked together, while the would-be rapist's panic became a frenzy. It was making ghastly, guttural noises now, its mottled tongue sticking straight out of its mouth. Spittle fell on her upturned face, stinging her eyes. She closed them, and kept on clutching, while the peacock clawed and flapped and thrashed.

The struggle had already gone on for three or four minutes, and her strength was giving out. The pain from her scratched breasts was excruciating, and her hands were numb. But by degrees the bird's rallies lessened. She didn't relax her grip on it however, suspicious that if she did so, it would recover itself somehow and renew its attack. She held on to its silken throat while its wings slowed their moronic flapping. She opened her eyes. The expression on the creature's face suggested that it was close to death. Its tongue lolled against its lower beak. Its gaze was unfocused. Most telling of all, its glorious tail had drooped to the earth.

Still she held on, pressing her thumbs hard against its windpipe until every last twitch had gone out of it. Only then did she let go; not with both hands, but with one, and started to pull herself up from beneath the body of the creature. She felt its semen cold on her belly, and her own blood hot on her breasts. A fresh wave of repugnance passed through her. But she had survived; that was the point. This creature had done its worst, and she'd overcome it. Grabbing hold of a branch she pulled herself to her feet. The peacock hung from her hand, its body sprawled on a bed of fallen blossoms. A spasmodic rattle passed through its gleaming tail feathers, but that was the last of it.

She let it go. It dropped to the ground, its head resembling some absurd little sock puppet that its owner had abandoned in the grass; the rest of its body a grotesque amalgam of forms.

'I killed you . . .' Tammy said softly. 'You sonofabitch.'

She lifted her gaze and surveyed the bushes around her. All this had been witnessed, she knew; the creatures that shared this beast's grotesque tribe were all out there in the twilight, watching their battle. She could not see those who were scrutinizing her, not even the gleam of a tooth or eye, but she knew they must be thinking twice about attacking her. On the other hand, she was seriously weakened. If they were to launch such an assault she would be lost; her energies were all but spent.

She looked down at her bosom. Her blouse was in rags and her skin had been deeply scored by the freak's claws. She touched the wounds. They stung, but the blood would soon start to clot. She wasn't a bleeder, luckily. But she was going to need something to clean the wounds if they weren't to become infected – God knows what kind of shit and dirt the creature had had beneath its claws – which meant finding her way, as quickly as possible, back to the house: to clean running water and fresh dressings.

But there was one other matter to deal with before she moved from this place: a bit of cleaning up that couldn't wait until she had water. She picked up a fistful of grass, and wiped her belly, removing as best she could the remnants of the creature's semen. It took more than one fistful to do the job; but when she had cleaned herself (and then cleaned her hands with a third portion of grass) she left the body where it lay, and went on her way.

She listened, as she went, for the sound of pursuit: the rustle of leaves, the snapping of twigs. But she heard nothing. Either the rest of the freakish clan had decided she was too dangerous to pursue, given that she'd just slaughtered one of their more fearsome members, or else the game of pursuit no longer amused them and they'd gone back to whatever crimes they committed in the stinking darkness.

Tammy didn't much care.

As long as they left her alone, she thought, they could do what the hell they liked.

'Tell me about all the stuff in the guest-house,' Todd asked Katya as they walked. 'Where does it all come from?'

'The large tapestry in the living room was made for *The Sorrows of Frederick*, which was a terrible picture, but the designs were magnificent. The castle they made for the banquet scene! You never saw anything so grand in your life. And all the Egyptian stuff was from *Nefertiti*.'

'You played Nefertiti?'

'No, Theda Bara played Nefertiti, because the front office said she was a bigger star than I was. I played her handmaiden. I didn't mind that much because in my mind it was a better role. Theda just vamped her way through her part. Oh Lord, she was bad! But I got a little chance to act. In the end Nefertiti had my lover killed because he was in love with me not her, so I threw myself off a boat into the Nile.'

'And drowned?'

'I suppose so. Either that or I was eaten by crocodiles.' She laughed. 'I don't know. Anyway, I got some of my best reviews for *Nefertiti*. Somebody said I could have stepped right out of history . . .'

The evening was beginning to draw on as they walked, taking the simple and relatively direct path which Todd had failed to find on his way up. It was the first night in a long time that Todd hadn't sat at his bedroom window, drinking, brooding and popping pills.

'What about the bed?' Todd said. 'Where did that come from?'

'That was from *The Devil's Bride*.'

'A horror movie?'

'No, it was this *strange* picture directed by Edgar Kopel. Very shocking for its time. The bed was supposed to have been owned by the Devil, you see. Carved to his design. And then the hero, who was played by Ronald Colman, inherits it, and he and his bride use it for the bridal bed. But the Devil comes for the bride, and then all Hell breaks loose.'

'What happened in the end?'

'The Devil gets what he wants.'

'You?'

'Me.'

'I don't think that would work for modern audiences.'

'Oh it didn't work in 1923. They stayed away in droves.'

They walked on for a while in silence. Finally Katya said: 'What's troubling you?'

'I can't make sense of what you're telling me. The pieces don't fit –'

'And it frustrates you.'

'Yes.'

'Maybe it's best you just don't think about it.'

'How can I *not* think about it?' he said. 'This place. You. The posters. The bed. What am I supposed to make of it all?'

'Make whatever pleases you,' she said. 'Why's it so important that you have an explanation for everything? I told you: things are different here.'

She caught hold of his hand, and they stopped walking. There were insects in the grass all around them, making music; overhead, the stars were coming out, their patterns as familiar as the din of cicadas; and tonight, as strange. His doubts were contagious. The fact that he didn't understand how it was possible this woman could have lived the life she claimed to have lived spread confusion into every other

263

sign the world brought him. What was he doing here, in between the music in the grass and the brightening stars? He suddenly seemed to understand nothing. His face throbbed, and his eyes stung.

'It's all right,' she said softly. 'There's nothing to be afraid of.'

'I'm not afraid,' he said.

It was the truth, in a way. What he felt was not fear, it was something far more distressing. He felt lost, cast off from every certainty.

But then he looked at her face, at her perfect face, and he felt a calm come over him. So what if he was adrift? So were they both. And wasn't it better to be with *her*, sharing her gentle madness, than to be alone in this unforgiving world?

He leaned towards her, and kissed her on the lips. Nothing overtly sexual; just a tender kiss.

'What was that for?' she asked him, smiling.

'For being here.'

'Even though you think I'm a lunatic?'

'I didn't say that.'

'No, but you think it. Don't you? You think I'm living in a fantasy land.'

'I'm taking your advice,' he replied. 'I'm making whatever I like of it. And I like being here, right now, with you. So the rest can go to hell.'

'The rest?'

'Out there,' he said, waving his arm in the general direction of the city. 'The people who used to run my life.'

'To hell with them?'

'To hell with them!'

Katya laughed. 'I like that,' she said, returning his kiss in the midst of their laughter.

'Where now?' he said.

'Down to the pool?' she replied.

'You know the way?'

'Trust me,' she said, kissing him again. This time he didn't let her escape so lightly, but returned her kiss with some force. His hand slipped up into her hair and made a cradle for her head. She put her arms around his waist, pressing so hard against him it was as though she wanted to climb inside his skin.

When they broke the kiss they gazed at one another for a little time.

'I thought we were going walking,' he said.

'So we were,' she said, taking his hand again. 'The pool, yes?'

'Do you want to go back to the house?'

'Plenty of time for that later,' she said. 'Let's go down to the pool while there's still some light.'

So they continued their descent, hand in hand. They said nothing now. There was no need.

Across the other side of the Canyon, a lone coyote began to yap; his voice was answered by another higher up on the ridge behind them, then another two in the same vicinity, and now another, and another, until the entire Canyon was filled with their glorious din.

When Todd and Katya reached the lawn there was a small, scrawny coyote loping across it, giving them a guilty backward glance as he disappeared into the undergrowth. As he vanished from sight, the pack ceased its din. There were a few moments of silence. Then the insects took up their music again.

'It's sad, the way things have declined,' Katya said, looking at the sight before them. The starlight was forgiving, but it couldn't conceal the general condition of the place: the statues missing limbs, or toppled over and buried in vines; the pavement around the pool cracked and mossy, the pool itself stained and stinking.

'What's that?' Todd said, pointing out the one-storey mock-classical structure half-hidden by the cypresses around the pool.

'That's the Pool House. I haven't been in there in a very long time.'

'I want to see it.'

It was a larger building than it had appeared from the front, and uncannily bright. There were several skylights in the ceiling, which ushered in the brightness of moon and stars, their light bouncing off the silky marble floor. In the centre stood a cocktail bar with mirrors of marbled glass behind the glass shelves. After all these years there were dozens of bottles on the shelves – brandies, whiskies and liqueurs.

'You used the pool a lot?' Todd said.

'We had the best pool-parties in Hollywood.'

Their voices echoed off the glacial walls as they spoke, coming back to meet them. 'And the people who came here, knew . . .' Katya said. 'They *knew*.' Letting the thought go unfinished, she moved past him to the bar.

'What did they *know*?' he said.

'Not to make any judgments,' she replied. She slipped behind the bar, and began to survey the rows of bottles.

'I don't think we should try drinking any of that stuff,' he said. 'I've got fresh booze in the house if that's what you want.'

She didn't reply; simply continued to survey the selection. Finally she decided upon one of the brandies, and taking the bottle by the neck she pulled it forward. There was a grinding noise from behind the mirror as some antiquated mechanism was activated. Then the mirror slid sideways three or four feet, revealing a small safe.

Todd was intrigued. He hopped over the bar to get a better look at what Katya was up to. She was working on the tumble lock; he could hear a faint clicking as she flipped it back and forth.

'What's in there?' he said.

'We used to have a book –'

'We?'

266

'Zeffer and I. We just kept it for fun.'

'A book of what?'

'Of party pieces,' she said, with a little smile. '*Who* did *what* to *whom*. And how many times.'

'You're kidding!'

She turned the lock one more time, and then pushed down on the handle and pulled the door. There was a cracking sound, as the decayed rubber seal broke. Then the door swung wide.

'Are there any candles?' she said to him. 'Look in the cupboard there between the columns, will you?'

Todd did as he was instructed, and found several boxes of plain white candles on the shelves. One was open, and the heat of many summers had turned the contents into a single box-shaped slab of white wax. But the contents of the other two boxes were in better condition: under the first layer, which was partially melted, there were salvageable candles. He set up six of them on the bar, seating them in their own dribblings so that they wouldn't fall over.

Their flickering yellow light flattered the marble interior; and by some strange arrangement of the walls it seemed he heard the whispering of the flames multiplied. Indeed they almost sounded like voices; uncannily so. He looked around, half-expecting to see somebody flitting between the columns.

'Ah, voilà!' said Katya, reaching into the depths of the safe.

She brought a small, thick book out of the little safe along with a sheaf of photographs and set them all down on the bar in the light from the candles. The book looked like a journal, bound in dark red leather. When she opened it he saw that its handwritten contents were arranged symmetrically; two columns to each page.

'Take a look,' she said, obviously delighted with her find.

He picked up the book and flicked through it. Almost

267

three-quarters of its pages were written on, sometimes in the two-column configuration, sometimes simply filled up from top to bottom. He turned to a page of the former variety. On the left hand side of the pages was a column of names; on the right hand, a column that was far harder to make sense of. Occasionally there were names, but more often letters and symbols, some of them resembling obscure mathematical equations. His puzzlement amused her.

'Think of it as a history book,' she said, offering a teasing smile along with the clue.

'A history of what?'

'Of better times.'

Todd flipped through the pages. Now and again, amongst the names, he came upon some he knew: Norma Talmadge, Theda Bara, John Gilbert, Clara Bow; all movie stars of another era.

'You knew all these people?' he said to her.

'Yes, of course. This was the place to come, when you wanted to have some fun. Every weekend, we'd have parties. Sometimes in the pool. Sometimes in the house. Sometimes we'd have hunts, all through the Canyon.'

'Animal hunts?'

'No. *People* hunts. People treated like animals. We whipped them and we chained them up and . . . well, you can imagine.'

'I'm beginning to. Wow. You had Charlie Chaplin up here, I see.'

'Yes, he came up here often. He used to bring his little girls.'

'*Little* girls?'

'He liked them young.'

Todd raised a quizzical eyebrow. 'And you didn't mind?'

'I don't believe in *Thou Shall Not*. That's for people who are afraid to follow their own instincts. Of course when you're out there in the world you've got to play by the rules, or you'll spend your life behind bars. They'd lock you up and throw away the key. But this isn't the world. This is my Canyon. They called it Coldheart Canyon, because they said I have a soul like ice. But why should I care what people say? Let them say whatever they want to say, as long as their money pays for the little luxuries in life. I want my Kingdom to be a place where people could take their pleasures freely, without judgment or punishment.

'This is Eden, you see? Only there's no snake. No angel to drive you out either, because you did a bad thing. Why? Because there were no bad things.'

'Literally none?'

She looked at him, her stare luminous. 'Oh you mean murder, perhaps? We had one or two murderers here. And we had sisters who'd fucked their brothers, and sons who fucked their mothers, and a man who liked having children suck him off.'

'What?'

'Ha! Now you're shocked. His name was Laurence Skimpell, and he was as handsome a man as I've ever met. He had a contract at Warner Brothers, and they were going to make him a star. A big star. Then this woman turns up at the studios with a child, who she said was Skimpell's. Warner Brothers have always been very loyal. They offered the woman money; said they'd put the child up for adoption. But as she got up and left she said: you don't understand, this isn't his offspring. This is his lover.'

'Oh Jesus Christ.'

'That was the last we ever heard of Laurence Skimpell.'

'That's a ridiculous story. I don't believe a word of it.'

She laughed, as though perhaps this time she was inventing a little. 'You're in here,' he said, coming to some mentions of Katya Lupi. 'And there's a long list of men . . .'

'Oh that was a competition we had.'

'You *had* all these men?'

'It was my Canyon. It still is. I can do what I like here.'

'So you let people do what they wanted?'

'More or less.' She returned to the book. 'You see the symbols beside the names?'

Todd nodded, somewhat tentatively. The conversation had taken a turn he was by no means certain he liked. It was one thing to talk about freedom in Coldheart Canyon; it was another to have her boasting about babies sucking dicks. 'All the symbols mean something different,' she said. 'Look here. That squiggle there, that means snakes. That knotted rope? That means being bound up. The more knots in the rope the more bound the person likes to be. So . . . here . . . Barrymore . . . his rope has six knots in it. So he liked to be very well tied up. And then there's a little flame beside him. That means –'

'He liked to be burned?'

'When he was sober. In the end, I stopped inviting him because he got so drunk and so abusive he wasn't any fun.'

'Ah! So you *did* make a judgment.'

She considered this for a moment. 'Yes. I suppose I did.'

'Did he spoil the secret? Once you didn't invite him any more. Did he start telling everyone about what it was like up here?'

'Of course not. What was he going to say? Even *he* had a reputation to keep. Besides, half of Hollywood swam in that pool at one time or another. And the other half wished they could. Nobody said anything but everybody *knew*.'

'What . . . exactly. That there were orgies here. That women got fucked with snakes?'

'All of that yes. But mostly that people came back from Coldheart Canyon spiritually changed.'

'You mean that? *Spiritually*.'

'Yes. Spiritually. Don't look so surprised. The flesh and the soul are tied together.'

Todd looked confused.

'Louise Brooks said to me once: *there's nothing they can give that would be worth my freedom*. She partied with the rest of us, but in the end she gave it all up, and moved away. She said they were trying to take her soul by boring her to death.'

'So she gave up making movies?'

'Indeed she did. But Louise was a rare example. *You* know what usually happens: you get addicted. And the studio *knows* you're addicted. You need your hit of fame every couple of years or you start to feel worthless. Isn't that right? So as long as they can keep giving you a little time in the spotlight, they've got you in their pocket.'

Todd continued to flip through the book as Katya spoke, as much because he didn't want to meet her gaze as because he was interested in the pages. All that she said was true; and it hurt to hear it: especially when he had done himself so much harm because of his appetite for the spotlight.

A sound, behind him. He looked up at the mirror behind the bar. It wasn't his wounded face that caught his eye, however, it was a motion of something, or somebody, passing by the door.

'I think there's somebody out there,' he whispered.

Katya looked unsurprised. 'Of course. They know we're here.' She took the book from his hand and closed it for him. 'Let me introduce you to them,' she said.

'Wait.' He reached for the photographs that Katya had also brought out of the safe. They still lay where she had put them, on the top of the bar.

'You don't need to look at those now,' Katya said.

'I just want to take a peek.'

He began to flick through the sheaf of photographs. There were probably forty or so; most in worse condition than the book, the prints made hastily, and poorly fixed, so that large parts of the image had faded to speckled sepia or to black. But there were still sizeable portions of many of the photographs visible, and the scenes they depicted confirmed every obscene or outlandish detail she'd offered. They weren't simply images of men and women coupling, but pictures of the most extreme forms of sexual gratification. In one, a naked man was bound to a metal chain, the cords that held him biting deep into his flesh. A woman wearing just a black brassiere was flogging his chest and his groin. Assuming this wasn't a set-up (and something about the quality of all the photographs suggested that all of these were the real thing), then the woman was doing her victim some serious hurt. There was blood running down his chest and stomach from blows she'd delivered there; and there appeared to be welts on his thighs and his dick, which stood testament to the pleasure he was taking in this. In another picture, some way down the pile, the same man (his face seemed vaguely familiar to Todd, though he couldn't put a name to it) had been redeemed from his bondage and lay on the paving stone beside the pool while another woman (this second completely naked) squatted over him and loosed a stream of urine on his wounds. To judge by the expression on the masochist's face, this hurt more than the whipping. His teeth were gritted, his body locked, as though he were only just holding back an unmanly scream.

'Wait. I know who that is,' Todd said. 'That's – Christ! It can't be.'

'It is.'

'He was always the Good Guy.'

'Well, sometimes Good Guys like getting pissed on.'

'And her? She was always so sweet in her movies. What's her name? Always the victim.'

'Well, that was part of the game you got to play in the Canyon. Up here you do the things the studios wouldn't let you do. Rub your face in the dirt for a while. And then on Monday morning you could brush your teeth and smile and pretend you were all-American again. That's all people want. An illusion. You can do what the hell you like out of sight. Just don't spoil their dreams. They want to believe you're perfect. And it's hard to put on a perfect face every day without going crazy. Up here, nobody was perfect, and nobody cared.'

'Jesus,' Todd said, coming across a picture of scatology. 'Who's the pooper?' Katya turned the picture round to get a clearer view of the woman's face. 'That was Edith Vine. At least that was her real name. I can't remember what they called her. She had a seven year contract with RKO, but they never made a star out of her.'

'Maybe they were afraid one of these would leak out and they'd lose their investment.'

'No, she just kept getting pregnant. She was one of those women who just had to look at a man and bam, she was eating anchovies and ice-cream. So she kept getting abortions. Two, three a year. And her body went to hell.'

'Where did she end up?'

'Oh she's here,' Katya said. 'We don't just take the famous up here in the Canyon. We take the failures, too.'

Without fully understanding what he'd just been told – perhaps not entirely wanting to – Todd moved on to another picture. A man who'd played cowboys most of his life was the centre of attention, all laced up in a girdle that made his waist as narrow as any showgirl's.

'That's one for the family album.'

'He liked to be called Martha when he was dressed like that. It was his mother's name. In fact, I think it was his mother's corset.'

Todd laughed, though he wasn't sure where the laughter was coming from. Perhaps it was simply that the parade of perversions was so excessive there was nothing to do, in the end, *but* laugh.

'Christ. What's that?'

'A jar of bees, and Claudette's breast.'

'She liked to get stung?'

'She would scream like her lungs were going to give out. But then she'd have somebody pick the stings out with their teeth.'

'Fuck.'

'And she'd be so wet you could fill a shot-glass from what came out of her.'

It was too much. He put the photographs down. Bees, piss, corsets. And they were only the pictures he could make sense of. There were plenty more that defied easy comprehension; arrangements of limbs and faces and artefacts which he had no appetite to interpret.

Before he left them where they lay there was one question remaining that he simply had to ask.

'Are you in any of these?'

'Well I'm in the book aren't I?'

'So all that stuff you were telling me in the Gaming Room, about offering yourself to the winner? All that was true?'

'All that was true.'

'Just how far did you go?'

She turned the photographs over, putting their excesses out of sight.

'As far as you want,' she said, smiling. 'Then just a *little* further.'

She unnerved him, and she knew it. She took hold of his hand. 'Come on,' she said. 'Let's go outside. We're missing the dusk.'

4

They were too late. It had been twilight when they'd entered the Pool House. Now it was night. But that wasn't the only change that had taken place in the time they'd lingered there. The air Todd breathed when he stepped outside again was something more than a little colder, a little darker, than it had been. Though there was no wind (at least the trees weren't moving) still he felt movement around and against him; a delicate touch on his arm, on his shoulder, something touching the back of his head. He looked at Katya. There was precious little light out here, but he could see her face with curious clarity, almost as though it were lit from within. Her expression was one of considerable pleasure.

'Say hello, Todd . . .' she told him.

'Who to?'

'Oh come on. Stop pretending to yourself. You know they're here.'

There was something brushing his cheek, lightly. He flicked it away, as though it might be a moth, though he knew it wasn't.

'I don't understand what's going on,' he said, his words a kind of plea. He'd thought earlier that he could do without answers; that having her here was enough. Now he was discomfited again; he wanted some explanations for these mysteries, which multiplied every time he turned round. First Katya and her stories of the Gaming Room, then the guesthouse and the life-masks and the posters, then the bath, and the Terror. Now this: the Pool House and its history of debaucheries, locked away for posterity; and as if all that weren't enough, they'd stepped out into these moth-wing touches against his cheek, his arm, his groin. He wanted to know what it all meant; but he was afraid of the answer. No, that wasn't it. He was afraid he already *knew* the answer.

'You don't need me to tell you what's going on here,' Katya said, echoing his thoughts. 'You can feel them, can't you?'

Oh God, yes, he could feel them. These weren't moths or mosquitoes around him. They were people. People, hidden in the air.

'Say it.'

'Ghosts.'

'Yes. Of course. Ghosts.'

'Oh, Jesus.'

'The Canyon's full of ghosts.'

'I don't believe in ghosts.'

'You don't have to believe,' she said. 'It's nothing to do with believing or not believing. *They're here*. All around you. Just let yourself see them. You know they're here.'

Of course he knew. In his gut, he'd known all along there was some mystery like this waiting in the wings. And what Katya said about belief was right. Whether he believed in the Life Everlasting or not was a grand irrelevance. The dead were here. He could feel their fingers, their breaths, their stares. And now, as they pressed closer, he began to see them. He had to work up some spit before he could speak again.

'Why can I see you and I'm only now seeing them?' he asked.

'Because I'm not dead, Todd. And if you're very good, in a little while I'll show you why. You're going to like it too. My special room –'

At the mention of the room, the air, or rather those who

276

moved invisibly through it, became agitated. The number of touches that Todd felt doubled, tripled. Apparently Katya felt them too, and she was somewhat irritated by them.

'Calm down, calm down,' she said.

There were subtle smears of light in front of Todd, as though the emotion the ghosts were feeling – spurred by Katya's mention of the room – was causing them to show themselves. He thought he saw a face in one of the smears, or some part of a face: a row of perfect teeth; the gleam of a bright blue eye. The more he thought he saw, the more there was to support his suspicion. The smears grew more cogent, painting the forms of faces and shoulders and hands. They lasted only a little time – like fireworks, bursting into glorious life then dying away – but each time one was ignited its life lasted a little longer, and the form it etched in the darkness made more sense to him.

There were people everywhere around him. Not just a few. Dozens of them; the ghosts of parties past, lining up to touch the living.

'You begin to see them, don't you?' Katya said.

'Yes,' he replied breathlessly. 'I do . . . begin . . . to see them.'

'Pretty people.'

More than pretty. Beautiful; and in many cases famous. One woman – was it Jean Harlow? – wandered in front of him with her glittering dress torn away to expose her breasts. She was come and gone so quickly it was hard for Todd to be sure, but she seemed to have bite-marks on her flesh, clustered around her nipples. She'd no sooner passed from sight than two figures, tied together with ropes that went from neck to neck, came into view. Both were male. Both were naked. Both shone with a mixture of sweat and blood. This would have been distressing enough; but it was their smiles, their lunatic smiles, which made Todd flinch.

'Sal and Jimmy,' Katya said. 'They fool around like that all the time. It's a little lynching game.'

He pulled his hand out of hers. 'This is too much.'

'It's all right,' she said. 'There's nothing to be afraid of.'

He waved them away, like a child trying to ward off nightmares. 'I don't want to see them.'

Laughter came out of the darkness to meet his demand. The ghosts were apparently much amused. Their laughing made faces blossom all round him. Several he could name: famous beauties, returned to their perfection in this bizarre after-life, as though they'd remembered themselves as their public would have willed them to be. Merle Oberon and George Sanders, Mary Pickford and Veronica Lake.

Todd started to retreat up the lawn, still waving them off. The phantoms came in giddy pursuit.

'All right, enough!' Katya yelled at them. '*I said enough!*'

Her word was apparently law, even in such stellar company as this. The laughter rapidly subsided, and the divine faces stopped pressing toward him.

He took the moment to hasten his retreat, turning his back on the assembly and hurrying back in what he hoped was the general direction of the house. His thoughts were in chaos. It seemed at that moment that his life since Burrows had been one long downward spiral into a kind of insanity.

'*Wait, love!*' Katya had come after him, her voice as pliant as ever. She caught up with him.

'I'm losing my mind,' he murmured. His hands went to his face, pressing his fingers into his tender flesh, as though the pain might help drag him back from the brink.

'You're not crazy, you're just seeing things clearly for the first time.'

'Well I don't want to see them.'

'Why not? Isn't it reassuring to know that death means nothing? That there's life after death? *Pleasure* after death.'

'Pleasure. You call that –' He glanced back at the Pool House, where he'd seen the excesses of so many of these people, recorded for posterity.

'We had no shame then. We have even less now.'

As if to prove Katya's point there was an eruption of libidinous laughter from somewhere nearby, and Todd followed the sound to see a woman tied up in the trees, naked but for a long string of pearls which ran like converging rivulets between her breasts. Her wrists were bound together, and her arms lifted high above her head, so that she hung, her pale body shaped like a bow, her toes grazing the ground. It was she who was laughing, despite the apparent vulnerability of her situation. There was a man on the ground between her legs, licking the base of her feet, while another, standing behind her and massaging her breasts, bit into the tender flesh of her shoulder and neck. The hands went from her breasts down to her groin, and parted the lips of her pussy, from which came a shimmering arc, raining down onto the man adoring at her feet

The recipient began to masturbate, obviously moved to fever-pitch by the shower.

Aware of Katya's gaze, Todd glanced over at her.

'Would you like to fuck her?' she said.

The girl *was* beautiful, with long red hair and that frothy laugh of hers, which sounded so very much more innocent than what she was up to.

'She's yours if you want her. Ava!'

The girl looked up.

'This is Todd,' Katya said.

'Hello, Todd.'

'Go on,' Katya said. 'Don't worry: I'm not going to get jealous. I'd like to see how you give pleasure to a woman.'

Despite the hint of judgement in this remark, Todd might have taken the opportunity to have the woman if the man at Ava's feet hadn't suddenly begun to moan, and raising his hips off the ground ejected a copious load of semen. The sight of this eruption was enough to keep Todd at bay.

'Another time,' he said to Ava, moving away.

279

She called after him, but he didn't look back.

'There's plenty more where she came from,' Katya said, catching up with him. Her hand casually brushed the front of his pants, as though to make the point that she knew he was aroused. 'You should go to one of them,' she said.

'Why?'

'Just to see what it's like . . .'

'Fucking a ghost?'

'If you want to put it that way.'

'I don't know. It's weird. I'm not sure –'

Her hand went back to his hard-on. 'Yes you are. You love the idea.'

Her hand went from his groin to his wrist, which she caught hold of, drawing him away from Ava into a kind of bower lined with honeysuckle and night-blooming jasmine, their mingled perfumes so strong they were practically intoxicating. It was darker here than it had been under the trees where Ava hung, but Todd could see bodies on the ground, in various combinations of coupling. Somebody reached down from a branch overhead, and ran his or her fingers through Todd's hair; someone else came up behind him and pulled his shirt out from his trousers. Again, he looked for Katya; and again found her close by, smiling.

'Katya?'

A girl's voice, off to the right, and Todd saw a naked young woman being carried towards Katya on the shoulders of three men, one at her head, the other two supporting her knees, in such a way as to hold her legs wide open. Even in the dim light Todd could see what a gloriously tender sight the girl presented. She had been shaved between her legs, making her look even younger than she was, which was surely less than twenty.

'Lick me, Katya,' she said, her voice dreamy. 'Will you please? Nobody does it to me like you. Lick me deep.'

Katya glanced round at Todd.

'Do you mind?'

280

'Help yourself,' he replied, as though the girl was a plate set before her.

Katya smiled, her hands going up to the insides of the girl's thighs, venturing up to the spot where they met but then before they quite reached the place and offered any satisfaction, retreated again. It was a tantalizing game, and it drove the girl crazy with anticipation.

'Oh *please*,' she said. '*Please*, Katya, *please*.'

Todd stepped a little to the side so as to have a better view of what was unfolding here. Katya had very quickly bared her breasts, so that now, as she approached the divide of the girl's legs, her nipples stroked her partner's thighs. Her hands were delicately parting the girl's labia, as though investigating the most exquisite of flowers.

Todd could feel the blood thumping at his groin. Was there no end to Katya's capacity to surprise him? Whenever he thought he was beginning to get a grasp of the woman, she changed the rules in some subtle fashion and found a new way to astonish him. Was this really the same woman he'd discovered in bed a while ago, looking like a dishevelled angel?

Katya glanced back at him one last time – just to be sure that he was indeed watching her – then she applied her mouth to the girl's flesh.

The recipient of this tonguing let out a long, contented sigh, stretching out on her bed of hands, opening her legs a little wider. Katya proceeded to press deeper into her, advancing with lickings and nibblings, occasionally seeming to murmur against the woman's sex. The girl was no longer relaxed. She had grabbed fistfuls of the hair of the men who supported her knees, pulling herself up almost into a sitting position one moment then falling back, her body convulsed with little shudders, her tiny nipples hard, her flat belly shiny with sweat.

Katya slowly escalated the sensations she was inducing in the woman's body until her victim (there was no other word for it) was thrashing and sobbing beneath the tiniest of touches.

Somewhere in the midst of this, another occupant of the bower, on her knees in the shadows beneath the spread-eagled girl, came forward and freed Todd's erection from his pants. He didn't attempt to dissuade her. The girl took him into her throat and kept him there. The mingling of the sight of Katya working on the girl, and this new sensation was almost too much for him. He had to gently ease himself out of the girl's mouth so as not to lose control too quickly.

She seemed to get the message because she crawled away, beckoning him to follow. He pulled off his shoes and socks, and then hauled down his trousers, stepping out of them as he followed. He doubted Katya had noticed what he was up to: she was too deeply engaged in driving her partner to distraction: the girl's sobs of pleasure were the loudest sound in the vicinity.

At ground level, beneath the spread shadow of the ecstatic girl, was a sub-world of shadowy bodies, touches and whispers. There were probably a dozen men and women down here, variously intertwined. Todd felt their hands at his backside, his face, his erection; heard an appreciative coo from someone who weighed the mass of his balls (a man's palm there, surely; but he was past caring); and the girl who'd beckoned to him grazing his lips with hers, saying something he couldn't catch.

He lost sight of her for a little while, then he heard her ahead of him, gasping with delight. Somebody had got their hands on her before him. He felt a spasm of possessiveness, and crawled on, over a couple of sweating bodies, to catch up with her. He'd got it into his head that the nameless girl was his for the having, and he wasn't about to be denied her.

She wasn't hard to find. In fact she found him: catching hold of his hand and drawing him towards her. The shadow of Katya's sobbing victim spilled across much of her body, but her face lay clear of it, and Todd saw that this girl who'd gobbled him down so gluttonously looked barely old enough to be out of her parents' charge. She was dark: dark skin, dark hair, dark eyes. And she was already lying back on a bed of bodies. She pulled him eagerly towards her and cupped his face with her hands, bringing his mouth to hers. There was some confusion of bodies around and beneath her, but he was too turned on to pay much attention to such details. He kissed the girl (wondering, indeed half-hoping, that Katya had paused in her ministrations to see what he was up to; wishing she'd feel just a little pang of jealousy), and the girl returned his kiss, lavishly.

Was there something in her kiss – some subtle tang to the juices of her mouth, some coldness to her lips – which would have given away the fact that she was a spirit? Not that he could tell. If anything she was hotter than most women he'd been naked with; almost feverish. And despite the fact that his eyes had for so long failed to see the ghosts in the Canyon, she – and all of those around him – now seemed absolutely solid.

His dick had lost none of its rigidity through this fumbling pursuit; the fact that the air was humid and pungent with the heat given off by these spirit-forms only aroused him more. Katya had prepared him well, with her talk of shamelessness. He wanted the girl, and she wanted him: what else mattered?

He put the head of his cock into her. She lifted her legs a little, to help him. There was undoubtedly somebody else beneath her, but he or she didn't seem to care that he was kneeling on them.

'All the way,' she insisted.

He slid into her, as she instructed, all the way to the root, and began to work his hips against her.

Her cunt was as agile as her throat; he felt a counter-rhythm moving beneath his dick, passing through the lower half of her vulva. The sensation was like nothing he'd ever experienced before; after just a few strokes he was brought to the edge. He slowly pulled out of her, to be sure he didn't ejaculate too quickly.

'You like that?' she said, putting her hand down between her legs, and guiding him back in.

'Yes. I like it a lot.'

'Good.'

'But go slowly. Please.'

He let her take him inside again and she threw back her head, expelling a sigh of satisfaction.

'Go on,' she said, her eyes fluttering closed. 'All the way. Both of you.'

Both? he thought, raising his head from her breast.

And as he formed the question he felt an arm, twice, three times as thick as hers, and deeply muscled, reach over and grab his neck.

He lifted his head as best he could, and saw the face of a man over the girl's shoulder. She was apparently lying on him, her back against his chest. He was black, and handsome, even in the shadows.

'She's good,' he said, smiling. 'Yeah?'

Tentatively Todd reached down into the moist muddle between their legs. He felt himself, hard as ever; and then, further back, buried in the girl's ass, the other man's dick. So that was what he had been feeling as he moved inside her. It wasn't a muscular contraction; it was the black man sliding in and out of her. In any other situation he would have been repulsed; would have pulled out and retreated. But this was the Canyon; Katya's Eden without the serpent. The part of him that would have been revolted had been sweated out of him. It only made him harder thinking about the woman being sandwiched between him and the other man; the fine sheath of her muscle dividing the two of them. He brought his hand up from the swamp between their legs and grabbed hold of the black man's wrist, tightening the three-way knot.

The man laughed.

'You like that?' he said.

'I like that.'

'Good,' he said, licking the girl's neck, but keeping his eyes fixed hungrily on Todd. ''Cause we like to get real crazy.'

Todd had found the rhythm of this now; and together they played her until she started to scream with ecstasy.

Somewhere in the midst of this, the girl Katya was pleasuring began to utter gut-wrenching cries. A little time later Katya must have had mercy on her, and allowed her to be carried off, because when Todd was next getting close to coming (for the fifth or sixth time) he looked away from the blissed-out faces beneath him, and saw Katya sitting amongst the jasmine and the honeysuckle, with a young man lying naked at her feet, covering them with reverential kisses.

She was watching Todd, her expression inscrutable. Somebody lit a cigarette for her. Todd smiled at her, and then – before she could choose either to return the smile or ignore it – he fell back into the bliss of his ménage-à-trois, thinking that if this was what sex with the dead was like, then the living had a lot to learn.

5

Tonight was one of those nights when Marco had decided to get drunk. 'An honourable occupation', as his father had always said. He didn't like to drink in company; in truth, he didn't much like company. People in this town were full of bullshit (his boss included, half the time) and Marco didn't want to hear it. He'd come out to Los Angeles after his career in professional wrestling had come to a premature conclusion, half-thinking he might have a crack at acting. Then someone had suggested that personal security might be a good job for a man like himself, since he not only looked intimidating, but had the moves to back up his appearance. So Marco had joined an agency, and after working for a succession of spoiled-brat movie stars who treated him as though he was something they'd just found on their shoe, he was ready to head for home. Then, within days of his planned departure, the job with Todd Pickett had come along.

It turned out to be a perfect match. He and Todd hit it off from the start. They had the same taste in girls, cars and whisky, which was more or less the contents of Marco's fantasy world.

Tonight, he wanted a girl, and was tempted to go out, hit the clubs on the Strip, see if he got lucky. If not there was always the credit card: he had no qualms about paying for sex. It certainly beat the five-fingered widow.

But before he went out he always liked to get mellow with a whisky or two: it made him more sociable. Besides, there was something strange about the house tonight, though he didn't know what. Earlier on, he'd been tempted to go out and take a look around, just to be sure they didn't have any intruders, but by now the whisky had got him feeling too lazy to be bothered. Fuck it, they should get another dog. Dempsey had been a great early warning system. As soon as anyone came anywhere near the house he'd go crazy. Tomorrow, Marco thought as he headed down from his bedroom to get a fresh bottle of whisky, he'd talk to Todd again about buying a pup, using the security angle to get past Todd's loyalty to Dempsey.

He found the whisky, and poured himself a glass, taking it neat in one swallow. Then he looked at his watch. It was eleven-twenty. He'd better get moving. Los Angeles was an early town, he'd discovered, especially mid-week. If he didn't hurry he'd be too late to catch any of the action.

He started back upstairs to fetch his wallet, but halfway up he heard a noise at the bottom of the stairwell. It sounded like a door opening and closing.

'Boss?' he yelled down. 'Is that you?'

There was no reply. Just the door, continuing to open and close, though there was no wind tonight to catch it.

'Huh,' he said to himself. He went up, found his wallet, picked up his whisky glass from the kitchen on the way back down, and descended the stairs.

There were plenty of places around the house he hadn't explored: one of them was the very lowest level of the house, which Jerry had told him were just store-rooms. Nor had he advised using them. They were damp and anything put down there would be mildewed in a month, he said.

A few steps from the bottom of the stairs, Marco emptied his glass, and set it down. He was now drunk, he realized as he stood upright. Not paralytically; just nicely, pleasantly toasted. Smiling a little smile of self-congratulation for having achieved this blissful state, he continued down.

It was cold here, in the bowels of the house. But it wasn't

the damp cold that Jerry had warned him about. This was an almost-bracing cold: like a late autumn night in his home town of Chicago. He went down the little corridor that led from the bottom of the stairs, at the end of which was the noisy door which had brought him down here. What the hell was making it open and close that way?

He felt the answer on his face the closer he got to the door. There was a wind blowing down here, unlikely as that seemed and it smelled not of small, mildewed rooms, but of wide green spaces.

For the second time in this journey, Marco said: 'Huh.'

He pushed open the door. There was complete darkness on the other side, but it was a high, wide darkness, his gut told him; and the wind that gusted against him came – though this was beyond reason – across a stretch of open land.

He wished he hadn't drunk the whiskies now. Wished he had his senses completely under his control, so that he could assess this phenomenon clearly.

He put his hand around the corner of the door, looking for a light switch. There wasn't one; or at least there wasn't one his fingers could find. Never mind. This would be a mystery for tomorrow. For now he'd just close the door and go back to his drinking.

He reached in and caught hold of the doorhandle. As he clasped it there was a flicker of light in the depths of the room. No, not of light, of *lightning*: a fragmentary flicker which was followed by three much longer flashes, in such quick succession they were almost a single flash.

By it, he saw the space from which the wind came, and had his instincts confirmed. Wide it was, and high. The thunderhead which spat the lightning was miles away, across a landscape of forest and rock.

'*Oh, Jesus,*' Marco said.

He reached out for the doorhandle, caught hold of it, and slammed the door closed. There was a lock, but no key. Still, it seemed firmly enough closed, at least until he'd found Todd, and shown him.

He started yelling Todd's name as he ran up the stairs, but there was no reply. He went to the master bedroom, knocked, and entered. The room was empty, the French doors to the balcony open, the drapes billowing.

He went to the balcony. The wind that was moving the drapes was a California wind: warm, fragrant, gentle. It was not remotely like the wind that had blown against his face in the room below. That was a wind from a different country.

Todd was not on the balcony. But once Marco was out there he heard the sound of voices from somewhere in the Canyon. Women's voices, mostly, laughing. And lights, running between the trees.

'Sonofabitch,' Marco said.

The boss was apparently having a party, and he hadn't invited Marco.

The evening was getting stranger by the minute. He went downstairs, through the kitchen and out to the back door. Anxiety had soured the drink in his stomach, and as he opened the back door a wave of nausea suddenly overcame him. He had no time to get outside. He puked on the threshold, the force of the feeling enough to fold his legs up beneath him.

He gazed weakly down at the splattered whisky and meatballs on the ground, his eyes vaguely comprehending the intricacy of five nails that were driven into the partially rotted wood of the threshold.

Then, from the darkness on the other side of the threshold there came a soft, infinitely sorrowful voice. The voice of a lost girl.

'Let me in,' she said.

Marco looked up, his head still spinning. There was more vomit gurgling in his belly; he could feel his system preparing to revolt again. He tried to make sense of the girl who just begged entrance to the house, narrowing his eyes to see if he could separate her from the shadows.

There she was: a young woman with a face that his sickened eyes could not entirely fix nor be certain of, but who seemed to be more than passingly pretty. She had long blonde hair and pale, almost white, skin; and as suited her tone of supplication she was on her knees, her pose a mirror image of his own. She was wearing what appeared to be a man's shirt, which was unbuttoned. Had Marco been feeling more like himself, he might have hoped to persuade her to take the shirt off before he took pity on her. But the nausea overwhelmed all other responses: the girl's near-nakedness only made his belly churn harder. He looked away from her, hoping to postpone the next bout of vomiting until she was out of sight.

She plainly took his averted eyes as a sign of rejection. '*Please*,' she said to him again, 'I just want to get back into the house. You have to help me.'

'I'm in no condition –' he started, looking up at her to try and communicate with the expression just how dire he felt, but the few words he'd begun to say were enough to bring about a sudden and calamitous change in her.

She let out a shriek of frustration and rage, volume and shrillness uncanny. He felt his gorge rising, and as the woman's din reached its inhuman height, he puked up what was left of his dinner.

The worst was over now; but there was more to come from the woman outside. Feeling his stomach settling, he chanced a look up at her. It was an error. She was still letting out the remnants of that godless shriek of hers, and it seemed – at least to Marco's sickened and bewildered eyes – that the noise was taking some grotesque toll on her body. Her face – which had been so beautiful just minutes before – had become a grey, smeared form: her forehead swollen so that she looked cretinous, her eyes pulled into empty slits, her mouth running with saliva from its turned down corners. Her oversized shirt had fallen open to reveal breasts that were grey scraps of dead flesh, hanging on the cage of her bones. Beneath them, he seemed to see her innards in frenzied motion, as though she had snakes nesting in her.

It was too much for Marco's already traumatized senses. He didn't give any further thought to finding Todd – *Christ, Todd was probably part of this insanity.*

With his heels sliding in the mess he'd made, he hauled himself to his feet – half expecting the abomination on the other side of the threshold to come after him. But for some reason she kept her distance, her transformation now so far advanced she was completely unrecognizable as the woman he'd first laid eyes on.

He retreated down the passageway – still assuming this nightmare might come after him. But she matched his retreat with one of her own, melting into the shadows. Marco wasn't reassured. She'd probably gone to find others; he didn't want to be here when they came back. He raced into the kitchen and picked up his car keys, which were on the table. He gave a moment's consideration to the possibility of lingering to wash his face and hands (maybe even to changing his puke-splattered shirt), but he decided to forego cleanliness in favour of making a fast exit.

He drove down the serpentine road that led out of the Canyon as if he were being pursued by a horde of demon-women, and without even thinking about it took the same route he'd taken with Todd countless times: up onto Mulholland Drive. He opened the window as he drove, so as to have a sobering breeze blowing against his face, but it had very little effect. There was too much alcohol in his blood, and too much panic inflaming that alcohol, to make him a safe driver on such a notoriously tricky and dangerous stretch of road. He didn't care. He just wanted to put some distance between himself and that damn Canyon as fast as possible.

On one of the hairpin bends his clammy hands slid on the wheel, and he momentarily lost control of the car. He was a good enough driver – even in his present state – to recover quickly, and things might have been fine had another speed-freak not come barrelling round the corner in the opposite direction. The other driver took quick evasive action, and was away round the bend before Marco lost what little control he had. The wheel slipped through his hands, and his drink-slurred foot was too slow on the brake to stop the car from skewing round, squealing loudly. There was no barrier between the road and the drop; not even a wooden fence. The front half of the vehicle went over the edge, and there it lodged for a moment, finely balanced between solid asphalt and oblivion. Marco muttered a little prayer, but God wasn't listening. The car tripped forward and slid off the road into darkness. It was a straight drop of perhaps forty or fifty feet.

The vehicle didn't hit solid ground, however. It fell into the massive boughs of a sycamore tree, which was large enough to hold the car, nose down, in its branches. Marco was thrown against the windshield. Through it he could see the yard in which the sycamore stood. There was a party going on down there. The pool was illuminated: its bright turquoise water twinkling. Lanterns hung in the bushes all around, swaying in the breeze. Marco had time to grasp the prettiness of all this, then something ignited in the engine, and the fume-filled air around him became a sheet of lurid orange flame. It enveloped him completely, the first burst of heat enough to sear the clothes from his body and set his hair and flesh alight.

Blindly, he fumbled for the handle of the door, and pulled on it. The rush of air only excited the flames further. Through the stench of gasoline and burning plastic he could smell the sickening tang of his own body being cooked. Still

292

he fought to escape, and gravity was on his side. The car was so positioned that he had only to lean forward and fall out through the open door. The sycamore's boughs slowed his descent, but once he was clear of them there was an eighteen foot drop to the polished Mexican pavers around the pool.

He scarcely felt the impact. The fire had completely traumatized his nerve-endings. Nor could he see anything: his eyelids had been fused shut by the heat. He could still hear, though he couldn't make much sense of the garbled cries of the people who had gathered to witness his agonies.

There was one person in the crowd who was willing to do more than stand and watch him burn. Marco felt arms grab hold of him; heard his saviour yelling something about the pool. Then he was in free-fall again, as the man who'd picked him up threw him into the water.

The flames were instantly extinguished. But the cure was too much for his flesh to endure. The sudden shock of cold after the blistering heat of the fire sent his body into systemic failure.

His last breath – a bubble of heated air – escaped from his cooked lungs. Then he sank to the bottom of the pool.

Even so, the people around the pool didn't give up on him. Three of the partygoers dived into the pool and brought his blackened, fire-withered body up from the bottom. He was tenderly lifted onto the side of the pool, where one of the girls attempted to breathe some life back into him. But it was a lost cause. The man who'd made such a dramatic entrance into the gathering was dead, and beyond hope of saving.

This was not quite the end of events along that stretch of Mulholland Drive, however.

Just a few hours later, as the first light of dawn was breaking, a jogger, who ran a two-mile route along the

Drive daily, rain or shine, saw a light on the road, close to the place where Marco's tyres had left their blackened imprint on the asphalt. Apparently aware that it had an unwanted witness, the mysterious luminescence rose up into the brightening air and was gone.

The following evening, Paul Booth, the man who'd had the courage to carry the burning body of Marco Caputo to the pool – went out into the back yard, alone. He was in a melancholy state of mind. The party he'd thrown the previous night had been in honour of his little sister's sixteenth birthday. Some celebration! Alice had barely stopped crying since. He could hear her now, sobbing in the house.

He took out the half-smoked reefer he'd been saving for a happier occasion, and lit it up. As he drew on the pungent smoke, he looked up and saw a patch of luminous air lingering at the edge of the pool. It had no discernible shape. It was simply a gentle brightness, which would have been invisible half an hour before, when the sun had still been up. He watched the brightness as it hung there for ten, perhaps fifteen seconds, then he nipped out his reefer, pocketed it, and went back inside to find someone to tell. He found his father; and together they emerged into the back yard.

The light had already gone from beside the pool.

'There!' Paul said, pointing up at something that could have been the light he'd seen, now up on Mulholland Drive. But it could just as easily have been the light of a car coming round the treacherous corner of the road. And anyway, it had gone in a heartbeat, leaving both father and son doubting what they'd seen.

6

In the depths of the Canyon, no more than half a mile
from the pool and the lawn and the tree where Ava
hung, Tammy lay in the earth, and waited for the end.
She'd done all she could do to survive: she had eaten
berries and licked the dew off leaves, she'd fought off the
fever-dreams which threatened to claim her consciousness;
she'd forced herself to walk when she had no strength left
in her limbs.

It had tricks, this Canyon: ways to lead you round and
round in circles, so that you burned up all your energies
coming back to the place you'd started from. It put colours
before your eyes that were so bewitching that you ended
up turning round and round on the spot to catch them,
like a dog chasing its own tail. And sometimes (this was its
cleverest trick) it went into your head and found the voices
there that were most comforting, then made them call to
you. Arnie (of all people to find comforting, Mr Zero Sperm
Count); and the man who used to do her dry-cleaning in
Sacramento, Mr O'Brien, who'd always had a smile and a
wink for her; and Todd, of course, her beautiful hero Todd,
calling out to her just to make her stumble a few more
steps. She hadn't quite believed any of these voices were
real, but that hadn't stopped her following them, back and
forth, around and about – voices and colours – until at last
she had no strength left in her body, and she fell down.

So now she was down, and she was too weak to get
up again; too damn heavy ever to get her fat ass up and

moving. At the back of her head was the fear that the freaks would come and find her. But they didn't come, at least by daylight. Perhaps, she thought, they were waiting for darkness. Meanwhile, there were plenty of things that *did* come: flies, dragonflies, hummingbirds, all flitting around.

As for the summonings from Arnie and Mr O'Brien and Todd, once she was down on the ground none of these came either. The Canyon knew it had her beaten. All it had to do was wait, and she'd perish where she lay.

The day crept on. In the middle of the afternoon she fell into a stupefied daze, and when she woke experienced a short and surprising burst of renewed ambition to save herself. After much effort she managed to get to her feet, and started to walk in what she thought was the direction of the house (sometimes she seemed to see the roof through the trees, sometimes not), but after ten minutes the Canyon seemed to realize she was up and walking, and it began its little tricks afresh. The colours came back. So did the voices.

She fell to her knees, crying, begging it to leave her alone. But it was merciless; the voices were louder than ever, yelling incoherently in her head; the sky was every colour but blue.

'Okay,' she said. 'Okay, okay. Just leave me alone to die. I won't get up again. I promise. I swear. Just leave me be.'

It seemed to get the message, because by degrees the yelling receded, and the colours dimmed.

She lay back in the foliage, and watched the sky darken, the stars emerge. Birds flew overhead, returning to their nests before the onset of night. She envied them, just a little, but then what did she have to go home to, in truth? A house in the suburbs she'd never really loved; a husband, the same. What a mess she'd made of her life! What a ridiculous, empty mess! All that time wasted doting on a man she'd seen on a screen; hours spent flicking through her treasures, fantasizing. Never really *living*. That was the horror of it. She was going to die and she'd never really lived.

The sky was almost lightless now. She could barely see her hand in front of her face. She let her eyes slide closed, draping the stars. In the grass around her, the cicadas sang a rhythmical lullaby.

Suddenly, somewhere not very far off, there rose an unholy din; part howl, part yelp, part laughter. Her eyes sprang open. The hairs at her nape stood on end. Was this a farewell performance by the Canyon? One last attempt to squeeze her wits dry?

No; no. This wasn't for her benefit. It was too far away. Up at the house. Yes, that was it; somebody up at the house was having one hell of a party.

Curiosity got the better of her fatigue. Tammy pushed herself up onto her knees, and attempted to figure out where the cacophony was coming from. There was light visible between the trees; flickering, but not flames. This was too cold a light to be fire.

Perhaps this wasn't a party after all. The din was as nasty as it was raucous. Who the hell could be making such a noise? The freaks perhaps? It seemed the likeliest source. She pictured them laying siege to the house. Oh God in Heaven, suppose they'd gone after Todd? Sniffed him out in his weakened state, and attacked him?

The thought of harm coming to him was unbearable, even now. It forced her to get up off the ground, something she couldn't have done on her own behalf. For a few seconds she stood with legs wide planted, uncertain whether she was going to fall down again. Then, she told herself to move, and much to her surprise her body obeyed the instruction. Her legs felt like lead and her head as light as a helium balloon, but she managed to stagger five or six steps without falling down.

The noise from the house had subsided somewhat, but

the lights were still visible between the trees. She paused for a moment to catch her breath, and while she did so she studied the lights, trying to make sense of them. Was it possible what she was seeing were people? Yes it was. Several of the figures had slipped away from the immediate vicinity of the house, and were coming closer to her. Some were zigzagging through the trees, as though they were engaged in a game of some kind. What sort of creatures were these, she wondered, that capered like children playing, but had such luminescence about them?

She stumbled on another two or three steps, but her body wasn't going to carry her much further, she knew. It was only a matter of time before she fell down again; and next time she knew she wouldn't have the strength to pick herself up.

Then, very close by, she heard the sound of something moving through the thicket. She looked in the direction of the sound. An animal perhaps? A coyote, or –

'Tammy?'

She held her breath, not quite daring to believe that she recognized the voice.

'It's Willem,' he said.

Her legs almost gave out from sheer gratitude. He came out of the bushes and caught hold of her before she fell.

'I'm heavy,' she warned him.

'I'm strong,' he said.

So she let him take her weight, sinking against his chest. As she relinquished herself to him she heard a little girl somewhere nearby, sobbing pitifully. She was about to ask who the hell it was making such a noise when she realized it was her own voice.

'It's all right,' Zeffer said. 'I'm here now. Everything's going to be fine.'

She wasn't sure that she believed him; it sounded like a bad piece of dialogue to her. But this was no time to be judgmental. He'd come to look for her, and she was grateful. She put her head on his chest, like a B-movie heroine snatched from the jaws of death, and laughing, then sobbing, then laughing again, let him put his arms around her, and rock her awhile.

7

Finally, it had not been Todd who'd lost control, but her other lover.

'I can't . . . hold back . . . much longer,' he said.

The girl was beyond giving even the most rudimentary instructions: she lay in a daze of pleasure, her legs hoisted up by Todd so that he could see the wonderful machinery of their interconnected anatomies.

'Are you ready?' the other man said to him. His face was liquid shadow, his eyes wild.

'You say the word.'

'Lift her legs higher.'

Todd did as he was instructed, noticing as he did so that their game had brought all the other games in the immediate vicinity to a halt. Everyone was watching the spectacle, their gazes ravenous.

The girl's eyes were closed but there was no doubt that she had achieved, and was sustaining, some state of sexual Nirvana. There was a Gioconda smile on her wet lips, and when on occasion her lids did flutter open, only the whites of her eyes were visible.

The girl's other lover had one hand on her face, a thumb pressed between her lips, but his other hand was gripping the muscle that ran from Todd's nape to his shoulder, gripping it so hard it hurt. Todd was glad of the pain. It was just enough to keep him distracted from emptying himself.

The man's eyes opened wide. 'Oh yeah!' he bellowed,

and Todd came the closest he'd ever come to feeling another man's orgasm.

The girl opened her eyes, and looked at Todd. 'You too,' she said.

'No,' said another voice.

Todd looked up. It was Katya who had spoken. She was looking at him with an appreciative smile on her face. Clearly she'd enjoyed watching the ménage-à-trois. But it was clear she now wanted Todd to leave the game.

'Gotta go,' he said to the girl.

She put her hand down between their legs, as though to hold him inside.

'Sorry,' he said, and pulled out of her.

As he stood up there was a light patter of applause from the vicinity of the bower.

'Quite the performer,' Katya said, as she stood up. She had his pants. He started to put them on, pressing his dick out of sight.

'You can come back and find them again another night,' Katya said, as she hooked her arm through Todd's, and escorted him away from the place.

It seemed the scene in the night-blooming jasmine had begun a chain reaction amongst the ghosts. As they walked through the warm darkness he saw orgiasts on every side, involved in pleasuring themselves and one another. Clothes had been shed in the grass or hung in the branches like Hallowe'en spooks; kisses were being exchanged, murmurs of passion. As he'd already discovered, death had done nothing to dim the libidos of these people. Though their dust and bones lay in cold tombs and mausoleums across the city, their spirits were very much in heat here. And, as Katya had told him, nothing was forbidden. It was only curious to see so many familiar faces amongst the orgiasts. Faces he associated with everything but this: comedians and adventurers and players of melodrama. But never naked; never aroused. And again, as had been true in the bower, what he would have turned away from in revulsion in the company of the living, intrigued and inflamed him here, amongst the famous dead. Was that Cary Grant with his trousers around his ankles; and Randolph Scott paying tribute below? Was that Jean Harlow lying on one of the lower boughs of a tree, with her foot running up and down the erection of a man standing devotedly by? There were others, many others, he only half-recognized, or didn't recognize at all. But Katya supplied names as they wandered back to the house: Gilbert Roland and Carole Lombard, Frances X. Bushman and Errol Flynn. A dozen times, seeing some coupling in progress, he wanted to ask, was that so-and-so? Three or four times he did. When the answer was consistently yes, he gave up asking. As for what was actually going on, well the pictures in the Pool House had given him a good idea of how wild things could get, and now he was seeing those excesses proved in the flesh, for just about every sexual peccadillo was being indulged somewhere in the Canyon tonight. Nor did Todd discount the possibility that even more extreme configurations than those he could see were going on in the murk between the trees. Given what he'd ended up doing after only a short night here, imagine the possibilities an occupant in the Canyon might invent with an indeterminate number of nights to pass: knowing you were dead but denied a resting-place?

What new perversions would a soul invent to distract itself from the constant threat of *ennui*?

At last the crowd of fornicators thinned, and Katya led him – by a path he hadn't previously seen, it being so overgrown – back to the big house.

'What I am about to show you,' she warned him as they went, 'will change your life. Are you ready for that?'

'Is it something to do with why you're here?'

'Why *I'm* here, why *they're* here. Why the Canyon is the most sacred place in this city. Yes. All of the above.'

'Then show me,' he said. 'I'm ready.'

She took a tighter hold of his hand. 'There's no way back,' she warned him. 'I want you to understand that. *There is no way back.*'

He glanced over his shoulder at the party-goers cavorting between the trees. 'I think that was true a long time ago,' he said.

'I suppose it was,' Katya replied, with a little smile, and led him out of the darkened garden and back into her dream palace.

8

'I'm hungry,' Tammy told Zeffer. 'Can't we get some food from the house before we leave?'

'You really want to find Todd,' Zeffer said. 'Admit it.'

'No, I don't care.' She stopped herself in mid-lie. 'Well, maybe a little,' she said. 'I just want to check that he's all right.'

'I can tell you the answer to that. He's not all right. He's with her. Frankly, that means you may as well forget about him. When Katya wants a man Katya gets him.'

'Were you married to her?'

'I was married when I met Katya, but I never became her husband. She never wanted me. I was just there to serve her, right from the start. To make her life easier. Todd's a different story. She's going to suck him dry.'

'Like a vampire, you mean?' Tammy said. After all she'd seen the idea didn't seem so preposterous.

'She's not the kind who takes your blood. She's the kind who takes your soul.'

'But she hasn't got Todd yet, has she?' Tammy said. 'I mean, he could still leave if he wanted to.'

'I suppose he could,' Zeffer said, his voice laced with doubt. 'But, Tammy, I have to ask you: why do you care about this man so much? What's he ever done for you?'

It took Tammy a few moments to muster a reply. 'I suppose if you look at it that way, he hasn't done anything . . . tangible. He's a movie star, and I'm one of his fans. But I

304

swear, Willem, if he hadn't been around over the last few years I would have had nothing to live for.'

'You would have had your own life. Your marriage. You're clearly a sensible woman –'

'I never wanted to be sensible. I never really wanted to be a wife. I mean, I loved Arnie, I still do I suppose, but it's not a grand passion or anything. It was more a convenience thing. It made things easy when tax-time came around.'

'So what did you really want for *yourself*?'

'For myself? You won't laugh? I wanted to be the kind of woman who comes into a room and instantly everybody's got something to say about her. That's what I wanted.'

'So you wanted to be famous?'

'I guess that was part of it.'

'You should ask Katya about fame. She's always said it was overrated.'

'How did we get off the subject of Todd?'

'Because it's impossible to help him.'

'Let me just go into the house and talk to him for a while. And maybe get something to eat while I'm there.'

'Haven't you seen enough of this place to be afraid of it yet?' Zeffer said.

'I'm almost past being afraid,' Tammy replied. It was the truth. She'd seen her share of horrors, but she'd lived to tell the tale.

They were twenty yards from one of the several staircases that ran up from the garden into the house.

'Please,' she said to Zeffer. 'I just want to go inside and warn him. If that doesn't work, I'll leave and I'll never look back, I swear.'

Zeffer seemed to sense the power of her will on the subject. He put up no further protest but simply said: 'You realize if you get in Katya's way, I can't step in to help you? I have my own allegiances, however foolish you may think they are.'

'Then I'll make sure I don't get in her way,' Tammy said.

'I'm not even supposed to go into the house, believe it or not.'

'Not allowed on the furniture, either?'

'If you're saying I'm little better than her dog, you're right. But it's my life. I made my choices just as you made yours.' He sighed. 'There are some days when I think hard about killing myself. Just to be free of her. But it might not work. I might slit my throat and wake up back where I started, her dead dog instead of her living one.'

Tammy's gaze slid past him to study the luminous people playing between the trees. The sight should have astonished her; but she'd seen too much in the last little while for this to impress her much. The scene before her was just another piece of the Canyon's mystery.

'Are they all dead?' she asked, in the same matter-of-fact way she'd sustained through much of their exchange.

'All dead. You want to go look?' He studied her hesitation. 'You do but you don't want to admit to it. It's all right. There's a little voyeur in everybody. If there wasn't there'd be no such thing as cinema.' He turned and looked towards the flickering figures weaving between the trees. 'She used to have orgies all the time in the Golden Age, and I liked nothing better than to pick my way amongst the configurations and watch.'

'But not now?'

'No. There's only so much human intercourse anyone can watch.'

'Do they look horrible?'

'Oh no. They look the way they looked at the height of their beauty, because that's the way they want to remember themselves. Perfect, forever. Or at least for as long as God allows this place to last.'

Tammy caught the apocalyptic undertone in this. 'What do you mean?' she said.

'That sooner or later there'll be an end to this endless indulgence. A Day of Judgment, if you will. And I think –'

he dropped his voice to a whisper, though there was no one nearby '– you may be its Deliverer.'

'Me?' She also dropped her voice. 'Why me?'

'It's just a hunch. A piece of wishful thinking if you like. They've had their time. And I think some of them know it. They're a little more desperate than they used to be. A little more shrill.'

'Why don't they just *leave*?'

'Ah. We had to come to that at last. The reason's very complex, and to tell you the truth I would not really know where to begin. Let me put it this way. They are afraid that if they leave this Canyon they may break the spell that keeps them in their strange state of perfection.'

'And do you believe that?'

'Yes, I believe it. They're prisoners here. Beautiful prisoners.'

A few minutes after Katya and Todd had left the party out on the night-lawn, a whisper went amongst the revenants, and one by one they gave up their pleasures, whatever they'd been, and turned their hollow gazes towards the house.

There are only so many times you can play out the old flesh games without losing interest in them. Yes, you could add piquancy if you introduced a whip, or some rope; you could mate with somebody of your own sex (or, if that was what you'd done in your lifetime, with somebody of the opposite gender). But all of it grew wearying with repetition. No feast can ever be so tempting that finally the act of eating doesn't lose its appeal. Sooner or later even the most ambitious glutton must crawl away and seek the solace of the vomitorium.

It was the same for the ghosts. They'd been here in the presence of their own perfection for decades; and now it meant nothing to them. They'd seen that beauty defiled and debauched, they'd seen it locked in every configuration lust could devise, and there was nothing left to surprise them. The presence of living flesh, in the form of Todd Pickett, might momentarily re-ignite some old flames, but the conflagration quickly died away once he was removed from their company.

Now their eyes went to the house, and though they said nothing, the same thought went through all their melancholy heads.

Maybe tonight, something would change. Maybe tonight, with this man in her company, the Queen of Sorrows would make a mistake . . .

A few of them began to move in the general direction of the house, attempting to seem casual, but fixing their silvery eyes on their destination.

A bank of cloud had come in off the Pacific and covered both moon and stars. On the ridge of the opposite side of the Canyon some of the grotesque offspring of these weary beauties began a wordless howling in the darkness. The sound was loud enough to carry down the hill to Sunset and the Beverly Hill flats. Several valets parking cars for a private party on Rexford Drive paused to comment on the weird din from up in the hills; a couple of patients, close to death at Cedars-Sinai, called for their priests; a man who lived next door to the house on Van Nuys where Lyle and Eric Menendez had murdered their mother and father, decided – hearing the sound – to give up screenwriting and move back to Wisconsin.

Todd heard it too, of course.

'What in God's name is that?'

He and Katya were deep in the bowels of the house, in a place he had never known existed, much less explored.

'Take no notice,' Katya told him, as the noise came again, even louder and more plaintive. 'Whatever it is, it's *out there*, it's not in here with us.' She took hold of his arm, and kissed his cheek. He could smell Ava on

308

her. His erection still throbbed. 'Are you ready?' she said to him.

'Ready for what?'

They were approaching a door just a little smaller than the front door; and similarly medieval in style.

'On the other side of that door is something that was given to me a long time ago. It changed my life. As I told you, it will also change yours. When you first get in there, it's bewildering. You just have to trust me. I'm going to be with you all the time, even if you can't always see me. And I swear no harm is going to come to you. You understand me, Todd? This is *my* house. Even this place, which will seem very *remote* from everything you've seen so far, is also *mine*.'

He didn't know quite what to make of any of this, but his curiosity was certainly piqued.

'So don't be afraid,' she told him.

'I won't be,' he said, wondering what kind of game she was playing now. She, who knew so many; what did she have up her sleeve?

As had happened so many times now, she read his thoughts. 'This isn't a game,' she said. 'Or if it is, it's the most serious game in God's creation.'

There was surely a trace of condescension here, but what the hell?

'I'm ready,' he said.

She smiled. 'In half an hour you'll realize what an absurd thing it is you've just said,' she told him.

'Why?'

'Because nobody can be ready for this.'

Then she pushed open the door.

Before Tammy went to find Todd, she had to eat. *Had to*.

So, while Todd was stepping over the threshold into a place that would change his life, Tammy was in the kitchen three storeys above, at the open fridge, gorging on whatever her hands found. Cold chicken, potato salad, some Chinese takeaway.

'Do we have to do this now?' Zeffer said, looking around nervously. 'She could come in here at any minute.'

'Yes, well let her. I'm *hungry*, Willem. In fact I'm fucking starving. Give me a hand here, will you?'

'What do you want?'

'Something sweet. Then I'm done.'

He dug around on the inner shelves of the fridge and found an almost-intact cherry pie, the sight of which made Tammy coo the way most women cooed when they saw babies. Zeffer watched her with an expression of bemusement on his face. She was too hungry to care. She lifted a slice of pie to her mouth, but before she could get it to her tongue, Zeffer caught hold of her wrist.

'What?' she said.

'Listen.'

Tammy listened. She heard nothing, so she shook her head.

'Listen,' he said again, and this time she heard what he was drawing her attention to. The windows were shaking. So were the doors. The cutlery on the sink was rattling; as were the plates in the cupboards.

She let the slice of pie drop from her fingers, her appetite suddenly vanished.

'What's going on?' she wanted to know.

'They're downstairs,' Zeffer said, his voice tinged with superstitious awe. 'Todd and Katya. They've gone downstairs.'

'What are they doing there?'

'You don't want to know,' Zeffer said hurriedly. '*Please*. I beg you. Let's just go.'

The windows were shaking with mounting violence; the boards creaked beneath their feet. It was as though the entire structure of the house was protesting about whatever was happening in its midst.

Tammy went to the kitchen sink, ran some cold water, and washed the food from around her mouth. Then she skirted around Zeffer and headed to the door that led to the turret and the staircase.

'Wrong direction,' Zeffer said. He pointed to the other door. 'That's the safest way out.'

'If Todd's down there, then that's the way I want to go,' Tammy said.

As she spoke she felt a blast of chilly air coming up from below. It smelled nothing like the rest of the house, nor of the gardens outside. Something about it made the small hairs at her nape prickle.

She looked back down at Zeffer, with a question on her face.

'I think I need to tell you what's down there before you take one more step,' he said.

Outside, the spirits of the dead waited and listened. They had heard the door that led into the Chamber of the Hunt opened; they knew some lucky fool was about to step into the Devil's Country. If they could have stormed the house and slipped through the door ahead of him, they would have gladly done so, at any price. But Katya had been too clever. She had put up defences against such a siege: five icons beaten into the threshold of each of the doors that would drive a dead soul to oblivion if they attempted to cross. They had no choice, therefore, but to keep a respectful distance, hoping that some day the icons would lose their terrible potency; or that Katya would simply declare an amnesty upon her guests and tear the icons out of the thresholds, allowing her sometime lovers and friends back inside.

Meanwhile, they waited, and listened, and remembered what it had been like for them in the old days, when they'd been able to go back and forth into the house at will. It had been bliss, back then: all you had to do was step into the

Devil's Country and you could shed your old skin like a snake. They'd come back to the chamber over and over, so as to restore their failing glamour, and it had dutifully soothed away their imperfections; made their limbs sleek and their eyes gleam.

All this was kept secret from the studio bosses, of course, and when on occasion a Goldwyn or a Thalberg *did* find out Katya made sure they were intimidated into silence. Nobody talked about what went on in Coldheart Canyon, even to others that they might have seen there. The stars went on about their public lives while in secret they took themselves up to Coldheart Canyon every weekend, and having smoked a little marijuana or opium, went to look at the Hunt, knowing that they would emerge rejuvenated.

There was a brief Golden Age, when the royalty of America lived a life of near-perfection; sitting in their palaces dreaming of immortality. And why not? It seemed they had found the means to renew their beauty whenever it grew a little tired. So what if they had to dabble in the supernatural for their fix of perfection; it was worth the risk.

Then – but inexorably – the Golden Age began to take its toll: the lines they'd driven off their faces began to creep back again, deeper than ever; their eye-sight started to fail. Back they went into the Devil's Country, desperate for its healing power, but the claim of time could not be arrested.

Terrible stories started to circulate amongst the lords of Tinseltown; nightmare stories. Somebody had woken up blind in the middle of the night, it was said; somebody else had withered before her lover's appalled eyes. Fear gripped the Golden People; and anger too. They blamed Katya for introducing them to this ungodly panacea, and demanded that she give them constant access to the house and the Hunt. She, of course, refused. This quickly led to some ugly scenes: people started appearing at the house in the Canyon in desperate states of need, beating at the door to be let in.

Katya hardened her cold heart against them, however. Realizing she would soon be under siege, she hired men to guard the house night and day. For several months, she and Zeffer lived in near isolation, ignoring the entreaties of her friends who came (often with magnificent gifts) begging for an audience with her; and for a chance to see the Devil's Country. She refused all but a very few.

In fact nobody truly understood what was happening in the bowels of the house. Why should they? They were dealing in mysteries even old Father Sandru, who had sold Zeffer the piece, did not understand. But their eager flesh had discovered what the dry intellect of metaphysicians had not. Like opium addicts denied their fix they went blindly after the thing that would heal their pain, without needing to understand the pharmacology that had driven them to such desperation.

For a time they had been happy in the Canyon, they remembered; happy in Katya's house, happy looking at the pictures of the Hunt on the tiled walls, which had moved so curiously before their astonished eyes. So it followed – didn't it? – that if they kept returning to the Canyon, and into that strange country of tiles and illusion they would be happy and healthy again. But Katya wouldn't let them; she was leaving them to suffer, denied the only thing they wanted.

Of course Katya was no more knowledgeable about the alchemy at work in her dream palace than those in her doomed circle. She knew that the gift of healing and the fever of need that followed was all brought about by being in the Devil's Country, but how it worked, or how long it would operate before its engines were exhausted, she had no idea. She only knew that she felt possessive of the room. It was hers to give and take away, as her will desired.

Needless to say, the more tearful visitors she had at her

gates, the more letters she received (and the more chaotic the tone of those letters) the less inclined she was to invite in those who'd written them, partly because she was afraid of the depth of addiction she had unleashed in these people, partly because she was anxious that the power of the Devil's Country might not be limitless, and she was not about to be profligate with a power that she needed as much as they.

There *might* come a time, she supposed, when she would need the healing effects of the house purely for herself, and when that time came she'd be covetous of every wasted jot of it. This wasn't something she could afford to be generous with; not any longer. It was her life she was playing with here; *her life everlasting*. She needed to preserve the power she had locked away below ground, for fear one day its sum was the difference between life and death.

And then – as though things were not terrible enough – they had suddenly got worse.

It began on Monday, the 23rd of August, 1926, with the sudden death of Rudy Valentino.

Only three weeks before he had managed to get past the guards in Coldheart Canyon (like one of the heroes he'd so often played, scaling walls to get to his beloved) and had pleaded with Katya to let him stay with her. He didn't feel good, he told her; he needed to stay here in the Canyon, where he'd spent so many happy times, and recuperate. She told him no. He became aggressive; told her – half in Italian, half in English – that she was a selfish bitch. Wasn't it time she remembered where she came from? he said. She was just a peasant at heart, like him. Just because she acted like a queen didn't make her one; to which she'd snappily replied that the same could *not* be said for him. He'd slapped her for that remark. She'd slapped him back, twice as hard.

Always prone to sudden emotional swings, Valentino had promptly started to bawl like a baby, interspersing his sobs with demands that she please God have mercy on him.

'I'm dying!' he said, thumping his gut with his fist. 'I feel it in here!'

She let him weep until the carpet was damp. Then she had had him removed from the house by two of her hired heavies, and tossed into the street.

It had seemed like typical Rudy melodrama at the time: *I'm dying, I'm dying.* But this time he'd known his own body better than she'd given him credit for. He was the first to pay the ultimate price for visiting the Devil's Country. Three weeks after that tearful conversation he was dead.

The hoopla over Valentino's sudden demise hid from view a series of smaller incidents that were nevertheless all part of the same escalating tragedy. A minor starlet called Miriam Acker died two days after Rudy, of what was reported to be pneumonia. She had been a visitor to the Canyon on several occasions, usually in the company of Ramon Navarro. Pola Negri – another visitor to the Canyon – fell gravely ill a week later, and for several days hovered on the brink of death. Her frailty was attributed to grief at the passing of Valentino, with whom she claimed to have had a passionate affair; but the truth was far less glamorous. She too had fallen under the spell of the Hunt; and now, though she denied it, was sickening.

In fact death took an uncommonly large number of Hollywood's luminaries in the next few months. And for every one who died there were ten or twenty who got sick, and managed to recover, though none were ever possessed of their full strength, or flawless beauty, again. The 'coincidence' was not lost on either the fans or the journalists. '*A harvest of death is sweeping Hollywood,*' *Film Photoplay* morbidly announced, '*as star after star follows the greatest star of all, Rudolph Valentino, to the grave.*'

The idea that there was some kind of plague abroad caught the public's imagination and was fed voraciously by those who'd predicted for reasons of their own that judgment would eventually fall on Tinseltown. Preachers who'd fulminated against the sinners of the New Sodom were now quick to point out the evidence in support of their grim sermons. And the public, who'd a decade before taken pleasure in crowning actors as the new Royalty of America were now just as entertained by the spectacle of their fall from grace. They were fakes and foreigners anyway, it was widely opined; no wonder they were falling like flies; they'd come here like plague-rats in the first place.

Hollywood was going to Hell in a hand-cart, and it didn't matter how rich or beautiful you were, there was no escaping the cost of the high life.

Up in the Canyon, Katya dared believe she was safe: she'd added three German Shepherd dogs to the retinue guarding her; and she had men patrolling the ridges and the roads that led to the Canyon night and day. It was such a strange time. The whole community was unsettled. There was talk of lights being seen in the sky; especially in the vicinity of death-sites. A number of small cults came into being, all with their own theories of what was happening. The most extreme interpreted these lights as warnings from God: the end of the world was imminent, their leaders announced, and people should prepare themselves for the Apocalypse. Others interpreted the lights more benignly. They were messengers from God, this faction claimed; angels sent to guide the deceased out of the coil of mortal confusions into the next life. If this was the case then these heavenly presences were not happy that Hell now had a stronghold in the Canyon. Though the dead came there, the lights did not. Indeed on several occasions they were seen at the bottom of the hill, three or four of them gathered in a cloud of luminescence, plainly unwilling to venture into the Canyon.

For her part, Katya took such reports as evidence that her

defences were working. Nobody could get into her precious Canyon. Or such was her conviction.

In fact her sense of security, like so much else in her increasingly fragile life, was an illusion.

One evening, walking in the garden, the dogs suddenly got crazy, and out of the darkness stepped Rudy Valentino. He looked entirely unchanged by death: his skin as smooth as ever, his hair as brilliantly coiffed, his clothes as flawless.

He bowed deeply to her.

'My apologies,' he said, 'for coming here. I know I'm not welcome. But frankly, I didn't know where else to go.'

There was no hint of manipulation in this; it seemed to be the unvarnished truth.

'I went home to Falcon Lair,' Rudy went on, 'but it's been trampled over by so many people, it doesn't feel as though it's mine any more. Please . . . I beg you . . . don't be afraid of me.'

'I'm not afraid of you,' Katya replied, quite truthfully. 'There were always ghosts in my village. We used to see them all the time. My grandmother used to sing me to sleep, and she'd been dead ten years. But Rudy, let's be honest. I know why you're up here. You want to get in to see the Hunt –'

'– just for a little while.'

'No.'

'Please.'

'*No!*' she said, waving him away, 'I really don't want to hear any more of this. Why don't you just go back to Sicily?'

'Castellaneta.'

'Wherever. I'm sure they'll be pleased to see the ghost of their favourite son.'

She turned her back on him and walked back towards the house. She heard him following on after her, his heels light on the grass, but solid enough.

317

'It's true what they said about you. *Cold heart.*'

'You say whatever you like, Rudy. Just leave me alone.'

He stopped following her.

'You think I'm the only one?' he said to her.

His words brought her to a halt.

'They're all going to come up here, in time. It doesn't matter how many dogs you have, how many guards. They'll get in. Your beautiful Canyon's going to be full of *ghosts*.'

'Stop being childish, Rudy,' she said, turning back to look at him.

'Is that how you want to live, Katya? Like a prisoner, surrounded by the dead? Is that the life you had in mind for yourself?'

'I'm not a prisoner. I can leave whenever I want to.'

'And still be a great star? No. To be a star you will have to be here, in Hollywood.'

'So?'

'So you will have company, night and day. The dead will be here with you, night and day. We will not be ignored.'

'You keep saying *we*, Rudy. But I only see you.'

'The others will come. They'll all find their way here, sooner or later. Did you know Virginia Maple hanged herself last night? You remember Virginia? Or perhaps you don't. She was –'

'I know Virginia. And no, I didn't know she hanged herself. Nor, frankly, do I much care.'

'She couldn't take the pain.'

'The pain?'

'Of being kept out of this house! Being kept away from the Devil's Country.'

'It's my house. I have a perfect right to invite whoever I like into it.'

'You see nothing but yourself, do you?'

'Oh *please*, Rudy, no lectures on narcissism. Not from you, of all people.'

'I see things differently now.'

'Oh I'm sure you do. I'm sure you regret every self-obsessed moment of your petty little life. But that's really not my problem, now is it?'

The colour of the ghost before her suddenly changed. In a heartbeat he became a stain of yellow and grey, his fury rising in palpable waves off his face.

'I will make it your problem,' he shrieked. He strode towards her. 'You selfish *bitch*.'

'And what did they call you?' she snapped back. 'Powder puff, was it?'

It was an insult she knew would strike him hard. Just the year before an anonymous journalist in the *Chicago Tribune* had called him 'a pink powder puff'. '*Why didn't somebody quietly drown Rudolph Guglielmi, alias Valentino, years ago?*' he'd written. Rudy had challenged the man to a boxing match, to see which of them was truly the more virile. The journalist had of course never shown his face. But the insult had stuck. And hearing it repeated now threw Valentino into such a rage that he pitched himself at Katya, reaching for her throat. She had half-expected his phantom body to be so unsubstantial that his hands would fail to make any real contact. But not so. Though the flesh and blood of him had been reduced to an urn full of ashes, his spirit-form had a force of its own. She felt his fingers at her neck as though they were living tissue. They stopped her breath.

She was no passive victim. She pushed him back with the heel of one hand, raking his features from brow to mid-cheek with the other. Blood came from the wounds, stinking faintly of bad meat. A disgusted expression crossed Valentino's face, as he caught a whiff of his own excremental self. The shock of it made him loose his hold on her, and she quickly pulled away from him.

In life, she'd remembered, he'd always been overly sensitive to smells; a consequence, perhaps, of the fact

319

that he'd been brought up in the stench of poverty. His hand went up to his wounded face, and he sniffed his fingers, a look of profound revulsion on his face.

She laughed out loud at the sight. Valentino's fury had suddenly lost its bite. It was as though in that moment he suddenly understood the depths to which the Devil's Country had brought him.

And then, out of the darkness, Zeffer called: 'What the hell's going on out –'

He didn't finish his question: he'd seen Valentino.

'Oh, Jesus Christ Almighty,' he said.

Hearing the Lord's name taken in vain, Valentino – good Catholic boy that he was – crossed himself, and fled into the darkness.

Valentino's vengeful prediction proved entirely accurate: in the next few weeks the haunting of Coldheart Canyon began.

At first the signs were nothing too terrible: a change in the timbre of the coyotes' yelps, the heads torn off all the roses one night; the next all the petals off the bougainvillaea; the appearance on the lawn of a frightened deer, throwing its glassy gaze back towards the thicket in terror. It was Zeffer's opinion that they were somehow going to need to make peace with 'our unwanted guests', as he put it, or the consequences would surely be traumatic. These were not ethereal presences, he pointed out, wafting around in a hapless daze. If they were all like Valentino (and why should they not be?) then they posed a physical threat.

'They could murder us in our beds, Katya,' he said to her.

'Valentino wouldn't –'

'Maybe not Valentino, but there are others, plenty of others, who hated you with a vengeance. Virginia Maple for one. She was a jealous woman. Remember? And then to hang herself because of something you did to her –'

'I did *nothing* to her! I just let her play in that damn room. A room which *you* brought into our lives.'

Zeffer covered his face. 'I knew it would come down to that eventually. Yes, I'm responsible. I was a fool to bring it here. I just thought it would amuse you.'

She gave him a strangely ambiguous look. 'Well, you know, it did. How can I deny that? It still does. I love the feeling I get when I'm in there, touching the tiles. I feel more alive.' She walked over to him, and for a moment he thought she was going to grant him some physical contact: a stroke, a blow, a kiss. He didn't really mind. Anything was better than her indifference. But she simply said: 'You caused this, Willem. You have to solve it.'

'But how? Perhaps if I could find Father Sandru –'

'He's not going to take the tiles *back*, Willem.'

'I don't see why not.'

'*Because I won't let him!* Christ, Willem! I've been in there every day since you gave me the key. *It's in my blood now.* If I lose the room, it'll be the death of me.'

'So we'll move and we'll take the room with us. It's been moved before. We'll leave the ghosts behind.'

'Wherever the Hunt goes, they'll follow. And sooner or later they'll get so impatient, they'll hurt us.'

Zeffer nodded. There was truth in all of this, bitter though it was.

'What in God's name have we done?' he said.

'Nothing we can't mend,' Katya replied. 'You *should* go back to Romania, and find Sandru. Maybe there's some defence we can put up against the ghosts.'

'Where will you stay while I'm gone?'

'I'll stay here. I'm not afraid of Rudy Valentino, dead or alive. Nor that idiotic bitch Virginia Maple. If I don't stay, they'll find their way in.'

'Would that be such a bad thing? Why not let them share the place? We could make a pile of them on the lawn and –'

'*No. That room is mine. All of it. Every damn tile.*'

The quiet ferocity with which she spoke silenced him. He just stared at her for perhaps a minute, while she lit a cigarette, her fingers trembling. Finally, he summoned up enough courage to say: 'You *are* afraid.'

She stared out of the window, almost as though she hadn't heard him. When she spoke again her voice was as soft as it had been strident a minute ago.

'I'm not afraid of the dead, Willem. But I *am* afraid of what will happen to me if I lose the room.' She looked at the palm of her hand, as though she might find her future written there. But it wasn't the lines of her hand she was admiring, it was its smoothness. 'Being in the Devil's Country has made me feel younger, Willem. It did that to everybody. Younger. Sexier. But as soon as it's taken away . . .'

'. . . yes. You'll get sick.'

'I'm never going to get sick.' She allowed herself the time for a smile. 'Perhaps I'm never going to die.'

'Don't be foolish.'

'I mean it.'

'So do I. Don't be foolish. Whatever you think the room can do, it won't make you immortal.'

The wisp of a smile remained on her face. 'Wouldn't you like that, Willem?'

'No.'

'Just a little bit?'

'I said *no*,' he shook his head, his voice dropping. 'Not any more.'

'Meaning what?'

'What do you think I mean? This life of ours . . . isn't worth living.'

There was a silence between them. It lasted two, three, four minutes. Rain began to hit the window; fat spots of it bursting against the glass.

'I'll find Sandru for you,' Willem said finally. 'Or if not

322

him, somebody who knows how to deal with these things. I'll find a solution.'

'Do that,' she said. 'And if you can't, don't bother to come back.'

PART SIX

THE DEVIL'S COUNTRY

1

Todd knew the mechanics of illusion passably well. He'd always enjoyed watching the special effects guys at work, or the stuntmen with their rigs; and now there was a new generation of illusionists who worked with tools that the old matte painters and model-makers of an earlier time could not even have imagined. He'd been in a couple of pictures in which he'd played entire scenes against blank green screens, which were later replaced with landscapes which only existed in the ticking minds of computers.

But the illusions at work in this room of Katya's were of another order entirely. There was a force at work here that was both incredibly powerful and old; even venerable. It did not require electricity to fuel it, nor equations to encode it. The walls held it, with possessive caution, beguiling him by increments.

At first he could make virtually no sense of the images. It simply seemed that the walls were heavily stained. Then, as his eyes became accustomed to reading the surface, he realized he was looking at tiles, and that what he'd taken to be stains were in fact pictures, painted and baked into the ceramic. He was standing in a representation of an immense landscape, which looked more realistic the longer he looked at it. There were vast expanses of dense forests; there were stretches of sun-drenched rock; there were steep cliff-walls, their crannies nested by fearless birds; there were rivulets that became streams, in turn converging into glittering rivers, which wound their way towards the horizon, dividing into silver-fringed deltas before they finally found the sea. Such was the elaboration of the painting that it would take many hours of study, perhaps even days, to hope to discover everything that the painters had rendered. And that would only have been the case if the pictures had been static, which, as he was now astonished to see, was not the case.

There were little flickers of motion all around him. A gust of wind shook the tangle of a thicket; one of those fearless birds wheeled away from the cliff-face, three hunting dogs sniffed their way through the undergrowth, noses to the ground.

'Katya . . . ?' Todd said.

There was no reply from behind him (where he thought she'd last been standing); so he looked back. She wasn't there. Nor was the door through which he'd stepped to come into this new world. There was just more landscape: more trees, more rocks, more birds, wheeling.

The motion multiplied with every flicker of his gaze. There were ripples on the rivulets and streams, there were clouds over the sea, being hurried along by the same wind that filled the sails of the ships that moved below. There were men, too, all around. Riders, moving through the forest; some solitary, some in groups of three or four; one procession of five horses mounted by richly attired men, parading solemnly between the trees. And fishermen on the banks of the streams; and on little boats, bobbing around the sandbars at the delta; and in one place, inexplicably, two men laid out naked on a rock, and in another, far more explicable, another pair hanging from a tree, while their lynchers sat in the shade of the old tree they'd put to such guilty use, and looked out at the rest of the world as they shared a flagon of beer.

Again he looked around for Katya, but she wasn't to be

seen. But she'd said she'd be close by, even if – as now – he couldn't see her. The room, he began to understand, had control of his eyes. He found his gaze repeatedly led away from where she might be, led skyward, to gawk at some passing birds (there were tiles on the vaulted roof, he saw; he could hear the squeak of the birds' wings as they passed overhead); led into the forest, where animals he could not name moved as if in some secret ceremony, and others fought; and others lay dead; and still others were being born. (Though like did not spring from like in this world. In one spot an animal the size and shape of a tiger was giving birth to half a dozen white lizards; in another a hen the size of a horse was retreating from her eggs in panic, seeing that they'd cracked open and were spilling huge blue flies.)

And still he kept looking. And still he kept seeing, and though there were horrors here, to be sure, nothing in him made him want to leave off his seeing.

There was a curious calm upon his soul; a kind of dreamy indifference to his own situation. If he'd reasoned this out perhaps he would have concluded that he wasn't afraid because none of this could possibly be real. But he did not reason it out. He was beyond reasoning at that moment. Beyond anything, indeed, but *witnessing*. He had become a living instrument; a flesh-and-blood camera, recording this wonderland. He kept turning on his heel, counter-clockwise, as sights caught his attention off to his left; and left again; and left again.

Everything here had a miraculous *shine* to it, as though whatever divinity had made it had an army of workers at His or Her command, perpetually polishing the world. Every leaf on every tree had its gloss; every hair on every mammal and every scale on every reptile had its sheen; every particle of earth, down to the shit from the flea-infested backside of a boar, had a glamour all of its own. A rat sniffing in the carcass of a gored hound came away

329

with drops of corruption on its whiskers as enchanting as a lover's eyes. The earth at his feet (yes, there were tiles there too, painted with as much love as forest or cloud) was a surfeit of glories: a worm his heel had half-killed was lovely in its knotted agonies.

Nothing was inconsequential here. Except perhaps, Todd Pickett. And if that was the case, then he wasn't about to dispute the point. He would not wish anything here other than the way it was, including – for the first time in his life – himself.

This thought – that he was finally at peace with himself – came over him like a breaking wave, cooling a long and exhausting fever. If he was nothing here, he thought, except the eyes with which these strangenesses could be glorified, then that suited him fine. And if in the end the witnessing burned him up, and made an end to him, that was fine too; perfectly fine, to die here, watching this shining world. It would hear no complaint from him.

'You like it?'

Ah, there was Katya. Off to his right, a little distance, staring up at the glamorous sky.

He followed her gaze, and saw something he'd missed until now: the sun was three-quarters eclipsed by the moon. That was why the light was so peculiar here; it was the light of a world in permanent semi-darkness; a murk which had inspired everything that lived here to catch its own particular fire. To snatch every last gleam of light out of the air and magnify it; to be its own exquisite advertisement.

'Yes,' he said to her, hearing something very close to tears in his voice. 'I like it very much.'

'Not everybody does, of course,' she said, glancing over at him. 'Some I brought here were so afraid that they *ran*. And of course, that's not a very smart thing to do here.'

'Why not?'

She wandered over to him, assessing him as she did so,

as though to see if he was telling the truth, and that he really liked what he saw. Apparently satisfied, she laid a light kiss on his cheek: it almost felt as though she was congratulating him. Coming here had been a test, he realized; and he'd passed.

'You see over there, just beyond the hill? The deep forest there?'

'Yes.'

'Then you also see the horsemen coming through the trees?'

'They're the reason we shouldn't run?'

'They are.'

'Why?'

'They're hunters. The Duke Goga, who leads them, counts all these lands as his own.'

'They're getting closer.'

'Yes they are.'

'How is that possible?'

'What do you mean?'

'I mean: how is it possible that they're getting closer to us? They're in the walls.'

'Is that what you think?' she said, coming closer to him. 'Is that what you *really* believe?'

He stood still for a moment, and listened to his heart. What did his heart tell him? The wind gusted, cold against his face. It was not a Californian wind. Overhead, the sun remained eclipsed, though he knew there was no possible way to see the sky from this deep a place in the house.

'I'm in another world.'

'Good,' she said.

'And it's real.'

'Again, good. And does it trouble you, to be in the middle of such a mystery?'

'No,' he said. 'I don't know why and I'm not sure I care.'

She put her arms around him, holding him tighter than

she'd held until now, and looked deep into his eyes, looking deeper than she'd ever looked. 'It doesn't matter, my love. Whether it's in my head, or your head, or the head of God –'

'– or the Devil?'

'– or the Devil. It doesn't matter. Not to us.' She spoke the last three words as a near whisper, close to his ear. He kissed her. He realized now how cannily she'd led him – teasing him with outlandish visions – ghosts and ungodly pleasures, slowly deconstructing his beliefs about what was real and what was not. All in preparation for this wonder of wonders.

'Nothing matters to us, huh?' he said between kisses.

'We're above it all,' she said. As she spoke she put her hand down between his legs. He was like a rock.

'You want to make love to me?'

'Of course I do.'

'You want to go back up to bed?'

'No. I want to do it right here.' He pointed to the hard ground at their feet.

Again, she laughed. This new-found fire in him seemed to entertain her. She lifted up her dress, so that he could have sight of her. She was naked.

'Lie down,' he told her.

She did so without a second instruction, lifting and parting her legs as she lay at his feet, so that he should have full disclosure of her. She ran her hand over herself. Into the groove, and out again, wet, to touch her anus.

He could hear the rhythm of the hunters' horses in the ground underfoot. Duke Goga and his party were getting closer. Todd glanced up towards the trees. He could no longer see the men: the forest had become too deep. But they were nearby.

No matter. He could watch the hunters another day. Right now he had sport of his own. He unbuttoned his pants and let his dick spring out. Katya sat up instantly and took it in her hand, rubbing it.

'So big.'

Maybe it was, maybe it wasn't. He liked the fact that she said it, and there was an appetite for it in her eyes, the likes of which he'd never seen on a woman's face before. She started to pull on his cock, not to pleasure him, simply to bring him down to her; *into* her.

He went down on his knees between her legs. Such was the lightness of her dress that it could be lifted up almost to her neck, to expose her belly and breasts. He put his face down against her flat stomach, licking her navel then going up to her breasts. It had always been a fantasy of his to wash a woman with his tongue, every inch of her, from the corners of her eyes, to the cleft of her buttocks, simply to be her servant, bathing her with his tongue. This was the woman he would realize that fantasy with, he knew. This was the woman he would realize *every* fantasy with, and hers was the body with which he could play freely, doing anything his heart desired; anything.

That was the only word of this sexual delirium that escaped him: '. . . anything.'

But she seemed to know what it meant because she raised his face from her breasts, and smiled at him. 'Yes, I know,' she said. 'Anything you want. And for me –'

'Anything *you* want.'

'Yes.'

She took hold of the collar of his shirt, and drew his face closer to hers. They kissed, while she moved beneath him, seeming not to care about the hard earth against her naked buttocks, her naked back. He had his hands either side of her, to support himself. But that was all he needed to do. She was perfectly capable of doing the rest. She lifted her hips a little and caught the head of his cock between her labia, then, sighing, she delivered herself up and upon it in one sweet motion.

Now she put her arms around his neck, and let out a most extraordinary sigh: a sound of complete abandonment.

Todd looked down at her face with something that began to feel like helpless adoration. The polishers who'd put a shine on everything in this strange world must have saved their best labours for her. The down on her cheek, the dark curve of her lashes, the fabulous hierarchy of lilacs and blues and turquoise in her eyes, all were perfect. She was almost unbearably beautiful: his eyes stung at the sight of her.

'I love you,' he said.

The words came out with such ease that they were said before he had chance to spoil them by making a performance out of them.

Of course he'd said it before, plenty of times (too many times, in truth) but never like this. It sounded, for the first time, simple. Simple and true. She raised her head from the ground, until her lips were almost touching his.

'I love you too,' she whispered.

'Yes?'

'You know I do. You're the one I've waited for, Todd. All these years. I've been patient, because I knew you'd come.'

She pressed her hips up towards him, sheathing him completely. Then, still holding onto him, she began to pull herself off him a little way, just until the head of his dick was about to find the air, then smothering it again, down to the root.

There was a heavy reverberation in the ground. Todd could feel it through his palms.

'The hunters . . .' he said.

'Yes,' she said, as though this was of little consequence. 'Goga's close. We should stay very still until he's passed by.'

She drew Todd down on top of her. He couldn't see the huntsmen yet, but the noise was getting louder nevertheless. The reverberations made the little shards of rock

334

around her head, decorated with tiny fragments of fossil, dance.

Finally, they came into view, rising over the crest of a hill some twenty-five or thirty yards from where they lay, locked together.

There were five of them in the Duke's party, and they looked as though they'd been riding for a very long time. Their horses shone with sweat, and the men – all of whom were dressed in tattered tunics – showed signs of extreme fatigue. But even their exhaustion had a kind of livid beauty to it. Their skin was as bright, or brighter, than the bone that it concealed; their eyes, which were sunk deep in their sockets, had a fevered brilliance in them. Todd wasn't surprised they looked so harried, given the orders of beast he'd glimpsed here. Yes, there were wild pigs and stags, but there were other kinds of creature, far less easily categorized; things that looked as though the Devil had had a hand in their design. Lethal quarry, no doubt. Indeed there were signs that the party had been recently attacked. One of the horses had a number of deep gashes on its rump, and its rider had clearly suffered in the encounter. His left arm hung limply, and a large dark bloodstain had spread from a place under his arm across a third of his upper body. His lips were drawn back from his teeth in pain, his eyelids drooping.

Even if Katya hadn't named the leader, it would have been clear to Todd that he was of a higher social standing than his companions, his horse a more finely bred animal than those the others rode, its mane and tail braided. As for the man himself, he was almost as beautifully coiffed as his mount, his full, dark beard well-shaped, his long hair a good deal cleaner than that of his companions. But these cosmetic polishes aside, he was in no better shape than his fellow riders. His eyes were sunk deep into his skull and his body, for all the upright position he held in his saddle, was full of little tics, as though he were uncomfortable in his

335

own skin. In his left hand he held the reins of his horse. His right rested on the golden pommel of his sword, ready to unsheathe the blade in a heartbeat.

Todd had never played in a medieval movie – his face was far too contemporary, and his acting skills too rudimentary for an audience to believe him as anything but a modern man. But he'd seen his share of epics: the kind Heston had made in the fifties and early sixties: all rhetoric and pose-striking. The men approaching them looked nothing like the well-fed heroes of those epics. Their bodies were wizened, their looks so intense they looked more like escaped lunatics than hunters.

Goga raised his right hand (which was missing two fingers) and with a silent gesture slowed the advance of the party. The men – sensing their leader's apprehension – proceeded to scan the landscape around them, looking for some sign of their enemy, whoever, or whatever, it was.

Todd stayed very still, just as Katya had instructed. Had these men been gun-slingers, he would have described them as trigger-happy. Plainly they were nervous and exhausted; not men to meddle with.

But even as he lay there, barely daring to breathe, he felt Katya reach down between his legs and proceed to stroke his balls. He gave her an astonished look, which she returned with a mischievous little smile. She stroked him back to full erection, and then subtly manoeuvred her body so that he was once again fully sheathed by her. The sensation felt even more extraordinary than it had a few minutes before. Without seeming to move her hips she contrived to make waves of motion move up and down her channel, massaging him.

All the while, the horsemen approached, and the closer they came the more desperate they looked. These were men who apparently lived in a constant state of fear, to judge by their expressions. One of the Duke's followers, the oldest and the most scarred, mumbled a prayer to himself as he rode, and in his hand he clutched a plain wooden cross, which more than once he kissed, for comfort's sake.

Todd was somewhere between ecstasy and panic. He didn't dare move, even if he'd wanted to. Katya, meanwhile was free to play havoc with his nerve-endings. He didn't move his hips; he didn't need to. She had all the moves. Her internal manipulations were becoming more elaborate all the time, driving him closer and closer to losing control.

Todd had always been a noisy lover; sometimes embarrassingly so. (A memorable night with a girlfriend in a suite at the Chateau Marmont had been brought to a premature halt when the manager had called up his room to regretfully report that the guests in an adjacent suite couldn't sleep for all his moans.) Now the best he could do was bite his lip until he tasted blood, and will himself not to let a sound escape him.

The horsemen were so close now that he did not dare move his head to look at them. But he could just see them from the corner of his eye.

The Duke gave an order, in Romanian: *'Stai! N-auzi ceva?'*

The men brought their horses to a halt, the Duke no more than four yards from where Todd and Katya lay on the ground. Had it not been for the fact that the eclipse rendered the light here so deceptive, the pair would surely have been seen, and dispatched: a single blade skewering them both in an instant. But as far as Todd's limited vision could tell, the men were looking further afield for their quarry, scanning the distant landscape rather than the ground yards from their horses' hooves.

There was another exclamation from the Duke, and this time a response from one of his men. Todd had the impression that they were listening for something. He listened along with them. What could he hear? Nothing out of the ordinary. The cry of birds, wheeling overhead; the coarse breathing and snorting of the horses; the slap

337

of the reins against their massive necks. And closer by, the breathing of the woman beneath him; and – a smaller sound still – the rhythmical click of a beetle as it made its clockwork way over the small stones close to his hand. In his mind's eye all of this around the tender place where their bodies met: the bird and the horse and the stones and the beetle, orbiting his pleasure.

He saw her smile beneath him, and with the tiniest contraction of her vulva she brought him to the point of no return. There was a flash of brightness in his head, which momentarily washed everything out. She came back out of the fog to meet him with her eyes half-closed, her pupils so full beneath them that they seemed to edge out the whites. Then her lids fluttered closed completely and he started to spurt into her. He could not have stopped crying out if his life had depended on it. No; it did. And still he let out a sob of relief –

There was a shout. The Duke was issuing an order. It made no sense to Todd, but he looked up anyway, as his body continued its spastic motion, emptying itself into her. The man who'd dismounted was now striding towards them, unleashing his sword.

The Duke spoke again:

'Cine sunt aceşti oameni?'

He obviously wanted to know who the hell these people were, because by way of reply there were shrugs from the other men. The last spasm passed through Todd's body, and with it went the idiot sense of his own inviolability. The bliss was gone. He was empty, and mortal again.

The man with the sword put his boot into Todd's side. It was a hard kick, and threw him off Katya. He rolled over in the earth, which got a laugh from the youngest of the men, seeing the lovers wetly parted thus.

The Duke was issuing further orders, and in response another of the riders dismounted, his sword drawn. Todd spat out a mouthful of earth, and made an attempt to push his rapidly wilting erection back into his pants before it became a target. Katya was still lying on the ground (though she too had managed to cover her nakedness); the first of the men who'd dismounted was standing over her, his sword dropped so that its point hung no more than two or three inches above her pale, slender neck.

The first word out of Todd's mouth was: *'Please . . .'*

The nobleman was looking at him with a strange expression on his face: part amusement, part suspicion.

'I don't know if you can understand me,' Todd said to him. 'But we meant no harm.'

He glanced down at Katya, who was staring up at the blade.

'He doesn't know what you're saying,' she said. 'Let me try.' She spoke now in the language of the lord. *'Doamne, eu şi prietenul meu suntem vizitatori prin locurile astea. N-am stiut că este proprietatea domniei tale.'*

Todd looked and listened, wondering what the hell she was saying. But her explanation, whatever it was, didn't seem to be making any great change in their circumstances. The sword was still at her throat, while the second horseman was now within two or three yards of Todd, waving his own blade around in a highly menacing fashion.

Todd glanced up at the Duke again. The trace of amusement Todd had thought he'd seen there had gone. There was only suspicion now. It crossed Todd's mind that perhaps it had been an error for Katya to speak in the man's tongue; that perhaps she'd only deepened his belief that these lovers were more than over-heated trespassers.

He felt a prick in the middle of his chest. The cold point of the sword was pressed into his skin. A small pool of blood was already coming from the spot, spreading through the weave of his shirt.

Katya had stopped talking for a moment – Todd thought perhaps she realized she was doing more harm than good

– but now she began again, making whatever pleas she could.

The man on the braided horse raised his hand.

'*Liniste,*' he said.

He'd obviously told her to shut the hell up, because that was exactly what she did.

There was a sound on the wind; and it instantly had all of the nobleman's attention. Somewhere not so far away a baby was crying: a mournful wail of a sound, that – though it was surely human – reminded Todd of the noise the coyotes would make some nights in the Canyon.

After a few moments of listening, the Duke let out a stream of orders: '*Lăsaţi-i! Pe cai! Ăla-i copilul!*'

The two men who'd been threatening Katya and Todd sheathed their swords and returned to their mounts. The baby's cry seemed to falter for a moment, and Todd feared it would fade completely and the swordsmen would return to their threats, but then the infant seemed to find a new seam of grief to mine, and the wail rose up again, more plaintive than ever.

The men were exchanging more urgent words; and pointing in the direction from which the sound was coming.

'*Este acolo! Grăbiţi-vă!*'

'*In padure! Copilul este in padure!*'

Katya and Todd were summarily forgotten. The horsemen were by now all re-mounted, and the Duke was already galloping away, leaving his weary company to follow in his dust.

Todd felt a curious sense of betrayal; the kind felt when a story takes an unanticipated turn. That he should have come into this half-eclipsed world and been made to bleed at the point of a sword seemed absolutely apt. That the man who'd threatened him had ridden away to pursue a crying baby did not.

'What the *hell* is going on?' he said as he bent to help Katya up off the ground.

'They heard Qwaftzefoni, the Devil's child,' she said.

'Who?'

She looked back in the direction of the riders. They were already halfway to the line of densely packed trees from which the pitiful summons had seemed to come, receding into the quarter-light as though being steadily erased.

'It's a long story,' she said. 'I heard it first when I was a child . . . and it used to frighten me . . .'

'Yes?' he said.

'Oh yes.'

'Well,' Todd said, a little impatiently, 'are you going to tell me?'

'I don't know if it'll frighten you.'

He wiped the blood from the middle of his chest with the heel of his hand. There was a deep nick in his chest, which instantly welled with blood again.

'Tell me anyway,' he said.

2

Though it had been Zeffer who'd offered the explanation of what lay down in the guts of the house, Tammy opened the conversation with a question that had been niggling at her since she'd first come into this place. She returned to the kitchen table, where she'd been eating her cherry pie, sat down and said: 'What are you afraid of?'

'I told you twice, three times: I shouldn't be in here. She'll be angry.'

'That doesn't answer the question. Katya's just a woman, for God's sake. Let her be angry!'

'You don't know what she can be like.'

'Why don't you try telling me? Then maybe I'll understand.'

'Tell you,' he said flatly, as though the request was impossible. 'How can I tell you what this place has seen? What I was? What *she* was?'

'Try.'

'I don't know how,' he said, his voice getting weaker, syllable on syllable, until she seemed sure it would crack and break. He sat down at the table opposite her, but he said nothing.

'All right,' Tammy said. 'Let me give you a hand.' She thought for a moment. Then she said: 'Start with the house. Tell me why it was built. Why you're in it. Why *she's* in it.'

'Back then we did everything together.'

'Who is she?'

'I'll tell you who she *was*: she was Katya Lupi, a great star. One of the greatest, some would once have said. And in its day this house was one of the most famous houses in Los Angeles. One of the great dream palaces.'

'And the rest of the Canyon is hers too?'

'Oh yes, it's all hers. *Coldheart Canyon.* That's what they called it. She had a reputation, you see, for being a chilly bitch.' He smiled, though there was more rue in the expression than humour. 'It was deserved.'

'And the *things* out there?'

'Which things?'

'Which things?' Tammy said, a little impatiently. 'The freaks. The things that attacked me.'

'Those? Those are the children of the dead.'

'You say these things so casually. *The children of the dead.* Believe it or not, the dead don't have kids in Sacramento. They just rot away quietly.'

'Well it's different here.'

'Willem, I don't care how different it is: *the dead can't have children.*'

'You saw them. Believe your eyes.'

Tammy shook her head. Not in disbelief, rather in frustration. How could it be that the rules of the world worked one way in one place, and so very differently in another?

'The truth is: I don't know,' Zeffer said, answering her unspoken question. 'Over the years the ghosts have mated with the animals, and the results are those *things*. Maybe the dead are closer to the condition of animals. I don't know. I only know it's real. I've seen them. You've seen them. They're hybrids. Sometimes there's a kind of beauty in them. But mostly . . . ugly as sin.'

'All right. So I buy the hybrids. But why here? Is it *her*?'

'In a roundabout way, I suppose . . .' He mused for a moment, and then – apparently with great effort, as though

343

since they'd come into the house a lifetime of suffering had caught up with him – he got to his feet. He went to the sink, and turned on the faucet, running the water hard. Then, cupping his hand, he took some up to his lips and drank noisily. This done, he turned off the faucet and looked over his shoulder at her.

'I know in my heart you deserve to know everything, after all you've been through. You've earned the truth.' He turned fully to her. 'But before I tell you, let me say I'm not sure I understand any of this much more than you do.'

'Well I understand nothing,' Tammy said.

He nodded. 'Well, then. How do I start this? Ah. Yes. Romania.' He put his hand up to his face, and wiped some water off his lower lip. 'Katya was born Katya Lupescu in Romania. A tiny village called Ravbac. And in the summer of 1920, just after we'd built this house, I went back with her to her homeland, because her mother was sick and was not expected to live more than another year.

'She'd been brought up in utter poverty. Abuse and poverty. But now she was a great star, coming home, and it was extraordinary really, to see how she had transformed herself. From these beginnings to the woman she'd become.

'Anyway, there was a fortress close to the village where Katya was born, and it was run by the Order of St Teodor, who made it their business to protect the place. When we arrived, Katya and myself had both been given a tour, but she wasn't very interested in the old fortress and priests with halitosis. Neither was I, frankly, but I wanted to leave her with her family to talk over old times, so I went back to the Goga Fortress a second day. The monk who took me round made it clear that the Order had fallen on hard times, and the brothers needed to sell off what they could. Tapestries, chairs, tables: it was all up for sale.

'Frankly, I didn't care for much of it, and I was about to leave.

344

'Then he said: *let me show you something special, really special*. And I thought: what the hell? Ten more minutes. And he took me down several flights of stairs into a room the likes of which I'd never seen before.'

'What was in there?'

'It was decorated with *tiles* – thousands of tiles – and they were all painted, so when you walked into the room it was almost as though – no; *it was as though* you were walking into another world.' He paused, contemplating the memory of this; awed by it still, after all these years.

'What kind of a world?' Tammy asked him.

'A world that was both very real and completely invented. It had space for sky and sea and birds and rabbits. But it also had a little pinch of Hell in the mix, just to make things more interesting for the men who lived in that world.'

'What men?'

'Well, one man in particular. His name was Duke Goga. And he was there in the walls, on a hunt that would last until the end of time.'

'The man on the horse,' Katya said, 'was the Duke.'

'I got that,' Todd said.

'He lived a long time ago. I'm not sure of *exactly* when. When you're a little child you don't listen to those kind of details. It's the story you remember. And the story was this:

'One day in autumn the Duke went out hunting, which he did all the time – it was his favourite thing to do – and he saw what he thought was a goat, trapped in a briar-thicket. So he got off his horse, telling his men that he wanted to kill this animal himself. He hated goats, having been attacked by one and badly hurt as a baby. He still had scars on his face from that attack, and they ached in the cold weather, all of which served to keep his hatred of goats alive. Perhaps it was a petty thing, this hatred; but sometimes little things can be the unmaking of us. There's

345

no doubt that Goga would not have pursued his goat as far as he did had he not been injured as a child. And then – to make matters worse – as he approached the animal history virtually repeated itself. The animal reared up, striking the Duke with its black hoof and cracking his nose. The goat then ran off.

'Goga was furious, beside himself with fury! To have been mistreated by a goat twice! He got straight back on his horse, blood pouring from his broken nose, and went after the animal, riding hard through the forest to catch up with it. His entourage went with him, because they were bound to follow the Duke wherever he went. But they were beginning to suspect that there was something strange about where they were headed and that it would be better for them all if they just turned round and rode back to the Fortress.'

'But Goga wouldn't do that?'

'Of course not. He was determined to chase down the animal that had struck him. He wanted revenge on the thing. He wanted to stick his sword through it, and cut out its heart and eat it raw. That was the kind of rage he was in.

'So he kept riding. And his men, out of loyalty, kept following, further and further from the Fortress and the paths they knew, into the depths of the forest. Steadily even the Duke began to realize that what his men were whispering was right: there were creatures here, lurking about, the likes of which God had not made. He could see things between the trees that didn't belong in any of the bestiaries he had in the Fortress. Strange, ungodly creatures.'

As Katya told her story, Todd glanced at the dark mass of trees into which Goga and his men had just ridden. Was that the Deep Wood she had just described? Surely it was. The same horsemen. The same trees. In other words, he was standing in the middle of Katya's story.

'So . . . the Duke kept riding, and riding, driving his poor horse as he followed the leaping goat deeper and deeper into the forest, until they were in a place where they were certain no human being had ever ventured before. By now, all the men, even the most loyal, the bravest of them, were begging the Duke to let them turn back. The air was bitter and sulphurous, and in the ground beneath the horses' hooves the men could hear the sound of people sobbing, as though living souls had been buried alive in the black, smoking earth.

'But the Duke would not be moved from his ambition. *"What kind of hunters do you call yourselves,"* he said to his men, *"If you won't go after a goat? Where's your faith in God? There's no danger to us here, if our hearts are pure."*

'So on they went, the men quietly offering up prayers for the safety of their souls as they rode.

'And eventually, after a long chase, their quarry came in sight again. The goat was standing in a grove of trees so old they had been planted before the Flood, in the tangled roots of which grew mushrooms that gave off the smell of dead flesh. The Duke got off his horse, drew his sword and approached the goat.

'*"Whatever thing you are,"* he said to the animal, *"breathe your last."*'

'Nice line,' Todd remarked.

'The animal reared up, as though it was going to strike the Duke with its hoof again, but Goga didn't give it the opportunity. He quickly drove his sword up into the belly of the animal.

'As soon as it felt the sword entering its flesh the goat opened its mouth and let out a pitiful wail . . .'

Katya paused here, watching Todd, waiting for him to put the pieces together.

'Oh Christ,' he said. 'Like a baby?'

'Exactly like a baby. And hearing this pitiful human sound escaping the animal, Goga knew something unholy

347

was in the air. Have you ever seen an animal slaughtered?'

'No.'

'Well there's a lot of blood. A lot more than you think there's going to be.'

'It was like that now?'

'Yes. The goat was thrashing around in a pool of red, its back legs kicking up the wet earth, so that it spattered Goga and his men. And as it did so, it started to *change*.'

'Into what?'

Katya smiled the smile of a storyteller who had her audience hooked by some unexpected change of direction.

'Into a little child,' she said. 'A boy, a naked little boy, with a nub of a tail and yellow eyes and goat's ears. So now the Duke is looking down at this goat-boy, twitching in the mud made of earth and blood, and the superstitious terror which his men had felt finally seizes hold of him too. He starts to speak a prayer.

' "Tătal Nostru care ne eşti în Ceruri, sfinţeasca-se numele Tău. Fie Impărătia Ta, facă-se voia Ta, precum în cer aşa si pe pământ." '

Todd listened to the unfamiliar words, knowing in the cadence that what Katya was reciting was not just *any* prayer; it was the Lord's Prayer.

' "Pâinea noastră cea de toate zilele dăne-o nouă azi si ne iartă nouă greselile noaştre." '

He scanned the landscape as he heard the prayer repeated; nothing had changed since he'd first set eyes on the place. The light of the eclipse held everything in suspension: the trees, the ships, the lynchers at their tree.

The rush of pleasure he'd experienced when he first arrived had diminished somewhere in the midst of Katya's tale-telling. In its place there was now a profound unease. He wanted to stop her telling her story, but what reason could he give that didn't sound cowardly?

So she continued.

'The Duke retreated, leaving his sword stuck deep in the body of the goat-boy. He intended to climb back onto his horse and ride away, but his steed had already bolted in terror. He called to one of his men to dismount, so that he might have the man's horse, but before the fellow could obey the rock beneath their feet began to shake violently, and a great chasm opened up in the ground in front of them.

'The men knew what they were witnessing. This was the very mouth of Hell, gaping in the earth beneath their feet. It was thirty, forty feet wide, and the roots of those ancient trees lined it like the veins of a skinned body. Smoke rose up out of the maw, stinking of every foul thing imaginable, and a good deal that was not. It was such a bitter stench that the Duke and his men began to weep like children.

'Half-blinded by his own tears, and without a horse, Goga had no choice but to stay where he was, on the lip of Hell's Mouth, close to where his victim lay. He tore his gloves from his hands and did his best to clear the tears from his eyes.

'As he did so he saw somebody coming up out of the earth. It was a woman, he saw; with hair so long it trailed the ground fully six feet behind her. She was naked, except for a necklace of white fleas with eyes that burned like fires in their tiny heads. Thousands of them, moving back and forth around the woman's neck and up over her face, busy about the business of prettifying her.

'She was not looking at the Duke. Her black-red eyes, which had neither lashes nor brows, were on the goat-boy. In the time it had taken for the mouth of Hell to open, the last of the boy's life had poured out of him. Now the child's corpse lay still in the wet earth.

'"You killed my child," the woman said as she emerged from the infernal mouth. "My beautiful Qwaftzefoni. Look at him. Barely a boy. He was perfect. He was my joy. How could you do such a heartless thing?"

'At that moment one of the horsemen behind the Duke attempted to make an escape, spurring his horse. But the goat-boy's mother raised her hand and at her instruction a gust of wind came up out of the depths of Hell, so strong that it drew her hair around her and forward, like a thousand filament fingers pointing towards the escaping man. He didn't get very far. The wind she'd summoned was filled with barbs; like the vicious seedlings of ten thousand flowers. They spiralled as they flew, and they caught the Duke's man in a whirling of tiny hooks. Blinded by the assault, the man toppled from his horse, and attempted to outrun the barbs. But they were fastened onto him, and their motion continued, circling his body, so that the man's flesh was unravelled like a ball of red twine. He screamed as the first circling took off his skin, and redoubled his shrieks when a second cloud of barbs caught his naked muscle, and repeated the terrible cycle. Having drawn off a length of the man's tissue, they described a descending spiral around him, leaving the victim clear for a third and fourth assault. His bone was showing now; his screams had ceased. He dropped to his knees and fell forward in his own shreddings, dead.

'Overhead carrion birds circled, ready to gorge themselves as soon as the body was abandoned.

'"This man is the lucky one amongst you," the woman said to the Duke. "He has escaped lightly. The rest of you will suffer long and hard for what you have done today."

'She looked down at the goat-boy's corpse, her hair crawling around her heels to fondly touch the body of the child.

'The Duke fell to his knees, knotting his hands together to make his plea. "Lady," he said to her, in his native tongue. "This was an accident. I believed the boy to be an animal. He was running from me in the form of a goat."

'"That is his father's chosen form, on certain nights," the woman replied. Goga knew, of course, what was signified

350

by this. Only the Devil himself took the form of a goat. The woman was telling him that she was Lilith, the Devil's wife, and that the child he had killed was the Devil's own offspring. To say this was not good news was an understatement. The Duke concealed his terror as best he could, but it was terror he felt. To be standing on the lip of Hell, accused of the crime before him, was a terrifying prospect. His soul would be forfeit, he feared. All he could do was repeat what he'd said: "I took the boy to be a goat. This was a grievous error on my part, and I regret it with all my heart –"

'The woman raised her hand to silence him.

'"My husband has seventy-seven children by me. Qwaft-zefoni was his favourite. What am I supposed to tell him when he calls for his beloved boy, and the child does not come as he used to?"

'The Duke had barely any spittle in his throat. But he used what little he had to reply. "I don't know what you will say."

'"You know who my husband is, don't you? And don't insult me by pretending innocence."

'"I think he is the Devil, ma'am," the Duke Goga replied.

'"That he is," the woman said. "And I am Lilith, his first wife. So now, what do you think your life is worth?"

'Goga mused on this for a moment. Then he said: "Christ save my soul. I fear my life is worth nothing."

'So,' said Zeffer, 'Goga's Hunt was painted on every wall of this room. Not just the walls. The ceiling, too. And the floor. Every inch of the place was covered with the genius of painter and tile-maker. It was astonishing. And I thought –'

'You'd give this astonishing thing to the woman you idolized.'

'Yes. That's exactly what I thought. After all, it was utterly unique. Something strange and wonderful. But

351

that wasn't the only reason I wanted to buy it, now I look back. The place had a power over me. I felt stronger when I was in that room. I felt more alive. It was a trick, of course. The room wanted me to liberate it –'

'How can a room want anything?' Tammy said. 'It's just four walls.'

'Believe me, this was no ordinary room,' Zeffer said. He lowered his voice, as though the house itself might be listening to him. 'It was commissioned, I believe, by a woman known as the Lady Lilith. The Devil's wife.'

This was a different order of information entirely, and it left Tammy speechless. In her experience so far, she'd found the Canyon a repository of grotesqueries, no doubt; but they'd all been derived from the human, however muddied the route. But the Devil? That was another story; deeper than anything she'd encountered so far. And yet perhaps his presence or the echo of his presence, was not so inappropriate. Wasn't he sometimes called the Father of Lies? If he and his works belonged anywhere, Hollywood was probably as good a place as any.

'Did you have any idea what you were buying?' she said to Zeffer.

'I had a very vague notion, but I didn't really believe it. Father Sandru had talked about a woman who'd occupied the Fortress for several years while the room was made.'

'And you think this woman was Lilith?'

'I believe it was,' Zeffer said. 'She made a place to trap the Duke in, you see.'

'No, I *don't* see.'

'The Duke had killed her beloved child. She wanted revenge, and she wanted it to be a long, agonizing revenge.

'But it had been an accident – an honest error on the Duke's part – and she knew the law would not allow her to take the soul of a man who killed her child.'

'Why would she care about the law?'

'It wasn't our *human* law she cared about. It was God's

352

law, which governs Earth, Heaven and Hell. She knew that if she was going to make the Duke and his men suffer as she wished to make them suffer, she would have to find some secret place, where God would not think to look. A world within a world, where the Duke would have to hunt forever, and never be allowed to rest . . .'

Now Tammy began to understand.

'The room,' she murmured.

'Was her solution. And if you think about it, it's a piece of genius. She moved into the Fortress, claiming that she was a distant cousin of the missing Duke –'

'And where was he?'

'Anybody's guess. Maybe she held him in his own dungeons, until the hunting grounds were ready for him.

'Then she brought tile-makers from all over Europe – Dutch, Portuguese, Belgians, even a few Englishmen – and painters, again, from every place of excellence – and they worked for six months, night and day, to create what awaits you downstairs. It would look like the Duke's hunting grounds – at least superficially. There would be forests and rivers and, somewhere at the horizon, there'd be the sea. But she would play God in this world. She'd put creatures into it that she had conjured up from her own personal menagerie: monsters that the painters in her employ would render with meticulous care. And then she'd take the souls of the Duke and his men – still living, so that she remained within the law – and she'd put them into the work, so that it would be a prison for them. There they would ride under a permanent eclipse, in a constant state of terror, barely daring to sleep for fear one of her terrible beasts would take them. Of course that's not all that's on the walls down there. Her influence invaded the minds of the men who worked for her, and every filthy, forbidden thing they'd ever dreamed of setting down they were given the freedom to create.

'Nothing was taboo. They took their own little revenges

as they painted: particularly on women. Some of the things they painted still shock me after all these years.'

'Are you certain all of this is true?'

'No. It's mostly theory. I pieced it together from what I researched. Certainly Duke Goga and several of his men went missing during an eclipse. The body of one of them was found stripped of its skin. That's also documented. The rest of the party were never found. The Duke had lost his wife and children to the plague so there was no natural successor. He had three brothers, however, and – again, this is a matter of documented history – they gathered the following September, almost five months to the day after the Duke's disappearance, to divide their elder brother's spoils. It was a mistake to do so. That was the night the Lady Lilith took occupancy of the Goga Fortress.'

'She killed them?'

'No. They all left of their own free will, saying they wanted no part of owning the Fortress or the land, but were giving it over to this mysterious cousin, in their brother's name. They signed a document to that effect, and left. All three were dead within a year, by their own hand.'

'And nobody was suspicious?'

'I'm sure a lot of people were suspicious. But Lilith – or whoever she was – now occupied the Fortress. She had money, and apparently she was quite liberal with it. Local merchants got rich, local dignitaries were rather charmed by her, if the reports are to be believed –'

'Where did you find all these reports?'

'I bought most of the paperwork relating to the Fortress from the Fathers. They didn't want it. I doubt they even knew what most of it was. And to tell the truth a lot of it was rather dull. The price of pigs' carcasses; the cost of having a roof made rain-proof . . . the usual domestic business.'

'So Lilith was quite the little house-maker?'

354

'I think she was. Indeed I believe she intended to have the Fortress as a place she could call her own. Somewhere her husband wouldn't come; *couldn't* come, perhaps. I found a draft of a letter which I believe she wrote, to *him* –'

'To the Devil?' Tammy replied, scarcely believing she was giving the idea the least credence.

'To her husband,' Zeffer replied obliquely, 'whoever he was.' He tapped his pocket. 'I have it, here. You want to hear it?'

'Is it in English?'

'No. In Latin.' He reached into his jacket and took out a piece of much-folded paper. It was mottled with age. 'Take a look for yourself,' he said.

'I don't read Latin.'

'Look anyway. Just to say you once held a letter written by the Devil's wife. Go on, take it. It won't bite.'

Tammy reached out and took the paper from Zeffer's hand. None of this was proof, of course. But it was more than a simple fabrication, that much was clear. And hadn't she seen enough in her time in the Canyon to be certain that whatever *was* at work here was nothing she could explain by the rules she'd been taught in school?

She opened the letter. The hand it had been written in was exquisite; the ink, though it had faded somewhat, still kept an uncanny lustre, as though there were motes of mother-of-pearl in it. She scanned it, all the way down to the immaculate and elaborate *Lilith* that decorated the bottom portion of the page.

'So,' she said, handing it back, her fingers trembling slightly. 'What does it say?'

'Do you really want to know?'

'Yes.'

Zeffer began translating it without looking at the words. Plainly he had the contents by heart.

'*Husband*, she writes, *I am finding myself at ease in the*

355

Fortress Goga, and I believe will remain here until our son is found –'

'So she didn't tell him?'

'Apparently not.' Zeffer scanned the page briefly. 'She talks a little about the work she's doing on the Fortress . . . it's all very matter-of-fact . . . then she says: *Do not come, husband, for you will find no welcome in my bed. If there is some peace to be made between us I cannot imagine it being soon, given your violations of your oath. I do not believe you have loved me in many years, and would prefer you did not insult me by pretending otherwise.'*

'Huh.'

Whatever the source of the letter, its sentiments were easily understood. Tammy herself might have penned such a letter – in a simpler style, perhaps; and a little more viciously – on more than one occasion. God knows, Arnie had violated his own vows to her several times, shamelessly.

Zeffer folded the letter up. 'So, you can make what you want of all this. Personally I think it's the real thing. I believe this woman *was* Lilith, and that she stayed in the Fortress to work on her revenge, where neither God nor her husband would come and bother her. Certainly somebody created that room, and it was somebody who had powers that go far beyond anything we understand.'

'What happened when she was finished?' Tammy asked.

'She packed up and disappeared. Got bored perhaps. Went back to her husband. Or found a lover of her own. The point is, she left the Fortress with the room still intact. And with Goga and his men still in it.'

'And that's what you bought?'

'That's what I bought. Of course it took a little time to realize it, but I purchased a little piece of Hell's own handiwork. And let me tell you – to make light of all this for a moment – it was Hell to move. There were thirty three thousand, two hundred and sixty-eight tiles. They all had

356

to be removed, cleaned, numbered, packed away, shipped and then put up again in exactly the same order that they'd been assembled in. I timed it so that the work could be done while Katya was off on a world tour, publicizing one of her pictures.'

'It must have driven you half crazy . . .'

'I kept thinking about how much pleasure Katya would derive from the room when it was finished. I was oblivious to the human cost. I just wanted Katya to be astonished; and then, to look at me – who'd given her this gift – with new eyes. I wanted her to be so grateful, so happy, she'd fling herself into my arms and say *I'll marry you*. That's what I wanted.'

'But that's not the way it turned out?'

'No, of course not.'

'What happened? Did she dislike the room?'

'No, she understood the room from the beginning, and the room understood her. She started to take people down there, to show the place off. Her special friends. The ones who were obsessed with her. And there were plenty of those. Men and women both. They'd disappear down there for a few hours –'

'These were people she was having sex with?'

'Yes.'

'You said both men and women?'

'Preferably together. That's what she liked best. A little of both.'

'And did everybody know?'

'About her tastes? Of course. Nobody cared. It was rather chic at the time. For women anyway. The nancy-boys like Navarro and Valentino, they had to cover it up. But Katya didn't care what people thought. Especially once she had the room.'

'It changed her?'

'It changed everyone who went into it, myself included. It changed our flesh. It changed our spirits.'

'How?'

'All you have to do is look at me to see how I changed. I was born in 1877. But I don't look it. That's because of the room. It has energies, you see, painted into the tiles. I believe it's Lilith's magic, in the tiles. She used her infernal skills to lock the Duke and his men and all those animals into the illusion: that's strong magic. The monks knew that. But they had the good sense to keep their distance from the place.'

'So did everyone who went down there stay young?'

'Oh no. By no means. It affected everyone a little differently. Some people simply couldn't take it. They went in for a minute, and they were out again in a heartbeat.'

'Why?'

'It's the Devil's Country, Tammy. Believe me, it is.'

Tammy shook her head, not knowing what to believe. 'So some people left, because they thought the Devil was in there?'

'That's right. But most people felt some extra burst of energy when they went in the room. Maybe they felt a little younger, a little stronger, a little more beautiful.'

'And what was the price of it all?'

'*Good question*,' he said. 'The fact is, everyone's paid a different price. Some people went crazy, because of what they saw in there. A few committed suicide. Most . . . went on living, feeling a little better about themselves. For a while at least. Then the effect would wear off, and they'd need to come back for another fix . . .

'I knew a number of opium addicts in my life. One of them was a Russian designer, Anatole Vasilinsky. Ever heard of him?' Tammy shook her head. 'No real reason why you should. He worked for the Ballet Russe, under Diaghilev. A brilliant man. But completely enslaved to "The Poppy" as he used to call it. He came to the house, only once, and of course Katya showed him the room. I remember the look on his face when he came out. He looked like a man who'd just seen his own death. He was stricken; clammy-white, shaking. "I must never come here again," he said. "I don't have enough room in my life for two addictions. It would be the death of me."

'That's what the room was, of course: an addiction. It addicted the flesh, by making you feel stronger, sleeker. It addicted the spirit, by giving you visions so vivid they were more real than real. And it addicted the soul, because you didn't want any other kind of comfort, once you'd been in the room. Prayer was no use to you, laughter was no use to you, friends, ideals, ambitions . . . they all seemed inconsequential in that perpetual twilight. When you were *here*, you thought all the time about being *there*.'

Again Tammy shook her head. There was so much here to try and make sense of. Her mind was reeling.

'Do you see now why you must leave, and forget about Todd? He's seen the room. That's where she took him.'

'Are you sure?'

'He's down there right now,' Zeffer said. 'I guarantee it. Where else would she take him?'

Tammy got up from the table. The food had done her good. Though she still felt a little light-headed, she was considerably stronger.

'There's nothing heroic about sacrificing yourself for him,' Zeffer pointed out. 'He wouldn't do it for you.'

'I know that.'

Zeffer followed her to the kitchen door. 'So don't. Leave, while you can. Tammy, I beg you. *Leave*. I'll lead you out of the Canyon and you can go home.'

'Home,' Tammy said. The word, the idea, seemed hollow, valueless. There was no home for her after this. Or if there was, it wasn't the one she'd had. Arnie, the little house in Sacramento. How could she even think of going back to that?

'I have to find Todd,' she said. 'That's what I came here to do.'

Without waiting for Zeffer to lead her or escort her, she left the kitchen and went to the top of the stairs. He called after her. Another attempt at persuasion, no doubt; or some more fancy story-telling. But she ignored him this time, and started down the stairs.

3

Katya had a little more of her story still to tell.

'"My life is worth nothing," the Duke had told the Devil's wife. He, who had led armies, and triumphed in his crusades against the infidel; now found his life was at an end. And why? Because he chased and killed what he took to be a goat?

'"It was an accident!" he said, his fury at the injustice of this suddenly getting the better of him. "I demand to be seen by some higher judge than you."

'"There is only one higher," Lilith replied. "And that's my husband."

'The Duke met her cold gaze, the profundity of his terror paradoxically making him brave.

'"There is a God in Heaven," he said.

'"Is there now?" said Lilith. "Are you certain? I saw him only once, the day He made me. Since then He has never shown his face. This is the Devil's Country, Goga. My Lord Lucifer rules here. Or in his absence, me. I doubt your God will stretch out his hand to save your soul."

'"Then I shall ride out of here," the Duke replied.

'"You saw what happened to your comrade. I'll do the same to you, before you reach your horse. I'll have you wailing like a baby at my feet."

'Goga wasn't a stupid man. He knew there was no use in contradicting the woman. He'd already seen one of his men horribly slaughtered by her. He would surely follow if he attempted to escape. All he could do was throw himself upon Lilith's mercy.

'He went down on his knees, and composing himself as best he could, he addressed her:

'"Please, gentle lady, listen to me."

'"I'm listening."

'"I have lost children of my own, all six of them dead by the plague. And my wife the same way. I know the pain you are suffering, and I'm sick that I was its cause. But what's done is done. I made a mistake, that I bitterly regret. But how can I take it back? Had I known I was on your husband's land I would not even have hunted here."

'Lilith looked at him for a long while, assessing the worth of his appeal.

'"Well, hereafter, my lord," she said finally, "it is my pleasure that you and your men will hunt here *always*."

'Another bitter breath came up out of Hell to accompany these words. The woman's long hair rose up around her body, a few of its strands grazing Goga's upturned face.

'"Get back on your horses, hunters," Lilith said. "Return to your hunt. There are boar in the thicket, waiting to be driven out. There are birds in the trees, ready to be shot while they sing. Kill them at will, as it pleases you to do so. There will be no charge for your sport."

'The Duke was astonished to hear this mild invitation, after all that had just taken place, and thinking perhaps his plea for clemency had carried some weight with Lilith, he very slowly got to his feet, thanking her.

'"It's most kind of you," he said, "to invite me to hunt. And perhaps another day I will come back here and accept your invitation. But today my heart is heavy –"

'"As well it might be," the woman replied.

'"So I think instead I will return to the Fortress and –"

'"*No*," she said, raising her hand. "You will not return to the Fortress. *You will hunt*."

'"I could not, madam. Really, I could not."

'"Sir," she replied, with a little inclination of her head. "You misunderstood me. *You have no choice*. You will hunt, and you will go on hunting, until you find my son a second time, and bring him back to me."

'"I don't understand."

'"*A second time.*"

'She pointed to the corpse of the goat-child, which lay in its cooling blood. Her hair drifted over the sprawled cadaver, lightly touching the boy's chest and stomach and private parts. Much to the Duke's astonishment the child responded to his mother's caresses. As the hair touched his chest his lungs drew a little breath, and his penis – which was disproportionately large for one his age – grew steely.

'"Take your sword out of him," Lilith instructed the Duke.

'But the Duke was too terrified at this scene of infernal resurrection to go near the boy. He kept his distance, filling his breeches in fear.

'"You men are all the same!" Lilith said contemptuously. "You find it easy enough to drive the sword *in*, but when it comes to taking it *out* you can't bring yourself to do it."

'She stepped into the puddle of her son's blood, and reached to take hold of the sword. The boy's eyes flickered open as he felt his mother's hand upon the pommel. Then he lifted his hands and caught hold of the blade with his bare palms, almost as though he were attempting to keep her from extracting it. Still she pulled, and it slowly came out of him.

'"Slowly, Mama," the goat-boy said, his tone almost lascivious. "It hurts mightily."

'"Does it, child?" Lilith said, twisting the blade in the wound as though to perversely increase her child's distress. He threw back his head, still looking at her from the bottom of his eyes, his lips drawn back from his little, pointed teeth.

"And this?" she said, turning the blade the other way. "Does this bring you agony?"

'"Yes, Mama!"

'She twisted it the other way. "And this?"

'Finally, it was too much for the child. He let out a hissing sound, and spat from his erection several spouts of semen. Its sharp stink made the Duke's eyes sting.

'Lilith waited until the boy had finished ejaculating, then she drew out the sword. The goat-boy sank back on the wet earth, with a look of satisfaction on his face.

'"Thank you, Mama," he said, as though well pleasured by what had just happened.

'The wound on his belly was already closing up, the Duke saw. It was as though it were being knitted by agile and invisible fingers. So too the wounds on his hands, incurred when he had seized the blade. In a matter of perhaps half a minute the goat-boy was whole again.'

'So if the child wasn't dead,' Todd said, 'why was the Duke guilty of murdering him?'

Katya shook her head. 'He'd committed the crime. The fact that the boy was an immortal was academic. He'd murdered the child, and had to be punished for it.'

Todd's gaze went again to the trees where the Duke and his men had disappeared, picturing the look of hope that had appeared on the men's faces when they'd heard the sound of the child's cries. Now all that made sense. No wonder they'd ridden off so eagerly. They were still hoping to find the boy, and earn their release from the Devil's Country.

A wave of claustrophobia came up over Todd. This was not the limitless landscape it had first appeared to be: it was a prison, and he wanted to be free of it. He turned, and turned again, looking for some crack in the illusion, however small. But he could find none. Despite the immensity of the vistas in all directions, and the height of heavens above him, he might as well have been locked in a cell.

His breath had quickened; his hands were suddenly clammy.

'Which way's the door?' he asked Katya.

'You want to leave? *Now?*'

'Yes, now.'

'It's just a story,' she said.

'No it's not. I saw the Duke. We *both* saw him.'

'It's all part of the show,' Katya said, with a dismissive little shrug. 'Calm down. There's no harm going to come to us. I've been down here hundreds of times and nothing ever happened to me.'

'You saw the Duke here before?'

'Sometimes. Never as close as we saw today, but there are always hunters.'

'Well ask yourself: *why* are there always hunters? Why is there always an eclipse?'

'I don't know. Why do you always do the same thing in a movie every time it runs –'

'So things are *exactly* the same, every time you come here, like a movie?'

'Not exactly the same, no. But the sun's always like that: three-quarters covered. And the trees, the rocks . . . even the ships out there.' She pointed to the ships. 'It's always the same ships. They never seem to get very far.'

'So it's not like a movie,' Todd said. 'It's more like time's been frozen.'

She nodded. 'I suppose it is,' she said. 'Frozen in the walls.'

'I don't see any walls.'

'They're there,' Katya said, 'it's just a question of where to look. *How* to look. Trust me.'

'You want me to trust you,' Todd said, 'then get me out of here.'

'I thought you were enjoying yourself.'

'The pleasure went out of it a while back,' Todd said. He grabbed her arm, hard. '*Come on,*' he said. '*I want to get out.*'

She shook herself free of him. 'Don't touch me that way,' she said, her expression suddenly fierce. 'I don't like it.' She pointed past him, over his right shoulder. 'The door's over there.'

He looked back. He could see no sign of an opening. Just more of the Devil's Country.

And now, to make matters worse, he once again heard the sound of hooves.

'Oh Christ . . .'

He glanced back towards the trees. The Duke and his men were riding towards them, empty-handed.

'They're coming back to interrogate us,' Todd said. 'Katya! Did you hear me? We need to get the hell out of here.'

Katya had seen the horsemen, but she didn't seem overly unnerved. She watched them approaching without moving. Todd, meanwhile, made his way in the general direction of the door; or at least where she had indicated it stood. He scanned the place, looking for some fragment – the corner of the doorframe, the handle, the keyhole – to help him locate it. But there was nothing.

Having no other choice he simply walked across the stony ground, his hands extended in front of him. After proceeding perhaps six strides, the empty air in front of him suddenly became solid, and his hands flattened against cold, hard tiles. The instant he made contact, the illusion of the painters' trompe l'oeil was broken. He could not believe he had been so easily deceived. What had looked like infinite, penetrable reality two strides before now looked absurdly fake: stylish marks on pieces of antiquated tile, plastered on a wall. How could his eyes have been misled for an instant?

Then he looked back over his shoulder, to call Katya, and the illusion in which she stood was still completely intact – the expanse of open ground between where they stood and the galloping horsemen apparently a quarter mile or more,

366

the trees beyond them twice that, the sky limitless above. *Illusion*, he told himself, *all illusion*. But it meant nothing in the face of the trick before him, which refused to bow to his doubt. He gave up trying to make it concede, and instead turned back to the wall. His hands were still upon it, the tiles still laid out under his palms. Which direction did the door lie in?

'Right or left?' he called to Katya.

'What?'

'The door! Is it to the right or left?'

She took her eyes off the riders, and scanned the wall he was clinging to. 'Left,' she said, casually.

'Hurry then –'

'They didn't find the child.'

'Forget about them!' he told her.

If she was attempting to impress him with her fearlessness she was doing a poor job. He was simply irritated. She'd shown him the way the room worked for God's sake; now it was time to get out.

'*Come on!*' he cried.

As he called to her he moved along the wall, a step to his left, then another step, keeping his palms flat to the tiles every inch of the way, as though defying them to play some new trick or other. But it seemed that as long as he had his hands on the tiles – as long as he could keep uppermost in his mind the idea that this was a painted world, it could not start its trickeries afresh. And on the third, or was it fourth? step along the wall his extended hand found the door-jamb. He breathed out a little sigh of relief. The door-jamb was right there under his hand. He moved his palm over it onto the door itself which, like the jamb, was tiled so that there was no break in the illusion. He fumbled for the handle, found it and tried to turn it.

On the other side, Tammy had found her way along the passageway and chosen that precise moment to turn the handle in the opposite direction.

'Oh Jesus –' Todd said. 'It's locked.'

'You hear that?' Tammy gasped. 'That's Todd? Todd!'

'Yeah it's me. Who's this?'

'Tammy. It's Tammy Lauper. Are you turning the handle?'

'Yeah.'

'Well let go of it. Let me try.'

Todd let go. Tammy turned the handle. Before she opened the door she glanced back at Zeffer. He was still one flight up the stairs, staring out of the window.

'The dead . . .' she heard him say.

'What about them?'

'They're all around the house. I've never seen them this close before. They know there are people passing back and forth through the door, that's why.'

'Do I open the door? Todd's on the other side.'

'Are you sure it's Todd?'

'Yes it's Todd.'

Hearing his name called, Todd impatiently yelled from the other side. *'Yes, it's me. And Katya. Will you please open the fucking door?'*

Tammy's hands were sweaty, and her muscles weary; the handle slid through her palm. 'I can't open it. You try.'

Todd struggled with the handle from his side, but what had seemed as though it was going to be the easiest part of the procedure (opening the door) was proving the most intractable. It was almost as though the room didn't want him to leave; as though it wanted to hold on to him for as long as possible, to exercise the greatest amount of influence over him; to addict him, second by second, sight by sight.

He glanced back over his shoulder. Katya was staring up at the sky, moving her hands down over her body, as though she was luxuriating in the curious luminosity of this enraptured world. For a moment he imagined her naked, cradled in the heavenly luminescence, but he caught himself in the midst of the fantasy. It was surely just another of the room's tricks to keep him from departing. The damn place probably had a thousand such sleights-of-mind: sexual, philosophical, murderous.

He closed his eyes hard against the seductions of the Country and put his head against the door. The tiles were clammy; like living things.

'Tammy?' he said. 'Are you still here?'

'Yes?'

'When I count three, I want you to push. Got it?'

'Got it.'

'Okay. Ready?'

'Ready.'

'One. Two. *Three!*'

She pushed. He pulled. And the door fell open, presenting Todd with one of the odder juxtapositions he'd witnessed in his life. In the hallway on the other side of the door stood a woman who looked as though she'd gone several rounds with a heavy-weight boxer. There were bloody scratches on her face, neck and arms; her hair and clothes were in disarray. In her eyes she had a distinctly panicked look.

He recognized her instantly. She was the leader of his Fan Club, a woman called Tammy Lauper. Yes! The *missing* Tammy Lauper! How the hell had she got up here? Never mind. She *was* here, thank God.

'I thought something terrible had happened to you,' Lauper said.

'Give it time,' he quipped.

Behind him, he heard the horsemen approaching. He glanced around, calling again to Katya.

'Hurry up, will you?'

When he returned his gaze to Tammy it was clear that she'd taken in, as best her disbelief would allow, the incredible sight over his shoulder. Her eyes were wide with astonishment, her jaw slack.

'So this is what it looks like.'

'Yes,' he said to her. 'This is it.'

Tammy threw a look back at a stooped, older man standing on the stairs behind her. He looked almost incapacitated with fear. But unlike Tammy, whose expression was that of someone who had never seen anything like this before, it was Todd's sense that her companion knew *exactly* what he was seeing, and would have liked nothing better than to have turned right there and fled.

Then Todd heard Katya calling from behind him, naming the man.

'*Zeffer*,' she said, the word freezing the man where he stood.

'Katya . . .' he said, inclining his head.

Katya came up behind Todd, pressing him aside in order to cross over the threshold. She pointed at the trespasser as she did so.

'I told you *never* to come back into this house!' she yelled at Zeffer. '*Didn't I?*'

He flinched at this, though it was difficult to believe she posed much physical threat to him.

She summoned him down the stairs. 'Come here,' she said. 'You worthless piece of shit! I said: *come here*!'

Before he could obey her, Tammy intervened. 'It's not his fault,' she said. 'I was the one who asked him to bring me down here.'

Katya gave her a look of complete contempt; as though anything she might have to contribute to the conversation was worthless.

'Whoever the hell you are,' she said, 'this is none of your business.'

She pushed Tammy aside and reached out to catch hold of Zeffer. He had dutifully approached at her summons, but now avoided her grasp. She came after him anyway, striking his chest with the back of her hand, a solid blow; and another; and another. As she struck him she said: 'I told you to stay outside, didn't I?'

The blows were relatively light, but they carried strength out of all proportion to their size. They knocked the breath out of him, for one thing, and she'd come back with a second blow before he'd drawn breath from the first, which quickly weakened him. Tammy was horrified, but she didn't want to interfere, in case she simply made the matter worse. Nor was her attention entirely devoted to the sight of Todd, or to the assault upon Zeffer. Her gaze was increasingly claimed by the sight visible through the open door. It was *astonishing*. Despite the fact that Zeffer had told her the place was an illusion, her eyes and her mind were wholly enamoured by what she saw: the rolling forest, the rocks with their thickets of thorn bushes, the delta and the distant sea. It all looked so real.

And what was that?

Some creature that looked like a feathered lizard, its coxcomb yellow and black, scuttled into view, and out again.

It halted, seeming to look back through the door at her: a beast that belonged in some book of medieval monsters than in such proximity to her.

She glanced back at Zeffer, who was still being lectured by Katya.

With the door open, and the visions beyond presented to her, she saw no reason not to step over the threshold, just for a moment, and see the place more plainly. After all, she was protected against its beguilements. She knew it was a beautiful lie, and as long as she remembered that, then it couldn't do her any harm, could it?

The only thing in the landscape that was real was Todd, and it was to him that she now went, crossing the earth and the windblown grass to go to him. The feathered reptile lowered its coxcomb as she crossed the ground, and slunk away, disappearing into a crack between two boulders. But Todd wasn't watching animal-life. He had his eyes on several horsemen who were approaching along a road that wound through a dense stand of trees. They were approaching at speed, kicking up clods of earth as they came. Were they real, Tammy wondered, or just part of the landscape? She wasn't sure, nor was she particularly eager to put the question to the test.

Yet with every passing second she was standing in this world the more she felt the power of the room to unknit her doubts. She felt its influence seeping through her sight and her skin into her mind and marrow. Her head grew giddy, as though she'd downed two or three glasses of wine in quick succession.

It wasn't an unpleasant sensation by any means, especially given the extreme discomfort of the last few hours. She felt almost comforted by the room; as though it understood how she'd suffered of late, and was ready to soothe her hurts and humiliations away. It would distract her with its beauty and its strangeness; if she would only trust it for a while.

'Tammy . . .' she heard Zeffer say behind her. His voice was weak, and the effect his summons had on her was inconsequential. She didn't even acknowledge it. She just let her eyes graze contentedly on the scene before her; the trees, the horsemen, the road, the rocks.

Soon, she knew, the riders would make a turn in that road, and it would be interesting to see how their image changed when they were no longer moving in profile, but were coming towards her.

She glanced back over her shoulder. It wasn't far to the door: just a few yards. Her eyes didn't even focus on whatever was going on in the passageway. It seemed very remote from her at that moment.

She looked back towards the horsemen. They had turned the corner in the road, and were now coming directly towards the spot where Todd and she stood. It was the oddest visual spectacle she'd ever witnessed, to see them growing larger as they approached, like illustrations emerging from a book. The landscape around them seemed to both recede and advance at the same moment as they approached, its motion throwing them forward as the ground beneath their horses drew back like a retreating wave. It was an utterly bewildering spectacle, but its paradoxical beauty enthralled her. All thought of Zeffer's summons, or indeed his safety, were forgotten: it was as though she was watching a piece of film for the first time, not knowing how the mechanism worked upon her.

She felt Todd throw her a sideways glance.

'Time to go,' he said.

The earth beneath their feet reverberated as the horsemen approached. They'd be at the door in thirty or forty seconds.

'Come on,' he said.

'Yes . . ,' she murmured. 'I'm coming.'

She didn't move. It wasn't until Todd caught hold of her arm and pulled her back towards the door that she eventually obeyed the instruction and went. Even then she kept looking back over her shoulder, astonished.

'I don't believe what I'm seeing,' she said.

'It's all real. Trust me on that,' he said. 'They can do you harm.'

They had reached the threshold now, and she reluctantly allowed herself to be coaxed back over it and into the passageway. She was amazed at the speed with which the room had caught her attention; made itself the centre of her thoughts.

Even now, it was still difficult to focus her attention on anything but the scene beyond the door, but finally she dragged her eyes away from the approaching horsemen and sought out Zeffer.

He had fallen to his knees three or four yards from the door, putting up no defence against Katya's assault.

'I told you, didn't I?' she said, slapping his head. 'I never wanted to see you in this house ever again. You understand me? *Ever again.*'

'I'm sorry,' he said, his head bowed. 'I just brought –'

'I don't care who you brought. This house is forbidden to you.'

'Yes . . . I know.'

His acquiescence did nothing to placate her. The reverse, in fact: it seemed to inflame her. She kicked him.

'You revolt me,' she said.

He bent over, as though to present a smaller target to her. She pushed him, hard, and he fell. She moved in to kick him again, aiming for his face, but at that moment Tammy saw what she was about to do, and let out a cry of protest.

'Leave him alone!' she said.

Katya turned. '*What?*'

'You heard me. *Leave him alone!*'

Katya's beauty was disfigured by the naked contempt on her face. She was breathing heavily, and her face was flushed.

'I'll do what it suits me to do in my own house,' she said, her lip curling. 'And no fat, ugly bitch like you is going to tell me otherwise.'

Tammy knew plenty about Katya Lupi by now, of course; her intimidating reputation went before her. But at that moment, seeing Zeffer lying on the floor, and hearing what the woman had just said, any trace of intimidation was burned away by a blaze of anger. Even the glories of the Devil's Country were forgotten at that moment.

She walked straight towards Katya and pushed her hard, laying her hands against the bitch's little breasts to do so. Katya was clearly not used to being manhandled. She came back at Tammy in an instant.

'*Don't you dare touch me!*' she shrieked. Then she back-handed Tammy; a clean, wide strike.

Tammy fell back, the metallic tang of blood in her mouth. There were three sickening heartbeats when she feared the force of Katya's blow was going to knock her unconscious. Darkness pulsed at the corners of her vision. But she was determined not to be floored by one blow, even if it did have something more than ordinary human force behind it, as she suspected it did.

She reached out for something to steady her, and her hand found the door-jamb. As she caught hold of it, she glanced back over her shoulder, remembering her proximity to the strange beauty of the Devil's Country. But the power of the room's illusion had been momentarily knocked from her head. The walls were simply covered in tiles now. There were trees and rocks and a painted river on those tiles, but none of it was so finely rendered that it could have been mistaken for reality. The only part of the scene before her that was real was Todd, who was still lingering at the threshold. Apparently he could see what Tammy could not because at that moment he threw himself over the threshold like a man in fear of something coming close on his heels. He caught hold of the doorhandle, and started to pull the door closed, but as he did so Katya came back into view and blocked the door with her foot.

'Don't close it!' she told Todd.

Todd obeyed her. He let go of the handle. The door struck Katya's leg and bounced open again.

Now the machinations of the room began to work on Tammy afresh. The gloomy air seethed, and the shapes of four horsemen appeared out of the murk, still riding towards the door.

The leader – *the Duke*, Tammy thought, *this is the Duke* – pulled hard on the reins to slow his mount. The animal made a din, as though its primitive gaze was failing to make sense of what was ahead of it. Rather than advance any further it came to a panicked halt, throwing up clods of earth as it did so. Goga jumped from the saddle, shouting a number of incomprehensible orders back at his men, who had also brought their animals to a stop. They proceeded to dismount. There were whispers of superstitious doubt

375

between the men: plainly whatever they were witnessing (the door, the passageway) they could make little or no sense of it. That fact didn't slow their advance, however. They dutifully followed their leader towards the door, swords drawn.

By now Tammy had recovered sufficiently to grab hold of Todd's arm and pull him back from the threshold.

'Come away,' she urged him.

He looked round at her. She was probably more familiar with his face, and with his limited palette of expressions, than she was with her own. But she'd never seen the look of stupefaction he wore right now. The veins at his temples were throbbing, his mouth was slack; his blood-shot eyes seemed to have difficulty focusing on her.

She tugged harder on his arm, in the hope of shaking him out of his stupor. Behind him she could see the horsemen approaching the door, their step more cautious now that they were almost at the threshold. Having stopped the door from being closed Katya had stepped away from it, leaving Todd the closest of them all to the horsemen. So close, in fact, that had the Duke so chosen, he could have lunged from where he stood, and killed Todd with a single stroke.

He did not do so, however. He hung back from the door, eyeing it with suspicion and awe. Though none of the light from the hallway seemed to illuminate the world on the other side of the doorway, Tammy could see the man's face quite clearly: his severely angular features, his long, braided beard, black shot through with streaks of grey; his dark, heavy-lidded eyes. He was by no means as beautiful as Todd had once been, but there was a *gravitas* in his physiognomy which Todd's corn-fed charm could never have approached. No doubt he was responsible for all manner of crimes – in such a landscape as he'd ridden who would not lay claim to their share of felonies? – but in that moment, in the midst of a dark journey of her own,

376

Tammy would have instinctively preferred the eloquence of this face for company than Todd's easy beauty.

Indeed, if she had ever been in love with Todd Pickett – which by many definitions she had – she fell *out* of love with him at that moment, comparing his face with that of Duke Goga, and finding it wanting.

That was not to say that she didn't want Todd safe from this place; from the house and all its inhabitants, especially Katya. So she hauled on his arm again, yelling for him to get away from the door, and this time her message got through to him.

Todd retreated, and as he did so Katya caught hold of Zeffer by the hair and lifted him up. Tammy was too concerned with reclaiming Todd from the threshold to do anything to save Zeffer. And Zeffer in turn did nothing to save himself. He simply let the woman he had adored pick him up, and with the same nearly supernatural strength Tammy herself had felt just moments before, Katya pitched Zeffer through the open door.

The horsemen were waiting on the other side, swords at the ready.

Only now, as he stumbled across the ground before them, did Zeffer raise his arms to protect himself against the swordsmen. Whether the Duke took this harmless motion as some attempt at aggression, and reacted to protect himself, or whether he simply wanted to do harm Tammy would never know. The Duke lifted his sword and brought it down in a great swooping arc that cut through the meat of Zeffer's right hand, taking off all four of his fingers, and the top half of his thumb. Blood spurted out from the wounds, and Zeffer let out a cry that was one part disbelief to two of agony. He stared at his maimed hand for a moment, then he turned from his mutilator and stumbled back towards the door.

For an instant, he lifted his eyes, and his eyes met Tammy's. They had a moment only to look at one another.

Then Duke Goga came at Zeffer again and drove his sword through the middle of his back.

There was a terrible sound, as the blade cracked Zeffer's breastbone and then the point emerged from the middle of his chest.

Zeffer threw back his head, and caught hold of the edge of the door with his unmaimed hand. He had his eyes fixed on Tammy as he did so, as though he was drawing the power to do whatever he was planning to do from her. There was a long moment when in fact he did nothing; only teetered on the threshold, his eyelids growing lazy. Then – summoning one last Herculean effort of will – he gave Tammy a tiny smile and closed the door in her face.

It was like being woken from a dream. One moment Tammy had been staring into Zeffer's stricken face, while the men closed in on him from behind, and the sky seethed overhead. The next the door had shut this terrible vision out, and she was back in the little hallway with Todd at her side.

The sight of Zeffer's execution had momentarily distracted Katya from any further mischief. She was simply staring at the door as though she could see through it to the horror on the other side.

Tammy didn't give her a chance to snap out of the trance. She started up the stairs, pulling Todd after her.

'Christ . . .' Todd muttered to himself. 'Christ oh Christ oh Christ . . .'

Five stairs up, Tammy chanced a backward glance, but Katya was still standing in front of the door.

What was she thinking, Tammy wondered. *What have I done*? Did a woman like that ever think *what have I done*? With Zeffer gone, she would be alone in Coldheart Canyon. Alone with the dead. Not a pretty prospect.

Perhaps she was regretting. Just a little.

And while she regretted, (if regretting was what she

was doing) Tammy continued to haul Todd after her up the stairs.

Six steps now; seven, eight, nine.

Now the escapees were on the half-landing. Through the window off to their left Tammy could see the sight that had held Zeffer's attention just minutes before: the occupants of Coldheart Canyon pressing against the glass.

Why didn't they simply break in, she wondered? They weren't, after all, insubstantial. They had weight, they had force. If they wanted to get in so badly, why didn't they simply break the glass or splinter the doors?

The question went from her head the next instant, driven out by a wail of demand from below.

'*Todd*?'

It was Katya, of course. She had finally stirred from her fugue state and was coming up the stairs after them. Speaking in her sweetest voice. Her come-hither voice.

'Todd, where *are* you going?'

Tammy felt nauseous. Katya could still do them harm. She still had power over Todd and she knew it. That was why she put on that little girl questioning voice.

'Todd?' Katya said again. '*Wait*, darling.'

If she let go of him, Tammy guessed, he would obey Katya's request. And then they'd be lost. Katya would never let him go. She'd kill him rather than let him escape her a second time.

There wasn't much advice Tammy could give to Todd except: 'Don't look back.'

He glanced at her, his expression plaintive. It made her feel as though she were leading a child rather than a grown man.

'We can't just leave her here,' he said.

'After what she just did!'

'Don't listen to her,' Katya said, her voice suddenly a siren-song, the little-girl lightness erased in favour of something more velvety. 'She just wants you for herself.'

Todd frowned.

'You can't leave me, Todd.'

And then more softly still: '*I won't let you leave me.*'

'Just remember what she did down there,' Tammy said to Todd.

'Zeffer was a nuisance,' Katya said. She was getting closer, Tammy knew; her voice had dropped to a sultry murmur. 'I never loved him, Todd. You know that. He hung around causing trouble. Listen to me. You don't want to go with this woman. Look at her, then *look at me*. See what a choice you're making.'

Tammy half-expected Todd to obey Katya's instruction. But Todd simply studied the stairs as they climbed, which under the circumstances was a minor triumph. Perhaps he still had the will-power in him to resist Katya, Tammy thought. He wasn't her object yet.

Even so the murdering bitch wasn't ready to give up.

'Todd?' Katya said, now casual, as though none of this was of any great significance. 'Will you turn round for a moment? Just for a moment? *Please*. I want to see your face before you go. That's not asking much, now is it? Just one more time. I can't bear it. *Please*. Todd . . . *I . . . can't . . . bear it.*'

Oh Lord, Tammy thought, she's turning on the tears. She knew how potent a well-timed flood of tears could be. Her sister had always been very quick to turn on the waterworks when she wanted something; and it had usually done the trick.

'Please, my love . . .'

It was *almost* believable; the words catching in her throat, the soft sob.

'. . . don't go. I won't be able to live without you.'

They were still a few strides from the front door. Then, once they were out, they had to get along the pathway and onto the street. Somehow she doubted Katya's power extended far beyond the limits of the house. The Canyon might have been hers once upon a time, but she'd lost control of it in the decades since her heyday. Now it belonged to the ghosts and the animals, and the bestial offspring of both.

Still coaxing Todd after her, Tammy made her way across the hallway to the front door.

Behind them, Katya kept up her tearful appeals: declarations of love, interspersed with sobs. Then more appeals for him to turn around and look at her.

'You don't want to go,' she called to Todd, 'you know you don't. Especially with *her*. Lord, Todd, *look at her*. You really want that?'

Finally, Tammy snapped. 'How the hell do you know what he wants, *bitch*?' she said, turning to look round at the woman on their heels.

'Because we're soul-mates,' Katya said.

Her eyes were swollen and red, Tammy noted with some satisfaction, and there were tears pouring down her face. Her mascara was running down her pale cheeks in two black rivulets. 'He knows it's true,' Katya went on. 'We've suffered the same way. Haven't we, Todd? Remember how you said it was like I was reading your mind? And I said it was because we were the *same*, deep down? Remember that?'

'Ignore her,' Tammy said. They were no more than three strides from the front door.

But Katya – realizing she was close to losing – had one last trick up her sleeve. One final power-play. 'If you step out of this house,' she said to Todd, 'then it's over between us. Do you understand me? If you stay – *oh*, if you stay, my darling – then I'm yours. I'm yours body and soul – *I mean it*: *body and soul*. But if you go it'll be as though you never existed.'

Finally, something she said carried enough weight to stop Todd in his tracks.

'Ignore her,' Tammy said. 'Please.'

'You know I can do that,' Katya went on.

Todd turned, and looked back at her, which was exactly what Tammy was praying he wouldn't do. Katya was standing in the darkness close to the top of the stairs but the shadows did not conceal the fierce brilliance of her stare. Her eyes seemed to flicker in the murk, as though there were flames behind them.

Now she had succeeded in making him look at her again, she softened her tone. She certainly had quite a repertoire, Tammy thought. First demands, then pleas and siren-songs; then tears and threats. Now what?

'I know what you're thinking . . .' she said.

Ah, *mind reading*.

'. . . you're thinking that you've got a life out there. And it's calling you back.'

Tammy was puzzled. This sounded like a self-defeating argument.

'You're thinking you want to be back in the spotlight, where you belong . . .'

While Katya talked, Tammy made a momentous decision. She let go of Todd's hand. She'd done all that she could. If after all this Todd decided that he wanted to turn back and give himself to the wretched woman, then there was nothing more Tammy could do about it. He was a lost cause.

She crossed swiftly to the front door, and opened it. The first tug was a little difficult. Then the door swung open easily, majestically. There were no ghosts on the threshold, only the refreshing night air, sweetened by the scent of night-blooming jasmine.

Behind her, in the house, Katya was finishing her argument. 'The fact is,' she said, 'there's nothing out there for you now. Do you understand me, Todd? There's nothing.'

Tammy stepped out onto the front steps. She looked back at Todd, in time to catch a look of pitiful confusion on his face. He literally didn't know which way to turn.

382

'Don't look at me,' Tammy said to him. 'It's your choice.'

His expression became still more pained. That wasn't what he wanted to hear.

'Look, you're a grown man,' Tammy said. 'If you want to stay with her, knowing what she's capable of, then you stay. I hope you'll be very happy together.'

'Todd . . .' Katya murmured.

She stepped out of the shadows now, choosing her moment, as ever, beautifully. The demonic Katya, the woman who'd thrashed Zeffer then thrown him to Goga, had vanished completely. In her place was a sad, gentle woman – or the appearance of such – who opened her arms to Todd like a loving mother.

'Come back to me,' she said.

He made the tiniest nod of his head and Tammy's heart sank.

He started to turn his back on the door, but as he did so there was a sudden and furious eruption of noise from the depths of the house. Somebody in the Devil's Country was beating on the door: a furious tattoo.

It came at the perfect moment. At the sound from below Todd seemed to snap out of his mesmerized state and instead of heading for Katya's open arms he began to retreat towards the door.

'You know what?' he said to Katya. 'I can't take this place any longer. I'm sorry. I've got to get out.'

Katya flew at him, her arms outstretched, her eyes wide. '*No*!' she cried. '*I want you here*!'

It was more than Todd could take. He backed away from her and stumbled out over the step.

'Finally,' Tammy said.

He grabbed hold of her hand. 'Get me the fuck out of here,' he said.

This time there was no hesitation in his voice, no turning back. They ran to the gate and out into the street, not stopping for a moment. Tammy slammed the gate loudly, not so much because she felt it would keep the bitch from following, but because it made the point to the entire Canyon that they were indeed out of the house and away.

'My car's up the road,' she told Todd, though of course it was now four days since she'd left it, and there was no guarantee it would still be sitting there. And the keys; what about the keys? Had she left them in the ignition? She thought she had; but she was by no means certain. So much had happened to her in the intervening time; she had no clear memory of what she'd done with the keys.

'I'm assuming you're going to come with me?' she said to Todd.

He looked at her blankly.

'To the car,' she said, for emphasis.

'Yes.'

'It's up the street.'

'Yes. I heard you.'

'Well, shall we go then?'

He nodded, but he didn't move. His gaze had drifted back to the house. Leaving him to stare, Tammy set off up the road to where she'd left the car. There was neither moon nor stars in the sky; just a blanket of amber-tinted cloud. She soon lost sight of Todd as she headed up the benighted road. Memories of her night-journey through the place, with all its attendant miseries and hallucinations, rose up before her, but she told herself to put them out of her head. She was going to be out of this damn Canyon in a few minutes, long before it got back into her mind again, and started its tricks.

The car, when she reached it, was unlocked. She opened the door and slipped into the driver's seat, fumbling for the ignition. Yes! The keys were there. 'Thank you, God,' she said, with a late show of piety.

She turned on the engine, and switched on the head-lights. They lit up the whole street ahead. She put the car into gear and brought it roaring around the corner. Todd had wandered out into the middle of the road, and she could have ploughed into him (which would have made an ignominious end to the night's adventures) had he not stepped out of her way. But at least the distracted look had gone from his face. When he got into the car there was a new and welcome urgency about his manner.

'We're out of here,' he said.

'I thought for a moment that you were planning to stay.'

'No . . . I was just thinking . . . about what a fool I'd been.'

'Well stop thinking for a while,' Tammy said. 'It'll slow us down.'

She put her foot down and they sped off down the winding street.

About halfway down the Canyon he said: 'Do you think she's going to come after us?'

'No,' Tammy said. 'I don't think her pride would let her.'

She had no sooner spoken than something sprang into the glare of the headlights. Todd let out a yelp of surprise, but Tammy knew in a heartbeat what it was: one of the hybrids she'd encountered on the slopes. It was ugly, even by the standards of its malformed breed: a loping, pasty thing with the flesh missing from the lower half of its face, exposing a sickly rictus.

Tammy made no attempt to avoid striking the beast. Instead she drove straight into it. The moment before it was struck the thing opened its lipless mouth horribly wide, as though it thought it might scare the vehicle off. Then the front of the car struck it, and its body rolled up onto the hood, momentarily sprawling over the windshield. For a few seconds, Tammy was driving blind, with the face of the beast grotesquely plastered against the glass. Then one of her more suicidal swerves threw the thing off, leaving just a smudge of its pale yellow fluids on the glass.

Very quietly Todd said: 'What the *fuck* was that?'

'I'll tell you some other time,' Tammy said. And leaving the explanation there she proceeded down the winding road in uncontested silence, bringing them finally to some anonymous but lamplit street, and so, out of the entrails of Coldheart Canyon, and back into the City of Angels.

PART SEVEN

THE A-LIST

1

In March of 1962 Jerry Brahms had bought a small two bedroom apartment a block or two within the gates of Hollywoodland, a neighbourhood created in the twenties which encompassed a large parcel of land in the vicinity of the Hollywood sign. The house had cost him nineteen thousand seven hundred dollars, a relatively modest sum for a place so pleasantly situated. Back then, he'd still indulged the fantasy that one day he'd meet a soul-mate with whom he would one day share the house, but somehow his romantic entanglements had always ended poorly, and despite three attempts to bring someone in, the chemistry had failed miserably, and each time he'd sent the man on his way, and he'd ended up alone. He no longer hoped for an end to his solitude: even the most optimistic of the cancer Drs who'd seen him gave him at best a year. The tumour in his prostate was now inoperable, and spreading.

For all his love of the dreamy far-off days of Hollywood, Jerry was a practical man, and – at least when it came to himself – remarkably unsentimental. The prospect of dying did not move him particularly one way or another: he was not afraid of it, nor did he welcome the eventuality. It would simply happen – sooner rather than later. Sometimes, when he got melancholy, he contemplated suicide, and in preparation for such a moment had amassed a considerable number of sleeping pills, sufficient, he felt sure, to do the job. But though he had very bad days now, when the pain (and, for a man as fastidious as himself, the practical problems of advanced bowel disorders) were so nearly overwhelming that he thought hard about tying up all the loose ends of his life and simply knocking back the pills with a strong Bloody Mary, somehow he could never bring himself to do it.

He had a sense of *unfinished business*, though he could not quite work out what the business might be. His parents were long since dead, his only sibling, a sister, also passed away, tragically young. Of his few friends there were few that he cared to say anything of any great profundity to. If he slipped away, there'd be little by way of tears: just some fighting over his collection of movie memorabilia – which he'd never had evaluated, but was probably worth half a million dollars at auction – and a few tear-sodden, bitchy remarks at Mickey's (his favourite bar) when he was gone. Lord knows, he'd made enough of those kinds of remarks in his life: he'd been the kind of queen with a feline answer to just about anything in his heyday. But there was no joy in that kind of thing any more. His style of queendom was long out of fashion. He was a dinosaur with prostate cancer; soon to be extinct.

Lately he'd found that his condition made him vulnerable to every little sadness that touched his world. The passing of Todd's dog, Dempsey, had left him in tears all day, though he barely knew the animal. And then the death of Marco Caputo: such a senseless waste of life. He hadn't ever been close friends with Caputo, but on those few occasions when he'd met the man, Caputo had always been polite and professional, rare enough in these days of mediocrity.

The funeral had not done justice to the man, in Jerry's opinion. It had been small (there were a couple of family members in from Chicago, but they looked as though they were more interested in what his will would say than in mourning their brother). Todd, of course, was not on hand, though Maxine was there as his representative. Jerry took the opportunity to ask her how much longer she thought the stalker business would be going on for. Were the police trying to catch this woman, and prosecute her, or was poor Todd just going to have to sit it out? Maxine said she didn't know. She wouldn't be dealing with Todd's affairs for very much longer, she told him: it was a waste of time and energy.

The conversation, the tiny, disinterested congregation, the coffin and the thought of its unviewable contents, all sent Jerry back home to his apartment in a blacker mood than usual. But even so, even on a day when it seemed that all decency and all hope had gone from the world, he found it impossible to take his stash of pills and finish the business.

Why, for God's sake? Something nagged at him; that was all he knew. Something told him: wait, just a little longer.

'It's not over,' the opera-queens of his acquaintance used to say, "til the fat lady sings.'

Well, somewhere deep in his soul, he knew that the fat woman still had an aria up her sleeve.

So he kept on living, which was often a wearisome business, all the while waiting for whatever it was that was nagging at him to make itself apparent.

Finally, it did.

The circumstances were peculiar: he had a dream so powerful that it woke him. This in itself was odd, because he usually went to bed with a couple of scotches to wash down his sleeping pills, and as a consequence seldom woke.

But he woke tonight, and the dream he'd dreamed was crystal clear.

He had dreamed that he was sitting on the toilet, of all places, in a state of agonizing constipation (which was in his waking life a consequence of the painkillers his doctor prescribed). As he sat there he realized that there were wooden boards on the floor of his toilet, not tiles as there were in life, and the cracks between the boards were so wide that he could see right down into the apartment below. Except that it wasn't another apartment, it was – in the strange logic of this dream – another house. Nor was it just any house. It was Katya's dream palace that was spread below him. And as he realized this, the gaps between the boards grew wider, so that he dropped down between them, slowly, as though he were feather-light.

And there he was, in Katya's house, in Coldheart Canyon. He pulled up his pants and looked around.

The dream palace was in a state of considerable disrepair. The windows were broken, and birds flew in and out, shitting on the fancy furniture. A coyote skulked around in the kitchen, looking for scraps. And outside in the tree there were dozens of little red-and-black-striped monkeys, chattering and screeching. This was not so fanciful a detail as it might have seemed to someone who'd not known the house, as he had, in its heyday. There *had* been monkeys there – escapees from Katya's private menagerie; and for a while it seemed the climate suited them and they would proliferate, but after a year or two some virus had decimated them.

Something about the place in its present condition made him want to leave. He knew, however, that he couldn't. Not without paying his respects to the lady of the house. So rather than wait for her to show herself, he went to look for her, figuring that the sooner he found her the sooner he'd be released from this dream. He started up the stairs. There were flies crawling on the ground beneath his feet, so densely assembled and so sluggish that they refused to move as he ascended, obliging him to crush them under his bare feet as he climbed.

The door to the master bedroom was open. He stepped inside, somewhat tentatively. He had only been into the room once before. He remembered it as being large; but here in his dream it was immense. The drapes were partially drawn, and the sunlight that streamed between them was a curious colour, almost lilac.

There was an enormous, but extremely plain, bed in the room. And sitting on the bed was the only woman, besides his mother, whom Jerry had loved: Katya. She was naked; or – more correctly stated – unclothed. Ninety percent of her body's surface was covered with large snails, the common tortoiseshell variety that every gardener curses. They were moving all over her skin. They were on her face, on her breasts and belly, on her thighs and shins. Her hair was matted with their silvery trails, and thirty or forty of them were arranged on her head like a grotesque crown. Her legs were open, and they were also investigating the crevice between her thighs. As is so often the case in dreams he saw all this with horrid particularity. Saw the way their boneless grey-green bodies extended from their shells as they moved over Katya's skin; their horns extending tentatively as they advanced, then retracting as they encountered an obstacle – a nipple, an ear, the knuckle of her thumb – only to stretch out again when they were certain there was no danger in the encounter.

Without speaking, Katya looked down and very delicately plucked one of the creatures off her breast. Then she spread her legs a little wider, so that Jerry had an even more intimate view of her private parts. He was no connoisseur, but even he could see that there was a certain prettiness to the configuration of her labia; she had the pussy of a young girl. Putting her hands down between her legs she spread her lips and delicately applied the snail she'd taken from her breast to the flesh there.

Jerry watched with a kind of appalled fascination as it responded to its new perch, expanding its horns and investigating her.

Katya sighed. Her eyes fluttered closed. Then, suddenly, they opened again. When they did they were fixed on him, with startling fierceness.

393

'*There* you are, Jerry,' she said, her voice full of the music he remembered from his childhood: the kind of bitter-sweet music by which he had judged the voice of every woman he'd met since.

Later he'd learned that silent movie stars had been notorious for having voices that precluded them from careers in the sound cinema: but Katya had been one of the exceptions to that rule. She had the slightest foreign inflection (nothing recognizable; just enough to add a certain poignancy to her sentences); otherwise she spoke with a beguiling elegance.

'I need help,' she said to him. 'Jerry, will you come to the house? Please. I am alone here. Utterly alone.'

'What happened to Todd?' he said to her.

'He walked out on me.'

'I can't believe that.'

'Well it's true. He did. Are you going to choose between him and me?'

'No, of course not.'

'He was just another empty shell, Jerry. There was no substance to him. And now I'm alone, and it's worse than death.'

His dream-self was about to get clever and ask her how she could possibly know what death felt like, but then he thought better of asking her. Perhaps she did indeed know. It wasn't beyond the bounds of possibility. He'd never understood exactly how her life had worked, up there in the house in the Canyon, but he suspected there were terrible secrets in that place.

'What do you want me to do?' he asked her.

'Come back up to the Canyon,' she said.

That was the end of the dream, at least as he remembered it when he woke. The image of her body covered with snails disgusted him, of course; especially its sexual details. Had she conjured that, in dispatching this dream, or had he dug it out of the recesses of his own

394

sub-conscious? Whichever it was, it had done its duty: making certain he understood the pitiful state she was in.

All through the following day, as he went about his chores – down to the market, back from the market, cooking himself chicken, eating the chicken, washing the plate from which he'd eaten the chicken, talking with Luis, who lived below, about how the apartments all needed painting, and who was going to talk to the manager because it had to be done soon; and so on, and so forth – through all of this he kept thinking about the dream, and whether it was really trying to tell him something or not. Out of the blue, he said to Luis: 'Do you believe in dreams?'

Luis, who was a plump, amicable man who'd been in Christopher Street the night of the Stonewall riots, in full drag, or so he claimed. 'Like how?' he said. 'Give me an example.'

'Like: you have a dream and it seems like it's telling you something.'

'Oh yeah. I've had those.'

'And were they?'

'Like I had a dream in which my mother told me to get out of this relationship I was in with a guy. I don't know if you met him. Ronnie?'

'I remember Ronnie.'

'Well he was a sonofabitch. He used to beat me up, he'd get drunk on tequila and beat me up.'

'What's this got to do with the dream?'

'I told you: my mother said throw him out. In the dream. She said throw him out or he'll kill you.'

'What did you do?'

'I threw him out. I mean, I was ready to do it anyhow. The dream just confirmed what I'd been feeling.'

'Did he just go?'

'No. He got physical, and we ended up fighting and –'

Luis pulled up his sleeve, exposing a six inch scar, pale against his mocha skin. 'It got nasty.'

'He did that?'

'We were fighting. And I fell on a glass-topped coffee-table. I needed sixteen stitches. By the time I got back from the hospital, the motherfucker had gone. He'd taken all my shoes. And they weren't even his size.'

'So you *do* believe in dreams?'

'Sure I believe. Why'd you want to know?'

'I'm trying to figure something out.'

'Well, you want my opinion? Dreams can be useful doing that sometimes. Then again, sometimes they're full of shit. It depends on the dream. You know how I know? My Momma got really sick with pneumonia, and she was in the hospital in New York. And I had this dream, and she was telling me she was fine, there was no need to spend the money and fly out East, because she was going to get better. Next day, she was dead.'

Jerry went back to his apartment and thought about his dream some more, and about what Luis had said. Gradually, it crept up on him why he was being so reluctant about the decision. He was afraid that if he went up to Coldheart Canyon (if he *sided* with Katya, knowing her capacity for cruelty), it would be the end of him. He'd seen so many movies in which the queen ended up dead in the second act, superfluous to the real heart of the story. Wasn't that him? Hadn't he lived his life at the edge of Katya's grand drama; never important enough to be at the heart of things? If events in Coldheart Canyon were indeed coming to an end – as it seemed they were – then what was the likelihood of his surviving to the final reel? Little or none.

And yet, if this was the inescapable truth of his life, then why fight it? Why lock himself away in his little apartment, watching game-shows and eating frozen dinners for one, when the only drama he'd ever really been a part of was playing out to its conclusion twenty minutes' drive away? Wasn't that just throwing more time away: waste on waste?

Damn it, he would go. He'd obey the summons of the dream, and go back to Coldheart Canyon.

This course determined, he set about preparing himself for an audience with the Lady Katya. He chose something elegant to wear (she liked an elegant man, he'd heard her once say); his linen suit, his best Italian shoes, a silk tie he'd bought in Barcelona, to add just a *touch* of colour to the otherwise subdued ensemble. With his clothes chosen, he showered and shaved and then – having worked up a bit of a sweat shaving – showered again.

It was late afternoon by the time he started to get dressed. It would soon be cocktail hour up in Coldheart Canyon. Tonight, at least, Katya would not have to drink alone.

2

About the time Jerry Brahms had been waking up
from his dream of Katya and the snails – which is
to say, just half an hour before dawn – Tammy
and Todd were slipping – 'quietly, quietly,' she kept saying
– into the little hotel where Tammy had been staying. The
last few days had provided Tammy with a notable range of
unlikely experiences but surely this was up there amongst
the weirdest of them – tip-toeing along the corridor of her
two-star hotel with one of the most famous celebrities in
the world in tow, telling him to hush whenever his heel
squeaked on a board.

'The room's chaos,' she warned him as she let him in.
'I'm not a very tidy person . . .'

'I don't care what it looks like,' Todd said, his voice so
drained by exhaustion it had no colour left in it whatsoever.
'I just want to piss and sleep.'

He went directly into the bathroom, and without bothering to close the door, unzipped and urinated like a race-
horse, just as though the two of them had been married
for years and he didn't give a damn about the niceties.
Telling herself she shouldn't be taking a peek, Tammy did
so anyway. Where was the harm? He was bigger than Arnie,
by a couple of sizes. He shook himself, wetting the seat (just
like Arnie) and went to the sink to wash, splashing water
on his face in a half-hearted fashion.

'I keep thinking –' he called through to her. 'Can you
hear me?'

'Yes, I can hear you fine.'

'I keep thinking this is all a dream and I'm going to wake up.' He turned the water off and came to the door, towel in hand. He patted his wounded face dry, very gently. 'But then I think: if this was a dream when did it begin? When I first saw Katya? Or when I first went up to Coldheart Canyon? Or when I woke up from the operation, and it had all gone wrong?'

He tossed the towel onto the floor of the bathroom; something else Arnie always did. It used to irritate the hell out of Tammy, forever chasing around after her spouse, picking up stuff he'd dropped: towels in the bathroom, socks and skid-marked underwear in the bedroom, food left out of the refrigerator, where the flies could get at it. Why were those habits so hard for men to change? Why couldn't they just pick things up and put them away in their proper place?

Todd was still talking about when his dream had begun. He'd decided it started when Burrows put him under.

'You're not serious?' she told him.

'Absolutely. All this . . .' he made an expansive gesture that took in the room and Tammy '. . . is part of the same hallucination.'

'Me, included?'

'Sure.'

'Todd, you're being ridiculous,' Tammy said. 'You're not dreaming this, and neither am I. We're awake. We're *here*.'

'Here, I don't mind,' Todd said, looking around the room. 'I can take being here. But Tammy, if this room exists then so does all that shit we saw up at Katya's house. And I'm not ready to believe in that.' He bit his nails as he spoke, pacing the floor. 'You saw what was in the room?'

'Not really. I mean I saw the man who killed Zeffer –'

'And the ghosts. You saw the ghosts.'

'Yes, I saw them. And worse.'

399

'And you believe all that's real?'

'What's the alternative?'

'I've told you. It's all just some hallucination I'm having.'

'I think I'd know if I was having an hallucination.'

'Have you ever done LSD? Really good LSD or magic mushrooms?'

'No.'

'See, you do some of that stuff and it's like you never look at the real world the same way again. You can never really trust it. I mean it's all *consensual reality* anyhow, right?'

'I don't know what the hell that is.'

'It's a phrase my dealer uses. Jerome Bunny is his name. He's a real philosopher. It isn't just drugs with him, it's a way of looking at the world. And he used to say we all just agree on what's real, for convenience sake.'

'I still don't get it,' Tammy said wearily.

'Well he used to explain it better.'

'Anyway, I thought you didn't do drugs. You said in *People* you were horrified to see what drugs had done to friends of yours.'

'Did I name anyone?'

'Robert Downey Jr was one. "A great actor," you said, "killing himself for the highs," you said.'

'Well I don't fry my brains every night like Robert did. I know my limits. A little pot. A few tabs of acid –' He stopped, looking a little irritated. 'Anyway, I don't have to justify myself to you.'

'I didn't say you did.'

'Quoting me –'

'Well that's what you said.'

'Well it's bullshit. It's his life. He can do what the hell he likes with it. Where did all this start anyhow?'

'You saying –'

'Oh yeah, we're having this dream together, because that way Coldheart Canyon doesn't exist. Can't exist. It's all something invented. I mean, how can any of that be real?'

'I don't know,' said Tammy flatly. 'But whatever you say about dreams or consenting reality or whatever it was: that place is real, Todd. It's up there in the hills right now. And she's there too. And she's planning her next move.'

'You sound very sure.' He was studying his reflection in the mirror of the dresser as he talked to her.

'I am sure. She's not going to let go of you. She'll find a way to get you back.'

'Look at me,' he said.

'I think you look fine.'

'I'm a mess. Burrows fucked it all up.' His hands went up to his face. 'It's gotta be a dream . . .' he said, returning to his old theme. 'I can't look like this in the real world.'

'I do,' Tammy said, considering her own unhappy reflection. 'I look like this.' She pinched herself. 'I'm real,' she said.

'Yeah?' he said softly.

'I know who I am. I know how I got here, where I came from, where my husband works.'

'Your husband?'

'Yes, my husband. Why? Are you surprised a woman with my dress size has got a husband? Well, I have. His name's Arnie, and he works at Sacramento Airport. And you don't know anything about him, do you?'

'No.'

'So you can't have dreamed him, can you?'

'No.'

'See? That's *my* life. My problem.'

'Why's it a problem?'

'Because he drinks too much and he doesn't love me and he's having an affair with this woman who works at the FedEx office.'

'No shit. Is he the violent type?'

'He would be if I let him.'

'But you don't.'

'I fractured one of his ribs the last time he tried something stupid like that. He was drunk. But that's no excuse.'

'So why do you stay with him?'

'You really want to know?'

'Yeah.'

'Sound like you mean it.'

'I mean it.'

'If I tell you, you've got to promise me one thing.'

'What's that?'

'Promise not to say anything.'

'Shit. I promise. Scout's honour. Why'd you stay with him?'

'Because being alone is the worst. Especially for a woman. I walked out on him two and a half years ago, when I found out about one of his women, but after a month I had to go back to him. Being on my own made me crazy. I made him tell me he was sorry for humiliating me and that he'd never do it again, but I knew that wasn't true. Men can't help being pigs. It's the way God made them.'

'And I suppose women are –'

'Bitches, most of us. Me included. But sometimes you need to be a bitch so you can get through the day.'

'And Katya?'

'I wondered how long it would take you to get round to her,' Tammy said. 'Well I'll tell you how much of a bitch she was. You know the man she threw into the room?' Todd nodded. 'His name was Zeffer. He was the man who made her into a movie star. That's the kind of woman she was.'

'There was another side to her, believe me.'

'Don't tell me: she loves dogs.'

'Wait . . .' he said wearily, waving away her cynicism. 'I'm trying to explain something here.'

'I don't want to hear about her kinder, gentler side.'

'Why not?'

'Because she's a bad woman, Todd. They named Coldheart Canyon after her, for God's sake. Did you know that? Anyway, we're neither of us going back up there. Agreed?'

Todd didn't reply. He simply stared at the faded photograph of the Hollywood sign that hung above the bed. 'Didn't somebody throw themselves off that?' he said finally.

'Yeah. Her name was Peg Entwistle. She was a failed actress. Did you hear what I said?' Tammy said.

'About what?'

'Neither of us is going back up to see Katya again, agreed? You're not going to try and sneak back up there the moment my back's turned?'

'Why? Would it matter so much if I did?' he said. His belief that all this was a dream seemed to have lost credibility in the last few minutes. 'You're never going to see me again after this anyway.'

It was true of course: this was the first and last time she'd sit in a motel room and have a conversation with Todd Pickett. But it still stung her to hear it said. Hurt, she stumbled after a response. 'It only matters because I want the best for you.'

'Then move over,' he said, coming to the bed, 'and let me lie down and sleep. Because that's what I want right now.'

She got up off the bed.

'You not going to sleep?' he said.

'There isn't room for both of us.'

'Sure there is. Lie down and get some rest. We'll talk about this when we've got some sleep.'

He slipped off his shoes and lay down, placing one of the paper-thin pillows beside the other so they'd both have somewhere to lay their heads.

'Go on,' he said. 'Lie down. I won't bite.'

'You do know how weird all this is for me, don't you?'

'Which part: the girl, the house, the Devil's wife –'

'No. You and me, together in one bed.'

'Don't worry, I'm not going to be making sexual advances –'

'I *know* that –'

'– I'm just suggesting we get some sleep.'

'Yeah. Well. Okay. But it's still weird. You know, you used to be somebody I idolized.'

'With a heavy emphasis on the *used to be*,' Todd said, opening one eye and looking at her.

'Don't be so sensitive.'

'No. I get the message. It was the same when I met Paul Newman, in the flesh.' He closed his eye again. 'I always used to think he was *the* coolest of all the cool guys. He had those ice-blue eyes, and that easy way of . . .' his words were getting slower, dreamier '. . . walking into a room . . . and I used to think . . . when I'm famous . . .' The words trailed away.

'Todd?'

He opened his eyes a fraction and looked at her between the lashes. 'What was I saying?'

'Never mind,' she said to him, sitting on the bed. 'Go to sleep.'

'No, tell me. What was I saying?'

'How much you wanted to be like Paul Newman.'

'Oh yeah. I just used to practise my Newman act for hours on end. The way everything he did was so *relaxed*. Sometimes he looked so relaxed you couldn't believe he was acting at all. It looked so . . . easy . . .'

While he talked Tammy took off her own shoes (her feet were filthy, and ached, but she didn't have the strength to get into a shower), and then lay down beside Todd. He didn't even seem to realize she was there beside him. His monologue continued, though it became less coherent, as sleep steadily made his tongue more sluggish.

'When I met him . . . finally met him . . . he was . . . so . . . *small* . . .'

His conclusion reached, he began to snore gently.

Tammy sat up on her elbows and looked at him, lying there, wondering how she would have felt if she'd been told a few days ago that she'd be sharing a bed with Todd Pickett. It would have made her heart jump a beat even to contemplate the possibility. And yet here she was, lying down beside him, and she felt nothing; nothing except a vague irritation that she was not going to get a fair share of the bed with him sprawled out over it. Oh well, she had no choice. She could either sleep on the bed with Mr Heart-throb, or take the floor.

She closed her eyes.

She was exhausted: sleep came in a matter of moments. There were no dreams.

3

While the two mismatched adventurers slept in the subterranean murk of Room 131 in the Wilshire Plaza Hotel, a sleep too deep to be called comfortable; too close to death, in fact – the city of Los Angeles got up and went about its daily business. There was profit to be made. There were movies being shot all over the city. Joyless little pornos being made in ratty motels, witless spectacles with budgets that could have supported small nations made on the soundstages of Culver City and Burbank; penniless independent films about the lives of hustlers, whores and penniless film-makers shot wherever a room could be found and the actors assembled. Some would go on to glory; even the pornos had their nights of prize-giving now, when the lucky lady voted Best Cock-Sucker was called to the podium to humbly thank her agent, her mother and Jesus Christ.

But the fictions, whether sex or science-fiction, were not the only dramas that would be played out today. This was a city that made its profit by selling dreams, not least of itself, and so every day young hopefuls arrived by bus and by plane to try their luck. And every day a few of those dreamers, having been here a few months (sometimes a few years) realized that their place in the food chain of fame was lower than a piece of week-old sushi. It was not going to happen for them: they weren't going to be the next Meryl Streep, the next Todd Pickett, the next Jim Carrey. They'd have to wait another lifetime for their slice of fame; or the lifetime after that, or the lifetime after that. And for some, it wasn't news they could bear to take home with them. Better to buy a gun (as Ryan Tyler, real name Norman Miles, did that morning) and go back to your one room apartment and blow out your brains. He'd had two lines in one of the *Lethal Weapon* movies, which he'd told everyone in Stockholm, Ohio, was the beginning of a great career. But the lines had been cut, and for some reason he'd never caught a director's eye ever again. Not once in six years, since he'd had those two lines, had he been called back for an audition. The bullet was kinder than the silent phone. His death didn't make the news.

The suicide of one Rod McCloud did, but only because he'd thrown himself off a bridge onto the 405 and brought the morning traffic in both directions to a halt for an hour. McCloud had actually won an Oscar; he'd been the co-recipient (with four other producers) of the coveted little icon fourteen years earlier. There hadn't been time for him to reach the microphone and thank his agent and Jesus Christ; the orchestra had started playing the exit music before the man in front of him had finished giving his thanks; then it was too late.

At noon, another suicide was discovered; that of a man who, unlike McCloud – who had been sixty-one – was still at the beginning of his life. Justin Thaw, who two years ago had been named by *Vanity Fair* the Most Powerful Agent In LA Under Twenty-Five (he was twenty-two at the time), and had been groomed by the greatest of the city's agent-deities as the inheritor of his chair, made a noose and hanged himself in his brother's garage, leaving a suicide letter that was arranged as a series of bullet-points (in the style his ex-boss had taught him), for maximum clarity. He could no longer fight his addiction, he said; he was too tired of feeling as though he was a failure, just because he was hooked on heroin. He was sorry for all the heartless things he'd said and done to those he loved; it had been the drug doing, the drug saying: but it was he who was sorry, and he who was glad to be leaving today, because life wasn't worth the effort any more. He was wearing the ten thousand dollar suit he'd had made for himself in Milan, the shoes he'd purchased in Rome, and (so as not to make as much of a mess of his death as he had of his life) a pair of adult diapers.

The news of Justin's death would spread quickly, and a few executives' doors would be closed for a while, giving the man behind them a moment to remember the occasions they'd got high with Justin, and wonder whether it wasn't time they asked for help from Narcotics Anonymous. Then the phones from their powerful contemporaries started to ring again, and the pressure of the day meant that meditation had to be put off for a while; they took a snort or two of coke, put Justin out of their minds, and got on with the deal-making. They could think about him again at the funeral.

Speaking of which: the ashes of one Jennifer Scarscella were on a Chicago-bound plane that afternoon, headed for interment in the city of her birth. Jennifer had died nine months ago, but her body had only recently been found and identified in the LA Morgue. She had left home seven years before, without telling her parents where she was headed, though it wouldn't have been hard for the Scarscellas to figure out that their daughter had left to try her luck in Tinseltown: all she'd ever wanted to do was be a movie star. She had been murdered by her boyfriend, because she'd refused, he said, to take a role in an X-rated movie. He was now in jail, and Jennifer was going home, having kept her ambitions high, and died for doing so.

And so the day went on, the shadows of the city lengthening as the sun began to drop from its high-point at noon.

At a little after four, there was a crisis at Warner's, when a set under construction caught fire, gutting an entire sound stage, and badly damaging two adjacent sound stages. Nobody was killed, but there were still grim faces in the boardroom that afternoon. Insurance would cover the reconstruction of the stages, but the set had been built for the Warner's Christmas offering *Dark Justice*. With an elaborate post-production schedule for the picture that required the main shoot to be over in a month's time, things looked bad. There had been a great deal of 'creative debate' about the script, which had no less than fourteen writers presently attached to it. Arbitration by the Writers' Guild would thin those numbers, but nothing would make the calculation look any better if the picture missed its Christmas release date, which it now looked likely to do. Two executives received calls from their superiors in New York, pointing out that if they hadn't warred so much about the script the picture would have been shot by now and the agonizingly slow post-production underway. Instead they had a smoking shell of a building where the big scenes were to have been shot, starting in two days. There was a fiscal disaster in the offing, and certain people should be ready to hand in their resignations before they were embarrassed into leaving by the imminent and unflattering analysis as to why ninety pages of dialogue about a man who dressed up as a jaguar to fight the villains of some fictional metropolis could not have been agreed on earlier, when there was four and a half million dollars' worth of writing talent on the job. The observation that 'we're not making fucking *Citizen Kane* here' dropped from several mouths that day; more often than not from men who had never seen *Kane*, nor would have cared for it even if they had.

By five, with the freeways bumper to bumper as people got out of town for the weekend, there were a plethora of accidents, but nothing of consequence. Scripts were delivered for the weekend read; writers crossed their fingers and hoped that somebody would read what they'd slaved over without kids fighting at their feet or their dick in somebody's mouth or a smudge of coke on their nose; plans were made for weekend adulteries; those letters of resignation were penned by smiling assistants.

And through it all Todd and the woman who had once idolized him slept side by side in the stale darkening air of Room 131.

4

Tammy woke first, rising up out of a dream of the very room in which she was sleeping, except that all the furniture had for some unfathomable reason been piled against one end of the room, including the frame of the bed in which she was sleeping, leaving her on a mattress on the floor. When she woke, of course, nothing had changed. It was still an ordinary room with one extra ordinary element, surreal in its lack of likelihood: the sleeping figure of Todd Pickett. There he was, sprawled across three-quarters of the bed, his head deep in the pillow, his face – his poor, wounded face – free, it seemed, of troubled dreams.

What she would have given, once upon a time, for a moment like this: a chance to lean over and kiss him awake. But she'd lost faith in such fairy-stories. She'd seen too much of their dark side, and she never wanted to go there again, even for the kissing of princes. Better to let them wake of their own accord, dragon-breath and all.

She glanced at the cheap digital clock on the bedside table. It was five-twenty-one in the afternoon. Surely that couldn't be right? That they'd slept for almost eleven hours? And Todd still sleeping?

Well, the latter she could believe. She knew from her years with Arnie how some men *loved* to sleep. In Arnie's case he'd loved it more than anything else. More than eating, more than drinking, certainly more than sex.

She left Todd to it, went into the tiny bathroom and

switched on the light. God, she looked terrible! How had he ever consented to get into the same bed as her? She started her clean-up by vigorously scrubbing her teeth, then ran the shower very hot, the way she liked it even when she felt clean, and got in. Oh, it felt good! The soap smelled flowery, and the cheap shampoo didn't work up a satisfying lather, but she was happy nevertheless, getting herself clean for the first time in days: washing off the freaks, the ghosts, the earth, the darkness. By the time she drew back the plastic curtain the steam was so dense she could barely see across the bathroom to the door. But it was being opened, that much she *could* see, and there was Todd, standing looking at her. She grabbed the towel off the sink where she'd left it, and used it as best she could to cover her considerable nakedness.

'Good morning,' he said.

'Good afternoon,' she replied.

'It isn't.'

'Almost five-thirty,' she said. 'There's a clock beside the bed. Why don't you go look? And close the door after you.'

'I gotta take a leak first. I'm sorry. But I gotta.'

'Let me get out first.'

'Just don't look,' he said, unzipping himself.

She drew the shower curtain back, and continued to dry herself, while for the second time in the last twelve hours she heard the solid splash of him emptying his bladder. He took an age. By the time he was finished she was almost done drying herself.

'Okay, I'm done,' he said, with evident relief. 'Does this place have room service?'

'Yes.'

'You want something to eat?'

This was no time to be ladylike, she told herself. 'I'm starving,' she said.

'What do you want?'

412

'Just *food*. Nothing fancy.'

'I shouldn't think there's much danger of that.'

She waited until she'd heard the door click closed, then she pulled the shower curtain back and finished off drying her nooks and crannies. She could hear his voice as he ordered food on the phone. It sounded like the soundtrack of a Todd Pickett movie playing on the television next door. Stepping out of the bath she cleared a hole in the steamed-up mirror with the ball of her hand and regarded her reflection balefully. She was cleaner, but that was about the only improvement. She opened the door a crack.

'I need some clean clothes.'

Todd was sitting on the bed. He'd finished making his order and had turned on one of the late afternoon chat shows.

'You can come in here and get dressed,' he said, not turning from the screen. 'I won't look.'

She discarded her sodden towel and ventured in, sorting through the meagre contents of her suitcase for something presentable.

'I ordered club sandwiches,' Todd said. 'That was pretty much all they had. And coffee.'

'Fine.'

As she pulled on her underwear she glanced up at the television. A woman in a red polyester blouse three sizes too small for her was complaining vociferously to the host of the show that her daughter, who looked about eleven, went out every night 'dressed like a cheap little slut.'

'I love this shit,' Todd said.

'People's lives,' Tammy replied.

'I guess they're happy. They get their fifteen minutes.'

'Did you like yours?'

'I got more than fifteen,' he said.

'I didn't mean to offend you. I was just asking.'

'Sure, I enjoyed it. Who wouldn't? The first few times you're in a restaurant and a waiter recognizes you, or

413

somebody sends over a drink, you get a buzz out of that. In fact, you feel like you're the only person who matters . . .' His voice trailed away. The daughter on the screen, who had the seeds of whoredom in her pre-pubescent features, was telling the audience that if she wanted to dress like a slut that was her business, and anyway who did she learn it from? She stabbed her finger in the direction of her mother, who did her best to look virtuous, but given what she'd chosen to do with her hair, makeup and outfit didn't have a chance. Todd laughed, then went back to what he was telling Tammy.

'The whole *"look at me, I'm a star"* thing gets old pretty quickly. And after a while you start to wish people didn't know who you were.'

'Really?'

'Actually, it's more that you want to be able to turn it on or off. Oh shit, look at this –'

The sluttish daughter was now up off her chair, and attempting to attack her mother. Luckily, there was a security man ready to step in and stop her. Unluckily, he wasn't quite fast enough to do so. The girl threw herself upon her mother with such violence the woman's chair toppled over, and the security man, who had by now taken hold of the girl to keep her from doing harm, fell forward too, so that chair, mother, daughter and security man ended up on the studio floor together. Todd continued to talk through it.

'There are days when you really want to feel good about yourself; you *want* to be recognized, you want people to say: I loved your movie so much I saw it six times. And then there are other days when it's a curse to have people know who the hell you are, because there's no privacy, no way to just go out and be yourself. Everything becomes a performance.' He pointed at the brawlers on television. 'Look at these stupid bitches. What are they going to say when their friends see this?' He pondered his own question

414

for a moment, then he said: 'Actually, I know *exactly* what they're going to say. They're going to say: did you see me on the TV? That's all that matters. Not: did you see me being smart or looking beautiful: just *did you see me*?'

He watched the women's antics for a while longer, shaking his head. Then he glanced over at Tammy and said:

'I've been thinking maybe I'm done with the movies. Or movies are done with me. It's time to buy a ranch in Montana and raise horses.'

'Really?' Tammy had finally got dressed, and came to sit down on the unmade bed beside Todd. 'You're going to retire?'

He laughed.

'What's so funny?'

'Oh, just hearing the word. Retire. At thirty-four.'

'I thought you were thirty-two. Your bio –'

'I lied.'

'Oh.'

'But I'm still young. Right? I mean, thirty-four is still young.'

'A mere kitten.'

'I just can't face the idea of that *circus* for one more day . . .' He turned off the television. The room was suddenly very silent.

After a few moments Tammy said: 'Are we going to talk about it or not?'

Todd stared at the blank television. She couldn't see his expression but she was certain it was just as vacant as the screen.

'The Canyon, Todd,' she said again. 'Are we going to talk about what happened in the Canyon or not?'

'Yes,' he replied finally. 'I suppose so.'

'Last night you said it wasn't real.'

'I was tired.'

'So?'

'It's real. I knew last night I was talking bullshit . . .'

415

He kept his back to her through this, as though he didn't want to let her see his incomprehension; as though it were something to be ashamed of.

'You saw more than I did,' she said to Todd. 'So you've probably got a clearer idea of what's going on. And you talked to –'

'Katya.'

'Yes. And. What did she tell you?'

'She told me the room downstairs had been given to her.'

'By Zeffer. Yes, I know that part.'

'Then what are you asking me for?' he said. 'You probably know as much as I do.'

'What about Maxine?'

'What about her?'

'She must have checked out the house for you –'

'Yeah. She took photographs –'

'Maybe she has some answers.'

'Maxine?' He got up off the bed and went to the table to pick up his cigarettes. He took one out of the packet and lit it, inhaling deeply. 'As soon as she'd moved me into that fucking house she told me she didn't want to manage me any longer,' he said.

There was a knock at the door. 'Room service.'

Tammy opened the door and an elderly man, who frankly looked as though this might be the last club sandwiches and coffee he delivered, tottered in, and set the laden tray on the table.

'I asked for extra mayonnaise,' Todd said.

'Here, sir.' The old man proffered a small milk jug, into which several spoonfuls of mayonnaise had been deposited.

'Thank you, it's all fine,' Tammy said.

Todd went into his jeans pocket and pulled out a bundle of notes. He selected a twenty – much to the antiquated waiter's delight – and gave it to the man.

'Thank you very much, sir,' he said, exiting rather faster than he'd entered, in case the man in the filthy jeans changed his mind.

They set to eating.

'You know what?' Todd said.

'What?'

'I think I should go and see Maxine. Ask her what she knows, face to face. Maybe this was all some kind of set up –'

'If you get her on the phone –?'

'She'll lie.'

'You've had that experience?'

'Several times.'

'Where does she live?'

'Well she's got three houses. A house in Aspen, a place in the Hamptons and a house in Malibu.'

'Oh how she must suffer,' Tammy said, teasing a piece of crispy bacon out of her sandwich and nibbling on it. 'Only three houses? How does she manage?'

'So eat up. We'll just drop in on her.'

'Both of us?'

'Both of us. That way she can't tell me I'm crazy. What I saw, you saw.'

'Actually, I saw some shit you didn't see.'

'Well, we'll be sure to get some answers from her.'

'Are you certain you want me to come?'

'There's safety in numbers,' Todd said. 'Drink your coffee and let's get going.'

5

Katya hadn't wasted any time weeping over Todd's departure. What was the use? She'd shed more than her share of tears over men and their betrayals across the years. What good had any of her weeping ever done her?

Besides, it wasn't as if she'd truly lost the man; he'd simply drifted away from her for a few hours, that was all. She'd get him back, humbled and begging to be returned into her company. After all, hadn't she let him kiss her? Hadn't she let him fuck her, there in the Devil's Country? He could never forget those memories.

Oh, he could try. He could put a hundred women, a thousand, between the two of them, but it wouldn't work. Sooner or later he'd come crawling back to her for more of what only she could give him, and nothing that fat bitch of a woman who'd coaxed him away could say would keep him from coming back. A man like Todd had nothing in common with a creature like that. He understood the world in ways she could not even guess at. What hope did she have of seeing with his eyes, even for a moment? None. She was a workhorse. Todd had lived with beauty too long to put up with the presence of something so charmless for very long. After a few hours of her clumsy company, he'd be off.

She had only one fear: that owing to the artful way her Canyon had been hidden, he wouldn't be able to find his way back to her.

The city had never been a simple place even during the years she'd lived in it; it was easy to get lost or distracted. How much more complicated would it be *now*, especially for someone like her poor Todd, whose soul was so muddled and confused. She knew how that felt, to have everyone falling over themselves to adore you one moment, and the next to find that those same people had given their devotions over to somebody else. It turned everything upside down when that happened; nothing made sense any more. You started looking around for something to hold on to; something firm and solid, that wouldn't be taken away. In such a mood of desperation, it was possible you could make a mistake: choose the wrong person to believe in, the wrong path to follow. Even now, he could be moving away from her.

The more she contemplated that prospect the more it became apparent that she was going to have to go and find him.

The idea of venturing out of her Canyon filled her with a mingling of fear and anticipation.

The world! The great, wide world!

It was three quarters of a century since she'd stepped beyond the bounds of the Canyon; and though she'd had plenty of clues as to the way things had changed, from those who'd come here after their decease, it would still be an intimidating experience for her to venture out there, even on a mission of love.

But what other choice did she have? Without him, her hopes were in ruins. She *had* to go and find him, it was as simple as that. And on the way back, once they were together again maybe she'd have the strength of heart to visit some of the places she'd known and loved in her youth; just to see how time had altered them. But then again perhaps that wouldn't be such a good idea. It troubled her enough to look out of the window and see the stretches of land that had been dust roads and shacks and orange groves in her time now completely transformed into towers of steel and glass. What if she were to discover that some precious place she'd loved had been desecrated; rendered unrecognizable? Though she liked to think she was fearless, in truth time was taking its toll on the resilience of her soul.

But then, of course, this whole quest was a test of her strength, wasn't it?

Venturing beyond the perimeters of her Canyon, beyond the reach of the magic that had preserved her perfection, was gambling with her life. She had no way of knowing for certain but she guessed that the further she ventured, and the longer she remained away from the Canyon, from the house and all it contained, the more vulnerable she'd be to the long-postponed indignities of old age. After all, beneath this veneer of youth she was a Methuselah. How long could she afford to be out in the raptureless world before the shell cracked and the crone inside, the hag that the Devil's Country had obscured with its magic, was unveiled?

It was terrifying. But in the end, it came down to this: finding Todd was worth the risk. If she survived the journey they would come back to the Canyon and initiate a new Golden Age. It wouldn't be like the previous Age of Gold, with its foolish excesses. This would be a more profoundly felt time, when instead of using the Devil's Country like a cross between a two-bit ghost-train ride and a fountain of youth, it would be respected as the mystery it was.

Despite the perverse pride she'd taken in showing Todd the orgiasts in the Canyon, and in letting him share their excesses, Katya's appetite for the witless hedonism of the twenties had long since passed away. And though Todd had happily played the sensualist, she was sure that he too had seen enough of the tawdriness of such spectacles. It was time they behaved as owners of something genuinely marvellous; and treated it respectfully. Together, they would

420

begin an exploration of the world Lilith had made. Katya had never possessed the courage to explore as it deserved to be explored, road by road, grove by sacred grove. Certainly she'd seen plenty there over the years that had inflamed her sexual self (women tethered to the underbellies of human-horses, in a constant state of ecstatic agony); and she would not scorn such spectacles if they came on them again. But there were other sights, designed to arouse the spirit not the loins; and it was to those places she wanted to take Todd.

There were enough diversions and wonders to keep them enchanted for decades to come. Though the heavens were fixed in the same configuration whenever she visited the Country, there was nevertheless evidence that the earth was still obeying some of its ancient rhythms.

There was, for instance, in the swamp, a manmade lake perhaps half a mile wide, which seemed to have been for many generations the place where a certain species of eel, the infants silver-blue, with great golden eyes, came in their millions – each no longer than her little finger – but sufficient in number that they filled the place of their birth to brimming when they spawned. For a day – when the larval eels appeared – this Genesis Bowl, as Katya had named it, was a feasting place for birds of every kind, who were literally able to walk on the squirming backs of their feast, taking all they could before lifting off (some so fat with food they could barely fly) and retiring to the nearest branch to digest their mighty meal. The next day (if the Country could be said to have days) the Genesis Bowl was empty, but for a few thousand runts that had perished in the exodus, and were being picked up by carrion crows and wild dogs.

She wanted to show this glorious spectacle to Todd; wanted to wade into the living mass of baby eels and feel them against her naked flesh.

On another day they might go to a place she knew where

there was a beast that spoke prophetic riddles; which had twice engaged her in conversation which she knew would make sense if she had the education to decode its strange poetry. It had the body of a huge bird, this riddler, with a man's head, and it sat, close to the ground, with a vast array of glittering gifts around the base of its tree, offered for its prophecies. She'd come to it a year ago, with some jewellery she had worn in *Nefertiti*.

'Is it real, the gift you give me?' the creature, whose name was Yiacaxis, had asked her.

'No,' she had admitted. 'I am an actress. These baubles are what I wore when I was an actress.'

'Then make them real for me,' Yiacaxis had said, clicking his old grey tongue against his cracked beak. 'Play me the scene in which you wore them.'

'It was silent,' she said.

'That's good,' he replied. 'For I am very deaf in my old age.'

She shed most of her clothes, and put on the jewellery. Then she played the scene from *Nefertiti* in which she discovers that her lover is dead by the order of the envious Queen, and she kills herself out of tragic longing for him.

The old bird-man wept freely at her performance.

'I'm pleased it moved you so much,' Katya had said when she was done.

'I accept your offering,' the creature had replied, 'and I will give you your answer.'

'But you don't even know my question yet.'

Yiacaxis clicked and cocked his head. 'I know you wonder if there will ever be a love worth dying for in your life? Is that your question?'

'Yes,' she said. She would perhaps not have asked it that way, but the prophet was notoriously short-tempered with those who attempted to press him.

'There are two multitudes,' he said. 'One within you.

422

One without. Should he love you enough to name one of these legions, then you will live in bliss with the other.'

Of course she desperately wanted to ask him what this meant; but the audience was apparently already over, for Yiacaxis was raising his black wings, which were lined with little knots of human hair, tied up in ribbons that had long-ago lost their colour. Thousands of locks of hair, in wings that spread perhaps twenty feet from tip to tip. Without further word, he closed them over his melancholy face, and the shadows of the tree seemed to close around him a second time, so that he was invisible.

Perhaps, if she had the courage, she would go back to Yiacaxis, with Todd, and ask him another question. Or this time Todd should do the asking.

And when they had questioned the Prophet Bird, and seen half a hundred other wonders in the Devil's Country, Katya would take Todd to a certain ship with which she was familiar, which had surely been made for a king, it was so finely wrought.

It had foundered on some rocks along the shore, and there it had been left, high and dry, many years ago. For some reason no looter had ever attempted to despoil this sublime vessel, perhaps because they feared some royal revenge. The only damage done to the vessel was the breaking of its hull by the rocks; and the inevitable deterioration of its exterior paintwork by wind and rain. Inside, it remained a place of incomparable luxury, its beautiful carved bed heaped with white furs, the wine still sweet in its flagons, the tinder in its fireplace still awaiting a flame. She had often fantasized about taking a lover to the ship, making love to him on the furs. If they were lucky, the wind would get up when they were cradled in the comfort of one another's arms. The wind would whistle in the ropes and the scarlet sails would billow, and they would imagine, as they made love, that they were on a voyage to the edge of the world.

It would be naïve to speak lovingly of the Devil's Country without allowing that it had its share of horrors.

There were species in the forests, and the ravines and the black silent pools between the rocks, that had been invented by some benighted mind. There were terrible arenas, where monsters were goaded to perform acts of horrible violation upon women, and sometimes upon men and even children. But having viewed several of these spectacles herself, she could not deny that they were perversely arousing. Some had the rigor of ceremonies, others seemed to be simple arenas of cruelty, where anything might be viewed if it was paid for.

The point was that she'd seen so little, and that there was so much for her to see; a private wonderland where she and Todd could go adventuring whenever they tired of the Canyon. They could explore it to its very limits; and when they were weary and needed to sleep, they could simply step through the door and lock it, and retire to bed like any loving pair, and sleep peacefully in one another's arms.

But first she had to find him; and to find him she needed a chauffeur. Only one man fitted that bill: Jerry Brahms. They had known one another for so many years. That was why she'd sent out the dream-summons to him. He was loyal; he would come without fail. It was only a matter of time before he turned up at the house, ready to do her bidding. He was probably on his way up, even now.

It didn't take her long to dress. She had wardrobes full of gowns designed by some of the greatest names in Hollywood history, but they were all too showy for this modest adventure. So she chose conservatively: an immaculately-tailored black dress. She kept her hair simple and her makeup discreet.

She was all dressed and ready to go, but there was still no sign of Jerry. Thinking that perhaps he'd mistakenly assume she would wait for him in the big house, she decided to wander down through the twilight to look for him. If he hadn't arrived then she'd wait for him at the front gate, so that there'd be no chance of their missing one another.

It was a walk she'd taken countless times, of course; though the pathway rose and dipped, she could have done it in safety blind-folded.

The night wasn't as clear as it had been when she and Todd had come out walking; there were rainclouds banked in from the north, and the air was sultry. It was going to be one of those nights when you longed for a heaven-and-earth-shaking thunderstorm, the kind she remembered from her childhood. But such events were rare in Los Angeles. All the great storms she'd seen here had been cooked up by lighting men and rain-machines; pure artifice.

She knew she was being watched as she walked. There wasn't a movement she made in the open air that the ghosts or their half-breed children did not observe. They had even made spy-holes in the walls of her little house, she knew. They watched her at her toilette; they watched her as she read and day-dreamed; they watched her as she slept.

She'd several times attempted to stop them and punish their voyeurism; but every time Zeffer plugged up the holes more appeared, and finally she'd given up the game as fruitless. If they wanted to watch her while she slept, then let them go ahead. Indeed until Todd had come into her life the idea of having somebody to watch over her – even if their motives were as hard to calculate as those of her voyeurs – was close to comforting.

Needless to say there was also a measure of danger in the proximity of these revenants. Katya didn't doubt that there was amongst their number some who would gladly have seen her dead, blaming her for the fact that their afterlife in Coldheart Canyon was a pitiful thing. Of course she didn't blame herself. If her guests hadn't been so hungry to taste the pleasures of the Devil's Country then they wouldn't be so obsessively drawn to it. But as long as they kept a respectful distance (why would they not, when she controlled the very thing they wanted for themselves?) then she would not persecute them.

They had their journey, she had hers.

She had reached the unkempt lawn, and paused there to take in the spectacle of the house. The wind-chimes rang on four or five balconies, lending their beauty to the grand façade. As she listened to their music she heard sounds from the thicket on the other side of the lawn.

She glanced back. There was still sufficient light in the evening sky to see the motion in the blossom-laden branches. There were several creatures following her, she guessed.

She watched the bushes for half a minute, until the motion died down. It wasn't unusual for creatures to follow her when she went out walking, but there was something different about this. Or was it that *she* was different? That tonight she was alive as she'd not been alive in many years, her heart quickened by love; and that they sensed a new vulnerability in her?

She didn't like that. The last thing she wanted was for them to imagine they could intimidate her, or somehow wrest a little power from her. Love might have made her step a little lighter, but she was still the Queen of Coldheart Canyon, and if they pushed her she would respond with her old severity.

As she watched the thicket, the last of the light went from the sky, and the darkness revealed several bright points of light in the bushes, where the revenants were standing, watching her. Even after all these years she could still be discomfited by a sight like this; by the fact that the dead were around her in such numbers.

Enough, she thought to herself, and turning on her heel hurried towards the stairs that led back up to the house.

As she did so she heard the swish of grass against

swiftly running limbs. They were coming across the lawn in pursuit of her.

She picked up her pace, until she reached the relative safety of the stairs.

Behind her, a soft voice, sounding as though it came from a palate full of pulp and disease, said: 'Let us in.'

There was a moment's silence. Then another said, 'We just want to come back into the house.'

'We won't do any harm,' said a third.

'Please, let us in . . .'

She'd been wrong about the numbers of revenants assembled here, she slowly realized. She thought there'd been perhaps ten, but there were two or three times that number out there in the darkness. Whatever the decayed and corrupted condition of their palates, they all attempted to say the same thing:

'Let us in. Let us in. Let us in.'

She would have ignored them, once upon a time: turned her back on their pleas and climbed the stairs. But she was changing. Katya the heartbreaker – the woman who'd never given a damn for what anybody wanted but herself – was rapidly becoming a thing of the past. If she was going to come back with Todd and live here, they couldn't live the idyllic life she had in mind while these hungry souls waited outside. Even with the five iron icons hammered into the threshold of each of the doors, and in the sills of even the smallest windows, their presence preventing the dead from ever setting foot in the house, the occupants were in a state of siege. It was no place to have a honeymoon.

She raised her hand to silence their murmuring.

'Listen to me,' she said.

The chorus began to subside.

'I'm going to be leaving the house for a few hours,' Katya said, her voice a little tentative at the beginning, but gaining strength as she proceeded. 'But when I come back I intend

427

to make some changes. I don't want you living in misery. That has to stop.'

She started to turn away, intending to leave the statement there. But some of her congregation didn't want to let her go without hearing something more specific in her reply.

'*What* changes are you going to make?' someone demanded.

'Is that you, Ramon?' Katya said, scanning the crowd.

The speaker didn't have time to identify himself. There were more questions. Somebody wanted to know why she was leaving; somebody else demanded to know how long they would have to wait.

'Listen to me, listen to me,' she said, quieting the rising hubbub. 'I understand that you all want to come into the house. But I don't think you understand the consequences.'

'We'll take them, whatever they are,' somebody said. There was a general murmur of agreement to this.

'If that's what you want,' Katya replied, 'I will consider it. When I get back –'

'What if you don't *come* back?'

'Trust me. I will.'

'Trust *you*? Oh please.' The mocking voice emerged from a bitter, painted face amongst the crowd. 'You tricked us all. Why the hell should we trust you now?'

'Theda,' Katya said. 'I don't have the time to explain right now.'

'Well you hold on, honey, because we want some answers. We've had years of waiting to go back into that room –'

'Then you can afford to wait a few hours more,' Katya replied, and without waiting for Theda Bara to come back with a retort she turned and headed on up the steps to the top of the flight.

There was a moment – just a quarter of a beat, there at

428

the top of the stairs – when she thought she'd misjudged her audience, and they'd come up the stairs after her, their patience finally exhausted. But they'd stayed below. Even Theda. Perhaps somebody had caught hold of her arm, to keep her from doing something stupid.

Katya opened the back door, stepping over the threshold. Occasionally, in the last several decades, one of the assembly outside had taken it into their heads to test the power of the icons Zeffer had brought back from Romania, and had personally hammered deep into the wood. The five icons were called, Zeffer had told her, the Iron Word. It was powerful magic designed to drive off anything that did not belong beside cot or hearth. Katya had never actually witnessed what happened when one of the phantoms had tested the threshold. She'd only heard the screams, and seen the looks of terror on the faces of those who'd goaded the victim. Of the trespasser himself, nothing remained, except a rise in the humidity of the air around the threshold, as though the revenant had been exploded into vapour. Even these traces lingered for only a moment. As soon as the air cooled the witnesses retreated from the door, looks of terror still fixed on their faces.

She had no idea how the Iron Word worked. She only knew that Zeffer had paid a member of Sandru's scattered brotherhood a small fortune to possess the secret, and then another sum to have the icons created in sufficient numbers that every door and window be guarded. It had been worth the investment: the Iron Word did its job. Katya felt like her mother, who'd always boasted that she kept a 'clean house'. Of course Mother Lupescu's definition of moral cleanliness had been purely her own.

You could fuck her twelve-year-old daughter for a small coin, but you could not say *Christ* when you were shooting your load between her tiny titties without being thrown out of the house.

And in her turn that twelve-year-old had grown up with

her own particular rules of domestic cleanliness. In short: *the dead did not cross the threshold.*

You had to draw the line somewhere, or all hell would break loose. On that Mama Lupescu and her daughter would have agreed.

She got herself a cup of milk from the refrigerator to calm her stomach, which always troubled her when, as now, she was unsettled for some reason or another. Then she went through the house, taking her time passing from one room to another, and as she came to the front door she heard the sound of a car coming up the street. She stepped outside, and walked along the front path until she reached the pool of light from the car's headlights.

'Is that you, Jerry?'

A car door opened.

'Yes, it's me,' he said. 'Was I expected?'

'You were.'

'Well, thank God for that.'

She went to the little gate, and stepped out onto the narrow sidewalk. Jerry had got out of the car. He had a barely-suppressed look of shock on his face, seeing her step beyond the bounds of her little dominion for the first time.

'Are we actually *going somewhere*?' he asked her.

'I certainly hope so,' she said, playing it off lightly. She could not completely conceal her unease, however. It was there in her eyes. But there was also something else in her glance, besides the unease: something far more remarkable. A kind of sweetness, even innocence. She looked like a girl out on her first Prom Night, tip-toeing to the edge of womanhood.

Amazing, Jerry thought. Knowing all that he knew about Katya – all that she'd done and caused to have done – to be able to find that look in her memory banks, and put it up there on her face, so that it looked as real as it did; *that* was a performance.

'Where will I be taking you tonight, ma'am?' Jerry asked her.

'I'm not exactly sure. You see we're going to be looking for somebody.'

'Are we indeed? And may I take a guess at who?'

Katya smiled. 'Too easy,' she said.

'We'll find him for you. Don't you worry.'

'You were the one who got him to come up here in the first place, Jerry. So you're the match-maker. And thank you. From both of us, thank you. It's been quite a remarkable time for me, Jerry. I never thought I'd ever fall in love again. And with an *actor*.' She laughed. 'You'd think I'd have learned by now.'

'I hope it's a happy mistake.'

'Oh it is, Jerry. It's perfect. *He's* perfect.'

'Is he?'

'For me. Yes. Perfect for me.'

'So will you be joining him somewhere?'

'Yes.'

'But you're not exactly sure *where*?'

'That's right.'

'Well, I'm going to hazard a guess and say he's at Maxine's, because I know she's having a big bash tonight. Do you want me to call her, and ask her if he's there? Maybe tell her I'm bringing a special guest?'

'No, I think it's best we just do this quietly, don't you?'

'However you prefer. Tonight's your night.'

'I don't want any big hoopla,' Katya said. '*I just want to find him.*'

For a moment the illusion disappeared completely, and reality showed itself: the desperate hunger of a woman who needed to find the love of her life. Not tomorrow, or the day after, but *tonight*. She had no time to waste, this woman; no time for error or procrastination.

'Shall we go?' she said.

431

'Ready when you are.'

She went to the car and started to fumble with the doorhandle.

'Please,' Jerry said. 'Allow me.' He came round to the passenger side and opened the door.

'Thank you, Jerry. How nice. Old-fashioned manners,' she said. She got into the car in one elegant movement. Jerry closed the door and went to the driver's side. She was *trembling*, he saw; just the slightest tremor.

'It's going to be all right,' he reassured her when he was settled in beside her.

'Is it?' she said, with a smile too tentative to survive more than a breath.

'Yes. It's going to be fine.'

'He's the one, Jerry. Todd is the one. If he were to turn me down –'

'He's *not* going to do that, now is he?' Jerry said. 'He'd be a fool to say no to you. And whatever else Todd is, he's no fool.'

'So find him for me. Will you?'

'Yes, ma'am.'

'Then I can start to live again.'

6

I t had taken Todd a few minutes to get used to sitting behind the wheel of the old Lincoln sedan which Marco had chosen, many years before, as the vehicle in which he preferred to anonymously chauffeur Todd around. Sitting in the seat adjusted for Marco's huge frame made him realize – for the first time in the chaotic sequence of dramas that had unravelled since Marco's sudden death – how much he would miss the man.

Marco had been a stabilizing influence in a world that was showing signs of becoming more unstable by the hour. But more than that: he'd been Todd's friend. He'd had a good nose for bullshit, and he'd never been afraid of speaking his mind, especially when it came to protecting his boss.

There would come a time, Todd had promised himself, when he would sit down and think of something to do that would honour Caputo's name. He'd been no intellectual, so the founding of a library, or the funding of the Caputo Prize for Scholastic Achievement, wouldn't really be pertinent: it would need some serious thought to create a project that reflected and honoured the complexity of the man.

'You're thinking about Marco Caputo,' Tammy said as she watched Todd adjust to the spatial arrangements of the driver's seat.

'The way you said that, it didn't sound as though you liked him very much.'

'He was rude to me on a couple of occasions,' Tammy said, making light of it now. 'It was no big deal.'

'The fact is he was more of a brother to me than my own brother,' he replied. 'And I'm only now realizing how much I took him for granted. Christ. First I lose my dog, then my best buddy –'

'Dempsey?'

'Yeah. He died of cancer in February.'

'I'm sorry.'

Todd turned on the ignition. His thoughts were still with Marco. 'You know what I think?' he said.

'What?'

'I think that the night he got killed he wasn't just drunk. He was panicked and drunk.'

'You mean he'd seen something?'

'Yes, that's exactly what I mean. He'd seen something up at the house and was running away.' He drew a loud breath through his nose. 'Okay. Enough of the detective work. We can do some more of that when all this is over. Right now, we're heading for Malibu.'

On the way down to the ocean, Todd provided Tammy with a little portrait of where they were going. She knew about the Colony, of course – the guarded community of superstars who lived in houses filled with Picassos and Miros and Monets, with the ever-unpredictable Pacific a few yards from their back door, and – just a jump across the Pacific Coast Highway – the Malibu Hills, which had been the scene of countless wild-fires in the hot season, and mud-slides in the wet. What she didn't know was just how exclusive it was, even for those who were powerful enough to write their own rules in any other circumstances.

'I was planning to buy this house next door to Maxine's place, way back,' Todd told her, 'but my lawyer – who was this wily old fart called Lester Mayfield said: "You're going to want to rip out that concrete deck and take off the old

434

shingle roof, aren't you?" And I said: "You betcha." And
he said: "Well, dream on buster, 'cause they won't let you.
You'll spend the next ten years fighting with the Colony
Committee to change the colour of your toilet seat."

'So I didn't buy the place. They've lightened up on the
rules a lot since then. I guess somebody must have pointed
out that they were preserving some pieces of utter shit.'

'Who ended up buying the house next door to Maxine?'

'Oh . . . he was a producer, had a deal with Paramount.
Made some very successful movies for them. Then the IRS
taps him on the shoulder and asks why he hasn't paid his
taxes for six years. He ended up going to jail, and the house
stood empty.'

'Nobody else bought it?'

'No. He wanted to be back making movies when he got
out of the slammer. Which is what he did. Went straight
back into the business. Made six more huge movies. And
he still snorts coke from between the tits of loose women.
Bob Graydon's his name.'

'Isn't he the one who had an artificial septum put in
his nose because he'd had the real thing eaten away by
cocaine?'

'That's Bob. Where'd you hear that?'

'Oh, the *National Enquirer* probably. I buy them all in case
there's something about you. Not that I believe everything
I read –' she added hurriedly.

'Just the juicy bits.'

'Well after a time you get a *feeling* about what's true and
what's not true.'

'Care to give me an example?'

'No.'

'Go on.'

'That's not fair. I'm screwed whatever I say. No! Wait!
Here's one! About two years ago they said you were going
into a private hospital in Montreal to have your ding-a-ling
enlarged.'

'My *ding-a-ling*?'

'You know what I mean.'

'Do you say ding-a-ling to Arnie? It *is* Arnie, isn't it?'

'Yes it's Arnie and no I don't say ding-a-ling.'

'Tell me about him.'

'There isn't much to tell.'

'Why'd you marry him? Tell me that.'

'Well it wasn't because of the size of his dick.'

'Dick! That's what you call it: dick.'

'I guess I do,' Tammy said, amused, a little embarrassed to have let this slip. 'Anyway, back to the story in *The Enquirer*. They said you were in Montreal getting your thingie – your dick – made bigger. Except I knew that wasn't true.'

'How come?'

'It just didn't make any sense. Not after the articles I'd read about you.'

'Go on,' Todd said, fascinated.

'Well . . . you know I read everything that's ever been written about you? Everything in English. And then if there's a really important interview in, say, *Paris Match* or *Stern*, I get it translated.'

'Jesus. Really? What for?'

'So I can keep up with your opinions. And . . . sometimes in the foreign magazines they write the kind of things you wouldn't read in an American magazine. One of them did a piece about your love-life. About all the ladies you'd dated, and the things they'd said about you –'

'My acting?'

'No. Your . . . other performances.'

'You're kidding.'

'No. I thought you knew about these things. I thought you probably signed off on them.'

'If I read every article in every magazine –'

'You'd never make another movie.'

'Exactly. So, go back to the article. The ladies, talking

436

about me. What does that have to do with the story in *The Enquirer*?'

'Oh just that here were all these women talking about you in bed – and a few of them were not exactly happy with the way you treated them – but none of them said, even vaguely intimated that . . .'

'I had a small dick.'

'Right. So I thought, there's no way he's gone to Montreal to have his ding-a-ling enlarged because it's just fine as it is. Now. Can we move on, or shall I throw myself out of the window from sheer embarrassment?'

Todd laughed. 'You are an education, do you know that?'

'I am?'

'You are.'

'In a good way?'

'Oh yeah, it's all good. It's all fine.'

'You realize, of course, that there's stuff being written about you right now, a lot of people upset and worried.'

'Why?'

'Because nobody knows what happened to you. There are plenty of people, fans of yours, like me, who think of you practically as a member of the family. Todd did this. Todd did that. And now, suddenly, Todd's missing. And nobody knows where he's gone. They start to fret. They start to make up all kinds of ridiculous reasons. I know I did. It's not that they're crazy –'

'No, look. I don't think you, or any of them, are crazy. Or if you are, it's a good crazy. I mean, what you did last night . . . none of my family would have done.'

'You'd be surprised how many people love you.'

'They love *something* but I don't think it's *me*, Tammy.'

'Why not?'

'Well for one thing, if you could get inside here, in my head with Todd Pickett, you wouldn't find much worth idolizing. You really wouldn't. I am painfully,

437

excruciatingly, ordinary. My brother, Donnie, on the other hand: he's worth admiring. He's smart. He's honest. I was just the one with this.' He turned on his smile as he drove and gave her the benefit of its luminosity. Then, just as easily, he turned it off. 'See, you learn to do that,' he went on. 'It's like a faucet. You turn the smile on, and people bathe in it for a while, then you turn it off and you go home and wonder what all the fuckin' fuss was about. It's not like I *deserve* the adulation of millions. I can't act. And I've got the reviews to prove it.' He chuckled at his self-deprecation. 'That's not mine,' he said, 'it was Victor Mature.'

'Okay, so you're not the best actor in Hollywood. You're not the worst either.'

'No. I grant you, there's worse.'

'A lot worse.'

'All right, a lot worse. Still doesn't make me a good actor.'

He obviously wasn't going to be moved on the subject, so Tammy left it where it was. They drove on in silence for a while. Then he swung the mirror round, and checked out his face. 'You know I'm nervous?'

'Why?'

'In case there's anybody at Maxine's place.' He went back and forth between studying his face and checking the road.

'You look fine,' Tammy told him.

'I guess it's not so bad,' he said, assessing his features.

'You just look a little different from the way you used to look.'

'Different enough that people will notice?'

Tammy couldn't lie to him. 'Sure they'll notice. But maybe they'll say you look better. I mean, when everything's properly healed and you've had a month's vacation.'

'You will come in with me, won't you?'

'To see Maxine? My pleasure.'

'Mind if I smoke?' He didn't wait for a reply. He just

438

rolled down the window, pulled out a battered pack of cigarettes, and lit up. The rush of nicotine made him whoop. 'That's better! Okay. We're going to do this. You and me. We're going to ask Maxine a lot of very difficult questions, and figure out whether she's lying to us or not.'

They had reached the Pacific Coast Highway, and the roar of the traffic through the open window made any further talk impractical for a time. They drove north for perhaps five miles, before coming off the PCH and heading west. The area wouldn't have been Tammy's idea of idyllic. Somehow she'd imagined Malibu being more like a little slice of Hawaii; but in fact it was just a sliver of real estate two or three houses deep, with the incessant din of the Pacific Coast Highway on one side and a narrow strip of beach on the other. They'd scarcely driven more than a quarter of a mile when they came to the Colony gates. There was a guard-house, and a single guard, who was sitting with his booted feet up beside a small television. The set went off as soon as they drove up, a broad smile appearing on the man's face.

'*Hey*, Mr Pickett. Long time, no see.'

'Ron, m'man. How goes it?'

'It goes good, it goes good.'

The guard was clearly delighted that his name had been remembered.

'Are you going to Ms Frizelle's party?'

'Oh . . . yeah,' Todd said, throwing a panicked glance at Tammy. 'We're here for that.'

'That's great.' He peered past Todd, at the passenger. 'And this is?'

'Oh, this is Tammy. Tammy, Ron. Ron, Tammy. Tammy's my date for the night.'

'Good goin',' Ron said, to no one and about nothing in particular. Just a general California yea-saying to the world. 'Let me just call Ms Frizelle, and tell her you're on your way down.'

'Nah,' Todd said, sliding a twenty dollar bill into Ron's hand. 'We're going to surprise her.'

'No problem,' Ron said, waving them by. 'Good to see you, by the way –'

It took Tammy a moment to realize that Ron was talking to her.

'It's always good to meet a new friend of Mr Pickett's.' There didn't seem to be any irony in this: it was a genuine expression of feeling.

'Well, thank you,' Tammy said, thrown a little off-kilter by this.

'Fuck. She's having a party,' Todd said to her as they left the guard-house behind them.

'So.'

'So there'll be lots of people. Looking at me.'

'They've got to do it sooner or later.'

Todd stopped the car in the middle of the street.

'I can't. I'm not ready for this.'

'Yes you are. The more you put it off the more difficult it's going to be.'

Todd sat there shaking his head saying: 'No. No. I can't do it.'

Tammy put her hand over his. 'I'm just as nervous as you are,' she said. 'Feel how clammy my hand is?'

'Yeah.'

'But we said we'd get answers. And the longer we take to ask her the more lies she'll have ready.'

'You do know her, don't you?' he said.

'She's my nightmare.'

'Really. Why?'

'Because she stood between me and you.'

'Huh.'

Silence.

'So what are we going to do?' Tammy said finally.

'Shit. I don't want to do this.'

'So that makes two of us. But –'

440

'I know, I know, if we don't do it now . . . All right. You win. But I will beat the living shit out of the first person who says one word about my face.'

They drove on, the houses they were driving past far more modest in scale and design than she'd expected. There was very little here of the kitsch of Beverly Hills: no faux-French chateaux sitting side by side with faux-Tudor mansions. The houses were mostly extremely plain, boxlike in most cases, with very occasional architectural flourishes. They were also very close to one another. 'You wouldn't get much privacy there,' Tammy commented.

'I guess everybody just pretends not to look at everybody else. Or they just don't care. That's more like it. They just don't care.'

'That's the connection between you and Katya, isn't it? You've both been looked at so much . . . and the rest of us don't know what that feels like.'

'It feels like somebody's siphoning out your blood, pint by pint.'

'Not good.'

'No. Not good.'

They rounded a corner, bringing their destination into view. The party-house was decorated with thousands of tiny white twinkle lights, as were the two palm trees that stood like sentinels to left and right of the door.

'Christmas came early this year,' Tammy remarked.

'Apparently.'

There were uniformed valets working the street; taking cars from the guests and spiriting them away to be parked somewhere out of sight.

'Are you sure you're ready for this?' Todd asked Tammy.

'No more than you are.'

'Want to go one more circle around the block?'

'Yes.'

'Uh-oh. Too late.'

Two valets were coming at the car bearing what must

441

have been burdensome smiles. As the doors were opened, Todd caught tight hold of Tammy's hand. 'Don't leave my side,' he said. 'Promise me you won't.'

'I promise,' she said, and raising her head she put on her best impersonation of someone who was rich, famous and belonged at Todd Pickett's side. Todd relinquished the keys to the valet.

'May I assume this is your first A-list Hollywood party in the flesh?' Todd said to Tammy.

'You may.'

'Well then this could be a lot of fun. In a grotesque, "there's a shark in the swimming pool" sort of way.'

7

There came a point, as Jerry's car was carrying Katya out of Coldheart Canyon for the first time in the better part of three quarters of a century, when her fears seemed to get the better of her. Jerry heard a voice, as dry as a husk, out of the darkness behind him: 'I'm sorry . . . I don't know that I can do this.'

'Do you want me to turn around?' he asked her. 'I will if you want me to.'

There was no reply. Just the soft sound of frightened weeping. 'I wish Zeffer was still here. Why was I so cruel to him?' None of this seemed to be for open discussion. It was more like a private confessional. 'Why am I such a bitch? Jesus. *Jesus.* Everything I've ever loved . . .' She stopped herself, and looked up at Jerry, catching his reflection in the mirror. 'Don't mind me. It's just a crazy old woman talking to herself.'

'Maybe we should go back and find Mr Zeffer? He could come with you. I realize there was some bad blood between you –'

'Zeffer's dead, Jerry. I lost my temper with him, and –'

'You killed him?'

'No. I left him in the Devil's Country. Wounded by one of the hunters.'

'Lord.'

Jerry brought the car to a halt. He stared out of the window, horrified. 'What would you like me to do?' he said after a while. 'If you can't go on without him, I mean.'

'Take no notice of me,' Katya said, after a short period of reflection. 'I'm just feeling sorry for myself. Of *course* I can go on. What other choice do I have?' She took another moment to study the passing world. 'It's just that it's been a long time since I was out in the real world.'

'This isn't the real world, it's LA.'

She saw the joke in that. They laughed together over the remark, and when their laughter had settled into smiles, he got the car going again, down the hill. At some unidentified point between the place where her faith had almost failed her, and Sunset Boulevard, they crossed the boundary of Coldheart Canyon.

Their destination was already decided, of course, so there wasn't much reason to talk as they went. Jerry left Katya to her musings. He knew his Hollywood history well enough to be sure that she would be astonished by what she was seeing. In her time Sunset Boulevard had been little more than a dirt track once it got east of what was now Doheny. There'd been no Century City back then, of course, no four lane highways clogged with sleek vehicles. Just shacks and orange groves and earth.

'I've been thinking,' Katya said, somewhere around Sepulveda.

'About what?'

'Me and my wickedness.'

'Your what? Your *wickedness*?'

'Yes, my wickedness. I don't know why it came into my mind, but it did. If I think about the women I've played in all my really important pictures, they were all wicked women. Poisonous. Adulterers. One who kills her own child. Really *unforgivable* women.'

'But don't most actors prefer to play bad characters? Isn't it more fun?'

'Oh it *is*. And I had a lot to inspire me.'

'Inspire you?'

'As a child, I saw wickedness with my own eyes. I

444

had its hands on me. Worse, it *possessed* me.' Her voice grew cold and dark. 'My mother ran a whorehouse, did I ever tell you that? And when I was ten or so, she just decided one night it was time to make me available to the customers.'

'Jesus.'

'That's what I said to myself. Every night, I said: *Jesus, please help me. Jesus, please come and take me away from this wicked woman. Take me to heaven.* But he never came. I had to run away. Three times I ran away and my brothers found me and dragged me back. Once she let them have me, as a reward for finding me.'

'Your own brothers?'

'Five of them.'

'Christ.'

'Anyway, I succeeded in escaping her eventually, and when you're a thirteen-year-old, and you're out in the world on your own, you see a lot thirteen-year-olds shouldn't have to see.'

'I'm sure you did.'

'So I put all that I saw into those women. That's why people believed in them. I was playing them for real.' She fumbled at the inside of the door. 'Is there some way to open this window?'

'Oh yes. It's right there. A little black button. Push it down.'

She pushed and opened the window a crack. 'That's better,' she said.

'You can have it all the way down.'

'No, this is fine. I'll take it in stages I think.'

'Yes, of course.'

'Going back to the pictures, I wonder if you'd do me a favour, when we get back to the house?'

'Of course. What?'

'In my bedroom in the guest-house there are six or seven posters from those early films of mine. I've had them up

445

there for so long, all around the bed. I think it's time I got rid of them. Will you burn them for me?'

'Are you sure you want them burned? They're worth a fortune.'

'Then take them for yourself. Put them up for auction. And the bed. You want the bed too?'

'There isn't room for it in my apartment, but if you want me to get rid of it for you –'

'Yes, please.'

'No problem.'

'If you make some money from it, then spend it. Enjoy it.'

'Thank you.'

'No, it's me who should be thanking you. You've been a great comfort to me.'

'May I ask you why?'

'Why what?'

'Why are you getting rid of all that stuff now?'

'Because everything's changed for me. That woman I used to be has gone. So are all the things she stood for.'

'They were just films.'

'They were more than that. They were my memories. And now's the time to let go of them. I want to start over with Todd.'

Jerry drew a deep breath to reply to this, but then thought better of it and kept his silence. Katya was acutely aware of every nuance in her immediate locality, however; even this.

'Say what's on your mind,' she said.

'It's none of my business.'

'Say it anyway. Go on.'

'Well. I just hope you're not relying too much on Todd Pickett. You know he's not all that reliable. None of them are, these younger guys. They're all talk.'

'He's different.'

'I hope so.'

446

'We can't ever know why things happen between two people. But when it feels right, you have to go with your instincts.'

'If he's so right for you, why did he run out on you?'

'That was my fault, not his. I showed him some things which were more than he was ready to see. I won't make that mistake again. And then he had some woman with him, Tammy Somebody-or-Other, who was just trying to steal him away. Do you know her?'

'Tammy? No. I don't know a Tammy. Oh wait. I do. I had a call from the police in Sacramento. She went missing.'

'And they called you. Why?'

'Because I know Todd. Apparently, this Tammy woman runs his fan-club.'

Katya started to laugh.

'That's all she is to him?' she said.

'Apparently.'

'She runs his fan-club?'

'That's my understanding.'

'So there's no romance between them?'

'No. I don't even think they really know one another.'

'Well, that solves that.'

'It does and it doesn't,' Jerry said cautiously. 'She still persuaded him to go with her.'

'Then it's up to me to persuade him to come home,' Katya purred. She pressed her window button, and kept it down until the window was entirely open. Jerry caught a glimpse of her in the mirror. The last of her caution and her fear had evaporated. She was luxuriating in the warm wind against her face; eyes closed, hair shining.

'How much farther?' she asked him, without opening her eyes.

'Another ten minutes.'

'I can smell the ocean.'

'Well, we're at Fourth Street. Four blocks over, there's the beach.'

'I love the sea.'

'Todd has a yacht, did you know that? It's docked in San Diego.'

'You see. Perfect.' She opened her eyes, catching Jerry's gaze in the mirror, demanding a response from him.

'Yes, it's perfect,' he said.

She smiled. 'Thank you,' she said.

'For what?'

'For everything. Bringing me here. Listening to me, indulging me. When things have settled down and Todd and I have made the Canyon a more civilized place, we're going to start inviting people over, just a few special friends, to share the beauty of the place. You never saw the house at its best. But you will. It is magnificent.'

'Oh I'm sure.'

'And that's how it's going to be again, after tonight.'

'Magnificent?'

'Magnificent.'

8

This was Tammy's Cinderella moment: her dream come true. All right, perhaps all the details weren't perfect. She could have looked a little more glamorous, and she would have liked to have lost another twenty-five pounds. And they could have been coming in through the front door instead of slipping in at the side to avoid the photographers. But she was happy to take what fate was giving her: and fate was giving her a chance to walk into an A-list party on the arm of Todd Pickett.

Everywhere she looked there were famous faces, famous smiles, famous gazes, famous figures swathed in gowns by famous designers, famous fools making jokes that had everyone in their circle breathless with laughter, famous power-brokers telling tales of how they'd made a million in a minute, and the less famous wives of these power-brokers listening with their lids half-closed because if they had a buck for every time they'd heard these tired old tales they'd be able to divorce their dead-weights of husbands.

And hanging on the arms of the famous (much as she was hanging on Todd's arm) were younger men and women who watched their companions with the kind of eyes Tammy was reserving for the hors d'oeuvres. There was appetite in those eyes. One day, those gazes seemed to say, I will have all that you have. I will own cars and yachts and palaces and houses. I will have a small vineyard in Tuscany and a large ranch in Big Sky Country. There will be no door that will be closed to me; no ear that will not attend to my concerns. When I drop my purse, somebody will pick it up for me. When my car is empty of gas, it will be miraculously filled (and the ashtrays emptied). If the drink in my hand is getting low, it will be replenished without my requesting it. When I am hungry, somebody will make food that will be so exquisitely shaped every mouthful is like a little meal unto itself.

In fact, the food was drawing her attention about as much as the famous faces. She'd never seen such exquisite little confections, and each one had a description, proffered by its server, much of which was so remote from Tammy's experience she didn't understand it. Slices of rare marinated this on slices of smoked that, drizzled with –

Oh what the hell? She'd take two. No make that three. It was only finger-food, for God's sake, and she was hungry.

To wash it all down she'd accepted a Bellini from a dazzling waiter as soon as she'd stepped inside, and it tasted so sweet and harmless she downed two-thirds of her glass before she realized how potent it was. In truth, however, it would scarcely have mattered if she'd downed five Bellinis and fallen flat on her face. She was invisible as far as these people were concerned. The glacial beauties and their handsome swains, the deal-makers and the word-splitters, none of them wanted to concede her ragged presence in their gilded midst: so they simply looked the other way. Once or twice she caught the tail of a mystified glance laid upon her, but these were from amateurs at the game. To the true professionals – which is to say most of the people in this assembly – she was simply a non-presence. She could have been standing right in their line of vision and somehow their gaze would have slid off her and around her; anything to avoid seeing her.

She caught tight hold of Todd's hand. So much for the Cinderella fantasy. It was a nightmare.

Much to her delight Todd clutched her hand in return. His palm was pouring sweat.

'They're all looking at me,' he said, leaning close to her.

'No, they're not.'

'Hi, Todd.'

'Hi, Jodie. Good to – see that? They say hi then they move on. She's gone already. Hi, Steven! When are you –? Too late. He's off. It's fucking uncanny.'

'Where's Maxine?'

'I haven't seen her yet. She's probably out back. She likes to sit and hold court at these things. She says only *hostesses* circulate.'

'And she's not the hostess?'

'Fuck, no. These aren't her guests. They're her supplicants.' Tammy had seen some attractive-looking hors d'oeuvres sailing by.

'I'll have one of those,' she said, tapping the waiter on the shoulder. 'If you don't ask in this place,' she explained, as she took three, 'you don't get.'

'Are they good?'

'What do I know? They're filling a hole. Very slowly. Doesn't anybody have any appetite around here?'

'Not publicly.'

To get to the back of the house he had led her into a larger room – which, despite the fact that it was packed with guests – was almost as hushed as a library. A few people looked round at Todd – a few even attempted tentative smiles – but nobody made any move to break off their whispered exchanges and approach him, for which Tammy was grateful. The density of famous faces was much the same in here as it had been next door. This really was the crème de la crème: the people who could get a studio to spend several million dollars developing a script by simply hinting that they might be in it when it was finished; the names above the title that audiences knew so well they only used an actor's given name when they were talking about the show: Bruce and Demi and Brad and Tom and all

451

the rest. Next year, some portion of the crowd would have slipped onto the B-list, after a dud or two. But tonight they were at the top of their game; famous amongst the famous. Tonight there wasn't an agency in the city that wouldn't have signed them on the spot; or a late-night talk-show that wouldn't have bumped Einstein, Van Gogh and the Pope to have them on. They were American royalty, the way that Pickford and Fairbanks had been royalty in the early years. Yes, there were more crowns now; more thrones. But there were also more fans, in every corner of the world, men and women ready to fawn and obsess. In short, none of these were people who hurt for want of admiration. They had a surfeit of it, the way the rest of the world had a surfeit of credit-card debt.

It was harder, in this more densely-populated space, for people not to concede the presence of Todd, who took hold of several unoffered hands and grabbed a couple of shoulders as he crossed the room, determined that nobody get away with pretending they hadn't seen him. And when a fragment of conversation did spring up, as it occasionally did, Todd very rapidly (and rather gallantly) made certain that Tammy was introduced into the exchange.

'You don't need to do that,' Tammy said, after the third such occasion.

'Yes, I do,' Todd replied. 'These sonsabitches think they can look the other way and pretend you don't exist. Well fuck 'em. I've starred in movies with some of these assholes. Movies you paid your seven bucks to see. And they were mostly shit pictures. So I figure they owe you a seven-buck-handshake.'

She laughed out loud, thoroughly entertained by his heretical talk. Whatever happened after this, she thought, (and no fairy-tale lasted forever) she'd at least have this extraordinary memory to treasure: walking arm-in-arm with the only man she'd ever really loved through a crowd of fools, knowing that even if they didn't look at

452

her they still knew she was there. And when she'd gone she'd be somebody they'd never be able to figure out, which suited her just fine. Let them wonder. It would give them something to do when they were studying their reflections in the morning.

'There's Maxine,' Todd said. 'Didn't I say she'd be holding court?'

It was a couple of years since Tammy had seen Maxine Frizelle in the flesh. In that time she had projected upon the woman an aura of power which in truth she didn't possess. She was smaller and more fretful-looking than Tammy remembered: the way she was perched in a high-backed chair, her bare feet off the ground, was presumably designed to give off the aura of childlike vulnerability, but in fact suggested just its opposite. The pose looked awkward and artificial; her gaze was woozy rather than happy, and her smile completely false.

Todd let go of Tammy's hand.

'Are you doing this on your own from here?' she said to him.

'I think I ought to.'

Tammy shrugged. 'Whatever you want.'

'I mean, it's going to be difficult.'

'Yeah . . .' she said, the observation given credence by the frigid stare they were getting from the patio.

'She's seen you,' Tammy said.

She smiled in Maxine's direction. The woman was getting up off her chair, her expression more bemused than angry. She leaned over and whispered something to the young man at her side. He nodded in response, and left the patio, heading indoors and weaving his way through the party-goers towards Tammy and Todd.

Tammy grabbed hold of Todd's hand again. 'You know what?' she said.

'What?'

'I was wrong. We're going to do this together.'

9

Out on the street, Katya let the valet open the car door for her, her eyes fixed on the house into which she was about to make an entrance. A hundred thoughts were crowding into her head at the same time, all demanding attention. Would anybody recognize her? Jerry had told her many times her films remained widely seen and appreciated, so it was inevitable somebody was going to figure out who she was. On the other hand it had been the style in those days to slather your face in makeup, so perhaps nobody would think to associate her with the high style of those movies. Nor, of course, would anybody assume that the Katya Lupi of *The Sorrows of Frederick* or *Nefertiti* could possibly resemble the young woman she still seemed to be. So again, perhaps her fears were groundless. And if somebody did recognize her, against all the odds, then she'd swiftly find some witty riposte about the brilliance of modern science, and let them wonder. If she sent a few admirers off shaking their heads, mystified by her untouched beauty, would that be such a bad thing?

She had nothing to fear from these people.

She was beautiful. And beauty was the only certain weapon against a brutal mind or a stupid world. Why should that power have deserted her?

She looked around, subduing a little burst of panic, to find that Jerry was not at her side.

'I'm here,' he said, sauntering over from a very handsome

and now well-tipped valet. 'I've been getting the scoop. Todd arrived a few minutes ago.'

Her face blossomed. 'He's here?'

'He's here.'

She was suddenly like a little child. 'I knew this was going to work!' she said. 'I knew! I knew!' Then, just as suddenly, a doubt: 'Is that woman with him?'

'Tammy Lauper? Yes she is.'

'I want you to separate them.'

'Just like that.'

'Yes,' she said, deadly serious. 'Do whatever you have to do. I just want you to part them, so that I can talk to Todd on his own. As soon as I get a chance to do that, the three of us can be out of here.'

'Suppose he wants to stay?'

'With *her*?'

'No. Amongst his friends.'

'He can't,' she said. 'He won't want to, when he sees me. He'll just come. You'll see.'

Her confidence was beguiling, whether it was fake or not. She took his arm, and they headed into the house. If Jerry had been expecting some grotesque echo of *Sunset Boulevard* he was pleasantly disappointed. Katya met the cameras at the door with an expression of familiarity on her face, as though she were saying to the world: *oh, there you are.* She let go of his hand at the threshold like a ship that suddenly finds the wind again, and remembers what it has to do effortlessly. She turned and the cameramen got greedy for her: the flashes a blinding barrage, and she bathing in the light as it glazed her bones and filled her eyes.

Of course none of them knew who the hell she was, so they were reduced to snapping their fingers and calling 'Miss uh –?! Over here, Miss –?' But she knew her job. She gave them all something wonderful, something miraculous, and just as the frenzy was approaching its height, abruptly

455

refused to continue, thanking them all and sweeping away into the house, leaving them begging for more.

This sudden burst of activity had attracted attention, of course. Half the faces in the room were turned towards the door when Katya entered, wondering who the hell could have just arrived. When it turned out to be a woman they did not even know the house became a gallery of whispers. Jerry stayed two or three steps behind Katya as she crossed the room, so he was able to see the range of responses her presence created. Envy, more than anything: particularly on the faces of women who assumed they were Katya's contemporaries. Who was this woman who was as young or *younger* than they were, *prettier* than they were, getting all the attention they should have been getting?

On the faces of the young men, there were similar questions being silently asked. Why is this damn woman more perfect than I am? Why does she have more eyes undressing her than I do? Then there was that other contingent of young men who were simply calculating their chances of getting across the room to her side with a drink or a witty pick-up line before the opposition.

Katya played it perfectly. She was careful not to lock eyes with anyone, so that she didn't get caught up in a conversation she wanted no part of. She looked back at Jerry, who pointed on across the room towards Todd.

And there he was, standing on the patio with Maxine. They were in the midst of what looked to be a very unpleasant exchange. She was shaking her head, turning away from him; he was following her, poking her in the shoulder like a kid who's not getting his mother's full attention.

She ignored his importuning, and headed down a flight of stairs, which led off the other side of the patio, down onto the beach.

*   *   *

The argument between Todd and Maxine had not gone unnoticed by the other occupants of the room. Ever since Todd's appearance at the party, all other subjects of whispered conversation had fallen by the wayside. It was Pickett the guests were talking about. They were chiefly debating his wounded appearance, of course, but now they were also discussing the way he stumbled in angry pursuit of Maxine, and the subject of their exchange, which had unfortunately now been taken out of ear-shot. There were plenty of people in the room who would have liked to have gone out onto the patio and followed Todd and Maxine down onto the sand, but the only one who did so was Tammy. She pushed through a group standing between her and the patio door, manoeuvred her way around a waiter and a sofa, and headed outside.

The wind had got up a little since she and Todd had arrived. It blew off the ocean, bringing with it the sound of raised voices. Tammy heard Maxine's voice first. She was demanding to know how Todd *dared* show his face —

Tammy crossed the patio to see if she could get a look at Todd. Did he need her help or not? As she approached the wooden railing an officious little man, with the improbable face of an ill-tempered troll, got in her way. 'Excuse me, but who the hell *are* you?'

'I'm a friend of Todd's. Are you the maître d'?'

There was a barely-suppressed guffaw from one corner of the patio. Tammy glanced round to see a young man, almost as well dressed as the troll, composing his face.

'My name's Gary Eppstadt. I'm the Head of Paramount.'

'Oh,' Tammy said. 'So?'

'So, *you* obviously don't belong on this patio.'

'In point of fact, I think she *did* come with Todd,' said another onlooker, a woman in black, who was lounging against the railing as she sipped her cocktail.

Eppstadt looked Tammy up and down as though he was assessing a particularly unappealing heifer. The nakedness

457

of his look so infuriated her that she simply shoved him out of her way, and went to the railing.

'Get security,' Eppstadt said. 'I want this bitch thrown out or I shall lodge charges for assault.'

'Oh, for God's sake, Gary,' the woman said, 'you're making a fool of yourself.'

Only now did Tammy recognize the woman's soft drawl. It was Faye Dunaway. Her weary glance fell momentarily on Tammy. 'She's not doing any harm.' Faye went on, 'Go inside and get yourself a drink.' Tammy glanced back over her shoulder. Eppstadt was obviously uncertain how to respond. He first threw a fiery glance at Dunaway, who promptly threw it straight back. Then he snapped at one of the three younger men doomed to be out here on the patio at the same time.

'Christian?'

'Yes, sir?'

'What did I just say?'

'That . . . you wanted security, sir?'

'And what are you doing?'

'Going to get them,' the man said, hurrying away.

'Christ!' Dunaway murmured. 'Didn't you hear what I said? She came in with Todd.'

'Well she doesn't belong in here,' Eppstadt said. 'With him or without him. She's up to no good. Mind you, so's he. He wasn't invited either. I should have security cart him away too.'

Tammy turned from her spot at the railings.

'What *is* your problem?' she said. 'This is nothing to do with you.'

'Where the fuck did you come from?' he asked. 'You look like a street-person. Is this Todd's idea of a joke? Bringing a street-person in here?'

'Who are you, honey?'

'My name's Tammy Lauper, and I'm a friend of Todd's.'

Eppstadt cut in here. 'Friend in the sense of –?'

'Friend as in friend,' Tammy said. 'Todd's been going through some hard times recently.'

'No? Do tell.'

'I'm afraid I'm not at liberty –'

'He's working you, honey,' Faye said. 'He knows all about the bad surgery. The whole town does.'

'As it happens I suggested the surgeon,' Eppstadt said. 'Bruce Burrows. He normally does first-rate work. Didn't he do some for you, Faye?'

'No,' said Ms Dunaway. 'I don't need it yet.'

'My mistake.'

'But when I do I'll be sure to avoid him, judging him by what he did to Todd. That boy used to be damn-near perfect. The way Warren was perfect fifty years ago. I mean, they were uncanny, both of them.'

Tammy didn't bother to listen to the rest of the conversation. Instead she slipped down the creaking wooden steps that led off the patio and down onto the sand. The wash of light from the house lit the beach as far as the surf, which was breaking quite boisterously. The beach, as far as she could see, was immaculately clean. No doubt the residents hired somebody to vacuum every morning, so that nothing unpredictable – a whisky bottle, a stray condom, a dead fish – be allowed to disfigure the perfection of their stretch of coastline.

The only items she could see on the beach were two human figures.

If either Todd or Maxine had realized that Tammy was there they gave no sign of it. They simply kept up what they'd been doing for the last ten minutes: arguing.

The wind carried most of their words away, but every now and again a phrase would reach Tammy's ears. Maxine called him a 'waste of time' at one point, 'all ego and no brains' at another. He called her 'a talentless bitch' and 'a parasite'. She mentioned, by way of response to one of his assaults that 'the whole town knows you got a face-lift, and that it went to hell.'

'I don't care,' Todd replied.

'Then you're even more of a fool than I thought you were,' Maxine yelled back, 'because that's your fucking reputation out the window.'

'Watch my lips,' Todd said, pointing to his mouth. '*I don't care.*'

Several exchanges followed of which Tammy did not catch a single word. She continued to approach the pair slowly, expecting at any moment to be seen by one or the other. But they were too deeply involved in expressing their rage at one another to take notice of her.

The conversation had definitely changed direction, however, because now, when the wind brought fresh words in Tammy's direction, the subject of the Canyon was under debate. And Todd was shouting.

'You set me up! You knew something weird was going on up there and you set me up!'

It was time to make this into a three-way conversation, Tammy decided, stepping into Maxine's line of sight. But Maxine wasn't going to be distracted from the subject at hand by Tammy.

'All right,' she said to Todd. 'So the house has a history. Is that such a big deal?'

'I don't like messing with that stuff, Maxine. It's not safe.'

'By that "stuff" you mean *what* exactly?'

Todd dropped his voice to a near-whisper, but Tammy was close enough to hear it. 'The Canyon's full of dead people.'

Maxine's response was to laugh; her laughter unfeigned. 'Are you high?'

'No.'

'Drunk?'

'No.' Todd wasn't about to be laughed off. 'I've seen them, Maxine. I've touched them.'

'Well then you should file a report to the *National Enquirer*, not come whining to me about it. As far as I'm concerned, this is our last conversation.'

'I want an explanation!'

'I'll give you one,' Maxine said: '*You're crazy.*'

'Jerry?'

Katya was at Jerry's side, her expression troubled. 'Is there a way down onto the beach along the side of the house?'

'I don't know. Maybe. Why?'

'Todd's down on the beach, being abused by that bitch of a manager.'

'I'm sure he can stand up for himself.'

'I just want to take him away, and I don't want to have to come back through the crowd when I bring him back.'

'Well let's see,' Jerry said. He took hold of Katya's arm and together they went back to the front door.

'I hate these people,' Katya said, when they reached the foyer.

'You don't know any of them,' Jerry said. 'With respect.'

'Oh believe me I do. They're the same old whores, fakes and fools. Only the names have changed.'

'Will you be leaving?' the valet wanted to know as they emerged from the house.

'No,' Jerry said. 'I was just showing my friend around the house. Do you know if there's a way down onto the beach?'

'Yes, of course. Just go back through the house –'

'We'd prefer not to go through the house.'

'Well. I guess there's a pathway which runs down the side of the house, which takes you to the beach. But it's much easier –'

'Thank you,' Katya said, catching hold of the man's

461

gaze and smiling at him. 'I'd just like to get away from the crowd.'

If the man had any objections they faded away on the spot. He blushed at the directness of Katya's look, and stood aside. 'It's all yours,' he said.

10

On the beach Todd looked up towards the house. The patio was now so crowded with spectators that people had gone into the kitchen and up to the bedrooms so they could look out at the beach and watch the exchange between himself and Maxine. A few of the partiers had wandered down the patio, and were watching intently from there. The general level of hubbub from inside had also dropped considerably. Word had got around that a war of words was being fought on the sand, and if everyone would just *shut up* for a minute or two, it would be more audible.

'You wish you'd never started this, now, don't you?' Maxine said.

'All I want is some answers.'

'No, you don't. You want to embarrass me in front of my friends because I let you go. Well, Todd, I'd had enough of you. It's as simple as that. I was tired. I wanted to be free of you and your endless demands.' Maxine closed her eyes as she spoke, and for the first time in her life Tammy had a morsel of sympathy for the woman. Despite her makeup and her immaculate coiffure, nothing could disguise her genuine exhaustion. When she said she wanted to be free of Todd, Tammy believed her.

'When I arranged for you to move into that house it was because it seemed to serve your comforts. That was all I cared about. Now, you come here yelling and swearing, and I think, to hell with your comforts. It's about time *they* all heard the truth.'

'Don't go there, Maxine.'

'Why not? Why the *hell* not? You came here to cause trouble. Well you're going to *get* trouble.' She had raised her voice, so that she was now plainly audible to the audience assembled on the patio and gathered at the windows.

Todd had nowhere to run. The closer she got to him, the more he was forced to retreat towards the house, and the more audible her words became.

'Just tell the damn woman you're sorry, Todd,' Tammy said. 'And let's get the hell out of here. This isn't the time or the place.'

Maxine glanced at Tammy, conceding her existence here with them for the first time. 'You think he's going to apologize? To me? He doesn't understand the word sorry. You know why? *He's never been wrong.* At least the way he tells it.'

'Well, he can make an exception, right, Todd?'

'Keep out of this,' Todd snapped.

'I hid you away in that house because you asked me to hide you away –' Maxine went on, her recollections delivered in the direction of the spectators. 'You needed time to heal.'

'I'm warning you,' Todd said.

Maxine went on, unintimidated. 'As I recall,' she said, 'your face looked like a piece of hammered steak, thanks to Dr Burrows.'

'All right, you win,' Todd said. 'Just stop right there.'

'Why? They already know the truth, Todd. The whole town's been gossiping about your Phantom of the Opera act for *weeks*.'

'Shut up, Maxine.'

'No, Todd, I will *not* shut up. I've kept your fucking secrets for years, and I'm not going to do it any longer.'

'Perhaps we should just go, Todd,' Tammy said.

'Don't waste your breath on him,' Maxine said. 'He's

not going to sleep with you. That's what you're hoping for, isn't it?'

'God,' Tammy said. 'You people.'

'Don't deny it,' Maxine snapped.

'Well, I am denying it. You think the world revolves around sex. It's pathetic.'

'Anyway, I didn't,' Todd said, as though he wanted to be sure that Maxine was not misled on the subject.

Something about his eagerness to have this particular fact set straight distressed Tammy. She knew why. He was ashamed of her. Damn him! Still concerned about his stupid reputation.

Maxine must have seen the anger and disappointment on Tammy's face, because the rage in her own voice mellowed. 'Don't let him hurt you,' she said. 'He's not worth it. Really he's not. It's just that he doesn't want *them up there* –' she jabbed her finger in the direction of the house '– thinking he'd ever sink so low as to sleep with the likes of you. Isn't that right, Todd? You don't want people thinking *you fucked the fat girl*?'

The knife turned a second time in Tammy. She wished the beach would just open up beneath her and swallow her, so she'd never have to see any of these people ever again.

But there was still enough self-esteem left in her to challenge the sonofabitch. What had she got to lose?

'Is that right, Todd?' she said. 'Are you ashamed of me?'

'Oh Jesus . . .' Todd shook his head, then made a furtive glance at the house. There were probably sixty people on the patio and balconies now, enjoying the spectacle below.

'You know what?' he said. 'Fuck *both of you*.'

With that he turned his back on Tammy and Maxine and started to walk off down the beach. But Maxine wasn't going to let him get away so easily. 'We didn't finish talking about your healing, Todd.'

'Leave it, Maxine –'

'The operation? The one to make you look a few years younger? The *face-lift*.'

He swung around at her 'I said: *leave it* or I will sue your fucking ass.'

'On what grounds? I'm just telling the truth. You're an arrogant, spoiled, talentless –'

Todd stopped his retreat. His face looked blotchy in the light thrown from the house; there was a tic beneath the left side of his mouth. The expression of empty despair on his mis-made face silenced Maxine. Todd looked past both the women at the crowd that was watching all this unfold.

Then he started to yell.

'Have you had enough? Well? Have you? She's right! It's all true! I did get a fucking face-lift. You know why? That cunt! Eppstadt! Yes, you, you fucking Quasimodo! You!'

Eppstadt had found a prime grandstand position to watch the encounter between Todd and Maxine, so there were plenty of eyes turned in his direction now. He didn't like the scrutiny any more than Todd had. He shook his head and waved Todd's accusations away, then turned his back and tried to disappear into the crowd.

But Todd kept on haranguing him. 'You're the freak here, you know that?' Todd yelled. 'You fuck with our lives, you fuck with our heads. Well, you're not going to fuck with me any more, because I'm not playing your game *any more. Hear me? I'm not playing!'*

Todd suddenly ran at the patio and reached up through the railing to catch hold of Eppstadt's pants leg. Eppstadt turned on him.

'Get your hands off me!' he shouted, kicking at Todd as though he were a crazed dog.

Todd simply pulled harder on his leg, so that Eppstadt had to grab hold of somebody beside him to stop himself falling over. His face was white with fury. The assault went

466

to the very heart of his dignity; this was a living nightmare for him, the mad dog actor, the audience of people who despised him, all drinking his embarrassment down like a fine champagne.

'You ain't getting away so easy, ugly-boy!' Todd said. 'We're all in this together.'

'*Pickett*! *Let go of me*!' Eppstadt demanded. His voice had become shrill with rage, beads of sweat popping out all over his face. 'You hear me? *Let me go*!'

'When I'm done,' Todd said. He pulled on Eppstadt again, dragging him a few inches closer. 'You miserable fucking shit. How many people have you told to get their faces fixed, huh?'

'You were looking old,' Eppstadt said.

'I was looking old? Ha! Look at you!'

'I'm not a movie star.'

'No, and neither am I. I'm over all that. You know why? I've seen where they go, Eppstadt. All the beautiful people, the stars. I've seen where they end up.'

'Forest Lawn?'

'Oh no. They're not in graves, Eppstadt. That's too easy. They're still out there. The ghosts. Still thinking some fuck like you will give them another chance.'

'*Will somebody get this crazy sonofabitch off me*?' Eppstadt shrieked.

One of the waiters went down on his haunches in front of the railing, took hold of Todd's hands and started pulling off his fingers one by one. 'You better let go, man,' the waiter quietly warned, 'or I'm going to start hurtin' you. And I don't want to do that.'

Todd ignored him. He simply hauled on Eppstadt, which threw the older man off-balance. The woman Eppstadt had been holding onto also toppled, and would have come down hard had the crowd around her not been so thick. Eppstadt was not so lucky, however. The people in his immediate vicinity had moved away as soon as Todd had caught hold of his leg. Down he went, catching the waiter a blow with his knee as he fell, so that the other man was also sent sprawling.

Todd dragged Eppstadt towards the edge of the patio. There wasn't a single witness to all of this who, knowing Eppstadt, didn't take pleasure in the indignity they saw being visited on the man. People he'd scorned and made to look like fools, were now all silently hoping this farce would escalate.

But Eppstadt was made of sterner stuff. He kicked at his attacker, the first blow striking Todd's shoulder, the second hitting his nose and mouth, a brutal blow. Todd let go of Eppstadt and fell back on the sand, blood pouring from both nostrils, like two faucets switched on full power.

Eppstadt scrambled to his feet, yelling: '*I want that man arrested! Right now! Right! Now!*'

Todd looked up from his sprawl, his hand going to his face, coming away red. A hundred faces now stared down at him. There wasn't a person at the party – whether bartender, guest, waiter, toilet attendant or valet – who had not forsaken the house to come out and see what all the hubbub was about. They were all staring down at the famous, bloody face on the sand, and the sprawled Eppstadt on the patio. Scandal didn't get much better than this; this was a story to dine out on for years.

A few people had come down onto the sand, on the pretext of helping Todd perhaps but actually, of course, to see better what was going on and so have a clearer account for later. Nobody lent Todd a hand; not even Tammy. She had retreated some distance, unwilling to provide these witless fools with something else to laugh at.

Todd scrambled to his feet without help, and instinctively turned his back on his audience. They'd already seen and heard far more than he wanted them to see or hear. All he wanted now was to get away from their snickering assessments.

468

'Fuck you all . . .' he muttered to himself, wondering which way he should go along the beach, left or right?

And then, straight ahead of him, he had his answer. Standing there at the water-line, watching him, was Katya.

At first he didn't believe it was really her. What was she doing so far from her sanctuary? But if it wasn't her, then who?

He didn't wait for his senses to catch up with what his instinct already knew. Without looking back at the ridiculous circus behind him he stumbled down the beach towards her.

Despite all that Katya had done, all that she was associated with in Todd's mind, her smile was welcome to him now: her madness infinitely preferable to that of Eppstadt and the mob behind him. He was done with them. Forever. This last humiliation was simply the final proof that he did not belong at this party any longer. For better or worse, he belonged in the Canyon, with the woman standing at the water's edge, beckoning to him.

'What are you doing here?' he asked.

She smiled. Oh that smile; still an astonishment!

'What do you think? I came to find you.'

'I thought you'd never leave the Canyon.'

'Sometimes I surprise myself.'

He put his arm around her. An ambitious wave came up around their legs and filled his shoes with cold saltwater. He laughed, snorting through the blood. It spattered her.

'God, I'm sorry. That's gross.'

He went down on his haunches and brought a handful of water up to wash his face, inhaling to cleanse his nostrils. The saltwater stung.

Katya came down to crouch in the surf beside him, her gaze going over his shoulder.

'They're coming down from the house to get you,' she warned.

'Fuck.' He didn't need to glance back to confirm what she was saying. Eppstadt would enjoy what came next, of course: having Todd arrested for assault, hauled up before a judge. It would be headlines tomorrow; and attached to it every detail of what Maxine had proclaimed to her guests. Burrows would be shooed out of hiding, wherever he was, to tell his half of the story; or – if he chose to stand by his Hippocratic oath and remain silent – then somebody would invent the details, or a nurse would spill them. However it was verified (as though anything needed verification) the secret was out.

But his story was only part of this. Katya? What about *her* secret? If they got her into the spotlight as well as Todd, then the mystery of Coldheart Canyon would become part of tomorrow's headlines. The sanctuary would be violated by police and press; and when they'd gone, by the public.

'I can't bear this,' he said. He was ready to weep, for them both.

She took hold of his hand. 'Then don't,' she said.

She stood up, facing the sea, pulling on his hand so that he stood with her. There were a few lights out there in the ocean, very remote. Otherwise it was completely dark.

'Walk with me,' she said.

She couldn't mean: *into the water*?

Yes she did.

She was already walking, and he was following, not because he liked the idea of striding off into the icy, roaring Pacific, but because the alternative – the mockery of the audience on the shore; all the interrogations that awaited him – was too much to contemplate. He wanted to be away from all that, and if the only direction he could take led him into the ocean, then so be it. He had her hand in his. That was all he needed. For the first time in his life, that was all he needed.

'There are currents . . .' he said.

'I know.'

'And sharks.'

'I'm sure.'

He almost looked back but stopped himself.

'Don't bother,' she said. 'You know what they're doing.'

'Yes . . .'

'Staring at us. Pointing at us.'

'Coming after us?'

'Yes. But not where we're going.'

The water was up to Todd's waist now; and higher still on Katya, who was a good six inches shorter than he. Though the waves weren't large tonight as they'd been at the height of the storm, they still had sufficient power to throw them backwards when they broke against their bodies. The force of one wave separated them, and Katya was carried back to shore a few yards. Todd turned and went back to get her, glancing up at the beach as he did so. Though they were probably less than twenty-five yards out, the land already seemed very distant: a line of sand scattered with people who'd come down to the water's edge to get a better view of whatever was going on. And beyond them, the houses, all bright with lights; Maxine's in particular. Down the path between the houses he could see the flashing yellow and blue of a police-car. It would only be a matter of time, he thought, before they sent a helicopter after them, with a searchlight.

He reached Katya and caught hold of her hand. The glimpse of land had filled him with new determination.

'*Come on,*' he said. '*I'll carry you.*'

She didn't protest this; rather let him gather her up in his arms so that they could continue their escape. He had become, he thought, a monster in an old horror movie: grabbing the girl and carrying her off into the night. Except that it was she who'd led him thus far. So that made them *both* monsters, didn't it?

She slipped her arms around his neck, and laid her head

471

against his chest. The water was so deep now that when the waves came and lifted them up, his toes no longer touched the bottom. Curiously, he wasn't afraid. They were going to drown, most probably, but what the hell? The water was so cold his body was already becoming numb, and his eyelids felt heavy.

'Keep . . . hold . . . of me . . .' he said to her.

She pressed her mouth to his neck. She was warmer than he was, which for some inexplicable reason he found amusing. She, who was so old, was the one with the fever. The thought of that, of her body's heat, made him voice his one regret.

'We . . . never did it properly . . . in a bed, I mean.'

'We will,' she said, kissing him on the mouth.

Another wave came, larger than most that had preceded it, and picked them both up.

They did not break their kiss, though the water closed over their heads.

On the shore, there was plenty of commotion, but Tammy kept away from the heart of it, moving off down the beach. She had watched Todd and Katya getting smaller and smaller, her panic growing. Now they were gone. Perhaps she just couldn't make them out any longer, and they'd reappear in a moment, but she didn't have very high hopes of that. There had been such determination in the way they'd headed out into the darkness; plainly they weren't going out to enjoy a little swim, then turn round and head back to shore. They were escaping together, in the only direction left for them.

She had a sick feeling in the pit of her stomach: part horror at what she'd just witnessed, part envy. He had made his choice, finally. And now, he was gone.

She heard the throb of rotor-blades, and she looked up to see a police helicopter coming from the south, following the line of the surf as it approached the place where the

472

lovers had disappeared. Its powerful spotlight illuminated the water with uncanny brightness.

Tammy looked back at the people assembled along the shoreline. Almost all the guests had vacated the house and were milling around on the sand. She couldn't see Maxine, but she could name a few famous folks, mainly from the colour of their clothes. Glenn Close was in white; Brad Pitt in a powder blue suit; Madonna was in red. They were briefly illuminated by the flood of the searchlight, then the helicopter veered off seaward, and Tammy followed its progress as it swooped down close to the water. Surely Todd and Katya couldn't have gone that far out. Even if the current had caught them, they couldn't have been swept more than a few hundred yards in the short time since they'd entered the water.

But then the current wasn't the only variable here, was it? There was also their own ambition. They had gone out intending to be lost. And lost they were.

Suddenly, she was crying. Standing outside the wedge of light thrown by the house, and beyond the presence of anyone who could possibly comfort her; dirty and cold and alone, she sobbed like a baby. She made no attempt to stop the flood. 'Better out than in,' her mother had always said; and it was true. She could never think straight when she had a bout of tears waiting in the wings. It was wiser to just weep them out, and be done with them.

At last her grief began to subside, and she cleared the tears from her cheeks with her hands. The helicopter was now some distance from the shore, and had dropped even closer to the water, hovering over one particular place. She tried to make sense of the waterscape. Had the men in the helicopter located the bodies? She stared at the spotlit water until her eyes started to ache, but she could make no sense of what she was seeing. Just the spume, being whipped up off the water, so that it looked like snow in the column of white light.

After a few minutes the helicopter moved away from that position, turning off its search-light for a while as it headed down the beach. When the light was turned on again and the brightness struck the water the search had moved much further out to sea. Still Tammy kept watching, desperately trying to make sense of the sight. But at last it simply became too frustrating, and turning her back on the water, she walked back up the side of the house to the street, where many of the same people she'd seen down by the water earlier, enjoying the spectacle along with their champagne, were now waiting to pick up their cars. They were quiet, eyes downcast, as though they felt just a tiny prick of guilt at having treated the death of one of their number as a spectator sport.

Whatever interest Tammy might once have had in these people was gone. The fact that she was practically rubbing shoulders with Brad and Julia and half-a-dozen other luminaries was a matter of complete indifference to her. Her thoughts were still out there in the dark waters of the Pacific.

Finally somebody spoke; some imbecilic remark about how valets were getting slower every day. It was all this air-headed company needed to throw off their show of introspection. Chatter sprang up, and on its heels, laughter. By the time Tammy's car had arrived the group was in a fine mood, exchanging jokes and telephone numbers; the scene on the beach – the tragedy they'd all just witnessed together – already a thing of the past.

11

Along the beach a hundred and fifty yards from where Tammy had been standing all eyes were also directed seaward, and, like Tammy's eyes, saw nothing but the uncanny, almost beatific, light from the hovering helicopter as it passed back and forth over the surface of the water.

Eppstadt had his lawyer, Jacob Lazlov, on the line while he watched the water. At his side, Maxine.

'I want this sonofabitch Pickett prosecuted to the full extent of the law, Jacob. What do you mean: what did he do? He practically tore off my leg, that's what he did. In public. Jesus, Jacob, it was an *attack*, a physical attack. And now the bastard's trying to drown himself.'

'Isn't this all a little premature?' Maxine remarked dryly. 'He's probably drowned by now.'

'Then I'll sue his fucking estate. I can sue the estate can't I, Jacob? Speak up, I can't hear you. The helicopter –'

'You are a piece of work, you know that,' Maxine said.

'I'll call you back, Jacob.' Eppstadt snapped his phone closed and followed Maxine back across the beach to the house. On the way they encountered the waiter who'd come to Eppstadt's aid during Todd's attack.

'What's your name, son?'

'Joseph Finlay, sir.'

'Well, Joe, I'd like you to do me a favour and stay within ten yards of me till I tell you otherwise. Will you do that? I'll pay you very well for your services. And if you see anything you don't like, son –'

'I'm there, sir.'

'Good. Good. But you can start by getting me a brandy. Be quick.' Joe hurried away. 'Didn't you have any security at this damn party, Maxine?'

'Of course!'

'Well where the fuck was it when I was having my leg torn off? Jacob's going to be asking some questions, Maxine, and you'd better have some damn good answers.'

'Todd wasn't some trespasser –' Maxine said. She had reached the patio, and now turned to face Eppstadt, tears filling her eyes. 'I've known him ten years. Everyone knows him.'

'Well apparently none of us knew him well enough. He was ready to kill me.'

'He was nowhere near killing you,' Maxine said, weary of Eppstadt's self-dramatization. She sank down into the chair where she'd been sitting when Todd had first arrived, turning it round so she could watch the beach.

'Your brandy, sir.'

Eppstadt took his brandy. Joe pulled a chair up, and Eppstadt sat down in it. 'Ten yards,' he said to Joe.

'I'm here.'

Joe stepped back a little distance to give Eppstadt and Maxine a measure of privacy. Eppstadt took out a pack of cigarettes; offered one to Maxine, who took it with trembling fingers. He lit both, and leaned back in his chair.

'Sonofabitch,' he said. 'Who'd ever have thought he'd pull a stunt like this?'

'I think it all got too much for him,' Maxine said. 'He cracked.'

'No doubt. What was he talking about: some house you put him in?'

'Oh yes, that *house*,' Maxine said. 'It all began with that *fucking* house. Where's Jerry Brahms?'

476

'Who?'

Maxine couldn't see Jerry, but she spotted Sawyer, her assistant, who was inside the house, eating. He came at her summons, mouth stuffed with canapés. She told him to find Jerry, pronto.

'I think we have to assume the current took them,' Eppstadt said, directing Maxine's attention at the helicopter, which had steadily moved further and further out from the beach in its search. There were now two Coast Guard boats bobbing around in the water, mounted with searchlights.

'Have people no *taste*?' Maxine said, surveying the condo on the beach. To make matters worse, something of the party atmosphere had returned to the gathering. The waiters were weaving amongst the guests, refreshing drinks or offering finger food. It was not being refused. People seemed to be of the opinion that the evening's drama was best viewed as part of the fun.

A waiter brought a platter to Maxine's side. 'Sushi?' he said. She looked at the array of raw fish with almost superstitious disgust.

'Oh God, why not?' Eppstadt said, a little too heartily. 'In fact you can leave the platter.'

'How can you *eat*?'

'I'm hungry. And if I were you, I'd keep me happy. Treat me *very* delicately.' He examined the piece of yellow-tail in his fingers. 'I suppose at this point I could get all stirred up wondering what the fish was eating before it was caught . . . but why wonder?'

Maxine got up from her chair and walked over to the railing. 'I always thought you liked Todd.'

'I thought he was acceptable company up to a point. But then he got full of himself, and he became impossible. Your handiwork, of course.'

'What?'

'Telling him he was the next best thing to sliced bread,

477

when all along he was just another pretty face. And now not even that, thanks to Dr Burrows.' He picked up a second piece of sushi. 'I tell you, if Todd *is* dead, then he's done the best thing he could do for his reputation. I know how that sounds, but it's the truth. Now he's got a crack at being a legend. If he'd lived, grown old, everyone would have realized he couldn't act his way out of a damp paper bag. And it would have made us all look like fools. You for representing him, me for spending all that money on him over the years.'

'Maxine?'

Sawyer was leading a stricken Jerry up onto the patio. At some point in the recent past his rug had become partially unglued and now sat off-centre on his head.

'Todd's gone,' he said.

'We can't be sure yet, Jerry. Sawyer, get Mr Brahms a scotch and soda. Light on the scotch. Jerry, this is Mr Eppstadt, from Paramount.'

'I'm familiar . . .' Jerry said, his gaze going from Eppstadt as soon as he'd laid eyes on him, and drifting off again towards the water. 'It's useless. I don't know why they keep searching. They've been swept away by now.'

'The house, Jerry.'

'What?'

'In the Canyon,' Eppstadt said. 'I've been hearing about it from Maxine.'

'Oh. I see. Well . . . there's not a lot I can tell you. I just used to go there as a child. I was an actor, you see, when I was much younger.'

'And were there other children there?'

'No. Not that I remember, at least. Just a woman called Katya Lupi – who took me under her wing. She's the one . . .' he pointed out towards the waterline '. . . who took Todd.'

'No, Jerry,' Maxine said. 'Whoever that woman was, she was *young*.'

478

'Katya was young.'

'This girl looked twenty-five.'

'Katya looked twenty-five.' He accepted his scotch and soda from Sawyer. 'She wasn't, of course. She was probably a hundred.'

'Then how the hell can she have looked twenty-five?' Eppstadt demanded.

Jerry had two words by way of reply.

'Coldheart Canyon.'

Eppstadt had no response to this. He just stared at Brahms, bewildered.

'She looks young,' Jerry said. 'But she isn't. That was her out there, no doubt about it. Personally, I think it was some kind of a suicide pact between them.'

'That's ridiculous!' Maxine snorted. 'Todd's got his whole life in front of him.'

'I think he may have been more desperate than you realized,' Jerry said. 'Perhaps if you'd been a little better as friends, he'd still be with us.'

'I don't think it's very useful to toss that kind of accusation around,' Eppstadt said. 'Especially when we don't know the facts.'

'I think the facts are very plain,' Jerry said. 'I still read *Variety*.' He pointed at Maxine. 'You decided to give up on representing him, when he was having difficulties with his career. And you –' now the accusatory finger went in Eppstadt's direction '– cancelled a movie which he had his heart set on. Not to mention the fact that you –' the finger returned to Maxine '– just made a public display of humiliating him. Is it any wonder he decided to put an end to his life?'

Neither accusee attempted a defence. What was the use? What Jerry had said was a matter of public record.

'I want to see this Canyon,' Eppstadt said. 'And the house.'

'The house has nothing to do with any of this,' Jerry

said. 'Frankly, I suggest you keep your distance from it. You've already –'

Eppstadt ignored him. 'Where is it?' he demanded of Maxine.

'Well I've never been able to find it on a map but the Canyon runs parallel with Laurel Canyon. I don't think it's even got a proper name.'

'Coldheart Canyon,' Brahms said again. 'That's what they used to call it in the Silent Era. Because she was supposed to have such a cold heart, you see.'

'You know your way there?' Eppstadt asked Maxine.

'I . . . suppose I *could* find my way . . . but I'd prefer somebody to drive me.'

'You,' Eppstadt said. It was his turn to point.

Jerry shook his head.

'It's either you taking me, or the police.'

'Why'd you want to call the police?'

'Because I think there's some kind of conspiracy going on. You. Pickett. The woman who went into the sea with him. You're all in this together.'

'To do what, for God's sake?'

'I don't know: promote that asshole's career?'

'I assure you –'

'I don't care to hear your assurances,' Eppstadt said. 'I just need you to take me to this Canyon of yours.'

'It's not mine. It's hers. Katya's. If we went there we'd be trespassing on her property.'

'I'll take that risk.'

'Well I won't.'

'Maxine, tell him he's coming.'

'I don't see why you want to go,' Jerry pleaded.

'Let's just make Mr Eppstadt happy right now, shall we?'

'I just don't want to trespass,' Jerry said again.

'Well you can blame me,' Eppstadt said. 'Tell this Lupi woman – if she ever surfaces again – that I *forced* you to take me. Where's the waiter? Joe!'

480

Eppstadt's makeshift bodyguard came over. 'We're going to make a little field-trip. I'd like you to come with us.'

'Oh? Okay.'

'Maxine, do you have a gun?'

'I'm not going with you.'

'Yes you are, m'dear. A gun. Do you have one?'

'Several. But I'm not going. I've had enough excitement for one night. I need some sleep.'

'Well here's your choices. Come now and let's find out what the hell's going on up there, *together*. Or sit tight and wait for my lawyer to call you in the morning.'

Maxine looked at him blankly.

'Do I take that as a yes?' he said.

There were five in the expedition party. Maxine's assistant Sawyer, armed with one of Maxine's guns, drove Maxine. And in a second car, driven by Jerry, went Eppstadt and Joe. The largest of Maxine's guns, a .45, was in Eppstadt's possession. He claimed he knew how to use it.

By the time they had left many of the party-goers had already drifted away, leaving a hard core of perhaps thirty-five people, many of them still on the beach, waiting to see if anything noteworthy was going to happen. About fifteen minutes after Eppstadt's expedition had departed for the hills the Coast Guard called off the helicopter. There had been a boating accident up the coast – nine people in the water – and air support was urgently needed. One of the two search boats was also called off, leaving the other to make wider and wider circles as any hope that the lost souls were still alive and close to the shore steadily grew more remote, and finally, faded entirely.

PART EIGHT

THE WIND AT
THE DOOR

1

The night was almost over by the time the two cars bearing Eppstadt's little expeditionary force made their way up the winding road that led into Coldheart Canyon. The sky was just a little lighter in the east, though the clouds were thick, so it would be a sluggish dawn, without an ounce of the drama which had marked the hours of darkness. In the depths of the Canyon itself, the day never truly dawned properly at all. There was a peculiar density to the shadows between the trees today; as though the night lingered there, in scraps and rags. Day-blooming flowers would fail to show themselves, even at the height of noon; while plants that would normally offer sight and scent of themselves only after dark remained awake through the daylight hours.

None of this was noticed by Eppstadt or the others in his party; they were not the sort of people who noticed things to which so little value could be readily attached. But they knew something was amiss, even so, from the moment they stepped out of their vehicles. They proceeded towards the house exchanging anxious looks, their steps reluctant. Even Eppstadt, who had been so vocal about seeing the Canyon when they'd all been down in Malibu, plainly wished he'd not talked himself into this. Had he been on his own he would undoubtedly have retreated. But he could scarcely do so now, with so many people watching. He could either hope that something alarming (though inconsequential) happened soon, and he was obliged to call a general retreat in the interest of the company, or that they'd get into the house, make a cursory examination of the place, then agree that this was a matter best left with the police, and get the hell out.

The feeling he had, walking into the house, was the same feeling he sometimes got going onto a darkened sound stage. A sense of anticipation hung in the air. The only question was: what was the drama that was going to be played out here? A continuation of the farce he'd been so unwillingly dragged into on the beach? He didn't think so. The stage was set here for some other order of spectacle, and he didn't particularly want to be a part of it.

In all his years running a studio he'd never green-lit a horror movie, or anything with that kind of supernatural edge. He didn't like them. On the one hand, he thought they were contemptible rubbish; and on the other, they made his flesh creep. They unnerved him with their reports from some irrational place in the psyche; a place he had fled from all his life. The Canyon knew that place, he sensed. No, he *knew*. There were probably subjects for a hundred horror movies here, God help him.

'Weird, huh?' Joe remarked to him.

Eppstadt was glad he'd brought the kid along. Though Eppstadt didn't have a queer bone in his body there was still something comforting about having a big-boned, Mid-Western dumb-fuck like Joe on the team.

'What are we looking for, anyhow?' Joe asked as Maxine led the way into the house.

'Anything out of the ordinary,' Eppstadt replied.

'We don't have any right to be here,' Maxine reminded him. 'And if Todd *is* dead, the police aren't going to be very happy that we touched stuff.'

'I get it, Maxine,' he said. 'We'll be careful.'

'Big place,' Joe said, wandering into the lounge. 'Great for parties.'

'Let's get some lights on in this place, shall we?' Eppstadt said. He'd no sooner spoken than Sawyer found the master panel, and flipped on every one of the thirty switches before him. Room after dazzling room was revealed, detail after glorious detail.

Jerry had seen the dream palace countless times over the years, but for some reason, even in its early days when the paint was fresh and the gilding perfect, he'd never seen the house put on a show quite like this. It was almost as if the old place knew it didn't have long to live and – knowing its span was short – was making the best of the hours remaining to it.

'The woman on the beach,' Eppstadt said. 'She built this place?'

'Yes. Her name was Katya Lupi and –'

'I know who she was,' Eppstadt replied. 'I've seen some of her movies. Trash. Kitsch trash.'

It was impossible, of course, that the woman who'd built this Spanish mausoleum was the same individual who'd escorted Todd Pickett into the surf. That woman might have been her grandchild, Eppstadt supposed, at a stretch; a great-grandchild more likely.

He was about to correct Brahms on his generational details when a chorus of yelping coyotes erupted across the Canyon. Eppstadt knew what coyotes sounded like, of course. He had plenty of friends who lived in the Hills, and considered the animals harmless scavengers, digging through their rubbish and occasionally dining on a pet cat. But there was something about the noise they were making now, as the sun came up, that made his stomach twitch and his skin crawl. It was like a soundtrack of one of the horror movies he'd never green-lit.

And then, just as suddenly as the chorus of coyotes had erupted, it ceased. There were three seconds of total silence.

Then everything began to shake. The walls, the chandelier, the ancient floorboards beneath their feet.

'*Earthquake*!' Sawyer yelled. He grabbed hold of Maxine's arm. She screeched, and ran for the kitchen door.

'*Outside!*' she shrieked. '*We're all safer outside!*'

She could move fast when she needed to. She dragged Sawyer after her, down to the back door. Jerry tried to follow, but the shaking in the ground had become a roll, and he missed his handhold.

Joe, Mid-Western boy that he was, had never experienced an earthquake before. He just stood on the pitching ground repeating the name of his saviour over and over and over again, in perfect sincerity.

It's going to stop any minute, Eppstadt thought (he'd lived through many of these, big and small), but this one kept going, escalating. The floor was undulating in front of him. If he'd seen it in dailies he would have fired the physical effects guy for creating something that looked so phoney. Solid matter like wood and nails simply didn't move that way. It was ludicrous.

But still it escalated, and Joe's calls to his saviour became shouts:

'*Christ*! *Christ*! *Christ*! *Christ*!'

'When's it going to stop?' Jerry gasped.

He'd given up trying to rise. He just lay on the ground while the rattling and the rolling continued unabated.

There was a crash from an adjacent room, as something was thrown over. And then, from further off, a whole succession of further crashes, as shelves came unseated, and their contents were scattered. A short length of plaster moulding came down from the ceiling and smashed on the ground a foot from where Eppstadt was standing, its shards spreading in all directions. He looked up, in case there was more to come. A fine rain of plaster-dust was descending, stinging his eyes. Meanwhile, the quake continued to make the house creak and crack on all sides, Eppstadt's semi-blinded condition only making the event seem all the more apocalyptic. He reached towards Joe, who was hoarse from reciting his one-word prayer, and caught hold of him.

'What's that noise?' the kid yelled over the din.

It seemed like a particularly witless question in the midst of such a cacophony, but interestingly, Eppstadt grasped exactly what the kid was talking about.

There was one sound, amongst the terrifying orchestration of groans and crashes from all over the house, that was deeper than all the others, and seemed to be coming from directly beneath them. It sounded like two titanic sets of teeth grinding together, grinding so hard they were destroying themselves in the process.

'I don't know what it is,' admitted Eppstadt. Tears were pouring from his eyes, washing them clear of the plaster-dust.

'Well I want it to fucking *stop*,' Joe said with nice Mid-Western directness.

He'd no sooner spoken than the noise in the earth started to die away, and moments later the rest of the din and motion followed.

'It's over . . .' Jerry sobbed.

He'd spoken too soon. There was one last, short jolt in the ground, which brought a further series of crashes from around the house, and from below what sounded like a door being thrown open so violently it cracked its back against the wall.

Only then did the noises and the deep-earth motion finally subside and die away. What was left, from far off, was the sound of car alarms.

'Everybody okay?' Eppstadt said.

'I'll never get used to those damn things,' Jerry said.

'That was a big one,' Eppstadt said. '6.5 at least.'

'And it went on, and on . . .'

'I think we should just get the hell out of here,' Joe said.

'Before we go anywhere,' Eppstadt said, venturing into

489

the kitchen, 'we wait for any aftershocks. We're safer inside than out there right now.'

'How do you figure that?' Joe said, following Eppstadt into the kitchen.

It was chaos. None of the shelves had come off the walls, but they'd been shaken so violently they'd deposited their contents on the tiled floor. A cabinet holding booze had been shaken down, and several of the bottles broken, filling the air with the sharp tang of mingled liquors. Eppstadt went to the refrigerator – which had been thrown open by the quake, and had half its contents danced off the shelves – and found a can of Coke. He cracked it carefully, letting its excitability fizz away by degrees, then poured it as though this sickly soda was a hundred year old brandy, and drank.

'Better,' he said.

'I'll take one of those,' Joe remarked.

'What colour do I look?'

Scowling, Joe kicked his way through the fractured crockery to the refrigerator, and got himself a Coke.

'What the hell happened to Maxine?' Eppstadt wondered.

'She went out back with Sawyer,' Joe said, averting his face from a fan of erupting Coke.

Eppstadt went out into a passageway that led down to an open door, kicking a few pieces of fallen plaster out of the way as he went.

'Maxine!' he called. 'Are you okay?'

There was no reply.

Without waiting for anyone to join him, he headed down to the back door. There was more plaster dust underfoot, and several large cracks in the walls and ceiling. Unlike other areas of the house this portion looked less solid to his eye, and very much less elegant. A hurried later addition, he guessed, and probably more vulnerable to shocks than the older parts of the house. He called out for Maxine again, but again there was no reply forthcoming. He wasn't surprised. The area just outside the door looked squalid; large masses of rotted vegetable matter covered the walkway on the other side of the threshold, giving off a sickly stench. The overhanging foliage was so thick that the area was practically benighted.

He went to the threshold, intending to call for Maxine again, but before he could do so he heard the sound of low, sibilant laughter. Since childhood he'd always been certain that laughter heard in his vicinity was laughter heard at his expense, and even though his therapist had worked hard for sixteen years to dissuade him of this neurosis, it lingered. He narrowed his eyes, trying to make sense of the shadows beneath the trees; dividing form from apparition. Obviously, the laughter had a source, perhaps more than one. He just couldn't make it out.

'Stop that,' he ordered.

But the laughter continued, which enraged him. They were laughing at him, he was certain of it. Who else would they be laughing at? Bastards.

He stepped over the threshold, ready to sue. The air was cold and clammy. This wasn't a very pleasant house, he'd decided very quickly, and this was a particularly unpleasant corner of it. But the laughter continued, and he couldn't turn his back on it, not until he'd silenced it.

'Who the hell *are* you?' he demanded. 'This is private property. You hear me? You shouldn't even –'

He stopped now because there, in the shadow of a humongous Bird of Paradise tree, he made out a human form. No, two. No, three. He could barely see their features, but he could feel the imprint of their stares upon him.

And then more laughter, mocking his protests.

'I'm warning you,' he snapped, as though he were talking to children. 'Get away from here. *Go on*! *Get away*!'

But instead of stopping, the addled laughter grew louder still, and its owners decided to step out from under the shade of the Bird of Paradise. Eppstadt could see them more clearly now. They were indeed trespassers, he guessed, who'd been up here partying the night away. One of them, a very lovely young woman (she couldn't have been more than seventeen, to judge by the tautness of her skin) was bare-breasted, her brunette hair wet and pressed to her skull. He vaguely thought he knew her; that perhaps as a child actress she'd been in a movie he'd produced over at Paramount, or during his earlier time at Fox. She was certainly developing into a beautiful woman. But there was something about the way she stepped out of the shadows – her head sinking down, as though she might at any moment drop to the ground and imitate some animal or other – that distressed him. He didn't want her near him, even with her tight skin, her lovely nubs of nipples, her pouty lips. There was too much hunger in her eyes, and even if he wasn't the focus of that appetite, he didn't want to be caught between such a mindless hunger and its object of desire, whatever it might be.

And then there were the others, still lurking close to the tree behind her. Wait, there were more than two. There were a host of others, whose gaze he now felt on him. They were everywhere out here, in this uncertain dawn. He could see the foliage moving where some of them had slunk, their naked bellies flat on the ground. And they were up in the branches too; rotted blossoms came down to add to the muck that slickened the Mexican pavers underfoot.

Eppstadt took a tentative backward step, regretting that he'd ever stepped out of the house. No, not just that. At that moment he was regretting the whole process of events that had brought him to this damned house in the first place. Going to Maxine's asinine party; having that witless argument with Pickett; then the interrogation of Jerry Brahms and the choice to come up here. Stupid, all of it.

He took a second backward step. As he did so the eyes of the exhibitionist girl who'd first appeared became exceptionally bright, as though something in her head had caught fire. Then, without warning, she broke into a sudden run, racing at Eppstadt. He turned back towards the door, and in the instant that he did so he saw a dozen – no, two dozen – figures who'd been standing camouflaged in the murk break their cover and join her in her dash for the door.

He was a step from reaching the threshold when the young bitch caught hold of his arm.

'Please –' she said. Her fingers dug deep into the fat where healthier men had biceps.

'*Let me go.*'

'Don't go in,' she said.

She pulled him back towards her, her strength uncanny. He reached out and grabbed the doorjamb, thinking as he did so that he'd got through the last twenty-five years of his life without anyone laying an inappropriate hand upon him, and here he was in the midst of his second such indignity in the space of twenty-four hours.

The woman still had fierce hold of him, and she wasn't about to let him go.

'Stay out here,' she implored.

He flailed away from her. His Armani shirt tore, and he seized the moment to wriggle free. From the corner of his eye he saw a lot of faces, eyes incandescent, converging on the spot.

Terror made him swifter than he'd been in three decades. He leapt over the threshold, and once he got inside, he turned on a quarter, throwing all his weight against the door. It slammed closed. He fumbled with the lock, expecting to feel instant pressure exerted from the other side.

But there was none. Despite the fact that the trespassers could have pushed the door open (smashed it open, lock and all, if they'd so chosen) they didn't. The girl simply called to him through the door, her voice well-modulated, like that of someone who'd been to a high-grade finishing school:

'You should be careful,' she said, in an eerie sing-song. 'This house is going to come down. Do you hear me, Mr? *It's coming down.*'

He heard; he heard loud and clear. But he didn't reply. He simply bolted the door, still mystified as to why they hadn't attempted to break in, and ran up the passageway back to the kitchen. Before he reached the door Joe rounded the corner, coming in the opposite direction, gun in hand.

'Where the hell were you?' Eppstadt demanded.

'I was just about to ask you the same –'

'We're under siege.'

'From what?'

'There are crazy people out there. A lot of crazy, fucking people.'

'Where?'

'Right outside that door!'

He pointed back down the passageway. There was nothing visible through the glass panel. They'd retreated in four or five seconds, taking refuge in the murk.

'Trust me,' Eppstadt said, 'there's twenty or thirty people waiting on the other side of that door. One of them tried to drag me out there with them.' He proffered his torn shirt and bloodied arm as proof. 'She was probably rabid. I should get shots.'

'I don't hear anybody,' Joe said.

'They're out there. Trust me.'

He went back to the kitchen, with Joe on his heels.

Jerry was running water into the sink, and splashing it on his temple. Joe went straight to the window to see if he could verify Eppstadt's story, while Eppstadt snatched a handful of water to douse his own wound.

'The line's down, by the way,' Jerry said.

494

'I've got my portable,' Eppstadt said.

'They're not working either,' Joe said. 'The earthquake's taken out the whole system.'

'Did you see Maxine or Sawyer out there?' Jerry said.

'I never got *out there*, Brahms. There are people –'

'Yes I know.'

'Wait. Turn off the water.'

'I haven't finished washing.'

'I said: *turn it off*.'

Brahms reluctantly obeyed. As the last of the water ran off down the pipes, another cluster of noises became audible, rising from the bowels of the house.

'It sounds like somebody left a television on down there,' Joe said, splendidly simple-minded.

Eppstadt went to the door that led into the turret. 'That's no television,' he said.

'Well what the hell else would it be?' Joe said. 'I can hear horses, and wind. There's no wind today.'

It was true. There was no wind. But somewhere, it was howling like the soundtrack on *Lawrence of Arabia*.

'You'll find this place gets crowded after a while,' Jerry said matter-of-factly. He patted dry the wound on his face. 'We shouldn't be here,' he reiterated.

'Who are they out there?' Eppstadt said.

'Old movie stars mainly. A few of Katya's lovers.'

Eppstadt shook his head. 'These weren't old. And several of them were women.'

'She liked women,' Jerry said. 'On occasion. Especially if she could play her little games with them.'

'What the fuck are you talking about?' Joe said.

'Katya Lupi, who built this house –'

'Once and for all –' Eppstadt said, 'these were not Katya Lupi's lovers. They were young. One of them, at least, looked no more than sixteen or seventeen.'

'She liked them very young. And they liked her. Especially when she'd taken them down *there*.' He pointed to the

495

turret door through which the sound of storm-winds was still coming. 'It's another world down there, you see. And they'd be addicted, after that. They'd do anything for her, just to get another taste of it.'

'I don't get it,' Joe said.

'Better you don't,' Jerry replied. 'Just leave now, while you still can. The earthquake threw the door open down there. That's why you can hear all the noise.'

'You said it was coming from some other place?' Joe said.

'Yes. The Devil's Country.'

'What?'

'That's what Katya used to call it. The Devil's Country.'

Joe glanced at Eppstadt, looking for some confirmation that all this was nonsense. But Eppstadt was staring out of the window, still haunted by the hungry faces he'd met on the threshold. Much as he would have liked to laugh off what Jerry Brahms was saying, his instincts were telling him to be more cautious.

'Suppose there *is* some kind of door down there . . .' he said.

'There is, believe me.'

'All right. Say I believe you. And maybe the earthquake did open it up. Shouldn't somebody go down there and *close* it?'

'That would certainly make sense.'

'Joe?'

'Aw shit. Why me?'

'Because you're the one who kept telling us how good you are with a gun. Anyway, it's obvious Jerry's in no state to go.'

'What about you?'

'Joe,' Eppstadt said. 'You're talking to the Head of Paramount.'

'So? That doesn't *mean* a whole heap right now, does it?'

496

'No, but it will when we get back to the real world.' He stared at Joe, with an odd little smile on his face. 'You don't want to be a waiter all your life, do you?'

'No. Of course not.'

'You came to Hollywood to act, am I right?'

'I'm really good.'

'I'm sure you are. Do you have any idea how much help I could be to you?'

'If I go down there –?'

'And close the door.'

'Then you make me a movie star?'

'There are no *guarantees* in this town, Joe. But put it this way. You've got a better chance of being the next Brad Pitt –'

'I see myself more as an Ed Norton.'

'Okay. Ed Norton. You stand a better chance of being the next Ed Norton if you've got the Head of Paramount on your side. You understand?'

Joe looked past Eppstadt at the doorway that led to the turret. The noise of the storm had not abated a jot. If anything the wind had become louder, slamming the door against a wall. If it had just been the whine of the wind coming from below no doubt Joe's ambitions would have had him halfway down the stairs by now. But there were other sounds being carried on the back of the wind, some easy to interpret, others not so easy. He could hear the screech of agitated birds, which was not too distressing. But there were other species giving voice below: and he could put a name to none of them.

'Well, Joe?' Eppstadt said. 'You want to close that door? Or do you want to serve canapés for the rest of your life.'

'Fuck.'

'You've got a gun, Joe. Where's your balls?'

'You promise you'll get me a part? Not some stinking little walk-on?'

'I promise . . . to do my best for you.'

Joe looked over at Jerry. 'Do you know what's down there?'

'Just don't look,' was Jerry's advice. 'Close the door and come back up. Don't look into the room, even if it seems really amazing.'

'Why?'

'Because it is amazing. And once you've looked you're going to want to go on looking.'

'And if something comes out after me?'

'Shoot it.'

'There,' said Eppstadt. 'Satisfied?'

Joe turned the proposition over in his head for a few more seconds, weighing the gun in his hand as he did so. 'I've been in this fucking town two, almost three, years. Haven't even got an agent.'

'Looks like this is your lucky day,' Eppstadt said.

'Better be,' Joe replied.

He drew a deep breath, and went out into the hallway. Eppstadt smiled reassuringly at him as he went by, but his features weren't made for reassurance. In fact at the sight of Eppstadt's crooked smile, Joe almost changed his mind. Then, thinking perhaps of what his life had been like so far – the casual contempt heaped on waiters by the famous – he went out to the head of the stairs and looked down. Reassuringly, the door had stopped slamming quite so hard. Joe took a deep breath, then he headed down the flight.

Eppstadt watched him go. Then he went back to the window.

'The people out there . . .' he said to Jerry.

'What about them?'

'Will they have harmed Maxine?'

'I doubt it. They don't want blood. They just want to get back into the house.'

'Why didn't they just push past me?'

'There's some kind of trap at the door that keeps them out.'

'I got in and out without any problem.'

'Well, you're *alive*, aren't you?'

'What?'

'You heard what I said.'

'Don't start with the superstitious crap, Brahms. I'm not in the mood.'

'Neither am I,' Jerry said. 'I wish I was anywhere but here, right now.'

'I thought this was your dream palace?'

'If Katya were here, it would be a different matter.'

'You don't really think that woman on the beach was Katya Lupi, do you?'

'I know it was her for a fact. I drove her down to Malibu myself.'

'What?'

Jerry shrugged. 'Playing Cupid.'

'Katya Lupi and Todd Pickett? Crazy. It's all crazy.'

'Why? Because you refuse to believe in ghosts?'

'Oh. I didn't say that,' Eppstadt replied, somewhat cautiously. 'I didn't say I didn't *believe*. I've been to Gettysburg and felt the presence of the dead. But a battlefield is one thing –'

'And an old Hollywood dream-palace is another? Why? People suffered here, believe me. A few even took their own lives. I don't know why I'm telling you. You know how people suffer here. You caused half of it. This miserable town's awash with envy and anger. You know how cruel LA makes people? How hungry?'

The word rang a bell. Eppstadt thought of the face of the woman at the back of the house. The appetite in her eyes.

'They might not be the kind of ghosts you think you hear moaning at Gettysburg,' Jerry went on. 'But believe me, they are very dead and they are very desperate. So the sooner we find Maxine and Sawyer and get out of here the better for all of us.'

'Oh dear God,' Eppstadt said softly.

'What?'

'I'm starting to believe you.'

'Then we've made some progress, I suppose.'

'Why didn't you tell me all this before we came up here?'

'Would it have stopped you coming?'

'No.'

'You see. You needed to see for yourself.'

'Well, I've seen,' Eppstadt said. 'And you're right. As soon as Joe's closed the door, we'll all go out and find Maxine and Sawyer. You're sure those things –'

'Use the word, Eppstadt.'

'I don't want to.'

'For God's sake, it's just a word.'

'All right . . . *ghosts*. Are you sure they won't come after us? They looked vicious.'

'They want to get into the house. It's as I said: that's all they care about. They want to get back into the Devil's Country.'

'Do you know why?'

'I've half a notion, but I don't fancy sharing it with you. Shall we not waste time standing around trying to guess what the dead want?' He returned his gaze to the expanse of green outside the window.

'We'll all of us know sooner than we care to.'

2

At 5:49 a.m., when the 6.9 earthquake (later discovered to have had its epicentre in Pasadena)
had shaken Los Angeles out of its pre-dawn doze,
Tammy had been standing on the nameless street outside
Katya Lupi's house in Coldheart Canyon, drawn back to
the place with an ease that suggested she had it in her
blood now, for better or worse.

She had left the party at the Colony a few minutes before
the departure of Eppstadt's expedition, having decided that
there was little point in her waiting on the beach. If Todd
and Katya were still in the water then they were dead by
now, their corpses carried off by the tide towards Hawaii or
Japan. And if by some miracle they had survived, then they
surely wouldn't go back to Maxine's house. They would
head home to the Canyon.

Her initial plan was to give up on this whole sorry
adventure, return to the hotel on Wilshire, shower, change
into some fresh clothes and then get the first available
flight out of Los Angeles. She'd done all she could for
Todd Pickett. More than he deserved, Lord knows. And
what had she got for her troubles? In the end, little more
than his contempt. She wasn't going to put herself in the
way of that ever again. If she wanted to cause herself pain
all she had to do was bang her head against the kitchen
door. She didn't need to come all the way to Los Angeles
to do that.

But as she drove back to the hotel, fragments of things

that she'd seen in the Canyon, and later in the house, came back to her; images that inspired more awe in her soul than terror. She would never get another chance to see such sights this side of the grave, certainly; should she not take the opportunity to go back, one last time? If she didn't go now, by tomorrow it would be too late. The Canyon would have found new protections against her – or anybody else's – inquiry; new charms and mechanisms designed to conceal its raptures from curious eyes.

And, of course, there was always the remote possibility that Todd had survived the ocean and made his way back up there. That, more than any other, was the strongest reason to return.

Her decision made, she drove on up to Sunset – forgetting about the shower and change of clothes – and made her way back to the Canyon.

No doubt it was foolhardy, returning to a place where she had endured so much but, besides her desire to see the spectacles of the place one last time, and putting aside any hopes she might have for Todd's survival, she could not shake the niggling suspicion that her business at the house was not at an end. She had no intellectual justification for such a feeling; just a certainty, marrow-deep, that this was the case. She'd know when it was over. And it was not.

It had been an eerie drive up the winding Canyon road in the pre-dawn gloom. She had deliberately switched off her headlights so as to attract as little attention as possible, but that made her feel even more vulnerable somehow; as though she was not quite real herself, here in this Canyon of a Thousand Illusions.

Twice something had moved across the road in front of her, its grey form unfixable in the murk. She put on the brakes, and let the creature cross.

Once she got to the house she realized she was not the first visitor. There were two cars already parked outside.

She was crossing the street to examine the other two when the earthquake hit.

She'd been in earthquakes before, but she'd never actually been standing so close to the bedrock while one took place. It was quite an experience. She almost lost control of her bladder, as the road idled under her feet, and the trees, especially the big ones, creaked and churned. She stood and waited for the first shock wave to pass, which seemed an eternity. Then, when her heart had recovered something approximating its natural rhythm, she headed towards Katya Lupi's dream palace.

Eppstadt was in the hallway, looking down the stairwell. It was dark at the bottom, but he thought he saw a motion in the darkness, like motes of pale dust, spiralling around.

'Joe?' he called. 'Are you there? Answer me, will you?'

The sound from below had died away: the din of beasts was now barely audible. All that remained was the sound of the wind, which was remarkably consistent, lending credence to the notion that what he was hearing was a soundtrack, not reality. But where the hell had Joe got to? It was fully five minutes since he'd disappeared down the stairs to close the slamming door.

'I wouldn't go down there if I were you.'

Eppstadt glanced over his shoulder to see that Brahms had forsaken his place at the window, and had come into the hallway.

'He doesn't answer me,' Eppstadt said. 'I thought perhaps he'd fallen, or . . . I don't know. The door's still slamming. Hear it?'

'Of course.'

'I don't suppose you want to go down there and close it for me?'

'You're big on delegation, aren't you? Do they teach you that in business school?'

'It's just a door.'

'So close it yourself.'

Eppstadt threw Brahms a sour look. 'Or don't. Leave him down there if that's what your instincts are telling you.'

'And if I do?'

'Put it this way: the longer you wait, the less chance there is you'll ever see him again.'

'I should never have sent him down there,' Eppstadt said.

'Huh. I never thought I'd hear that from you.'

'Hear what?'

'Regret. This place is changing you. Even you. I'm impressed.'

Eppstadt didn't reply. He simply stared down the long curve of the stairway, still hoping he'd see Joe's well-made face emerging from the shadows. But the only motion down there was the dust stirred up by the wind, circling on itself.

'*Joe*!' he yelled.

There wasn't even an echo from below. The bowels of the house seemed to consume the shouted syllable.

'I'm going upstairs,' Jerry said, 'to see if there's anybody up there.'

'Is Maxine still out back?'

'I assume so. And if I remember from previous quakes she'll stay out there a while. She doesn't like being under *anything*, even a table, during a quake. She'll come in when she's ready.'

'Thanks.'

'You're welcome.'

'You don't like me, do you?' Eppstadt said out of nowhere.

Jerry shrugged. 'Hollywood's always had its share of little Caligulas.'

So saying, he left Eppstadt to his dilemma, and went on up the stairs. He knew the geography of the house pretty well. There were three doors that led off the top landing. One went to a short passageway, which led in turn to a large bedroom, with *en suite* bathroom, which had been occupied, until his death, by Marco Caputo. One was a small writing room. And one was the master bedroom, with its astonishing view, its immense closet and sumptuous, if somewhat over-wrought, bathroom.

Jerry had only been in the master bedroom two or three times; but it held fond memories for him. Memories of being a young man (what had he been, twelve, thirteen at the most?) invited in by Katya. Oh, she'd been beautiful that night; it had been like lying in the bed of a goddess. He'd been too frightened to touch her at first, but she'd gently persuaded him out of his fears.

As his life had turned out, she'd been the only woman he'd ever slept with. In his early twenties he was certain his queerness was a result of that night. No other woman, he would tell himself, could possibly be the equal of Katya Lupi. But that was just self-justification. He'd been born queer, and Katya was his one grand exception to the rule.

As he reached the door of the master bedroom, there was an aftershock. A short jolt, no more; but enough to set the antiquated chandelier that hung in the turret gently swaying and tinkling again. Jerry waited for a few moments, holding onto the banister, waiting to see if there were going to be any more shocks coming immediately upon the heels of this one. But there were none.

He glanced down the stairwell. No one was in view. Then he tried the bedroom door. It was locked from the inside. There was only one thing to construe from this: the room had an occupant, or occupants. He glanced down at the shiny boards at his feet, and saw that there were a few droplets of water on the polished timber.

It wasn't hard to put the pieces of this puzzle together; nor to imagine the scene on the other side of the locked door. Todd and Katya had survived their brush with the

Pacific. They were alive; sleeping, no doubt, in the great bed. The voyeur in him would have liked very much to have slid through the closed door and spied on the lovers as they slept; both naked, Todd lying face up on the bed, Katya pressed to his side. She was probably snoring, as he'd heard her do several times when she'd cat-napped in his presence.

He didn't blame Katya for her covetousness one iota. If being hungry for life meant being hungry for an eternity of nights wrapped in the arms of a man who loved you, then that was an entirely understandable appetite.

And there was just a little part of him which thought that if he stayed loyal to her long enough – if he played his part – then she would let him have a piece of her eternity. That she would show him how the years could be made to melt away.

He retreated from the door, and headed downstairs, leaving the sleepers to their secret slumber.

When he got to the mid-level landing Eppstadt had gone. Apparently, he'd made the decision to go downstairs and look for Joe. Jerry looked over the balcony. There was no sound from below. The wind had died away to nothing. The door was no longer slamming.

He went from the stairs to the front door, which stood ajar.

Perhaps this was his moment to depart. He had nothing more to contribute here. Katya had her man; Todd had found some measure of peace after his own disappointments. What else was there for Jerry to do, but make his silent farewells and slip away?

He stood at the front door for two or three minutes, unable to make the final break. Eventually, he convinced himself to just linger here a little longer, simply to see the look on Maxine's face when she realized Todd was still alive. He went back into the kitchen, and sat down, waiting – like anyone who'd spent their time watching other lives rather than having one of their own – to see what happened next.

Eppstadt had been two steps from the bottom of the stairs when the aftershock hit. He was by no means an agile man, but he leapt the last two steps without a stumble. There were ominous growlings in the walls, as though several hungry tigers had been sealed up in them. This was, he knew, one of the most foolish places to be caught in an earthquake, especially if (as was perfectly possible) the aftershock turned out not to be an aftershock at all, but a warm-up for something bigger. It would be more sensible – *much* more sensible – to ascend the stairs again and wait until the tigers had quieted down. But he wasn't going to do that. He'd been sensible for most of his life; always taking the safe road, the conservative route. For once, he wanted to play life a little dangerously, and take the consequences.

That said, he didn't have to be suicidal. There was a door-lintel up ahead. He'd be safer under there than he was in the open passageway. He made a dash for the spot, and as he did so, the aftershock abruptly ceased.

He took a deep breath.

Then he glanced over his shoulder into the room behind him. Presumably this was the place Joe had disappeared into; there was nowhere else for him to go.

He went to the door. Looked inside. He could see nothing at first, just undivided gloom. He reached in, as many had done before him, to fumble for a light switch, and failing to find one, allowed a little surge of curiosity to take hold of him. Hadn't he said to himself he wanted to live a little more riskily? Well, here was his opportunity. Stepping into this strange room at the bottom of this lunatic house was probably the most foolish thing he'd ever done, and he knew it.

A cold wind came to greet him. It caught hold of his

elbow, and drew him over the threshold into the world –
yes, it was a world – inside. He looked up at the heavens;
at that three-quarter blinded sun, at the high herringbone
clouds that he remembered puzzling over as a child, wondering what it was that laid them out so carefully, so
prettily. A star fell earthward, and he followed its arc
with his eyes, until it burned itself out, somewhere over
the trees.

Far off, many miles beyond the dark mass of the forest,
he could see the sea, glittering. This was not the Pacific,
he could see. The ships that moved upon it were like
something from an Errol Flynn flick, *The Sea Hawk* or
some such. He'd loved those movies as a kid; and the
ships in them. Especially the ships.

It was twenty-six seconds since the man from Paramount,
who'd spent his professional life keeping the dreamy, superstitious child in him silenced by pretending a fine, high-
minded superiority to all things that smelt of grease-paint
and midnight hokum, had entered the Devil's Country;
and had lost himself in it.

'Come on, don't be afraid,' the wind from the sea
whispered in his ear.

And in he went, all cynicism wiped from his mind by
the memory of wheeling ships beneath a painted sky, still
young enough to believe he might grow up a hero.

3

Todd stirred from a state closer to a stupor than a
sleep. He was lying on the immense bed of the master
bedroom in the house in Coldheart Canyon. Katya
was lying beside him, her little body gathered into a tight
knot, pressed close to him. One arm was beneath him, the
other on top, as though she'd never let go of him again.
She was snoring in her sleep, as she had been that day he'd
found her in her bedroom at the guest-house. The human
touch. It was more eloquent now than ever, given what
they'd gone through together.

There had been some terrifying moments for them both
in the last few hours; fragments of them played in Todd's
head as he slowly extricated himself from her embrace,
and slid slowly out of the bed. First, there'd been that
breath-snatching moment when he'd turned his back on
the Malibu house and headed out into the dark waters of
the Pacific with Katya. He'd never been so frightened in his
life. But then she'd squeezed his hand, and looked around
at him, her hair blowing back from her face, showing off
the glory of her bones, and he'd thought: even if I die now,
I will have been the luckiest man in creation. I will have
had this woman by my side at the end. Who could ask for
more than that?

It hadn't been quite so easy to hold on to those feelings
of gratitude in the chaotic minutes that followed. Once they
were out of their depth, and in the grip of the great Pacific,
the bitter-sweet joy of what they were doing became a

shared, instinctive attempt to survive in the dark, bruising waters. Fifty yards out, and the big waves, the surfers' waves, started to pick them up and drop them down again into their lightless troughs. It was so dark he could barely see Katya's face, but he heard her choking on seawater, coughing like a frightened little girl.

And suddenly the idea of just dying out here, beaten to death by the waves, didn't seem so attractive. Why not try to *live*, he found himself thinking? Not the kind of life he'd had before (he wouldn't want that again, ever) but some other kind of life. Travelling around the world, perhaps, incognito; just the two of them. That wouldn't be so bad, would it? And when they were bored with travel they could find some sunny beach down in Costa Rica and spend every day there drunk amongst the parrots. There they could wait out the years until the big, glossy world he'd once given a shit for had forgotten he even existed.

All these thoughts came in flashes, none of them really coherent. The only thought that took any real shape was the means by which they could escape this dark water alive.

'We're going to dive!' he yelled to Katya. 'Take a deep breath.'

He heard her do so; then, before another pulverizing wave could come along and knock them out he drove them both into a teetering wall of water, diving deep into the placid heart of the wave. They must have done this half a hundred times; diving down, rising up again gasping, then watching for the next monstrous wall to be almost upon them before diving again. It was a desperate trick, but it worked.

It was clearly preventing them from getting a terrible beating, but it was steadily taking its toll on their energies. He knew they couldn't continue to defy the violence of the water for very much longer. Their muscles were aching, their senses were becoming unreliable. It would only be a matter of time before the force of the water got the better of them, and they sank together, defeated by sheer fatigue.

But they had counted without the benign collusion of the tide, which all this time had been slowly bearing them south, and – as it did so – had been also ushering them back towards the shore. The tumult of waters around them began to die down, and after a few minutes their toes began to brush some of the taller coral towers. A few minutes later they had solid ground beneath their feet, and a few minutes after that they were stumbling ashore at Venice.

For five minutes or so they lay on the dark sand together, spitting up water and coughing, and then eventually finding it in them to laugh, and catch each other's hands.

Against all the odds, they'd survived.

'I guess we . . . we weren't ready . . . to die,' Todd gasped.

'I suppose so,' Katya said. She dragged her head over the sand, to put her lips in reach of his. It wasn't a kiss, so much as a sharing of breath. They lay there, mouth to mouth, until Katya's teeth began to chatter.

'We have to get you back to the Canyon,' he said, hauling himself to his knees. The lights of the Venice boardwalk seemed impossibly remote.

'I can't,' she said.

'Yes you can. We're going home. We're going back to the Canyon. You'll feel stronger and warmer once we're walking. I promise.'

He helped her get to her knees and then practically lifted her to her feet. Arms around one another they stumbled towards the boardwalk, where the usual tourist-trap entertainments were still going on, despite the lateness of the hour. They wove between the people, unrecognized, and in a back street Todd found a kid with a beaten up Pinto to whom he offered three hundred waterlogged bucks if he'd take them back home, and another three hundred, dry, if he promised not to mention what he'd done and where he'd been, to *anyone*.

'I know who you are,' the kid said.

'No you don't,' Todd said, snatching the three hundred back from the kid's hand.

'Okay, okay. I don't,' the kid replied, gently reclaiming the money. 'You gotta deal.'

Todd knew that there wasn't much chance that the driver's promise would last very long, but they had no choice in the matter. They made their makeshift chauffeur close all the windows and turn up the heating, and they clung together in the back of the car trying to get some warmth back into their blood. Todd got him to drive as fast as the vehicle was capable of going, and twenty minutes later he was directing the kid up the winding road into Coldheart Canyon.

'I've never been up here before,' the kid said when they were outside the house.

Katya leaned in and stared at him.

'No,' she said. 'And you never will again.'

Something about the way she said it made the kid feel very nervous.

'Okay, okay,' he said. 'Just give me the rest of the money.'

Todd went inside for another three hundred dollars in dry bills, and a few minutes later the guy drove off six hundred bucks the richer, and none the wiser, while Todd and Katya dragged themselves up the turret stairs to the master bedroom, sloughing off their cold damp clothes as they crept towards the bed they'd thought they'd never see again.

It took Todd a long time to get across the bedroom to the closet: his body ached to his marrow, and his thoughts were as sluggish as his body. Only as he was pulling on a clean pair of jeans did he realize there were voices in the house.

512

'Shit . . .' he murmured to himself.

He decided not to wake Katya. Instead he would try to get rid of these people himself, without unleashing her righteous fury on them.

He went back across the bedroom. Despite the hulla-baloo from below Katya showed no sign of waking. This was all to the good. She was obviously healing the hurts of recent days. He lingered at the bed-side, studying her peaceful features. The seawater had washed every trace of rouge or mascara from her face; she could have been a fifteen-year-old, lying there, dreaming innocent dreams.

Of course that innocence was an illusion. He knew what she was capable of; and there was a corner of his brain that never completely ceased warning him of that fact. But then hadn't she come to the beach to save him? Who else would have done that, except perhaps for Tammy? All anybody had ever done for him was use him, and as soon as they'd got what they'd needed, they'd moved on. But Katya had proved she was made of more loyal stuff. She'd been ready to go all the way with him; to death if necessary.

So what if she *was* cruel? What if she had committed crimes that would have had her behind bars if anybody knew about them? Her sins mattered very little to him right now. What mattered was how she'd taken his hand as they'd turned their back on the lights of the beach and faced the dark waters of the Pacific; and how hard she'd struggled to keep holding onto it, however much the tide had conspired to divorce them.

The voices below had quieted.

He pulled on a white T-shirt, and went to the door. As he did so there was a small earthquake. The door rattled in its frame. It was a short jolt, and he guessed it was probably an aftershock. If so, then perhaps what had woken him in the first place was the big shaker. Why else would he have woken? He was still very much in need of sleep, God knows. Nothing would have given him more pleasure than to strip off his jeans and T-shirt and crawl back into bed beside Katya for another three or four hours of blissful slumber.

But he could scarcely do that with a search party in the house. He heard Eppstadt's voice amongst the exchanges. Fuck him! It was typical that the little prick would get his nose in their business sooner or later. Todd had hoped that he and Katya would get some quiet time together to plan their next move: to search the house (and of course the Pool House) for incriminating evidence of scandal, and destroy it; then to hide in the depths of the Canyon until the investigators were satisfied that there was nothing here worth investigating, and left, taking Eppstadt and whoever the hell else was here (Maxine, no doubt) back with them. But Eppstadt had ruined that hope. Before these interlopers left they were going to search every damn room, no doubt of that: the master bedroom included. He was going to need to find a way to spirit Katya and himself out of the house and away before they came looking.

He listened at the door and then very gingerly unlocked it and opened it an inch. He could hear an exchange from below, which seemed to be led by Eppstadt. Jesus, of all people to be up here amongst Katya's mysteries: Mr Bottom-line himself, Gary Eppstadt. There was no sign of an opinion from Maxine, which was unusual. She was normally vocal in any debate, however little she knew about the subject. Then Todd remembered her phobia about quakes. She always fled for the open air at the first sign of a trembler, and no doubt she'd done exactly that. He was tempted to go onto the balcony and see if he could spot her in the back yard – just to see the bitch in a state of agitation – but there wasn't time. There was too much going on downstairs. He ventured out of the bedroom a step, and peered over the rail, in time to see somebody – it was a young man, either a waiter brought from the party, or one of Maxine's new boys (or both), heading down the spiral into the darkness down there, where a door was banging.

Next he heard footsteps, and felt certain that Eppstadt was about to appear from the kitchen door. Before he was spotted, Todd gently closed the door. It made a barely perceptible click; certainly nothing audible with so much else going on in the vicinity.

He knew what that banging door was all about. The earthquake had thrown open the door to the Devil's Country, and it looked as though Eppstadt had convinced some dope to go down and close it. Idiots! Didn't they have any *instincts*? Didn't something whisper at the back of their heads that when a door slammed in this house, you *let* it slam, you let it slam till it chose to stop. What you didn't do was head on down the stairs to close it. That was suicide, or the next best thing.

He peered behind him, but Katya was still fast asleep. He briefly contemplated waking her, then thought better of it. All her life she'd had men following her around asking what they should do next. He wasn't going to be numbered amongst them.

No, he would deal with this on his own. After all, the house was going to be his home as much as it was hers. His word should be law here. He just had to work out how best to proceed, and without a shot of espresso to quicken his sluggish thoughts, it might take a while. No matter, the answer would come to him, in time.

He sat with his back against the wall, and tried to put out of his head the image of the innocent stranger heading down the spiral staircase to close the door to the Devil's Country.

4

Todd stayed put behind the door for several minutes, his thoughts describing vague circles. In truth he was still hoping that it would not take any action on his part to fix the problem. The preferable solution would be this: somebody (perhaps Maxine, out there in the back yard) would encounter something that would raise the panic-level in the house, and there would be a mass exodus. Perhaps it was too much to hope for, but every other option (diversions, locating keys to side exits) required a higher degree of wit than he possessed in his present exhausted state.

He finally got up from behind the door and returned through the bedroom, past his sleeping beauty, to the balcony. He stepped out. The dull dawn had ushered in a dull day. Later, perhaps, the marine layer would burn off and they'd have some sun, but for now, the sky was a wall of dead cloud. He looked down into the greenery, hoping to spot Maxine, but the thickness of the jungle all around the house – especially the gigantic Bird of Paradise trees – made it virtually impossible to see very much.

And then, out of the corner of his eye, he glimpsed a motion. Somebody was running through the thicket, throwing panicked backward glances as he went. It wasn't Maxine, it was her assistant Sawyer, who'd been with her for the last three years. He wasn't any more than thirty, but he'd let his body get out of shape. Too many hurried lunches, snatched because Maxine had more work for him than he could ever possibly finish; too much after-work socializing, knocking back his single malts and beluga at fancy premieres; not to mention the Bavarian crème-filled donuts he would bring into the office in boxes of six, to help him through his day with a well-timed sugar rush.

Thanks to the donuts and hamburgers, and his neat scotches, he couldn't run very fast. And he certainly couldn't yell for help while he was running: he didn't have enough breath for both. All he could do was sob between gasps, throwing panicked glances over his shoulder. His pursuers were closing on him. Todd could see the bushes thrashing around immediately behind him; and something else – something smaller and more nimble – was throwing itself from branch to branch overhead, to keep up with its quarry.

'M . . . Max . . . Maxine!' he managed to get out, in between gasps.

'I'm over here!' Maxine yelled. 'Sawyer! I'm at the cages!'

Todd followed the sound of Maxine's voice, and located her. She was a considerable distance from the house, and had clambered up on top of one of a series of cages. There she was kneeling, with a gun in her hand. She'd always kept guns around the house, Todd knew, but this was the first occasion he'd seen her using one.

'Keep following my voice,' she yelled to Sawyer. 'Look for a tree with bright yellow flowers, like big bells –'

'I'm looking!' Sawyer sobbed.

From his vantage point on the balcony, Todd felt like a Caesar at the Colosseum, watching the lions and the Christians. He could see the Christians perfectly clearly, and now – as the gap between the pursuer and the pursued closed – he began to glimpse the lions too.

In the bushes no more than a yard or two behind Sawyer was one of the dead's children: a foul hybrid of ghost woman and – of all things – jaguar. The latter must have been a prisoner in Katya's menagerie, but the marriage of anatomies had turned its sleek perfection into something rougher, uglier and entirely more bizarre. The human element had been female; no doubt of that. The face – when Todd glimpsed it – was two-thirds humanoid. The high cheekbones, the icy stare: it was surely the face of Lana Turner. Then the creature opened its mouth, and the bestial third showed itself: vast teeth, top and bottom, a mottled throat, a black tongue. It let out a very unladylike roar, and pounced on Sawyer, who threw himself out of its path with inches to spare.

'Are you okay?' Maxine yelled.

All that Sawyer could manage was: 'No!'

'Are you close to me?' Maxine said.

'I can't see you,' he cried. The branches over his head were shaking violently.

'Look for the yellow flowers.'

'. . . yellow . . . flowers . . .'

It would have been easy for Todd to direct Sawyer through this maze, but that would have taken all the fun out of it. Better to keep his silence and let the man find his own way. It was the kind of game he knew Katya would love. He was tempted to wake her, but it would be over in the next few seconds, he guessed. Sawyer was a few yards from the cages, and safety. Having failed to catch its victim on its first pounce, the Lana, as Todd had mentally dubbed the creature, had returned to her stalking. Todd caught glimpses of her mottled back as she slid through the thicket. Her intentions were clear, at least from Todd's point of view. She was moving to cut Sawyer off from the gallery of cages. Sawyer and Maxine kept a banal exchange going meanwhile, so that Sawyer could find his way to her.

'You're getting louder.'

'Am I?'

'Sure. You see the yellow flowers, yet?'

'Yeah. I see them.'

518

'You're *really* close.'

'I'm under them –'

He stopped talking because he heard the low growl of the Lana. Todd could hear the creature too, though he couldn't see it. He silently willed Sawyer not to make any sudden moves; just stand still, shut up, and maybe the animal would lose interest. Sawyer could stand still without any problem, but could he shut up? No, he could not. Sawyer was a gabber. 'Oh God, Maxine. Oh God. It's close to me.'

'Shush,' Maxine advised.

He stopped talking, but it was too late. The Lana knew exactly where Sawyer was positioned. She launched herself out of the thicket, striking Sawyer so that he fell sideways, through the very patch of yellow flowers which had been his beacon.

He was now in view of Maxine, who yelled to him to *get up, get up quickly* –

He started to do so, but the breath had been knocked out of him by the blow, and before he could get to his knees the creature was on him a second time, her claws digging deep into the mass of his shoulder-muscle.

From her perch on the cage Maxine was attempting to get a clear shot, but it would have been difficult for anyone, however sophisticated their skill with guns, to put a bullet in the animal and not wound Sawyer in the process. But Maxine was ready to give it a try. She'd been taking lessons from an ex-cop from the LAPD for several months; she knew to keep a steady hand and her eye fixed on the target.

Sawyer couldn't have moved if his life had depended upon it. The creature had him held in a death-grip.

Maxine fired. The sound was sharp in the still air of the Canyon, like a whip-crack. It echoed off the other wall of the Canyon, the blow of the bullet throwing Sawyer's attacker off her victim. She lay, this not-so-distant relation to the exquisite Miss Turner, on the ground beside

Sawyer, whom she'd loosed as soon as she was hit. Blood ran copiously from them both, mingling on the ground between them.

'Get up,' Maxine said to Sawyer.

It was good advice. The Lana was still alive, her breathing quick and shallow.

Sawyer wasn't so badly injured that he failed to realize the danger he was still in. He rolled away from his attacker and started to get to his feet. As he did so the creature suddenly sat up beside him and opening her sizeable jaws, lunged. She took a chunk from Sawyer's leg, twisting her head to take away the bulk of his calf. He screamed, and fell forward onto his hands.

Maxine had a clear shot at the beast, and took it. But her second shot was not as efficient as her first; it struck the creature's shoulder, passing through the muscle without appearing to significantly slow the animal, which threw itself on top of Sawyer as though she were attempting to mount him.

Seconds later, the Lana opened her mouth and sank her teeth into the bones of Sawyer's skull. The man's sobs ceased instantly, and what little strength his limbs had possessed fled. He hung beneath the Lana's body like a zebra's corpse from the jaws of a lion, glassy-eyed and lifeless.

Todd heard Maxine say, 'Oh Christ . . . oh Christ . . .'

But the horror wasn't over with yet. The creature apparently wanted to get her teeth into her wounder, because having dispatched Sawyer she let the body drop from her jaws and began to move towards the cage on which Maxine was crouched. Even in her hurt state there was no doubt that she had the physical power to get up onto the cage and attack Maxine. In fact, the wounds she had sustained didn't seem to be hurting her that much; her hybrid face carried a look that was somewhere between an animal snarl and a human smile. Maxine didn't hesitate. Taking a bead on the animal, she fired. The bullet struck the creature in the middle of her face, taking out the flat nose and the top half of the mouth.

For one long moment she seemed not to comprehend the fatal damage she had sustained. She lifted her front leg, which ended in a hand which erupted into claws, towards her face, almost as though she intended to explore the damage. But before her corrupted limb could reach her face the creature's system closed down, and she fell forward, dead.

There had been a good deal of motion in the foliage throughout this episode; Todd had the sense that there were several other creatures watching to see how this proceeded before they showed their own faces. Now, with the death of Lana, the thicket was still. Nothing moved; nothing breathed.

The only sound Todd could hear was the very soft sound of Maxine saying *Oh God* to herself, over and over. She quickly got control of her horror and her fear and started to clamber down off the cage where she'd been perched.

Todd was half-tempted to call down to her, to offer some word of encouragement, but he refrained from doing so. For one thing, he didn't want to admit that he'd stood as a spectator to this whole drama; second, he was afraid of distracting Maxine while she was down there. Certainly her killing of the creature had silenced its brethren in the thicket, but their silence didn't mean they'd given up their stalking. They were simply sitting in the shadows waiting for Maxine to make a mistake, when no doubt they would fall upon her in a vengeful mob.

Thus, keeping his silence, Todd watched Maxine make her way between the cages, glancing back at the house constantly, as though she was trying to find a path that would lead her back to safety but was at present only able to find one that ran parallel to the house. She was now thirty or forty yards from the cages, which was a good thing, because that meant she couldn't see what was happening on the walkway beneath them.

A minute or two after her exit, a few of Lana's family members appeared from the thicket where – as Todd had known – they'd been waiting. Now about six of them came out of hiding. They had no interest in the corpse of their sibling. It was Sawyer they wanted. Surrounding his body they began to play with the corpse like children with some gruesome toy. They tore off his clothes, and bit off his penis and balls. They followed that by biting off fingers, knuckle by knuckle, and spitting the pieces out. They seemed to take infantile pleasure in the mess they were making. Todd was horribly disgusted by the spectacle, but he kept watching, until they were finished with the fingers and began to disembowel the man. Only then did he retreat from the balcony railing and go back inside.

It would not necessarily be easy for Maxine to find her way back up to the house, he realized. Many of the pathways were overgrown, and in her present, no doubt panicked, state of mind, she could easily lose her way and keep on losing it. He would have to go outside and find her.

Katya was still sleeping. The shots hadn't even stirred her. Indeed, she seemed to have scarcely moved, so profound was her slumber. Her hand was still up at her mouth, limply curled round on itself.

He kissed her, saw that this did not wake her either, and left her to her slumbers.

5

Eppstadt was in the Devil's Country. A fine drizzle, almost a mist, was drooping from the bloated clouds; it came in soft waves against his face, cooling his flushed skin. If he doubted the reality of this place, its chill seemed designed to undo his doubt.

He hated the idea that what he was witnessing was real; doing so violated all his logical faculties. But what was the alternative? That he'd slipped and fallen, and was now lying at the bottom of the stairs in a semi-comatose state, imagining all this? It was a pretty solution, but as he had no way of knowing whether it was true or not, his only option was to find Joe, and get the hell out of here before the place began to get even crazier than it already was. The less he knew about this country – the less its grotesqueries lodged in his psyche – the happier the rest of his life would surely be.

With that thought he began a three hundred and sixty degree scanning of the landscape, calling Joe's name as he did so. His din (even his simple presence) was enough to stir life in the bushes and trees. He felt himself watched by several species of unlikely animal, their eyes huge and luminous, their postures, and in some cases the details of the physiognomies, vaguely human, as though this twilight world had witnessed all kinds of criminal couplings.

Finally, he heard a response from Joe.

'Who's there?'

'Eppstadt.'

'Come over here. Quickly. You gotta help me.'

He followed the sound of the man's shouting. There was a small copse ahead, and Joe had clambered a few feet into a tree by means of a crude wooden ladder which had been propped against one of the trunks.

'What the hell are you doing?' Eppstadt wanted to know.

Joe simply repeated his plea: 'You gotta help me.'

'There's no time, Joe,' Eppstadt said. 'You've got to come back with me. *Right now*. Christ, I sent you down to close the door. Why'd you come in?'

'For the same reason you did,' Joe said. 'I couldn't believe what I was seeing. Are you going to help me or not?'

Eppstadt had pressed his way into the midst of the thicket as he and Joe spoke, snagging his suit on the briars that grew in profusion here several times as he did so. The tableau that now came into view appalled him.

There was a man crucified amongst the higher branches of the tree Joe had climbed, the deed done with both rope and nails. Joe had already managed to remove a couple of the nails (spattering his arms and face with blood in the process) and was now pulling at the knotted rope with his teeth. He was desperate to get the man down from the tree, and he had reason. The branches around the man's head were bustling with birds, the Devil's Country's version of carrion crows: bigger, crueller versions. They'd clearly made several assaults on the man's face already. There were deep gouges around the victim's sockets where the birds had gone after his eyes. Blood from the wounds poured down his face. He might have resembled Christ but for the brightness of his blond hair, which fell in dirty curls to his shoulders.

'I need a stone!' Joe yelled down at Eppstadt.

'What for?'

'Just find me a fucking stone, will you?'

524

Eppstadt didn't like to take orders – especially from a waiter – but he saw the urgency of the situation, and did as he was asked, looking around until he laid his hands on a long, sharp stone, which he passed on up to Joe. From his perch on the ladder, Joe took aim at the closest of the carrion crows. It was a good throw. The stone struck the most ambitious of the flock – who had apparently decided to come in for the kill – and messily smashed open the bird's head, but its companions did not fly off, as Joe had hoped. They simply retreated up the tree a branch or two, squawking in fury and frustration, while the dead bird dropped from the perch.

As if awoken from a grateful sleep by the din of the birds, the crucified man raised his head, and opened his mouth. A black snake, no thicker than a baby's thumb, slid out from between his lips in a thin gruel of blood, spittle and bile. The snake dangled from the man's lower lip for a few moments, hooked by its tail. Then it fell to the ground, a foot from Eppstadt.

He stepped away in disgust, throwing a backward glance at the door, just to reassure himself that his means of escape from this insanity was still in view. It was. But the snake had changed his perspective on this mercy mission.

'The guy's on the way out,' Eppstadt said to Joe. 'You can't do anything for him.'

'We can still get him down.'

'And I'm telling you he's beyond help, Joe. Look at him.'

There did indeed seem little purpose in labouring to depose the man; he was obviously close to death. His eyes had rolled back beneath fluttering eyelids, showing nothing but white. He was attempting to say something, but his mind and his tongue were beyond the complex business of speech.

'You know what?' Eppstadt said, glancing around the landscape. 'This is a set-up.' There were indeed dozens of

525

hiding places for potential attackers – human or animal – within fifty yards of them: rocks, holes, thicket. 'We should just get the hell out of here before whoever did this to him tries the same on us.'

'Leave him, you mean?'

'Yes. Leave him.'

Joe just shook his head. He had succeeded in getting this far, and wasn't going to give up now. He pulled on the rope that held the man's right hand, The arm fell free. Blood pattered on the leaves over Eppstadt's head, like a light rain.

'I'm almost done,' Joe said.

'Joe, I –'

'*Get ready*,' Joe said again, leaning across the victim's body to untie the other hand. 'You're going to have to catch him,' he warned Eppstadt.

'I can't do that.'

'Well who else is going to do it?' Joe snapped.

Eppstadt wasn't paying attention, however.

He'd heard a noise behind him, and now he turned to find that a freakish child, naked and runty, had appeared from somewhere, and was looking up at him.

'We've got company,' he said to Joe, who was still struggling to free the crucified man's other hand.

When Eppstadt looked back at the freak, it had approached a few steps, and Eppstadt had a clearer view of it. There was something goatish in the gene-pool, Eppstadt decided. The child's bandy legs were sheathed with dirty-yellow fur, and his eyes were yellow-green. From beneath the pale dome of his belly there jutted a sizeable erection, which was out of all proportion to the rest of his body. He fingered it idly while he watched.

'Why are you taking the man down?' he said to Joe. Then, getting no answer from Joe, directed the same question at Eppstadt.

'He's in pain,' was all Eppstadt could find to say, though

526

the phrase scarcely seemed to match the horror of the victim's persecution.

'That's the way my mother wants him,' the goat-boy said.

'Your mother?'

'Lil-ith,' he said, pronouncing the word as two distinct syllables. 'She is the Queen of Hell. And I am her son.'

'If you're her son,' Eppstadt said, playing along for time until a better way to deal with this absurdity occurred, 'then it follows, yes . . . she would be your mother.'

'And she had him put up there so I could see him!' the goat-boy replied, the head of his pecker echoing his own head in its infuriated nodding.

The angrier he became, the more the evidence of his extreme in-breeding surfaced. He had a hare-lip, which made his outrage harder to understand, and his nose – which was scarcely more than two gaping wet holes in his face, ran with catarrhal fluids. His teeth, when he bared them, were overlapped in half a dozen places, and his eyes were slightly crossed. In short, he was an abomination, the only perfect piece of anatomy he'd inherited that monstrous member between his legs, which had lost some of its hardness now, and hung like a rubber club between his rough-haired legs.

'I'm going to tell my mother about you!' he said, stabbing a stunted forefinger in Eppstadt's direction. 'That man is a crinimal.'

'A crinimal?' Eppstadt said, with a supercilious smirk. The idiot-child couldn't even pronounce the word correctly.

'Yes,' the goat-boy said, 'and he's supposed to hang there till the birds fluck out his eyes and the dogs eat out his end tails.'

'Entrails.'

'End tails!'

'All right, have it your way. End tails.'

'I want you to leave him up there.'

During this brief exchange, Eppstadt's gaze had been drawn to the goat-boy's left foot. The nail of his middle toe had not been clipped (he guessed) since birth. Now it looked more like a claw than a nail. It was six, perhaps seven, inches long, and stained dark brown.

'Who the hell are you talking to?' Joe yelled down from the top of the ladder. The density of the foliage made it impossible for him to see the goat-boy.

'Apparently he's up there as a punishment, Joe. Better leave him there.'

'Who told you that?'

Joe came down the ladder far enough to have sight of the goat-boy. '*That*?'

The boy bared his teeth at Joe. A dribble of dark saliva came from the corner of his mouth and ran down onto his chest.

'I really think we should just get going . . .' Eppstadt said.

'Not until this poor sonofabitch is down from here,' Joe said, returning up the ladder. 'Fucking freak.'

'This isn't our business, Joe,' Eppstadt said. There was something about the way the air was rolling around them; something about the way the clouds churned overhead, covering the already depleted light of the sun, that made Eppstadt fearful that something of real consequence was in the offing. He didn't know what this place was, or how it was created; nor, at that moment, did he care. He just wanted to be out through the door and upstairs again.

'Help me!' Joe yelled to him.

Eppstadt went to the bottom of the ladder and peered up. The crucified man had dropped forward over Joe's broad shoulder. Even in his semi-comatose state he could still beg for some show of compassion. 'Please . . .' he murmured. 'I meant no offence . . .'

'He wouldn't fuck my mother,' said the goat-boy, by

way of explanation for this atrocity. He was just a foot or two behind Eppstadt, staring up at Joe and the man he was attempting to save. He turned briefly; surveyed the sky. The wind was getting gusty again, slamming the door and then throwing it open.

'She's coming,' the goat-boy said. 'Smell that bitterness in the air?'

Eppstadt could indeed smell something; strong enough to make his eyes water.

'That's her,' the goat-boy said. 'That's Lil-ith. She's bitter like that. Even her milk.' He made an ugly face. 'It used to make me puke. And me? I *love* to suckle. I love it.' He was getting hard again, talking himself into a fine little fever. He put his thumb in his mouth, and pulled hard on it, making a loud noise as he did so. He was every inch an irritating little child, excepting those inches where he was indisputably a man.

'I'd put him back if I were you,' he said, pushing past Eppstadt to stand at the bottom of the ladder.

Eppstadt's gaze returned to the heavens. The sky was the colour of cold iron, and the bitterness the child had said was his mother's stench was getting stronger with every gust of the cold wind. Eppstadt looked off into the distance, to see if there was any sign of an arrivee on the winding roads. But they were almost deserted. The only person on any of the roads right now was a man some two or three miles away, who was lying sprawled, his head against a stone. Eppstadt had no logical reason to believe this, but he was somehow certain the man was dead, his brains spattered on the stone where his head lay.

Otherwise, the landscape was empty of human occupants.

There were plenty of birds in the air, struggling against the increasingly violent gusts to reach the safety of their roosts; and small animals, rabbits and the like, scampering through the roiling grass to find some place of safety.

Eppstadt was no nature-boy, but he knew enough to be certain that when rabbits were making for their bolt-holes, it was time for human beings to get out of harm's way.

'We've got to go,' he said to Joe. 'You've done all you can.'

'Not yet!' Joe yelled. The wind was strong enough to make even the heavy branches of the tree sway. Dead leaves were shaken down all around.

'*For God's sake, Joe*. What the fuck is wrong with you?'

He took a step up the ladder and caught hold of Joe's belt. Then he tugged. 'You're coming, or I'm going without you.'

'Then go –' Joe began to say. He didn't finish because at that instant the ladder, which was presently bearing the weight of Eppstadt, Joe the Samaritan, and the crucified man, broke.

Eppstadt was closest to the ground, so he sustained the least damage. He simply fell back in the sharp stones in which the copse and its briar thicket were rooted. He scrambled to his feet to find out what had happened to the other two men. Both had fallen amongst the thorns, the crucified man spread-eagled on top of Joe. Only now were the man's wounds fully displayed. Besides the peckings around his eyes, there were far deeper wounds – certainly not made by birds – in his chest. Somebody had had some fun with him before he was nailed up there, cutting star-patterns around his nipples.

Joe struggled to get himself out from under the man, but his flailing only served to catch him in the thorns.

'Help me,' he said, throwing his hand back over his head towards Eppstadt. 'Quickly. I'm being pricked to death here!'

Eppstadt approached the thicket and was about to take hold of Joe's hand when two of the largest wounds on the crucified man's chest gaped, and the flat black heads of two snakes, each ten times the size of the serpent that had slipped out of his throat, pressed their blood-soaked snouts out of the layers of flesh and yellow fat, and came slithering out of his torso. One of them trailed a multitude of what Eppstadt took to be eggs, suspended in a jellied mass of semi-translucent phlegm.

Eppstadt stepped away from the thicket, and from Joe. The serpents crisscrossed as they emerged, their beady white eyes seeking out some new warm place to nest.

'Are you going to help me or not?' Joe said.

Eppstadt simply shook his head.

'Eppstadt!' Joe wept. 'For God's sake get me out.'

Eppstadt had no intention of getting any closer to the snakes than he already was: but the goat-boy had no such scruples. He pushed past Eppstadt and grabbed hold of Joe's outstretched hand. His strength, like his member, was out of all proportion to his size. One good haul, and he had Joe halfway freed from the thorn bushes. Joe screamed as his back was scored by the thorns, which had been pressed deep into his flesh by the weight of the man on top of him.

'Ah now, shut up!' the goat-boy yelled over Joe's complaints. Hanging out of the thicket, poor Joe looked half-dead. The pain had made him vomit, and it was running from the side of his mouth. His demands had become pitiful sobs in the space of a few seconds. Horrified though he was – and guilty too (he'd come down here to help Joe; and now look at him) – Eppstadt still couldn't bring himself to intervene. Not with the snakes raising their heads from the body in which they'd nested, still eager for another victim.

Ignoring Joe's weak protests, the goat-boy pulled on him a second time, and then a third, which was the charm. Joe fell free of the thicket, landing heavily on his pierced back. Sheer agony lent him the strength to throw himself over onto his stomach. His back was nearly naked; the violence of the goat-boy's haulings had torn open his shirt. He lay face down in the earth, retching again.

'That'll teach you,' the goat-boy said. 'Playing with crinimals! You should get some of your own!'

While he was addressing Joe in this witless fashion, Eppstadt chanced to look up at the man still sprawled on the bed of thorns. The two snakes had slithered over his chest and were now entwined around his neck. He was too close to death to register this last assault. He simply lay there, eyelids fluttering over sightless eyes, while the life was throttled out of him.

'See that?' the goat-boy said. 'So much for you and your tricks. Now I lost my toy and your little friend is dead. Why couldn't you stay out of it, huh? He was mine!' The boy's fury had him jumping up and down now. 'Mine! Mine! Mine!'

And suddenly he was up on Joe's back, dancing a tarantella on the mess of thorns and wounds and blood. 'Mine! Mine! Mine!'

It was a show of petulance; no more nor less. Joe rolled over and threw the boy off. Then he started to get to his feet. But before he could do so, the goat-boy came at him, his step still reminiscent of some peculiar little dance.

'*Get up!*' Eppstadt yelled to Joe, not certain what the goat-boy was up to, but certain it was mischief. '*Quickly!*'

Despite his agonized state, Joe started to push himself off his knees. As he did so the goat-boy made a high slashing kick. Joe's hand went up to his neck, and he fell back in the earth.

The foot which had struck Joe was the one with the long middle nail, and what had looked to Eppstadt like a glancing blow had in fact slashed open Joe's windpipe.

Both Joe's hands were at his neck now, as blood and air escaped his throat. He turned his gaze towards Eppstadt for a moment, as though the Head of Paramount might know why Joe was lying in the earth of a place he couldn't even name while his last breath whined out between his fingers.

Then the look of incomprehension went out of his eyes, to be replaced with a blank stare. His hands dropped away from his neck. The whining sound died away, and he rolled forward. All the while the goat-boy went on dancing, out of pure pleasure.

Eppstadt didn't move. He was afraid to draw the murderer's attention. But then the boy seemed to take it into his half-witted head to go find some other plaything, and without looking back at Eppstadt again, he ran off, leaving Joe dead in the earth and the man who'd come to save him alone in the darkening air.

6

Tammy had come into the house cautiously, not at all certain what she was going to find. In fact what she found was Jerry Brahms. He was standing in the hallway, looking down the stairwell, his face ashen – except where it was bloody from his fall – his hands trembling. Before he could get a word out of his mouth there came a din of shrieks from below.

'Who's down there?' Tammy asked Jerry.

'Some boy we came up here with from Maxine's party. A waiter. And Eppstadt. And God knows what else.'

'Where's Maxine?'

'She's outside. She fled into the backyard when the earthquake hit.'

There were more noises from below, and then a rush of wind, coming up the stairwell. Tammy peered down into the darkness. There was somebody down at the very bottom, lying on the floor. She studied the figure. It moved.

'Wait a minute,' she said, half to herself. 'That's Zeffer!'

It was. It was Zeffer. And he was alive. There was blood all over him, but he was definitely alive. She went to the top of the stairs. He'd heard her calling his name, and his shining eyes had found her; were fixed on her. She started down the stairs.

'I wouldn't go down there . . .' Brahms warned her.

'I know,' she replied. 'But that's a friend of mine.'

She glanced up at Brahms as she took her second step. There was a look of mild astonishment on his face, she wasn't sure why. Was it because people didn't have friends in this God-forsaken house; or because she was going down the stairs despite the cold, dead smell on the wind?

Zeffer was doing his best to push himself up off his stomach, but he didn't have the strength to do it.

'Wait,' she called to him, 'I'm coming.'

She picked up her speed to get to him. Once she reached the bottom she tried not to look towards the door through which he'd crawled, but she could feel the wind gusting through it. There was a spatter of rain in that wind. It pricked her face.

'Listen to me . . .' Zeffer murmured.

She knelt beside him. 'Wait. Let me turn you over.'

She did her best to roll him over, so he wouldn't be face to the ground and managed to lift him so that his head was on her lap, though his lower body was still half-twisted around. He didn't seem to notice. He seemed, in fact, to be beyond comfort or discomfort; in a dreamy state which was surely the prelude to death. It was astonishing that he'd survived this long, given the wounding he'd sustained. But then perhaps he had the power of the Devil's Country to thank for that.

'Now,' she said. 'What do you want to tell me?'

'The horsemen,' he said. 'They're coming for the Devil's child . . .'

'Horsemen?'

'Yes. The Duke's men. Goga's men.'

Tammy listened. Zeffer was right. She could hear hooves on the wind, or in the ground; or both. They sounded uncomfortably close.

'Can they get *out*?' she asked Zeffer.

'I don't know. Probably.' His eyes closed lazily, and for a terrible moment she feared she'd lost him. But they opened again, after a time, and his gaze fixed on her. His hand reached up and took hold of Tammy's arm, though his grip was feeble. 'I think it's time the dead came in, don't you?' he said to her. His voice was so softened by weakness she was not sure she'd heard it right at first.

'The dead?' she said.

He nodded. 'Yes. All the ghosts, outside in the Canyon. They want to come into the house, and we've kept them out all these years.'

'Yes, but –'

He shook his head, as if to say: *don't interrupt me, I don't have time*.

'You have to let them in,' he told her.

'But they're afraid of something,' Tammy said.

'I know. The threshold. Remember how I told you I went back to Romania?'

'Of course.'

'I found one of the Brotherhood there. A friend of Father Sandru's. He taught me a method of keeping the dead from coming into your house. What you have to do is *un*do what I did. And in they'll come. Believe me. In they'll come.'

'How?' she said. If time was so short, and he was so certain, why waste a breath on argument?

'Go into the kitchen and get a knife,' he told her. 'A strong knife, one that's not going to break on you. Then go to the back door and dig in the threshold.'

'The threshold?'

'The wood frame you step over to go outside. There are five icons, in the wood. Ancient Romanian symbols.'

'And all I have to do is remove them?'

'You just remove them. The dead will be ready, as soon as the threshold is clear. They've waited a very long time for this. Been very patient.' He allowed himself the smallest of smiles as he spoke; clearly the prospect of the dead invading the house pleased him. 'Will you do this for me, Tammy?'

'Of course. If that's what you want.'

'It's what's *right*.'

'Then I'll do it. Of course I'll do it.'

536

'You only need open one door, they'll all find their way in. I suggest the back door, because it's rotting. The threshold will be easier to . . .' He stopped, his lips drawn back from his teeth in a grimace. The wound was taking its terrible toll. Fresh blood came between his fingers.

'You don't need to tell me any more,' she told him. 'You just lie quietly. I'll go get some help.'

'*No*,' he said.

'You need help.'

'*No*,' he said again, shaking his head. 'Just get to work.'

'Are you sure?'

'Yes. This is more important.'

'All right, I'll –'

She was about to repeat her reassurance when she realized he'd stopped breathing. His eyes were still open, and there was still a lively gloss in them, but no life there; nothing. Willem Zeffer's long and agonizing life was at an end.

On the floor above, Jerry looked up as the door to the master bedroom opened and Todd emerged.

'Hello, Jerry,' he said as he started down the stairs. 'You got hurt?'

'I fell during the quake.'

'We need to get outside and find Maxine.'

'Really?'

'She's lost out there. And Sawyer's dead. I'm afraid if somebody doesn't get to her –'

'I heard the shouts,' Jerry said vaguely, looking and sounding like a man who'd lost all interest in the drama that was being played out around him.

'Who else is here?' Todd asked him.

'Eppstadt's downstairs with some kid he brought from the party –'

'Yes, I saw him. Is he one of Maxine's new superstars?'

'No. He's just a waiter,' Jerry said.

537

Todd looked down the rest of the flight. There was a body at the bottom of the stairs, and somebody else, a woman, bent over, touching the face of the dead man. With great gentleness, she closed the dead man's eyes. Then she looked up the stairwell.

'Hello, Todd,' she said.

'Hello, Tammy.'

'I thought you were drowned.'

'Sorry to disappoint you.' He started down the stairs towards her. She turned her face from him, returning her gaze to the body.

'Did you see Eppstadt?' he asked her as he came down the flight.

'You mean that sonofabitch from the studio?'

'Yes. That sonofabitch.'

'Yes, I saw him.' She glanced up at Todd. There were tears in her eyes, but she didn't want to shed them in front of him. Not after what had happened on the beach. He'd been so horribly careless of her feelings. She wasn't going to show any vulnerability now, if she could help it.

'Where did he go?' Todd asked her, as if there was much choice in the matter.

She nodded down the passageway towards the door to the Devil's Country.

'He went in there, I think. I didn't see it. Jerry told me.'

'How long ago?'

'I don't know,' she said. 'And frankly, I don't really care right now.'

Todd put his hand on Tammy's shoulder 'I'm sorry. This is a bad time. I never was very good expressing my feelings.'

'Is that supposed to mean you're sorry?' she said.

'Yeah,' he replied, the word hardly shaped; more like a grunt than an apology. She made the tiniest shrug of her shoulder, to get him to take his hand off her, which he

538

did. There was so much she wanted to say to him, but this was neither the time nor the place to say it.

He got the message. She didn't have to look back to see that he'd gone; she heard his footsteps as he headed off down the passageway. Only after ten or fifteen seconds did she look up, and by that time he was stepping through the door.

Suddenly, the tears she'd held back broke: a chaotic cluster of feelings battling to surface all at once: gratitude that Todd was alive, sorrow that Zeffer was dead, anger that Todd had no better way to show his feelings than to grunt at her that way. Didn't he know how much he'd hurt her?

'Here.'

The voice at her shoulder was that of Jerry Brahms. He was offering her a cleanly pressed handkerchief: a rather old-fashioned gesture but very much appreciated at that particular moment. 'Which one are you crying over?'

She wiped her tears from her eyes.

'Because if it's Todd,' he went on. 'I wouldn't bother. He'll survive this and go on and forget all of us. That's the kind of man he is.'

'You think so?'

'I'm sure of it.'

She wiped her nose. Sniffed.

'What was he talking to you about?' Jerry asked.

'He wanted to know about Eppstadt.'

'Not Todd. Zeffer.'

'Oh. He . . . he had something he wanted me to do for him.'

She wasn't sure she wanted to share Zeffer's proposal with Jerry. This was a world filled with people who had extremely complicated allegiances. Suppose Jerry, out of some misplaced loyalty to Katya, tried to stop her? It was perfectly possible that he might try. But then how the hell did she get rid of him, so that she could go upstairs and do what she had to do?

One obvious way presented itself, although it was playing with fire. If she went to the door of the Devil's Country, Jerry would probably follow her. The place had a way of holding your attention, she knew. And if it held his for long enough, then she could slip away upstairs into the kitchen. Find a knife. Go to the threshold, and get to work.

It wasn't her favourite plan (the further she stayed away from that door the happier she was) but she had no alternative to hand at that moment. And she needed to act quickly.

Without saying anything she got up and walked off down the passageway towards the door. The wind came out to meet her, like an eager host, ready to slip its arms through hers and invite her in. She didn't need to look over her shoulder to know that Jerry was coming after her. He was talking to her, just a step behind.

'I don't think you should go any further,' he said.

'Why not? I just want to see what's in here. Everybody talks about it. I think I'm the only one who hasn't actually seen it properly for myself.'

As she spoke she realized that there was more truth to this than she was strictly admitting. Of course she wanted to see. Her little plot to lure Jerry's attention away was also a neat opportunity to excuse her own curiosity. Talk about muddied allegiances. She had some of her own. One more glimpse into that other world was on her own subconscious agenda, for some reason.

'It's not good to look in there for too long,' Jerry said.

'I know that,' she replied, a little testily. 'I've been in there. But another peek can't hurt, can it? I mean, *can it?*'

She'd reached the door, and without further debate with Brahms, pushed it open and stared at the landscape before her with eyes that had recently been washed with tears. Everything was in perfect focus; and it was beautiful. She didn't hesitate to debate the matter with her conscience, Brahms or God in Heaven. She just stepped out of the passageway and followed where Todd had gone just a couple of minutes before.

7

I t wasn't difficult for Todd to find Eppstadt. Unlike his first visit to this little corner of hell, when his eyes had taken some time to become used to the elaborate fiction that the tiles were creating for him, this time everything was warmed up and ready to go. He looked through the door and there it was, in all its glory, from the spectacle of the eclipse overhead to a single serrated blade of grass bent beneath the toe of his shoe, along which a little black beetle was making its way.

And standing in the midst of all this, looking as appropriate as a hard-on in the Vatican, was Eppstadt. He'd obviously had some problems while he was here. The man who'd been several times cited as the 'best-dressed man in Los Angeles' was looking in need of a tailor. His shirt was torn and severely stained with what looked like blood, his face was covered in sweat, and his hair which he obsessively combed over the bald patch (where the hair plugs hadn't taken) – had fallen forward, exposing an area of shiny pink scalp, and giving him a ridiculous fringe.

'*You*!' he said, pointing directly at Todd. 'You fucking lunatic! You did this deliberately! And now people are dead, Pickett. Real people. Dead because of your stupid games.'

'Hey, hey, slow down. Who's dead?'

'Oh, as if you give a damn! You trick us all into following you into this . . . this . . . *obscenity* . . .'

Todd looked around as Eppstadt ranted. Obscenity? He saw no obscenity. Given the shortness of his acquaintance with this place he had certainly felt a lot of different things about it. He'd been enchanted here, he'd been so terrified that he'd thought his heart would burst, he'd been absurdly aroused and close to death as he ever wanted to get. But obscene? No. The Devil's Country was simply the ultimate E-Ticket Ride.

'If you don't like it,' he said to Eppstadt, 'why the hell did you come in here?'

'To help Joe. And now he's dead.'

'What happened to him?'

Eppstadt glanced over his shoulder, dropping his voice to a whisper. 'There's a child around here. Only it's not a child. He's a goat.'

'So he's the Devil's kid?'

'Don't start with that Devil shit. I never made one of those movies –'

'This isn't a movie, Eppstadt.'

'No, you're quite right. It isn't a movie. It's a fucking –'

'Obscenity. Yeah, so you said.'

'How can you be so casual?' Eppstadt said, taking a stride towards Todd. 'I just saw somebody sliced to death.'

'What?'

'The goat-boy did it. Just opened up Joe's throat. And it's your fault.'

Eppstadt's stride had picked up speed. He was getting ready to do something stupid, Todd sensed; his terror had become a capacity for violence. And even though there'd been times (that lunch, that long-ago lunch, over rare tuna) when Todd had wanted to beat the crap out of Eppstadt, this was neither the time nor the place.

'You want to see what you caused?' Eppstadt said.

'Not particularly.'

'Well you're going to.'

He caught hold of the front of Todd's T-shirt.

'Let go of me, Eppstadt.'

Eppstadt ignored him. He just turned and hauled Todd

after him, the volatile mixture of his fear and rage making him impossible to resist. Todd didn't even try. Katya had given him a lesson in how to behave here. You kept quiet, or you drew attention to yourself. And somehow – it was something about the way the wind seemed to be blowing from all quarters at once, something about the way the grass seethed at his feet and the trees churned like thunderheads – he thought it wasn't just Eppstadt who was in a state of agitation. This whole painted world was stirred up.

By now the hunters' dogs probably had their scent, and the Duke was on his way.

'Just chill,' Todd said to Eppstadt. 'I'm not going to fight you. If you want me to see something then I'll come look. Just stop pulling on me, will you?'

Eppstadt let him go. His lower lip was quivering, as though he was about to burst into tears, which for Todd's money was worth the price of admission.

'You follow me,' Eppstadt said, 'I'll show you something.'

'Keep your voice down. There are people around here you don't want to have coming after you.'

'I met one of them already,' Eppstadt said, walking on towards a small group of trees. 'And I never want to see anything like it again.'

'So let's get out of here.'

'No. I want you to see. I want you to take full responsibility for what happened here.'

'I didn't make this place,' Todd said.

'But you knew it was here. You and your little lover. I'm putting the picture together now. Don't worry. I've got it all.'

'Somehow I doubt that.'

Eppstadt was searching the ground now, his step more cautious, as though he was afraid of treading on something.

'What are you looking for?'

He glanced back at Todd. 'Joe,' he said. And then, returning his gaze to the ground, he pointed. 'There,' he said.

'What?'

'There. Go look. *Go on.*'

'Who was he?' Todd said, staring down at the maimed body in the earth, its throat gaping.

'His name's Joe Something-or-Other, and he was a waiter at Maxine's party. That's all I know.'

'And goat-kid did this to him?'

'Yeah.'

'Why, for Christ's sake?'

'Amusement would be my closest guess.'

Todd passed a clammy hand over his face. 'Okay. I've seen him now. Can we get the hell out of here and find Maxine?'

'Maxine?'

'Yeah. She went outside with Sawyer –'

'I know.'

'And now Sawyer's dead.'

'Christ. We're being picked off like flies. Who killed him?'

'Some . . . animal. Only it wasn't any kind of animal I ever saw before.'

'All right, I'm coming,' Eppstadt said. 'But you listen to me, Pickett. If we survive this, you've got a fuck of a lot to answer for.'

'Oh, like you don't.'

'Me? What the hell do I have to do with this?'

'I'll tell you.'

'I'm listening.'

'I wouldn't be here and nor would you or Maxine or any other poor fuck –' He glanced at Joe's corpse. 'If you hadn't sounded off at the beach. Or – if you *really* want to go back to the start of things – how about a certain conversation we had, during which you suggested I get my face fixed?'

545

'Oh, that.'

'Yes that.'

'I was wrong. You should never have done it. It was a bad call.'

'That was life. My flesh and –' He froze, for something had emerged from the undergrowth: a beast that was a vague relative of a lizard, but shorter, squatter, its back end having, instead of a long and serpentine tail, an outgrowth of two or three hundred pale, bulbous tumours. It went directly to the remains of Joe.

'No, no, no,' Eppstadt said quietly. Then suddenly, running at the creature the way he might at a dog who'd come sniffing at his gate. 'Get away!' he yelled. 'For God's sake, *get away*!'

The lizard threw the yellow-blue gaze of one of its eyes up in Eppstadt's direction, was unimpressed, and returned to sniffing around the sliced-open neck. It flicked the wound with its tongue.

'*Oh Jesus. Oh Jesus*,' Eppstadt gasped.

He picked up a rock and threw it at the animal, striking its leathery hide. Again, the cold, reptilian assessment, and this time the creature opened its throat and let out a threatening hiss.

Todd caught hold of Eppstadt, wrapping his arms around him from behind, to keep him from getting any more belligerent with the animal. They were lucky the beast was so interested in the remains of Joe, he knew; otherwise it would have turned on them.

The lizard averted its gaze from Eppstadt again, and started to tear at the raw meat around Joe's neck so that Joe's head was thrown back and forth as it secured itself a mouthful.

Eppstadt was no longer attempting to free himself from Todd's bear-hug, so Todd let his hold slip a little, at which point he turned on Todd, slamming the heel of his hand against Todd's shoulder.

'That should have been you!' Eppstadt said, following the first blow with a second, twice as strong.

Todd let him rant. Over Eppstadt's shoulder he saw the lizard retreating into the undergrowth from which it had emerged, dragging the remains of Waiter Joe after it.

'You hear me, Pickett?'

'Yeah, I hear you,' Todd said wearily.

'That's all you're good for: lizard food. *Lizard*! *Food*!' The blows were coming faster and harder now. It was only a matter of time before Todd hit him back, and they both knew it. Knew it and wanted it. No more innuendo; no more lawyers; just fisticuffs in the mud.

'All right,' Todd said, bitch-slapping Eppstadt for the fun of it. 'I get it.' He struck him again, harder. 'You want to fight?' A third blow, harder still, which split Eppstadt's lip. Blood ran from his mouth.

And then suddenly the two of them were at it, not exchanging clean neat blows the way they did in the movies but knotted up together in a jumble of gouges and kicks; years of anger and competition emptying in a few chaotic seconds. They could not have chosen a less perfect place or time to settle a personal score if they'd looked a lifetime, but this wasn't about making sensible decisions. This was about bringing the other sonofabitch down. As it was they *both* went down, having wrestled their way into muddy terrain. Their feet slid from under them and down they went, locked together, like two boys.

Tammy saw them fall.

'Oh no,' she said, half to herself. 'Not here. Don't do it here.'

'I wouldn't go any closer if I were you,' Brahms advised her.

'Well you're not me,' Tammy said, and without waiting for any further response she pressed on over the uneven ground towards the two men in the mud. There were sounds of birds overhead, and she glanced up at the sky as she walked towards the men. It was spectacularly beautiful, and for a moment her thoughts were entirely claimed by the piled cumulus and the partially-blinded sun. The darkness of the heavens between the clouds was profound enough that the brightest of the stars could be seen, set in velvet grey.

When she looked back at Todd and Eppstadt, they were virtually indistinguishable from one another physically – both liberally coated in mud. But it was still clear which one was Eppstadt. He was letting out a virtually seamless monologue about Todd. The general sense of which was that Todd was a vapid, over-paid, talentless sonofabitch. Furthermore, when all this insanity was over he, Eppstadt, was going to make certain that everybody knew that Todd had caused the death of a number of innocent people with his arrogance.

As Tammy got closer to the fight it became evident to Tammy that this wasn't going to end quickly or easily. Neither man was going to be talked down from their fury; it had escalated too far. She could only hope they exhausted each other quickly, before they attracted unwanted attention.

There seemed little hope of that. Though they'd fought to their feet again, it was becoming harder and harder for either man to land a solid blow in this slippery environment. Finally Eppstadt swung wide and went down in the mud, falling heavily. He struggled to get up, the heels of his hands sliding in the mud, but before he could succeed, Todd clambered on top of him, and straddled him, his hands at the man's throat. There was no fight left in Eppstadt. All he could do was gasp and shake his head.

'You fuckhead,' Todd said. 'None of this would have happened . . . if you . . . had made my fucking movie.'

Eppstadt had by now recovered enough energy to speak.

'I wouldn't put you in a movie if my fucking *life* depended on it.'

At which point, Tammy made her presence known. 'Todd?'

It was Eppstadt who looked up first. 'Oh Jesus,' he said. 'I wondered when you were going to show your fat ass.'

Tammy wasn't in the mood for long speeches. 'Leave the shithead in the mud, Todd,' she said, 'and let's just get out of here.'

Todd grinned through his mask of mud; the megawatt smile. 'It would be my pleasure.'

He got to his feet and stepped away. Eppstadt pulled his rather ungainly bulk to his knees. He had lost one of his choice Italian shoes in the mêlée, and now began to search for it. In fact, it had been flung wide of mud, close to where Tammy was standing.

'Looking for this?' she said.

'Yes,' he glared, beckoning with his fingers.

She tossed it in the thorn bushes.

'Cunt.'

'Faggot.'

'No. I am many things but a bugger I am not. Right, Brahms?'

'Don't bring me into this,' Jerry said. 'I just want us all out of here.'

'We're coming, Jerry!' Todd said, not looking at him. 'You go on and take Tammy.'

'Not without you.'

'Oh, how touching,' Eppstadt said. 'The fat girl is loyal to the end, even though she doesn't have a hope in hell of getting a fuck out of it.'

Tammy had kept her fury limited to that one casual toss of the Italian shoe, but now it erupted; all her fury towards Eppstadt and his kind. The Mr-High-and-Mightys who thought that fat fan-girls were less than shit.

'You are such scum!' she said. 'You nasty-minded tiny-peckered little piece of excrement!'

She approached him as she yelled, but after the fight with Todd the last thing Eppstadt wanted was this woman laying her hands on him.

'Keep her away from me, Jerry,' he demanded, raising his hands, palms out. As he did so he retreated towards the copse of trees. 'Jerry? You hear me?'

'Leave him, Tammy.'

'Well, he's scum.'

'And tell her to cover herself up,' Eppstadt fired back. 'The sight of her cellulite makes me gag.'

Jerry had caught hold of Tammy's arm.

Luckily for him, Tammy had suddenly lost interest in all this score-settling. She was studying a group of horsemen who were following a winding road that would eventually bring them, she quickly realized, to this very spot. 'Todd . . .' she said.

'Yes, I saw.'

'We have visitors.'

The Duke of Goga, of course, along with his entourage.

They still had plenty of time to get to the door, Tammy reckoned. The hunters were still some distance away, and it didn't seem that they'd yet spotted the interlopers. Jerry was already on his way to the exit. Todd had found some clean water to wash his wounds but he could be up and gone in a couple of seconds.

Eppstadt was the exception. He'd gone into the thorn-thicket to fetch his Italian shoe, and as he did so, something moved in amongst the mass of thorny branches off to the left of him.

He stopped reaching for his shoe, and studied the shadows. Whatever it was seemed to have become snagged in there, because it shook itself. Then it let out a kind of mewling sound and shook itself again, this time more violently. The manoeuvre worked however. Freed of the thicket it stumbled out into view. It was the goat-boy. He started to pull thorns out of his flesh, the pain of it making him weep, softly, to himself.

Eppstadt knew what this creature was capable of from his previous encounter and he had no desire to draw the attention of the beast. He gave up on his shoe and set his eyes on the door. Jerry Brahms was right: it was time they got the hell out of here.

The goat-boy had stopped weeping now, and for some reason had fixed his gaze upon Tammy. Or more particularly, upon her breasts. There was no equivocation in his stare; no attempt to pretend he was looking elsewhere. He simply stared lovingly at the upper part of Tammy's torso, and licked his lips.

Tammy had heard the boy's sobbing complaints, and was staring at him. So was Todd.

'Come on, Tammy,' Todd said.

Tammy let her gaze go from the boy to the approaching hunters. Plainly they'd also heard the sound of the child's wails because they'd picked up their speed and were approaching at a hard gallop.

Tammy looked back at Lucifer's child, in all his goaty glory. His tears had dried now, and he was less interested in picking thorns out of his flesh. They'd done some damage, she saw; little rivulets of dark red blood ran down his limbs from the places where he'd been pierced. There was one spot that looked particularly tender, deep in the groove of his groin. He worked the thorn out a little, but not once did he take his eyes off the objects of his present devotion. He didn't even glance over at the horsemen, though he must have heard their approach. He obviously knew how to out-manoeuvre them. He'd been doing it for centuries. He had a warren of hidey-holes to tuck himself away.

Tammy glanced up at the sky: at the moon locked in its unnatural position in front of the sun. Then she looked around at the landscape which that half-clouded light illuminated: the road and the approaching horsemen, the cluster of boulders where Todd was standing, stripped of his torn T-shirt, doing his best to lift handfuls of clean water up to his wounded face.

The goat-boy would be gone in a moment, Tammy knew. And when it was gone the Hunt would, as Zeffer had told her, continue in the same weary way it had been going for centuries.

Perhaps it was time to bring the whole sorry thing to an end, once and for all: to see if she, little Tammy Lauper from Sacramento, couldn't deliver the Devil's child back into the hands of the Duke, who could then return him to his mother, and bring an end to this long, weary chase.

She knew of only one, desperate method by which she might do this. She didn't waste time enacting it. She unbuttoned her torn blouse, starting at the top. She had every jot of the goat-boy's attention from the moment her fingers touched the first button. He forgot about removing thorns from his flesh. He simply watched.

'Like them?' she said to him so softly she was certain nobody would hear.

The goat-boy heard her, as she knew he would. He had an animal's ears.

By way of reply he nodded; very slowly, indeed almost reverentially.

There were two buttons remaining. Two buttons, and her blouse would fall open, and he'd have a feast of her, hanging in front of his eyes. She stopped unbuttoning. He made a little growl in his throat. The smile suddenly went from his face. Perhaps she was imagining it, but there seemed to be a flicker of fire in his eyes.

She stopped her teasing and put her hands back up to the first of the remaining buttons. He rewarded her with a little smile, which showed her a detail she'd missed until now. His teeth, though small, were all sharpened to a fine point. He had the smile of a piranha. She literally felt the flesh around her nipple tighten up at the prospect of those needles coming anywhere near her.

She chanced a quick look in the direction of the horsemen, but they had disappeared from sight for a time. The road that was bringing them here had wound into an expanse of pine forest. She looked back at the goat-boy. He was tapping his left foot, which appendage boasted a nail that would not have shamed a raptor. Plainly he was just a little anxious about the proximity of the Duke and his men: he did not wish to be caught. But just as plainly he was not going to leave. Not yet; not until he'd seen what Tammy had to offer.

He pointed at her. Made a little waggling motion with his forefinger. 'Show me,' he said.

She smiled at him, but she didn't move to oblige.

'*Show*,' he said again.

She continued to smile at him, all the while assessing how many strides of his flat little feet it would take for him to reach her, should he take it into his head to run. He could be on her in five strides, she guessed. Four if he pushed it.

She slipped one of the two buttons out of its hole. The blouse fell open a little, giving him a peek at her left nipple. She flashed, suddenly, on some hot summer's day in her fourteenth year, when she'd crept into her parents' room in the middle of the afternoon, and played striptease in the mirror. She had more to boast about than any of the other girls in her class. Bigger breasts, and hair down between her legs. Her life would have been a lot happier if her breasts had stopped growing that day. But they'd had a long way to go. By the time she was fifteen she was like a young Shelley Winters; and it just got worse from there.

Strange how things came round. How something that had become a source of shame for her was now, out of nowhere, redeemed. She let her fingers slip down to the last button, knowing that the goat-boy's gaze would go

553

with them, and she would have a chance, however slim, to look up past him and see whether the horsemen had emerged from the forest.

The news was bad. There was no sign of the Duke and his men. Had they perhaps taken a wrong turning in the forest? Surely not. Surely they knew this entire territory, after so many years of riding it.

'Show me your tits,' the goat-boy demanded.

As he spoke he lifted his left leg and struck a stone with his raptor claw. A bright spark leapt from the place and landed on a tuft of grey grass, where it erupted into a little fire. It had too little fuel to keep it sustained for long, but in the five or six seconds that it took for the cycle of spark, fire and extinction to play out Tammy heard the sound of the Duke's horses, and from the corner of her eye saw them emerging from between the trees.

The goat-boy narrowed his eyes to golden slits. The corners of his mouth turned down, showing the lower row of monstrous teeth.

'Show me,' he said again.

Plainly he wasn't going to be toyed with any longer. He wanted to see what she had, and he wanted to see them *now*.

She didn't pretend that the horsemen's proximity was not of interest to her. What was the use? Everybody was in on this ridiculous game, the goat-boy included. He dropped his head a little, which should have been a sign for Tammy as to what he would do next, but she was too busy thinking about how long the Duke would take to get off his horse to realize that the goat-boy was making a run at her. And by the time she *did* realize, he was already halfway there, and there was nothing between her bare breasts and his hands, his mouth, his teeth, but a prayer.

8

earing the worst, Todd let out a yell, and started racing across the muddy, bloody ground to do whatever he could to stop the goat-boy attacking Tammy. But before he could get there she had taken matters into her own hands. She let the last of the six buttons slip, and her blouse fell open, unveiling her breasts. The sight of them literally stopped the Devil's child in his tracks. He opened his mouth and drool ran from it.

Tammy was smart enough not to reject this sign of adoration, however crude. Instead, she opened her arms, inviting him into her embrace. Todd would have betted against the wisdom of this. The goat-boy was no sentimentalist. He wanted to play rough. But had he made that bet, he would have lost it.

The Devil's child fell to his knees, laughing. Then he crawled – yes, crawled – into Tammy's arms. His hands went greedily up to one of her breasts, and he held the unwieldy bubble of flesh before his eyes for a moment of devotion. His mouth was slick and wet; the saliva glinted off his terrible teeth.

'Please God . . .' Todd murmured.

It was very possibly the strangest sensation of Tammy's thirty-four years, the feeling of the Devil's child's mouth around her left nipple. There had been a moment – as he closed his mouth around her – when it had crossed her mind that she should be *afraid*; that with one chomp he could give her an instant mastectomy if he so chose. But somehow she knew he would not. He was in love with her breasts. Instead he worshipped them, in his way. Though his mouth was tight around her flesh, she felt not so much as the lightest of scratches from those shark-like teeth. In fact she suspected he'd somehow sheathed them, the way a snake sheathed its fangs, because as he sucked and sucked all she felt was a slightly guilty rush of pleasure as his suction drew the blood to the nipple, and the flesh surrounding the nipple, sensitizing the entire area.

Then, as though all this weren't peaceful and domestic enough, the Devil's child closed his eyes, his fat little hands holding the source of his bliss, and Tammy gently rocked him in her arms.

Goga had been searching for Lilith's child for many centuries now, under a sky that – though it was sometimes cloudy, sometimes clear – always showed the sun eclipsed. He had no real idea of how long his imprisonment in the Devil's Country had lasted; his mind had long ago lost any grasp on the passage of time. He and his men had passed the centuries in a kind of fugue state. Sometimes, when they rested and ate what they'd hunted – rabbit on occasion, or venison, or wild pig – they would talk about what had happened to them that day on the hunt, and where they now were. It was the Duke's opinion that this was not a real place at all, but a kind of dream that the Devil was dreaming, and they were trapped in it. How else to explain the curious limitations of their condition? The same ships forever heading towards the horizon, the same roads haunted by the same beasts; the same sun in the same heaven, half-blinded by the same black moon?

But in the last few days – if days and nights could truthfully be said to pass here – there had been signs that things were changing in what had been hitherto a virtually changeless place. There had always been strangers coming and going (trapped, the philosophizing Duke surmised, in the same infernal dream they found themselves in). But whereas in the past visitors had little or no effect upon the world they were wandering through, the trespassers of recent times had not been quite so guileless or so lucky. Several had perished in the region around the forest.

And now – as if all this were not strange enough – a new spectacle, stranger by some measure than all that had preceded it:

Sitting beside the road – nursing the object of their long search as though he were a commonplace baby – was a bare-breasted woman.

The Duke dismounted a few yards from where Tammy sat in the dirt, rocking the goat boy in her arms. His lieutenants had dismounted several horse-lengths away, and were now creeping around the nursing woman, swords drawn.

Tammy saw all of this, but she registered nothing – not a word, not the raising of a finger – for fear of alerting the contented child to the fact that his time in this idyllic state was about to end.

Very cautiously, the Duke approached the woman and child, beckoning to his men to take their final positions. One of the men had brought a wooden box; clearly his own crude handiwork which he now opened and positioned behind the pair.

The goat-boy didn't open his eyes, but he pulled his mouth away from Tammy's breast long enough to say: 'You don't all have to creep around like that. I know what you're up to.' He'd no sooner spoken than his interest in the Duke's men was forgotten again and he was back to stroking the ample flesh in front of him. 'Beautiful,' he said to Tammy. 'Do you have names for your tits?'

'Names?' Tammy said. 'Actually, no.'

'Oh you should. They're amazing.' He kissed them, first left, then right, then left again, tender, affectionate kisses:

'May I name them myself?' He asked this question with the greatest delicacy, stumbling over the words. Plainly the last thing he would have wished to do was cause offence.

'Of course,' she said.

'I may? *Oh thank you*. Then this must be Helena, who I sucked on, and this one I'll call Beatrice.' He looked at Tammy, framed by her breasts. 'And you? Who are you?'

'Tammy.'

'Just Tammy?'

'Tammy Jayne Lauper.'

'I'm Qwaftzefoni,' the goat-boy said. 'Are you on the run from somebody, Tammy?'

'I was, I suppose, in a way.'

'Who?'

'My husband Arnie.'

'He doesn't appreciate you?'

'No.'

The goat-boy began to lick Helena and Beatrice, again big sloppy tonguings that made Tammy shudder with pleasure.

'No children?' he said in the middle of a stroke.

'No. Arnie can't . . .'

'But you could, Tammy.' He laid his head against her pillows. 'Believe me, I know about these things. You're fertile as the Nile. As soon as you get pregnant these beautiful mammaries will become milk-machines. And your children will be strong and healthy, with strong, healthy hearts, like you.' Finally, he opened his eyes just a slit, his gaze first settling on her face then slipping sideways, to get a glimpse of the cage. 'So what's your opinion?' he said to her.

'About what?'

'Should I give myself up, or let the chase go on?'

'What happens if you give yourself up?'

'I go home. With my mother, Lilith. Back to Hell.'

'Isn't that where you should be?'

558

'Yes, I suppose so. But how would you feel if I said you should be back with Arnie?'

'Oh no . . .'

'So, you understand,' he said, running an appreciative palm over the smooth globes, then putting his head down between them, his chin in the groove. 'Sometimes you just have to get *away*, at least for a while. But you know, now that I lie here, I think, maybe it's time to give up. I've been running for years. Never let anybody lay a finger on me. Until you.' His voice, already low, went to a barely audible whisper, almost a hiss. 'Are they very close now?' he said.

'Yes,' she told him. 'They're very close.'

He toyed with her hardened nipple. 'If I give myself up, what will happen?'

'I think we'll all leave this country, one way or another.'

'And . . . in your opinion . . . would that be such a bad idea?'

'No,' she told him. 'In my opinion it would be a very *good* idea.'

'And they won't hurt me?'

'They won't hurt you.'

'You promise?'

She looked into his eyes, brown into gold. 'I promise they won't hurt you.'

'All right,' he said, lifting his arms up and putting them round her neck. 'It's time we put an end to this. But first you have to kiss me.'

'According to who?'

'According to me.'

She kissed his grizzled lips. And as she did so, he leapt out of her arms, as though he'd been slick with butter; a jump that carried him three or four feet above her head.

'*Prindeţi-l!*' the Duke yelled.

His men weren't about to come so close to their quarry and lose him again. They each caught hold of an arm and

559

leg of the child, and carried him, squealing more like a pig than a goat, to the wooden crate.

Before they could get him safely locked away, however, there came a shout from Eppstadt. 'Where are you going with that thing?' he demanded.

'They're taking it away,' Todd explained.

'Oh, no they're not. Absolutely not. I saw it commit murder. I want to see it tried in a court of law.'

He started towards the two men who had taken hold of the creature. The Duke, sword drawn, instantly came to stand between them.

Tammy, meanwhile, even before she'd buttoned herself up, was ready to add her own voice to the argument. 'Don't you interfere,' she told Eppstadt. 'You'll fuck up everything.'

'Are you crazy? Well, yes, why am I asking? Of *course* you're crazy. Letting that thing suck on you that way. You obscene woman.'

'Just do it!' Todd urged the men, hoping his miming of the boy's imprisonment would help the men understand his meaning.

It did. While the Duke held Eppstadt at swordpoint, his men put the goat-boy into the crate, the wooden bars of which were decorated with small iron icons, hammered into the timber. Whatever their meaning, they did the trick. Though Qwaftzefoni was easily strong enough to shake the crate apart he did not so much as lay his hands on the bars, but sat passively in his little prison, awaiting the next stage of the proceeding.

The Duke issued a new round of orders, and the men lifted the crate onto the back of one of the horses, and started to secure it there.

While they did so the Duke made a short, but apparently deeply sincere, speech to Tammy, thanking her, she assumed, for her part in this dangerous enterprise. All the while he kept an eye on Eppstadt, and his sword

raised should the man attempt to interfere. Eppstadt was
obviously equally aware that the Duke meant business,
even if he didn't understand the exchange, because he
kept his hands raised throughout, and his mouth shut.

Todd, meanwhile, stood watching the sky. There was,
it seemed, a subtle change in the configuration of the
heavens. The moon was very slowly moving off the face
of the sun.

Suddenly, there was a shriek from one of the Duke's
men. The goat-boy had found a place where his hand and
arm could fit through the bars without touching the icons,
and using a moment of the man's distraction, had reached
out and was digging his short-fingered hand into the meat
around the man's eye. He had firm hold of it; firm enough to
shake the man back and forth like a puppet. Blood gushed
from the place, splashing against the goat-boy's palm and
running down his victim's face.

The horse on which the crate was set reared up in panic,
and the crate which had not yet been firmly fixed to the
saddle, slid off. The creature did not let go of his victim.
He hung onto the man's face as the crate crashed to the
ground. It did not break open, as no doubt the goat-boy
had hoped; and in a fit of frustration he started to tear the
man's flesh open still further.

The Duke was swift. He came to the place in two
strides and with a single swing of his sword separated
the goat-boy's hand from his wrist. The creature let out
a sickening, shrill wail.

Tammy – who'd watched all this in a state of horrified
disbelief (how could this cruel monster be the same childish
thing she'd had sucking on her moments ago?) – now
covered her ears against the noise of *both* victims, man
and boy. Though she'd muted the scene she couldn't
take her eyes off it: the hunter, dropping to his knees
with the child's hand still fixed in his face like some foul
parasite; the goat-boy in his crate, staunching his stump

561

with his other hand; the Duke, wiping the blood off his blade –

There was a short moment of calm as the goat-boy's sobs became subdued and the wounded man, having pulled the hooked finger out of his flesh, covered his wound with a cloth, to slow the flow of blood.

The calm lasted no more than twenty seconds. It was broken by a grinding sound in the earth, as though a machine made of stone and iron was on the move down there.

'What fresh hell is this?' Jerry murmured.

Tammy's eyes were on the crate, and its contents. The goat-boy had given up all his complaints, and was peering between the bars with his mouth open and slack. He knew exactly what was about to happen.

'Earthquake?' Eppstadt said.

'No,' Tammy replied, reading the look on the goat-boy's face. '*Lilith*.'

PART NINE

THE QUEEN
OF HELL

1

The ground opened up as though it was going to bring forth some fantastic spring: red shoots, as fine as needles, appeared in their tens of thousands, pierced the ground. A V-shaped crack, each side perhaps twenty feet in length, then erupted into the burgeoning ground, the apex no more than a yard from the spot where the goat-boy's crate sat.

The steady reverberation of immense machinery increased, and it now became apparent what purpose this machine had, for an opening appeared in the earth, resembling the upper part of some vast reptilian snout. The red needles continued to grow, both in size and number, especially around the lip; and at a certain point, when they were perhaps a foot tall, or taller, they produced hosts of tiny purple-black flowers, which gave off a scent no one in the vicinity (except, of course, Qwaftzefoni) was familiar with. It was pungent, like a spice, but there was nothing about it which would ever have persuaded a cook to use it: the smell, and thus presumably the taste, was so powerful that it would have overwhelmed even the most robust dish. It made everyone feel faintly nauseated by its forcefulness. Eppstadt, who had the weakest stomach, actually threw up.

By the time he'd done with his retching the extraordinary growth-cycle of the plant had carried it past its peak, however. The small black blossoms were in sudden decay, their petals losing their colour. And now, in its autumnal mode, the odour of the plant changed. What had been an almost unbearable stench a minute before became transformed by the process of corruption, its foulness entirely evaporated.

What remained was a scent that somehow conspired with the souls of everyone present to put them in mind of some sweet memory: something lost; something sacrificed; something taken by time or circumstance. Nor, though their bodies were held in the embrace of these feelings, could they have named them. The scent was too subtle in its workings to be pinned to any one memory. All that mattered was the state of utter vulnerability in which it left everyone. By the time Hell's Mouth had opened, and Lilith herself had stepped out of its long, sharp shadows, her flora had enraptured the souls of everyone who stood before her. Whatever they saw from now on, whatever they said and did, was coloured by the way the scent of her strange garden had touched them.

Was she beautiful? Well, perhaps. The scent was beautiful, so it seemed she – who was shaped by the scent, as if her body were carved from perfumed smoke – was surely beautiful too, though a more logical assessment might have pointed out how curiously made her face was, close in colour and texture to the blossoms in their corrupted phase.

Her voice, that same less dreamy assessor might have said, was unmusical, and her dress, despite its great size and elaboration (tiny, incomprehensible motifs hand-sewn in neat rows, millions of times) more proof of obsession, even of madness, than of beauty.

Even allowing that there can be not one good and reliable report of Lilith, the Devil's wife, some things may still be clearly said of her. She was happy, for one. She laughed with almost indecent glee at the sight of her caged child, though she plainly saw that he was missing a hand. And her manner, when dealing with the Duke, was nothing short of exquisite.

'You've suffered much for your crime against my household,' she said, speaking in cultured English, which – by some little miracle of her making – he understood. 'Do you have any idea how many years have passed since you first began to hunt for *that* idiot child of mine?' She stabbed a finger at the creature in the crate, who started to moan and complain, until she shushed him by slapping the bars.

The Duke replied that no, he did not know.

'Well, perhaps it's best you don't,' Lilith told him. 'But what you *should* know, because it will shape what happens when I have taken this imp of mine back, is that your natural life-span – your three score years and ten – was over centuries ago.'

The Duke looked puzzled at this; and then aghast, as he realized the consequences of what she was telling him: that he and his men had ridden their lives away in this fruitless Hunt; around and around and around, chasing a baby who'd put on perhaps two years in the period of the pursuit.

'My father?' he said. 'My brothers?'

'All dead,' Lilith said, with some little show of sympathy. 'All that you knew and remembered has gone.'

The Duke's face remained unchanged, but tears filled up his eyes and then spilled down his cheeks.

'Men and your hunts,' Lilith went on, addressing, it seemed, some larger error in the Duke's sex. 'If you hadn't been out killing healthy stags and boars in the first place, you could have lived and loved. But,' she shrugged, 'we do as our instincts dictate, yes? And yours brought you here. To the very edge of your own grave.'

She was telling him, it seemed, that he'd run out of life and now, after all the sacrifices of his Hunt, his reward would be death: pure, simple and comfortless.

'Let me have my child then,' she said. 'Then we'll have this wretched business over and done with.'

It was at this point that Eppstadt spoke up once more.

He'd had a twitching little smile on his face for a while, the reason for which was simple enough: this latest spectacle (the earth opening up, the flowers, the scent that toyed with memory) had finally convinced him that one of his earlier explanations for all of this was most likely the correct one. He was lying unconscious somewhere in the house (probably having been struck by a falling object during the earthquake) and was fantasizing this whole absurd scene. He very seldom felt as self-willed in dreams as he felt in this one; indeed, he seldom dreamed at all; or at least remembered his dreams. But now that he had this nonsense in his grasp, he wasn't ready to let it go just yet. Ever the negotiator, he stepped forward and put out his hand, to prevent the Duke passing over the child.

'I don't suggest you do that just yet,' he said, not sure whether the man understood him or not, though the gesture was clear enough. 'The moment you hand over the brat, you're dead. You understand?'

'Don't do this, Eppstadt,' Todd advised.

'Why the hell not? It's just a dream –'

'It's not a dream,' Jerry said. 'It's real. Everything down here is as –'

'Oh Christ, Brahms, *shut up*. You know what I'm going to do when I'm finished sorting this out? I'm going to kick your faggot ass.' He grinned, obviously hugely satisfied to be so politically incorrect.

'You're going to regret this,' Todd said. 'Jerry's right.'

'How *can* he be right?' Eppstadt said, his voice dripping contempt. 'Look at this place! How can any of this fucking idiocy be *real*? It's all going on in my head! And I bet you thought I had the dull little mind of a business school executive!'

'Eppstadt,' Todd said. 'This is *not* going on in your mind.'

Eppstadt made the donkey-bray buzz that accompanied the wrong answer on a quiz show. He was riding high on his

568

newfound, comprehension of his situation. 'Wrong, baby. Fuck! So very, very wrong. Can I say something, while we've got this moment, and it's my dream so I'll fucking say it anyway? You are a terrible actor. I mean, we would get the dailies in at Paramount and we would *howl*, I mean we would *fucking* howl, at some of the takes. Tears pouring down our faces while you attempted to *emote*.'

'You are such a cunt.'

'That I am. And you're a millionaire many times over because I persuaded a bunch of losers who wouldn't know a crass commercial decision from a hole in their asses to pay you an obscene amount of money to parade your God-given attributes.' He turned to Lilith, who had been watching this outburst as though amused by the cavorting of an antic dog. 'Sorry. There I go mentioning the G-word. Probably doesn't sit well with you?'

'God?' Lilith said. 'No. *God sits perfectly well with me.*'

Eppstadt was clearly about to make some boorish reply to this but Lilith ignored him.

She let out a rhythmical whistle, and up from the dark throat of the earth came two women, bald and bare-breasted. At the sight of either faces or breasts, perhaps both, the goat-boy in the crate started to get voluble again, wailing and chattering.

'This is the end, then,' Lilith said to the Duke. 'I'm taking him. Do you have any final words?'

The Duke shook his head, and raised his sword – jabbing it in Eppstadt's direction in order to persuade him to stay out of these proceedings. Eppstadt stood his ground, until the point of the Duke's sword pierced his mud-caked shirt. Then he yelped and duly stepped back to prevent worse coming his way.

'Hurt, did it?' Jerry said.

'Shut the fuck up,' Eppstadt snapped.

He made no further attempt to agent the exchange between Lilith and the Duke, however. The crate was unbolted, and Lilith reached in, grabbing her one-handed offspring by his dick and balls.

'Take him, ladies,' she said to the women, and in a most unmotherly fashion she threw him into the arms of her maidservants, who seized him between them and carried him off down the slope and into the darkness.

'So it finishes,' Lilith said to the Duke.

She turned on her heel, catching hold of her insanely embroidered garment, and lifting it up to clear her step. Then she glanced back. 'Did you have children?' she asked the Duke.

He shook his head.

'Then you'll lie with those who went before you but not with any that came after. That's good. It would be mournful to meet your children in the grave tonight.' She inclined her head. 'Farewell then, my lord. It seems to me you've earned your rest.'

She had said all she intended to say, and again made to depart, but Eppstadt wasn't quite done.

'You're good,' he said. 'I mean, real *gravitas*. I don't see that a lot. And you're beautiful. You know, it's usually one or the other. Tits or brains. But you've got both. I almost wish I wasn't dreaming.'

Lilith gave him a stare which would have sent wiser men running. But Eppstadt, still believing himself the master of his own dream, was not going to be cowed by any of its cast.

'Have I met you somewhere before?' he said. 'I have, haven't I? I'm conjuring you up from a memory.'

'Oh don't do this,' Todd murmured.

'Don't what?' Eppstadt snapped.

'Play. Not here. Not now.'

'It's my sand-box. I'll play if I want to. But the rest of you can get the fuck out! That means you, faggot, and her –' He pointed at Tammy. 'And you, Pickett. Out! Go on! I want you out!'

570

For some reason, Todd looked to Lilith for permission to depart. She nodded, first at Todd, then at Tammy, finally at Jerry.

'Are you sure you don't want to make a graceful exit?' Todd said to Eppstadt.

'Fuck you.'

Jerry had already turned away from the Hell's Mouth, and was heading back towards the threshold. Tammy had also turned, but had halted, caught by the sight of the Duke and his men, who were lying on the ground at the edge of the trees. How they had got there – what instinct had driven them to lie down like this – she didn't know.

Their bodies were already in advanced states of corruption, even though they were still alive and they were gazing up at the slowly-changing sky, their faces cleansed of any expression of resentment or need or pain. They seemed perfectly resigned to their decease, as though after all these years trapped in a circle they could not break, they were simply grateful to be leaving it. So there they lay, maggots at their nostrils, beetles at their ears, their sight drowning in pools of rot.

She didn't watch to the end. She wasn't that brave. Instead she turned away and followed Jerry to the door.

As she came to his side he said: 'Look.'

'I saw.'

'No, not there,' Jerry said. 'That's too sad for words. Look up. It's almost over.'

2

So it was.

The sun was now over halfway uncovered, and with every passing moment the landscape it had lit with so miserly a light for several hundred years was growing brighter. The thinnest clouds – those most susceptible to heat – had already evaporated. Now the cumuli were in retreat, showing a bank of blue through which clusters of falling stars came blazing down, as though to celebrate the passing of the Hunt. Some of the braver beasts in this extraordinary landscape – creatures that had lived contentedly in the perpetual twilight but were curious to see what change the sun would bring – were venturing out of their dens and caves and squinting up at the spectacle overhead. A lion blessed with wings strong enough to carry it aloft rose from its imperial seat amongst the branches of a Noahic oak, as though to challenge the sun itself. It was instantly overcome by the incandescence that filled the heavens, and tumbled back to earth, shedding feathers the size of swords.

Jerry saw the lesson clearly enough. 'It's all going to change very quickly now,' he said.

There was indeed a general sense of panic in the landscape. Every species that had learned to prosper in the silver-dim light was in a sudden terror, fearful that whatever the sun was shedding – light, heat or both – it would be their undoing. In every corner of this painted world, creatures were scuttling and scampering, fighting over the

merest sliver of shadow. It was not just the lion that had
been brought down. Several flocks of birds, confounded by
the sudden blaze, panicked in mid-flight, and descended
in squawking confusion. On the roads, wild dogs went
noon-day crazy, and set on one another's throats in bursts
of overheated rage; the air was suddenly populated with
myriad tiny gnats and dragonflies, which rose from the
grass in such swarming abundance they could only have
been born that moment, their eggs cracked by the abrupt
rise in temperature. And where there were flies, of course,
there were fly-*catchers*. Rodents leapt up out of the grass to
feed on the sudden bounty. Lizards and snakes swarmed
underfoot.

It was an astonishing transformation. In the four or
five minutes since the child had been passed back to his
mother and the Duke's curse had been lifted, the landscape
through which Goga and his men (their flesh and bones
now indistinguishable from the swampy earth in which
they'd lain down to die) had ridden had undergone a
sea-change: falling stars and falling lions, the air filled
with the flutter of a million dragonflies and the howling
of a thousand sun-blinded dogs; trees coming into sudden
blossom, their buds so fat and fruitful they exploded like
little bombs, so that a blizzard of petals drenched the air
with perfume.

And in the same moment as the dragonflies rose up, and
the trees blossomed, Death caught a million throats, and
with howls and shrieks and crazed cavorting, the Reaper
claimed both the common dog and the fanciful beasts Lilith
had hatched to make the Hunt more purgatorial for her
victims. The chicken that had laid eggs filled with serpents
was devoured by its brood in its dotage. A lizard with a
dragonfly still fluttering in its jaws was taken by a beast only
Lilith could have conjured: its back a shameless homage to
the cunt, from its glorious labial head to the enormous
golden eye buried in its depths like an opulent egg.

A thousand, thousand witnesses could not have catalogued what happened to the Devil's Country in those minutes. An army of chroniclers could not have caught a quarter of the stories here; they came and went too fast: birth, death and the madness between filling the senses to overflowing.

At the door, Tammy had time to wonder if perhaps Eden had been like this. Not the calm hand of a placid creator moving over the dappled grass of paradise and leaving the lion, the lamb and all that lived in between where it passed, but rather this: the sun turned up as though by an impatient cook, frying life into being, in one frenzied, blazing carnival, its most exquisite beasts no more likely to survive the heat than its basest creations. Beauty of no importance, in the heat of the moment; nor poetry; nor intelligence. Just things rising and falling without judgement or consideration; the loveliest of beings dying before they had time to speak, while veils of flies descended to pump their eggs into the bed of their quickened rot.

No wonder Lilith had said, so knowingly, that God sat perfectly well with her. Hadn't she been his first female creation; the bride for Adam which Yahweh had rejected? Hers the first womb, hers the first egg, hers the first blood shed in pain because a man had made it so.

Tammy looked to see if she could catch a glimpse of the woman one last time, with this new notion in her head.

But the air between where she stood and where the Queen of Hell had been standing was a maze of petals, flies, birds, seeds, scales and flakes of cooked corruption. Lilith was out of sight, and Tammy knew that if she was lucky she would never have occasion to look into the woman's eyes again.

3

Upstairs, in the great bed in the master bedroom, Katya had woken from one of the most restorative slumbers she'd enjoyed in years. No nightmares; not even dreams. Just a deep sense of well-being, knowing that she had finally found the man with whom to share the years in the privacy of the Canyon.

A moment later, the comforts of her waking-state were dashed. The bed beside her was cold and empty and she heard voices; strangers in her house. That there might be people in the kitchen or the dining room would have been bad enough, but she knew instinctively where the voices were coming from. They were way downstairs, in *that* room, and given that Todd was not beside her, he was probably down there with them. The thought did not comfort her.

She understood all too well the claim that place had. Nor did it play favourites. It beguiled, with equal eloquence, the genius and the dullard, the intellectual and the sensualist. She'd seen it happen over and over again. Lord knows, she'd had fixes enough from it herself over the years. It had kept her beautiful, kept her strong. But for her being in the room was merely a function of cosmetics: it wiped away the years. Though perhaps it was truly the Devil's Country, she attached no great metaphysical significance to the place. It was her beauty parlour, nothing more. And if there were people in there now, using up her dwindling sum of perfection, then she wanted them out! *Out!*

She got up and started to dress, going over the events of the previous evening as she did so. There was only one person she knew who might have seduced Todd away from her side: Tammy, the bitch who'd taken him away last time. For some reason Todd felt some sentimental attachment to Tammy. There was nothing wrong with that, in principle. It proved he had a heart. But the woman had no place in the scheme of things from this point on. She'd served her minor purpose; it was time she was removed.

Dressed now, Katya went to the mirror. The sleep had done her good. There was a luminosity in her eyes that had not been there for many years. She could even bring herself to turn on a smile.

It was unfortunate, she thought as she stepped out onto the landing, but there were bound to be these little challenges at the outset. Nothing, however, was going to get between her and her paradise. Zeffer had tried, and Zeffer was dead. This woman would probably try too, but she'd end up the same way he had. And, if things really went well, the killing blow would come from Todd. That would make things perfect: if he found the weapon and struck her down. It was essential to make him understand that anyone who endangered their little paradise would have to be killed. And there was nothing better for the cementing of a relationship than to spill a little blood together.

Eppstadt had sent Pickett, the woman and Brahms running; but he'd stayed awhile to torment the strange woman he'd conjured up.

It wasn't often he tangled with a woman whose intellect he respected. For a time Columbia had been run by just such a woman, Dawn Steel, and Eppstadt had always enjoyed a good debate with her. But she'd died of brain cancer, at some absurdly young age, the loss had saddened him. True, there were a couple of actresses who had the wit to hold his attention for more than a sentence – Jamie

Lee Curtis was surprisingly sharp, Susan Sarandon and Jodie Foster were worth his time; but mostly they were little more than bodies to him. So where, as he'd already asked himself, had he found the raw material for this baroque fantasy called Lilith? It wasn't just the beauty and eloquence of the woman, it was the whole implausible world that surrounded her, like an MGM musical designed by Hieronymus Bosch.

'What are you staring at?' Lilith asked him. She had long ago begun her slow descent into the Underworld, but now – caught by Eppstadt's scrutiny – she had halted, and turned to face him again.

'You,' he said bluntly.

'Well don't.'

So saying, she again turned her back and continued to descend into the earth.

'Wait!' he demanded. 'I want to talk with you.'

He caught hold of the rear of her trailing gown. 'Didn't you hear me? I said *wait.*'

If there had been any trace of indulgence left on Lilith's face it had now disappeared. She assessed him with a merciless gaze.

'Wait?' she said, her tone withering. 'What makes you think I would obey any instruction of yours?'

As she spoke she glanced down at Eppstadt's feet and he felt a motion under his heel. *Odd*, he thought. He stepped aside, only to find that a new crop of the shoots had sprung up before the opening of the Hell-Mouth. This time, however, they were more densely planted than before, and they were only growing in his immediate vicinity.

'What is this?' he said.

He felt the first needle-pricks in his ankles; little more than irritations really. But when he lifted his leg, he dragged the shoots out from under his skin, and they hurt. He yelped with pain. Hopping on one leg, he hoisted up his trouser leg. There were dozens of tiny wounds around his ankle where the shoots had entered his skin; all were bleeding.

'Fuck,' he said.

There was nothing remotely entertaining about this dream now. He wanted it to stop. Meanwhile he felt the crop of shoots entering his other leg. He had no intention of repeating his error, so he stomped down the area of the shoots with his injured foot, and planted it there while he gingerly hoisted up his other trouser leg to examine the damage. Impossible as it seemed, the shoots had already advanced through the muscle of his calf. He could see their trajectory through his skin; they were getting steadily more ambitious as they climbed; dividing and dividing again, forming a network through his flesh. He caught hold of one at his ankle, where it pierced his skin. It was no thicker than a few braided hairs, but it wriggled around between his finger and thumb as though determined to keep on climbing, keep on growing. He tried to pull on it but a spasm of pain ran up through his leg, following the path of the shoots' advance. It had almost reached his knee.

There were tears of agony in his eyes now. He looked up at Lilith, blinking them away so as to see her better. She was still watching him.

'All right,' he said. 'You made your point.'

She didn't reply.

'Make it stop,' he told her.

She seemed to consider this for a moment, biting lightly on her lower lip as she turned the option over. As she did so he glanced down at his other foot. The plants he'd ground beneath his heel had been replaced by new growths, which were already four or five inches high, and piercing him afresh.

'Oh God, no,' he said, returning his gaze to his tormentor's face. 'Please. I was *wrong*.' He was barely able to get the words out, the pain was so intolerable. '*Make it stop!*'

Though his vision was blurred he could see her response to his plea. She was shaking her head.

'*Damn you*!' he said. 'I made one fucking mistake! I've said I'm *sorry*. That should be good enough.'

Something burst just above his knee. He tore at his trouser leg, ripping the fabric with such pain-inspired force that it tore all the way up to his groin. There were *flowers* blossoming from the meat of his knee: six or seven small florets, each giving off a stink so pungent it made him giddy to inhale it. He glanced up at the woman who'd done this to him just one last time, hoping his tongue would be inspired to make her merciful. But she'd plainly already decided she knew how this would end. She had turned her back on him, and was continuing her descent into the underworld.

Eppstadt felt a new series of eruptions in his legs, leading all the way up from his knee to his groin. The large, pale muscle of his thigh had become a veritable garden; upwards of twenty flowers had blossomed there. Blood ran from the places where they'd come forth, and it coursed around the back of his leg, soaking into the tatters of his trousers. The collected scent of the blossoms all but made him swoon. He toppled backwards, and sprawled in the shoots that were waiting for him, like a death-bed welcoming him into its final comfort.

'What the hell happened to Eppstadt?' Todd said, looking back.

The brightening day had put a layer of haze between the Hell's Mouth and the door that led up into the house. The details of Eppstadt's condition were impossible to fathom. All they could see was that for some reason the man was lying back amongst flowers.

'I thought he was in trouble a few moments ago,' Jerry said. 'He seemed to be crying out.'

'He's not crying out now,' Tammy said. 'Looks like he's taking a nap.'

579

'Crazy . . .' Todd said.

'Well leave him to it, I say,' Jerry remarked. 'If he wants to stay, that's his damn business.'

There was no argument from the other two.

'After you,' Jerry said, stepping aside to let Tammy cross the threshold. He followed quickly after her, with Todd on his heels.

Todd glanced back one last time at the transforming landscape. The ships had disappeared from the horizon, as though some long-awaited wind had finally come and filled their sails, and borne them off to new destinations. The little gathering of houses beside the river, with its two bridges, had been eroded by light, and even the snaking shape of the river itself was on its way to extinction. Though he'd doubted the tale Katya had told him it seemed now that it was true. This had been a prison painted to hold the Duke. Now that his Hunt was over and the Devil's child had been returned, the place no longer had any reason to exist.

Age was catching up with it. The heat of its painted sun was undoing it, image by image, tile by tile.

'*Eppstadt*?' he yelled, 'Are you *coming*?'

But the man in the long grass didn't move, so Todd let him lie there. Eppstadt had always been a man who did what he wanted to do, and to hell with other people's opinions.

Sprawled on the ground, Eppstadt heard Todd's call, and half-thought of returning it, but he could no longer move. Several shoots had entered the base of his skull, piercing his spinal column, and he was paralysed.

The greenery pushing up through his brain, erasing his memories as they climbed, had not yet removed every last shred of intelligence. He realized that this was the end of him. He could feel the first insinuations of shoots at the back of his throat, and an itching presence behind his eyes, where they were soon to emerge and flower but it concerned him far less than it might have done had he imagined this sitting in his office.

It wasn't the kind of death he'd had in mind when he thought of such things, but then his life hadn't been as he'd expected it to be either. He'd wanted to paint, as a young man. But he'd had not the least talent. A professor for the Art School had remarked that he'd never met a man with a poorer sense of aesthetics. What would they have thought now, those critics who'd so roundly condemned him, if they'd been here to see? Wouldn't they have said he was passing away prettily, with his head full of shoots and colour and his eyes were

He never finished the thought.

One of Lilith's flowers blossomed inside his skull, and a sudden, massive haemorrhage stopped dead every thought Eppstadt was entertaining, or would ever entertain again.

Indifferent to his death, the plants continued to press up through his flesh, blossoming and blossoming, until from a little distance he was barely recognizable as a man at all: merely a shape in the dirt, a log perhaps, where the flowers had grown with particular vigour, hungry to make the most of the sun now that it was shining so brightly.

4

Tammy knew there was trouble brewing the moment she set eyes on Katya. The woman was smiling down at them beatifically, but there was no warmth or welcome in her eyes; only anger and suspicion.

'What happened?' she said, straining for lightness.

'It's over,' Todd told her, coming up the stairs, his hand extended towards her in a placatory manner. No doubt he also read the signs in the woman's eyes, and didn't trust what he saw there.

'Come on,' he said, laying his palm against her waist in a subtle attempt to change her direction.

'No,' she said, gently pressing past him so as to go down the stairs. 'I want to see.'

'There's nothing *to* see,' Jerry said.

She didn't bother to sweeten her expression for Brahms. He was her servant; nothing more nor less. 'What do you mean: *there's nothing to see?*'

'It's all gone,' he said, his tone tinged with melancholy, as though he were gently breaking the news of a death to her.

'It can't be gone,' Katya snapped, pushing on past Jerry and Tammy and heading down the stairs. 'The Hunt goes on forever. How could Goga ever catch the Devil's child?' She turned at the bottom of the stairs, her voice strident. *'How could any man ever catch the Devil's child?'*

'It wasn't a man,' Tammy piped up. 'It was me.'

Katya's face was a picture of disbelief. Obviously if the

idea of a man bringing the Hunt to an end wasn't farcical enough, the notion that a woman – especially one she held in such plain contempt – had done so, was beyond the bounds of reason.

'That's not possible,' she said, departing from the bottom of the stairs and heading along the passageway.

She was out of Tammy's view now; but everyone could hear Katya's bare feet on the floor, and the doorhandle being turned –

'*No*!'

The word was almost a shriek.

Jerry caught hold of Tammy's elbow. 'I think you should get out of here –'

'*No! No! No!*'

'– that room was the reason she stayed young.'

Now it made sense, Tammy thought.

That was why Jerry had sounded as though he were announcing a death: it was Katya's demise he was announcing. Denied her chamber of eternal youth, what would happen to her? If this was a movie, she'd probably come hobbling back along the passageway with the toll of years already overtaking her, her body cracking and bending, her beauty withering away.

But this wasn't a movie. The woman who strode back into view at the bottom of the stairs showed no sign of weakening or withering: at least not yet.

'*That bitch*!' she yelled, pointing at Tammy. 'I want her killed. Todd? You hear me? I want her dead!'

Tammy looked up the stairs to where Todd was standing. It was impossible to read the expression on his face.

Meanwhile Katya ranted on. 'She's spoiled everything! *Everything*!'

'It had to end eventually,' Todd said.

As Todd spoke Tammy felt the pressure of Jerry's hand on her arm, subtly encouraging her to head on up the stairs while there was still time to do so. She didn't wait for a second prompt. She began to ascend, keeping her eyes fixed on Todd's face. What was he thinking?

Look at me, she willed him. *It's me, it's your Tammy. Look at me.*

He didn't, which was a bad sign. It would be easier to obey Katya if he didn't think of Tammy as a real human being; didn't look into her eyes; didn't see her fear.

'*Don't let her go*!' Katya said.

She was coming up the stairs now, taking them slowly, her pace casual.

Todd just stood there, and for once Tammy was glad of his passivity. She slipped by him without being apprehended, and headed on to the top of the stairs.

'*Todd*!'

The cry was from Jerry, not from Katya. Tammy looked back. For some reason, Todd had caught hold of him, and was preventing him from following Tammy.

From the expression on his face, it was clear Jerry knew he was in trouble. He struggled to pull himself away from Todd, but he was much the weaker man.

'I looked after you, didn't I?' Katya said to Jerry. 'When you didn't have a friend in the world, I was there for you, wasn't I? And now you let this happen.'

'It wasn't my fault. I couldn't stop it.'

Katya was right in front of him now, her palm flat against his chest. She didn't seem to be exerting any pressure, but whatever power she was exercising through her hand was enough to make him sink back against the wall.

'It wasn't your doing?' Katya said incredulously. 'You could have killed her. That would have stopped her interfering.'

'Killed her?' Jerry said, plainly horrified at the idea; as though he'd not realized until now that the stakes were so high, or that the prospect of murder – casual, inevitable – was so close. Perhaps, most of all, not realizing that the woman he'd obviously fallen in love with should now show herself to be as cold as the Queen of Hell.

'You little fake!' Katya said, putting her hand on Jerry's head and ripping at the hair glued to his scalp. She dug her nails in, and a flap of skin came away in her hand. Blood ran down over Jerry's face.

'*Jesus*, Katya,' Todd said. 'There's no need –'

'*No need to what?*' she broke in, her face perfect in its fury, those wonderful bones, that exquisite symmetry, finding in rage its best purpose. 'No need to *punish* him? He knows what he did.'

She tossed away the flap of hair and skin and slapped Jerry across his face. Tammy had witnessed this kind of cruelty from her before; the last time Zeffer had been its target. And, just like Zeffer, Jerry seemed almost mesmerized by her show of fury, powerless to defend himself against her.

But Tammy wasn't about to watch him kicked half to death the way Zeffer had been kicked, even if in some twisted way Brahms was ready to accept that fate.

'You know how pathetic you are?' she said to Katya. 'Slapping around old men? *Pathetic*. He didn't do anything down there. I did *it*. I did it all. Tell her, Todd.'

'It wasn't Jerry's fault. It wasn't Tammy's, either.'

'Yours, then?' Katya said, shifting her burning gaze to Todd.

As she spoke she put her hand on Jerry's face and pushed him. He reached out to stop himself tumbling back down the stairs, but there was nothing to catch hold of. Down he went, head over heels.

Tammy peered over the stairwell. Jerry was sprawled at the bottom, still breathing, but apparently unconscious. She was almost grateful. Better Katya dismiss him, and come after her instead. She could still run; she could still defend herself. And she certainly wasn't about to be hypnotized by the bitch's gaze.

She didn't wait for Katya to start up the flight in

pursuit of her. She left the banister and headed into the kitchen.

'She's crazy.'

It was Todd. He'd followed her in, shaking his head. 'You gotta go!' he said to Tammy.

'Catch her!' Katya yelled. She was obviously taking her sweet time coming up the stairs, confident, even now, that she had this under control. 'Todd? You hear me? Catch her!'

'What are you: her *dog*?' Tammy said. 'Is that what she's reduced you to?'

'Just go,' Todd said. 'She's all I've got left.'

'She'll kill you too if it suits her,' Tammy said. 'You know it.'

'Don't say that,' Todd begged. 'I've got to stay with her. If I don't, what have I got? You were at the party! You heard what they said. It's all over for me. I don't have anything left, except her. She loves me, Tammy.'

'No she doesn't.'

'She does.'

'*No*! She's just using you. That isn't love.'

'Who the hell are you to say –'

'– as good as anybody else. Better, where you're concerned. The *years* I wasted thinking about you.'

'Wasted?'

'Yes, wasted. I wanted you to love me. But you never did. Now you want *her* to love *you*. And she won't. Not ever. She's incapable of love.'

It hurt him to hear that. It hurt because he believed her, much as he didn't want to. It was the truth. She knew it, and so – to judge by those despairing eyes of his – did he. His gaze went to the window. He studied the glass for a time.

'Do you think they're still out there?' Todd said.

'What? The dead? Yes . . .'

Even as she was speaking she was thinking about Zeffer's

586

last request. The madness of the Devil's Country had put it out of her head.

'Suppose I said I knew a way to get them into the house?' Tammy said.

'Is that possible?'

'It's possible,' Tammy said cautiously.

He went back to the door he'd just stepped through. 'How?' he asked, lowering his voice.

Tammy was still uncertain of his allegiances. She didn't want to tell him everything in case he was still going to side with Katya. But on the other hand, she needed his help.

'It's just something somebody told me,' she said. She wanted to believe she had him on her side, but she was far from certain.

Katya was calling from the stairs again. 'Todd? Have you got her?'

'Close the door,' Tammy said. 'Keep her out.' She started to look around the kitchen. Which of the drawers was most likely to contain a knife? A good strong steak knife. No, better, a fat-bladed chopping knife. Something that wouldn't snap under pressure.

'Todd?' Katya sounded as though she was in the hall-way.

'Close the door,' Tammy said. 'Please.'

Todd glanced back in Katya's direction. Then, God bless him, he closed the door.

'What are you doing?' Tammy heard her say.

'It's all right!' Todd called back to her.

Tammy started going through the drawers, as quickly as possible. There seemed to be dozens of them. Did she want aluminium foil and plastic bags? No. Spoons and ladles? No. Cutlery? There were a few knives in here, but they were too flimsy for her purposes. She needed a blade she could use to dig at the wood. If she didn't get the icons out of the threshold, the ghosts would stay out there.

'Todd! Let me in!'

'You have to go,' Todd said to Tammy.

'Not until I've got a –'

Yes! A knife! The ninth drawer she opened was a treasure trove of knives; large, small, middle-sized. Knowing she could only have a few seconds left before Katya came in, Tammy simply gathered up a handful of knives – five or six – and headed back to the passageway.

As she reached the door, she heard Katya's voice from across the room.

'You think you're going to save yourself with those?'

Tammy looked back over her shoulder. Katya had pushed the door open, and shoved Todd aside, raising her hands as she approached, ready to take Tammy by the throat.

Todd raced ahead of her to stand between the two women.

'Hey now,' he said. 'Let's just calm down. Nobody's going to hurt anybody.'

Katya seemed to listen to him. Her agitation quieted. 'All right,' she said, looking at Todd with wide, dark eyes. 'What do you suggest?'

Tammy didn't trust this little performance at all; but it gave her time to back off towards the door. As she reached it, one of her hastily-collected knives slipped from her hand. She bent down to pick it up, and in attempting to do so, lost her grip on all the others. She cursed as they went spinning across the polished tiles in all directions.

'Pick them up, Todd,' Katya said.

'Later,' Todd replied, his tone still mellow.

In response she slapped him, hard, across his already-wounded face, striking blood from it. 'I want them picked up.'

He stared at her for a minute. Then, very calmly, he caught hold of her hand and said: 'Don't do that.'

'You want to hit me back?' Katya said. 'Go on. If that's what you want to do, then do it! No, you won't will you? You're too damn weak. All you men. *Too damn weak.'*

As if to prove the point she pulled her hand out of Todd's grip and pushed past him, heading straight for Tammy.

Faced with the choice of waiting a few seconds to see if Todd would come to her rescue, or making an escape while she could, Tammy snatched up the first knife to hand, which was neither the largest nor toughest of the blades, and made a run for the door.

Katya came after her; Tammy stumbled as she got up, and Katya would probably have caught up with her if Todd hadn't finally found the courage to put his arms around Katya from behind, and hold her back.

'All right!' he yelled to Tammy. *'Go!'*

Tammy didn't need a second invitation. She ran out into the passage and slammed the door after her. It had a lock but regrettably no key.

She looked down the passageway to the back door. There was a glass panel in it. The glass wasn't flawless, but it was clear enough for Tammy to see the shapes of the ghosts, assembled like a pack of hungry dogs eager to be let into the house. She could hear the odd, listless murmuring they made, the words like objects that had been used so many times they had lost all their shape.

Did they know, somehow, that she was on her way to let them in? Was that why their murmuring became a little more urgent as she opened the door, and the silvery stare in their eyes a little brighter?

'Wait,' she said to them. 'I'm going to do this. But you have to wait.'

There was noise from the kitchen behind her. Plainly Katya was attempting to persuade Todd to go and fetch her – probably kill her. Tammy couldn't make sense of the words, and that was probably for the best. She couldn't afford to be panicked any more than she already was, or she'd screw this up.

Tammy glanced back over her shoulder, to check that Katya wasn't already in the passageway, then she went down on her hands and knees and examined the threshold. The wood was worn with time, and rot had got into it, softening it. She ran her fingers over the full length of it, clearing away the dirt. The area smelt vaguely of vomit, but she supposed that was the rot she was smelling. At three or four inch intervals along the length of the threshold there were metal markers, like nails with large, elaborately configured heads, hammered into the timber. She dug around one of them with the nail of her forefinger. It seemed very solidly imbedded in the wood. But she had no doubt she was on the right track, meddling with these things, because as soon as she started to do so the ghosts' murmuring became almost reverent in tone; worshipful.

She looked up at them. The light they emitted had grown brighter; either that or they'd narrowed their eyes. Yes, that was it; they narrowed their eyes to study what she was doing.

'This is it, isn't it?'

They answered the only way they could: they fell completely silent. This was not a procedure they wanted to put at risk by making so much as a single sound.

There were five icons in the threshold, the middle one slightly bigger than the other four, which was a circle with two irregularly-shaped 'arms' coming from it, at noon and seven o'clock on its dial.

She dug her knife into the centre of the symbol. 'Okay,' she said softly to it, 'out you come.'

The wood was so wormy it crumbled beneath her knife-point. She dug deeper, exposing parts of the icon that were still clean. It gave off a subtle iridescence, like mother-of-pearl. Her confidence growing, she kept digging until she had cleared the wood away around the whole thing. Then she put her knife-tip under the rim and tried to lever it out.

Much to her disappointment, it wouldn't budge; not even a little bit.

'Damn,' she said softly.

She worked at it a little more, then remembered the old school adage, trotted out before every test. 'If you can't answer the first question, don't waste time on it. Move on to the next one.'

That's what she did. She moved left, and started to stab at the wood around the icon at the far end of the row. If anything, the threshold was even more rotted here than it was at the centre; the wood came away in fat splinters.

There was more noise from the kitchen now, but she ignored it. Just kept digging. Bigger splinters flew. She felt a rush of certainty. She was going to *do* this. She pressed the knife under the edge of the icon. There was a moment of resistance, then the pressure of the blade on a nerve in her hand sent a spasm of pain up her arm. She yelped. And in the same moment the icon jumped free of the wood, landing on the tiles outside.

The din from the kitchen suddenly became very specific. She heard Todd say:

'Don't do that.'

It was a voice she'd never heard from him before, not even in a movie. There was fear in his voice. Something Katya was doing, or was *about* to do, had made him afraid. Not a very comforting thought.

Without wasting time looking over her shoulder, she quickly went to the other end of the threshold, and started to work there. Though there was plenty of light between the trees, she was cold. There was a length of clammy flesh down her spine, and another across her shoulderblades, as though somebody had painted a cold cross on her skin. Her teeth chattered lightly.

But again, she was in luck. The wood around the icon came away in three or four large pieces. She pressed the knife as deep under the device as it would go and levered.

591

The thing shifted instantly; and as it did so the same spasm she'd felt before ran up her arm. It wasn't a nerve she was striking, she realized. It was a jolt of energy given off by the metalwork as it was levered out. It hurt so much she dropped the knife for a moment, to massage her hand. Her fingers were getting numb.

She looked up at her silent witnesses. 'Yes, I know,' she said. 'Hurry up. I know.'

She picked up the knife again, and moved left. Long strips of splinters had already come out of the wood at that end, so some of the work was done. And now she had a technique. She ferreted around with the knife-point close to the metal, looking for a weakness; then she dug out a few large pieces of wood, and went in for the kill. The third one was the easiest so far, except for the pain, which was excruciating. It ran all the way up to her shoulder joint, and into her neck. Her hand was beginning to feel stupid with numbness. Still, there were only two icons left to move. Surely they weren't beyond her capabilities.

Some instinct made her go back to the middle icon, thinking that she might get lucky. But it was a waste of time. The damn thing was as immovable as it had been previously. She went on to the right of it, and dug around the second of the remaining pair. The wood was just as vulnerable as it had been on the other side, but her numbed muscles were nowhere near as strong now as they'd been a minute ago. She took both hands to the blade, but she wasn't as smart with her left hand as she was with her right, and it added little by way of leverage. Her breath was coming in short gasps, her frustration mounting.

She glanced up at the ghosts, as though the fierceness of their need to be inside would lend her some strength. To her surprise she found that one of them had come forward and crouched down to examine one of the icons. It apparently carried no power now that it was out of its place in line, like a letter lifted from a curse-word, and rendered harmless.

The man was so close to her she could have touched him if she'd raised her hand.

Very quietly, the dead man spoke.

'The bitch is coming,' he said.

Tammy glanced over her shoulder. There was nobody in the passageway behind her, *yet*; but now, nor was there any sound from the kitchen. Still she didn't doubt that what the man had said was true.

She willed her hands to grasp the knife a little harder, and they seemed to oblige her, just a little. She pushed the blade deeper into the wood and the icon shifted. She twisted and felt what was by now a familiar jolt of power from the metalwork. This time it passed through both hands. The icon was spat from the wood, and fell, spinning, on the tiles.

But she had no reason to celebrate. Her hand was now so weak that the knife fell from her grip and clattered on the floor between her knees. There was now no feeling remaining in her right hand; and her left was not going to be much use to her on the remaining icon.

Still, what choice did she have? She picked the knife up in her left hand anyway, and using the numbed wrist of her right, guided it to the hole she'd dug around the central icon. Perhaps if she just wriggled the point of the blade around for long enough, she'd locate a weak spot. She leaned forward, to put the weight of her body into the calculation.

'Come on,' she murmured to it, 'you sonofabitch . . . move for Momma.'

There was a sound behind her. A soft sound. A groan.

She looked back, fearing the worst, and the worst it was.

Todd had swung around the doorjamb coming from the kitchen, his hand clutching his lower belly. There was blood running between his fingers; and blood on his trousers, a lot of it.

'She stabbed me,' he said, his tone one of near disbelief. He kept his eyes fixed on Tammy, as though he couldn't bear to inspect the damage. 'Oh Jesus, she stabbed me.'

He leaned forward, and for a moment Tammy thought he was simply going to fall over. But he reached out and caught hold of the lips of one of the four alcoves carved into the walls of the passageway.

'You have to get out of here,' he said to Tammy.

She got to her feet, ready to help him, but he waved her away.

'Just go! Before she –'

Comes, he would have said. But it was academic. Katya was there already, coming round the corner, the knife in her hand, his blood on it. Todd turned back to look at her.

She was moving at her old, leisurely pace, as though they had all the time in the world to play out the last reel of this tragedy.

Todd reached into the alcove and found an antique pitcher there. His body blocked what he was doing from Katya's view, but even if she'd seen what he was up to, Tammy thought, she would have still kept coming. She had the knife, after all. And more than that, she had the certainty that Todd had nowhere else to go; nowhere to fall, finally, except into her arms; into her knife. That was what the pace of her approach announced: that she expected him to die in her embrace.

Todd grasped the pitcher and swung it round. It caught Katya's shoulder, and shattered, shards of ceramic flying up into her face.

The impact was sufficient to throw her back against the wall, and the knife dropped from her hand, but the effort had used up a significant part of what was left of Todd's energies. He stumbled across the passageway, his arms outstretched, and fell against the opposite wall.

His face was ashen, his teeth clenched – his eyelids lazy with pain.

'Let them in,' he murmured to Tammy. 'What are you waiting for? *Let. Them. In*!'

At the other end of the passageway, Tammy felt Katya's gaze fix on her. A ceramic chip had nicked the skin beneath her eye; a single drop of blood ran down over her flawless cheek. She didn't trouble herself to wipe it away. She simply dropped to her haunches and casually picked up the knife.

Even in the chaos of her thoughts, the symmetry of all this was not lost on Tammy. Two women, each with a knife. And dying between them, the man they'd both loved; or imagined they had.

As Tammy's mother had been fond of saying, when the subject of love had come up in conversation, as it would from time to time: *it'll all end in tears*.

Well, so it had. And more to come, no doubt. Plenty more to come.

She tore her gaze from Katya, picked up the knife with her left hand and guided it with her right back to the assaulted wood around the middle icon.

Again, she leaned into the task, put every pound to work. She twisted the knife to the left. A few small splinters came away. She twisted again, this time to the right, wanting nothing in the world as much as she wanted that sickening jolt through her bones. She could see more of the icon's depth now, embedded in the wood. It went far deeper than the others, she saw. That was why it refused to budge. It wasn't just wider, it was longer.

She glanced up at the ghosts. They'd missed nothing of what was going on in the passageway. Eyes like slits, they'd all come a little closer to the threshold, daring its consequences.

Behind her, Todd said: 'Tammy?'

He was sliding down the wall, his gaze fixed on her. Katya had apparently used the knife on him again, but hadn't lingered to finish him off. She was moving past him, her eyes on Tammy.

'*It'll all end in tears . . .*' Tammy murmured to herself, and then turned one last time to the challenge of the central icon.

For the last time, she threw her weight down upon it, using her weakened left hand and her benumbed right to twist the knife-blade in the groove beneath the metal ridge.

Another two or three small splinters came away.

'*Come on*,' she begged. '*Please God. Move.*'

Katya was right behind her now. She could feel her presence at her back. And of course Tammy was a perfect target, right now, but there wasn't a thing in Hell she could do about that, not if she wanted to keep going, keep pushing, keep hoping the damn thing would –

It moved!

She looked down at the icon, and yes, God love it, the thing had lifted out of the wood a little. Scarcely at all, in truth, but movement was movement.

She twisted again, using what little strength her left hand had. And suddenly the jolt came up out of the icon with such force that it threw her backwards, so that she landed in front of Katya, deposited before her like a sacrificial lamb.

The pain in her hands and her arms was so severe this time that she had difficulty staying conscious.

The image of Katya loomed above her, knife in hand. Blotches of darkness invaded it from the corners of her sight. But she held on by force of will, determined not to lie there passively while Katya leaned over and slit her throat.

'You interesting bitch,' Katya said, raising the knife. She took hold of Tammy's hair, pulling back her head to expose her throat.

But before she could deliver the cut, something else drew her attention. It seemed she had not realized until this moment that all her defences had been breached.

'Jesus Christ,' she said.

596

Weak as she was, Tammy was still capable of feeling a little satisfaction as she saw the look on Katya's face go from murderous intent to puzzlement, and then – very suddenly – to fear.

'What have you done?' she murmured.

Tammy didn't have the energy or the wit for a pithy reply. But she didn't really need one. Events would speak for themselves now.

The door was open and the threshold cleared.

After years of frustration and exile, Katya's long-neglected guests were coming back to reacquaint themselves with the mysteries of the Devil's Country.

PART TEN

AND THE DEAD CAME IN

1

They came almost silently at first, and cautiously, as though even now they suspected Katya had laid some trap to catch them once they were inside the house. But as soon as four or five of them were safely over the threshold, and it became obvious that there were no traps, their silence erupted into a horrid din of triumph, and their caution turned into an ungainly torrent of desperate spirits, all struggling to get through the door at the same time.

Though Tammy's consciousness was still slippery, she had enough strength left to protect her face from the feet of those coming through, rolling herself into a semi-foetal position to avoid the worst.

There were so many revenants, and the door through which they were attempting to pass was so narrow, that impatience soon ignited amongst the crowd. Arguments became physical assaults, as the stronger pushed the weaker aside so they could be the first down the stairs, the first through the door that would take them into the Devil's Country. Tammy had her hands over her face, but between her fingers she saw Katya put up a vain protest against this invasion. She shouted something, but it was lost in the din of triumph and argument. A moment later, she too was lost, as the wave of exiles threw themselves against her and carried her away. This time Tammy *did* hear her, though it was not a word she uttered but a scream, a furious scream.

They were in her dream palace –

These *things*, which had once been her friends, her beautiful friends, the virile and the beautiful deities of a lost Golden Age, reduced by hunger and despair to the filleted, smeared, wasted dregs of humanity now bore her away.

The noises they made as they came – *and came, and came* – were some of the most distressing sounds Tammy had ever heard.

Slaughterhouse shrieks and plague-pit moans, chattering and curses that were more like the din out of a padded cell than anything that should have come from an assembly of once-sophisticated souls.

Finally, however, the noise and the kicking of her body by passing feet, slowed and ceased.

The procession of the dead had passed over the threshold, along the corridor and into the house. It had taken perhaps five minutes to get the entire assembly inside. Now they were gone. The passageway was deserted, except for Tammy and Todd.

Tammy waited another minute or two before gathering the strength to unknot her weary limbs and roll herself over. She gave thanks, as she did so, to her mother, of all people, who had been an unpleasant piece of work (especially in her latter years) but had possessed the constitution of a horse, which Tammy had inherited. Most of the women Tammy knew would not have survived the brutal physical assaults and violations that had punctuated the adventures of her last few days. Thanks to Momma, Tammy had.

She fixed her gaze on Todd, who had apparently also survived both Katya's attack and the revenants' tide.

He was half-sitting, half-slumped, against the wall further down the passageway, staring at the alcove from which he'd grabbed the antique pitcher. His breathing was ragged, but at least he was still alive. It was a short drive to Cedars-Sinai from here, if she could get help to carry him to the car.

She crawled over to him. He was doing nothing to staunch the wounds (Katya had stabbed him at least twice, possibly three times); the blood was pulsing out of him. He saw her coming from the corner of his eye. Very slowly, he turned his head towards her. 'You let them in,' he said.

'Yes. I let them in.'

'You . . . had it planned all along then?'

'Not really. It was Zeffer's idea.'

He made a long, soft moan, as he saw the neatness of this. Zeffer, the first exile from the dream palace; Zeffer, who'd been the bitch-goddess's dog, finally became her undoer. And Tammy, his agent.

'So you were in this together,' he said.

'I'll tell you about it later. Right now we should get out of here.'

He made a very small, very weary shake of his head. 'I don't think . . . I'll be going anywhere anytime soon.

'She meant to kill me. And I'm afraid . . . she has. She knew in the end I'd sided with you. And that meant I'd betrayed her.'

'You didn't –'

'*Yes, I did*. I knew the last thing she wanted was that the ghosts get in.' He shook his head, his eyes sliding closed. 'But I had to. It was the right thing.' He opened his eyes again, and looked down at the blood. 'And her killing me, that was right, too.'

'Christ, no . . .'

'It's all . . . ended up . . . the way it should.'

'Don't say that,' Tammy murmured. 'It's not over yet.' She pushed herself up onto her knees, then grabbed hold of the edge of one of the alcoves, and hauled herself to her feet. The numbness was passing from her hands. Now they simply tingled, as though they'd been trapped under her while she slept.

From outside, she heard the sound of footsteps, and she looked round to see Maxine stumbling up the steps

603

from the garden, in a state of total disarray. In any other circumstance, Tammy might have found the sight funny; Maxine's clothes were torn, her face scratched and grimy. But right now she was just one more victim: of Katya, of the house, of the Canyon.

'My *God*,' she said, seeing Todd sitting there, the blood pooling on the floor. 'What the hell happened?'

'Katya . . .' Tammy said. It was all the explanation she had energy for.

Once over the threshold, Maxine closed the door and locked it, her hands trembling.

'There's *things* out there –'

'Yes, I know.'

'They killed Sawyer.'

For a moment it looked as though she was going to succumb to tears, but she fought them off, and came along the passageway, her expression turning from one of imminent tears to shock.

'Wait . . .' she said. 'Is that *Todd*?'

Was he that unrecognizable? Tammy thought. It seemed he was. In the hours since Maxine had last set eyes on him Todd had taken a hell of a beating. By the sea, by Eppstadt, by Katya. Now he looked like a boxer who'd gone twenty rounds with a man twice his strength: both his eyes puffed up, his lower lip was swollen and jutting, his whole face a mass of colours, bruises old and new, cuts old and new, all spattered with dried mud.

Looking at him afresh, with Maxine's appalled gaze, Tammy realized that she could have shown this poor broken face to a thousand members of the Todd Pickett Appreciation Society and not a single one would have known who they were looking at; and that probably included herself. How far they'd all fallen; the Gods and their admirers both.

'We have to get an ambulance up here,' Maxine said. She bent down to speak to Todd. 'We're getting an ambulance.'

'No,' he said weakly, lifting his hand. 'Stay with me.'

Maxine looked at Tammy, who gave her a small nod. Maxine took hold of Todd's hand.

'What happened to Eppstadt?' Maxine asked.

'Last time I saw him he was in Hell,' Tammy replied.

There was something rather satisfying about being able to say that, even if she didn't really know what they'd all experienced behind that door downstairs. Whatever it was, it was real. Her breast still tingled from the goat-boy's suckling.

'And the woman? Katya?'

'I don't know where she went. But if you'll take care of Todd, I'd like to find out.'

Todd gave his own, misshapen reply to this suggestion. 'Be . . . careful.'

As he spoke he raised his free hand in Tammy's direction. It was impossible to interpret the expression on his face, but the fact that he was afraid for her spoke volumes. And she in her turn was afraid; afraid that if she didn't find some excuse to leave now, she'd be left here watching him die.

She pressed his fingers, and he returned the pressure. 'It's good,' he said. 'Better see. That bitch.'

She nodded, and headed off back down the passageway. As she went she heard Maxine dialling 911 on her portable phone, which had apparently survived the traumas of her journey through the wilderness behind the house.

There was a calamitous din coming from the centre of the house. It sounded as though a hurricane had been loosed down there, and was moving from room to room, getting stronger as its frustration mounted.

Tammy went to the stairwell and stood there for a few moments, letting the tears fall. Why not? Why the hell not? What crazy person *wouldn't* weep, when they'd turned over the rock of the world, and they'd seen what was there, crawling around: the dead, the nearly dead, and the sorrow of every damn thing.

It wasn't just Todd she was weeping for. She was shedding a tear, it seemed, for everyone she'd ever known. For Arnie, for God's sake, who one night had told her how his grandfather, Otis, when he was in his cups, would burn the eight-year-old Arnie's knuckles with cigarettes 'for the fun of it', and how Arnie had said it was good they'd never have children because he was afraid he'd end up doing the same.

For the dead who'd waited outside this insane asylum for so long, waiting for their chance to get back over the threshold, and now they were in, they weren't happy, because what they'd come in search of was gone. That was their noise, she knew, their fury, circling below; their frustration, mounting with every turn.

For Todd, and all the imperfect people who'd loved him because they'd thought he was made of purer stuff than they. All the worshippers who'd sent him messages through her, begging him just to drop them a note, pick up the phone, tell them that he knew they existed.

She'd been one of those people herself, once upon a time.

In a way she'd been the worst of them, in fact, because although she'd got so close to understanding the ways of this grotesque town, and known it was a crock of deceits and stupidities, instead of turning her back on it all, burning Todd's pictures and getting herself a life worth living, she'd let herself become a propagator of the Great Lie. She'd done it in part because it made her feel important. But more because she'd wanted Todd to be the real thing, the dream come true, alive in the same imperfect world she'd lived in, but better than that, dirty, disappointing world. And having once decided to believe that, she had to keep on believing it, because once he fell from grace, there was nothing left to believe in.

It'll all end in tears, as her mother had been wont to say, and Tammy had been distressed by her lack of faith in things; by her calm certainty that everything was bound to sorrow. But in the end she'd been right. Tammy was standing in the creaking, raging ruins of that terrible truth: tears on her own face, shed for just about everything she'd ever known.

She wiped her cheeks, and looked down the stairwell. The last time she'd looked she'd seen Jerry sprawled at the bottom; another one of Katya's victims. But now he was gone. She didn't want to call his name. That risked drawing Katya's attention, if she was in the vicinity, and Tammy had already had enough of her to last several lifetimes.

She ventured cautiously down the stairs, holding the banisters with both hands. The wood reverberated beneath her palms, shaken by the noise of the dead.

About halfway down she felt a rush of icy air erupt from the stairwell, and a heartbeat later a flood of forms returned from the passageway that led to the Devil's Country. The revenants – or at least some of them – were coming back the way they'd come.

Tammy let go of the banister and threw herself against the wall as half a dozen of the phantoms came roaring up the stairs.

'*Gone . . .*' she heard one of them saying, its voice a mournful howl, '*. . . gone . . .*'

More revenants were emerging from the Devil's Country now, all in a similar state of fury. One of them began to dig at the ground at the bottom of the stairs with his bare hands, attacking the boards with such violence they cracked. Then he tore them up, obviously looking for what was already lost.

Tammy stayed glued to the wall, and in that state slid down to the bottom of the flight, to see if she could spot Jerry. Zeffer's body had been shoved aside by the passage of the ghosts, and lay face down in the corner of the stairwell. Looking in the other direction she saw that the door to the Devil's Country was throwing itself open and closed, slamming with such violence that its framework had cracked. So had the plaster overhead. The light had dropped out of its fixture, and was dangling, along with a clod of plaster, from a bare wire, describing a figure of eight in the air as it swung.

It wouldn't have been Tammy's first preference to venture any closer to the slamming door than she'd already come but as she'd left the responsibility of Todd with Maxine, she knew it fell to her to protect Jerry.

The ghosts wouldn't hurt her, she hoped, as long as she didn't get in their way. She'd done nothing to harm them. If anything, she should be their heroine. But in their present state of high frustration she wasn't sure they knew the difference between those who were on their side and those who weren't. They simply wanted to know where their long-awaited paradise had gone. Apparently some of them were certain it had been removed to some other part of the house to trick them: hence this crazy tearing up of the floor, and smashing of the walls. It was here *somewhere*, and they were going to tear up the fabric of the house until they found it.

Two of these berserkers emerged from the room, their faces smears of fury, and raced past her up the stairs. She waited until they'd disappeared and then she went to the door. With the light swinging giddily overhead the passageway pitched like a fun-house ride. She closed her eyes to snatch a much-needed moment of stillness, then opened them, and without waiting for the door to stop its lunatic slamming, she pushed it open and stepped into the space that had once been called the Devil's Country.

Maxine had had occasion to lie to Todd many times over the course of their working life together, but she had never lied more profoundly than when she'd told him – that day she'd announced she was no longer working for him – that there were more like him available on every plane. The image of hordes of potential Todd Picketts just waiting to be picked out of the hopefuls who flew into LAX every hour had been cruel nonsense. Sure, there were always good-lookers in any bunch; sometimes beauties. And sometimes – though very rarely – a beauty had some innate talent. But very few who came to Tinseltown hoping to snatch the brass ring had what the young Todd had possessed: the kind of effortless charm that an entire generation, men and women both, could fall in love with. He'd been that rarest of things: a universal object of desire.

Of course it didn't take much to taint such purity. But Todd had been lucky. Though in private he'd often been sour, envious and scornful, Maxine had successfully kept all that from the fans. Todd's image had remained damn near perfect. His only enemy was time.

And even that, in the end, wouldn't have mattered, if he'd allowed it to take its toll without shame. Look at Paul Newman, practically sainted at seventy. It would have been the same for Todd. People would have loved him as he grew old the way they loved certain songs: because he was part of *who they were*.

Maxine could have said all of this to him on the beach, if she'd been prepared to eat enough humble pie. Her words might have even persuaded him not to go into the water with Katya, and what a lot of grief that would have prevented.

But instead she'd been stupid and let the lie stand. And now they were here at the end of it all, and what had their petty warring earned them? Well, a lot of things she'd have preferred never to have experienced. Being out in the back yard with the ghosts, for one: that had been almost more than her sanity could endure. Seeing Sawyer torn apart that way was a horror she'd never be able to get out of her head. And then to make her way back through the undergrowth while some of his mutilators stalked her, sniffing after her as though they were dogs in heat and she the local bitch. There were no words for the horror of that.

And finally, *this*. Coming back inside the house to find Todd as near dead as made no difference, his face covered in wounds, his body all cut up. The emergency services were on their way, but even if the Canyon had been easy to find, which of course it wasn't, she didn't have much hope that they'd make it in time to help him.

He made a noise, his eyes fluttering.

'Can you hear me, Todd? There's an ambulance on its way.'

For a moment his eyes opened a little wider, and he seemed to be making an effort to concentrate on the face in front of him.

'It's *Maxine*,' she said. 'Remember me?'

There was no recognition in his eyes. His breathing, which had steadily become shallower, was now so shallow she could scarcely see his chest rising and falling.

She dropped her head towards his, and spoke softly into his ear, as if to a child.

'Please don't go,' she said to him. 'You're strong. You don't have to die here if you don't want to.'

He opened his mouth a little; his breath smelt metallic, as though he'd just swallowed a mouthful of old pennies. She thought he intended to tell her something, and put her ear to his lips. His mouth continued to move, but no sound came out, except the wet sounds of his throat and tongue working. She was bent forward for perhaps half a minute, hoping for something from him, but the posture was making her back creak, so she sat up again.

In the fifteen seconds it took her to lift herself up from her bowed position and sit up straight, the man she was tending died.

It was only when she started to speak to him – just repeating his name, in the hope that she might get some response from him – that she realized every trace of animation had gone out of him.

Very tenderly, she put her hand up to Todd's battered face, and touched his cheek. Many times over the years she'd gone on set to find that the makeup people had given him swellings or wounds that had looked grotesquely realistic. But they'd always been 'movie wounds'; however bloody they got – and however much he was supposed to have suffered in their getting – they were never disfiguring. The Todd Pickett whom audiences had come to see, with his blue-green eyes, his dark, lush hair, his symmetry – his smile – none of that was ever spoiled.

But this, lying before her, this was a different spectacle entirely. Once she had closed his eyes, there was nothing left visible of the Todd Pickett the world had loved.

She extricated herself from beneath his corpse with some difficulty. It bothered her to be leaving his body just sprawled here in the passageway in such an undignified manner, but she didn't know what else to do. She needed to find Tammy, Jerry, and a vodka, not necessarily in that order. Anyway, she thought, as she looked down at the corpse, what the hell did Todd care where he was lying? He was gone, hopefully about some better business than the rest of the ghosts who lingered around this damnable house.

The thought of them – of the undeniable *fact* of them, which she'd witnessed just a few minutes before – made her heart quicken. If the dead lived on after their demise, did that mean that Todd's spirit was in the vicinity right now, hovering around before he decided where he was headed?

She could feel herself blushing with self-consciousness, wondering what she'd done in the few minutes since his passing that he might have witnessed. Had she said anything asinine; or let go of some gas, in her nervousness?

Feeling a little foolish, but knowing she couldn't take a step without speaking, she said:

'Todd? Are you here?'

Then she waited, looking around.

A fly had buzzed in from the back yard where the door was now open, and it now landed in the pooling blood between Todd's legs, where it supped eagerly.

She bent down and shooed it away. It rose giddily into the air, as though stupefied by the sheer scale of the feast that lay below. She swatted at it with the back of her hand and, to her surprise, she struck it. Down it went on its back, its buzz suddenly manic, as it careened around on the tiles beside Todd's body.

Had Maxine been a deeper thinker she would perhaps have hesitated to kill the thing. But there'd never been any room for metaphysics in her life, and though she might once have heard in conversation that in some cultures a fly attending on a corpse must be treated reverentially, in case it carried the soul of the deceased, such possibilities were very remote from her way of thinking.

She put her foot down on the upturned fly without a moment's hesitation, and headed back into the kitchen.

2

The tiled room was hazy when Tammy stepped inside. Though the walls were now quite solid – she could see the grout between the tiles, and the cracks on the surfaces of the tiles – there was a dense, cold fog in the place which made deep breathing difficult, and seeing any great distance more difficult still.

The air smelt rank; like a very intense mildew. Apparently one of the illusions the room had been capable of creating was the illusion of smell. There had been the fragrance of greenery in here when she'd last entered; the smell of rain on leaves, and damp earth, and the pungent aroma of horse manure from a dump left by one of the Duke's horses. But apparently all that had been masking the real smell of the place, which was this smothering fungoid stench.

She advanced cautiously, fearful of suddenly encountering somebody in the fog, and not leaving herself time to retreat. She could hear the ghosts now and again; their howls and their complaints strobed through the fog-thickened air, making it hard for her to judge their distance. For safety's sake she kept one of the walls in sight to her left, as a point of reference.

It possessed only a shadow of its former genius for deception. The landscape that had once seemed so real was now reduced to outlines. Even these were not complete. In some places they had deteriorated to near abstractions, in others they'd gone entirely. But then in other places there were still large expanses of paintwork intact, where she could make out the whole visual structure of a picture. In one place there were tufts of grass and small white flowers spreading from the bottom of the walls across the ground, creating the illusion that the visitor was walking over fertile ground. In another, rocks and boulders were strewn about, some cracked open by ambitious shrubs which had settled in their cracks as seeds. And more distantly, here and there she could still see copses and forests, roads and rivers, which cloud-shadows had once passed over most convincingly; and beasts had haunted; and men lived and died in.

The hues of all these fragments of the Country had faded, needless to say, burned away by the unveiled sun. All the richness of the rendering, all the detail of the painters' craft, was lost. What remained was almost as simple as the outlines in a child's colouring book.

Once in a while, as she walked, the fog would become a little thinner overhead, and she'd catch a glimpse of the ceiling. It was in much the same state as the walls and floor. The outlines of cloud formations were still visible, but without the brushwork and colour to lend them life they looked even more abstracted than the landscape: just meaningless shapes.

Only the sun, whose appearance had begun the process of destruction, retained some lifelike qualities. The brightness it shed was sickly however, as though it was blazing too brightly to stay aloft and alight for long, and would soon be consumed by its own fever.

And still she walked, with the wall on her left, certain that she'd soon come to the corner of the room. But the journey went on, and on, much to her astonishment. The room must truly have been enormous, as Zeffer had boasted. She remembered the pride on his face when he'd described how they'd built the room. How the tiles had been numbered so that they could be put up in the exact order he'd found them in. Only now, with the deceptions of the room removed, did she better understand why he'd felt such pride. The achievement had been substantial. Lunatic, but substantial.

Finally, the wall turned a corner, leading away from her, which was a surprise. She began to wonder if this search wasn't becoming foolhardy. How much further should she explore, hugging the wall for security's sake but getting further and further away from the door? Should she take a chance and step out into the dark, featureless fog, hoping her sense of direction would guide her back to the place she'd come from? No, that wasn't sensible. She decided on the more conservative option. She simply turned on her heel and, putting the wall that had been on her left on her right, returned the way she'd come. Her only concession to risk was to venture perhaps six or seven yards from the wall, which put it at the limit of her sight, given the density of the mist. In this manner she proceeded tentatively back the way she'd come.

The trek back to the door was not the uneventful journey the outward bound trip had been. She'd taken perhaps five strides from the turnabout spot when she heard the whooping clamour of ghosts, and a *body* of them – smeared together in their grief, melded, it seemed, into one furious being – appeared from the fog. Their faces were bitter: turned-down mouths and burning, cold blue eyes like the luminous eyes of deep-sea fish.

She'd not been terrified of them at the threshold, but she was terrified now. Not because they would see her and recognize her and blame her for the absence of their consolation, but because they could catch her up in their momentum, and carry her away with them. She instinctively dropped to the ground as they approached, and they moved on past her, wailing and cursing. She heard cracking sounds as they passed by, and when they'd gone she saw that the tiles which they'd passed over had shattered.

She stayed pressed on the ground, while the fog roiled around her, afraid that they'd come back.

They didn't return, thank God; but it was clear that this wasn't a safe place to be. She could hear other packs of ghosts roving around in the fog, making their own terrifying din. The fog, she assumed, had delayed their full realization that this place was a shadow of its former self. That was why some of them kept on searching, hoping that the power they'd fed on in the good old days was still here somewhere. Of course it was not; and by degrees the bitter word was spreading, so that each of the groups searching the room slowly grasped the disastrous truth. And as soon as they did they went crazy.

'Tammy?'

She looked up. Close to the ground the fog thinned somewhat, and she could see twice as far as she could see when standing. And there, at the limit of her vision, lying on the ground like her (and probably for the same reason) was Jerry Brahms.

'Oh thank God . . .'

There was a dark smear on his face, which she guessed was blood. Otherwise, he seemed to be all right. He crawled towards her on his belly, like a soldier under fire. As she approached she saw that the smear was indeed blood, its source the patch of skin which Katya had torn out of his scalp. When he reached her he caught hold of her hand.

'My dear, thank the Lord you're still alive. I feared the worst, I truly did. Somebody let the ghosts in.'

'That was me.'

'In God's name *why*?'

'Because Todd wanted me to,' she said. It wasn't the whole truth, of course, but it was enough for now.

'Where *is* Todd?'

She looked away from him, just for a moment. It was all she needed to do.

'Oh Lord, no. Not my Todd.'

'She stabbed him –'

'Katya stabbed him? Why?'

'It's too complicated . . .'

'Well, later then. Where's Katya now?'

'I think she's in here somewhere.'

'So why did you come down?'

'Why'd you think? To find you.'

'Oh you sweet . . .' He grasped her hand hard.

'Now can we *please* go?' she said.

'Do you know the way to the door?'

She glanced over her shoulder. The wall she'd strayed from was still visible. 'Yes. I think so. Back to the wall. Make a right. And then we follow it until we reach the door, which will be on the left.'

'Very organized.'

'I hope I'm right,' Tammy said. She started to get to her feet. Jerry tried to persuade her back down on the ground.

'I'm too big to be crawling around like this,' she said.

Jerry nodded. 'And you know what? I'm too old,' he said. 'If she sees us, she sees us. Yes?'

He scrambled to his feet, and together they headed back to the relative security of the wall. There were noises from every direction. Some were the by-now-familiar cries of frustrated ghosts; but there were now also sounds of mounting destruction. The revenants were venting their fury by taking the room apart. Tammy could hear them tearing at the walls, bringing down waves of tiles. And after the shrill crash of breaking tiles came the deeper din of wood beams being smashed, timber wrenched from timber with the squeal of unseated nails.

Tammy and Jerry stayed close to the wall; but the air was quickly filling with particles of dust, which suggested the destruction was getting closer to them. It was impossible to tell from which direction: perhaps from all.

'May I?' Tammy said, slipping her hand into Jerry's.

617

'Be my guest.'

The door was in sight now, and though the din was sickening, Tammy dared to think they might get out of this alive, with a little luck.

No sooner had it crossed her mind than there was a massive disturbance in the fog close by – so large a disturbance that the fog actually parted like a pair of drawn drapes.

Tammy dragged Jerry back the way they'd come, two or three steps, no more.

As she did so the ghosts came out of the gaping fog, and flung themselves at the door. They tore at it – and at the wall surrounding it – with such force that part of the ceiling above the door came crashing down. Pieces of shattered tiles, splintered wood and plaster flew in all directions. Tammy and Jerry turned away and shielded their faces. A barrage of shards peppered their backs.

When the noise of the demolition ceased and Tammy looked back, a haze of plaster dust had replaced the fog. She inhaled and it caught in her throat, reducing her to a coughing, tearful mess. Jerry was in the same, or worse, condition.

Tammy spat out a mouthful of the white soot, and wiped her eyes with the heel of her hand. Not the smartest thing to do. She felt plaster particles scrape between her irises and her lids; a new flood of tears came. As she wiped them away she felt Jerry catch hold of her arm, seizing her so hard that she stopped coughing, and blinked the tears out of her eyes to cleanse them. Then she looked round at him.

The ghosts who'd demolished the wall were now tearing at the exposed sub-structure of the wall, reducing it to splinters. But it wasn't the scene of destruction Jerry was looking at. He was staring ahead, back towards the centre of the room.

'She always knew how to make an entrance,' he whispered.

618

Tammy followed his gaze.

The drapes of mist were beginning to close again slowly. But walking up between them, like a diva preparing to take her place centre-stage, and armed for this final scene with the knife she'd used to stab Todd, was Katya Lupi.

'Hello, Tammy,' she said. 'I suppose you thought you were going to get out of here alive. Well you're not. Sorry to disappoint you.'

'Enough's enough, Katya,' Jerry said, doing his best to sound authoritative.

'Oh you know me better than that, Jerry,' Katya replied. 'Enough's never been enough for me.' She looked at Tammy. 'Did he tell you I took his virginity? No? He didn't. Well I did. He was a sad little thirteen year old, with a dick about as big as this.' She waggled her pinkie. 'Do I exaggerate, Jerry?'

Jerry said nothing.

'All that I've done for you, and you're ready to creep away, ready to leave me alone. That's all you men ever do, isn't it? You creep away.'

'Not Todd,' Tammy said. 'Todd wanted to trust you.'

'Shut up. You couldn't possibly understand what was between us.' She pointed the bloody knife at Jerry. 'But you. You understood. You knew how I'd been deserted in the past.'

This was the big scene, Tammy thought; no doubt about that. And she was playing it for all she was worth, as though she could finally be absolved of all she'd done, in the name of deserted womanhood.

'You're pathetic!' Tammy cried. 'Why don't you do something useful with that knife and slit your fucking wrists!'

'Oh no. This isn't the end for me,' Katya replied calmly. 'This is the end for him. And for you –' She poked the knife in Tammy's general direction. 'Your miserable lives are certainly over. But not me. I was always a chameleon. Wasn't I, Jerry? From picture to picture, didn't I *change*?' He didn't reply to her, but she pressed the point, as though she simply sought verification of the truth. '*Well didn't I?*' she said. 'Grant me that much.'

'Yes . . .' he said, as though to silence her.

'So I'll change again. I'll go out into the world and I'll be somebody new. *There's a whole new life, still waiting to be lived.*'

'Not a hope in Hell,' Tammy said.

'What?'

'Let it go, Tammy,' Jerry said.

'Why? She may look like a million dollars but she's just a slice of the same stale ham that she ever was. You know what? I love movies. Even the silent ones. Like *Broken Blossoms*. I love *Broken Blossoms*. It still makes me cry. There's some heart in it. Something real. But your . . . flicks?' She laughed, shaking her head. 'They're dead. You see, that's the paradox. Mary Pickford's gone, and Fairbanks and Barrymore. They're all gone. But they live on because they made people laugh and cry. Whereas you? You're alive, and the shit you made isn't worth a damn.'

'That's not true,' Katya said. 'Jerry, tell her.'

'Yes, Jerry,' Tammy said, quietly. 'Tell her.'

'The truth is that you're not remembered quite as well as I may have –'

'Let's not tell any more lies,' Tammy said grimly. She looked at Katya. 'Nobody knows who the fuck you are.'

Katya looked at Tammy for a moment, and then back to Jerry, who shook his head.

'If they knew,' Tammy said, 'don't you think *somebody* would have recognized you, when you came to get Todd?'

Katya looked down at the cracked floor. She was absolutely still, except for her right hand, which was idly judging the heft of the knife. When she looked up again, her face carried a radiant smile.

'All right. Enough recriminations. We've said our hard words. Now we must begin to forgive.'

Tammy looked at her with incredulity. How many faces did this woman have? 'There's going to be no forgiving here,' she said.

'*Will you shut up,*' Katya snapped, passing her hand over her brow. The smile dropped away for a moment, and there was a terrible vacuity in its place. As though the masks, however many there were, concealed nothing at all.

But she put the smile on again, a little more tentatively, and looked at Jerry.

'I'm in need of your help,' she said. 'Your help and your forgiveness. Please.' She opened her arms. 'Jerry. For old times' sake. I gave you a life. Didn't I? Being up here with me, wasn't it something to live for?'

Jerry took a long time to answer. Then he said: 'You smell of death, Katya.'

'Please. Jerry. Don't be cruel. Yes, I've hurt a lot of people. I realize that. Nobody regrets that necessity more than I do. But right from the beginning, I was trapped. What could I do? Zeffer was the one who brought the Hunt into this house, not me. I knew nothing about it. How can I be blamed for that?'

'I think *they* blame you,' Jerry said, nodding past Katya at the now-stilled fog; or rather, at what it concealed.

At some point in this exchange, the revenants had left off their demolition, their fury momentarily calmed as they listened to Katya's self-justification. Many of them had been physically intertwined earlier, but they had separated themselves from one another, and, shrouded by the fog, listened to the woman play her parts.

622

'They were your guests,' Jerry said to Katya. 'Some of them were great actors.'

'If they were so great, why did they become addicted so easily?'

'So did you,' he reminded her.

'But the room was *mine*. They were just people who just passed through. Yes, some of them were casual friends. Some of them were even casual lovers. But once they were dead? *They were nothing.*'

'I knew you were going to say that eventually,' Tammy said. 'You selfish bitch.'

'*Jesus,*' Katya said. 'I have heard enough of you.'

She lifted her knife and came at Tammy. In two seconds she would have had the blade buried in Tammy's heart, but before she could reach her target somebody stepped out of the mist, and knocked the knife from her hand. It spun on the tiles, but Katya was quick. She ducked down and snatched it up again, her gaze going to the figure who had stepped into her path.

He had opened his arms, as though to formally present himself to her.

'Rudy?' she said.

The man in front of her bowed his gleaming head.

'Katya,' he replied.

Tammy couldn't see his face but she thought there was some sorrow in the syllables; whether for her, or for himself, who could say?

He'd no sooner spoken than from another spot, close to the door, somebody else spoke her name. This second voice was heavier than Valentino's; there was more anger in it than melancholy. 'Remember me?' he said. 'Doug Fairbanks?'

Katya turned. 'Doug? I didn't realize you were here too.'

'And me?' came a third voice, this time a woman.

'Clara?' Katya said.

'Of course.'

The speaker walked up to Katya as she spoke, her stride remarkably confident. She was a shadow of her former self, but Tammy would still have recognized the face of Clara Bow. The bee-stung lips. The high, curved brows. The wide eyes, once filled with innocent high-spirits. But not now. Now they burned.

Katya glanced over her shoulder. 'Please, Clara,' she said. 'Don't come so close.'

'Why should you care how close we get?' Clara Bow said.

'Yes,' came a fourth voice. 'You're not to blame, remember?'

'Anyway,' came a fifth voice, 'we're nothing.'

'Nothing,' said a sixth voice. And a seventh.

Katya turned, swinging her weapon in a wide arc. Even so, it missed its several marks. The ghosts were too quick for her; she was sluggish, even in her fury. Besides, Tammy thought, what possible harm could a kitchen knife do upon these creatures? Yes, they had a corporeal existence; no question of that. But they were – as far as she understood it – spirit presences made of ether and memory. These people couldn't die. They were already dead; long, long dead.

And they were assembling now in even greater numbers, having apparently given up on looking for the Devil's Country.

It was gone; the evidence of which was the fading lines on the walls of this melancholy chamber. All that remained by way of satisfaction, if that was the word, was to punish the woman who had kept them outside in her joyless Canyon for so many seasons, holding on to the hope that they would one day be let back in to the house to satisfy their craving for the solace of their addiction.

Katya was well aware that she was in jeopardy, and hopelessly outnumbered. While still holding the knife she raised both hands in a vague gesture of surrender.

624

The dead seemed not to care. Their pale faces, which had always looked impersonal, were now – in the presence of the woman who had once been their confidante – assembling fragments of forgotten particularities. It was like a room full of Alzheimer's patients, recovering in the presence of some person they'd known well what they'd previously lost: themselves. Their eyes, which had been little more than lights in their heads, took on a specific shape and colour. Their mouths, which had been slits, bloomed into sensuality.

Tammy didn't think any of these reconfigurations were good news for Katya. Unobtrusively, she caught hold of the back of Jerry's shirt, and gently eased him out of Katya's immediate vicinity.

She moved him not a moment too soon.

An instant later one of the ghosts came barrelling out of the mist and caught hold of Katya. Tammy didn't see the attacker's face, but she heard the guttural cry which escaped him as he swung his captive around to face the fog.

Katya struggled, but he had her arms pinned behind her, and despite her considerable strength, he was the stronger.

'*Fuck you, Ramon*!' she screamed.

She made a second attempt to wrest herself free of Novarro's grip, and by sheer vigour succeeded in liberating one of her arms; the one with the knife. She then stabbed wildly at the man who had hold of her: Ramon Novarro. The knife slid into his side, and there it lodged.

Before she could retrieve it he had caught hold of her flailing arm and had pinned it again. Though he had very firm hold of her she still continued to struggle and curse, giving up on English in favour of Romanian. And then, after perhaps thirty seconds of Romanian curses, she gave up completely, and fell silent.

For a moment Tammy thought Novarro had killed her, her silence was so sudden and complete. But – as had always been the case in this house – the truth was not so simple.

The curtain of fog shifted, as though several breezes had pierced it at the same moment. And then, like a troupe of actors appearing to take their final bow, the rest of the revenants began to appear from the mist; four, five, six, seven, eight, ten, twelve –

Their eyes were on Katya; all of them, on Katya.

Now she began to struggle with fresh fervour, her movements chaotic and panicky, like those of a trapped animal. Much to Tammy's surprise, Novarro let her go. She turned on him, instantly, reaching for the knife that was still protruding from his side. But before she could catch hold of it he reached out and grabbed the front of Katya's dress. Then he pulled, tearing the light pink fabric away from her body and exposing her breasts.

The look on her face changed, her fury apparently mellowing. Novarro bent forward and put his face between her breasts.

She let out a light laugh, which was surely artificial, but nevertheless passed for the real thing well enough. He responded by licking the passage of flawless skin up to her throat, wetting it until it shone. Her nipples, aroused by his touch, were hard. Her eyes flickered closed, murmuring something in Romanian; words of appreciation to judge by their tone. Encouraged he moved his mouth down from her throat to her left breast; and as he did so he slipped his arms beneath her legs, and lifted her up.

The ghosts still assembling behind her raised their heads, watching her elevation.

She was laughing for real now, her head thrown back in abandon. Novarro was no longer licking her; he was putting all his effort into lifting her up, higher and higher still, until Katya and her laughter and her shining breasts were above his head.

Katya opened her eyes. The laughter suddenly passed away from her face, as she realized what he'd done. Again, she spoke in Romanian, but this time the words were not so appreciative. Nor did she have long to speak them, before Novarro threw her to the assembled crowd.

She seemed to hang for a long moment in the space between her deliverer's arms and the hands of those who were ready and eager to receive her.

Then she fell.

Down, down into their open arms; down to be caught by her dead, patient friends, who'd waited so very long to enjoy her hospitality again, and had been so bitterly disappointed.

Finally, after all these years – all her cruelties, all her games, all her indifference – *they had her*.

She screamed as they laid their cold hands on her flesh; shrieked like a little girl being violated. They ignored her protests, as she had ignored them over the years.

They pulled her hair, so that it came out at the roots. They ripped at her smooth, sweet flesh, that showed no sign of the toll the years had taken on the rest of the world. They bit off her nipples, they tore off her labia, like shreds of tender meat, and shoved the pieces down her throat to silence her.

Death had not made them kind. Time had not made them kind. Years of sitting in the Canyon – the Santa Anas in one season, rain in another, crucifying heat in another: none of it had made them kind.

They pulled at her as though she was a perfect little doll that they'd been given, and were now fighting over. The trouble was, she wasn't designed for such careless handling. She tore too quickly.

In a matter of seconds what had once been Katya Lupi was a ruin: they broke her arms so that the bones poked through; they tore at her sex so that the gaping, lipless slit ran halfway up her stomach. She had spat out her labia and now attempted to call them by name, to eke out a little mercy.

But they had none to give.

627

They had planned this martyrdom for years; each playing his or her horrid part. Someone got their fingers beneath the skin of her face and worked it off, inch by ghastly inch, leaving only the pinkness of her eyelids in a mass of red muscles. Two others (women, working together in smiling harmony) unseated her breasts from the bone, so that they hung down like sacs of fat, while the blood poured from the wounds where her nipples had been.

And then – perhaps sooner than they'd wanted or planned – her body gave out.

Her shrieks ceased. Her death-dance ceased.

She hung in their arms like something that had once made sense but would never make sense again.

Just to be sure there was no more fun to be had with her, Virginia Maple, who'd been the second victim of the scourge of stars that had begun with the death of Rudolph Valentino, drove her hand into the dead woman's mouth, and with the strength death and hatred had lent her, clawed out a fistful of the woman's brains, which she threw at the tiles.

There it spattered, holding for a moment before sliding to the ground. Meanwhile someone else had gone in through her womb and pulled out her innards, like a magician's coloured handkerchiefs coming one after the other (yellow, purple, red, brown), the coils of her guts, her stomach, and all the rest attached with loose strings of tissue and fat.

Tammy saw it all.

It was a good deal more than she wanted to see; but no less than her eyes could take in. Not once did she look away, though every second that it continued she told herself she should do so, because this was just a common atrocity now. It was nothing to look at, and nothing to be proud of to be looking.

But when it was over, and the ghosts dragged Katya's

disembowelled remains away into the fog, to put to whatever grotesque purpose their anger still demanded, she at least knew that the bitch was finally dead. She voiced that opinion, and of course Jerry – never one to sweeten things unnecessarily – replied:

'Things are never the way you think they'll be in Coldheart Canyon. We'll see how dead she really is.'

When they went upstairs, Maxine was in the kitchen, squatting in the corner with a blank expression on her face. She looked extremely weary, as though the toll of recent events had taken fifteen years off her life. She wouldn't get up, so Jerry went down on his haunches and started to talk quietly to her.

Finally she spoke. She'd had every intention of coming downstairs to help them, she told him, tears streaming down her face, but then the noises started, those *terrible* noises, and she could no longer bring herself to do it. She went on in the same fashion for a while, circling on herself.

'Why don't you try and get her to get up?' Tammy suggested to Jerry. Then she went to pay her respects to Todd.

The Golden Boy was lying where he'd fallen, more or less; looking peaceful, more or less. Eyes closed, mouth open; blood shining on the ground around his head.

During the early years of her infatuation, Tammy had dreams in which she would touch him. There'd been nothing sexual in these touches; or at least nothing explicitly so. Just his being there in an ordinary room, and saying to her, it's okay, you can come over here, you can touch me. That had been the sum of it.

She'd always woken from those dreams with such a profound *yearning* in her heart: a yearning to confirm his existence in her waking world, simply by one day getting the chance to really touch him. Just to know that he wasn't simply a game played with light, but a real thing, of flesh and blood.

Now here she was, and here *he* was, and she could touch him all she liked, but nothing on earth could have persuaded her to do so.

What she'd been looking for in that touch was no longer there to be found. He'd gone, and what remained, as she'd just seen in the room below (yellow, purple, red), was not worth her attention.

She turned from his corpse, fighting the instinct to say goodbye to it, and finally – unable to resist the force of instinct – saying it anyway. Then she returned to the kitchen where she found that Jerry had succeeded in coaxing Maxine to her feet, and was now rummaging in the fridge for something cold for her to drink.

'I'm afraid there's only beer,' he said. 'Oh no, wait. There's some milk here too. You want some milk?'

'Milk,' she said, her eyes suddenly brightening, like a child's eyes. 'Yes. A glass of milk.'

Jerry carefully poured a brimming glass for her, and she drank it down, staring out of the window between gulps. 'As soon as you're ready,' Jerry prompted her, 'we should go. Yes?' She nodded as she drank.

There were new dins from below, suggesting that the ghosts were up to fresh mischief. Nobody wanted to be around when they finally tired of their labours downstairs, and decided to ascend.

'Eppstadt?' Maxine said, her mind apparently sharpened by the milk. 'What happened to Eppstadt?'

'I told you,' Tammy reminded her.

'Oh yes. He's dead, isn't he?'

'Yes, he's dead.'

'And the waiter?'

'Joe?'

'Yes, Joe.'

'He's dead too.'

630

There was a long silence between them then, while Maxine emptied her glass, which gave Tammy an unhappy moment to picture the bodies that were littered around the house. Todd in the hallway, Sawyer somewhere in the garden, Joe the Waiter and Eppstadt in the bowels of the house; and Katya? Many places, by now.

'We should be thankful,' Jerry said.

'For what?' Maxine wanted to know.

'For getting out of here alive.'

'Let's be thankful when we see Sunset Boulevard,' she said, a little of the old Maxine showing, 'not before.'

The noise in the house was still escalating as they left, and when Tammy looked back she saw that there was a crack over the front door, two inches wide, which zigzagged all the way up to the eaves, like a bolt of black lightning.

They got into Tammy's car, and drove down the hill. Maxine's spurt of fortitude gave out halfway down, and she began to cry pitifully, but Tammy was having none of it.

'Shush,' she said, half gently, half not. 'We're not having any of that, you hear? It's over, Maxine. It's over.'

Of course that wasn't strictly true. Her mind turned to the creatures she'd encountered in the Canyon during the night; the children. What would happen to them? And what other perverse miracles had the Devil's Country worked upon the anatomies of those who'd ventured there? She vaguely wondered if perhaps she or Jerry, both of whom had spent some considerable time in that godless place, would have something to show for their presence there. She would have to watch herself closely, at least for a while.

By now they were almost at the bottom of the hill.

'We have to go and report all this to the police,' Tammy said. 'Together.'

'Now?' Maxine said. 'I couldn't possibly.'

'We have to, Maxine. There are bodies up there. We don't want to be accused of murder.'

631

'They're going to think we're all crazy,' Maxine commented.

'Well, that's easily solved,' Jerry said. 'We'll bring them up here, and they can see it all for themselves. That'll change their minds.'

'Suppose they *do* think we're responsible?' Maxine said. 'People like to point fingers in this damn town.'

'Well they won't be pointing any fingers at us,' Tammy said. 'We'll explain.'

'Explain?' Maxine said. 'How the hell will we ever *explain*?'

'We'll start at the beginning and go on until we're done. We've got nothing to hide.'

'There'll be no end to it,' Maxine said. 'Now Todd's dead, the press is going to be all over us. They're going to be digging up every sordid little story about him, whether it's true or not. They'll print any piece of garbage that floats down the sewer. It's going to go on for months. And you think in the middle of all this the truth is going to be heard? Forget it. It's going to be a circus.'

'You don't have to be a part of the circus,' Jerry said. 'None of us do. We can just say no, and walk away. Let them write whatever they want to write. They're going to do it anyway.'

'True enough,' Maxine sighed. 'I just wanted to try and guard his reputation.'

'Maybe if you'd guarded him a little better when he was still around we wouldn't be in this mess,' Tammy said. She caught Maxine's reflection in the mirror; the corners of her mouth turned down in misery. 'I'm sorry,' Tammy said. 'Maybe that was a bit sharp.'

'No,' Maxine replied. 'I let him down. He needed me and I walked in the opposite direction. *Mea culpa.*'

'What does that mean?'

'I'm responsible?' Maxine said. 'And I am. Don't think I don't know it.'

632

Her reply brought an end to the exchange. They drove on in silence until they reached Langley Road, which in turn brought them on to Doheny Drive, and finally down onto Sunset Boulevard.

It was a busy intersection, the lights slow. They had to wait through three changes, creeping closer to the main tide of traffic; but there was a simple contentment for all three in sitting in the car and watching the buses and the messenger bikes and the Beverly Hills' Rolls Royces drive on past. Life going on, in other words, in its usual way. People going east, people going west, all oblivious to the fact that just a short drive from this loud, bright place was a cleft in the rock of the City of Angels which was deep enough to conceal miracles.

PART ELEVEN

THE LAST CHASE

1

News, like a life-form, is divided into orders and classes and kinds. Thus, what was deemed worthy of note on the front page of *Variety* (the grosses of Todd Pickett's last four pictures, the fact that his agent Maxine Frizelle had been present at the death-scene, some sketchy details about the history of the house in the Canyon) was not thought appropriate for the front page of the *LA Times* (the fact that there were multiple bodies at the scene, suggesting some vague connection with the horrors of the Manson Murders; a brief synopsis of Todd's career; elsewhere, an obituary, and elsewhere again a sincere, if hastily edited, appreciation of Pickett's contribution to cinema); none of which was again deemed appropriate for *The National Enquirer*, which put together a special edition centred on the deaths of Todd, Gary Eppstadt and – as they put it – *'the unfortunate, unnamed victims who were pulled down into the same spiral of decadence and death that claimed the Hollywood power-players'*, but padded the issue out with the Old Faithfuls: Haunted Hollywood, The Tragic Deaths of the Young and the Beautiful – Marilyn; James Dean; Jayne Mansfield – *'Doomed Souls Who Paid The Ultimate Price For Fame!'*; and all this gutter journalism of a high order by comparison with the real bottom-feeders, the journalists of *The Globe*, who printed, amongst countless lurid absurdities which they had clearly invented at their editorial meetings, a number of facts that were paradoxically closer to the truth of the events than anything in any other newspaper or magazine. Given their notoriously low standards of veracity, however (*The Globe*'s editors considered crudely-Dred pictures of Pyramids hovering over the Pentagon hard news), the publication of these reports made the truest parts of the story unprintable in any other journal. The facts became tainted by association; poisoned, in fact. If it appeared in *The Globe*, how could it be true?

The only items of the story that appeared in every location were those that were related to the hard facts of death in Tinseltown.

Todd Pickett, everyone agreed, had been on some kind of downward spiral. The cause might be disputed, but the fact that he was no longer the Most Beautiful Man in the World (*People* Cover, Jan. 1993) or the Most Successful Male Star of the Year (ShoWest, five years running), was not. In the eternal game of snakes-and-ladders that was Hollywood, Todd Pickett had done all the climbing he was ever going to do. If he'd survived, it would all have been downhill from here.

There was in fact a widely-held opinion which stated that in dying young – even dying violently – Todd had made the best career move of his life. He'd gone while the going was relatively good; and in a fashion that would assure his name was never forgotten.

'For Todd Pickett fans the world over,' Variety opined, *'today's tragic news brings the curtain down on a stellar career filled with glorious moments of pure cinematic magic. But there must be many of those admirers who are relieved that their hero will never disappoint them again. His run of spectacular successes (many of which were produced by Keever Smotherman, who died less than a year ago), was plainly drawing to an end. All that remained was the sad, and regrettably all-too-common spectacle of a great star eclipsed.'*

638

2

Tammy saw that word everywhere now: *eclipsed*. It sat hidden in otherwise innocent sentences, waiting to mess with her mind. The instant she saw it she was back in the Devil's Country, staring up at the shape of that black moon obscuring the face of the sun. She could feel the contrary winds against her face. She could hear the sound of horses' hooves, or worse, the wailing of Qwaftzefoni.

When that happened, she would have to put down whatever it was she was reading that had concealed the treacherous word and direct her attention back to the real world: the room in which she was sitting, the view through the window, the weight of the flesh on her bones.

Of course, the word wasn't the only trap. Though she'd come back to the house on Elverta Road and valiantly tried to pick up the rhythm of her briefly forsaken life, she knew it would be a long time until the bad times passed away. She'd simply seen too much; and the threads of what she'd seen were intimately woven into the world she'd returned to. Though she'd put all the objects around the house that were connected to Todd (and there were a lot of them) away in the big front bedroom with the rest of her memorabilia, out of sight was not out of mind. She knew she was going to have to deal with all that stuff in a more thorough way before too long; and the prospect weighed heavily upon her.

Meanwhile, she was alone in the house. Just under three weeks after her return to Sacramento, Arnie had announced that he was moving out in order to move in with Maureen Ginnis, a bottle-blonde who worked as a dispatcher at the FedEx offices at the airport. In a way, Tammy was glad. She knew Maureen a little, and she was a nice woman; a better match for Arnie than Tammy had ever been. And having the house to herself – knowing that when she got up in the morning she didn't need to see anybody or speak to anybody if she didn't want to (and there were days, sometimes four or five in a row, when her mood fell into a kind of trough, and she was so sluggish she could barely keep her eyes open; then others when she would turn on the television and some stupid quiz show would make her bawl like a baby) that made the craziness she felt itching inside her a little easier to cope with, because she didn't have to conceal it from anyone. She could just take the phone off the hook, lock the doors, draw the drapes and act like a crazy lady.

She got a bad cold a couple of weeks after Arnie left, and bought up a cabinetful of over-the-counter cold, flu, congestion and expectorant medications. They usually made her feel so dopey that she avoided taking them, but in her present situation it scarcely mattered if she felt half-comatose. Having bought the medicines she dosed herself to the gills with cure-all syrups the colour of fancy French liqueurs, and went to bed in the middle of the afternoon to sweat it out. It was a bad move. She woke about one in the morning from a dream in which she'd been lying in bed with the goat-boy clamped to her breast, suckling noisily. She could smell the meaty sweetness of her breast-milk as it seeped from the corner of his hairy mouth, and heard the long middle nail of his foot catching on the comforter as he jerked around in animal bliss.

With the weird logic of dreams she had very reasonably told Qwaftzefoni that she felt feverish and he would have to stop. She had pulled him off her breast with some difficulty, only to discover that he had hold of her hand, the sharp nail of his thumb pressed hard against the pulsing vein in her wrist as though threatening to pop it at a moment's notice. Then he had guided her palm down to the clammy place beneath the curve of his stomach, where his prodigiously veined prick stuck out from folds of infant fat. She felt a row of tiny objects down the underside of his shaft.

'They're black pearls,' he said, before she asked the question. 'They'll increase your pleasure.'

In her fever-dream, she barely had time to register what the little bastard was proposing before he was climbing up onto her, her tit spurting in his fist as he milked her, her screams going for nothing. In the hellish heat of the room the spilt milk went bad in a heartbeat, souring on the sheets. It stank as if they'd been soaked in vomit, the stench rising around her with physical weight, as though it might smother her.

She had begged for the goat-boy to leave her alone, but he clutched her hand so tight she was afraid he'd break the bones if she didn't obey him. So she had taken hold of his pearl-lined ding-a-ling and proceeded to jerk it.

'You want it over with quickly?' he had said to her.

'Yes . . .' she had sobbed, hoping he'd let her go. Men knew how to do it better than women anyway. Arnie had always turned up his nose at the offer of a hand-job. 'You never do it right. I'd prefer to do it myself.' But there were no easy get-outs here.

'Then stay still!' the goat-boy had said, flipping over backwards, still keeping his grip on her fountaining breast, but relinquishing the enforced masturbation for a grosser game. He was straddling her head now, his thick little legs just long enough to raise the cushy divide of his ass six or seven inches above her nose. The coarse hair on his goaty legs pricked her face. It thickened around his buttocks, and he'd long since given up trying to clean it. The stench made her gag.

'Open your mouth. Put out your tongue.'

641

She could bear it no longer. She reached up and grabbed his balls hard, throwing the little fuck forward, so that he was sprawled on the milk-soaked bed. Then she lifted his tail and started to beat his ass with her palm, for all the world like a mother chiding a monstrous child. He started to sob, and shit, the groove of his buttocks filling up with the turd he would have dumped on her face if he'd had the chance. She was past caring about how dirty her hands were. She just kept beating the little fucker, until he had no more tears left, and he was reduced to hiccups.

No, the hiccups weren't his, they were hers.

Her eyes fluttered open. The fever had broken, and she was alone in a bed that was damp with all the sweat she'd shed, but otherwise sweet-smelling. The cretinous horror she'd brought from the Devil's Country was gone; shit, hair and all.

She got up out of bed and flushed all the medicines down the toilet, determined to let the flu pass from her system of its own accord. She was crazy enough, without the aid of medication.

3

'Jerry.'

'Tammy. My *dear*. Whatever happened to you? I wondered when you were going to call.'

'You could have called me.'

'Well, to be perfectly honest,' he said, 'I didn't want to trouble you. Unlike me, you've got a life to live.'

'Well actually, Arnie left me.'

'Oh, I am sorry.'

'Don't be. It's for the best.'

'You mean it?'

'I mean it. We weren't meant for one another. It just took us a long time to find out. What about you?'

'Well, since we made the news I've been invited out to a few more fancy dinners than I used to be. People are curious. So they wine me and dine me and then they casually interrogate me. I don't mind, really. I've met a lot of people, mostly young men, who have a faintly morbid interest in what went on up in the Canyon, which they pass off as an interest in me. I play along. I mean, why not? At my age, you don't argue. Interest is interest.'

'And what do you tell them?'

'Oh, bits and pieces. I've got quite adept at figuring out who can take what. You know, the ones who say *tell me everything* are the ones who go clammy when they're told –'

'Everything?'

'No. Never everything. I don't think anybody I've met is ready for everything.'

'So how do people respond?'

'Well, they're usually ready for something fairly wild. If they sought me out in the first place it's because they know *something*. They've heard some rumour. Some little piece of gossip. So it keeps the conversation interesting. Now: you. What about you? Have you been sharing our adventures with anybody?'

'No.'

'Nobody?'

'No. Not really.'

'You should, you know. You can't keep it all bottled up. It's not healthy.'

'Jerry, I live in Rio Linda, Sacramento, not Hollywood. If I started spouting off about going to the Devil's Country my neighbours would probably never talk to me again.'

'Would you care? Be honest.'

'Probably not.'

'What about Rooney?'

'Who?' Tammy frowned.

'Rooney. The detective who interviewed us, remember? Over and over.'

'His name was Rooney? I thought it was Peltzer.'

'No, that's one of Maxine's lawyers. Lester Peltzer.'

'Okay. So Peltzer's a lawyer, and Rooney's who?'

'You haven't heard from him? He's the detective at the Beverly Hills Police Department who first talked to us. Have you been checking your messages?'

She hadn't but she said she had.

'Strange,' Jerry said. 'Because he's called me six or seven times, pressing me for details. Then I called the Department, replying to one of his calls, and you know what? He was fired two weeks ago.'

'So why's he calling you?'

'I think the sonofabitch is writing a book.'

'About what happened to us?'

'I guess we'll find that out when it's published.'

'He can do that?'

'Maybe he'll change the names. I don't know.'

'But it's *our* story. He can't go round telling our story.'

'Maybe we should all talk to Peltzer and see if we can stop him.'

'Oh God,' Tammy said softly. 'Life used to be so simple.'

'Are you having a hard time?' Jerry said.

'Yeah. I guess. No, what am I saying? I'm having a horrible time. Really bad dreams.'

'Is that it? Dreams? Or is there more?'

She thought about her reply for a moment, wondering if she should share the problems she'd been having, with him. But what was the point? Though they'd been through hell together she didn't really know him all that well. How did she know he wasn't planning to write a book too? So she said: 'You know all things considered, I'm doing just fine.'

'Well that's good,' Jerry said, sounding genuinely pleased. 'Have the reporters stopped bothering you?'

'Oh I still get the occasional journalist on the doorstep, but I had one of those little spy-hole things put in the door, and if I think he looks like a reporter then I just don't open the door.'

'Just as long as you're not a prisoner in your own house.'

'Oh Lord, no,' she lied.

'Good.'

'Well . . . I should let you go. I've got a thousand –'

'One other thing.'

'Yes.'

'This is going to sound a little wacko.'

'Oh. Okay.'

'But I wanted to tell you about it. Just . . . for old times' sake, I suppose.'

645

'I'm listening.'

'You know we never really discussed what happened to us in the house.'

'No. Well I figured we all *knew* –'

'I didn't really mean what happened to *everybody*. I meant you and me, down in that room. You know that there was a lot of *power* in those tiles. Visiting the Devil's Country kept Katya looking perfect all those years . . .'

'What are you getting to?'

'As I said, it's going to sound wacko, but I guess we're both used to that by now, yes?' He took a deep breath. 'You see, I had prostate cancer; inoperable. The Drs gave me nine months to a year to live. That was December of last year. Christmas Eve, actually.'

'God, Jerry, I'm so sorry.'

'No, Tammy, you're not listening. I said, I *had* a tumour.'

'What?'

'It's gone.'

'Completely?'

'Every detectable trace. Gone. The Drs can't believe it. They've done the scan five times to be absolutely sure. And now – finally – they are absolutely sure. Jerry Brahms' brain tumour has disappeared, and according to them that simply can't happen. Ever.'

'But it has.'

'It has.'

'And you think it's got something to do with us being in the room?'

'Put it this way: I went *into* that house with a malignant tumour, and when I came out again the tumour had gone. What can you say about a thing like that? It's either a coincidence or it's a miracle.'

'And you think it's a miracle?'

'You know what?' He paused. 'Now I *am* going to sound wacko, but I prefer to think of it as Katya's last present to me.'

'She didn't seem the gift-giving type.'

'You only saw the darkness, Tammy. There was another side to her. I think there always is, don't you? There's always some light in the darkness, somewhere.'

'Is there?' Tammy replied. 'I guess I'm still looking.'

4

Tammy desperately wanted to believe that she had indeed profited somehow from the madness-inducing journey she'd taken through the wilds of Coldheart Canyon. She didn't need anything as monumental as Jerry's healed tumour; just some modest sign to prove to her that, despite all the death and the suffering she'd witnessed, some palpable good had come of it.

Every waking hour her thoughts circled on what she'd experienced, looking for some sign of hope. Not miracles, just hope. A light in the darkness; a reason to live. But the more she searched, the more absurd the search seemed to be.

Common sense told her she should venture out into the world and start trying to live a normal life again. Perhaps if she joined a couple of women's clubs, or maybe even tried to find herself a lover – anything to change her focus; get her out of her head and back into a normal way of thinking. But she always found some reason to put off anything too adventurous. It was almost as though she'd used up her capacity for adventure during her time in the Canyon. Her trips into the dangerous territory over her front door step became briefer and briefer by the day. She started to get panicky when she got into her car, and the panic escalated so quickly that by the time she got to the end of the block she often had to turn round and head straight back home again. Going to the market had become impossible; she took to ordering essential food-stuffs by phone, and when the supplies arrived she'd make the exchange with the delivery guy as short as possible. She'd just take the stuff, pass over the money, and close the door, often not even waiting for the change.

She realized that this odd behaviour was beginning to get her a reputation around the neighbourhood. More than once she peeped out between the closed drapes and saw that people were lingering outside her house, some on the sidewalk, some in cars, pointing or staring. She'd become, she supposed, the local eccentric; the woman who'd come back from the wilds of Hollywood in a state of mental derangement.

All of this, of course, only added to her spiralling sense of anxiety, mingled with more than a touch of paranoia. If she answered the door to the delivery boy and caught sight of somebody in the street outside she naturally assumed the passer-by was spying on her. At night she heard noises on the roof and woke more than once certain that one of Katya's *los niños* had found its way to Rio Linda and was scrambling over the eaves, trying to get down to her bedroom window.

In saner moments (which became fewer and fewer), she knew all this was nonsense. But the very fact that she *had* saner moments implied that she was slowly giving herself up to lunacy. It was all very fine for Jerry Brahms to talk about having his cancer cured by the power of the room (and maybe he had; she didn't discount the possibility), but she felt as though whatever *she'd* been given in the Devil's Country it was affecting her mind not her body, and it was not doing anything *remotely* healing. Quite the reverse. It was deconstructing her grip on reality, piece by piece. Some days when she woke the dreams remained attached to her all day like pieces of lint. She'd go through her waking hours in a half-stupefied state, coming into rooms and not knowing why she was there; leaving them again and remembering, then forgetting as she turned round. She

649

was in a constant state of exhaustion. Her lids were like lead. Once, in the middle of the day, she found herself on her hands and knees in the bathroom, working at the tiles with her bare hands and Ajax, attempting to remove some spidery sketches of a certain country that she'd day-dreamed into creation. Another time, she'd gone into the kitchen to find the faucet running, and a shape in the sink that looked like a piece of road-kill; a matted pelt, two rows of sharpened teeth set between black leathery lips. The force of the hot water slowly turned the cadaver over and showed her the broken head of something she'd seen in the Canyon, or in her dreams of the Canyon, foul beyond words.

She turned off the faucet. Steam rose from the mouth of the thing, like a last breath. Then it melted, fur and teeth and all, and was gone down the plug-hole.

'Hmm,' she said to herself, unimpressed by this ugly little show. Somehow she'd always imagined madness to be a more dramatic thing than this. Again the movies had it wrong. There was no grandeur in it; no exquisite folly. Just a pile of teeth and dirty fur in the kitchen sink.

That said, she knew that her mental decline was gathering speed. She needed to do something about it soon, or this journey she was taking was going to take her away from herself completely. She would be a blank-eyed thing sitting at the kitchen table, wiped clean by banalities.

5

While Jerry was giving thanks for his new life, and Tammy was dealing with the grim illusions in her kitchen sink, Maxine was in a very different frame of mind. Her injuries were remarkably slight, given all that she'd gone through. Within a week she was physically ready to return to her offices and attempt to pick up business. But most of the calls she got in the first week weren't business calls at all but gently inquiring conversations that rapidly gave way to interrogation. It seemed as though everyone in Hollywood wanted to know about events at the house in Coldheart Canyon.

In truth, she had no desire to tell her story to anyone, not even her closest friends. Ghosts and rooms laid with tiles providing visions of another world – this was not the stuff she could have shared with any of her contemporaries without being mocked. But she had to say something, or she was going to start making even more enemies than she already had. So she concocted a version of events without supernatural elements. In the censored version, Todd had indeed been hiding away because of work done to his face (it was no use lying about that any longer: he'd admitted to the surgery at her party), and there he'd been stalked and finally – sadly – murdered by his stalker. Most of the people she talked to accepted this bowdlerized version of events, at least for the duration of the conversation. But those few loyal sources she still had around town reported something very different back to her. Everyone had their own version of what had happened in Coldheart Canyon, ranging from the ludicrous to the actionable, and they were spreading it around freely. Whatever the version of the story – and they ranged from murder mystery to ghost-stories – they had this in common: Maxine was the villain.

She was to blame for knowingly putting her innocent client in a house that was haunted; she was to blame for not warning him that a close friend was a murderer (this version had started in *The Enquirer*, and required another star as murderer. *The Enquirer*, of course, claimed to know who it was, and would soon be in a position to reveal the name of the guilty party. What they could already say with confidence was that Maxine Frizelle had known of the plan against Todd's life, but simply hadn't taken it seriously). She, in short, was the reason he was dead. It seemed that nothing she could say or do persuaded people that this wasn't the case. Years of resentment towards her surfaced now as her enemies elaborated version after version of what had gone on in the Canyon, each one less flattering to Maxine than the one before.

She eventually gave up attempting to put people straight on such matters. People would believe what the hell they wanted to anyway. She'd learned that after twenty-two years in the business. You could sometimes guide people's opinions, but if they didn't want to buy what you had to sell you could shout yourself hoarse trying to make them do it and it would never work.

After a few days of fruitless endeavour she became curiously immune to all the gossip flying around, and just got on with trying to get to see some new talent. She was an agent without a major client, which meant that as far as the town was concerned there was no reason to take her calls, especially as she wasn't playing ball and offering up the inside scoop on what a psychic hired by the Fox Channel to wander round the Canyon called '*the most haunted piece of real estate in Hollywood.*'

In other words, everybody knew there was more to this – a lot more than they had been told so far – and it was only a matter of time before somebody started to talk.

That somebody was Patrick Rooney, the detective at the Beverly Hills Police Department who'd done the initial work on the Pickett case. At fifty-eight he was very close to retirement, and was looking at a life on a middle-ranking detective's pension. Life would not be lush, he knew. Although he didn't have an expensive life-style he had all the normal outgoings: alimony, a mortgage, car payments (he ran three cars, one of his few concessions to self-indulgence), plus a well-stocked bar and a habit of smoking between forty and fifty cigarettes a day. He'd already calculated the dip in his standard of living he'd have to take when he left the force. It was going to be substantial.

But here – dropping into his lap like a gift from God – was the answer to all his problems. He'd been told the story first by the Lauper woman, and later by Maxine Frizelle. Though their accounts had been outlandish, to say the least, they had also been remarkably consistent. Something weird had happened up in the Canyon and whether it was true in part or not at all scarcely mattered. What mattered to Rooney was that people loved this kind of thing. There was profit to be made here. Enough to make his retirement look a lot more cosy.

He began to make surreptitious copies of the interviews and smuggle them out of the station, with an eye to assembling them all into book form. It wasn't hard to do; if he asked for copies of a record in order to advance some particular aspect of the case then nobody challenged the request. In a short time he had amassed at home eleven bulging files of material on the 'Canyon' case: enough to start editing and collating.

What he needed was a point of view, other than his own. After all, he wasn't at the heart of all this: he was simply an onlooker, coming in after the drama was over. What his book needed was an insider whose story would become its backbone. He decided to approach Maxine Frizelle.

'You want to do what?'

'I'm going to write a book about events in Coldheart Canyon, as everyone insists on calling it. I was hoping I could count on your involvement. Your point of view, Miss Frizelle, would make the book a good deal stronger.'

'You've had all the facts you're going to get from me, Detective.'

'Wait, *wait*!' Rooney said. 'Before you put the phone down on me, think about it. Todd Pickett was your client for how long?'

'Eleven years.'

'So think of this as your chance to set the record straight once and for all. The good, the bad and the ugly.'

'If I were ever to choose to set the record straight, Mr Rooney, it would not be with a cop as a co-author.'

'Oh, I wasn't going to *write* any of this. I was going to get a ghost-writer in to do that.'

'Then I'm really missing something here, Rooney,' Maxine said, summoning up her most withering tone. 'What exactly *is* your contribution to this project?'

'My experience of almost four decades in the LAPD. I worked on the Manson case –'

'This is *nothing* like Manson. Not remotely –'

'Will you let me finish? I'm not saying the cases are identical. But we still have a lot of parallels. The brutal deaths of several high-profile Hollywood people, all with some connection to the occult.'

'Todd never had anything to do with that kind of thing. And you can quote me.'

'Well somebody in that house did. I have copies of photographs of every inch of the place. There are occult symbols hammered into all the thresholds, did you know

654

that? Several symbols – probably East European in origin – were removed from the area around the back door around the time Mr Pickett died. He may even have been responsible for their removal. Do you have any comment to make about any of that?'

'Yes. It's preposterous. And if you try to tie Todd to any of that kind of stuff you're going to be in deep trouble.'

'That's a risk I'm willing to take. But I *am* going to write the book, Ms Frizelle, with or without your assistance.'

'I doubt you can do that, Rooney. You got that information because you were a cop. You can't go using it to make money.'

'I wouldn't be the first and I won't be the last,' Rooney said. 'Frankly, I don't see what the hell your problem is, unless you were planning to do it yourself. Is that it? Am I rainin' on your parade here?'

'No. I have no intention of writing my own version of events.'

'Then help me do mine,' Rooney said, his tone perfectly reasonable. 'I'll throw a piece of the action your way if that's what this is about. How does five percent sound?'

'Don't make this any worse than it already is. I don't want your blood money. Have a little decency, for God's sake. Todd is dead. So are a lot of other people. This isn't the time to be thinking about making a profit.'

'I'm not going to do a hatchet job on him. I swear. Your ex-client's reputation is perfectly safe with me. Okay, so I hear he did a few drugs. A lot of coke, I hear, especially when he worked with Smotherman. And the plastic surgery. Again, no big deal. I mean, I'll have to write about it, but I won't make him look bad. I promise you.'

'Why the hell would I rely on your promises, Rooney?'

There was a brief silence.

'So that's a no?' Rooney finally said.

'Yes. That's a big, fat no.'

'Well, don't say I didn't ask.'

'And for the record, Mr Rooney, let me say this: if you *do* want to try and write this book, you go ahead and try. I promise you will have so many lawyers crawling up your ass you'll think they're breeding up there.'

'Very nice. Very ladylike.'

'Nobody ever mistook me for a lady, Rooney. Now get the hell off my phone. I need to call my lawyer.'

6

The call from Rooney stirred Maxine up. She contacted her lawyer, Lester Peltzer, as she said she would, and organized a conference call with several other lawyers in town whom she respected, so that everyone could give her the benefit of their very expensive opinion. Unfortunately, they all agreed on one thing: she didn't have a hope in hell of stopping Rooney going ahead. When the book was written and being set for publication, that was a different matter, one of the lawyers pointed out. If he wrote something libellous, then they could go after him, and if it was obvious that he'd got access to police files then LAPD Internal Affairs might get riled up and take him to court. But there was no guarantee. The LAPD had a lousy record when it came to policing themselves.

'So right now he's free to say whatever he wants to say?' Maxine raged. 'Just for profit?'

'It's the Constitution,' one of the lawyers pointed out.

'It's not against the law,' Maxine's lawyer pointed out lightly. 'You've made a good deal of money yourself over the years.'

'But I didn't *lie* to do it, Lester.'

'All right, Maxine, don't get your blood pressure up. I'm merely pointing out that this is America. We live and die by the rule of Mammon.' He drew a deep breath; put on his most rational tone. 'Maxine, ask yourself whether taking this guy to court over some book that'll be off the shelves in two, three months is worth your time and temper. You may end up giving him more publicity by suing him than he would ever have got if you hadn't. You'll make an issue of it and suddenly everybody's buying his damn book. I've seen it happen so many times . . .'

'So you're saying I should let him do it?' Maxine said. 'Let him write some shit about Todd –'

'Wait, wait,' Lester said. 'In the first place, you don't know he's going to write shit. Maybe he'll be respectful. Todd was a very popular actor. An American icon for a while.'

'So was Elvis,' Maxine pointed out. 'It doesn't mean some sonofabitch didn't write about every dirty little secret Elvis ever had. I know, because I read the book.'

'So what are you afraid of?'

'That the same will happen to Todd. People will write bullshit, and in the end it'll be the bullshit that's remembered, not the work.'

Lester was usually quick with an answer, but this silenced him. Finally, he said: 'Okay, let me ask you something. Do you think there's anything Rooney knows – as a matter of *fact* – which could be really destructive to Todd's long-term reputation?'

'Yes. I do. I think –'

'Don't,' Lester said. 'Please. Don't tell me. Right now, I think it might be simpler for everyone if I didn't know.'

'All right.'

'Let's all go away and think about this, Maxine. And you do the same thing. I can see your concern. You've got a legacy here you want to protect. I think the question is – do you do that best by drawing attention to Rooney with a lawsuit, or by letting him publish and be damned?'

The phrase caught Maxine's attention. She'd heard it before, of course. But now it had new gravity, new meaning. She pictured Rooney publishing his book, and then having his soul dragged away to the Devil's Country for his troubles.

'Publish and be damned?' she said. 'You know, *that* I could maybe live with.'

Tammy hadn't seen a human face, real or televised, in four days; not even heard a voice. The Jacksons, her next-door neighbours, had gone off for a long weekend the previous Thursday, noisily departing with the kids yelling and car doors being slammed. Now it was Sunday. The street was always quiet on Sunday, but today it was particularly quiet. She couldn't even hear the buzzing of a lawn-mower. It was as though the outside world had disappeared.

She sat in the darkness, and let the images that had been haunting her for so long tumble over and over in her head, like filthy clothes in a washing machine, over and over, in a gruel of grey-grimy water; the madness she'd seen and heard and smelled; over and over. The trouble was, the more she turned it all over, the dirtier the washing became, as if the water had steadily turned from grey to black, and now when she got up to go to the bathroom, or to climb the stairs, she could hear it sloshing around between her ears, the muck of these terrible memories, darkening with repetition.

So this was what it was like to be crazy, she thought. Sitting in the darkness, listening to the silence while you turned things over in your mind, going to the kitchen sometimes and staring into the fridge until she'd seen everything that was in there, the rotted things and the unrotted things, then closing it again without cleaning it out; and going upstairs and washing the bathroom floor then going to lie down and sleeping ten, twelve, fourteen hours straight through, not even waking to empty your bladder. This is what it was. And if it didn't go away soon, she was going to be a permanent part of the madness; just another rag turning in the darkness, indistinguishable from the things she'd worn.

Over and over and –

The telephone rang. Its noise was so loud she jumped up from the chair in which she was sitting and tears sprang into her eyes. Absurd, to be made to weep by the sudden sound of a telephone! But the tears came pouring down, whether she thought she was ridiculous for shedding them or not.

She had unplugged the answering machine a while ago (there'd been too many messages, mostly from journalists) so now the phone just kept on ringing. Eventually she picked it up, more to stop the din than because she really wanted to speak to anyone. She didn't. In fact she was perfectly ready to pick up the receiver and just put it straight down again, but she caught the sound of the woman at the other end of the line, saying her name. She hesitated. Put the receiver up to her ear, a little tentatively.

'Tammy, are you there?' a voice said. Still Tammy didn't break her silence. 'I know there's somebody on the line,' the woman went on. 'Will you just tell me, is this Tammy Lauper's house?'

'No,' Tammy said, surprised the sound her own voice made when it finally came out. Then she put the receiver down.

It would ring again, she knew. It was Maxine Frizelle, and Maxine wasn't the kind of woman who gave up easily.

Tammy stared at the phone, trying to will the damn thing from ringing. For a few seconds she thought she'd succeeded. Then the ringing started again.

'Go away,' Tammy said, without picking up the receiver. The syllables sounded like gravel being shaken in a coarse sieve. The telephone continued to ring. '*Please* go away,' she said.

She closed her eyes and tried to think of the order in which she would need to put the words if she were to pick up the receiver and speak to Maxine, but her mind was too much of a mess. It was better not to even risk the conversation, if all Maxine was going to hear in

Tammy's replies was the darkness churning around in her washing-machine of a head.

All she had to do was to wait a while, for God's sake. The telephone would stop its din eventually. Maybe five more rings. Maybe four. Maybe three –

At the last moment some deep-seated instinct for self-preservation made her reach down and pick up the receiver.

'Hello,' she said.

'*Tammy*? That *is* you, isn't it?'

'Maxine. Yes. It's me.'

'Good God. You sound *terrible*. Are you sick?'

'I've had the flu. Really badly. I still haven't got rid of it.'

'Was that you when I called two minutes ago? I called two minutes ago. It was you, wasn't it?'

'Yes it was. I'm sorry. I'd just woken up and as I say, I've been so sick . . .'

'Well you sound it,' Maxine said, in her matter-of-fact manner. 'Look. I need to talk to you urgently.'

'Not today. I can't. I'm sorry, Maxine.'

'This really can't wait, Tammy. All you have to do is listen. The flu didn't make you deaf, did it?'

This drew a silent smile from Tammy; her first in days. Same old Maxine: subtle as a sledgehammer. 'Okay,' Tammy said, 'I'm listening.'

She was surprised at how much easier it was to talk once you got started. And she had the comfort that she was talking to Maxine. All she'd have to do, as Maxine had said, was listen.

'Do you remember that asshole, Rooney?'

'Vaguely.'

'You don't sound very sure. He was the detective we talked to when we first went to the police. You remember him now? Round face, no hair. Wore too much cologne.'

For some peculiar reason it was the memory of the

cologne, which had been sickly-sweet, which brought Rooney to mind.

'Now I remember,' she said.

'Well he's been on to me. Did he call you?'

'No.'

'Sonofabitch.'

'Why's he a sonofabitch?'

'Because the fuckhead's got me all stirred up, just when I was beginning to put my thoughts in order.'

Much to Tammy's surprise, she heard a measure of desperation in Maxine's voice. She knew what it was because it was an echo of the very thing she heard in herself, night and day, awake and dreaming. Could it be that she actually had something in common with this woman, whom she'd despised for so many years? That was a surprise to say the least.

'What did the sonofabitch want?' she found herself asking. There was a second surprise here. Her mouth put the words in a perfectly sensible order without her having to labour over it.

'He *claims* he's writing a book. Can you believe the audacity of the creep –'

'You know, I *did* know about this,' Tammy said.

'So he talked to you.'

'He didn't, but Jerry Brahms did.' The conversation with Jerry came back to her remotely, as though it had happened several months ago.

'Oh good,' Maxine said, 'so you're up to speed. I've got a bunch of lawyers together to find out if he can do this, and it turns out – guess what? – he can. He can write what the hell he likes about any of us. We can sue of course but that'll just –'

'– give him more publicity.'

'That's exactly what Peltzer said. He said the book would last two months on the shelves, three at the outside, then it would be forgotten.'

662

'He's probably right. Anyway, Rooney's not going to get any help from me.'

'That's not going to stop him, of course.'

'I know,' Tammy said, 'but frankly –'

'You don't give a damn.'

'Right.'

There was a pause. It seemed the conversation was almost at an end. Then, rather quietly, Maxine said: 'Have you had any thoughts at all about going back up to the Canyon?'

There was a second pause, twice, three times the length of the first, at the end of which Tammy suddenly found herself saying: '*Of course.*'

It felt more like an admission of guilt than a straightforward reply. And what was more, it wasn't something she'd consciously been thinking about. But apparently somewhere in the recesses of her churned-up head she'd actually contemplated returning to the house.

'I have too,' Maxine confessed. 'I know it's ridiculous. After everything that happened up there.'

'Yes . . . it's ridiculous.'

'But it feels like . . .'

'Unfinished business,' Tammy prompted.

'Yes. Precisely. Jesus, why didn't I have the wit to call you earlier? I *knew* you'd understand. *Unfinished business*. That's exactly what it is.'

The real meat of this exchange suddenly became clear to Tammy. She wasn't the only one who was having a bad time. So was Maxine. Of all people, Maxine, who'd always struck Tammy as one of the most capable, self-confident and unspookable women in America. It was profoundly reassuring.

'The thing is,' Maxine went on, 'I don't particularly want to go up there alone.'

'I'm not even sure I'm ready.'

'Me neither. But frankly, the longer we leave it the worse

663

it's going to get. And it's bad, isn't it?'

'Yes . . .' Tammy said, finally letting her own despair flood into her words. 'It's worse than bad. It's terrible, Maxine. It's just . . . words can't describe it.'

'You sound the way I look,' Maxine replied. 'I'm seeing a therapist four times a week and I'm drinking like a fish, but none of it's doing any good.'

'I'm just avoiding everybody.'

'Does that help?' Maxine wanted to know.

'No. Not really.'

'So we're both in a bad way. What do we do about it? I realize we're not at all alike, Tammy. God knows I can be a bitch. Then when I met Katya – when I saw what kind of woman I could turn into – that frightened me. I thought: *fuck*, that could be me.'

'You were protecting him. You know, in a way, we both were.'

'I suppose that's right. The question is: have we finished, or is there more to do?'

Tammy let out a low moan. 'Do you mean what I think you mean?' she said.

'That depends what you think I mean.'

'That you think he's still up there in the Canyon? Lost.'

'Christ, I don't know. All I know is I can't get him out of my head.' She drew a deep breath, then let the whole, bitter truth out. 'For some stupid reason I think he still needs us.'

'Don't say that.'

'Maybe it's not *us*,' Maxine said. 'Maybe it's you. He had a lot of feeling for you, you know.'

'If that's you trying to talk me into going back to the Canyon, it's not going to work.'

'So I take it you won't come?'

'I didn't say that.'

'Well make up your mind one way or another,' Maxine

664

replied, exhibiting a little of the impatience which had been happily absent from their exchange thus far. 'Do you want to come with me or not?'

The conversation was making Tammy a little weary now. She hadn't spoken to anybody at such length for several weeks, and the chat – welcome as it was – was taking its toll.

Did she want to go back to the Canyon or not? The question was plain enough. But the answer was a minefield. On the one hand, she could scarcely think of any place on earth she wanted to go *less*. She'd been jubilant when she'd driven away from it with Maxine and Jerry; she'd felt as though she'd escaped a death-sentence by a hair's-breadth. Why in God's name would it make any sense to go back there now?

On the other hand, there was the issue she herself had raised: that of unfinished business. If there was something up there that remained to be done then maybe it was best to get up there and do it. She'd been hiding away from that knowledge for the last several weeks, churning her fears over and over, trying to pretend it was all over. But Maxine had called her bluff. Maybe they'd called each other's: admitted together what they could not have confessed to apart.

'All right,' she said finally.

'All right, what?'

'I'll go with you.'

Maxine breathed an audible sigh of relief. 'Oh, thank God for that. I was afraid you were going to freak out on me and I was going to have to go up there on my own.'

'When were you planning to do this?'

'Is tomorrow too soon?' Maxine said. 'You come to my office and we'll go from there?'

'Are you going to ask Jerry to come with us?'

'He's gone,' Maxine replied.

'Jerry's dead?'

665

'No, Key West. He's sold his apartment and moved, all in a week. Life's too short, he said.'

'So it's just the two of us.'

'It's just the two of us. And whatever we find up there.'

7

On several occasions in the next twelve hours Tammy's resolve almost failed her and she thought about calling and telling Maxine that she wouldn't be coming to Los Angeles after all, but though her courage was weak it didn't go belly up. In fact she arrived at Maxine's office twenty minutes earlier than they'd arranged, catching Maxine in an uncharacteristic state of disarray, her hair uncombed, her face without blush or lipstick.

She'd lost weight; shed perhaps fifteen pounds courtesy of the Canyon. So had Tammy. Every cloud had a silver lining.

'You look better than you sounded,' Maxine said. 'When we first started talking I thought you were dying.'

'So did I, on and off.'

'It was that bad, huh?'

'I locked myself in my house. Didn't talk to anyone. Did you talk to anybody?'

'I tried. But all people wanted to know about was the morbid stuff. I tell you, there's a lot of people who I thought were friends of mine who showed their true colours over this. People I thought cared about Todd, who were about as crass as you can get. "Was there a lot of blood?" That kind of thing.'

'Maybe I did the right thing, locking myself away.'

'It's certainly given me a new perspective on people. They like to talk about death: as long as it's not theirs.'

Tammy took a look around the office while they chatted.

It was very dark, very masculine: antique European furniture, Persian rugs. On the walls, photographs of Maxine in the company of the powerful and the famous: Maxine with Todd at the opening of several of his movies, Maxine with Clinton and Gore at a Democratic fundraiser, when the President-elect still had colour in his hair, and a reputation to lose; Maxine with a number of A-list stars, some of whom had fallen from the firmament since the pictures had been taken: Cruise, Van Damme, Costner, Demi Moore, Michael Douglas (looking very morose for some reason), Mel Gibson, Anjelica Huston, Denzel Washington and Bette Midler. And on the sideboard, in Art Nouveau silver frames, a collection of pictures which Maxine obviously valued more highly than the rest. One in particular caught Tammy's eye: in it Todd was standing along side a very sour, very old woman who was ostentatiously smoking a cigarette.

'Is that Bette Davis?'

'Five months before she died. My first boss, Lew Wasserman, used to represent her.'

'Was she ever up in the Canyon, do you think?'

'No, I don't think Bette's ghost is up there. She had her own circle. All the great divas did. And they were more or less mutually exclusive. At a guess a lot of Katya's friends had an interest in the occult. I know Valentino did. That's what took them up there at the beginning. She probably introduced them to it all very slowly. Maybe tarot cards or a ouija board. Checking out which ones were in it for the cheap thrills and which ones would go the distance with it.'

'Clever.'

'Oh she was clever. You can never take that away from her. Right in the middle of this *man's* city, where all the studio had men at the top, she had her own little dominion, and God knows how many people wrapped around her little finger.'

'It sounds like you admire her a bit.'

'Well I do. I mean she'd broken every commandment, and she didn't give a shit. She knew what she had. Something to make people feel stronger, sexier. No wonder they wanted to keep it to themselves.'

'But in the end it drove some of them crazy. Even the ones who thought they could take it.'

'It seems to me it affected everyone a little differently. I mean, look at us. We got a taste of it, and it didn't suit us too well.'

'I should tell you, I thought I was heading for the funny farm.'

'You should have called me. We could have compared notes.'

'My mind was just going round and round. Nothing made sense any more. I was ready to do myself in.'

'I don't want to hear that kind of talk,' Maxine said. 'The fact is: you're here. You survived. We both did. Now we have to do this one last thing.'

'What if we get up there and don't find anything?'

'Then we just leave and get on with our lives. We forget we ever heard of Coldheart Canyon.'

'I don't think there's very much chance of that, somehow.'

'Frankly, neither do I.'

It was hot. In the Valley, the temperature at noon stood at an unseasonal one hundred and four, with the probability that it would climb a couple of degrees higher before the day was out. The 10 freeway was blocked for seven miles with people trying to get to Raging Waters, a water-slide park which seemed like a cooling prospect on a day like this, if you could only reach the damn thing.

Later that afternoon in a freak mirror-image of the fire at Warner's, there was a small conflagration at a warehouse in Burbank, which had been turned into a mini-studio for the making of X-rated epics. By the time the fire-trucks had wound their way through the clogged traffic to reach the blaze, there'd already been five fatalities: a cameraman and a ménage-à-trois whose versatility was being immortalized that afternoon, along with the male star's fluffer, had all been cremated. There was very little wind, so the sickly smell of burning flesh and silicon lingered in the air for several hours.

Even if that particular stench didn't reach the Canyon, there were plenty that day that did. Indeed it seemed the Canyon had become a repository for all manner of sickening stenches in the weeks since its sudden notoriety, as though the rot at its heart was drawing to it the smell of every horror in the heat-sickened city. Every unemptied dumpster that concealed something for forensics to come look at; every condemned apartment or lock-up garage where somebody had died (either accidentally or by their own hand) and had not yet been discovered; every pile of once-bright flowers collected from the fresh graves of Forest Lawn and the Hollywood Memorial Cemetery, and were now piled high in the corner, along with their tags carrying messages of sympathy and expressions of loss, rotting together; all of them found their way into the cleft of the Canyon, and clung to the once healthy plants, weighing them down like a curse laid on the air itself.

'It's so damn quiet,' Tammy said as she got out of Maxine's car in front of what had once been Katya Lupi's dream palace.

There were a few birds singing in the trees, but there wasn't much enthusiasm in their trilling. It was too hot for music-making. The birds themselves sat in what little shade they could find beneath the leaves, and stayed still. The only exception to this were the falcons, which rode the rising tides of heat off the Canyon, their wings motionless, and the ravens, who dipped and banked as they chased one another overhead, landing in argumentative rows on the high walls around the house.

The dream palace itself was in a shocking state, the damage the ghosts had done to the vast chamber on which the house sat throwing the whole structure into an accelerated state of decay. The once-magnificent façade, with its highlights of Moroccan tile, had not only cracked from end to end but had now fallen forward, exposing the lath-and-timber below. The massive door – which Tammy had imagined belonging to an Errol Flynn epic – had split in three places. The metal lock, which had been as vast and medieval as the rest of the thing, had been removed, sawn away by a thief with an electric saw. He'd made an attempt to take the antique hinges too, but the size of the job had apparently defeated him.

Tammy and Maxine squeezed through the mass of debris which had gathered behind it. The turret into which they stepped was still intact, all the way up to its vault, with its painted images of once-famous faces peering down. But the plaster on which the fresco had been made was now laced with cracks, and cobs of the design had fallen away, so that the vault looked like a partially-finished jigsaw. Underfoot, the missing pieces: fragments of Mary Pickford's shoulder and Lon Chaney Senior's crooked smile.

'Is this earthquake damage?' Maxine said, looking up at the turret. There were places where the entire structure of the turret, not just the inner, painted layer, but the tiles too, had dropped out of place, so that the Californian sky was visible.

'I don't see why the house would survive all these years of earthquakes without being substantially damaged, and then practically come apart in a 6.9.'

'It's weird,' Maxine agreed.

'Maybe the ghosts did it?'

'Really? They got up there?' she said, pointing at the vault.

'I bet you they got *everywhere*. They were pretty pissed off.'

Tammy stepped into the kitchen and had her thesis proved correct. The kitchen had been comprehensively ripped apart; shelves torn down, cutlery pulled out of drawers and scattered around. Plates smashed, frying pans used to beat at the tiled work-surfaces so that they were shattered. Food had been pulled out of the fridge and deep-freeze, both of which stood open – rotted fruit and uncooked steaks scattered around, broken bottles of beer and cartons of spoiled milk. Everything that could be destroyed had been destroyed. The tops of the faucets had been twisted off, and water still gurgled from the open pipes, filling up the clogged sink until it overflowed, soaking the floor.

But all this was cosmetic. The ghosts had been working on the structure too, and they'd had the supernatural strength to cause considerable damage. Ragged holes had been made in the ceiling, exposing the support beams, some of which – through a massive effort by the phantom demolition team – had been unseated and pulled through the plaster façade, jutting like vast broken bones.

Tammy waded through the filthy water to the second door, and opened it. A scummy tide had preceded her out into the passageway where Todd had died. It was considerably darker than the kitchen. She instinctively reached round and flicked on the light. There was a sharp snap of electricity in the wall. The lights came on, flickered for a moment, then went out again. After a beat there was another noise and an eruption of sparks from one of the light fixtures further down the wall. She thought about trying to switch the electricity off, but that didn't seem very smart under the circumstances: she was standing in half an inch of water with the power crackling in the walls. Better just leave it alone.

The only reason she'd come out here was to be certain

that the place where Todd had lain had been cleaned up. In fact, it hadn't been touched. The water from the kitchen had not reached as far as the spot where he had died, so the pools of blood that had come from his body were now dry, dark stains on the floor. There were other stains, too, where his body had lain, that she didn't want to think too much about.

Further down the passageway, beyond the bloodstains, was the back door and the threshold where she'd dug out the icons. The nerves in the tips of her fingers twitched as she thought about those terrible minutes: hearing Todd and Katya fighting in the kitchen, while the ghosts waited on the threshold, bristling but silent; waiting for their moment. Her heart quickened at the thought of how close she'd come to losing the game she'd played here.

Something crunched beneath her sole, and she stepped aside to find one of the icons was lying on the tiles. She bent down and picked it up. There was nothing left of the force it had once owned so she pocketed it, as a keepsake. As she was doing so she caught sight of a body lying outside, in the shadows of the Noahic Bird of Paradise trees.

'*Maxine*!' she called, suddenly alarmed.

'I'm coming.'

'Be careful. Don't touch the light switches.'

As soon as she heard Maxine's footsteps splashing through the kitchen, Tammy ventured to the threshold, and stepped over it. The greenery smelt pungent back here; she was reminded of those dark parts of the Canyon where she'd almost lost her life. The jungle had crept closer to the house it seemed; there were mushrooms and fungi growing out of the wall, and the Mexican pavers were slick with green algae underfoot.

'What's wrong?' Maxine wanted to know.

'That.' Tammy pointed to the body, which lay face down in the middle of a particularly fertile patch of fungi. Tammy wondered if perhaps he'd been trying to make a meal of them, and died in mid-swallow, poisoned.

'Help me turn him over,' Tammy said.

'No thanks,' Maxine said. 'I'm as close as I need to get.'

Undaunted, Tammy went down on her haunches beside the body, pressing her fingers into the damp, sticky groove between the body and the tiles upon which it lay. The corpse was cold. She lifted it up an inch or two, peering down to see if she could get a better glimpse of the dead man. But she couldn't make out his features. She would have to turn the cadaver over. She pushed harder, and hoisted the body onto its side. Rivulets of pale maggots poured from its rot-bloated underbelly. She let it fall all the way over, lolling on the ground.

Not only was it not a man, it was not strictly speaking, a human being but one of what Zeffer had called the children, the hybrid minglings of ghost and animal. This one had been a female: part coyote, part sex-goddess. It had six breasts, courtesy of its bestial side, but two of them had gone to jelly. The four that remained however, were as lush as any starlet's, adding a touch of surrealism to this otherwise repulsive sight. The creature's head was a mass of wormy life, except – for some reason – its lips, which remained large, ripe and untouched.

'Who is it?' Maxine hollered from the interior of the house.

'It's just an animal,' Tammy said. 'Sort of. The ghosts fucked the animals. And sometimes the animals fucked the ghosts. And these *things*, the children, were the result.'

Obviously Maxine hadn't known about this little detail because a look of raw disgust came over her face.

'Jesus. This place never fails to . . .' She finished the sentence by shaking her head.

Tammy wiped her hands on her jeans and surveyed the steps that led down to the garden.

674

'There's more of them down here,' she called back to Maxine.

'More?'

By the time Maxine's curiosity had overcome her revulsion and she'd reached the first body, Tammy had already moved on to the second, third and fourth, then to a group of four more, all lying on the steps leading down to the lawn or at the bottom, and all in roughly the same position, face down, as though they'd simply fallen forward. It was a curiously sad scene, because there were so many different kinds of animals here: large and small, dark and striped and spotted; lush and bony.

'It looks like Jonestown,' Maxine said, surveying the whole sorry sight.

She wasn't that far off the mark. The way bodies had all dropped in the grass, some lying alone, others in groups, looking as though they might have been hand in hand when the fatal moment came. It had the feel of a mass suicide, no question. Had the sun been on them directly, no doubt the stench would have been nauseating. But the air was cool beneath the heavy canopy; the smell was more like that of festering cabbages than the deeper, stomach-turning stench of rotting flesh.

'Why so few flies?'

Tammy thought on this for a moment. 'I don't know. They weren't properly alive in the first place, were they? They had ghosts for fathers and animals for mothers. Or the other way round. I don't think they were flesh and blood in the same way you and I are.'

'That still doesn't explain why they came here to die like this.'

'Maybe the same power that ran through Katya and the ghosts ran through them too,' Tammy said. 'And once it was turned off –'

'They came back to the house and died?'

'Exactly.'

'And the dead?' Maxine said. 'All those people. Where did they go?'

'They didn't have anything to keep them here,' Tammy said.

'So maybe they're out wandering the city?' Maxine said. 'Not a very reassuring thought.'

As Maxine talked, Tammy plucked some large leaves from the jungle all around, and then went back amongst the corpses, bending to gently lay the leaves – which she'd chosen for their size – over the faces of the dead.

Maxine watched Tammy with a mingling of incomprehension and awe. It would never in a thousand years have occurred to her to do something like this. But as she watched Tammy going about this duty she felt a surge of simple affection for the woman. She'd endured a lot, and here she was, still finding it in her heart to think of something other than her own comfort, her own ease. She was remarkable in her way: no question.

'Are you done?' she asked, when Tammy was all but finished.

'Almost,' she said. She bowed her head. 'Do you know any prayers?'

'I used to, but . . .' Maxine shrugged, empty-handed.

'Then I'm just going to make something up,' Tammy said.

'I'll leave you to it then,' Maxine said, turning to go.

'No,' Tammy said. 'Please. I want you to stay here with me until I'm finished.'

'Are you sure?'

'Please.'

'Okay,' Maxine said.

Tammy bowed her head. Then after taking a few moments to decide what she was going to say, she began. 'Lord,' she said. 'I don't know why these creatures were born, or why they died . . .' She shook her head, in a kind of despair, though whether it was about the words or the situation she

676

was attempting to describe, Maxine didn't know; perhaps a little of both. 'We're in the presence of death, and when that happens we wonder, it *makes* us wonder, why we're alive in the first place. Well, I guess I want to say that these things didn't ask to be alive. They were born miserably. And they lived miserably. And now they're dead. And I'd like to ask you, Lord, to take special care of them. They lived without any hope of happiness, but maybe you can give them some happiness in the Hereafter. That's all. Amen.'

Maxine tried to echo the *Amen*, but when she did so she realized that these hesitant, simple words coming from so unlikely a source, had brought on tears.

Tammy put her arm around Maxine's shoulder. 'It's okay,' she said.

'I don't even know why I'm crying,' Maxine said, letting her head drop against Tammy's shoulder while the sobbing continued to wrack her. 'This is the first time I've cried like this, *really* cried, in Lord knows how long.'

'It's good to cry. Let it come.'

'Is it really good to cry?' Maxine said, recovering herself slightly, and wiping her nose. 'I've always been suspicious when people say crying's good for you.'

'Well it is. Trust me.'

'You know, Tammy, I don't know if anyone has ever told you this, but you're quite an amazing lady.'

'Oh really?' she said. 'Well that's kind of you. It's not the sort of thing Arnie used to say.'

'Well then, Arnie was a fool,' Maxine said, recovering a little of her old edge.

'Are you ready to go back inside now?' Tammy said, a little embarrassed by Maxine's compliment.

'Yeah. I guess so.'

They made their way through the dead to the steps, and started to climb. As they did so it occurred to Maxine that in laying the leaves on the dead, and offering up a prayer on their behalf, Tammy had brought the idea

677

of forgiveness into Katya Lupi's loveless domain. It was probably the first time the subject had been broached in this vicinity in three-quarters of a century. Katya hadn't seemed too big on forgiveness. You erred against her, you suffered for it; and you kept suffering.

'What are you thinking about?' Tammy asked her.

'Just this place.' Maxine looked up at the house, and turned to take in the rest of the Canyon. 'Maybe the tabloids had it right.'

'About what?'

'Oh you know: the most cursed piece of real estate in Hollywood.'

'Bullshit,' Tammy said.

'You don't think that room downstairs was made by the Devil, or his wife?'

'I don't want to know who made it,' Tammy said. 'But I know who *fed* it; who made it important. People. Just like you and me. Addicted to the place.'

'That makes sense.'

'Places can't be good or bad,' Tammy said. 'Only people. That's what I believe.'

'Did that make you feel better, by the way? What you did out there?'

Tammy smiled. 'Bit crazy, huh?'

'Not at all.'

'You know, it did make me feel better. Much better. Those poor things didn't have a hope.'

'So now, we can go look for Todd?' Maxine said.

'And if we don't find him in –' Tammy looked at her watch '– shall we say, fifteen minutes, we give it up as a bad idea? Agreed?'

'Agreed.'

'Where do you want to look first?' Tammy said.

'The master bedroom,' Maxine replied. 'Whenever things didn't go well, he used to go to his bedroom and lock the door.'

678

'Funny, Arnie would do the same.'

'You never told me anything about Arnie,' Maxine said, as she led the way through the chaos of the kitchen to the hallway.

'There wasn't that much to tell. And there's even less now he's gone.'

'Do you think he'll come back?'

'I don't know,' Tammy said, sounding as though she didn't care that much. 'Depends on whether his new woman puts up with him or not.'

'Well, put it this way: do you want him back?'

'No. And if he tries to make nice, I'm going to tell him to go fuck himself. Excuse my French.'

They stepped out into the hallway. 'You want to go up there first?' Tammy said. 'He was your friend, or client, or whatever.' Maxine looked doubtful. 'Go on,' Tammy urged her. 'You go on up and I'll try downstairs.'

'Okay,' Maxine said, 'but stay in shouting distance.'

'I will. And if I don't find anything down there I'll come straight up and find you.'

Maxine started up the stairs two at a time. 'I'm not spending another hour after dark in this Canyon,' she called as she went.

She watched Tammy descend as she ascended, and then, when the turn in the stairs put them out of sight of one another, she concentrated her attentions on the doorway in front of her. The landing she was crossing was creaking with every footfall: no doubt the damage the ghosts had done up here was as thorough as it had been below. God knows how profoundly they'd affected the sub-structure of the place. Another reason – if any were needed – to be out of here quickly. She'd read her Poe; she knew what happened to houses as psychotic as this had been. They came tumbling down. Their sins finally caught up with them and they collapsed on themselves like tumorous men, burying anyone and everyone who was stupid enough to be inside when the roof began to creak.

'Tammy!'

'I can hear you.'

'The place is creakin' up here. Is it creakin' down there?'

'Yep.'

'So let's make this short an' sweet, huh?'

'We already agreed –'

'Even shorter and sweeter.'

Maxine had reached the door of the master bedroom. She knocked, lightly at first. Then she called Todd's name. There was no reply forthcoming so she tried the handle. The door was unlocked. She pushed it open. It grated over a scattering of earth; and there was the sound of several irregular shaped objects rolling behind it. She investigated. Besides the earth there were some rocks behind the door, and several clods of earth, some with grass attached. Somebody appeared to have hauled a sack of earth up from the garden and it had split open behind the door.

'Todd?' she called again.

This time there was a mumbled reply. She stepped into the room.

The drapes were almost completely drawn, keeping out nine-tenths of the sunlight. The air smelt stale, as though nobody had opened the door in days, but it also smelt strongly of fresh earth. She studied the gloom for a little time, until she saw the figure sitting up on the bed, his knees raised under what she took to be a dark coverlet. It was Todd. He was naked from the waist up.

'Hello, Maxine,' he said. There was neither music nor threat in his voice.

'Hello, Todd.'

'Couldn't stay away, huh?'

'Tammy's with me,' she said, shifting the blame.

'Yes, I heard her. And I expected her. No. *Half*-expected

her. But I didn't expect you. I thought it was all over with us once I was dead. Out of sight . . .'

'It's not as simple as that.'

'No, it isn't is it? If it's any comfort, it's true in both directions.'

'You think about me?'

'You. Tammy. The life I had. Sure. I think about it all the time. There isn't much else to do up here.'

'So why are you up here?'

He moved in the bed, and there was a patter of earth onto the bare boards. What she'd taken to be a blanket was in fact a pyramid of damp earth, which he'd piled up over the lower half of his body. When he moved, the pyramid partially collapsed. He reached out and pulled the earth back towards him, so as not to lose too much over the edge of the bed.

His body, she saw, looked better than it had in years. His abdominals were perfectly cut, his pectorals not too hefty, but nicely defined. And his face was similarly recovered. The damage done by time, excess and Dr Burrows' scalpels eradicated.

'You look good,' she said.

'I don't *feel* good,' he replied.

'No?'

'No. You know me. I don't like being on my own, Maxine. It makes me crazy.' He wasn't looking at her any longer, but was rearranging the mound of earth on his lap. His erection, she now saw, was sticking out of the middle of the earth.

'I wake up with this,' he said, flicking his hard-on from side to side with his hand. 'It won't go down.' He sounded neither proud of the fact, nor much distressed by it: his erection was just another plaything, like the earth heaped over his body.

'Why did you bring half the back yard up here?'

'Just to play,' he replied. 'I don't know.'

'Yes you do,' she said to him.

'Okay I do. I'm dead, right. Right?'

'Yeah.'

'I knew it,' he said, with the grim tone of a man who was having bad news confirmed. 'I mean, I *knew*. As soon as I looked in the mirror, and I saw I wasn't fucked up any more, I thought: I'm like the others in the Canyon. So I went out to look for them.'

'Why?'

'I wanted to talk to somebody about how it all works. Being dead but still being *here*; having a body; *substance*. I wanted to know what the rules were. But they'd all gone.' He stopped playing with himself and stared at the sliver of light coming between the drapes. 'There were just those things left –'

'The children?'

'Yeah. And they were droppin' like flies.'

'We saw. They're all around the house.'

'Ugly fucks,' Todd said. 'I know why too.'

'Why what?'

'Why they were droppin'.'

'What?'

He licked his lips and frowned, his eyes becoming hooded. 'There's something out there, Maxine. Something that comes at night.' His voice had lost all its strength. 'It sits on the roof.'

'What are you talking about?'

'I don't know what it is, but it scares the shit out of me. Sitting on the roof, shining.'

'Shining?'

'Shining, like it was a piece of the sun.' He suddenly started to make a concentrated effort to bury his erection, like a little boy abruptly obsessed with some trivial ritual: two handfuls of earth, then another two, then another two, just to get it out of sight. It didn't work. His cock-head continued to stick out, red and smooth. 'I don't want it

682

to see me, Maxine,' he said, very quietly. 'The thing on the roof. I don't want it to see me. Will you tell it to go away?'

She laughed.

'Don't laugh at me.'

'I can't help it,' she said. 'Look at you. Sitting in a sackful of earth with a hard-on talking about some *light* –'

'I don't even know what it is,' he said. Maxine was still laughing at the absurdity of all this. 'I'll tell Tammy to do it,' he said. 'She'll do it for me. I know she will.' He kept staring at the crack of light between the drapes. 'Go and get her. I want to see her.'

'So I'm dismissed, am I?'

'No,' he said. 'You can stay if you want or you can go if you want to. You've seen me, I'm okay.'

'Except for the light.'

'Except for the light. I'm *not* crazy, Maxine. It's here.'

'I know you're not crazy,' Maxine said.

He looked straight back at her for the first time. The light he'd been staring at had got into his eyes somehow, and was now reflected out towards her – or was that simply the way all ghosts looked? She thought perhaps it was. The silvery gaze, that was both beautiful and inhuman.

'I suppose we both could be dreaming all this,' he went on. 'They don't call these places *dream palaces* for nothing. I mean . . . I *was* dead, wasn't I? I know, I was dead. That bitch killed me . . .' His voice grew heavy, as he remembered the pain of his final minutes; not so much the physical pain, perhaps, as the pain of Katya turning on him, betraying him.

'Well, for what it's worth,' Maxine said, 'I'm sorry.'

'About what?'

'Oh, a thousand things. But mainly leaving you when I did. It was Tammy who pointed it out. If I hadn't gone and left you, perhaps none of this would have happened.'

'She said that to you?' Todd replied, with a smile.

683

'Yep.'

'She's got a mouth on her when something strikes her.'

'The point is: she was right.'

Todd's smile faded. 'It was the worst time of my life,' he said.

'And I made it worse.'

'It's all right,' he said. 'It's over now.'

'Is it really?'

'Yes. Really. It's history.'

'I was so *tired*,' Maxine said.

'I know. Tired of me and tired of who you'd become, yes?'

'Yes.'

'I don't blame you. This town fucks people up.' He was looking at her with that luminous gaze, but it was clear his thoughts were wandering. 'Where's Tammy, did you say?'

'She went downstairs.'

'Will you please go get her for me?'

'Oh *please* now, is it?' she said, smiling. 'You have changed.'

'You know what starts to happen if you stay here long enough?' he said, apropos of nothing in particular.

'No, what?'

'You start to have these glimpses of the past. At least I do. I'm sitting here and suddenly I'm dreaming I'm on a mountain.'

'On a mountain?'

'Climbing, this sheer cliff.'

'That can't have been a memory, Todd. Or at least it can't have been a real mountain. You hated heights, don't you remember?'

He took his gaze off her and returned it to the crack between the drapes. Plainly, this news made him uncomfortable, questioning as it did the nature of his recollections.

'If it wasn't a real mountain, what was it?'

'It was a fake, built on one of the soundtracks at Universal. It was for *The Big Fall*.'

'A movie I was in?'

'A movie. A big movie. Surely you remember?'

'Did I die in it?'

'No, you didn't die in it. Why do you want to know?'

'I was just trying to remember last night, what movies I'd made. I kept thinking if the light has to collect me, and I have to leave, and I have to tell it what movies I made –'

He glanced at the wall beside the bed where he'd scrawled a list – in a large, untutored scrawl – of some of the titles of his films. It was by no means comprehensive; proof perhaps of a mind in slow decay. Nor were the titles he *had* remembered entirely accurate. *Gunner* became *Gunman* for some reason, and *The Big Fall* simply *Fallen*. He also added *Warrior* to the list, which was wishful thinking.

'How many of my pictures did I die in then?'

'Two.'

'Why only two? Quickly.'

'Because you were the hero.'

'Right answer. And heroes don't die. *Ever*, right?'

'I wouldn't say ever. Sometimes it's the perfect ending.'

'For example?'

'*A Tale of Two Cities*.'

'That's old. Anyway, don't quibble. The point is: I don't care about what the light wants. I'm the hero.'

'Oh, I get where this is headed.'

'*I'm not going*, Maxine.'

'Suppose it wants to take you somewhere better?'

'Like where?'

'I don't know . . .'

'Say it. Go on. You see . . . you can't even say it.'

'I can say it. *Heaven. The afterlife.*'

'Is that where you believe it wants me to go?'

'I don't know where it wants you to go, Todd.'

685

'And I'm never going to find out because I'm not going to go. I'm the hero. I don't *have* to go. Right?'

What could she say to this? He had the idea so very firmly fixed in his head that it wasn't going to be easily dislodged.

'I suppose if you put it that way,' she said, 'you don't have to go anywhere you don't want to.'

He put his heel behind a small portion of earth and pushed it off the edge of the bed. It rattled as it rained down on the bare boards.

'It's all bullshit anyway,' he said.

'What's bullshit?'

'Movies. I should have done something more useful with my life. Donnie was right.'

'Donnie?'

'Yes.' He suddenly looked hard at her. 'Donnie was real, wasn't he? He was my brother. Tell me I didn't dream him.'

'No, you didn't dream him.'

'Oh good. He was the best soul I ever met in my life. Sorry, but he was.'

'No, he was your brother. It's good you love him.'

'Hmm.' A silence; a long silence. Then: 'Life would be shit if I'd just dreamed him.'

8

At the bottom of the stairs Tammy discovered that the entire sub-structure of the house – the floor once occupied by the Devil's Country – was now reduced to heaps of rubble, with a few support pillars here and there, which were presumably the only things keeping the house from collapsing upon itself completely. Seeing the tenuous state of things, Tammy was tempted to go straight back upstairs to warn Maxine, but then she figured that there was probably no tearing urgency. The house had managed to stay upright in the weeks since the ghosts had wreaked this havoc, and wasn't likely to collapse in the next five minutes: she would risk looking around for a little while, just to be sure she'd understood as much of this mystery as was comprehensible before she turned her back on it forever.

The last few steps of the stairway had been torn away by the revenants' assault, but there was a heap of its own rubble directly beneath it, so it wasn't much of a leap for her. Even so, she landed awkwardly, and slid gracelessly down the side of the heap, puncturing her ankles and calves on the corners of the shattered tiles.

She stumbled away from the bottom of the stairs and through the doorway, the naked framework of which was still standing, surprisingly enough, though the walls to the right and left of it were virtually demolished, and the ceiling brought down, exposing a network of pipes and cables. There was very little light, beyond the patch in which she stood, which had leaked in from the turret. Otherwise, it was murky in every direction. She strayed a little distance from the doorway, taking care not to hobble herself on a larger piece of masonry, and careful too not to lose her bearings.

Every now and again something on a higher floor would creak or grind, or somewhere in the darkness around her she'd hear a patter of dry plaster-dust. Then the creaking would stop, the pattering would stop, and her heart would pick up its normal rhythm again.

Of one thing she was pretty certain: there were no ghosts here. They'd wreaked their comprehensive havoc and gone on their melancholy way, leaving the house to creak and settle and eventually, when it could no longer support its own weight, collapse.

She'd seen enough. She moved back to the doorway and returned through it to the stairs, climbing over the rubble onto the lowest step. The staircase swayed ominously as she heaved herself onto it, and she saw that it had become disconnected from the wall a few feet up and was therefore 'floating', a fact she had failed to grasp during her descent. She ascended with a good deal more caution and reached the relatively solid ground at the top of the stairs with an inwardly spoken word of thanks.

The door to the master bedroom was open, she saw. A moment later, Maxine emerged and beckoned for her to come up.

'Todd's here and he wants to see you,' she explained.

'Is he all right?' Tammy asked, fully realizing, even as she said this, that it was a damn-fool question to ask about a man who'd been recently murdered.

By way of reply Maxine made a strange face, as though she didn't have the least clue what the man in the master bedroom was up to.

'You should just come up and see for yourself,' she said.

As they crossed on the stairs Maxine took the opportunity to whisper: 'I hope to hell you can make more sense of him than I could.'

'Hello, Tammy.'

Todd was lying in the bed, with a pile of earth covering his lower half. There was earth on the floor too; and on his hands.

'You're a mess,' she remarked brightly.

'I've been playing in the mud.'

'Can I open the drapes a little, or put on a lamp? It's really gloomy in here.'

'Put on a lamp if you really must.'

She went to the table in the corner and switched on the antiquated lamp, doing so tentatively given her problem with the electricity on the lower floor. Then she went to look out of the narrow gap between the drapes. Maxine had been right; the evening was coming on quickly. Already the opposite side of the Canyon was purple grey, and the sky above it had lost all its warmth. There were no stars yet, but the moon was rising in the north-eastern corner of the Canyon.

'Don't look out there,' Todd said.

'Why not?'

'Just close the drapes. Please.'

She obviously wasn't quite quick enough for him, because he sprang out of bed, scattering earth far and wide. His sudden movement startled her a little. It wasn't that she was afraid of him exactly; but if death emphasized people's natural propensities, as it seemed it did, then there was a good chance he'd be wilder in death than he had been alive. He took the drape from her hand – snatched it, almost – and pulled it closed.

'I don't want to see what's out there,' he said. 'And neither do you.'

She looked down at his groin. How could she help herself? He was as hard as any man she'd laid eyes on, his dick moving even though he was standing still, bobbing to the rhythm of his pulse.

It would be ridiculous, she thought, not to mention it. Like his standing there with a pig under his arm, and making no reference to *that*.

'What's that in honour of?' she said, pointing down at the pulsing length. 'Me?'

'Why, would you like it?'

'It's covered in dirt.'

'Yeah.' He took hold of the lower four inches of his dick and began to brush the soil off the top four, twisting his dick round (in a manner that looked painful to Tammy) so that he could fetch out the particles of earth in the ridges of his circumcision scar.

'I didn't think I'd see you again,' he said, as he worked. He let his dick go. It thumped against his belly before settling back into its head-high position. 'I was beginning to think this was my only friend,' he said. He knocked his dick sideways with a little laugh.

'I'm sorry,' Tammy said. 'I wasn't feeling well enough to come before now.'

Todd wandered back over to the bed and sat down on the edge of the mattress. More earth fell onto the floor. He folded his arms, bunching the muscles of his shoulders and chest.

'Are you mad at me?' she said.

'A little, I guess.'

'Because I didn't visit?'

'Yeah.'

'I wouldn't have made very good company. I thought I was going crazy.'

'You did?' He was interested now. 'What happened?'

'I locked myself up in my house. I wouldn't see anybody. I was just about ready to kill myself.'

'Oh shit,' he said. 'There's no reason to do that. All the bad times are over, Tammy. You can go off and live your life.'

'*What life*? I don't have a life,' she sighed. 'Just that stupid little home filled with Todd Pickett memorabilia.'

'You could sell it all.'

'I'm going to, trust me. Maybe take a cruise around the world.'

'Or better still, stay up here with me.'

'I don't think –'

'I mean it. Stay here.'

'Have you been downstairs?'

'Not recently. Why?'

'Because this house is going to fall down, Todd. Very soon.'

'No it isn't,' he said. 'Did you know there are dozens of small earthquakes in California every day? Well there are. And this place is still standing.'

'It doesn't have any bottom floor left, Todd. Katya's guests dug it all up.'

He turned to the bed, and started to pull armfuls of the earth off the sheet.

'What are you doing?'

'Persuading you to stay,' he said, still pulling at the earth. When he had almost all the earth removed from the bed he pulled the sheet out and went around the other side of the bed, throwing the corners of the sheet into the middle, and then bundling up both sheet and earth. He pushed the bundle off the bed, and got up onto the clean mattress, sitting with his head against the board, and his legs crossed. His balls were tight and shiny. His dick was hard as ever. He gave her a lascivious grin.

'Climb aboard,' he said.

Here, she thought, was an invitation in a million. And there would have been a time, no doubt, when she would have swooned at the very idea of it.

'I think you should cover yourself up,' Tammy said, keeping the tone friendly, but firm. 'Haven't you got a pair of pants you can wear?'

'You don't want this?' he said, running his fingers over the smooth head of his cock.

'No.' she said. 'Thank you.'

'It's because I'm dead, isn't it?'

She didn't reply to him. Instead she wandered through to the closet, which was enormous; barely a tenth of it was filled, and started to go through the trousers and jeans on the hangers, and found an old, much-patched pair of jeans, their condition suggesting that he was fond of them, because he'd had them fixed so often.

As she pulled them off the hanger she heard a sound on the roof, like something scraping over the Spanish tiles.

'Did you hear that?' she called through to Todd.

There was no answer from the room next door. Bringing the jeans with her she made her way back into the bedroom. Todd was no longer on the bed. He had snatched the earth-stained sheet up off the floor and had wrapped it haphazardly around his body the result being something between a toga and a shroud, and was now crawling around in the corner of the room in this bizarre costume, his eyes turned up towards the roof. He beckoned Tammy over, putting his forefinger to his lips to ensure her silence. There were more noises on the roof; scraping sounds that suggested the animal, whatever it was, had some considerable bulk.

'What is it?' she said. 'That's not a bird.'

He shook his head, still staring up at the ceiling.

'What then?'

'I can't see what it is, it's too bright.'

'Oh so you *have* looked.'

'Yes of course I've looked,' he said, very softly. 'Shit, this always happens. It's like they're its chorus.'

He was referring to the coyotes, which had begun a steady round of almost panicked yelpings from the other side of the Canyon. 'Whenever the light appears, the damn coyotes start up.'

692

He had begun to shudder. Not from the cold, Tammy thought, but from fear. It crossed her mind that this was very far from the conventional image of ghost-hunting. The phantom naked and afraid; her proffering a pair of jeans to cover him up.

'It's come here for me,' Todd said, very quietly. 'You know that.'

'How can you be sure?'

'Because I can feel it. In my chest. And in my balls. The first time it came here it actually got into the house. I was asleep, and I woke up with this terrible ache in my balls. And that –' he pointed down between his legs '–was so hard it hurt. I was terrified. But I yelled at it to go away, and off it went. I think I must have startled it.'

'How many times has it been back since that first time?'

'Six or seven. No, more. Nine, ten times. Sometimes it just waits in the garden. Sometimes it sits on the roof, like it is now. And then once it was in the pool.'

'There's no water in the pool.'

'No, I know. It was lying at the bottom, not moving.'

'And you couldn't see any shape in it?'

'No, no shape. I mean, do angels even have shapes?'

'An angel? That's what you think it is?'

'I'm pretty sure. I mean, it came to get me. And I *am* dead. So that's why it's hanging around. And it almost had me once –'

'What happened?'

'I looked at it. And my head started to fill up with all these memories. Things I hadn't thought about for years and years, literally. Me and Donnie as kids. Cincinnati. Nothing important. Just things you might think of in a daydream. And it said to me –'

'Wait. It speaks? This thing speaks?'

'Yes. It speaks.'

'What sex is it?'

'I don't know. Sometimes it sounds more like a guy . . .' He shrugged. 'I don't know.'

'I'm sorry. I interrupted you. What did it say?'

'Oh. It said: *all this is waiting for you.*'

'"All this," meaning what?'

'All the memories, I suppose. My past. People. Places. Smells. You know how sometimes you wake up from a dream and it's been so *real*, so strong, everything in the real world seems a bit unconvincing for the first half-hour? Well, it was like that after I saw the memories. Nothing was quite real.'

'So why the hell are you fighting it? It doesn't want to hurt you.'

'I'll tell you why I'm fighting. Because it's a one-way street, Tammy. I go with the light, there's no way back.'

'And is being here so wonderful?'

'Now don't –'

'I mean it.'

'Don't argue with me,' he said. 'I've thought about this a lot. Believe me. It's *all* I've thought about.'

'So what do you want to do?'

'I want you to stay right here with me until the damn thing goes away. It won't try any tricks if you're here.'

'You mean giving you the memories?'

'It's got others. Once it appeared on the lawn looking like Patricia, my mother. I knew it wasn't really her, but it's crafty that way. You know, she was telling me to come with her, and for just a few seconds –'

'It had you fooled?'

'Yeah. Not for long, but . . . yeah.'

At this juncture there was a rapping sound on the door. Todd jumped.

'It's only Maxine,' Tammy said, getting up, and turning from Todd. He caught hold of the jeans she was carrying, not because he wanted to wear them but to stop her escaping him.

694

'Don't answer it,' he said. 'Please stay here with me. I'm begging you, stay: *please*.'

She held her breath for a moment, listening for the presence on the roof. It was no longer audible. Had the creature – whatever it was – simply departed, or was it still squatting up there, biding its time? Or – a third possibility, just as plausible as the other two – was she falling for some fictional fear that Todd, in his confused, post-mortem state, had simply created out of thin air? Was she just hearing birds on the roof, skittering around, and letting his imagination work her up into a frenzy about it?

'Put your jeans on,' she said to him, letting go of them.

'Tammy. Listen to me –'

'I am listening,' she said, crossing to the door of the bedroom. 'Put your jeans on.'

She heard the rapping sound again. This time she thought perhaps she'd been wrong. It wasn't Maxine at all. It was somebody outside the house beating on the front door.

She went to the bedroom door and cautiously opened it. She was in time to see Maxine retreating across the hallway from the front door.

'What is it?' she whispered. Maxine looked up at her; by the expression on her face something had unsettled her. 'I heard this knocking. Went to the door. And, Tammy, there was a *light* out there, shining in through the cracks in the door.'

'So he's not having delusions,' Tammy said.

She headed downstairs to comfort Maxine. As she did so she reported what she'd just heard Todd tell her. 'Todd said there was something out there waiting for him. That's his turn of phrase: *waiting for him*. Apparently it sits on the roof a lot.' She put her hand on Maxine's trembling shoulder. 'Are you okay?'

'I am now. It just freaked me out.'

'So you didn't open the door?'

695

'Well you can't open it, can you? It's cracked. But it's not much protection.'

'Stay here.'

So saying, Tammy crossed the hallway, gingerly slid through the broken door and stepped out onto the doorstep.

'Oh Jesus, be careful,' Maxine murmured.

'There's nothing,' she said.

'Are you sure?'

Maxine stepped out through the cracked door and they stood together on the step.

The last light of the afternoon had by now died away; but the moon had risen and was shedding its brightness through the trees to the right of the front door.

'Well, at least it's a beautiful evening,' Maxine remarked, staring up at the light coming between the branches.

Tammy's thoughts were elsewhere. She stepped out of the house and onto the pathway. Then she turned around, running her gaze back and forth along the roof, looking for some sign, *any* sign whatsoever, of the creature that had made the noise up there. As far as she could see the roof was completely deserted.

'Nothing,' she said to herself.

She glanced back at Maxine, who was still staring up at the moon. She was alarmed to see that the sight of the moonlight seemed to have brought Maxine to tears.

'What's wrong?' she said.

Maxine didn't reply. She simply stared slackly up at the tree.

A few leaves fluttered down from the branches where the moonlight was sourced, and to Tammy's amazement the light began to slowly descend.

'Oh fuck,' Tammy said very softly, realizing that this was not the moon.

Todd had been right. There *was* some entity here, its outer form consisting of raw light, its core unreadable.

Whatever it looked like, it apparently had eyes, because it could see them clearly; Tammy had no doubt of that. She felt its scrutiny upon her. Not just upon her, in fact, *in* her. She was entirely transparent to it; or so she felt.

And as its study pierced her, she felt it ignite other images in her mind's eye. The house on Monarch Street where she was born appeared in front of her, its presence not insistent enough to blot out the world in which she was standing, but co-existing with it, neither sight seeming to sit uncomfortably beside the other. The door of the Monarch Street house opened, and her Aunt Jessica, her father's sister, came out onto the stoop. Aunt Jessica, of all people, whom she hadn't thought about in a very long time. Jessica the spinster aunt, smiling in the sunshine, and beckoning to her out of the past.

Not just beckoning, speaking.

'Your papa's at the fire station,' she said. 'Come on in now Tammy. Come on in.'

She'd not liked Aunt Jessica over-much, nor had she had any great fear of her father. The fact that Aunt Jessica was there on the stoop was unremarkable; she used to come over for supper on every Tuesday, Thursday and Saturday, often taking care of Tammy when her parents went out to see a movie or go dancing, which they'd liked to do. Even the line about Papa being at the fire station carried no especial weight. Papa was always at the fire station for one thing or another, because he wasn't just a fireman, he was the union organizer, and a fierce advocate for better pay and conditions. So there had always been meetings and discussions, besides his diurnal duties.

In short, the memory carried no particular measure of significance, except for the fact that it was a memory of hers, and that somehow this creature – angel or whatever it was – had got into her head to set it in motion. Was its purpose that of distraction? Perhaps so; being so perfectly common-place. Tammy could slip into its embrace without protest, because it evoked neither great joy nor great regret. It was just the past, there in front of her: momentarily real.

She thought of what Todd had said, about how the angel had appeared as his mother. Somehow the way Todd had described the process it had sounded altogether more sinister than this: more like a trap for his soul.

'Tammy?'

'Yes, I see it,' she said to Maxine.

'What do you see?' Maxine said.

'It's just my Aunt Jessica –'

'Well if I were you I'd look away,' Maxine advised. Tammy didn't see why it was so important that she looked away.

'I'm okay, just watching,' she said.

But Maxine had taken hold of her arm, and was gripping it so hard that it hurt. She wanted to turn and tell the woman to let go of her, but it was easier said than done. The image of the clapboard house on Monarch Street had in fact caught her up in its little loop. It was like a short length of film, running round and round.

The door would open, Aunt Jessica would beckon and speak her three lines:

'Your papa's at the fire station. Come on in, Tammy. Come on in.'

Then she'd beckon again and turn round to step back into the house. The door would close. The dappled sunlight, falling through the branches of the old sycamore just to the right of number 38 Monarch Street, would move a little as a gust of summer wind passed through its huge, heavy branches. Then, after a beat, the door would open once again, and Auntie Jessica would reappear on the stoop with exactly the same smile on her face, exactly the same lines to speak.

'Look away,' Maxine said again, this time more urgently.

The urgency got through to Tammy. *Maybe I should do as she says*, she thought; *maybe this little picture-show isn't as innocent as it seems. Maybe I'm going to be stuck in this loop with the door and Jessica and the shadows coming through the sycamore forever.*

A little spasm of panic rose in her. She made a conscious effort to avert her eyes, thinking of what Todd had said. But her mind's eye had become glued to the scene the angel had conjured, and she couldn't shake herself free of it. She forced herself to close her eyes but the loop was still there behind her eyelids. Indeed it carried more force there because it had nothing to compete with. She began to shake.

'Help me . . .' she murmured to Maxine.

But there was no answer forthcoming.

'Maxine?'

There were beads of brightness in the image she could see in her mind's eye, and they were getting stronger. In spite of her panicked state, Tammy didn't have any difficulty figuring out what they signified. *The angel was getting closer to her.* It was using the cover of the looped memory to approach her, until she was within reach of it.

'*Maxine!*' she yelled. '*Where the hell are you?*'

In her mind's eye, the green door on Monarch Street was opening for perhaps the eleventh or twelfth time: smiling Aunt Jessica appearing to beckon and speak –

'*Maxine?*'

'Your papa's at the fire station –'

'*Maxine!*'

She'd gone; that was the bitter truth of it. Seeing the angel approaching, and unable to pull Tammy out of its path, she'd done the sensible, self-protecting thing. She'd retreated.

The light in the scene on Monarch Street was getting brighter with every passing moment. She could feel its corrosive energies on her skin. What would the angel's luminescence do to her if it touched her? Cook her marrow in her bones? Boil away all her blood? *Oh, God in Heaven.*

This wasn't a game: it was life or death. She had to find something to break the loop, before the light of the angelic projector got so hot it cremated her.

There was to be no help from Maxine, that was clear; so she was left with Todd. Where had he been the last time she'd seen him? Her thoughts were now so chaotic she couldn't even remember that.

No, *wait*; he'd been upstairs, hadn't he? She couldn't picture him (the loop was too demanding, the brightness too sickeningly strong: it overwhelmed every other image in her head, real or imagined) but she remembered that he'd been up in the master bedroom.

Oh, and he'd been naked. She remembered that too. Todd the naked ghost, slapping his hard dick around as though it was a toy that he'd suddenly discovered was unbreakable. For a moment the image of Jessica on the doorstep juddered, as though the sprockets had become caught in the gate for a moment. Her mind had found a tool to thrust into the mechanism. Actually, Todd's tool, bobbing at his groin, giving her its slit-eyed gaze.

Yes! She could almost see it –

Aunt Jessica's smiling image juddered a second time, then the brightness behind the picture started to press through her eyes, burning away the pupils, making her look momentarily demonic.

'Yoyo yoyo you-your–Papas-as-as-as-atat-atat-atat-the-the-the-the –'

The woman was jerking round like a puppet being manipulated by someone in the early stages of a *grand mal*. The loop flipped back, and she was beckoning again, with the first syllable of her speech caught on her tongue.

Tammy ignored it. She had Todd's beautiful rod in her mind's eye, and it was strong enough to break the angel's back.

'*Go away*,' she told Aunt Jessica.

'Yo-yo-yo-yo –'

'*I said: Go away*!'

There it was now: Todd's erection, clear as day. She made an intellectual assessment of it, to give solidity to the memory. It was a good eight inches long, circumcised, with a slight left-hand drift.

The light behind Aunt Jessica grew blindingly bright, burning away not only the old lady's figure, but the stoop and the summer tree. The image of Todd's manhood was getting stronger all the time, as though Tammy's pulse beats were feeding it blood; fattening it, glorifying it.

The angel's brilliance still made her skin itch, but she had the better of it now. Two, three more seconds and Monarch Street had disappeared completely, overtaken by the image of Todd's manhood.

'*Maxine*!' she yelled again.

There was still no reply. She put her head down, so when she opened her eyes she would be staring at the ground not at the angel's light. She half-expected to see Maxine sprawled on the ground at her feet, overcome by the angel's power. But no. There was nothing below her but the cracked pathway that led from the front door.

She turned on her heels and lifted her gaze a little. The front door was open; the light the angel shed washed the entire scene before her, taking its colour out, and throwing Tammy's shadow up against the wall.

She felt a perverse imperative to glance back over her shoulder; to put the weapon she'd summoned to the test one more time. But she persuaded herself from such nonsense, and stumbled back the way she and Maxine had come just a little while before.

Even before she reached the steps she heard Maxine sobbing inside. Enraged that she'd been left to face the enemy alone, but at least grateful that Maxine was alive, she climbed the steps, pushed the cracked front door closed as far as it would go, and went back into the house.

Maxine was sitting on the stairs, shaking.

701

On the floor above, Todd had just emerged from the master bedroom. He'd put on the jeans Tammy had fetched for him, and he was carrying a large gun.

'It won't do you any good,' Tammy said, slamming the door behind her.

'I'm sorry,' Maxine said, 'I left you out there.'

'So I noticed.'

'I was yelling for you to come, but you wouldn't move. And that thing was just getting closer and closer.'

'It wants me. It doesn't want you two.'

'Well then,' Tammy said, staring at the front of Todd's straining jeans and giving up a silent prayer to the efficacy of their contents. 'We have two options. We either give you to the angel, and let it take you wherever the hell it intends to take you –'

'Oh God no. Please. I don't want to go with that thing. I'd rather die.'

'Stop waving the gun around and listen to me, Todd. I said we had two options.'

'What's the other one?'

'We make a run for it.'

9

I t wasn't really a choice, given their circumstances.

They had to make a run for it, and the way Tammy looked at it, the sooner they did so the better for everybody. The angel could afford to play a waiting game, she assumed. Did it need nourishment? Probably not. Did it sleep or take private little moments in which to defecate? Again, probably not. It could most likely afford to lay siege to the house for days, weeks, even months, until its victims had no strength left to outwit it or outmanoeuvre it.

Maxine had gone to the guest bathroom to wash her ashen face. She didn't look much better when she got back. She was still pale and shaking. But in her usual straightforward manner she demanded that everyone agree to what was being contemplated here, in words of one or, at most, two syllables.

'Let's all get this straight,' she said. 'The thing outside is definitely an angel. That is to say, an agent of some divine power. Yes?'

'Yes,' Todd said. He was sitting at the top of the stairs, only partially visible in the light from the dining room, which was the only light that now worked.

'And why's it here? Exactly. Just for the record.'

'We know why it's here, Maxine,' Tammy said.

'No, let's just be very clear about this. Because it seems to me we are *playing with fire*. This thing, this light –'

'*It wants my soul*,' Todd said. 'Is that plain enough for you?'

'And you,' Maxine said, glancing at Tammy to see how

she was responding to all this, 'are blithely suggesting we try and *outrun* it?'

'Yes.'

'You're crazy.'

Before Tammy could reply, Todd put in a final plea. 'If we fail, we fail. But at least let's give it a try.'

'Frankly, I realize I'm outvoted on this, but I think this is insanity,' Maxine said. 'If you really believe in your immortal soul, Todd, why the hell aren't you letting this divine agent come and get you?'

'I'm not saying I don't believe in my soul. I do. I swear I do. But you know me: I've never trusted agents,' he chuckled. 'Joke. Maxine, lighten up. It was a joke.'

Maxine was not amused.

'Suppose it's the real thing,' she said. 'Suppose it's God, looking at us. At *you*.'

'Maybe it is. But then again, maybe it isn't. This Canyon's always been full of deceits and illusions.'

'And you think that's what it is?'

'I don't know. I just don't trust it. I'd prefer to stick around here a little longer than go off with it.'

'*Here*? You want to stay in this dump? Todd, it's not going to be standing for more than another week.'

'So maybe I'll set off across America, I don't know. I just got more living to do. Even though I'm dead.'

'And suppose we're pissing off higher powers?' Maxine said. 'Have you thought about that?'

'You mean God? If God really wants me, He'll find a way to get me. Right? He's God. But if He doesn't . . . if I can slip off and enjoy myself for a few years . . .'

Maxine threw a troubled glance at Tammy. 'And you go along with all this?'

'If Todd doesn't feel –'

'You were the one saying prayers out there.'

'Let me finish. If Todd doesn't feel he's lived his full life, it's his choice.'

'The point is: you've had all the life you're going to get,' Maxine said to him. Then to Tammy, 'We're talking to a dead man. Something we would not be doing outside Coldheart Canyon.'

'Things are different here . . .' Todd murmured, remembering what Katya had told him.

'Damn right they are,' Maxine said. 'But the rules of this place end somewhere north of Sunset. And it's only because of the power that was once in this house that you're getting a chance to play this damn-fool game with God.'

'A game with God,' Tammy said, so quietly Maxine barely heard what she'd said.

'What?'

'I was just saying: *a game with God*. I didn't think you'd care about something like that. Aren't you an atheist?'

'Once, I might have –'

Todd stood up. 'Hush. *Hush*.'

The women stopped talking. Todd looked up towards the vault of the turret, with its holes that showed the night sky.

'Stay very still,' he said.

As he spoke, the light came over the top of the turret, its motion eerily smooth and silent. Three beams of its silvery luminescence came in through holes in the roof. They slid over the walls, like spotlights looking for a star to illuminate. For a moment the entity seemed to settle directly on top of the turret, and one of the beams of light went all the way down the stairwell to scrutinize the debris at the bottom. Then, after a moment's perusal, it began to move off again, at the same glacial speed.

Only when it had gone completely, did anybody speak again. It was Maxine who piped up first.

'Why doesn't it just come in and get you?' she said. 'That's what I can't figure out. I mean, it's just a body of light. It can go anywhere it chooses, I would have thought. Under the door. Down through that hole –' she

705

pointed up to the turret. 'It's not like the house is burglar-proof.'

Tammy had been thinking about that very question. 'I think maybe this place makes it nervous,' she said. 'That's my theory, for what it's worth. All the evil this house has seen.'

'I don't think angels are afraid of anything,' Maxine said.

'Then maybe it's just repulsed. I mean, it's like a dog, right, sniffing out souls? Its senses are really acute. Think how this place must stink. Especially down there.' She glanced down the stairwell, where the angel's light had lingered for a moment before moving on. 'The Devil's Country was down there. People suffered, died, horrible deaths. If I was an angel, I'd stay out.'

'If you were an angel, my love,' Maxine said, 'God would be in a lot of trouble.'

This won a laugh out of Tammy. 'All right, you've heard my theories –'

'I think you're both right,' Todd said. 'If the light wanted to come inside the house it could. It did once, remember? But I think between my not wanting to go and the smell of what this house has seen, it's probably figured it'll wait. Sooner or later the house is going to start falling down. And then I'll come out and it'll have me.'

'That's why we should surprise it,' Tammy said. 'Go now, while it's least expecting anyone to leave.'

'You don't know *what* it's expecting,' Maxine put in. 'It could be listening to every damn word we say, as far as you can tell.'

'Well I'm going to try for it,' Todd said, pushing his gun into his trousers, muzzle to muzzle. 'If you don't want to come, that's fine. Maybe you could just divert it somehow. Give me a chance to get to the car.'

'No, we're going,' Tammy said, speaking on behalf of Maxine, whose response to this was a surrendering shrug.

706

'It *is* preposterous,' she pointed out however. 'Who the hell ever outran an angel?'

'How do we know?' Todd said. 'Maybe people do it all the time.'

They stood together at the door and listened for twenty, twenty-five minutes, seeing if there was some pattern to the motion of the light. In that time it went up onto the roof twice, and made half a circuit of the house, but then seemed to give up for no particular reason. It made no sound. Nor did its light at any point seem to alter in intensity. It was – perhaps predictably – constant and patient, like a hunter sitting by a burrow, knowing that sooner or later its occupant must show its nose.

About nine fifteen or so, Tammy went up to the master bedroom to scan the view across the Canyon and down towards Century City. She'd scoured the kitchen for dried goods and tinned goods that had survived either the ghosts' rampages or the passage of time and had found many tins had been punctured, and the food inside was rotten; but she collected up a few cans of edible stuff: baked beans, peaches, hot-dogs in brine. And then, after some digging around, found an opener, and made up a plate of unlikely gastronomic bed-fellows; and took them upstairs to the balcony.

The Canyon had gone pin-drop quiet. If she hadn't already known they had an agent of Creation's Maker in their vicinity, the spooked silence of every cicada, coyote and night bird would have confirmed the fact. It was eerie, standing there, watching the dark hollow of the Canyon, and the few stars that were visible above it, and listening to the empty dark. She could hear the click of the fork against her teeth, the noise of her throat as it swallowed the beans and bites of hot-dogs.

'I used to love hot-dogs,' came a voice from the dark room behind her. It was Todd. 'You know, ordinary food. I never really got a taste for the more sophisticated stuff.'

707

'You want some of this?' she asked him, glancing round as she proffered the plate.

'No thanks,' he said. 'I haven't really got an appetite any more.'

'Maybe ghosts aren't supposed to eat.'

'Yeah that's what I figured,' he replied, coming out onto the balcony. Then, 'Do you think they fuck? Because if they don't I'm going to have to find some other way to get this down.' He glanced down at the lump beneath his bath-towel.

'Cold showers.'

'Yeah.' He chuckled. 'Everything comes full circle, doesn't it? Cold hot dogs for you. Cold showers for me. Nothing really changes.'

'I don't know,' she said. 'This isn't normal for me. Conversations with – if you'll excuse the phrase – *dead* movie stars in million dollar houses . . .'

'– with an angel waiting on the front door step –'

'Right.'

She'd finished her ad hoc meal, and went back into the bedroom to set the plate down. While she was doing so she heard Todd call her name, very softly.

She went back out onto the balcony.

'What is it?'

'Look.'

She looked, following the direction of his gaze. There was a glow of light in the densely-forested cleft of the Canyon. It looked as though it had settled in the fork of a tree.

'I guess Raphael must have got bored.'

'Is that his name? Raphael?'

'I don't know. It's just the only angel's name I know. Angels aren't my strong point. His real name's probably Marigold. The point is: it's wandered off. We should go while we've got the opportunity. It may not stay down there very long.'

'Right. I'll go and find Maxine.'

'Wait,' Todd said, catching hold of her arm. 'Just one thing before you go.'

'What's that?'

'I want your honest opinion . . .'

'On what?'

'Do you think she's right? Am I screwing with my immortal soul, trying to escape this thing?'

'You know, I was wondering about that when I was eating my hot-dogs. My Aunt Jessica was a church-lady all her life. She used to go and arrange the flowers on the altar three times a week. And she used to say: God sees everything. This was when I was a little girl and she thought I'd been naughty. *God sees everything*, she'd say, wagging her finger. So you can't ever hide from Him. I think He can hear us right now. And at least she would have believed He could.'

'And you?'

'Who knows? I used to believe her. And I suppose there's a little part of me that still thinks wherever I am, whatever I'm doing – good, bad or indifferent – God's got His eye on me. Or Her eye.'

'So . . .'

'So if He doesn't want something to happen He can stop it.'

'Oh, we're back to that. If God doesn't want me to get out of here, He'll make sure I don't.'

'Right.'

Todd allowed a little smile to creep onto his face. He looked like a mischievous six-year-old. 'So what do we think when we see *that* . . .' He nodded to the light in the distance. 'Isn't it like it's looking the other way?'

Now Tammy smiled.

'Maybe,' she said. 'Maybe God's saying: I'll give you a chance. Just this once.'

Todd leaned forward and kissed Tammy on the cheek. 'Oh I like that,' he said. 'Just this once.'

'It's just a theory.'

'It's all I need right now.'

'So you want to go?'

He paused a moment and studied the light in the Canyon below. The angel had apparently paused down there, either to contemplate the loveliness of Creation, or to fall asleep for a while. Whatever the reason, it was no longer moving.

'If we're going to go,' Todd said, 'this is the time. Agreed?'

'Agreed.'

'I'll go get dressed.'

They found Maxine (who had in turn found a bottle of vodka, and had drunk a third of it on an empty stomach, which wasn't perhaps good for her state of mind, but what the hell? It was done). Tammy explained to her what she and Todd had seen from the balcony, and that it was time to try and make a getaway. Pleasantly lubricated by the vodka, Maxine was ready for an escape, in fact she was first to the door, bottle in hand, remarking that the sooner they were all out of this fucking house the better for everyone.

Tammy led the way, clutching Maxine's car-keys tightly in her palm, to keep their merest tinkle from reaching the ears of the angel. The Canyon was now completely dark. Even the few stars that had been lit overhead earlier were now covered by cloud, as though – Tammy thought – the angel had extinguished them. It was the kind of notion she wouldn't have given room to on any other night but this, in any other place but this; but who knew where the bounds of possibility lay tonight? It was ridiculous, in a way, to imagine that an angel could blow out stars. But wasn't it equally bizarre that there should be a dead man walking in her footsteps, planning to outrun heaven? Incident by incident, wonder by wonder, her adventures in the Canyon had escalated in outlandishness; as though in preparation for this night's excesses. First the ghosts and their children; then the Devil's Country; now this.

They moved without mishap to the gate; paused there to be sure the coast was clear and then moved on – again without incident – out into the street. Nobody said a word.

If the silence of the natural world had been uncanny from the balcony, it was ten times stranger now they were out on the road, where there would usually be a chirping carpet laid out all around them, and trilling songs in the darkened canopy. But here, now, nothing. It made what was already strange enough, stranger still. It was as though every living thing from the most ferocious coyote to the tiniest flea, was intimidated into silence and stillness by the scale of power in their midst. The only things foolish enough to move were these three human beings, stumbling through the darkness.

All was going well until Tammy caught her foot in a pothole and fell sideways. Todd was there to catch her, but he wasn't quick enough to stop the short cry of alarm that escaped her as she slipped. It was the loudest thing that had been heard in the Canyon in a long while; its echo coming back off the opposite wall.

She silently mouthed the word *damn*; then, taking a deep breath, she went to the car, adrenaline making her a little more efficient than she might have been otherwise, and opened the door. The car announced that there was a door open with an irritating little *ping, ping, ping*. Well, hell, it scarcely mattered now. They were committed to this. The angel was already pricking up its ears, no doubt.

'Get in,' she hissed.

Todd ducked into the back. Maxine opened the passenger door and slid in with something less than grace. Then she slammed the door so hard it was probably audible in Santa Barbara.

'Sorry,' she slurred. 'Force of habit.'

Todd leaned over from the back seat and put his hand on Tammy's shoulder.

'Give it all you've got,' he said.

'I'll do what I can,' she said, and slipped the key into the ignition.

Even as she was instructing her fingers to turn the key, the moon came out above Coldheart Canyon. Except, of course, that it wasn't the moon, it was the messenger of God, roused from its meditations, and climbing a silent ladder into the dark air over their heads.

'Fuck and double fuck,' Todd said.

It moved straight towards the house, and – perhaps because the evening was a little damp, and the marine layer had come in off the ocean – it had collected around it a cloak of mist. Now, instead of simply being a light, it looked like a cloud with a white fire burning at its core; trailing a tail like a comet.

Tammy wasn't intimidated. She turned on the car engine. It roared, reassuringly loud.

'Handbrake!' Maxine said. 'Handbrake!'

'I've got it,' Tammy said. She took off the handbrake, and put the vehicle into gear. Then she slammed her foot down, and they took off.

'Todd!' she yelled over her shoulder. 'I want you to keep an eye on that sonofabitch for me.'

Todd was already doing just that, peering out of the back window. 'It's still above the house,' he reported. 'Maybe it thinks we're still in there.'

'I don't think it's that dumb somehow,' Maxine said.

Tammy drove the car up the street, and around two wide curves, before she found a place where it was possible to turn round. It was a squealing, messy five or six point turn in the narrow street, and the last manoeuvre delivered the back end of the car into the shrubbery. No matter. Tammy hauled the wheel round and accelerated. Todd went to the other side of the back seat, and looked out.

712

'Huh,' he said.

'What?'

'The damn thing *still* hasn't moved.'

'Maybe it's lost interest,' Tammy said.

It was a forlorn hope, of course, scarcely worth voicing. But every moment the thing failed to come after them was blessed.

'By the way,' she said, as she turned the first wide corner south of the house, 'I got a little taste of what that thing does to you, Todd –'

'You mean the memories?'

'Yeah.'

'Did it freak you out?'

'No. It was just sort of banal, really. It has a memory of my Aunt Jessica –'

'*It's coming.*'

'Oh shit!'

Tammy glanced in her rear view mirror: nothing. Looked over her shoulder: nothing.

'I don't see it!'

'It's after us.'

'I don't see it!'

She caught a glimpse of Todd's face in the mirror, his eyes turned directly upwards; and she knew where it was. The next moment there was a light on the road all around the car, as though a police helicopter had appeared over the ridge with a spotlight, and caught them in it.

There was a turn up ahead. She took it at sixty-five miles an hour, wheels shrieking, and for a moment the cloud overshot the road, and she was driving in near darkness. Losing the light so suddenly left her utterly disorientated and she took the next curve, which came fifteen yards after the previous one, so tightly that the lefthand side of the car was clawed by twigs and branches. Todd whooped.

'Hell, woman! You're quite a driver! Why didn't you tell me?'

'You never asked!' Tammy said, steering the car back into the middle of the road.

'We could have gone drag-racing together. I always wanted to find a woman I could go drag-racing with.'

'Now you tell me.'

Another curve came up, as tight as the one before. But this time she took it without any problem. They were halfway down the hill by now, and Tammy was beginning to think that maybe, just maybe, they were going to reach Sunset Boulevard without their pursuer catching up with them.

'If we *do* get to Sunset,' she said, 'what happens then? Do you think the damn thing will give up?'

She'd no sooner spoken than the light reappeared on the street ahead of them. It was no longer hovering in the air above the street but had descended to block the road from one side to the other.

Tammy slammed on the brakes, but as she did so a sliver of the angel's light came through the windshield to meet her mind, its freight familiar from their previous encounter. The road ahead of her was instantly erased, replaced with the façade of the house on Monarch Street. She heard Maxine, somewhere to her right, let out a yell of panic, and then felt her reaching over to wrest control of the car from her. There was a brief, chaotic moment when Tammy's panic overwhelmed the angel's gift of memory, and she saw, to her horror, that the car had swerved off the road and was speeding into the dense thicket that grew between the trees. The image lasted for a moment only. Then it was gone, the approaching trees, Maxine's fumbling hands, her curses: all of it erased.

In its place, Tammy was standing at the door of her house on Monarch Street, in the dappled sunlight, and Aunt Jessica was telling her that her papa had gone down to the fire station –

The car struck a tree, and the windshield smashed, but

714

Aunt Jessica smiled on. They hit another tree, and another, though Tammy saw none of it. She didn't hear the splinter of wood, or the shrieks from Maxine. Nor did she hear the din of tearing metal as a door was torn off. Her foot was still jammed on the brakes but they didn't seem to be slowing the vehicle's momentum. What eventually brought the car to a halt was a boulder, which lifted it up and threw it over on its left side.

At the instant of impact the angel's vision faltered again, and Tammy saw the world as it really was – a blur of tumbling trees and raining glass. She saw her arms in front of her, her white-knuckled hands still seizing the wheel. She saw blood on her fingers, and then a little storm of shredded leaves coming in through the broken window, their sweetness reminding her, even in the midst of this chaos, of quieter times. Mown lawns on a Sunday afternoon; grass in her hair when she'd been play-wrestling with Sandra Moses from next door. Pieces of green memory, which flickered into her mind's eye between the tumbling view through the windshield and the last, brief appearance of Aunt Jessica on the doorstep.

She knew it was the last because this time, as the car came to a halt, and Tammy slumped in her seat, her consciousness decided to forsake the pain of her broken bones (of which there were many) or the sound of Maxine's screaming (of which there was much) and just go away into the reassuring gloom of the house.

'Why did you not come when I called?' Aunt Jessica demanded. Kindly though she was, she didn't like to be disobeyed.

Tammy looked at the woman through her eleven-year-old's eyes, and fumbled for an answer to the old lady's question. But nothing she could say to Jessica would make any sense, now would it? Canyon, car, angel, crash. How could she possibly understand?

Anyway, Aunt Jessica didn't really want an answer.

715

She had her niece inside the house where she wanted her, and that was all that was really important. Tammy walked down the hallway, into this brown comfortable memory, and let Aunt Jessica close the door behind her, so that the screaming and the raining glass and the world turned upside down could be forgotten, and she could go wash her hands before sitting down to a plate of Aunt Jessica's special meatloaf.

10

It was night in Coldheart Canyon, and though it was the wrong season for the Santa Anas proper to be blowing, the wind that came up about a quarter to midnight was warm for a night in early spring. It carried away the smell of burned rubber and spilled gasoline; it even took away the stench of the vodka-laced vomit Maxine had ejected. With the vodka out of her system, she found she could think a little better. With trembling fingers she unfastened her seat-belt and fell through the open door, out of the seat in which she'd been hanging and on to the grass.

She lay there for a long time, alternately sobbing and being stern with herself. Luckily – if this can be said to be luck – she'd had two previous experiences with car wrecks, the second of which had been substantially worse than this one, in that it had happened on the 101 in the middle of the morning rush, and involved nineteen vehicles and eight fatalities (one of them a passenger in the same stretch limo in which Maxine had been travelling). She had suffered a hairline skull fracture, a dislocated shoulder, and back problems that her chiropractor had blithely announced would be with her for the rest of her life.

Unless she was very much mistaken, she was not in anything like as bad a condition after this little fun-ride as she'd been on that occasion. Shaken up, yes; dizzy, sick and a little hysterical, certainly. But when she finally crawled away from the car, and got to her feet, she was pleased to discover that she could stand up quite well, and that nothing hurt with that piercing hurt that suggested something had been broken or punctured.

'You must have had an angel watching over you.'

She looked round at the wit who'd spoken. It was Todd. He was close to the car, trying to wrench open the door on the driver's side.

'Is Tammy still in there?' Maxine said.

'Yeah. I'm afraid she is.'

'How does she look?'

'How the hell do I know?' Todd remarked. 'It's too dark to see.'

Yes, it *was* dark. And though that wasn't good for finding out how Tammy was doing, it did suggest the absence of their pursuer.

'It's still here,' Todd said. 'Just in case you were wondering.'

'Where?'

He pointed up. Maxine followed his finger. The angel's light brightened the high branches of a nearby pine. It wasn't as steady as it had been up at the house. In fact, it was fluttering nervously, which made Maxine picture a flock of luminous birds up there, all shaking out their feathers after a rainstorm, and hopping from bough to bough in their agitated state.

'Hey you!' Maxine yelled up at the light, too frustrated and angry to care about the protocol of what she was doing. 'Tammy could be bleeding to death in there. How about a hand down here?'

'I don't think it's interested in helping anyone but me. I had to beg it to let me get you two sorted out before it . . . you know . . . came and took me.'

'You mean you talked to it?'

'Yeah. While you were unconscious.'

'And you promised –'

'I promised I'd go with it, as soon as you two were safe. That was the deal.'

718

'Huh. You made a deal with an angel.'

'What else was I going to do? I had to do something. And it was my stupidity that got us into this mess.' He put his head through the broken window. 'At least she's still breathing. But she's also bleeding.'

He lifted his hands and displayed his palms for Maxine. They were blood-soaked.

'Oh God.'

'You know what?'

'What?'

'You're going to have to go for help. Because that sonofabitch isn't going to let me out of its sight. Can you do that?'

'Can I walk? Yes I can walk. Can I walk as far as Sunset?' She drew a deep breath. 'I don't know. I can try.'

'Okay then. You go get someone to help Tammy. And for God's sake be quick about it. I don't think she's got much time. I'll stay here with her. Not that I've got much choice.'

'A deal's a deal.'

'A deal's a deal.'

'Have you got a cigarette?'

Todd stood up and dug in his jeans pocket. 'Yep.' He pulled out a crushed packet, and examined its contents. 'Two Marlboro Lights. One each.'

'Matches?'

'Never without.' He came over to Maxine, and gave her the better preserved of the cigarettes.

'You light it,' she said.

He put both the cigarettes in his mouth and lit them from a single flame. Then he handed Maxine's back to her.

'Didn't somebody do that in a movie?' he said.

'God, you are an ignoramus. Yes, *of course*. Paul Henreid, in *Now, Voyager*. I showed it to you.'

'Yeah,' he smiled. 'I remember. Maxine Frizelle's Ten Favourite Moments.'

719

She drew on the cigarette, and started to walk back along the path carved through the thicket by the car, to the street.

'Hurry,' Todd said.

Tammy ate her meatloaf in silence, thinking of nothing in particular. Aunt Jessica busied herself in the kitchen, coming in now and again to be sure that Tammy was eating all her vegetables. If the plate wasn't cleaned, there'd be no dessert. No pie or cake. Aunt Jessica wasn't a very good cook but she knew what her niece liked. Pie and cake, preferably with ice cream.

'You're going to be a big girl,' she said to Tammy when she brought through the slice of peach cobbler and ice cream. 'Big all over. And that can get a girl into a lot of trouble.'

'Yes, Auntie.'

'Especially with the boys.'

'I know, Auntie.'

'So you have to be extra careful. Boys take advantage of big girls, and I don't want to see you hurt.'

'I won't let them, Auntie.'

'Good,' Aunt Jessica said, though she didn't sound much convinced. Back into the kitchen she went, leaving Tammy to enjoy her cobbler à la mode.

The first couple of mouthfuls tasted good. She ate them thinking of nothing in particular. The clock ticked on the mantelpiece. The canary chirped in its cage.

She took a third mouthful. For some reason it didn't taste as good as the first two; almost as though there was a piece of bad fruit in it. She put her napkin up to her mouth and spat out whatever it was, but the taste of earth, and the gritty texture of it, remained on her tongue and in her throat.

She put down her spoon, and put her fingers into her mouth.

'Wait . . .' somebody said.

It wasn't Aunt Jessica who spoke to her, however. It was a man's voice. A gentle man.

'There's . . . something . . . in my mouth . . .' she said, though she wasn't quite sure who she was talking to.

'Dirt,' the man told her. 'It's just dirt. Can you spit it out? Spit hard.'

She glanced back towards the kitchen. Aunt Jessica was at the sink, washing pans. She wouldn't approve of Tammy spitting in the house.

'I should go outside,' she said.

'You *are* outside,' the man replied.

As he spoke to her she felt the room lurch sideways – the table, the mantelpiece, the canary in his cage.

'Oh no –' she said. 'What's happening?'

'It's all right,' the man said, softly.

'Auntie!' she called.

'No, honey. I'm not your auntie. It's Todd. Now *spit*. You've got dirt in your mouth.'

The world lurched again, only this time there was somebody's arms to catch her, and she opened her eyes to see the face of the handsomest man in the world looking down at her. He was smiling.

'There you are,' he said. 'Oh thank God. I thought I'd lost you.'

As the last morsels of Aunt Jessica's peach cobbler melted away she remembered where she was and how she'd got here. The angel on the road, the trees, the car overturning and glass shattering.

'Where's Maxine?'

'She's fine. She went to get help. But she's been away a long time so I had to drag you out of there myself. It took a little doing. But I did some bandaging. There was a first aid kit in the trunk. I got the bleeding to stop.'

'I was eating peach cobbler.'

'You were hallucinating is what you were doing.'

721

'Only there was dirt in it.' She spat, with as much gusto as she could manage. It made her body hurt to do it, though. Her stomach, her head. She winced.

'You did good,' Todd said, 'Maxine got out with scrapes.'

'It was pure luck,' she said. 'I was driving too fast, and that damn angel got in my way.' She dropped her voice. 'Did it leave?'

Todd shook his head, and directed her attention up at the tree where the angelic presence still sat. It was quite composed now. It had made its arrangements, and it was waiting.

'I'm afraid it's going to want me to go with it very soon,' he said. 'I promised I'd go.'

'You did? You didn't try and make a run for it?'

'How could I? You were in there, hurt. I couldn't just run out on you.'

'But you might have escaped.'

'Ha. You know, I think I did,' he said.

'I don't understand.'

'Oh . . . not quite the way I thought I was going to. But I escaped being a selfish fuck-up.' He looked into her eyes. 'You think I would have had an angel come to fetch me before I met you? No way. It would have been straight down to hell for Todd Pickett.'

He was making a joke of it, of course; but there was something here that came from his heart. She could see it in his eyes, which still continued to stare deep into hers. 'I want to thank you,' he said, leaning down and kissing her cheek. 'Maybe next time round it'll be our turn, eh?'

'Our turn?'

'Yeah. You and me, born next-door to one another. And we'll know.'

'I want you to stop this now,' she told him gently. There were tears blurring her vision, and she didn't like that. He'd be gone soon enough, and she wanted to have him in focus for as long as possible.

He looked up. 'Uh-oh. I hear the cavalry,' he said. Tammy could hear them too. Sirens coming up from the bottom of the hill. 'Sounds like I should make my exit,' Todd said. The sirens were getting louder. 'Damn. Do they have to come so quick?' There were tears in *his* eyes now, dropping onto Tammy's cheek. 'Shit, Tammy. I don't want to go.'

'Yes, you do,' she said. She fumbled for his hand, and finding it, squeezed it. 'You've had a good time. You know you have.'

'Yeah. Oh yeah. I've had a great time.'

'Better than most.'

'True enough.'

The light was descending from the tree, and for the first time – either because the angel was close to finishing its business, or because Tammy herself was hovering on the edge of life – she saw the contents of the light more clearly. There was no attempt to confuse her with memories now; no Monarch Street, no Aunt Jessica at the door. There was a human shape, neither male nor female, standing in the light, and for a moment, as it came to stand behind Todd, she thought it *was* Todd – or some other face of his, some gentle, eternal face that no camera would ever capture, nor words would ever show.

He stroked her face with the back of his fingers, and then he stood up.

'Next time,' he murmured.

'Yeah.'

Then his smile, that trademark smile of his which had made Tammy weak with infatuation when she'd first seen it, dimmed a little; its departure not signifying sadness, only the appearance of a certain ease in him, which his smile had concealed all these years. He didn't need to try so hard any longer. He didn't need to charm or please.

She tried to catch his eye one last time – to have one last piece of him, even now. But he was already looking away; looking at where he was really headed.

She heard him speak one last time, and there was such happiness in his voice, she began to cry like a baby.

'Dempsey?' he said. 'Here boy! Here!'

She turned her head towards the light, thinking she might glimpse him even now, but as she did so, she heard – or thought she heard – the angel utter a word of its own; a seamless word, like a ribbon wrapped around everything she'd ever dreamed of knowing or being. It wasn't loud, but it erased the sound of the sirens, for which she was grateful; then it moved off up into the darkness of the Canyon.

Knowing she was safe in the hands of those who would take care of her, and one, Maxine, who loved her, she followed the ribbon of the word up the flanks of Coldheart Canyon, skimming the darkened earth.

And as the woman and the word passed over the ground together, the creatures of the Canyon forgot their fear. They began to make music again; cicadas in the grass, night-birds in the trees; and on the ridge, the coyotes, yapping fit to burst. Not because they had a kill, but because they had life.

AND SO, LOVE

1

Although every medical expert who paraded by Tammy's bed in the next many weeks – bone-specialists and skull-specialists, gastroenterologists and just good old-fashioned nurses – invariably pronounced the opinion that she was a 'very lucky woman to be alive' there were many painful days and nights in that time of slow, slow recovery when she did not feel remotely lucky.

Quite the reverse. There were times, especially at night, when she thought she was as far from unmended as she'd been when Todd had first pulled her out of the car. Why else did she hurt so much? They gave her painkillers of course, in mind-befuddling amounts, but even when she'd just taken the pills or been given the injection, and the first rush of immunity from pain was upon her, she could still feel the agony pacing up and down just beyond the perimeter of her nerves' inured state, waiting for a crack to appear in the wall so that it could get back in and hurt her again.

She was in the Intensive Care Unit at Cedars-Sinai for the first seventy-two hours, but as soon as she was deemed fit to be removed from the ICU, her insurance company demanded she be taken to the LA County Hospital, where she could be looked after at fifty percent of the price. She was in no state to defend herself, of course, and would have undoubtedly been transferred had Maxine not stepped in and made her presence felt. Maxine was close friends with several of the Hospital Board, and made it clear that she would unleash all manner of legal demons if anyone even *thought* of moving Mrs Lauper when she was in such a delicate state. The hospital authorities responded quickly. Tammy kept her bed, complete with a private room, at Cedars-Sinai. Maxine made it her business to be sure that the room was filled with fresh orchids every day, and that fresh three-layer chocolate cake from Lady Jane's on Melrose was brought in at three every afternoon.

'I want you well,' she instructed Tammy during one of her first visits after Tammy had been released from ICU. 'I have a list of dinner parties lined up for the two of us that will take every weekend for the next year, at least. Shirley MacLaine called me; claimed she'd had a vision of Todd passing over, wearing a powder blue suit. I didn't like to spoil the poor old biddy's illusions so I told her that was *exactly* what he was wearing. Just as a matter of interest what was he wearing?'

'Jeans and a hard-on,' Tammy replied. 'He'd torn up his T-shirt for bandages.' Her voice was still weak, but some of its old music was starting to come back, day by day.

'Well, I'll leave you to tell her that. And then there's all these friends of Todd's who want to meet you –'

'Why?'

'Because I told them about what an extraordinary woman you are,' Maxine said. 'So you'd better start to get seriously well. As soon as you're ready to be moved I want you to come down and stay with me in Malibu.'

'That'd be too much trouble for you.'

'That's exactly what I need right now,' Maxine replied, without irony. 'Too much trouble. The moment I stop to think . . . that's when things get out of hand.'

Luckily, Tammy didn't have that problem. In addition to the heavy doses of painkillers she was still being given, she was getting some mild tranquillizers. Her thoughts were dreamy, most of the time; nothing seemed quite real.

'You're a very resilient woman,' her doctor, an intense, prematurely-bald young fellow called Martin Zondel observed one morning, while scanning Tammy's chart. 'It usually takes people twice as long as it's taking you to bounce back from these kinds of injuries.'

'Am I bouncing? I don't feel like I'm bouncing.'

'Well perhaps bouncing is too strong a word, but you're doing just fine!'

It was a period of firsts. The first trip out of bed, as far as the window. The first trip out of bed, as far as the door. The first trip out of bed as far as the en-suite bathroom. The first trip outside, even if it was just to look at the construction workers on the adjacent lot, putting up the new research block for the hospital. Maxine and Tammy ogled the men for a while.

'I should have married a blue-collar worker,' Maxine said when they got back inside, 'Hamburgers, beer and a good fuck on a Saturday night. I always overcomplicated things.'

'Arnie's blue-collar. And he was a terrible lover.'

'Oh yes, Arnie. It's time we talked about Arnie.'

'What about him?'

'Well for one thing, he's a louse.'

'Tell me something I don't know. What's he been up to?'

'Are you ready for this? He's been selling your life-story.'

'Who to?'

'*Everyone*. You're hot news, right now. In fact I had a call from someone over at Fox wondering if I could sell you on the idea of having your life turned into a Movie of the Week.'

'I hope you said no.'

'No. I just said I'd talk to you about it. Honestly, Tammy, there's a little window of opportunity in here when you could make some serious money.'

'Selling my life-story? I don't think so. I don't have one to sell!'

'That's not what these dodos think. Look at these.'

Maxine went into her bag and brought out a sheaf of magazines, laying them on the bed. The usual suspects: *The National Enquirer* and *The Star* plus a couple of more up-market magazines, *People* and *US*. Tammy was still too stiff to lean forward and pick them up, so Maxine went through them for her, flicking to the relevant articles. Some carried photographs of Todd at the height of his fame; the photographs often emblazoned with melodramatic questions: *Was Fame too much for the World's Greatest Heart-throb?* on one; and on another: *His Secret Hideaway became a Canyon of Death*. But these lines were positively restrained in contrast with some of the stuff in the pages of *The Globe*, which had dedicated an entire '*Pull-out Special your family will treasure for generations*', to the subject of *Haunted Hollywood*; or, in their hyperbolic language: '*The Spooks, the Ghosts, the Satan-worshippers and the Fiends who have made Tinseltown the Devil's Fanciest Piece of Real Estate!*'

There were pictures accompanying all the articles, of course: mostly of Todd, occasionally of Maxine and Gary Eppstadt, and even – in the case of *The Enquirer* and *The Globe*, pictures of Tammy herself. In fact she was the subject of one of the articles which was led off by a very unflattering picture of her; the article claiming that '*According to her husband Arnold, obsessive fan Tammy Jayne Lauper, probably knows more about the last hours of superstar Todd Pickett's life than anybody else alive – but she isn't telling! Why? Because Lauper (34) is the leader of a black magic cult, which involves thousands of the dead star's fans worldwide, who were attempting to psychically control their star, when their experiment went disastrously and tragically wrong.*'

'I was of two minds whether to show you all this,' Maxine said. 'At least yet. I realize it probably makes your blood boil.'

'How can they write such things? They're just making it up . . .'

'There were worse, believe me. Not about you. But there's a piece about me I've got my lawyers onto, and two pieces about Burrows –'

'Oh, really?'

'One of them was a very long list of his . . . how shall I put this? His "less than successful" clients.'

'So Todd wasn't the first?'

'Apparently not. Burrows was just very good at buying people's silence. I guess nobody really wants to talk about their unsuccessful ass-lifts, now do they?'

Maxine gathered all the magazines up and put them into the drawer of the bedside table. 'That's actually put some colour back into your cheeks.'

'It's indignation,' Tammy said. 'It's fine to read all that nonsense in the supermarket line. But when it's about you, it's different.'

'So shall I not bring any more of them in?'

'No, you can bring 'em in. I want to see what people are saying about me. Where are the magazines getting my photographs from? That one of me looking like a three-hundred-pound beet –'

Maxine laughed out loud. 'You're being a *little* harsh on yourself. But, you're right, it's not flattering. I guess the photographer himself gave them the picture. And you know who that was?'

'Yes. It was Arnie. It was taken last summer.'

'He's probably gone through all your family photographs. But look, don't get stirred up. He's no better or worse than a thousand others. Believe me, I've seen this happen over and over. When there's a little money to be made – a few hundred bucks even – people come up with all these excuses to justify what they're doing with other people's privacy. *America deserves to be told the truth*, and all that bullshit.'

731

'That's not what Arnie thought,' Tammy said. 'He just said to himself: *I deserve to make some money for putting up with that fat bitch of a wife all these years.*'

There was no laughter now; just bitterness, deep and bleak.

'I'm sorry,' Maxine said. 'I really shouldn't have brought them in.'

'Yes, you should. And please, don't apologize. I'm not really all that surprised. What are they saying about you . . . if you don't mind me asking?'

Maxine exhaled a ragged sigh: 'She was exploitative, manipulative, never did anything for Todd except for her own profit. That kind of stuff.'

'Do *you* care?'

'It's funny. It used not to hurt. In fact, I used to positively wallow in being people's worst nightmare. But that was when Todd was still alive . . .' She let the thought go unfinished. 'What's the use?' she said at last, getting up from beside the bed. 'We can't control any of this stuff. They'll write whatever they want to write, and people will believe what they want to believe.' She leaned in and kissed Tammy on the cheek. 'You take care of yourself. Dr Zondel – is that it, Zondel?'

'I think so.'

'Sounds like a cheap white wine. Well, anyway, he thinks you're remarkable. And I said to him: "*this we knew.*"'

Tammy caught hold of her hand. 'Thank you for everything.'

'Nothing to thank me for,' Maxine said. 'We survivors have got to stick together. I'll see you tomorrow. And by the way, now that you're *compos mentis* – I warn you – there's a chance you're going to have nursing staff coming in to ask you questions. Then selling your answers. So say nothing. However nice people are to you, assume they're fakes.'

*　　*　　*

Maxine came every day, often with more magazines to show. But on Wednesday – three weeks and a day after Tammy had returned to consciousness – she had something weightier to place on her bed.

'Remember our own Norman Mailer?'

'Detective Rooney?'

'Ex-Detective Martin Patrick Rooney. The same. Behold, he did labour mightily and his gutter publishers saw that it was publishable and they did a mighty thing, and put it in print in less than three weeks.'

'No!'

'Here it is. In all its shoddy glory.'

It wasn't a big book – a mere two hundred and ninety-six pages – but what it lacked in length it made up for in sheer bravura. The copy described it as a story too horrific for Hollywood to tell. On the cover was a photograph of the house in Coldheart Canyon, with the image of a glowering demon superimposed on the clouds overhead.

'He says you, me and a woman called Katya Lupescu were in it together. Like the three witches in Macbeth.'

'You mean you actually read it?'

'Well, I skimmed. It's not the worst thing I've read. He spells all our names right, most of the time, but the rest? Oh God in Heaven! I don't know where to begin. It's a big sticky mess of Hollywood myths and Manson references and completely asinine pieces of detective work. Basically, he's convinced everyone is in on this massive conspiracy –'

'To do what?'

'Well . . . that's the thing. He's not really sure. He claims Todd found out about it, so he was murdered. Same with Joe. Same with Gary Eppstadt, though of course *everybody* in Hollywood had a reason to murder Gary Eppstadt.'

'I didn't know books could be published so fast.'

'Well it's just hack-work. It'll be off the shelves in a month. But Rooney got a quarter of a million dollars advance for it. Can you believe that?'

Tammy picked the book up – which was called *Hell's Canyon* – and flicked through it.

'Did he interview Arnie?'

'Well I didn't read it *that* closely, but I didn't see his name.'

'Oh, there's pictures,' Tammy said, coming to the eight-page section in the middle of the book. To give him his due, Rooney – or somebody working on his behalf – had done a little research. He'd turned up two photographs from the archives of some silent movie enthusiast. One was a picture of Katya Lupi, dressed in a gown so sheer it looked as though it had been painted on, the other a much more informal photograph which showed Katya, Mary Pickford, Douglas Fairbanks, Theda Bara, Ramon Navarro and a host of other luminaries at a picnic in the shadow of the dream palace in Coldheart Canyon. At the back of the crowd – separated from Katya by several rows of smiling, famous faces, was Willem Zeffer. Tammy closed the book.

'Don't want to see any more?'

'I don't think so. Not today.'

'I've been thinking . . . Dr Zinfandel –' Tammy laughed at Maxine's perfectly deliberate error '– has told me you'll be out of here in a week, ten days at the most. I don't want you going back to Rio Linda, at least not yet. I want you to come and stay with me at the house in Malibu, if it doesn't have too many distressing memories.'

Tammy had been worrying about how she'd cope when she was released from the hospital; the offer made her burst with tears of relief.

'Oh Christ, I hadn't realized you hated the place *that* much!'

Laughter appeared through the tears. 'No, no, I'd love to come.'

'Good. Then I'm going to send Danielle – she's my new

734

assistant – to Sacramento and have her pick up some of your things, if that's okay with you.'

'That would be perfect.'

Nine days later, Tammy moved out of Cedars-Sinai and Maxine ferried her down to the beach-house. It looked much smaller by day; and somehow more ordinary without the twinkle lights in the trees, and the cars driving up, full of the great and the good. Perhaps it was simply that she'd come to know Maxine so well in the past few weeks (and how strange was that?; to have become so fond of this woman she'd despised for years, and to have her sentiments so sweetly returned?), that the house didn't seem at all alien to her. It was very far from her taste of course (or more correctly, far from her pocketbook) but it was modestly stylish, and the objects on the shelves were elegant and pretty. Sitting on the patio on the second or third evening, sipping a Virgin Mary, the wind warm off the Pacific, she asked Maxine if she'd decorated the place herself, or had it done professionally.

'Oh I'd love to say I chose every object in the house, but it was all done for me. Actually Jerry selected the paintings. He's got a good eye for art. It's a gay thing.'

Tammy spluttered into her drink.

'He's flying back to California next weekend, to see a friend in the hospital. So I said he should call in. That's all right, yes? If you don't feel up to it, you don't have to see him.'

'I'm fine, Maxine,' Tammy said. 'Believe me, I'm fine.'

2

As it turned out, the following Saturday, when Jerry came to visit, Tammy was feeling anything but fine. Dr Zondel had warned her that there would be some days when she felt weaker than others, and this was certainly one of those. She only had herself to blame. The previous day she had decided to take a walk along the beach and, as the day was so sunny, and the air so fresh, she'd completely lost track of time. What she'd planned as a twenty-minute stroll turned into an hour-and-a-quarter trek, which had not only exhausted her, but made her bones and muscles ache. She was consequently feeling frail and tender when Jerry came by the following day, and in no mood for intensive conversation. It didn't matter. Jerry had plenty to talk about without need of prompting: mainly his new and improved state of health.

'I'm trying not to be too much of a Pollyanna about it all in case something goes horribly wrong and the tumour comes back. But I don't think it's going to. I'm fine. And you, honey?'

'I have good days and bad days,' Tammy said.

'Today's a bad day,' Maxine said, chucking Tammy under the chin to get a smile.

'Look at you, Maxine. If I didn't know better I'd say you had a gay gene in you someplace.'

Maxine gave him a supercilious smile. 'Well if I did I certainly wouldn't tell *you* about it.'

'Are you implying I gossip?'

'It was not an implication,' Maxine dead-panned. 'It is a fact of life.'

'Well I'll keep my mouth closed about this, I promise,' Jerry said, with a mischievous glint. 'But were you not once a married lady, Tammy?'

'I'm not getting into this,' Tammy said.

'All right, I will say no more on the subject. But I see what I see. And I think it's very charming. Men are such pigs anyway.'

Maxine gave him a fierce look. And beneath her makeup, Tammy thought, she was blushing.

'You said you had pictures to show us?' Maxine said.

'I did? Oh yes, I did.'

'Pictures of what?' Tammy said, her mind only a quarter committed to the subject at hand, distracted as she was by the exchange that had just taken place between Maxine and Jerry. She knew exactly what Jerry was implying, and although she couldn't remember thinking that she and Maxine had been nesting just like a couple of lesbians, she could see that his innuendo was not without plausibility, from the outside, at least.

And besides, men *were* pigs; or at least most of the men it had been her misfortune to become attracted to.

Jerry had brought out his pictures now, and passed them over to Maxine, who started to look through them.

'Oh my Lord . . .' she said softly. Maxine handed the photographs over to Tammy one by one, as she'd looked at them.

'They were just taken by my old camera, so they're not very good. But I stayed all day, to watch the whole thing from beginning to end.'

'The thing' Jerry had watched, and had photographed (rather better than his disclaimer suggested) was the Los Angeles Public Works' demolition of Katya Lupi's dream palace.

'I didn't even know they were going to knock it down,' Maxine said.

'Well apparently there was a fierce lobby from your gang, Tammy –'

'My gang?'

'The Appreciation Society.'

'Oh.'

'– to keep the place as some kind of Todd Pickett shrine. You didn't hear about that?' Tammy shook her head. 'My, my, you two have had your heads in the sand. Well, there was a petition, saying that the house should be left standing, but the authorities said no, it had to come down. Apparently, it was structurally unsafe. All the foundations had gone. Of course we know why but nobody else can figure it out. Anyway, they sent in the bulldozers. It was all over in six hours. The demolition part at least. Then it took another five or six hours to put the rubble in trucks and drive it away.'

'Did anybody come to watch?' Tammy asked.

'Quite a few, coming and going. But not a crowd. Never more than twenty at any one time. And we were kept a long way back from the demolition which is why the pictures are so poor.'

The women had been through all the pictures now. Tammy handed them back to Jerry, who said: 'So that's another piece of Hollywood history that's bitten the dust. It makes me sick. This is all we've got faintly resembling a past in this city of ours, and we just take a hammer and knock it all down. How sensible is that?'

'Personally, I'm glad it's gone,' Tammy piped up. Another wave of weakness had come over her as she looked at the pictures, and now she felt almost ready to pass out.

'You don't look too good,' Maxine said.

'I don't feel too good. Would either of you mind if I went to lie down?'

'Not at all,' Jerry said.

Tammy gave him a kiss and started towards her bedroom.

738

'Aren't you going to tuck her in, Maxine?' Tammy heard Jerry say.

'As it happens: yes.' And so saying, she followed Tammy into the bedroom.

'You know, you mustn't let anything Jerry says bother you,' Maxine said, once Tammy was lying down. She stroked the creases from the pillow beside Tammy's head.

'I know.'

'He doesn't mean any harm.'

'I know that too.' She looked at Maxine, seeking out her grey eyes. 'You know . . . just for the record . . .'

'No, Tammy. We don't have to have this conversation. You don't have a lesbian bone in your body.'

'No, I don't.'

'And if I do . . . well, I haven't discovered it yet. But, as you raised the subject, I could quite happily take care of you for as long as you'd like. I like your company.'

'And I like yours.'

'Good. So let's have the world believe whatever it wants to believe.'

'Fine by me.'

Tammy made a weak little smile, mirrored on Maxine's face.

'Who'd have thought?' Maxine murmured.

She leaned forward and kissed Tammy very gently on the cheek. 'Go to sleep, honey. I want you well.'

When she'd gone, Tammy lay beneath the coverlet, listening to the reassuring rhythm of conversation between Maxine and Jerry from next door, and the draw and boom of the Pacific.

Of all the people to have found such comfort with: Maxine Frizelle. Her life had taken some very odd turns, no question about that.

But somehow it still seemed right. After the long journeys of late, the pursuits and the revelations, the terrors that could not speak, and those that spoke all too clearly, she felt as though Maxine was somehow her reward; her prize for staying the terrible course.

'Who'd have thought?' she said to herself.

And with Maxine's words on her lips, she fell asleep.

'I want to go back to Rio Linda,' Tammy announced two days later. They were sitting on their favourite spot, out on the patio, and today there was a splash of the vodka mixed with tomato juice in Tammy's glass.

'You want to go home?' Maxine said.

Tammy took her hand. 'No, no,' she said. Then, more fiercely: 'God, no. That's not my home any longer.'

'So –?'

'Well, I had this huge collection of Todd Pickett memorabilia. And I want to get rid of it. Then I want to think about selling the house.'

'Meaning you'll move in with me?'

'If it isn't too sudden?'

'At our age, nothing's too sudden,' Maxine said. 'But are you sure you want to go through all that stuff yourself? Can't you get one of the fans to do it?'

'I could, I suppose,' Tammy said. 'But I'd feel better doing it myself.'

'Then we'll do it together.'

'It'll be boring. There's so much stuff. And Arnie's been using the house on and off so it'll be a pig-sty.'

'I don't care. When do you want to go?'

'As soon as possible. I just want to get it over and done with.'

Tammy tried to find Arnie, first at the airport and then at his new girlfriend's house, just to warn him that they were coming into town, but she didn't get hold of him. Part of her was glad that Maxine was accompanying her, when there were so many variables she couldn't predict; but there was another part of her that felt a little uncomfortable at the prospect. Maxine lived in luxury. What would she think

740

when she laid eyes on the scruffed, stuffed, little ranch-house where Tammy and Arnie had lived out the charmless farce of their marriage for fourteen-and-a-half years?

They got an early plane out of Los Angeles, and were in Sacramento by nine-thirty in the morning. Maxine had arranged for a chauffeured sedan to meet them at the airport. The chauffeur introduced himself as Gerald, and said that he was at their disposal. Did they want to go straight to the address he'd been given? Tammy gave Maxine a nearly panicked look: the moment was upon her, and suddenly she was anxious.

'Come on,' Maxine said. 'We'll face the horror together. Then we'll be out of here by the middle of the afternoon.'

Arnie hadn't bothered to mow the front lawn, of course, or weed the ground around the two rose bushes that Tammy had attempted to nurture. The bushes were still alive, but only just. The weeds were almost as tall as the bushes.

'Of course he may have changed the lock,' Tammy said, as they approached the front door.

'Then we'll just get Gerald to shoulder it in,' Maxine said, ever practical. 'It's still your house, honey. We're not doing anything illegal.'

In fact, the key fitted and turned without any problem; and it was immediately apparent from the general state of the place that Arnie hadn't after all been a very regular visitor here in a while. But the heating had been left turned up so it was stiflingly hot in all the rooms; a stale, sickly heat. In the kitchen there was some food left out and rotting: a half-eaten hamburger, a pile of fruit which had been corrupted into plush versions of the originals, two plates of pizza crusts. The stink was pretty offensive, but Tammy got to work quickly clearing up the kitchen, while Maxine went around the house opening the windows and turning down the heating. With the rotted food bagged and set outside, and bleach put down the sink to take away the stench, the place was a little more hospitable, but Tammy made it very clear that she wanted to stay here for as short a time as possible, so they set to work. Given the size of the collection it was obviously not going to be sorted through and disposed of in a day; all Tammy wanted to do was collect up all the stuff that was personal, and either burn it or take it away. The rest she would let members of the Appreciation Society come in and collect. They'd end up fighting over the choicest items no doubt; all the more reason not to be there when they came.

'I didn't realize you had so much *stuff*,' Maxine said, when they'd looked through all the rooms.

'Oh I was a top-of-the-line obsessive. No question. And I was organized.' She went over to one of the filing cabinets, opened it, and fingered through it till she found the file she wanted.

'What's this?' Maxine said.

'Letters from you to me. Usually *Dictated but not read*.'

'I was a bitch, I know. I was just trying to protect him the only way I knew how.'

'And it worked. I never really got near him. Nobody did.'

'Maybe if I had been less paranoid, he'd have been less paranoid. Then we wouldn't have tried to hide him away, and none of this –'

Tammy interrupted her. 'Enough of that,' she said. 'Let's start a bonfire out in the back yard, and get this done.'

'A bonfire? For what?'

'For things like *these*.' She proffered the Maxine Frizelle file. 'Things it's nobody's business to ever see or read.'

'Is there much like that?'

'There's enough. You want to start a fire with these, and I'll bring some more stuff out?'

'Sure. Anywhere in particular?'

'Arnie built a barbecue pit to the right of the back door. Only he never finished it. We could use that.'

'Done.'

Maxine took the papers outside, leaving Tammy to go through the cabinets collecting up other files that for one reason or another she didn't want people to see. She wasn't proud of what her over-bearing tendencies had led her to do or say on occasion; this was the perfect time to clean up her past a little. It wasn't so much the thought of posterity that drove her to do this (although she was aware that she had become a part of a footnote to Hollywood history), rather it was the desire to keep these unflattering missives and notes out of the hands of the members of the Appreciation Society who would come in here after they'd gone to cast dice and divide the lots.

When she took the first armful out to the back yard she found that Maxine had made quite a healthy fire with the copies of her own letters.

'Is that all?'

'No, no,' Tammy said, studying the fire. 'There's a lot more.' She kept staring. 'You know that's what I used to think ghosts were like?' she said. 'Flames in the sun. Invisible, but there.'

Maxine took the files from Tammy, and proceeded to feed them to the flames.

'Are we ever going to set the record straight?' Tammy wondered aloud.

'Like how?'

'Write our own book.'

'Lauper and Frizelle's Guide to the Afterlife?'

'Something like that.'

'It'd just be another opinion,' Maxine said, poking at the fire with the stick she'd picked up. 'People would go on believing their favourite versions.'

'You think?'

'For sure. You can't change people's opinion about stuff like that. It's imbedded. They believe what they believe.'

'I'll go get some more stuff.'

'Historians of the future are going to curse us for this, you know that?'

'Probably,' Tammy said, catching a thin, black smut that was spiralling up from the fire like some bizarre insect. It crumbled in her hand. She brushed her palms together briskly, to clean it off. Then she went back inside for some more fuel for the fire.

Three or four trips out into the back yard and she'd done all she needed to do. She stood in the front bedroom, where she'd always kept her special treasures, and assessed the contents. She could only imagine how many fights there would be over the contents of this room: how much bitching and bargaining. Her gaze went to the back of the room, where – out of sight behind several boxes of film stills – she had hidden the holy of holies: the box of photographs of Todd that she and she alone owned. The idea that these would become bargaining material like all the other bits and pieces they were leaving was repugnant. It was fine for the fans to have their petty arguments over crew-jackets and scraps of costuming, but not her precious photographs.

She carefully negotiated her way through the piles of bric-a-brac (her legs, still mending, were beginning to ache) to where her treasure lay hidden. Then she slipped her hand down into the hiding-place, and pulled the box out into view.

The rest could go to the fire or the fans, but this, and this alone, she would keep, she decided. She put it under her arm and went outside to see how her fire-stoker was doing.

'Is that the last of it?' Maxine said, looking at the box under Tammy's arm.

'No, I'm keeping this.'

'Oh? Okay.'

'It's just pictures of Todd.'

The fire was still burning strongly; waves of heat rose

744

up out of the half-finished pit, making the air undulate. While she stared at the fire Tammy opened the box of photographs, and as she did so some instinct – a kind of repugnance for the woman who had obsessed so often on these pictures – made her toss the box lid aside, and with one unpremeditated movement, pluck the pictures and the little roll of negatives out of the box and toss them into the middle of the fire.

'Changed your mind, huh?' Maxine said.

'Yep.'

The flames were already curling around the first of the series, but Maxine could see him clearly enough.

'He was younger then.'

'Yeah. They were taken on *Life Lessons*.'

'Are those the negatives you're burning?'

'Don't ask.'

'That must have cost you a small fortune. But he surely was a good-looking man.'

The first of the photographs had been consumed. Now the second and the third.

'Are these the last of it, then?'

'I think so,' Tammy said. 'They can argue over the rest.'

'Only I'm parched. Watching fires is thirsty work.'

'You want me to get you a coke or a beer?'

'No. I want us to get back in the car and go home.'

'Home,' Tammy said, still looking at the fire. The sixth, seventh and eighth pictures were being consumed. The roll of negatives had already curled up into a little black ball.

'Yes, home,' Maxine said.

She took Tammy's hand, and kissed the back of it. 'Where you belong.'

The last of the photographs had come into view, preserved from the heat of the flames on which it sat by the bottom of the box. This was always the picture she'd stared at most often, and most intensely; the one in which she'd often willed Todd's gaze to shift, just a few degrees, so he would look out at her. The fire had caught it now. In a few seconds it would be ashes.

Suddenly, just as impetuously as she'd delivered the pictures into the fire, she now reached down and plucked this one out. She blew on the flames, which only encouraged them.

'Here,' Maxine said, and snatching the photograph from Tammy's hand dropped it to the ground and quickly stamped out the flames.

'You left it a bit late for a change of mind.'

Tammy picked the picture up, nipping out the last orange worms of fire that crawled around its charred edges. Three-quarters of the image had been consumed, and the remaining portion was browned by the heat and earth of Maxine's stamping, but Todd's face, shoulder and chest had survived. And his eyes, of course, just one second from meeting the gaze of the camera. Imminent, but permanently averted.

'You really want to keep that?'

'Yes. If you don't mind. We'll frame it and we'll find a place in the house where we can say hello to him once in a while.'

'Done.' She headed back to the house. 'I'm going to call the airport. Find out when the next plane back to Los Angeles is. Are you ready to go?'

'Just say the word.'

Tammy looked down at the picture in her hand. Maxine was right; she had left it a little late to salvage it. But there might come a time when she and Maxine needed the comfort of this face; when they were no longer young, and the imminence of his gaze would carry with it the promise of a reunion in another, kinder place.

She glanced up, to be sure Maxine had gone inside, then she gave the bitter-smelling scrap of photograph a quick kiss. Having done so she smiled at the man in the picture, and at herself for all her years of vain adoration. Well, she'd made her peace with it, at least. She slipped the photograph into her pocket and went inside, leaving the fire to burn itself out in Arnie's half-finished handiwork.

3

It is night in Coldheart Canyon, and the wind is off the desert.

The Santa Anas they call these winds. They blow off the Mojave, bringing sickness, on occasion, and the threat of fire.

But tonight the Santa Anas are not blisteringly hot. Tonight they are balmy as they pass through the Canyon. Their only freight is the sweet fragrance of flowers.

They make the young palms that are growing wild on the flanks of the Canyon sway, and the banks of bougainvillaea churn. They raise dust along the road that winds up the Canyon.

Once in a while somebody will still make their way up that winding road, usually to look for some evidence of scandal or horror. But nature, abhorring a vacuum, has blanketed with green vine the deep pit that marked the location of Katya Lupi's house. So the visitors, coming here in the hope of finding bloodstains or Satanic markings scrawled into the sandstone, dig around for a while in the hot sun and then give up. There's nothing here that gives them gooseflesh: just flowers and dragonflies. Grumbling to one another that this was all a waste of time, they get back in their rental cars, arguing as to who suggested this fool's errand in the first place, and drive away to find something that will give them something morbid to talk about once they get back in to Tulsa or New Jersey.

When people finally ask them whether they went up

to that God-forsaken Canyon where all those Hollywood folks died, they say that yeah, they went and had a look, but it was a waste of gas and temper, because there was nothing to see. Not a thing.

And so, over the next few summers, as people come and look and go away disappointed, word slowly spreads that Coldheart Canyon is a sham, a fake; not worth the effort.

So people come less and less. And eventually the tourists don't come at all.

There's only one kind of visitor who will still make the effort to find the place where Katya Lupi built her dream palace, and for this sort of sight-seer, the Canyon will still put on a show.

They come, always, in expensive vehicles, designed to be driven over rough, undomesticated land. They come with rolls of geological maps and surveyors' equipment, and talk proprietorially about how the Canyon would look if it had a five-star hotel, seven or eight storeys high, built at the top end, with three swimming pools and a dozen five-grand-a-night bungalows, all arranged so that everybody has a little corner of the Canyon walled off for their private spa, the contours of the land altered so that it feels like a world within a world; an escape into paradise, just two minutes' drive from Sunset Boulevard.

The Canyon has heard all this idle nonsense before of course. And it has promised itself: *never again*.

Hearing these men talk about the money they're going to make once they've done their digging and their planting, the Canyon loses its temper, and starts to show its displeasure as only earth and rock given something close to consciousness by the magic worked in its midst, can do.

At first it simply shakes the ground a little, just enough to send some stones skipping down the Canyon's flanks to shatter the windshields on every vehicle on the road. Very often, a tantrum like this is enough to make the developers turn tail. But not always. Once in a while, there's somebody who refuses to be so easily intimidated, and the Canyon must escalate its assault.

It shakes its flanks until it uncovers certain horrid forms: the mummified remains of the children of the ghosts and the animals who mated here in the dark days of the Canyon's shameful past.

The revelation is brief. Just enough to say: *this is the least of it, my friend. Dig and you will regret what I will show you for the rest of your life.*

The show works every time.

Pragmatic though these men are, they feel the cold presence of the uncanny all around them, and suddenly they want no more of this place. In their panic they don't even bother to clear the granulated glass off their leather seats. They just get into their cars and drive away in clammy haste, leaving their maps and artists' renderings to decay in the earth, and their ambitions to rot beside them.

So the Canyon sits in the middle of the sprawling city, inviolate. Nobody will touch it now. All it has to do is wait; wait for a certain summons.

There's no telling when it will come.

Perhaps it's a hundred years away, this call. On the other hand, perhaps it will come tomorrow.

All the Canyon knows is this: that at some point in the future a whisper will pass through its cracks and its vaults, and with one almighty heave, the canyons and the hills and the flatlands as far as the shore will stand up on end, and all the towers and the dams and the dream palaces that were built here, along with their builders and their inheritors, will drop away into the deep, dark Pacific.

The land will shake for a year or so, as it lays itself down again. Tremors will continue to convulse it. But by degrees, things will return to the way they were in an earlier time. The Santa Anas will blow in their season, and they'll carry into the Canyon the seeds of the flowers whose scents they bear, dropping them carelessly in the newly-churned earth.

After a few weeks of warm winter rain, the naked ground will be covered with grass and the shoots of young flowers; even the first spears of palm trees and bamboo. In the months to come they will flourish, transforming the land out of all recognition.

And in time it will be as though men had never come to this perfect corner of the world – never called it paradise on earth, never despoiled it with their dream factories; and in the golden hush of the afternoon all that will be heard will be the flittering of dragonflies, and the murmur of hummingbirds as they pass from bower to bower, looking for a place to sup sweetness.